THE
FROZEN
FIST

ADAM SUNDERMAN

Fulton Books
Meadville, PA

Published by Fulton Books 2024

ISBN 979-8-88982-985-0 (paperback)
ISBN 979-8-88982-986-7 (digital)

Printed in the United States of America

PART I

CHAPTER 1

Her journey proved bitter, even upon entering the free waters of the north. The ship taking Demosyna and her fellow traveling companions was sluggish with a teeming load of bodies and cargo. Despite the air turning crisp with the first snowflakes, passengers continued to gather on deck to gaze along their northern route. Excited puffs of chatter blew away in the frozen wind as the trees grew thinner with each passing day.

A signal horn sounded from where the captain stood next to her great wheel. Demosyna looked toward the open waters, searching for the ship that had been spotted. The sun was sinking low in the sky, and cold fog had already formed as they sailed into arctic waters.

"I do hope that is not a pirate ship," the elaborate elf standing beside Demosyna muttered, removing a collapsible telescope from her robes. "I was told to be wary of such once we reach the free waters."

"Do you really think pirates would attack us right after crossing the border, Klai?" the other figure standing with Demosyna called, taking the offered telescope. "Besides, I think I can make out the sails."

He flipped up his visor and put the telescope to a compound eye.

"What is it, Bhreel?" the elf asked, nervously picking at the fur cuffs on her coat.

"It's the Empress's colors all right, and it's coming up fast," Bhreel responded with his deep, clicking voice.

His rigid skin was hardly visible in the helmet's shadow, but his eyes caught the fading light. Bhreel collapsed the small telescope with a clack, causing Klai to wince and pull a little bit of fur from the cuff she fiddled with.

"Give that back at once, you brute," Klai exclaimed, extending her arm expectantly. "That particular piece of equipment costs more for me to make than your payment. I would remind you to know your place once again, but I feel it will fall on deaf ears to an Orc like you."

"May I see, Wise Mother?" Demosyna asked, not wanting this to turn into another argument.

"No," Klai responded flatly, eyeing her fellow Wizen with barely concealed disdain. "I don't like flashing my equipment around where any urchin can make a mark of me. I do not trust any of these filthy seeders, especially in the wild."

Klai peered suspiciously at the other passengers gathering to watch the approaching imperial ship. Horns called between the two, and crew members dropped anchor to slow the overloaded passenger ship. Klai slipped the telescope back into her sleeve and found a vacant spot on the railing.

The imperial ship cut swiftly through the water on an intercept course with their civilian craft. Dark sails fluttered in the wind, bearing the crimson and white gold colors of the Empress. Oars on both sides rose and fell, their splashes barely noticed in the dark. Other than the vivid colors of the sails, the small ship bore no symbols or decorations on its hull.

"You can know the Empress's colors by their unique properties," Klai said, adopting a dry, lecturing tone. "Observe how the silver shines. That is because the thread is white gold woven into the silk. As for the crimson, each member of the unit contributes blood that is cursed by Wise-women to never fully dry," the Wise Mother finished, looking at her assigned pupil with a sharp expression.

Demosyna nodded before turning to watch the ship approach through the deep blues of the water. The dark red of the sails glistened, and Demosyna now knew it wasn't just from the icy spray.

There were only three people on the deck of the Empress's ship, leaving the craft looking barren to the thickly populated boat taking Demosyna north. The very short general stood at the wheel clad in silvery armor that shone in the remaining light, each movement sparkling with adjustments. The second figure stood at the mast and watched the cargo ship. A heavily armored cannon operator, at the front of the long deck, stood ready in deep-black armor matching the imposing cannon on a set of rails.

While still barely visible in the fog, all the oars stopped their rhythmic dance. They pulled into the ship at the silent command of the captain, letting the boat coast. The armored general walked to the telescope while issuing orders to those on deck via hand signals. The cannoneer at the front adjusted the artillery while the larger figure saluted and went belowdecks. A hush had fallen over the deck of her ship, and Demosyna held her breath as she awaited inspection.

The silence grew worse as the entire ocean seemed to still with the anxiety of the passengers. Demosyna, shifting back onto the flats of her feet, placed a hand gently on Klai's hand.

"I think it's just an inspection, Wise Mother," Demosyna said hopefully, glancing at their hired guard for confirmation.

Before the Orc answered, the apprentice felt Klai's hand shudder and pull away. As Klai took a sharp breath, she glared at the younger Wise-woman.

"How dare you!" Klai exclaimed, her voice shaky. "I cannot stand the feel of your slimy scales, as I have told you when we started this fool's errand. I am here as an observer only, because that is how you will be tested. I do not care that you have only one chance to prove your worth, Scale. I do not wish to interact with you unless it is mortally necessary."

Klai stood glaring at the apprentice before straightening up, brushing her robes.

Demosyna lowered her head, putting her hands in the pockets of her leather coat. The intimate quarters on the ship had enlightened Demosyna to her Wise Mother's view of herself as a student and as a person as well.

There was silence among the three, broken when Bhreel pointed at the captain walking back to the wheel.

"It looks like they just wanted to know who we were. Watch what happens next if you want," Bhreel said, shaking his head. "But that's enough excitement for me. I'm gonna go talk with the first mate. The next few days should prove interesting once we reach the ice shelves."

Klai turned and grabbed her own staff, carved with many intricate symbols. The entire inspection had taken only minutes and was carried out with eerie, silent precision. The deck slowly emptied the population of the ship, who had come up for the inspection and had grown bored.

A flat note sounded from the sleek military craft as the oars churned the icy waters. Even before the adjacent ship had gotten out of sight, two more blasts sounded in rapid succession. More ships came from the same southern direction the first had as the echoes faded. These transport boats were slightly larger than the commander's but moved without any sign of slowing.

Dark shapes in the water around the soldiers' boats signaled trailing aquatic troops—dolphins and great ring-toothed fish supporting the navy. Harnesses and reins soaked the water as chained Scales rode atop hovering moon squid. Before long, they caught up to the first ship, sleek and dark in the water.

As she leaned over the railing of her low ship, slow in unfurling its sails, Demosyna saw her reflection for the first time in the free waters. As far as she could tell, she didn't look any different despite now being free. She still had the same light-purple scales, the same sharp smile, and the curious yellow eyes she always had. The only difference in her reflection was the gold hoops on Demosyna's horns, picked from the endless supply in her apprentice hall.

Small waves lapped the side of the boat and sent her image swirling off into sparkling colors, rising in a cold spray. The foamy ocean stung her cheek with its touch, shocking the apprentice with the chill. Turning around as she pulled her outer cloak tighter, Demosyna scanned the deck of the ship she had been riding for weeks.

A sea of faces moved past her as she strode toward the center of the soaked deck. It was feeding time for the masses, and they clamored for a ration of food the ship's crew handed out. The crew and first class were in the front of the line, with many from the lower decks making up the rear.

It has been refreshing, Demosyna thought as she descended the stairs, *to simply be another body among so many others. At least their attention is on their own concerns and not on my ineptitude.*

"Not hungry again today, eh?" the first mate asked as Demosyna entered the mid deck.

The simple gold hoops adorning her horns trembled as the apprentice Wise-woman shook her head. Demosyna stood for a moment to dust off the snow from her outer coat, replying further once defrosted.

"No, ma'am. Thank you, but I ate this week already. Besides, the water is still not too cold for me to catch my meals."

Demosyna shrugged, shivering from the cold metal earrings.

"The last time I fished, there were only a few icebergs after all."

"Aye!" the first mate said, winking. "We've all seen how you go fishing! It's the only entertainment we get on seeder jobs."

This got a laugh from most of those belowdecks, along with a few whistles. The apprentice wasn't the only one of her kind on board the cargo liner. Many of her fellow passengers were also Scales. But she was the only one who still fished naked. Whenever Demosyna was craving food, she would remove her Wise-woman–issued clothes before crouching on the railing. A strong tail kept the apprentice balanced, leaving her sharp eyes to watch for fish. Then, with a flash, she would jump from the ship, her scaled body contrasting with the sky. Demosyna would become a soft-purple arc as she dived to fish, free of restrictions for that time.

Demosyna excused herself and pulled her coat tighter while passing through the boisterous crew. The sounds of laughter and the steady, creaking sway of the boat followed her. It had been a change to be thrust into close quarters with a diverse group, and such talk had begun to be expected. The majority of her peers had always been statuesque elves, living as she had in the Wise Orders, which held all knowledge in the world.

Demosyna adopted a gentle sway as she moved toward the back, with lower-class passengers and storage. Finding her cabin, she quietly slipped inside and saw her cabinmates asleep on the hard floor. She stepped carefully over the figures, sitting down on the apprentice chest. Her mind drifted away, feeling the carved surface and its time-smoothed symbols of crystal.

The apprentice remembered the day she was told of this journey and how happy she was to be afforded the opportunity.

* * * * *

Demosyna would now learn directly from her Wise Mother instead of behind all the others she trailed. Sitting alone in the empty apprentice housing, Demosyna had been reciting her lessons. The apprentice was again trying to channel something, a vague and hopeful anything, through her staff. So far, in her years as an adopted Wizen, Demosyna had not yet been able to perform any magic.

Over ten years had gone by in her formal training, and there had yet to be more than a passing word between her and Klai. Demosyna had watched students come and go, being transferred to higher levels of study. Sadly, Demosyna had yet to be proved as a Wizen and was viewed as a burden. Determined to change her novice skills, Demosyna once again recited the mantras taught to her by Klai.

Demosyna closed her eyes, feeling the smooth wood staff, and let her thoughts reach outward. She was familiar with each grain of the wood and began to recite passages learned from her lessons. After hours of this, sitting in meditation with her staff, Klai opened the wide door. Klai was dressed in extravagant finery, golden hair falling in an impeccable bob, and walked to where Demosyna was seated.

"I have an assignment that would be perfect for someone like you," the Wise Mother told her, a now familiar, sly look in her eye. "So many like you have already had the good sense to ship out without being told. At least you can be useful to the Orders and not continue to embarrass me."

"I want to help in any way I can, Wise Mother," Demosyna said earnestly, tilting her head. "Thank you for the opportunity even though I know there are more deserving students."

"There are indeed. But as I recall, you claimed you would do whatever it took to improve, did you not?"

Klai's voice echoed on the jade walls.

"The Wisest have decided to contact our lost northern Order. Apparently, mere decades are required for them to care about those seeder Wizen hiding in the north. Since the Wisest are in such a hurry, we are to set sail by the end of the season."

Demosyna was speechless upon hearing that she would go on such an important adventure. The Wise-woman Order established in the north lands had remained silent for over seventy years. No word had come from the Battle Wizen sent decades ago to contact the lost Order, nor did they return. A seemingly perpetual civil war, according to Demosyna's studies, had claimed the team, along with many other lives.

"I didn't agree, but due to the nature of the task, the Order has assigned equipment. I will handle the gold, naturally, and you will be responsible for everything else," Klai said, her arms crossing to remove a gold coin. "Use this to hire any strong arm who wants to join us on the last boat."

Klai gave the shocked young woman a single round coin before turning to walk away.

"Thank you, Wise Mother, for the chance to learn under you personally," Demosyna said, looking up from the golden coin in her hand with excitement. "I will try my best to make you and the other Wise Mothers proud!"

Klai's sharp elven face formed a thin smile.

"No, thank you. We leave in hardly any time. Be at the docks with the apprentice chest by the final changing of this season."

The rest of the year before getting on the boat was a blur of happy, frantic errands. The ship stood vivid and surreal, looming into view as she sat steering the cart. It had been a challenge, due to her unpopular position, for Demosyna to get another training Wizen to help. She convinced a short human man to assist her and thanked him again despite his complaints.

Chains rattled on flesh and rope strained against wood as the bustle of docks ebbed. Finding a space for their cart among the sweltering crowd, Demosyna left Klai at the elf's instructions. The young Wizen sought out the tavern where Bhreel was, having been hired to escort Klai. Her Wise Mother gave a hushed warning of cutthroats who followed Demosyna as she made her way through the crowd.

The fall weather was starting to turn frigid, and the coats of those around shone with brilliant patterns. This town had been an often-sought place, and Demosyna felt she would miss the wooden port. Long winter months would prevent any travel, leaving Demosyna in the Fist without contact to her home in the southern Orders. Because of this natural phenomenon, most referred to a year as season in reference to the frozen months cutting the calendar in half.

Dirty faces moved past Demosyna as the Gemini Maiden tavern appeared around a corner. She saw the Orc in his worn steel armor, leaning against a smoky chimney. Bhreel's long legs held the man over six feet tall, common among the Orcs Demosyna had encountered.

"Let me collect my gear, smooth scale," Bhreel said, eyeing the young woman before downing his cup.

Having only two bags, it was a simple matter for Bhreel to gather his things and follow her. Stopping at the barkeep, Bhreel filled four empty skins he removed from his pack. The sturdy man placed some tiny coins on the counter before motioning to the bartender.

"I'll be using the alley before I go," Bhreel said, tapping the bar and nodding toward Demosyna.

The two left the tavern but stopped shortly after when Bhreel called out. Curious, Demosyna followed to see the Orc removing his chest plate before picking up a large axe. She approached more cautiously as the figure looked over his shoulder, taking a step forward. Shadows hid the face of the powerful Orc, and Demosyna stopped with her heart racing.

Turning to fully face the figure approaching, the bare-chested Bhreel nodded toward a hollow. To Demosyna's fearful eyes, the buildings seemed to lean inward, swallowing her in darkness. Even without the heavy armor, the man was still covered in a solid mass of plates that looked impervious. Orcs often were compared to locusts from their look, but Demosyna found the chitin unique like her own scales.

"One last thing before we go," Bhreel said, producing a piece of wood. "It is surprising how fast a fire will deplete your kindling when traveling."

Both laughed, breaking the tension, and took turns splitting wood with the axe.

The walk back was sped along by the crowd eager to watch the last ship depart. Klai walked aboard without a word to seek out the captain once seeing Demosyna. The Wise Mother strode away to discuss the barrels that the Wizen was providing, leaving their wagon full.

Demosyna and Bhreel shouldered the contents aboard, Bhreel being strong enough to haul nearly everything. Demosyna sent the horse back with the grumbling human apprentice, waving goodbye to a retreating back.

"I see you have managed to find a seeding brute," Klai said, eyeing the Orc with distaste. "Even though you are an Orc, I expect you can understand what you were hired for. I require you to carry my instructions out to the letter and guard my person with your life."

Bhreel simply nodded.

"I understand completely. Despite being a male Orc, I am fully instructed in imperial hierarchy. I can also read three languages, if you wish to send the instructions in any formal manner."

Klai raised an eyebrow and held his gaze before nodding, satisfied. Demosyna breathed a sigh as the deck below her lurched forward with a start. The ship sailed out into the blue north, awash with fortune. A wide deck was broken up by masts and the raised back of the ship. One central staircase allowed travel to the lower decks, and all the wood smelled of adventure.

* * * * *

Returning from her thoughts with a sigh, Demosyna removed the soft leather she wore and put it away. The few possessions allowed to apprentices were also stored in the box, and Demosyna smiled at the items. Recent days had forced her to wear the coat more frequently than she cared to, but she wished to be cold even less. Apprentice robes hung long enough to scrape the ground, covering Demosyna's strong purple legs most times. With the thin garments stored away, the apprentice was able to wash her limbs as she hummed softly in her underclothes.

Demosyna felt better after the soft cloth had shined her bright scales with water from a skin, as she usually did when making her legs look softer. The apprentice was careful to not let the claws on her feet click against the floor, tucking a tail between her legs. The floor was cold and wet, but the heat of her traveling companions soon quieted her chilled scales. Demosyna was able to let the free waters rock her to a fitful sleep, the deep snores of her roommates like a mournful lullaby.

CHAPTER 2

Shivering herself awake, Demosyna watched her breath curl away to the ceiling. This was the first time the morning chill had been deep enough to show vapor, and the night sleeping on the unforgiving floor put knots in her joints. No worry was given to waking alone, as that had become a staple of the young woman's life. Even before the journey, Demosyna had found that the other Wizened cared little to wait for her to wake before starting their days.

Her companions must have gone to the deck for food, she thought while dressing. Demosyna tightened her belt and began her sunrise meditations. It was a habit, ingrained by the strict instruction of the Wise Mothers, to practice their channeling techniques. After seasons of practice, Demosyna felt no closer to what she wished for in life. She desired of herself to be a powerful Wizen, able to help others with her wisdom like the Wise Mothers she grew up under.

A knock at the door caused Demosyna to jump, having been lost in the morning's breathing exercises.

"Fine day for a swim, eh, Demosyna?" a fellow passenger asked, her green scales wet in the low light.

"Perhaps, once I am finished with my duties," Demosyna replied, looking up from her crouched position.

"We already went once but can go with you when you're ready," the smaller figure with orange-and-gold scales said, his hand never leaving the green-scaled woman's.

Demosyna smiled at the two as they walked away, thinking of her nearly empty stomach. The pair was among the humble few passengers whom Demosyna got to know during the journey and the only two who deigned to converse with her. Both had risked everything, selling their property and using their entire savings, to purchase tickets into icy lands of freedom and fable.

The cold drains my energy faster than I would have guessed if I am hungry again, Demosyna thought as she resumed her mental exercises.

After another hour, Demosyna stood and stretched her sore joints. The light of the morning sun shone down on the vast expanse of water surrounding the boat. Morning fog was dissipating grudgingly, giving way to a clear line of sight. The shore was to the right, always within visual range, showing the impassable dwarf-wood forests.

Cloaked figures with thick, reptilian tails crouched together against the cold. While approaching the group, her staff tapping in time with her steps, Demosyna's stomach began complaining. It was the smell of fresh fish reaching her nose that made her lick her dry lips eagerly with a long tongue.

"Anyone want to fish with me?" Demosyna asked, looking at the figures eating.

Many didn't look up from their meals, but the two Demosyna talked with earlier stood up.

"The water is getting so cold. It's going to be harder to fish soon. Rrra here didn't even want to after feeling the sea," the large green female Scale said, shivering in the wind.

Demosyna removed her outer cloak and instantly felt what the green woman meant. The arctic wind was constant, and the spray of the water stung with ice upon passing into free waters. After wrapping her cloak around her staff, Demosyna removed her remaining clothes and set them aside where they wouldn't get too wet.

Rrra looked at his orange-scaled hands.

"I wish I had the courage to swim like you do, Demosyna. Jui says she will do it with me, but I'm too shy."

Chuckling softly, Demosyna climbed up onto the railings of the deck to view the waters. The other two stepped up beside her and dived almost at once, wearing only their underclothes. Twin splashes rose in the clean light and glittered before turning into a spray, blanketing those who had begun gathering. Demosyna's purple scales glistened in the sun as she balanced, searching for a likely diving spot.

Taking a steadying breath, Demosyna leaped outward and dived nose first into the water. She pierced the churning waves with each limb tucked tightly, splashes forming at her entry. Chilly needles dug into her body while freezing skin and numbing bones. The touch of the sea was so unexpected that the apprentice sat frozen in shock, the pain of the cold filling her.

The last time she had gone fishing, the water had been chilled enough to make her shiver upon climbing back into the boat, a fresh catch between her teeth. The water now, however, was frigid beyond what she had felt in her life. Sunlight did nothing to warm Demosyna despite the bright glare of the midmorning light.

Bobbing in the clear water, she noticed shadows circling below. The two who had gone fishing with her were motioning the apprentice to follow, grinning. All three Scales swam off underwater together, leaving the boat behind as they moved into the open sea.

Once you get used to it, Demosyna thought, *the cold is not so bad. I just need to keep moving.*

Noticing a school of fish, Demosyna swam after the enticing mass. The two mates in the distance turned and swam back to join her. While blowing air from their nostrils, the three circled the school and took turns darting into the mass of food. Each scaled figure aided the other while trying their hand at catching a meal.

In little time, Demosyna had eaten several fish from the frenzied school. The young Wise-woman backed off the buffet while the other two continued. The confused fish huddled together in a tightly packed ball, the gator-like fishers keeping a circle on the prey. Once the other two had eaten their fill, Demosyna made one last pass through the teeming ball.

A bright sun shone in ribbons through the water as the three swam toward the surface, full and happy. Demosyna broke through the churning waves and blinked the salty water from her eyes. The wind had kicked up while they fished, pushing the clouds and boat farther north.

"Let's catch up to the ship," Demosyna said through clenched teeth when the other two broke the surface.

"What did you say?" Rrra asked, laughing, his bright scales shining.

Demosyna pointed toward the ship and opened her mouth to reply, but the fish held in her teeth seized the moment for escape. It thrashed its body off the needles impaling it, splashing back into the water. Demosyna dived under the water again in search of the lost fish, smiling to herself. The cold of the water was broken in small pockets as she swam, smelling dark blood left behind by the fleeing prey.

It took Demosyna longer than she liked to catch the ship due to its added speed given by the wind. The cold drained her energy, forcing her to rest, gripping the hull. Being carried through the water still felt foreign to her, but Demosyna was adapting to the new style of fishing.

Once she caught her breath, Demosyna climbed up the side with her strong hands and feet. The wind sliced into her during the ascent, and the young apprentice was shivering by the time she reached the railing. Finding her belongings, Demosyna sat down upon the small bundle and tore the fish in half.

After eating the tail in a few bites, Demosyna put the gasping head aside. She began wiping the water off her scales with her coat, careful to dry her horns. The wind ran over her already cold, sensitive body, causing her nipples to harden and teeth to chatter uncontrollably. Demosyna had to avoid the air trying to take her clothes but soon stood in her bright-green robes.

"Catch anything good, Demosyna?" Bhreel's deep voice called as he approached. "It took longer for you to fish today, little Scale, but I watched you swim back."

Demosyna held out the fish head to the approaching Orc before replying.

"I wouldn't forget about you, Bhreel. I don't look forward to fishing again, but the weather makes me hungrier than normal," she said as Bhreel ate the offered fish.

Bhreel responded with a sympathetic expression, "Thank you for the fresh meat. The food they serve the passengers here is just shy of horrible, but I guess it beats having to swim."

Demosyna shrugged and looked out toward the wall of trees along the shore. The ship required all her kind to find their own food, forcing amphibious people to swim for meals. Despite being a Wizen, albeit an apprentice, and having a government ticket, Demosyna was expected to forage.

During the silence while Bhreel brought out a pipe, Demosyna watched those on deck retreat to the warmth below. Strong clouds rose into the sky as the Orc smoked thoughtfully. Demosyna sighed, drawing her hood and rubbing her arms.

"I did prefer fishing when I was younger, feeling the warm water and the soft mud. This ocean is too cold to swim in long, but at least I can fish with others. That way, I am not looking for hours, hoping to find a slow fish!"

Exhaling a thick cloud of smoke, Bhreel moved behind the shivering Wizen. The man rubbed her upper arms while holding the pipe with strong jaws. Demosyna felt that his fingers were rigid with jointed chitin like the man's entire frame. Unlike her kind, who had scales, Orcs often had an exoskeleton of natural armor. She laughed and thanked Bhreel, who smoked with his pipe in his mandibles.

"That is much warmer, thank you. I won't say a word, not after you got yelled at by Klai. I'm glad you decided to come with us even though it means being in the Fist for years," Demosyna said, turning to look at Bhreel. "Even though the ticket was free, you were the only one wishing to join us."

Bhreel grunted sadly and looked around at the bundled figures on deck. The passengers traveled north in hope of being granted the chance to gain citizenship. This final boat of the season carried mostly noncitizens during the dangerous voyage. Even though Demosyna was a Wizen, she was relegated to the lower tiers of society as a seeder kind.

"I spent fourteen years as a bodyguard for a politician. She fired me when I asked to be made head of security, just like that," Bhreel said, snapping his fingers. "Fourteen years of knocking heads, and not so much as two coins to rub together. When you offered me the chance to get a fresh start with your Orders, I couldn't pass it up. The land I will get to buy for being a citizen is a good bonus as well! I waited fourteen for nothing, but the next ten years will be worth it."

"Well, getting those fish heads you like is another bonus for your troubles," Demosyna said, smiling widely.

Bhreel laughed and tapped his pipe over the side to send hot ash into the water with a hiss.

"Klai ordered me to return once I got food, but I waited to check on you. You should see a fort at some point soon, if this wind keeps up," Bhreel said as he walked away.

After stamping her booted feet, Demosyna walked to the other side to Jui and Rrra. A game of dice was already in progress, and as Demosyna approached, a losing roll caused travelers to groan in frustration. The dice were old wooden cubes and clearly not weighted correctly from the shoddy production.

"I told them not to gamble their food. The water was so cold, I don't want to swim again. Lucky most of our cabinmates have small appetites, or we would be swimming every hour of the day!" Jui said, chuckling and holding Rrra.

Demosyna sighed at the gamblers as a few edible scraps were taken. Two of the group shuffled off and began eating their prizes. The remaining of the bunch grabbed the dice and began placing bets again.

"My outer coat is wet, but it may warm you better than the soaked clothes I see you in," Demosyna said, removing her coat.

"Thank you," the mates said in unison with looks of hopeful gratitude on their shivering faces.

The brightly scaled couple communally wrapped it around themselves, becoming a mass of light-green leather. Demosyna smiled and propped her staff against the railing to let the thin strip of securing cloth arc with the steady winds.

"My pleasure. The more I get used to the cold, the better I can serve the Orders. If it's this cold here, it will be much colder when we disembark," the young apprentice said, her yellow eyes gleaming.

Jui and Rrra soon warmed beneath the coat and turned to peer north. A shape loomed on the horizon, almost invisible in the fog. Each passing moment, the ship moved closer until Demosyna could make out what obscured the view of unending cliffs.

"A fort!" Rrra said, excitement in his voice. "We can finally make a fire and have hot food again."

Demosyna shaded her eyes with a hand and peered at the distant spec ahead of them.

"Unless the fort is built in the water, we may be dealing with something else," Demosyna said with curiosity, studying the gigantic shape through the fog.

A wall of ice stretching from the shore into the ocean materialized, and the ship slowed to avoid a collision. Once the glacier came into view, Demosyna saw the massive cliff of ice sitting frozen in her path north. The solidified ocean stood in near-dead stillness, rising into the air and shadowing the deck. Many pieces fell before breaking and splashing down from the weight of the frozen waves.

Pulling herself from the chilled spectacle, Demosyna saw crewmates wheeling barrels up from belowdecks. Recognizing the symbols, she walked with the aid of her staff to watch. Bhreel was moving the last of the barrels into a rowboat as Demosyna observed with interest.

"Only one thing to do now—not blow yourselves up," Bhreel said to the crew, wiping his brow with a cloth.

After two sailors climbed aboard the rowboat, five crewmates began lowering the boat into the water.

Bhreel walked over to where Demosyna stood watching, stretching his arms.

"If they can avoid capsizing, we should be in for quite a show over the next few days," Bhreel said as he rested next to Demosyna. "We have reached the frozen coasts, and this is going to be something to get used to."

"Those were the hardest part of loading the cargo," Demosyna said, reflecting on the lessons Klai gave. "The Orders only allowed us access to such quantities because Klai is a master alchemist. She fretted about how the captain stored them, enough that the first week, she slept with the cargo."

Both travelers shared a laugh at the worrying of the Wise Mother. Klai's fretting hands had wrung themselves raw over the thought of her precious barrels.

"Once the air turned cold, she changed her tune," Bhreel said, chuckling. "She may not be fond of me, but she is grateful I am so warm."

As the rowboat reached an icy wall, the crowd shifted for a better view. Demosyna stood on the railing and watched them place the barrels in hollows carved using pickaxes. Whatever storm froze these waves also churned them dozens of feet above the water, solidifying the mass into an angular iceberg.

Moving with delicate speed, the rowboat returned to the cargo ship. Demosyna crouched to watch through the railing as the rowboat pulled alongside. The first of the crew was just beginning to climb when a thunderous boom shook the air, surprising the sailor. Heat bloomed orange, and Demosyna turned, startled, toward a cloud of steam. Cries of dismay from the crowd were drowned out by two more deafening explosions that sent chunks of ice scattering.

As the second explosion sounded, Demosyna looked back down at the water to avoid the glare. The expression of shock on the crewmate's face didn't change as a huge piece of ice tumbled in the third explosion. Ice tore the top half of her body off in its screaming path, not slowing in its arc. A great rending sound accompanied the piece of ice gouging holes in the ship, which rocked wildly from impact. Mist hung in the air as the crewmate's limp legs fell into the water with a crimson splash.

Shards of ice splintered the deck, where the crowd huddled to shelter themselves against the needles. Both of the masts had their sails damaged with several hanging uselessly in the breeze. Moments after the last splashes signaled the end of danger, a collective roar filled the air.

The newly bloodied crewmate remaining in the small boat was yelling with a hole now in the place of the ladder. Demosyna saw faces, also covered in freshly flowing blood, emerge from the hole. They were frightened, along with Demosyna, and she turned her attention around numbly. Some of the passengers on deck when the icy debris rained down were struck and lay scattered among the crowd.

Working her way through the bodies, Demosyna walked to the front of the ship with ringing ears. The young woman saw the straight channel sheared through the ice, barring their path no longer. One of the frozen waves crashed into the water and began floating north as a jagged iceberg.

"If those two had secured them properly, the reaction would have happened as planned," Klai informed the first mate. "I tried on numerous occasions to enlighten you about the delicate nature of the barrels. I relayed clear and detailed instructions, and I am not responsible for the undisciplined rabble you call crew."

"Look at the damage you caused with three barrels. How many others did you bring aboard? Seven? Ten?" the first mate asked, her face almost as red as her hair. "I haven't seen the hole you put in the side, but I'm told it will prevent us from sailing."

"I have made a path despite the unintended side effects," Klai said in a loud voice. "I suggest you remind your captain that..."

Both the first mate and Klai were shouting and simply not to be heard over the noise. The captain, an average-looking woman with a large stomach and bowed legs, ordered the deck cleared for repairs. The first mate stood still for a moment before meeting the captain at the large wheel.

Demosyna brushed melting shards off her light-green robes and followed Klai. A room directly across from theirs was exposed from the damage, Demosyna saw on the worried faces in the hallway.

Once Klai had locked the door, she turned angrily to Demosyna.

"Did you touch any barrels?" Klai asked, her voice hushed.

Demosyna shook her head, eyes widening in confusion. It was not like her Wise Mother to show such open aggression, even toward Bhreel. The apprentice had not been near the barrels since loading them, as her Wise Mother instructed. The furious elf got the same response when Klai asked Bhreel about tampering with the barrels.

"Where is your coat?" Klai asked sharply, turning back to Demosyna and cutting her off. "If you have lost it, we cannot get you a new one this far north. Go get it back, as I will have no more mistakes on this trip."

Demosyna walked from the cabin in a daze to the sound of Klai pacing. Thinking back, Demosyna had yet to see her Wise Mother so angry about anything. Demosyna let slow feet carry her along while finding Jui and Rrra among the lower levels. Their cabin, it turned out, had nearly half the wall torn off when the ice hit the ship. Already, the shared cabin was frigid, and the two sat huddled in the warmest available corner. They had wrapped themselves in the jade cloak Demosyna loaned and smiled at the woman.

"Oi, Demosyna," Jui said as she saw the light-purple figure approach through the snow.

Any ground nearest the open wall was covered with water, making that corner slippery and unusable. Several passengers attempted to block the incoming spray with blankets, but the flimsy barrier failed to resist the cold. The cloth flexed in the wind as a poor replacement for the wood taken by ice.

Demosyna greeted the two as she crouched, feeling the cold begin to bite into her scales. Noticing a small barrel between the mates, Demosyna gestured.

"Why don't you start a fire in that barrel? If you avoid letting the flames get too tall, it should provide a good amount of heat," Demosyna said, brushing a bit of snow from her tail.

Rrra bent closer to Demosyna.

"We were going to share this with you for being kind to us, especially Jui. We have been nesting on this. Just promise not to share with that elf!"

Rrra winked slyly and used a claw to remove the lid. Strong vapors arose, and Demosyna smelled the bitter fruit scent. Smiling herself, the apprentice leaned back to avoid having the fumes bring tears to her eyes. Closing the lid again, Jui reached over and pulled the coat to hide it from view.

"I would like to try that! Did the captain say when the repairs would be started?" Demosyna asked, motioning to the large hole inadequately covered.

Jui shook her head.

"The last anyone heard, they were still discussing it in their dining room. If it is not soon, I am not sure what we can do about this cold."

Nodding slightly, Demosyna broached the subject she had come to see the two about.

"I am sorry to have to take it back so soon, but I need the coat that I lent you," the apprentice said, watching a gust of wind make a blanket flap.

Rrra looked at his mate with big eyes, and the two exchanged hushed words before unwrapping the coat. Before Demosyna could open her mouth, Jui held up her hand.

"Thank you for your kindness, Demosyna. Do not be sorry you are collecting what is yours," Jui said with a slight smile, kissing Rrra. "We may just have to finish the barrel tonight instead of when we arrive at New Empress City."

Jui hugged Rrra, causing him to snuggle closer into her arms while laughing.

Demosyna held a flask out to Jui with a smile.

"We can use this to try it!"

A round crystal window showed the flask was empty, so Jui and Rrra huddled together while filling the jade container. Several others in the room looked over, and Demosyna stood to deliberately fold her large coat. The rough shield worked, and those looking their way went back to their own interests. Sitting back down, Demosyna saw Jui take a sip from the flask. Jui's eyes widened, and she pushed the drink into Rrra's hand while stifling a cough.

Rrra smiled and took a sip of the refined wine for himself. His reaction to the mouthful was exactly that of Jui's—struggling to hold a cough while passing it to Demosyna.

As the tempting smell of the drink rose to her nostrils, Demosyna took a small sip. The liquor burned at the first touch of the liquid, and she swallowed quickly. This proved to be the mistake the other two made, and the warm burn caused Demosyna to cough. An initial fire was replaced by the biting flavors of homemade wine, and Demosyna enjoyed her first drink with friends.

The three passed the small flask around the circle, and the second time, they all were able to avoid choking. Demosyna asked Rrra how the wine was so strong, having never smelled anything like it.

Rrra took the flask.

"That is my family's recipe, Demosyna. Besides starting a nest, that is one of the reasons we need to become citizens. With the land we are allowed to buy, I will start a brewery with Jui!"

Rrra's eyes took on a faraway sheen as the orange-scaled man spoke. Jui kissed Rrra, who sighed and blushed shyly as he returned from his thoughts.

Demosyna smiled and took the flask again as Rrra passed it to her. Finishing the wine off, Demosyna had begun to store the flask back in her coat sleeve when Jui smiled crookedly.

"Let me give you some for later," Jui said, taking the opaque jade vessel and filling it. "Rrra was raised to brew, but I was schooled on numbers and ledgers! Our books are always tidy since I taught myself written words to sell the liquor."

"If I am able, I will lend my jacket again," Demosyna said, standing and tucking the leather under her arm.

Jui whispered, laughing with Rrra, "If the cold doesn't get us, we welcome that. Hopefully, by tomorrow, the crew will have decided how to fix the hole in their ship."

Demosyna walked carefully over the prone bodies, each wrapped in many layers to avoid the chill. She passed the first mate while returning to Klai, busy gathering tools. The young woman noticed the activity and walked on to tell her Wise Mother about the repairs starting. Bhreel, sitting in a corner of the common area, was approached by the first mate, holding tools.

As Demosyna walked the narrow hallway toward the shared cabin, she saw the door was open. Klai was pacing alone in the cabin, but the lock being cracked alarmed Demosyna. Once she reached the door, Demosyna saw something that made her worry.

As Klai walked the room, her hands clutched together, she shook her head in sharp motions. On Klai's face was an expression Demosyna had never seen on any elven face—one of uncertainty. Then with a violent twist of her slender neck, Klai changed her expression from confusion to anger and back again. As the door was slowly pushed open, Klai instantly regained composure.

"Good. You seem to have located the rest of your uniform. What news of the repairs?" Klai asked shortly.

"The repairs have begun, it seems. I saw the first mate getting things underway," Demosyna said, quietly sitting down. "She was talking to Bhreel earlier."

Klai nodded and remained facing away with the snow drifting through the window. Crisp light cast thin shadows in the fading day, and Demosyna saw a bird make its fleeting profile. For a long moment, there was silence in the room with small puffs of breath lingering in the still air.

Heavy footsteps approached their cabin in a familiar hopping stride, and Bhreel knocked on the door.

"Enter," Klai said, viewing the small window high in the wall.

Bhreel walked in and set down two flagons on the single chest serving as the room's table. Bhreel motioned for Demosyna to take one before turning in a formal posture to Klai.

"I have been assigned to collect wood to aid in the repairs. The first mate said that any nonessential wood is to be delivered to the deck," Bhreel said, removing his helmet. "I have also filled these with water, as you requested."

"Very well. You may accompany me to the captain to hear her explanation," Klai said, finally turning to face the two. "I have your contract, and that will be that."

"As you say, ma'am. I will need to take our wood with me, as each cabin is responsible for their own portions."

Bhreel bowed quickly, holding up a small tool.

"That is ridiculous. This cabin doesn't have any extra wood. If the captain means my chest, then she is out of line," Klai said, anger rising in her voice.

"No, ma'am, not the chest. The door and the shutter are the shipmaster's property," Bhreel informed, turning to gesture at the metal clasps with the tool he was holding.

Klai stood silently for a moment before ordering Bhreel to follow her. People in the hall jumped aside, and Klai stormed down the hallway at a near jog.

Sitting on the floor, Demosyna heard those gathering in the hallway discussing the new situation. Several of the crewmates were shouting what the captain had decided—that all wood was to be brought up to the deck. Demosyna spotted Rrra coming from around the corner while working her way through the crowd. Rrra was in near panic when Demosyna reached him and clutched her robes with tears in his eyes.

"They found our smuggled barrel when they came to tell our cabin," Rrra said, his eyes wide. "Now Jui is in trouble."

Demosyna put her hands on the trembling man's arms and tried to steady him. She walked up for fresh air, holding an arm around Rrra's shoulder. Crewmates were busy running between workbenches to deliver the raw wood. Others took the cut planks to damaged areas of the ship, so the two avoided the clamor.

"Tell me what happened," Demosyna said. "I'm sure it isn't as bad as you are saying."

Rrra wiped his eyes and shook his head.

"Because we smuggled it in, they destroyed the barrel for repair wood. That wouldn't be so bad if the punishment for smuggling wasn't ten lashings."

"Ten lashings?" Demosyna cried in dismay. "Rrra, there must be some mistake."

"No mistake," he said, beginning to cry again.

From across the deck, one of the crew shouted for Demosyna to get to work. With a final promise to return for Rrra, Demosyna walked back to her cabin. Using the tool to pry the studs out was no easy feat, but with a little effort, they began to come loose.

For nearly an hour, she wrested the hinges apart, straining against the tool. It was tiring work, and Demosyna took a break to watch her breath drift in the air. It was still a new thing to see, as she had never seen snow till weeks into the trip. A sudden cold drop had caused the rain to explode into ice, and the excited woman had rushed onto the deck.

Demosyna was picturing the way the sun caused the world to sparkle, a thousand rainbows of sleet, when Klai came back to the cabin. Klai noticed the work Demosyna had done on the hinges, smiling slightly at the young woman.

"Your efforts prove in vain once again," Klai said, pulling down her hood. "I have reminded the captain of why she has us on the ship. In light of these facts, we have been permitted to keep our door and shutters."

"I see, Wise Mother. Will there be enough wood for the repairs, then?" Demosyna asked, gathering the hinges.

"That isn't my concern, and I didn't ask," Klai said, turning to the window with a serene expression on her face.

Bhreel helped Demosyna put the door back together, and as they finished, a crewmate yelled the news that all passengers were to come onto the deck at the captain's orders. Klai remained with her back to them, saying nothing, and Bhreel replied by shrugging.

Demosyna made her way to the deck while Klai and her bodyguard trailed behind. Once the damaged deck was crowded with people, the captain called for silence.

"There were smuggled goods found in a cabin," the captain yelled, her voice carrying over the hushed crowd. "The punishment is ten lashings. Guards, seize the representatives of cabin 14 and tie them to the railing for punishment."

With that, the captain stepped back to the wheel, and armed crew began rounding up passengers. Watching in dismay, Demosyna saw Rrra grasping at his mate as Jui was dragged off. A loud murmur was running through the crowd, and many were openly begging the captain. Seven passengers were dragged to the front of the ship with their shirts removed, exposing their backs. Their hands were tied, and the women stood struggling in the sun.

The first mate came with a small whip, and the crowd parted. Demosyna watched, shocked, as each of the women received ten quick lashings. Cries of pain echoed in the afternoon air, and then the civilians were taken back to their cabin. Many had to be carried, as they had fainted from the cruel whip that had scarred their backs. The crowd dispersed, and the crew began to speed along with the repairs once again.

As a crew member came with a mop for the blood, Demosyna made her way slowly back to her cabin. She was sickened by the brutal sight just witnessed and wanted to be alone. Low grumbles of displeasure resonated from around the young woman as the passengers took down their doors. Demosyna wanted desperately to check on Jui, but her way was blocked by men whose mates were punished.

"You and those two drank and lied. You knew they had the contraband, and you didn't warn us," one of the angry men shouted. "And now I hear you get to keep your door, stuck-up things you are. Leave us be, you apprentice snake."

Demosyna opened her mouth to reply but closed it again when she saw the expressions on their faces. Anger mixed with deep hopelessness swam over them, so Demosyna offered no word of protest. It was likely true, what they said, she thought sadly, since disappointment was all she had caused her whole life. Demosyna walked away with her head down and a new ache in her heart.

CHAPTER 3

It wasn't until sunset before the ship was repaired enough to continue through the gap made by the explosives. As the sail was readied, many of the crew went back to their posts. A select few remained to finish the repairs, but the captain ordered the ship moving. Not many of the passengers left their cabins, preferring instead to huddle for warmth inside the hull. Windows and doors now offered no protection and left most cabins frigid and damp.

The large ship began moving with a jolt and navigated the wide cut in the wall of frozen sea. In the faint light of the setting sun, the ice became a deep red purple of blood. Once the sun was gone, much of the sky was obscured by the deadly walls on each side.

The lack of light gave the captain pause, and she sent for the only Wise-women on board. Both Demosyna and Klai protested the apprentice's involvement, to no success.

"We need you two to light the path, Madams Wizened," the captain said, motioning. "Please illuminate the way, and we can be through this channel you made before morning."

"It will not be an issue for me. However, this apprentice has shown no aptitude for magic. She will try of course, but I have little faith that she will succeed," Klai said.

"Is this true?" the captain asked, frowning at Demosyna.

"Yes. I have been studying hard for years but have yet to perform magic," Demosyna said, gazing at her staff.

"Well, that was unexpected," the captain sighed, running a hand across her brow. "I've never heard of any Wizen in your position. Let our cargo serve as motivation, shall we?"

Without waiting for a response, the captain turned on her heel and strode away. The first mate returned control to the captain before helping with a crew member tugging a rope. Demosyna looked over to where Klai was straightening her robes, statuesque and motionless. The elf placed her staff at an angle against the deck of the ship before untying the securing cord.

Concentrating hard on a glyph from her studies, Demosyna tried to bring light into the world. For several moments, it was as it always had been with the staff cast in shadow and no hint of magic. Suddenly, Demosyna felt drained in a way she hadn't experienced while trying to summon. It was as if her energy was being lost at an alarming rate. Yet the staff had no change at all.

Klai watched from across the deck before turning back to her own staff. The cloud Klai exhaled followed a blinding beam into the night sky, scattering the shadows. A magical light began small, just the diameter of the staff. But after a heartbeat, the energy began pulsing erratically. Demosyna had been removing her own staff's tethers, mirroring Klai, when the magic was cast.

The glowing beam formed into a sphere, causing Klai to cry out in surprise. Demosyna turned from the sudden light and had to cover her eyes as well. Spots of bright afterimages filled her vision, and Demosyna heard those on the deck fall to their knees. The ball of searing light vanished as Klai dropped her staff to sever connection.

There was a commotion as the crew began stumbling around, having been watching closely to see magic. The captain was yelling for all sailors to remain still, but it was too late. One of the crewmates fell over the side while searching for a handhold with her eyes dazzled. A broken railing wasn't repaired, and the poor woman dropped from sight.

Demosyna wasn't facing her Wise Mother when the spell was cast and had only a bright dot blocking her sight. The apprentice heard the crewmate's cry and rose to unsteady feet.

"My staff!" Klai yelled. "We are lost without it."

Demosyna saw the rod rolling along the deck, even with spots in her vision. She began running and kicked at it while leaping over the boat. Her Wise Mother was powerful, Demosyna knew, and the staff would allow aid with healing spells. There was no time to undress, and jade-green robes fluttered in the cutting wind.

"Here, Wise Mother," Demosyna called out, the staff skittering across the deck after a kick.

Her vision was returning, but even without clear eyes, Demosyna could see where to jump. Torches on the ship let her catch a glimpse of the blinded woman who struggled against the churning waters. A wave caused the woman's head to be driven into the ice with a sickening crack. Her heavy coat soaked up water and began to drag the crew member under, so Demosyna swam onward with more vigor. As she approached the helpless woman, the unfortunate crewmate vanished under the surface.

Powerful waves jostled the apprentice this way and that before smashing the woman into a broken ice wall, rattling her greatly. It took only seconds to recover, but pain was seeping into her body as the silver-haired figure sank. Demosyna dived frantically after the sailor, but the strip of night above provided no sign of the drowning deckhand. Looking all around her, Demosyna swam deeper toward the last place she had seen the sinking body. Her muscles ached when pushed deeper into the frigid water after the woman was lost from view.

I can stay under forever, but how long can she hold her breath? Demosyna thought, straining for any light.

Desperation had begun seeping into her, a frustrated resignation of her weaknesses, when the sky above shone with a brilliant light. The darkness was beaten back in an instant, showing the sinking form of the crewmate. She was meters away but being swallowed by the deep ocean. Demosyna rushed toward her with muscles straining in the soaked clothing now threatening them both.

Clawed hands tore through the sailor's clothing as Demosyna grabbed the motionless woman. She began swimming up as fast as her tired frame allowed, leaving a trail of blood behind. As she approached the surface, Demosyna could see the ball of blinding light held at the front of the ship. This allowed the light to be blocked by the prow and avoid blinding anyone with its brilliance.

Swimming toward the back of the ship to avoid the magic, the apprentice rose to the surface. Demosyna held the limp sailor above the water while desperately clawing at the boat. All the panicking woman could muster was a loud croak with water filling her mouth as Demosyna tried to get help.

Klai, while holding her staff, was hastily wrapping a cloth around her eyes. The radiance of the spell washed the Wise Mother in clean light, setting the jewels on her robes ablaze with color.

Crew members responded to Demosyna's calls, and the young woman tied ropes around the drowning sailor. The first mate joined the rescue with her muscular arms straining to pull them up. The work was slow due to the illuminated walls of ice on either side of the boat. Several of the blinded crew had the rope slip, but the first mate continued pulling. The first mate had blood coming from between her white knuckles but pulled without noticing the severe rope burns.

Even keeping her eyes open was a challenge, with the sparkly walls threatening to overwhelm. Demosyna held desperately to the rope, a helpless body during the slow trip. Crewmates joined from belowdecks to assist with their uncompromised vision, but most were still blind.

Panting after climbing onto the deck, Demosyna unclenched her frozen hand from the sailor. The young woman watched as the crewmate was revived by the first mate, providing a skilled display of sailor craft. Demosyna collapsed on the deck of the ship before beginning to shiver uncontrollably. With stiff hands, one of which had freezing blood on the nails, Demosyna removed her green robes.

Each numb step was exhausting, and the wind howling through the ice channel pierced into her. Demosyna saw her shadow dance crookedly while it limped along the wall, frail and useless. The larger shadow cast by Bhreel rushed to join Demosyna's, and he helped her downstairs.

"That was a great thing you did, little Scale," Bhreel whispered to Demosyna. "You saved a life tonight."

Demosyna reached out to grab a piece of firewood, but her arm was shaking too much. She dropped the wood with a clatter and sighed in frustration. Bhreel retrieved the dropped piece of kindling to deposit it into the kitchen embers before rushing to get a blanket. Bhreel gave Demosyna the wrap once she had stopped shivering, with the fire beginning to calm her violent body.

During the few minutes he was gone, Demosyna heard the cheers as the rescued woman was carried down. The captain herself approached the two huddled figures, putting a hand on each of their shoulders.

"If your Wise Mother hadn't healed our eyes, we may have been in trouble. At least you didn't nearly get people killed with your magic," the captain said, silhouetted from behind. "Thank you for rescuing our sister here. You will have double rations for your bravery."

Still too cold to speak, Demosyna smiled weakly while nodding. For the next few hours, Demosyna warmed herself and rested from the strenuous ordeal. The woman she had rescued was carried away, but Demosyna stayed near the fire. A curfew that the ship observed ensured Demosyna remained undisturbed, thawing in the belly of the craft.

Resting her chin on cold hands, she chided herself for yet again failing to perform magic. It had seemed so close this time that the apprentice could almost see the end of her staff begin to shine. The draining sensation was an exciting development for Demosyna, as her observations of magic often left her fellows exhausted. Yet for all the feelings of being on the edge of a crucial step, she had failed to make the jump to understanding.

A small consolation she found was the fact that she saved a life. Aided by her familiarity with swimming in the frozen ocean—for fish over the past weeks—the young Wizen hadn't given a second thought before jumping.

The boat left the massive ice walls, and the light streaming into the lower deck cut off. Demosyna walked back to her cabin while holding her clothes in a wet bundle. Laying them out to dry beside the mat serving as a bed, Demosyna covered herself with the blanket. The apprentice was so tired that she was asleep before Klai returned.

The Wise Mother set her staff against the wall and collapsed into a seated position in a corner. Sweat matted her typically pristine blonde hair till Klai's magic fixed it the next morning. Klai wrapped herself in voluminous robes, and she, too, fell asleep at once. The ship sailed on through the starlight, and its passengers slept uneasily. Wind howled pain from the hasty repairs, and many found rest impossible.

Demosyna remained in her cozy room for the next several days, having eaten recently and not desiring any cold stares. Many of the other passengers had taken to glaring at her about the ship with anger stamped on their faces. She instead sent all the rations of food the captain allowed to Jui and Rrra. It wasn't much, but Demosyna hoped it could serve to help during the last part of this journey.

The captain allowing her to keep the basic warmth provided by shutters and a door proved invaluable for recovery. Demosyna quickly regained her energy, resting her strained body in relative privacy. The apprentice also lost the persistent chill that had haunted her after rescuing the sailor, with Klai's potions. The few times Demosyna did venture out of her cabin, she was met with alarmingly opposite reactions.

Many of the passengers were angry with her, yet the crew was overjoyed by her heroic presence. Whispered insults would follow behind Demosyna as smiling crew passed with friendly waves. Demosyna tried once to visit with her friends a deck below but found the way still blocked by furious passengers. The near-hostile people were among those who had also felt the captain's wrath, so Demosyna left with a resigned sigh.

Klai, too, rarely left the cramped room, save to oversee the detonation of her barrels. Twice, another ice wall was encountered, halting the boat with a resounding horn. Klai insisted she oversee everything from here on out to avoid further damage to the boat. Once the ship stopped a safe distance from the ocean wall, the crew would detonate the barrels to cut a path. Upon returning the second time, Klai had a pleased expression on her face as the boat began moving again.

"It was simply a matter of portion," Klai said, turning to Demosyna with a flourish of robes. "The error was caused by the potency of the reagents. Perhaps the deplorable storage conditions of the barrels are to blame."

Nodding in thought at the lesson, Demosyna stood to stretch her back. Bhreel moved his legs to allow this and looked up when addressed.

"How close are we to the First Fort? I am anxious to go for a walk on dry land!" Demosyna said, her eyes alight.

"We should see it with your spyglass by sunset, I'd say. It's the best one I've seen."

Bhreel nodded toward Klai.

"But it'll still be another day before we reach it. That spyglass can see farther than you would believe, but the favorable wind is dying."

Demosyna gathered her coat to go above deck after bowing to her Wise Mother. Passing empty doorframes, she tried to avoid the unhappy stares of the occupants inside. Removing a spyglass from her robes, Demosyna looked along the route the boat sailed.

Sure enough, far in the distance, there was a wide circular tower on a rare low area. A harbor fanned out near the base, and two boats were tied up on the docks. Demosyna couldn't make out any people moving around, so she closed the telescope and returned it to her robes. As she did, Rrra came from belowdecks onto the sun-bleached planks.

"Rrra, over here," Demosyna called, waving.

Demosyna sat beside Rrra, resting her staff across her lap to sit closer.

"How are you and Jui?" Demosyna asked, putting her arm around the small man beside her.

"We have basic salves we made from aquatic plants. She is in a lot of pain, and the cold water from the walls isn't helping," Rrra said, sighing deeply and trying to maintain his composure. "I really appreciate the food you have given us, as it helps calm our cabinmates. They are so angry, though. I'm not sure we should continue after the fort. Jui agrees and just wants to recover in a bed."

The two sat in silence for a long moment and watched the coast float by.

If Jui and Rrra disembark, I will only have Bhreel for company, Demosyna thought before she shook her head. *No, it will be best for her to recover on land. I shouldn't be so selfish. And we can always stay in touch. Jui said she can write and teaches Rrra too!*

To break the silence, Demosyna removed her spyglass and offered it to Rrra as his orange scales shone in the light.

"You can see the fort from here, Rrra, but we will get there tomorrow sometime, I think," Demosyna said, pointing northward.

Rrra stood and focused the glass until he let out a cry of joy, sighting the tower in the far distance. It was still invisible to the naked eye, but the multiple lenses could be adjusted to see beyond the horizon.

"It is there, just there! What a tiny dot!" Rrra exclaimed, smiling for the first time since he sat. "I'll go tell Jui how close we are. Thank you, Demosyna. See you on shore!"

He handed the telescope back, and Demosyna smiled as he ran across the deck. Seeing Rrra again had brightened the young woman's day, and Demosyna continued smiling to herself. Looking through the glass one last time in the fading light, she saw dots on the two ships. The apprentice gently collapsed the delicate tool and put it away into a sleeve of her light-green robes.

As Demosyna walked slowly back to her cabin, the wind did indeed begin to slow its piercing battery. After several hours, however, the wind died out altogether, and the captain ordered the anchor dropped. For the first time in weeks, Demosyna slept without the rhythmic rocking motion that the ship provided. It was odd at first, as she seemed to have gotten used to the sensation, but Demosyna fell asleep after her evening meditations, eager to reach the slaver fort.

CHAPTER 4

Demosyna slept well for the majority of the evening, her rest only broken when horn blasts sounded. Footsteps and muffled voices filled the still air as the first rays of sun began to filter through the shuttered window. Their cabin was cramped, a chest taking up an entire corner, but the three threw off the blanket they shared to rouse themselves.

Awaking with a shivering start, Klai wrapped herself in her elaborate robe before addressing Demosyna.

"What new wonder has the captain formulated? We were anchored all night, so we cannot have reached port already. Follow me when you have finished your duties," Klai ordered while frowning and motioning impatiently at Bhreel.

Winking at the seated young Wizen, Bhreel left the apprentice with her thoughts in the chorus of horn blasts. After finishing the morning stretches in her modest cabin, Demosyna gathered the blankets. Sitting down with her staff across her knees, Demosyna tried to concentrate on the meditations her Order taught. The horns that awoke the ship were answered by a louder horn slowly approaching.

Demosyna wrapped an outer coat with a sigh, her concentration broken. She quickly passed a few passengers discussing the sudden turn of events while squeezing by in the tight hallway. In the low light of the rising sun, Demosyna could just make out a ship approaching from the north. A general feeling of disorder hung about everybody on deck, contrary to all Demosyna had seen from the crew thus far.

The captain barked orders to her crew while the first mate oversaw the others. Looking through her spyglass, Demosyna saw many shadowed figures on the deck of the approaching military ship. The dark sails pushed the sleek craft closer to the halted transport with horns calling all the while.

Demosyna was unable to see fine detail through her spyglass, so she returned it to her pocket. Bhreel was standing several paces away as Klai spoke to the first mate, smoking a long pipe through the slits in his helmet. Klai was motioning emphatically with her arms, and as Demosyna drew closer, Klai began nearly shouting.

"That is what I am trying to tell you, seeding dullard. The captain must be informed immediately," Klai cried, speaking frantically at the stone-faced first mate.

"The captain will not risk her imperial approval for your paranoia. We are being inspected by the Empress's navy, so we are stopping. That is the end of it, ma'am," the first mate responded, shaking her head.

Klai stood silent for a moment before seeing that Demosyna had joined her. Her Wise Mother looked at Demosyna with an odd, frantic expression on her elven face. The young woman was about to break the silence when Klai motioned for Bhreel and Demosyna to follow. Bhreel exchanged a confused look and followed the retreating Wise Mother with hurried strides.

"Listen to my words with mortal attention, as time is against us now. Bhreel, go to the cargo and get my locked chest," Klai commanded and pointed to the wide stairs leading belowdecks.

Bhreel said nothing and began striding away, his large frame parting the growing numbers. As with the previous inspection, all hands were required on the damp deck. The sun rose steadily in the breezy morning air and pushed back the misty darkness to reveal the approaching ship. Demosyna squinted north to make out the boat, but Klai stamped her staff impatiently.

"If you want to be useful for once in your life, do nothing but what I tell you," Klai said in a harsh whisper. "Return to the cabin and pack all our things into the apprentice chest."

Taking the uneasy tone her Wise Mother had with worry, Demosyna rushed down to their cabin with wide eyes. Conflicted thoughts raced through her head as Demosyna collected the few belongings kept in the shared cabin. Her Wise Mother often spoke unkindly due to the young woman's incompetence, but it had never been so harsh. As Demosyna put the thin blankets away, finishing her task, Klai opened the cabin door.

"I collected the—" Demosyna began before Klai interrupted.

"Silence," Klai said, motioning Bhreel to the chest Demosyna was seated on. "I suspect that the majority of those aboard are likely to be killed. Bhreel, go find a lifeboat at the back with those chests."

Bhreel shuffled around the cramped room to maneuver the two bulky chests. With the door closed again, Klai strode to the window and peered out to scan the coastline. Demosyna, aghast at the proclamation just heard, watched the dust filter through the rays of sunlight in contemplation.

Jui and Rrra are on deck with everyone else and must be warned, Demosyna mused with growing foreboding.

A knock gave her a start, and Demosyna opened the door to see a crewmate.

"Captain ordered all aboard up onto the deck," the crewmate said, rubbing sleep out of her eyes, "even private tickets, Wise Mother. You can discuss it with the first mate."

Klai's staff glowed from magic along the inlaid runes, making the crewmate jump away in fear. Demosyna followed as the sailor moved to the next doorless room.

Bhreel stood examining the control for the lowering cranks as the coast loomed alongside. The chests were stored in the back of a lifeboat that looked just big enough for the three travelers.

"Lower us down at once," Klai said upon getting in.

"Wise Mother, I trust your words to be true, but are we to abandon all these people?" Demosyna asked, thinking of her friends' ignorance to the danger.

The ship was close enough for one to see the dark brown of the sails and the numerous crew members running around on the deck of the armored boat. Demosyna recognized the shape of the sleek vessel as the smaller of the ships that had passed not long ago, yet the sails had lost their luster in the bloodred half.

"If you do not board the lifeboat this instant, you will be left behind."

Klai motioned for Bhreel to start lowering.

Confusion clouded her mind, causing thoughts to chase one another to no clear end, so Demosyna followed her Wise Mother's instructions. Demosyna looked up at Bhreel as he lowered the pair into the frigid water. His gray-green face was set in a frown, and he strained to lower the rowboat.

As the two sat rocking gently in the water, Bhreel remained on deck and was lost from view. Klai handed Demosyna an oar as the apprentice sat balancing in the tiny craft. The frantic elf pointed to the shore some distance away with a long, delicate finger.

Nearly a mile away, at a northern angle, there were the beginnings of a rocky beach. It widened eventually to form a proper coastline that the First Fort stood on, just beyond her aid.

"As fast as you can, head for that spot," Klai said impatiently and closed her large eyes.

Demosyna nodded, and the lifeboat slowly drifted away from the stuffed craft she had called home. Those on the deck were gathered on the far railing, watching the imperial ship approach, unaware of the lifeboat moving away. She tried to push her friends' faces from her mind, alternating the oar between the sides of the small craft. The apprentice hadn't been able to warn them, and a deep weight dragged the young woman into a cold despair.

The smaller ship slowed as it approached and began turning so that it was broadside to the passenger craft. A horn blasted from the commander's ship, and the cannon mounted on the deck rang out. Her back was turned while she rowed, so Demosyna jumped in surprise at the deadly sound from the cannon.

A chunk of the larger mast exploded, and panic erupted on the passenger ship. Yells of distress reached Demosyna in her small lifeboat, and she stood up, giving a cry of dismay. Horns signaled from both boats as more cannon shots rang out ruthlessly.

"Don't stop rowing, you Scale," Klai yelled at her.

"Ma'am," Demosyna said weakly, watching a fast reload.

"Row!"

Klai prodded Demosyna with her staff.

Demosyna numbly sat back down and returned to her rowing as a cannon shot tore into the helpless ship. The makeshift repairs were splintered and flung into the ocean, along with screaming bodies. Remembering her lessons, Demosyna tried to calm her terrified mind with steadying breaths.

Smoke billowed into the clear morning sky from both ships, and Demosyna saw Bhreel at the side of the damaged vessel. He was pouring something over the edge and calmly standing while many passengers were jumping overboard. As another shot rang out across the water, the captain dived away just before the wheel was hit. The attack left a dark hole in the deck where the wheel used to be and no sign of the captain.

Lifeboats were being filled, and crew aboard the helpless ship worked to lower them down. As the distance grew between Demosyna and the ships, more cannon shots tore holes into the side. A mast began falling with a groaning wooden scream, causing people to be crushed under the timber. One lifeboat was capsized by frantic bodies as they clawed at the sides while screaming for assistance.

Three more of the filled lifeboats were in the water and making their way directly to the shore. Demosyna continued to steadily row toward the spot indicated, now only hearing the carnage behind her. The sight of the attack was lost to the panicked young woman, but bright flashes reflected in the water. The smell of smoke reached her nose, and Demosyna turned to see the deck of the ship burning in places.

Bhreel and many others abandoned hope of getting into a lifeboat and jumped overboard. His heavy armor sparkled in the sunrise against the blue water as he splashed into the ocean. His metal armor prevented him from swimming, and Bhreel didn't surface, bubbles rising to show where he sank.

Figures swam toward the shore to escape the onslaught, crying out all the while. Demosyna turned her eyes away to focus on the shoreline. For many minutes, she tried to block out the booming cannon fire and desperate shrieks. From behind her, Demosyna heard Klai gasp and felt the boat rock to one side. Waves battered the rowboat as a cannonball splashed into the water barely a foot beside them.

Looking around wildly, Demosyna saw the hostile ship turn to intercept the lifeboats. Many jumped into the water from the escape boats upon seeing the cannons turn again, and the passenger craft was fully ablaze. A steady reloading had taken place, and the cannon was periodically firing shots at the lifeboats.

Armored dark figures fired arrows and slung rocks into the water, killing many swimming desperately away. Klai stood to balance on the sides of the lifeboat while gripping her staff in both hands. The Wise Mother glanced from the approaching ship to the shore several times with uncertainty in her eyes.

Klai opened her mouth to say something to Demosyna, but it was drowned by the latest cannon fire. Demosyna watched in horror as one of the other lifeboats was torn apart by the cannonball barely a hundred yards behind. Screams of pain rang out as the passengers were thrown into the water with a spray of blood. All her thoughts turned to escape as Demosyna resumed paddling toward the shore with all her strength.

Another splash caused icy needles of spray to cover Demosyna's face as a cannonball barely missed hitting their lifeboat. Demosyna didn't turn to see how close their pursuers were and rowed without restraint toward shore. She knew it was too far to reach with her exhausted arms working the oar, but the apprentice refused to give up.

Klai, standing astride the lifeboat, aimed her staff at the attacking boat and yelled. Demosyna saw from the reflection in the ocean that lines of light raced up the length of the staff, gathering into a large ball of color. In an instant, the ball grew to be several feet in diameter and rocketed away from the staff.

Demosyna didn't see the magic being cast directly but did feel a sharp pain all down her back when the ball launched away. She also felt the boat violently whipped to the right, capsizing the small craft and spilling everything aboard. It happened so suddenly that for a moment, Demosyna lost all sense of the world. The apprentice's wide eyes saw only swirling blue-white ocean as she was thrown into the frigid water.

As her vision cleared, Demosyna saw two dark shapes rapidly sinking into the ocean with a trail of bubbles. She swam toward the surface and tasted blood in the water from her Wise Mother. Swimming hurriedly toward the gently bobbing figure, Demosyna began removing her leather coat. The cold of the water bit into her each moment, but Demosyna was determined to get to Klai.

Holding the bundled coat in her teeth, Demosyna grabbed Klai under her arms and swam to the surface. Klai moaned weakly, and Demosyna looked around for sign of the approaching ship. When she didn't immediately see it, Demosyna grew even more confused as to what had just happened. Swimming toward the nearby shore with agonizing slowness, Demosyna saw the remains of the ship that had attacked them.

The last of the dark sails sank into the murky depths while turning the brown fabric a brighter red as they did. Bits of wood planking bobbed casually on the surface, and broken pieces of the bow sank into darkness. Closing her eyes and straining her muscles, Demosyna continued her arduous swim to the temporary safety of the land.

The next minutes were a blur of salt water as Demosyna labored to get her Wise Mother to shore. Icy waves buffeted her from all sides, and the added deadweight made each foot gained a grueling task. Pain in her back slowly worsened, and the frigid sea Demosyna swam through did little to ease the burn. Finally, with one last pull, both Wise-women lay gasping on the shore.

Turning onto her stomach, Demosyna pushed herself up to vomit seawater onto the dark stone. A wave crashed over both figures and drove Demosyna into the sharp rocks, cutting her slightly. Klai opened large eyes and looked down at the torn garments before gently probing the damage across her face and chest.

Klai croaked something that was too hoarse for Demosyna to understand. Many of the wooden pieces impaling the Wise Mother were lodged in her throat and face, so talking looked painful.

"Staff," Klai said hoarsely.

"I didn't see where your staff went, Wise Mother. I'm sorry, but one moment, I was rowing. And the next, we capsized," Demosyna said between labored breaths.

Klai shook her head and once again assessed the damage she had sustained. One by one, Klai began removing the splinters that covered the front of her body, some as big as a finger. Demosyna found her outer coat on a nearby rock and tore off one of the sleeves before making long bandages.

Demosyna sat down next to Klai and felt to discover many splinters of wood lodged into her back. Wincing at the extent of the damage, Demosyna steadied herself and began removing the impaling wood. Warm blood trickled down her back in places where the shards had penetrated the deepest, but the young woman persisted.

The cold of the air combined with the dampness of her clothes came to aid Demosyna in being numb to much of the pain. By the time she was done, Demosyna had over a dozen splinters of various sizes. A wave crashed upon her legs and took the shards into the ocean as Demosyna stood to slowly remove her soaked clothes.

Klai, too, had finished removing her shrapnel, standing groggily as she took in her surroundings. Demosyna used the long strips to wrap around her torso, wincing at the pain the movements caused. The young woman had never seen her Wise Mother so disoriented before and worried she was gravely injured. Hay-colored hair clung in salty tangles from the ocean, making the elf look waterlogged and haggard.

"Here, Wise Mother," Demosyna said, offering the strips.

Klai shook her head, pointing to the staff bobbing in the water. Demosyna grabbed the cord around her waist and reeled in her staff, thankful she had remembered to secure it. The wood was soaked with seawater and was heavier than normal, but even with her exhausted arms, Demosyna handed Klai the staff.

Klai's breath was ragged, but she steadied herself with the aid of the pole. Once she had regained her composure, Klai waved the staff above her head to draw a halo of light. Demosyna forgot her pain for a moment as the ring of brilliant light split, with Klai pointing the smooth wooden staff. Klai motioned the staff downward, dropping it to the rocky ground.

As the ring traveled forward, Demosyna saw that the halo above Klai had begun descending. No sooner had her ring of glowing energy reached Demosyna than it began the same procedure of lowering itself. When the ring moved over her head, Demosyna closed her eyes against the bright energy. The wind stopped in the places the halo passed, leaving behind a scent of familiar surroundings.

Demosyna exhaled in relief as her muscles relaxed and felt her wounds stop crying out. The ring reached Demosyna's knees as the golden circle Klai was surrounded by reached the shore, dispersing into glowing dust. It was like embers in a breeze with the light scattering into nothingness once the spell was finished. Klai breathed deeply before stretching her limbs and striding confidently farther north up the beach. It took several more seconds for Demosyna's halo to complete its descent, leaving her body feeling whole.

After gathering up her things from the ground, Demosyna followed behind on the uneven terrain. The larger vessel had sunk below the surface, no longer filling the sky with smoke, and Demosyna felt a pang of sorrow. Many bodies dotted the surface till pulled under by tentacles, and Demosyna looked away with her heart heavy. Two rowboats tried to turn against the current, and cries rang out as they were dashed onto the rocks by unfeeling waves.

Klai called to Demosyna, drawing her attention from the huddles of survivors when the young Wizen caught up.

"That slope appears gentle enough for us to ascend into the forest. Follow and step only where I step, apprentice Wizen," Klai said as she secured the staff's tether.

"Yes, Wise Mother. Thank you for healing me, and we can hope the others catch up soon," Demosyna said. "May I swim and help them get here?"

"No. Enough chatter for now. Many dangers await us in the forest, and we must be on constant alert," Klai whispered, facing Demosyna with a stern expression.

Demosyna nodded in response and carefully followed her companion up the slope into the shade of massive dwarf-wood trees. The sun was rising into the sky, and Demosyna turned to view the scene from new heights. She could no longer see the fortress in the north or the small landing party that was all that survived from her place atop the bluffs.

Frowning and wondering at the attack, Demosyna walked briskly behind Klai. Several paces into the space between two trees, the apprentice saw why there was a rare gap in the living wall. Trees lay uprooted in different directions, leaving a small clearing of soft earth. The wind was cut off in the tiny pocket of forest, so Demosyna set her clothes down.

"There appears to be a supply of kindling scattered around. Once your pants are dry, see to gathering it," Klai instructed Demosyna without looking at her. "I must meditate."

Without another word, Klai sat down and closed her eyes, leaving Demosyna alone. Steam began rising from the damp clothes the Wise Mother wore, and Klai ignored the young Wizen. Even Klai's hair dried with magical speed, being combed by invisible fingers into a smart bob again.

Once the jade robes hanging from a limb next to her were dry enough to put on, Demosyna dressed. Even with a dozen yards of space the trees uprooting provided, Demosyna found precious little wood.

"I see," Klai said once Demosyna had piled the sticks.

Klai assembled the skeleton of a campfire with a practiced hand by stacking the wood carefully. Klai stood and casually touched the bottom of the borrowed staff into the campfire. At once, a flame burst from a gout of fire pouring into the wood. Klai withdrew the staff and wiped ash off the bottom before walking to the entrance of the small clearing.

For hours, Demosyna was alone while listening to the unfamiliar sounds of the northern forest. Exhausted from the series of events that morning, Demosyna tried to understand what had happened. The speed at which the day turned deadly was shocking, and she turned the events over again and again in her mind.

"It appears the other survivors are making their way up the shore. They should be here by sundown," Klai proclaimed as she crested the rise, many of the sewn jewels gone from her robes.

Demosyna sat up as Klai knelt down on the opposite side of the fire. Klai put the simple wooden staff across her knees and gazed into the embers.

"Wise Mother, what happened to our lifeboat?" Demosyna asked sadly.

"Foolishness and stupidity is what happened. If the captain had just done the sensible thing, we may have saved our supplies," Klai responded, frowning as she stared into the fire. "As it stands, I was unable to see them as I combed the shore and assume they are lost. The journey forward will be very perilous, and we have no supplies to give the Order."

Demosyna lowered her eyes to the ground as she contemplated her Wise Mother's words.

"Did you see Bhreel? Or my new friends Jui or Rrra?" Demosyna asked.

"No. However, there were around thirty, and your seeder friends are more likely to have survived than most," Klai said as she shook her head. "Beyond that, we must hope that some of the crew survived to aid me. I am unsure how well a mass of seeders will fare in these untamed lands."

Demosyna furrowed her brow and thought of the people she had grown close to. Bhreel had jumped overboard, but Demosyna didn't recall seeing him in the ensuing chaos. Rrra and Jui could have swum, but Demosyna feared the lashings would make swimming too difficult for the whipped passengers.

"Our priority should be to contact the imperial army. It will likely be a journey of days now since our boat is no longer viable," Klai said, speaking softly, breaking the silence. "Tomorrow, we should get beyond these impassable trees and into the start of the evergreens."

Demosyna reflected on her studies of dangerous wildlife in preparation for the journey. Books on the subject were sparse in the apprentice library, and the facts presented were mostly conjecture. Few survived in the vast, untamed woods while those who did came back in varying states of mutilation and sanity.

"I will use your staff until I craft you a replacement," Klai said, running her hands over the unadorned stick. "My staff exploded from the power of the spell, which will take me time to understand. That is also what capsized us, as it seems that the canoe was not able to absorb the spell either."

"What does that mean, Wise Mother?" Demosyna asked, worry in her voice.

Demosyna had observed her powerful Wise Mother perform numerous different magics, and the enchanted staff had never so much as gotten dirty. For a long time, Klai sat in silence while doing little to curb Demosyna's fears. So many unexpected things had already happened during the glaring morning that Demosyna's mind raced, trying to process it all.

"I do not know anymore," Klai finally responded in a low tone as if to herself. "I may have once, but this is novel for the current me, and that is what gnaws my mind."

Demosyna calmed her thoughts, as she had been instructed all her life. Rather than worry over possibilities, she crossed her legs and began meditating on the day's events.

We have days of hard marching ahead, Demosyna thought. *I will do what I can to help those that survived the shipwreck. I can always fish for food or gather medicines from the forest if I don't stray far.*

Hours passed, and the steady roar of the ocean was a constant metronome. The young Wizen did her best to avoid thinking the worst for her friends and found little success.

Shadows began to lengthen as the sun sank toward the horizon before the clamor of survivors approached. Demosyna looked the group over and saw many were injured and being carried on wooden sledges. To her relief, Bhreel was pulling the first mate behind him with Jui and two other injured figures.

"Bhreel!" Demosyna cried with a smile on her long face, hugging the man. "I am so happy you survived. Both of you."

Demosyna placed a hand on her friend's shoulder, but Jui wasn't conscious. A grimace of discomfort was stamped on Jui's green face, and her shirt had spots of fresh blood. With a sigh, Demosyna stood and faced Bhreel, who removed his helmet.

"I saw you sink in the ocean, Bhreel. I was so worried," Demosyna said shyly, passing a nearly empty waterskin.

"I understand, little one."

Bhreel laughed softly and put his hand on her shoulder.

"I figured out long ago how to deal with heavy armor in water. I emptied my wineskins and used them as air bladders."

Shocked, Demosyna thought about that before laughing as well in relief.

Rrra found the two after the first mate had begun issuing orders and dried the tears on his cheek as he lay down with Jui.

"Thank you, Bhreel," Rrra said, looking up at the Orc with gratitude. "I will carry Jui now, but thank you for the help."

"How is she?" Demosyna asked quietly to Rrra, his orange scales glittering.

"She is in a lot of pain. Two of the others that got lashings drowned right next to us because they couldn't swim fast enough," Rrra told her, holding back tears. "I had to carry her the whole swim since we weren't allowed to use lifeboats."

Aghast, Demosyna looked around in confusion at the small group who survived the attack. Already, the figures were divided as they had been on the ship, the crew together with the first-class passengers. Klai was talking with the first mate, who stood with the aid of a fallen branch.

"She is breathing but hasn't woken up this morning. What will I do without her?" Rrra sighed and wiped a tear.

"I don't know, Rrra, but I will help however I can," Demosyna replied as she looked at Jui. "The Orders will get us any supplies and medicine we need."

Anger flashed across Rrra's face for a moment but was replaced with weary sadness. Rrra took his mate's hand while Demosyna walked to where Klai stood talking. As the apprentice approached, the first mate was describing the distance they must travel to reach safety. The once pristine clothes the first mate wore clung to her bloody body, stained with mud from the naval escape.

"With the injured being dragged behind at a snail's pace, we are sitting ducks," the first mate said, her red hair still matted.

"That is why I suggest I go with my ward to seek aid. A smaller party will travel quicker than forty people, a third of whom are injured," Klai responded promptly. "We will take the necessary supplies, and you may wait for a few days—"

"We may not have a few days," a passenger interrupted. "Without food, we are more likely to die before you get back. You can't just decide how provisions are used, Wizen!"

"Or get eaten in the meantime," proclaimed a crewmate with a broken arm. "Who knows what beasts roam these lands? And you want to leave us without a Wise-woman?"

The talk began overlapping till no sense could be made of the discussion. Klai stamped her staff into the dirt, and her voice filled the clearing. It boomed with magic, causing the lower-class passengers to look over.

"Time is of the utmost import for all, but I cannot be delayed any further," Klai boomed around the clearing. "I am not subject to the whims of seeders, and I will escort you on my terms. If my advice had been taken by our esteemed first mate, we would not be in this mess."

For a moment, there was silence as the woods around them stilled. Klai pointed north with a borrowed staff, and her voice returned to a normal volume.

"Whoever it was that attacked us is of no concern, as the imperial navy will surely take care of the bandits. Assuming I didn't earlier today, that is," Klai said, surveying the group.

"We can't travel at night. It's suicide," the first mate spoke up after looking at her leg. "We will wait till morning, and if you want any of the supplies, you will wait as well. If the captain ever turns up, it will be different, but I am in charge of these supplies, Wise-woman."

Klai turned on her heel and walked off with Bhreel behind her, saying nothing.

Demosyna looked at the grim faces of the crew and first-class passengers to see no love, so she, too, walked away. Yells of anger followed, accusing them of cowardice for taking a lifeboat with only two people. Klai walked to an empty area of the clearing and was starting another fire when Demosyna sat.

The remainder of the evening was spent with Klai silently fuming while the humble number of survivors tried to rest. Stars were nearly obscured by the dense canopy, and the wind groaned against the impenetrable dwarf-woods. Demosyna couldn't sleep, however, and was still shaking. She clenched her hands in an attempt to stop the trembling, but when she relaxed her fist, it was still twitchy.

For the remaining hours of the night, as the moon rose, Demosyna walked along the shore in the slicing wind. Walking helped to relieve the jittery energy that had overcome her ever since the first cannonball splashed close. During a shady part of the night, Demosyna watched in wonder as the wind kicked up in strength. A bitter cold spun across the water, pulling the ocean into the air as it did. Before her eyes, the surface of the ocean was frozen solid from the arctic winds.

Demosyna shivered in the cold and jumped as loud, cracking noises echoed, calls from the ice breaking apart in the current. The apprentice rubbed her arms for warmth before returning to the camp from her first sleepless night on northern soil. Witnessing the sudden freezing that caused the massive glacier walls was something wondrous that Demosyna would reflect on for many years.

Klai meditated silently before laying down to rest for the evening. Bhreel had moved Jui to the new campsite.

* * * * *

After the sun rose and the camp stiffly awakened from the cold ground, the first mate gathered all those in the clearing around.

"We are lucky enough to have two lifeboats of rations left, but we have used all the medications. As always, crew and first class get a portion first. All the rest can go looking for anything they want to eat," she said, having to raise her voice over the protests.

The first mate waved her hands for order, and the angry crowd of lower-class passengers quieted.

"Things aren't going to change just because we have a setback. Make ready the cots for those that can't walk," the first mate said in a loud voice. "Now let's eat."

There was laughter from the remaining crew, and they walked over to the assortment of boxes.

Demosyna had no appetite with the visions of the previous day's events still fresh in her mind. Having not slept that evening, she was also mildly sluggish in going about her morning routine.

The food was quickly depleted, and nearly half the people didn't get any. This caused fights among the slower eaters who did get food and those who did not. The crew got the tussles under control, and the band set out down the steep slope with the wounded carried on sledges.

The first mate walked to the shoreline to get their attention. Then she grew deathly pale, and her eyes opened wide. A few of the others on the beach screamed and pointed at the trees above the small clearing they had camped within. Strung between the trees, around a hundred feet up, were large, opaque webbing in a clearly patterned design.

Demosyna looked at the webs in horror and began searching the trees for any sign of movement. The cables that made up the trap were thick as her arm and over twenty feet in diameter for the smallest. A chill ran up Demosyna's spine when remembering no spiderwebs present when Klai found the spot.

The group moved away from the clearing as quickly as the surf and rocks would allow after that, stopping only once their camp was hours behind. Nobody complained about the dangerous retreat, for each wished to leave the horrible webs in their wake.

CHAPTER 5

The coast Demosyna walked along consisted of a thin shore of uneven rock, with sea on one side and sheer cliffs on the other. This left no room for walking without going single file, especially at times when the water came closer to the rocks. A tidal wind was ever present and threatened to knock the stumbling group off their feet at all times.

Little talk was had by the people walking up the coast, but a general silence was broken by cries of the wounded. Jui was still unconscious, Demosyna saw as she looked back from beside Klai. The few times the young apprentice glanced back, Rrra was looking at the ground and trying to make his mate's hauling smooth. Those behind Demosyna glared with weary anger while some even cursed her outright, sending clouds of hatred away.

For hours, the progress was slow with the water splashing around their ankles. Everybody who survived the naval assault did their best to avoid falling, but twice, different people fell and caused a halt. Whether by wind or the slippery nature of the shore, the second person to fall broke an arm. This stopped the group for a long time while soaking everyone with surf.

Just after noon, the first mate called a stop to the group, who let out a groan. The water had risen to the point that they would have to swim, and the first mate was organizing teams to carry the wounded.

Soon enough, the first group was swimming with two of the injured on a makeshift raft.

Klai seemed distant the entire walk but frowned at the prospect of swimming. Demosyna removed her clothes and bundled them with her wide belt before crossing. Swimming on her back with the clothes in one upraised arm proved effective, and others started doing the same. Once she got to the far side, Demosyna dressed again while shivering in the windy atmosphere. It took over an hour for all the people to swim across, and after a short rest to dry, the first mate ordered them to move on.

The remainder of the daylight passed without incident, and Demosyna tried to distract herself from the ache in her feet. Without her staff, the apprentice found walking difficult, but she watched the sun drop toward the horizon for the second time on free land with hope. Demosyna's attention was torn away from the sight when the first mate sounded a soft horn blast, warning from around a corner.

"Halt the march!" several voices called from around the slight bend in the shore.

Panic began circulating the group while Klai strode forward with Bhreel and Demosyna close behind. The crowd parted as cries of complaint rose on the narrow beach, and Demosyna stopped in her tracks. The larger of the ships that had passed them days ago was anchored north of where the group was on the beach. From her position, Demosyna could see people already on the shore.

"Is it the imperial army?" Demosyna asked, hope in her voice.

Klai didn't respond, as she was looking through her spyglass. Bhreel removed his helmet and sat down to catch his breath from hauling. A soft clack followed Klai finishing her scan of the distant bodies. The spot where they had landed was several hundred yards ahead, where the imposing trees lining the cliffs turned to evergreens.

"We must talk to the first mate," Klai said, moving forward.

Bhreel helped part the bodies ahead of Klai with his wide frame, and Demosyna scurried after the Wise Mother.

"Those are not soldiers. They are bandits," Klai announced to the first mate as Demosyna got within earshot.

"How can you tell? Even with my spyglass, I see the red sails and the red stripe on their armor," the first mate said.

"The sails are dry, meaning the Battle Wizen was killed," Klai responded quickly. "I assume that they took the soldiers' armor. If that is true, we are in worse trouble than I had dared to think. If the armor is taken, the fort may be as well."

The first mate pondered this carefully and shook her head in indecision. Klai grew impatient and walked forward boldly, raising her staff.

"Give me your shield, boy."

Klai motioned for Bhreel.

With the metal shield in hand, Klai walked farther and covered her face with the disc. Klai channeled a stream of magic while holding the staff out in front of her.

"Wait," the first mate began, but it was too late.

A huge ball of energy began expanding from the staff pointed toward the ship in the north. The crowd fell back in terror, and a clamor of protests fell on deaf ears as the ball continued to grow. After nearly ten seconds, the spell shot forward with a cracking noise, and Klai lowered the shield.

The ball of glowing light sped across the water, waves lapping and sizzling into steam. Klai watched the sphere sail directly toward the ship parked in the water and impact the side. A hole appeared straight through the boat as the ball of energy passed without slowing. After exiting the side of the anchored ship, the magic exploded into fiery chunks that splattered destruction everywhere.

Many of the projectiles hit the ocean and sizzled out in vapor, but enough hit the deck to set it ablaze. Those from the boat that had landed ashore were knocked over, dancing flips with limp bodies. Seconds later, a wall of force passed over Demosyna, almost knocking her to the pointed stones. Klai addressed the first mate while handing the shield to Bhreel.

"What have you done?" the acting captain asked Klai.

Several of the crew around the first mate shouted their agreements at the prompt actions.

"I may have saved many of your lives. With only a few already ashore, we might be able to make for the trees," Klai responded calmly and turned to Demosyna. "We must make haste across the stretch if we are to seek shelter in the passable woods."

Those of the group on the same side of the cliff turned from Demosyna and began murmuring. Klai jogged carefully away, tucking the staff under an arm. Demosyna motioned Rrra to join, and they carried Jui's sledge.

"Are you sure about this?" Rrra asked, scrambling over the beach debris.

"I trust my Wise Mother, even when I don't understand all that she does," Demosyna replied as she hopped over a jagged rock threatening her shins. "I want to keep you two safe however I can, as I told you."

Rrra stopped for a moment and glanced back with a suspicious look. Demosyna cocked her head, but Rrra didn't say anything and started moving again. From down the widening beach, Demosyna heard the fading sounds of the group arguing. Eventually, the waves overpowered those noises as Demosyna jogged toward the armored figures.

Before reaching the fallen group of people, Bhreel hopped ahead at a gesture from Klai. He knelt at the figures strewn about, some of whom were drenched when the waves crashed into the shore.

"They are out cold, whatever you did," Bhreel told the party. "If the others hurry, they should be able to make it."

Klai considered for a moment before responding.

"Who are these two? Your low-class friends, no doubt."

Demosyna nodded before she introduced Jui and Rrra. Rrra bowed slightly while balancing his end of the sledge, and Jui lay painfully unconscious. Klai peered down at them and raised the staff in her hand to inspect it. Two large cracks ran nearly the length of the shaft, and Klai frowned.

Demosyna watched the band of survivors in the distance as they approached the small group.

"They seem to be coming, Wise Mother," Demosyna said while turning to face Klai.

"Indeed, but we will not await their arrival. Come, before these creatures wake up," Klai responded.

Demosyna got at the back of the wood carrying Jui. Together, she and Rrra followed at a good clip. A final glance behind her showed Demosyna that survivors of the previous encounter were approaching from the south.

As she passed by the prone women on the ground, it was clear to Demosyna that the armor was ill-fitting and mismatched. From her studies of the imperial armies, Demosyna was aware of the pride each soldier took in their bespoke armor. Passing among the fallen bandits, Demosyna also noticed the varying lengths of hair from the figures prostrate on shore. That was contrary to regulations for the Empress's army, and Klai had surely noticed such details.

The trees on the right changed from dense, impassable dwarf-wood trees to large evergreens in an instant. These ancient trees were still densely spaced but far more passable. Several bodies twitched as Demosyna and Rrra stepped over them, but all appeared knocked out.

The thinner forest loomed ahead of Demosyna as she raced behind Rrra, keeping the platform holding Jui steady. As they reached the shade, the panting group stopped and turned to catch their breath. A large mass led by the first mate was approaching the spot of beach with the laid-out bandits. Some of the slavers were beginning to stir, and Demosyna waved one arm to encourage their progression.

The gesture seemed to work, as the group picked up pace toward the shady forest. Two of the bandits on the beach had sat up and were rubbing their heads. For a moment, the first mate barked orders, and the group was careful to avoid any lively bodies. It took almost ten minutes for the entirety of the passengers to reach Demosyna on the tree line. Nearly a dozen of the bandits on the beach had recovered enough to try their feet, and Klai was impatient to continue.

"We must journey on if we are to escape these lowlifes," Klai exclaimed to the first mate.

"Whatever you did, we don't need to worry about these lot," the first mate replied, sitting down.

"No," Klai said simply, showing the split staff.

"What is that supposed to be?" asked the first mate, crossing her arms. "If you can do that, it shouldn't be a problem to reach the fortress."

Klai didn't respond at first and instead held the staff out to Demosyna. Once Demosyna had grasped it, Klai looked at the seated first mate and folded her hands.

"You are welcome to stay here as the bandits regain their composure, but that staff cannot withstand another spell," Klai said calmly as though talking to a toddler.

The first mate's face darkened, and she stood up to face Klai. Bhreel took a stride forward and placed himself between Klai and the furious first mate. A hush fell over the group who had assembled around the scene, leaving only distant waves crashing. Klai turned and began traversing the uneven forest behind her without another word.

The first mate about-faced and addressed the crowd, explaining the plan to avoid these bandits. Many of the shivering figures protested the continued march, but the commanding voice of the first mate settled the murmur. Demosyna followed her Wise Mother deeper into the dark as the worried talk turned to acceptance. Crew and passengers alike followed Klai's lead, and the wounded were muffled with their shirts.

Behind the group of shipwrecked passengers, the sound of threats was heard from the bandits who had recovered. The next hour was spent trekking through the forest and gaining distance from the shoreline for Demosyna and those following.

Sounds of their pursuers grew intense at times, prompting the exhausted group to push themselves. The woods called threats in cruel, laughing voices all the while. Klai was leading in a wandering course through the dense woods but ever northward. As the sun finally fell, the shadows made running a treacherous affair, but sounds of the bandits behind them also faded.

Taking shelter in the darkness, Demosyna placed Jui onto the ground and fell to her knees. The apprentice had never been so winded, not even after carrying her Wise Mother from the sea. Klai steadied herself against a tree with her breath heavy in the air. Bhreel joined the majority of the party and sat on the ground in exhaustion, having carried the wounded for nearly a day.

The first mate had her hands on her knees for several minutes before walking over to Klai.

"Thank you, Wizen," the first mate whispered breathlessly, with restrained anger. "You may well have saved our lives."

Klai nodded at the acting captain and opened her mouth to reply, but angry shouts from passengers interrupted.

"You killed us all!" one lady yelled from the wounded.

Shouts of agreement were heard from many of the survivors, and another yelled out at Klai.

"They may have only wanted money, but now they will kill us for sure," a lady said frantically, looking around at those standing nearby. "Why do you decide what is best?"

Klai shook her head and tried to speak again, but many people were angrily pointing. Demosyna saw desperation on the faces of those shouting their grievances. The first mate waved her arms wildly and blew a horn for attention, which was restored after a second soft blast.

The woods were still after the second horn, and as the first mate talked to the mob, Demosyna heard a faint sound. At first, it was low and distant, but it was rapidly approaching. Klai seemed to have sensed the noise and held her near-broken staff up. Magic produced a ball of light that hovered fifty feet above Klai. Bhreel put his helmet back on after wiping his face and brandished an axe in preparation.

Four large wasps, each the size of a pony, were buzzing toward the group through the canopy. Screaming passengers began running in all directions, ignoring the first mate's cries to rally on her. Two of the remaining crew ran to engage but were impaled on stingers with cries of agony. The wasps flew skyward, and the bodies slid off the barbs with nauseating thuds. Demosyna shrank back at the sight while stepping behind Klai and Bhreel. One wasp flew up to investigate the orb, but the others began darting among the terrified people.

Klai raised her staff as one approached, and blue-green orbs flew from both ends. Upon touching the wasp, the spheres stuck to it before expanding and combining. Bhreel jumped with his axe in both hands and swung at the ball, grunting in effort. The light dissipated as the axe cleaved into it, but the wasp was cut in half.

A loud sound interrupted the praise Demosyna was going to express, and a third crack appeared on the staff. Klai unwrapped the tether while handing the pole to Demosyna. Taking it from her Wise Mother, Demosyna examined the familiar wood and saw it was falling apart. The once smooth surface was broken with splinters and deep splits in the grain.

"What happened, Wise Mother?" Demosyna asked.

"We have to move," Klai said, loudly enough for the first mate to hear.

The first mate turned from watching the wasps buzzing above those who didn't bolt. Any wounded were gathered up and carried two strong. Almost as soon as they started fleeing the aerial attack, two of the group fell off a dirt cliff. Cries of pain followed, and Demosyna saw the two impaled on a large tangle of thorns dripping a dark poison.

Demosyna watched as the two writhed for seconds before their skin began to turn a hot red, and they ceased. Klai called out to keep running, and Demosyna pulled her eyes away from the horrific sight to follow her Wise Mother.

* * * * *

Swords flashed in the unnatural light Klai produced while figures retreated into the darkness. Demosyna and Rrra supported the unconscious Jui as they followed doggedly behind Klai. The remaining eighteen shipmates fled through inky blackness, several crying in terror.

A sharp cry of pain from the back brought fresh screams, begging them to hurry. Demosyna ran as fast as her worn legs would permit, and they soon began to burn from fatigue. Rrra stumbled momentarily but found his footing when Demosyna planted her broken staff to hold the man up. A dark shape buzzed by her, and Demosyna felt the wind of the wasp as it passed.

"Wise Mother!" Demosyna shouted in warning.

Bhreel halted at the call to see the approaching wasp in the scarce light through the canopy. Klai spun quickly and, with a dexterous maneuver, cartwheeled to the left. Despite the acrobatics the elf displayed, the fat thorax of the wasp struck her midair to spin Klai to the ground.

Demosyna ran toward her fallen Wise Mother as Bhreel jumped at the wasp, tackling it from the sky. Its buzzing grew frenzied as Bhreel wrestled on the ground while hacking with his axe in one hand. Demosyna fell to her knees beside Klai and saw she was winded but unhurt. Refusing the outstretched hand, Klai rose to her feet as the first mate helped finish killing the large wasp.

The ball of conjured light was a speck in the distance, and the buzzing couldn't be heard anymore. Normal sounds of the forest returned after tense moments, when the few remaining from the ship listened desperately. No danger appeared, so the first mate announced the plan.

"It is too dangerous to run through the forest. We must camp here for the night," the acting captain said, turning to peer at Klai.

Klai said nothing at first, only stood in the shadow of the tree where she had been flung.

"Without a staff, I cannot protect myself, much less anyone else," Klai explained. "We must find a suitable tree to fashion a replacement."

"I will go. Just tell me what you need," the first mate said, ignoring her injured leg.

A second crewmate agreed, and Klai explained what was needed, sending them off. Those left with the group placed the wounded under a nearby tree and rested in heaps. Only a handful of the wounded was left, many being unable to defend themselves from the wasps.

Rrra lay down beside Jui and cradled her still form while Demosyna asked how she was.

"I don't know. She is better at medicine than me," Rrra whispered sadly. "She hasn't woken up in two days."

"Once we get a new staff, I will ask my Wise Mother to heal her," Demosyna said, placing a hand on his shoulder.

As the two sat in silence, Jui began to stir and moan weakly. Rrra jolted up and called out to his mate with tears flowing. Jui turned onto her back and opened her eyes slowly in the starlight.

"Rrra," Jui croaked, reaching for her mate.

"Jui, you've come back to me!" Rrra said through tears.

Jui swallowed painfully and asked for water. Her lips were terribly dry, having been crusted in salty ocean for days.

"I will find some if there is any in camp," Demosyna told the two Scales while standing.

Demosyna asked several people if they had any water, but many refused to even converse. Ten minutes of searching yielded no hydration, and Demosyna was returning with the bad news when the first mate appeared. Klai walked quickly over to inspect the pieces, and Demosyna sat down next to the friends she had made.

"Nobody had any water," Demosyna said. "Or if they did, they weren't sharing. I'm sorry."

"No, it was probably because of my liquor," Rrra exclaimed, wiping a tear. "The rest of the trip, the passengers turned against us."

Demosyna didn't respond and simply considered Rrra's words. Jui tried to say something, but Rrra hushed her.

"Save your strength, my love," he said tenderly, kissing her on the mouth.

Jui smiled weakly and nodded, turning on her side with a grunt. Rrra lay down, and Jui put her arms around him. Demosyna wished them a good night and found where Klai stood with the first mate.

"The other crew member has not returned, but these should do," Klai told the first mate. "I must not be disturbed while I form the staff."

The first mate agreed, and she walked off to organize the precious few survivors. Klai searched the immediate area for a spot where the stars shone clear, running her hands along the length of a branch. After several passes, the bark fell off to reveal intricate filigree the length of the pole.

Gasping in wonder, Demosyna saw the finished staff was identical to the original Klai wielded. Klai noticed the interest in Demosyna's tired face and addressed her.

"If you ever show aptitude for magic, you will be able to do that as well," Klai instructed. "Tomorrow, I will make you a new apprentice staff, but I must rest. Disturb my meditations only if there is another attack."

Bhreel followed as Klai walked away without looking back. Demosyna lay down and looked at the few stars that were visible through the dense leaves. Demosyna fell asleep in piles of nettles with an ever more frequent frown on her face.

* * * * *

At the first sign of light, the acting captain woke everyone, and all headed north through the forest. Jui was able to walk, albeit slowly, on her own after she finally woke. Demosyna lingered at the back with Rrra to help if needed, searching the woods for any healing plants. This drew angry looks from the group in front of her, but Demosyna ignored them with darting searches.

After hours of steady marching, the remaining survivors, many of whom were first class, began complaining loudly. The small procession was halted while the first mate tried to restore order. Jui leaned against a tree and breathed ragged breaths, painful sounding to Demosyna. Rrra looked on in worry, and Jui asked for water.

"Go swimming for it," one of the passengers called angrily.

"Jui is hurt, and she needs water," Rrra yelled at the woman.

"Just leave the wounded behind. They are only slowing us down," the lady said, hands on hips.

"We are not leaving anyone behind," the first mate yelled, her voice bellowing. "Now move out and quit complaining. We are just a few hours from the fortress."

The weary travelers marched on with Demosyna helping Rrra carry Jui when she collapsed again. Rrra had a worried expression on his face for over an hour before fatigue replaced it.

Cold gnawed at her strength, and hunger was beginning to become a discomfort for Demosyna on the long walk. The burn in her legs was a welcome motivation, for Demosyna felt rising hope at getting Jui to safety.

Soon enough, the trees gave way to a sweeping view of rolling hills leading to the coast. In the far distance, the fort could be seen next to the shore, and weary travelers gave a collective cry of relief. Demosyna smiled in tired joy and adjusted Jui's arm on her shoulder.

"Onward, ladies," the first mate said, laughing. "The first drink is on me!"

Gentle hills were a relief after the dense forest, and they crossed the plains with renewed energy. The drawbridge of the fortress was lowered as they approached, and riders galloped closer. Klai stopped in her tracks and produced the spyglass to see clearly.

"What is it now?" the first mate asked, fear in her voice.

"It looks like the imperial army at last!" Klai proclaimed.

A cheer rose from all around, and Klai replaced the spyglass into her sleeve. From her place in the back of the line, Demosyna saw the riders slow and circle the group before the lead rider climbed down.

"Hello," the horsewoman began in a cheery voice. "Where might you be headed?"

"Our ship was attacked, and we barely escaped," the first mate said, stepping forward and offering a hand. "I am the acting captain, and they had an imperial scout ship, madam soldier."

"We know about those bandits," the lead rider said. "They have been trying for weeks to take the fortress, but days ago, they took the craft from us."

Several of the mounted riders laughed as well, and Klai stepped forward.

"Take us to your commander at once, soldier," Klai demanded.

The figure regarded Klai carefully before responding in a flat tone.

"Are you the Wizen from the ship?" asked the stranger, her face hardening.

Klai did not answer, and there was silence before one of the passengers called out that she was. Demosyna excused herself quietly before making her way to the front of the group. The woman by the horse nodded and took a step toward Klai. With a practiced motion, the woman drew her sword and sliced out at Klai, cutting through the staff. The blade embedded itself into the Wise Mother's neck, sending red streams onto the soft grasses.

Demosyna screamed in shock as Klai gasped, and blood began streaming down her robes. Bhreel yelled and raised his axe, but a mounted horsewoman thrust a spear. She stabbed him in the armpit, and Bhreel yelled in pain. There was a cracking noise before the Orc fell beside Klai. The woman who had hacked into Klai yanked the sword back, kicking the Wizen into the crowd.

"Now, everyone, calm down," the lady said, wiping the blood off her sword. "If nobody else does anything stupid like this Orc, we can all get this over with."

The lead rider stepped forward and chopped at Klai's body, holding a severed head for the group to see. Shining golden hair fell like thread onto the bloody grasses from the rough handling. Demosyna watched numbly, her ears ringing, as riders tied Bhreel to their horses. Armored mounts dragged him back to the fortress, his limp body bouncing sickeningly.

Maybe Klai can heal Bhreel, Demosyna thought wildly. *She must be playing possum.*

Her attention was drawn from the morbid display by a harsh shout. Demosyna slowly turned to the voice, feeling her legs grow weak.

"This Wizen bitch attacked my soldiers. She would have been too much trouble, just like all the rest of you if you aren't useful. Now on your knees," the lead rider shouted.

Crying in fear at this sudden turn, the remaining survivors did as they were bidden. Another of the riders dismounted with manacles to bind the group. The cold steel closed around her wrists, but Demosyna hardly took notice. Klai lay dead before her, and the apprentice stared at the lifeless body before fainting.

When she came to, Demosyna saw that the last of the surviving passengers was being shackled to a long chain. Demosyna sat up slowly, unsure where she was. Rrra was pleading with the lead rider to take Jui with them.

"Why would we want half-dead bodies?" the lead rider asked, laughing, seeing Rrra's distress.

"Please, soldier. She will die if you leave her," Rrra begged, falling to his knees.

"She won't be alone, boy," the lead rider responded. "The other wounded will keep her company. She can't even walk, and I don't think anyone wants to carry her."

"I will," Demosyna called out, tearing her eyes from Klai. "She needs water, and I'm sure she will recover."

The leader approached Demosyna with a frown and looked at the Wizen.

"Another Wise-woman, I see. What happened to your staff, little Scale?" she asked Demosyna while punching her in the face.

Demosyna's vision went blurry for a moment as she recovered from the sudden blow.

"Stupid Wizen. Shut up," a passenger hissed. "You'll get us all killed."

Two of the riders began gathering up all the obvious possessions, clubbing any who resisted. The process took little time and ended for Demosyna as she handed over her marred staff. The leader took it and eyed it suspiciously before breaking the pole against the first mate. She fell to the ground with a cry and blood flowing from her face.

"I suppose we could take that one with us, if you carry it," the woman said, standing above Demosyna. "Besides, it would be a nice treat for the girls! We are always looking for something fresh. The other wounded stay."

Demosyna watched with a bloody snout as the woman walked away and mounted up. The other riders all cheered as they marched the prisoners across the field toward the fort. Rrra and Demosyna carried Jui between them, and she mercifully passed out before entering the tower. This spared Jui the sting of the whips used to encourage the prisoners and the growing dread of the approaching enslavement.

CHAPTER 6

T he large bricks of the tower Demosyna was taken to seemed ready to swallow her up, along with the fellow prisoners. Their march took an hour, and her back was quickly sore from whip marks. A wide moat encircled the walls with stagnant water that reeked of disease. The riders talked among themselves casually during the trip but preferred to bark orders to their new prisoners.

Demosyna did her best to keep pace while carrying Jui, but the windows of the tower glared like empty sockets. Many soldiers patrolled a second-story wall encircling the tower with bows ready. The lead rider crossed the thick drawbridge and dismounted before leading the prisoners. Any remaining riders stayed outside the court-yard, talking with those atop the walls.

As she cleared the arched entryway, Demosyna was once again shocked at the developments. All the walls inside the courtyard were decorated with bodies, most in states of decay. The smell hit her too, and someone behind the young apprentice retched. The unfortunate man received a club to the back, and he yelped in pain. Carrion birds pecked at the fresher cadavers, and on one wall, Bhreel was hung without armor.

His chitinous skin was shiny in the afternoon light, impaled on hooks under the arms. Bhreel's wings were spread wide against the wall, extending from his back in translucent scales of color.

Demosyna felt bile rise at the sight of his decapitated body slowly being dismantled by prying tools. The Orc's delicate wings were also impaled on hooks, and skin separated from muscle with wet sounds. Demosyna had to look away as the lead rider took the group of survivors along.

"We were lucky with that one," the lead bandit exclaimed upon seeing the flaying. "Winged Orcs are rare, even in the north. His skin will make fine armor."

The slaver laughed coldly and walked farther into the depths of Demosyna's imprisonment. Dozens of bandits milled around the open courtyard, some with cowering men following in chains. Many people were shackled while ordered about, and Demosyna began fearing she would never see freedom. A majority of the bandits were gathered around barrels containing pills that were full to the brim.

Laughter came from that corner, and Demosyna saw young teens being fed the pills. Nearly ten women clustered around the chained boys, gathering closer after all had taken the pills. No banners could be seen adorning the tower, and only the grisly display of bodies hung as visible decoration.

The lead rider escorting them paused and moved to an elf strung up on the wall. The rider took a dagger from her belt and made a long cut, stopping just short of the elf's hip. She laughed at the prisoners' reactions, and the elf's cries of anguish rang across the hourglass courtyard.

"This little beauty was a guard. Weren't you?" the rider asked as the blade cut. "You can keep watch from there."

She was led down a flight of stairs before Demosyna was directed into a cell with the women. The few men who had survived till this point were taken into an adjacent room. Demosyna lost track of Rrra when the heavy wooden door closed, giving no sound from beyond. Demosyna was left with her fellow shipmates to await their fates as doubt gnawed at her mind.

Jui awoke after the jailers left them in the cell, built as an arc into the stones. Demosyna tried to comfort her friend, but there was no water in the grimy cell. No blankets to lay upon were found either, and the filth made Demosyna gag. Many of the women in the prison were yelling for mercy from the absent bandits while others stared at the ground.

"Rrra," Jui said weakly from beside Demosyna.

"They took him through that door with the other men," Demosyna replied.

Jui opened her eyes wide and sat up onto her elbow to scan their surroundings. Demosyna saw first dismay, then outright panic as Jui confirmed her mate wasn't present.

"No, no!" Jui croaked, slamming her hand against rusty metal. "I promised I'd protect him."

Jui began to stand but fell with a cry of pain. Demosyna lifted up the back of her friend's shirt to see the wounds. Deep whip marks were not healing correctly and remained a puffy red. The rough trip to the fortress had reopened the cuts, and Jui tried to endure the pain when Demosyna tested the skin.

"The wounds are warm, Jui," Demosyna said quietly. "We need medicine for healing."

Jui sighed her understanding.

"How can I protect him like this? It's all my fault. I convinced Rrra to keep a sample of liquor to sell while the new batch is brewing. I had to be a trader and keep a little on the side."

Demosyna said nothing and waited for Jui to continue with her hand on her shoulder. Jui didn't speak again, and Demosyna leaned back against the bars. The young Wizen curled up for warmth while lying beside her shivering friend to share heat. Her outer coat had been taken, and the cold stone floor chilled the apprentice through her thin robes.

There was no window in the underground prison, and the only light came from torches. Shadows danced in the flickering flame and showed half-decomposed bodies. Demosyna and the other women were the only other living occupants of this room of the prison, it seemed.

"What are they going to do with us?" one of the passengers asked the first mate.

"Work us to death as slaves, if I make my guess," the first mate said, clearly still disoriented.

There were cries of distress at this proclamation, and the two remaining crewmates began shaking the door to the cell. Offers of gold and power were shouted, but after an hour, it became clear that nobody was coming.

It was impossible for Demosyna to say how long she was sitting in silence, listening to the desperate whimpers. A lack of natural light prevented accurate estimations, and the torches burned with an ever dimming flame. Demosyna watched Jui pass out while the first mate paced the cell. The injured sailor examined the joints of the bars with blood caking her face.

The smell of decay and excrement was ever present in the stale basement air, and Demosyna covered her nostrils with a sleeve. Their cell had no furniture, not even a bucket, and the handful of prisoners restlessly sought a place to sit. Little sound reached Demosyna through the thick stone, and the noises that did was muffled to the point of mystery. Demosyna reflected that her mind no longer raced and tried to meditate.

No matter how hard she concentrated, she couldn't remain focused and gave up on that. The young apprentice instead sat in thoughtless silence with a numb body resting against the bars. The door the men had been taken through was thrown open, and the lead rider stumbled out. She steadied herself on the bars of a cell while grinning loosely. The woman laughed to herself and ran a hand through black hair.

"It is lucky we found you. My mates were getting bored!" the lead rider proclaimed.

"Hey, Helen!" a voice from the open door yelled. "Get back in here. They are in quite the mood!"

"Don't go anywhere, little Wizen," Helen called as she walked drunkenly back and closed the door behind her.

It was timeless hours later that the door opened again, and the men were marched out. They walked into the cell without resistance, led with no chains. After the men were in the cell, they vaguely tried to view their surroundings. Heads bobbed this way and that while their eyes refused to focus. The slavers walked sloppily up to the courtyard with Helen staying behind.

70

"Well, that was fun!" Helen exclaimed in slurred speech. "I can see why you were so attached to that orange Scale."

Demosyna furrowed her brow and looked up at Helen. The rider who had captured Demosyna's party was swaying slightly, holding herself up against the bars.

"We need water," Demosyna responded quietly. "Jui won't last much longer without it."

Helen looked at the sleeping form of Jui.

"You've caught me in a generous mood after meeting your boys."

Helen removed a skin and held it out to Demosyna. When the scent of water reached her nostrils, the apprentice took a mouthful of the liquid. The young Wizen tasted water for the first time in days, lighting her eyes up. Several other women in the cell eyed the skin while gathering around the purple-scaled woman.

Kneeling down and shaking Jui gently, Demosyna gave her friend sips of water.

"Thank you," Jui whispered.

"Of course."

Demosyna passed the skin to the others.

Helen walked with a sleepy smile while leaving the prisoners in the stale dungeon. Demosyna watched the men in their cell as they sat dully looking around at nothing.

"Rrra!" Demosyna called toward the seated figure.

No response was seen from Rrra as he looked at his hand with rapt attention and a vacant face. The other men had similar reactions when those who knew them tried to engage the males. The women gave up trying to talk with the men and eventually fell into fitful sleep.

Demosyna sat on the rough stone floor and tried to process the last days. She felt untethered, lost, since her Wise Mother was killed. For the first time in her life, she was nearly alone, and the thought disturbed Demosyna beyond previous fears. Living in the Wise-woman Order, she was surrounded by peers despite her lack of innate talent.

Demosyna got little sleep, and she only knew she did sleep because of her tail. One moment, she was staring at the bars of her cage; and the next, a sharp pain was stabbing through her. Yelling in surprise, Demosyna tried to scramble forward. This proved only to increase the pain, as she was held in place by the tip of her tail. Demosyna cried out again from the crushing force but heard a laugh from behind her.

"Well, look who woke up. Here I was, just walking by, and you happened to awaken," Helen proclaimed in a mocking tone. "What are the odds?"

"Please, my tail," Demosyna cried out through the pain.

"Tail?" Helen asked and adopted an exaggerated face. "Oh, I'm stepping on your tail, am I?"

Helen pressed down on the sensitive tail harder, and there was a loud crack. Yelling wildly, Demosyna tried again to scramble away and was successful. She crawled on all fours to a corner and curled up around her screaming tail. The fellow cellmates were awakened by the apprentice's yells of pain, watching in silent horror. Helen laughed again while packing a pipe, one Demosyna recognized as Bhreel's.

Three more bandits, in full leather armor, walked down the stairs armed with crossbows. Helen unlocked the cage containing the men, who shrank away when the door opened. Two of the guards with crossbows ordered the men to follow.

"Please, ma'am, my family is wealthy and will…" one of the frightened men began before the guard grabbed him.

"We have a volunteer!" she called to the others.

"Time to earn your keep while these men earn theirs," Helen said, smoking a pipe. "Hand everything to Sklia here."

Sklia stepped forward and raised a crossbow as encouragement. Slowly, all stripped to their underclothes and walked to turn them over. Sklia laughed and turned to Helen.

"Every time, am I right? Underwear and jewelry too, stupids," Sklia told the fearful cellmates.

Demosyna, who was staying in the back of the cell, removed the rest of her clothes. Her green robes weren't made for a Scale and once again got tangled on the apprentice's tail. The gold hoops in her horns were removed with a sigh, and the young woman looked at the earrings without expression. Holding her bundle of clothes to her stomach, Demosyna meditated as the rest were stripped of their last possessions.

One by one, they shuffled forward and handed their clothes over, along with any remaining items. Covering themselves uselessly with their arms, the group waited near the bottom of the stairs. Demosyna stood without thinking much about it with her attention on the end of her tail.

"Well, you aren't bashful, are you?" Helen asked, watching each prisoner squirming before seeing Demosyna.

The young Wise-woman didn't look up and shook her head in response. Helen walked up the stairs when the first mate, still in shackles, rushed one of the bandits. The acting captain launched herself at the unaware guard and wrestled the crossbow from her hands.

"Stop!" yelled the first mate as she aimed the weapon.

Helen turned from her place on the stairs and raised her arms, palms out. A silence fell over the room, and Demosyna stood paralyzed with indecision.

"What seems to be the problem?" Helen asked.

"Let us go, or this bolt goes through your eye," the first mate barked at Helen, eyes darting.

Helen smiled broadly and continued to hold her hands up.

"There's no need for such rash actions. Put down the crossbow, and you die quickly."

The first mate backed up and glanced at the surviving crew. The passengers also cowered, and resignation registered in the acting captain's eyes. Two more armed women came bounding down the steps while aiming their bows. Lowering the weapon, the defeated sailor was overtaken by the bandits.

Demosyna watched the standoff in silence, vaguely observing the events. Even after the first mate slipped into unconsciousness, the guards took turns kicking her prone form. The other prisoners were led up to the courtyard with a smoke-filled grin when Helen grew bored of the violence. The scene inside the large courtyard was similar to the previous day, with hanging bodies on the walls.

Several bandits were sleeping in a pile with the teenage slaves, and a group of half-armored women were eating at a table. The drawbridge was up, and the prisoners were marched across the courtyard. Slavers' catcalls echoed across the stones, mocking the destitute women.

Helen called to Sklia to get rags, and she hurried off into a shack against the wall. The prisoners rubbed themselves and shuffled, yet Demosyna focused on her morning meditations. As she stood with her eyes vacant, Demosyna became aware that a young slave dressed only in his loincloth was watching her secretly.

"Looks like you have an admirer, Scale," a woman called through a mouthful of food.

The Wizen's attention was thankfully taken away from the fragrant dishes when Sklia returned with fabrics. Sklia threw the pile to the ground, and the prisoners grabbed a piece. They were rectangles of cloth, much like sacks for grain, with holes cut to allow it to be worn as a top. Several of the prisoners complained about the clothes and were clubbed for their back talk. Demosyna donned her shirt and found it came to mid-thigh. Once she scratched her shoulders, she saw it was stained with various dubious patches and reeked of decay.

At least it avoids my tail, unlike my Wizen robes, Demosyna thought.

"You lot are going down," Helen announced, motioning to the trapdoor. "Those pompous soldiers didn't think one of their own would turn, but the profit I found was too tempting! Now get down there and make me coin, you moles."

A ladder leading down into the earth was exposed once the door was opened.

"Talk to Timothy about where to work," Helen said as she walked away.

Demosyna was near the last to descend the ladder into the earth. Upon reaching the bottom, a small man was directing prisoners to their assignments.

"You, soft scale, grab a pickax and get to work," the frail man with balding brown hair said.

Demosyna broke her concentration and saw a rack of pickaxes near the man. Demosyna grabbed one, surprised by the heft of the dull metal pick.

"Follow the torches and mine ore," Timothy said with boredom. "We work until we are told to stop."

Demosyna watched those who protested be beaten by the guards. One of the passengers didn't rise again, and her body was dragged with ropes up the hole. Demosyna watched this brutality with detachment, having become numb to her surroundings.

Jui was leaning against the wall and breathing with a grimace on her lean face.

"Is there any water?" Demosyna asked the small man.

"Sure. Each piece of ore will earn you a mouthful," Timothy replied without turning around.

The handful of prisoners left did not complain and walked the paths lined with torches. Demosyna trudged along next to Jui and helped the injured woman move. Shackles around her hands were a frigid reminder of reality, and thoughts of loss threatened to overcloud Demosyna's mind. Her head was calmed by meditation as she felt indignation creep into her heart.

After many yards into the tunnel, it branched into three directions, with two lit by torches. Some discussion was had among the ragged band, and Demosyna didn't wait. She elbowed Jui to follow and headed down the rightmost path. Demosyna had never been in a mine and had no knowledge of what to look for. Jui found the first vein, and Demosyna began chipping at the crystalline ore. Each strike of the pickax sent reverberations up the apprentice's arms, rattling her bones and making her sore.

As with her night in the prison cell, time meant little underground while Demosyna tried to pry ore from the earth's grip. Demosyna's arms ached, and her fingers bled from missing scales while handling the prismatic ore.

"I'll get water, Jui. Rest a moment," Demosyna said.

Jui's eyes were closed, but she nodded and continued her haggard breathing. One final look at the shivering form motivated

Demosyna to hurry. Timothy was at the table near the ladder with sunlight streaming down in a spotlight.

"Here is some ore, Timothy," Demosyna said, offering the double handful.

He motioned to the empty barrel underneath the table, and Demosyna deposited the ore. Timothy handed Demosyna a waterskin and said nothing while she took a mouthful. Walking back to Jui with the skin, Demosyna passed people scanning the walls that glared. Jui stirred as the Wizen neared, and her eyes lit up for the first time in days.

"Drink it slowly, Jui. Otherwise, you may not keep it down," Demosyna recommended as she passed the skin.

Quickly uncapping the top, Jui upended it while she drank the stale water. Panting slightly after removing the skin from her lips, Jui handed it back. Demosyna took a pair of nourishing sips, and her body calmed from the small drinks.

"Thank you for the help, Demosyna," Jui said, her voice a whisper. "My poor Rrra. I can't stand to be apart from him."

"We will make it through this, Jui. I was taught to always find the answer no matter how obscene the task," Demosyna replied distantly, standing and helping Jui up. "I have to trust in that, if I can't use magic to help us."

Together, they worked in the hateful light to extract any ore noticed. A small group who had seen the water began milling around in a rough following, giving looks of longing.

Glancing over to see how her friend was, Demosyna noticed Jui's bright eyes were unfocused. Resting the pickax against the wall, Demosyna reached out to place a hand on Jui's shoulder. The green-scaled woman hadn't spoken in some time, and Demosyna felt a fever from Jui's body.

"Do you need a rest?" Demosyna asked softly.

"No," came the flat reply from Jui. "I need to get Rrra out of here. This place will kill us."

Demosyna said nothing and only lowered her head to ponder her own fate. There was silence for a moment before the padding of naked footsteps broke the unease. A few prisoners from the ship were approaching with an air of desperation and anger broiling.

"Hello," Demosyna said, vaguely recognizing two faces.

"Enough of your fancy talk," one of the women interrupted. "Give us the water, you entitled Wise-woman. We know you can't do magic without a staff. That elf was worthy of our fear, but you're not, and she is dead!"

There was agreement from those around her, and Demosyna blinked at the force of tone. Jui backed up a few inches to the mine wall and slid down to hide her face while sobbing. This got laughs from the mob, and Demosyna tried to comfort her friend. As she saw Jui sit on the dirty ground, the woman who demanded water grabbed Demosyna's wrist. The grip was cold despite the already chilled scales covering Demosyna.

With a series of quick blows, the woman holding the apprentice struck her eye, jaw, and stomach. The last strike took the breath from her lungs, and Demosyna slumped to the ground. The young Wise-woman lay gasping in the dust near her terrified friend. White dots danced wildly, partially obscuring the feet of the women as they kicked Demosyna. Jui cried out while dragged away and was also driven unconscious by the assault.

Time became meaningless as Demosyna drifted in the cold. The daylight passed as the two women lay, swollen and bleeding, in the dust after being robbed. When Demosyna did regain her senses, Jui was already up.

"Jui, are you okay?" Demosyna asked, then swallowed dryly.

There was no response from Jui and no indication the prone woman heard the question. As soon as Demosyna attempted to move, pain radiated from places all over her body. Gingerly, Demosyna began prodding her injured body while lying stiffly on the floor. Before any good accounting of her wounds could be acquired, there was a clamor from the entrance. Raising her head to see, Demosyna spied Helen strolling toward the two Scales.

"Get up and get out," Helen yelled. "Be happy you got captured when you did. Once the snows fall, you wouldn't get to eat once a week like you will now. The storms can kill with just the air, so be thankful we found you lost lambs."

Helen's laughter echoed as she walked past to step over Jui, who didn't acknowledge the kidnapper. Demosyna got onto all fours before approaching her injured companion. The apprentice called to Jui, but there was no sign of understanding, and Jui continued staring. Demosyna heard Jui's labored breathing and a phrase repeated over and over.

"Jui, we have to go see Rrra," Demosyna whispered.

When there was no response, Demosyna stood on trembling legs. Jui rose without any resistance, trotting forward at the gentle nudge on her damaged back. Watching on in concern, Demosyna saw Jui walk with a disturbingly blank expression. Rays of red light cast themselves into the mine as a last attempt to illuminate the world. Jui went up the ladder first, swaying in the breeze flapping at her burlap top.

The oppressively high walls around her were still decorated with torment, like the first time Demosyna was marched into the Fort. Few bandits milled around the hourglass courtyard, and Helen escorted the group back to the cells with armed guards. As she was walked toward the yawning frame, Demosyna glanced frantically for a glimpse of anything hopeful. The sight of Bhreel's mangled corpse, wings hanging limply, turned Demosyna's stomach.

The apprentice closed her eyes to steady herself and heard laughter from a corner. The outlaws were talking with a short figure carrying a flower basket. Sensing the Wise-woman's gaze, the small shadow caught eyes with the Wizen. Any time before the boat now seemed like a lifetime ago, and Demosyna wondered at the girl. Demosyna tilted her head slightly and saw elvish features under the orange hood.

I haven't seen a flower girl since leaving the Orders, Demosyna thought, turning away with a sigh. *I even sold my fair share when I was too young for schooling.*

Demosyna tried to remember her days of wandering the streets, just barely able to walk. The apprentice would be found selling flowers to anyone who noticed her for coins, which she handed to Klai.

Glancing back at the cloaked figure, Demosyna did her best to smile at the girl. The flower vendor's expression changed, and Demosyna didn't know what the look meant. It was gone as the face turned from Demosyna, leaving her in captivity once more.

The small figure said something to the bandits before handing each a flower. Demosyna watched this display with confusion but didn't have time to dwell.

Her line of chained prisoners reached the top stair, giving the apprentice a moment of respite. One by one, the captives were unchained and put back into an open cell. None resisted the orders given, having seen the consequences for noncompliance.

Demosyna paced around, trying to calm her mind when not seeing the men. Thoughts raced through her head while fatigue and anger coursed through her veins. The door atop the stairs was left open when the guards locked the women away, with shoves to encourage them. Fading light showed the figures in the cell, and Demosyna felt her mind churning with dawning reality. The beating from her fellow prisoners had shattered any illusion of comradery, and Demosyna avoided their eyes. That small street vendor had jarred loose emotions, and Demosyna was forced to see the bars as more than just metal.

Jui sat in a heap once the jailers tossed her into the cell and was by the door of the cage. When the wood door opened again, Jui turned her head to see Rrra. The men were put into a cell on the other side without restraints. Jui clasped her hands to her mouth at the sight, and tears welled up. Demosyna gasped as Rrra, along with the other men, stumbled drunkenly forward. It was clear from their gait they were intoxicated, but darkened eyes made it obvious each was about to pass out.

Shadows in the darkening cell room slid over the men as they walked naked, none resisting in the slightest. The guards ordered the men to sleep it off, and one of the men responded incomprehensibly. This caused both the guards and men to laugh while the swaying prisoners had to clutch the bars for support. Still laughing, the women walked back through the wood door, and the lock was heard turning.

"Rrra," Jui called weakly, her voice harsh.

There was a moment where Rrra continued chuckling, but finally, he turned to face Jui. Demosyna saw the expression on Rrra's face and was immediately concerned at the vacant look. Jui gasped and began crying in earnest as Rrra stepped forward, and his erect penis stuck out a few inches. Looking at the other men, Demosyna saw that they, too, had erections as they blinked mutely. The other males smiled at the roof while absently rubbing their bodies.

"Rrra, are you okay?" Demosyna asked, coming to the bars and removing her top.

Rrra leaned his head against the cold bars and smiled. He blinked rapidly and squinted with his face forming a quizzical expression. Jui called to him again, but he didn't seem to hear. Rrra's eyes went to a spot behind the two. Rrra giggled to himself and leaned his whole body against the bars, moaning slightly.

Demosyna held out her garment through the bars and tried to get Rrra's attention. Demosyna had seen people who were deep in their cups, but the way Rrra was swaying gave her great alarm. The other two men had sat down clumsily, lowering in sloppy stages. Laughing softly to themselves, each of the seated men leaned against a surface with a drooling grin.

Rrra, while singing to himself, began stroking his tail as Demosyna waved the shirt. It seemed to get his attention, as Rrra reached at the movement. Demosyna tossed the shirt toward the outstretched hands, and it landed over his forearm. Rrra laughed and took a wobbling step back into his cell. The hanging cloth got caught on the bars, dropping to the floor as he moved. Rrra stood with a puzzled look while trying to balance.

After a long moment, he started to bend down, but his horns hit against the bars with a clang. Rrra jolted back at the loud noise, shouting something too garbled to understand. Losing balance, he hit the back of the cell and slid down. Rrra lay groaning with his head and shoulders resting against the stone wall. Rrra's legs moved weakly as if through tar while he tried to sit up or turn over. Demosyna watched in shock as this played out, with Jui crying softly.

The thrown clothing Demosyna had offered Rrra lay forgotten, and the men slept after barely five minutes. Many of the women around her had watched with little interest, preferring to scowl at the Wizen. As the men lay naked and snoring across the tower, weary prisoners tried to rest. They avoided making noise to not draw more ire from the captors, and deep silence fell in the room.

Jui was once again whispering to herself as she watched her mate sleep in such an awkward position. Demosyna saw the hurt in her friend's eyes, and all thought of her own aching body left her. Jui was shaking and crying as Demosyna held her in the dark of their prison. With both of their heads closer, Demosyna could make out the words Jui was muttering.

"Far away. How can I hold you?" Jui was whispering. "You're so far away. How can I hold you?"

Demosyna heard her repeat the phrases and couldn't ease the grief. Looking from Rrra to the other two men, Demosyna felt a foreign, white-hot heat building. Sharp eyes felt prickly in her skull from the outrage and seemed to vibrate in Demosyna's head. It reminded her of when she thought a glow was on her staff, but this was more primal, as it danced in the apprentice's spine. Closing her eyes, she looked toward the sky that had been taken from her.

Demosyna felt the rolling waves of passion threaten to consume her rational thought and tried to hold on to herself. One by one, the events of the previous days began surfacing in her mind with clear and brutal reality. From the frantic rowing to the hostile survivors on the jagged shores, Demosyna saw the events anew. For the first time, she was without a Wise Mother, and a deep sadness loomed like a mental thunderhead. Memories of her early days ran in uncontrollable streams, and Demosyna saw Wise Mother Vessa walking through a garden.

Ever since Klai had taken Demosyna into her instruction, Vessa had been lost to memory. Now the words of the old Wise Mother echoed in the apprentice's mind from her earliest lessons.

* * * * *

The elder Wise Mother passed by slowly with her signature expression as she cast magic to make flowers.

"Hello, little thing," Vessa said, her voice singsong as each step grew flowers. "Walk with me as I tend my garden."

Demosyna, having been in her Orders for less than a season, laughed with Vessa and skipped through the fresh wildflowers in her wake. Marveling at the display, Demosyna ran giddily through fragrant blooms and heard Vessa laugh.

"I always make the most beautiful flowers for you, little one," Vessa said as though to herself. "Just goes to show you, the basic teachings still ring true for me!"

Demosyna, not understanding what her earliest teacher meant, ran to Vessa and held on to her coat. She laughed at the flowers before craning her neck to look up in adoration at the elf. Smiling gently, Vessa extended two long fingers for the toddler to hold as they walked.

*　*　*　*　*

Vessa had used her lyrical voice to teach the young Demosyna her earliest lessons, yet the memory surfaced with clarity. The teachings of her Order, Demosyna decided after having the memory rise, were all she had to rely on. Her apprentice library had been a second home, and the young woman scanned her memories. Anything that would help was recalled—from metal and stonework to crossbows and horses. The answer was there, Demosyna knew in her heart, and it was up to her to find safety for her friends.

The cold of the underground air was hardly noticed by Demosyna despite her lack of clothing. With her mind now turning to her situation with a new resolve, Demosyna knew sleep would not come for her. Giving a large sigh at the freshly remembered day of summer, Demosyna looked at Jui next to her and almost smiled.

"Together, everyone thrives," Demosyna whispered to Jui. "A linked chain is strong."

The injured green-scaled woman remained rocking and mumbling, so the young Wizen stood to ponder escape. Without magic, her mind would be her only tool available. Things seemed hopeless, but Demosyna refused to let her heart burn with anything but anger for her captors. Even the dismay at being robbed melted from the apprentice's mind, leaving a clear and focused goal of escape for her friends.

CHAPTER 7

The night passed achingly slow for all the prisoners, and stifled cries of sorrow were the only sounds. The apprentice stood and worried at getting her friends their freedom while fretting at options. Jui had passed out at an early-morning hour, shivering quietly in a corner. The three men remained erect and muttered for nearly an hour after they fainted. Whatever the captors had done to them was not obvious to Demosyna, as such behavior was unknown in her young life as a Wise-woman.

Demosyna was beginning to feel the first stabs of hunger, a bad sign in this desperate place. Hours of shivering contemplation passed in a fog, and now her body had exhaustion creeping over it. Demosyna had refused to acknowledge the last days, but it seemed to be catching up. Crying softly, most of the women huddled together and took glances around the shadows.

The heavy door atop the stairs opened, and Helen descended with three armored figures.

"You know the drill, little worker bees," Helen said, lighting the stolen pipe. "What happened here?"

Helen walked to where Demosyna stood rubbing her forearms while running fingers through the untidy black hair atop her head. As Demosyna opened her mouth to respond, Helen punched her in the cheek. Several of the women stifled cries at the violence, but many glared with approving hatred. Helen walked to the men's cell and picked up the discarded garment. The three men slept, drooling slightly, as Helen threw the cloth to a guard.

"If she doesn't need it, we can use it tonight!" Helen said to the soldier. "They should have slept it off by then."

Demosyna blinked tears of pain away as she gently felt her cheek for damage. Already swelling slightly, it seemed unbroken, but her snout remained bleeding. For the second time, Demosyna felt a raw wave of emotion sweep along her spine, illuminating her nerves. The new pain in her face fell into obscurity as Demosyna breathed deeply to calm herself.

Helen saw the young woman steadying herself and smiled.

"Looks like you are made of stronger stuff than you seemed! Cheers."

Helen clapped shackles onto Demosyna's wrists while the other guards bound the weakened prisoners. Demosyna kept her eyes down while she was walked toward the mine entrance by the drawbridge. It was raised, blocking her view of the fields, so the young woman didn't tease herself with sights of freedom. The blood-drenched walls and gore were things Demosyna didn't wish to view either, so she focused on her claws.

Jui walked a few people behind Demosyna, and Helen addressed the sorrowful woman.

"Looks like we need to dry you out."

Helen grabbed Jui's shackles. Several bandits in the courtyard cheered as Helen found an empty hook. Demosyna watched in wonder as Jui didn't resist this cruel treatment and only cried softly. The shabby cloth that served as a shirt was pulled above her bright-green hips, but Jui didn't seem to care. Jui's eyes were distant as she hung against the bloody wall. The hook Helen chose was in the path of the rising sun, and Jui had to squint to not be blinded.

"That should be good in a few days, eh?" Helen asked loudly to a group lounging with slaves.

The bandits laughed, and Demosyna found herself taking a step forward without thinking. As she took another step toward Jui, Demosyna was stopped by a hand grabbing her horn. The hand yanked with enough force to stagger her, but the apprentice kept her eyes on Jui. Managing to maintain her footing from the grapple, Demosyna felt a steel boot strike her knee.

The Wise-woman went face-first into the dirt and curled up into a ball while expecting further attacks. When none came, Demosyna glanced around and saw Helen walking back. All the slaves had backed up to as near the bloody walls as they dared. A small group of bandits at the tables watched the scene, shoving aside the small flower girl.

You shouldn't be here, little one. Run from here with those flowers and never look back, Demosyna thought while Helen produced a dagger.

Helen walked confidently toward the cowering Wizen with a smile plastered on her face.

"What did you want?" Helen asked. "You want to take her place?"

Demosyna looked at the fresh blood from her nose and shook her head, not trusting her voice. The flower girl was gathering a basket that was dropped as the guards walked past. The approaching women raised crossbows, readying them as they did. Fear gripped Demosyna as she saw the group of bandits encircle her while pulling her upright. The young apprentice was held facing Helen by her horns and unable to turn her head.

"I thought the first mate would be the last problem, but I see this Scale is trouble." Helen barked at the prisoners, "Watch and understand."

Helen took a step toward Demosyna and raised her knife to eye level. Demosyna saw the keen, glinting edge shine in the new sun as Helen inched it closer. Panic threatened to overwhelm Demosyna as her blindness drew near. Demosyna cried out but only succeeded in drawing laughter from the bandits around her.

The long dagger was inches from her left eye, and Demosyna braced herself. The orange-cloaked flower girl stood near a dining table, her bundles of flowers colorful reminders of better days. Demosyna remembered her walks with Vessa in the flower gardens the Wise Mother loved to make. Memories of flowers filled her mind and eyes as Demosyna focused on what would be a pleasant last sight.

The girl holding the flowers to her chest caught Demosyna's eye, tilting her small head questioningly. Breaking eye contact with the short flower girl, Demosyna let the image of the flowers fill her. The helpless woman tried to ignore the shiny steel touching her eyelid and the gleeful smile Helen wore. The sharp pain of the knife piercing her flesh was not enough to break Demosyna away from looking at the flowers.

Helen paused for just a moment when she saw Demosyna's gaze drift, and the flower girl disappeared. In an instant, the bright-orange cloak was gone, leaving only a falling bouquet. Demosyna widened her eyes in disbelief, and Helen's grin faltered. Helen withdrew the knife from Demosyna's eye and began turning to follow her gaze.

As suddenly as the flower girl was gone from view, Demosyna heard cries of pain ring out. The air grew thick with tension and the metallic smell of blood from beyond her vision. Panic seemed to grip all those in the curved courtyard as overlapping noises formed a chorus of anarchy. Yells of pain were overshadowed by the tinny clang of metal, and Demosyna turned her head dully.

The sight that met her eyes took Demosyna a moment to understand. The courtyard that she had passed through not ten minutes ago was strewn with dismembered bodies. Decapitated torsos were lying in pools of dark mud, and others twitched as life flowed from amputated limbs. Fifteen bodies littered the once bustling courtyard as Helen ran.

The blur of an orange cloak darted from a decapitated bandit, nearly too fast to track. Demosyna tried to follow the dot, but the fluttering motion was too swift. Every time the cloak came near one of the slavers, they lost an appendage.

Anguished cries rose to a fever pitch as the remaining bandits rushed the blur that was obliterating them. Helen jumped at where the smear had just removed Sklia's right leg. A loud clang rang out, jarring Demosyna into action.

"I'll finish what I started with your soldiers," Helen yelled in a fury. "This is my fort now, you arrogant bitch!"

As the dust settled from the leap Helen took, Demosyna saw the small flower girl again. She was holding a sword to block the downward swing while using only one arm. Demosyna furrowed her brow in utter confusion at the sight of the four-foot figure holding back the ferocity Helen displayed.

Yet again, the apprentice found herself walking toward Jui. It was less than a dozen paces before she reached Jui, but in that time, Helen's duel continued. As her body moved of its own accord, Demosyna watched the flower girl throw Helen's blade aside. The orange cloak was a blur of dark blood, and Demosyna couldn't look away.

Jui watched Demosyna approach with the bandits beginning to form a shield circle around the flower girl. The bashing of swords rang in time with Demosyna's heartbeat, and she found a foothold. She clawed between the joined stones and climbed up awkwardly with her bound hands.

Demosyna was quite fond of climbing the rocky cliffs and walls of the country around her original Orders. Many Scales shared the love of using strong limbs in tandem when scuttling. Even in this dire time, her body remembered, and she scurried up the wall.

Demosyna tried to lift Jui off the cruel hook while gripping the seams of the wall. Jui was gaunt from malnutrition but still larger in size than Demosyna was herself. Demosyna strained, and her first attempt at raising the shackles high enough to clear the hook failed. Shield bearers now surrounded the flower girl with Helen pressing forward. The door to the basement prisons prevented further retreat, and Helen charged confidently with a yell.

Demosyna watched the cornered flower girl stand still as the large, armored Helen bore down. In a blur that seemed invisible, Helen was thrown through the door with a crash of rending metal. When Helen didn't reappear in the doorway, all the bandits seemed hesitant to continue.

As Demosyna turned her attention back to Jui, the cloaked elf jumped and impaled a bandit through the head. The flower girl rode the toppling body before blurring out of sight. Not wanting to waste any more of this opportunity, Demosyna grabbed the chain again. Using her legs too this time, the apprentice hoisted Jui up and dropped her. Jui looked up at Demosyna gripping the wall with her belly pressed against the bloody stones.

"We can't leave Rrra," Jui said, barely audible.

Demosyna opened her mouth to respond but lost her grip. Clawing desperately for a moment, she pushed off the wall and landed next to Jui. Demosyna stood as quickly as her shackled state permitted and faced her friend. Over Jui's shoulder, there were seven bandits standing against the flower girl, all behind grand shields. Nodding in acknowledgment, Demosyna felt waves of passion forming in her spine.

Time seemed to slow for Demosyna, and the air felt cool and moist against her naked scales. The strong wind that had followed her for months whipped around the apprentice's eyes. Power and emotion surged up her spine and down her tail as Demosyna looked at her hands. Her shackles were rattling in the wind and smacking against her wrists painfully. Jui glanced suddenly at her own chains, which had also begun jerking violently.

As the wind continued to increase, debris from a meter around began circling like a cyclone. Jui opened her mouth to speak, but the words were lost in the gale. Demosyna could no longer see the bandits or the assaulting elf through the dusty wall of wind. After another heartbeat, her shackles began vibrating and hovered above the apprentice's wrists.

Looking down with wide eyes, Demosyna saw the clasp holding the bands snap open. The chains fell to the ground with a puff of dust, liberating the shocked apprentice. A moment later, Jui's shackles joined hers, and Demosyna looked up in disbelief. The young Wizen saw Jui with a similar look on her panicked face.

Whatever was happening around her seemed to have stopped, as the fierce wind was gone from enclosing them. Time returned to a normal pace for Demosyna after receiving a flash of half-understood clarity.

"What..." Jui began, but a bolt shot between the two.

Crouching instinctively, Demosyna turned to see guards coming up from the stairwell. They were in various states of undress and firing to lay down cover. This new danger caused Jui and Demosyna to ignore the strangeness that just happened. The important issue was their new freedom, so they both scrambled weakly up the wall. Shouts and bolts bounced off the stones as they climbed the defenses, indifferent to their injured bodies.

Once at the top, both women lay on their backs and breathed heavily. The thick walls allowed both to lay side by side, hearing the shouts and clangs. As Demosyna rose to her feet, she was taken aback by the sight beyond the walls. Standing silently in formations were hundreds of imperial soldiers. Squad leaders bore large poles with banners tied down to avoid noise. The shining armor glittered as Demosyna and Jui gaped, momentarily forgetting the danger.

From atop the twenty-foot-high walls, Demosyna saw the ranks standing as orderly rows of death. Crouching back down behind the cover of the spaced stones, Jui and Demosyna both froze at the silence that fell. Wind whistled in the courtyard, but no other sound was heard from the First Fort. No more cries of pain disturbed the morning air, and it frightened the apprentice more than the killing. Demosyna was hesitant to peek over the edge but readied herself.

Jui looked with fearful eyes, and Demosyna knew without her saying that Rrra was what mattered. Steadying herself with a breath, Demosyna crawled flat against the wall to the edge. Pondering on the fate of the shackled prisoners, Demosyna assumed the worst from the unnerving stillness. The apprentice cried out despite herself as the sound of two horn blasts erupted from the silence below.

In response to the horn, one long note was sent from the silent army. The noise of thunderous footfalls followed once the deep blast finished echoing across the fields. A rumbling atop the wall signaled the army moving inward to Demosyna's prison. Jui stiffened, and Demosyna froze in place, unable to peek at the carnage.

Several moments passed in this manner, with the steady rhythm of the marching army behind and the ringing stillness below. Demosyna found that no thoughts but fleeing filled her head, and sweat formed on her purple scales. She momentarily considered flight over the wall and into the sea via the docks beyond.

"No," Demosyna said aloud, angry at the thought.

Demosyna resolved to stay and see things through, hoping for Rrra's safety.

Just as the young Wise-woman was moving to peek an eye over, a voice called out, and she froze.

"You two up there"—the voice sounded strong in the morning air—"climb down and present yourselves before me."

The voice clapped with a steady calm, from years of commanding others, up at the two women. They glanced between themselves, and both nodded before peering over the side. A solitary figure stood in the shattered doorway, dwarfed by the frame due to her stature. Before the flower girl was a fanning spread of corpses, many in full armor. All the defeated bandits were missing at least one appendage and bleeding out into the dirt. Every single one of the slavers was bloody and dead on the filthy floor they had called home.

CHAPTER 8

The deadly flower girl approached the two Scales as they descended, marching the courtyard with a confident stride. Her dark robes had the hood down, revealing a youthful face with short-cropped hair. Demosyna reached the bottom of the wall before Jui, who went slower due to illness. The panting young woman saw the prisoners sitting silently near the mine entrance. The small elf crossed the gore of the courtyard while effortlessly avoiding her carnage.

When the two were at the bottom of the wall again, they knelt before the figure, who stopped paces from them. The soldier regarded them silently with hands behind her back. After eyeing the two in terrifying glances, the elf spoke with a voice older than her youthful body would denote.

"Who are you two?" the short figure asked, her eyes level with the kneeling women.

"My name is Demosyna, and this…" Demosyna began, but the soldier held up a hand.

"Has she a tongue?" the youthful elf asked sharply.

"Jui, soldier," Jui rasped, clasping her hands.

Demosyna had seen Jui act this way with other imperial officers on the ship, always addressing them formally.

The short figure motioned to the cowering prisoners.

"Are you prisoners with them?" she asked, eyeing the two with suspicion.

"Yes, soldier," Demosyna replied, mirroring Jui's posture.

"I am Sai Aeri," the elf said, never breaking eye contact with Demosyna. "Lie to me again, and I will remove your head. A Wizen wouldn't be taken prisoner easily, and I saw that whirlwind."

Demosyna shivered from the intense glare before tilting her head in confusion.

"I speak true, ma'am," Demosyna replied, dread falling over her again. "I was with Jui and the other prisoners there and the boys below."

Sai Aeri glanced at Jui before craning her neck to gaze atop the wall. A stern, thoughtful look remained upon her young face as her eyes searched. Long moments passed in silence, broken by the sound of approaching footsteps.

"Where are your bindings and her clothes?" Sai Aeri asked Jui finally.

For a moment, Jui didn't answer, and Demosyna saw that Jui was frozen in terror. Jui remained deadly still, pointing toward the pair of crude shackles. Following Jui's pointing hand, Sai Aeri turned on her heels, which were armored boots of elven design. Held behind her back in one fist was a filigreed sword, lying flat along Sai Aeri's spine.

Bending slightly to pick up the iron handcuffs, Sai Aeri addressed the huddling group of survivors.

"Are they with you as prisoners?" Sai Aeri asked with her voice rising to overcome the approaching army.

Demosyna glanced from the imposing orange cloak to her fellow prisoners with a look of pleading. Those who huddled across the courtyard looked fearfully toward the soldier. Masks of contempt formed like a tide across their faces in the silence. With dismay, Demosyna waited for them to answer, but none did.

After more than a minute, Sai Aeri tapped the sword against her back several times. Sai Aeri removed her orange cloak to reveal a familiar set of armor, one Demosyna had seen not so long ago. It had shone aboard the small imperial boat that passed during her trip. The figure had been at the wheel of the sleek craft, Demosyna recalled, and likely was the general of the army outside. Sai Aeri sparkled with the impressive filigree of her supremely high rank in the imperial army.

"It matters not either way," Sai Aeri said to those in the court-yard. "Helen was tricky, but I have destroyed her utterly. We will hear your fable in time, so put these on."

Sai Aeri tossed each of the Scales their shackles as she strode toward the drawbridge at the far side of the double courtyard. In numb silence, the two women obeyed the instructions and once more felt metal against their wrists. Sai Aeri sheathed her sword and removed a pair of armored gloves from her belt. Using the simple controls for the drawbridge, Sai Aeri slowly lowered the banded door to reveal the army.

Sai Aeri strode out across the bridge created and addressed the first officer. After only a few stressful minutes, Sai Aeri returned. A stream of soldiers marched silently three wide across the courtyard toward the stairs.

"Please, my mate, Rrra, he is down with the other men," Jui cried, her voice breaking.

Demosyna looked toward the retreating Sai Aeri and once more thought of Rrra. It worried Demosyna how helpless he had seemed the previous night from whatever was done to him. Sai Aeri didn't answer at first, and instead, she directed those following to begin unhooking the bodies.

As the soldiers began removing the corpses from their grisly impalement, Sai Aeri walked back to Demosyna.

"Hang Helen outside to warn any left on raids," Sai Aeri told the first officer. "Take the prisoners below and see them clothed and fed. Keep a special eye on these two as you do. This one crawled the wall in shackles."

Demosyna saw Sai Aeri motion in her direction at that remark, and she looked back silently. With one final quizzical look, Sai Aeri walked away without another word.

The mask in the first officer's helmet was bright gold. She barked orders to the soldiers. Removing her mask from the helmet, the officer looked much older than the general appeared.

"Follow me please," the first officer said flatly.

Jui and Demosyna complied, trailing the monotone soldier to the other prisoners. After rejoining her deniers, Demosyna was led down into the cells. The first officer directed them to the males' cell, which had all the men sitting against the wall. They had recovered their faculties but were crouched, looking scared and confused.

When Jui saw Rrra, her eyes filled with tears, and she shuffled over to him. Demosyna joined them in the cell and took a seat, her knees pressed to her chest.

"My beautiful boy, I have you again," Jui whispered, rocking Rrra while they wept.

Rrra moaned distantly, not seeming to be able to articulate yet. In minutes, armored soldiers brought the prisoners clothes of thick cloth and simple rations. None complained as the provisions were passed over, with all now dressed and chewing. Demosyna fetched enough for her friends, happily reunited at last. Jui smiled as Demosyna returned with the supplies, and the green-scaled woman wrapped Rrra in robes before offering food.

He turned his head away when Jui did, and she sadly bit into the offered cheese. Rrra had his hand over closed eyes as though the light hurt the orange-scaled man. As Demosyna, too, clothed and began eating, she noticed the passengers were avoiding them. Demosyna marveled at the previous night spent in contemplation over her dry bread, having not formed a viable escape plan.

The terror of being blinded had left the apprentice nearly hopeless, for without sight, escape would have been impossible. Fortune was with them, as their rescue had come from a most unlikely source. Reunited couples paired off as the hours passed, and Demosyna could hear the vague sounds of work from above. No soldier visited them in their subterranean jail, even when several of the more affluent prisoners rallied to be heard.

When a soldier did arrive to address the prisoners, the first officer came with buckets. After placing them beside the locked cell door, the officer glanced at the prisoners.

"We will see you one at a time," the soldier said in a bored tone, flipping through her keys, "starting with the crew and first class."

Kicking the buckets inside the cell, the first officer told the group to use them as toilets. Hours passed, and many of the prisoners were taken to be debriefed. Eventually, Demosyna saw she was being pointed at and walked past the others. Marching Demosyna ahead of her, spear ready, the officer led the shackled woman into the blinding sun. Her eyes adjusted to the blue sky, and Demosyna was shocked to find the courtyard pristine.

The bodies of the bandits and the tortured adorning the walls were gone. No trace remained of the viscera that decorated the fort, with even the dirt swept thoroughly. Demosyna saw banners unfurled at intervals by guards atop the walls to cover the engravings. The courtyard was likewise populated by trios of soldiers at the perimeter or standing in rapt attention at stations.

Demosyna was taken to one of the shacks that lined the walls, ushered inside by the first officer. The golden-masked elf remained outside after closing the door, saluting before leaving. Seated at a wooden desk was Sai Aeri, writing with a quill when Demosyna entered. After resting her pen, the general stood and greeted the young apprentice.

"Have a seat, Demosyna."

Sai Aeri remained standing as Demosyna obeyed.

"Tell me how you came to be in my realm."

Demosyna looked with a confused expression at Sai Aeri before bringing a hand to her chin, glancing away to gather her thoughts. Beginning with the uneventful voyage, she recounted the story of her shipwreck. Demosyna held back tears when telling the subsequent hardships of the beaches and forest. Sai Aeri remained silent, sitting down and taking notes only after Demosyna recalled the imperial inspection.

When Demosyna told of Klai and Bhreel dying before entering the Fort, Sai Aeri made a quick note and narrowed her eyes at the news.

"Bhreel was skinned on the wall," Demosyna said, remembering the sight with disgust. "They kept us down in the cells without food and only got water if we mined."

Sai Aeri nodded absently at this, and Demosyna swallowed with a dry throat. Once Demosyna had told of her surprise at the sudden attack from the flower girl, she fell silent and waited for a response.

"You gave me the distraction I needed," Sai Aeri told Demosyna, who nodded in confusion. "For days before you arrived, I was waiting for the opportunity to take back my fort. Helen thought herself smart, but I knew she would rise against me while I was away."

Demosyna was taken aback by her involvement in the slaughter and felt shame rising in her mind. Sai Aeri studied the seated woman carefully and rose to stand eye to eye.

"Where did your Orders' chest sink?" Sai Aeri asked in a clipped tone. "If you are not working with Helen to steal my lands, you will know."

Demosyna responded, thinking hard, "It was about two days' march through the woods. The shore turned to rock where the boats sank, and that's why so many people died."

Demosyna shook back tears, remembering the chaos that had engulfed her that day. After placing papers on the desk, Sai Aeri glared at Demosyna with sudden contempt.

"You seek protection as a Wise-woman, yet none of your mates claim that you are magically gifted," Sai Aeri said sternly. "I have taken back my fort, and I will not have you jeopardize that. I accept the mystery surrounding you for now since I will investigate your claims. Even without official papers, if you prove yourself an apprentice by lighting that candle, I will unbind you."

Fear gripped its teeth into her heart, and Demosyna felt a cold sweat form. Sai Aeri stood at attention with her hand on the hilt of a deadly blade. Even with her staff, she was unable to do what the new captor asked, and the thought of her powerlessness filled Demosyna.

"I am but an apprentice Wizen, soldier," Demosyna said humbly, trying to steady her voice. "I have not been able to do magic yet."

A shadow passed over Sai Aeri's face when Demosyna responded, and she called for the guards. Two entered the small space at once, and each placed a hand on Demosyna's shoulders.

"I do not tolerate lies. Take her to her friends," Sai Aeri ordered as she stared with a withering expression. "I will find who you are despite what you think of me."

Demosyna looked from the guards to the small general before her, growing despair filling her heart. The apprentice was led back to the cells and sat numbly down next to her sleeping companions. All proof of her identity was lost in the sinking of her boat, frustrating the apprentice greatly. Despite being saved from the blood-thirsty slavers, Demosyna found that her future was still dangerously unknown.

* * * * *

Morning brought little comfort, but fresh bread and water were provided by unarmed soldiers. After being marched out to the courtyard, the small group of remaining survivors shivered in the cold air. Every ten feet along the wall, both on the ground and atop, shiny-armored soldiers stood at attention while Sai Aeri spoke.

"Jui, Rrra, Demosyna," Sai Aeri called, reading from a scroll, "you are given the worker's path into the Fist. Seven years indentured servitude to gain citizenship, so say I, and so says my Empress."

Jui and Rrra both looked shocked at the news before clutching each other tightly. Knowing the word of the Empress was law, all three understood Sai Aeri had just declared their fates in no uncertain terms. Demosyna looked from her friends' grief to the general before her.

"I do not understand. We were to be given entry with our seeder tickets," Demosyna said weakly. "As a Wise-woman, am I—"

Sai Aeri cut her off before she could continue, silencing the sobs of her friends.

"I will not hear any more lies from you, Demosyna. You claim to be an impotent Wizen, yet I watched you slip shackles with a powerful magic. Since I cannot prove you are not working with Helen, unless you take my offer, you all will be executed as enemies of my Empress."

Demosyna opened her mouth, but no words came to her in her distress. Demosyna did remember the gale of helplessness that had surrounded her, freeing them from their bindings. How it had happened was beyond her, and the apprentice frowned at the general in frustration.

"You still look at me like I am nothing," Sai Aeri sighed, turning from the group. "Take them away, and send word that the rest are to be released. Once proof of identity is confirmed, they will mine till a rescue debt is paid."

Before she or any other prisoner could voice a single protest, Demosyna and her two friends were chained together. Seven soldiers were assembled to take the shaking prisoners north, to the nearest outpost, for processing into servitude.

Marching forward slowly with her numb body, Demosyna heard the muted cries of the remaining prisoners fade. Gently rising hills guided the party along, nearly leaving the First Fort in their bloody past. Looking toward the west, Demosyna recalled the ocean that had borne her to this fate and the frigid nature that now held her in its grasp.

CHAPTER 9

Jui struggled to march through the gentle hills despite the leisurely pace the mounted soldiers took. Demosyna was behind
the woman and saw that Jui's posture revealed dark lines on the
fresh clothes. It had been days since medicine had been applied, and
the shuddering figure before Demosyna was worse off than ever.

"Jui, do you need to rest?" Demosyna whispered.

"No. There is nothing we need from you."

Jui didn't turn as she responded, her horned head looking at the
ground.

The anger she heard in her friend's voice quieted any further
questions for Demosyna, who glanced back at Rrra. A last dot of
the Fort that had held them prisoner was behind the man, and he
glowered. The memory of imprisonment already seemed a dream, as
the troops Demosyna now dealt with were a familiar presence from
childhood. Hardly a day passed when an imperial soldier wasn't there
to enforce the will of the Empress, and the young Demosyna came to
feel such was valuable.

The speed at which she and her new friends' fates had been
decided over the days was exhausting for Demosyna, who tried to
avoid stumbling. Flashes of clubs and laughing faces would dissolve
into the stern mask of imperial authority at the Fort. If only she could
have done even a simple spell to prove herself, Demosyna thought as
she watched the soft grasses spring around purple feet.

Failing to identify herself as a Wise-woman was the latest in a long string of failures Demosyna recalled during the arduous march north. Pain bit into her scales from the arctic winds and occasional jagged rock, along with the injuries she carried. Her latest Wise Mother's voice rang through her mind like a bell, tolling Demosyna's ineptitude with each frozen breath. The ache in her chest was worse than before, and Demosyna clutched a hand to her shirt.

Each of the seven soldiers who escorted the slaves was mounted with bespoke armor, seeming to flow like water with the slightest twitch. Their horses walked so quietly that even feet away, Demosyna heard only soft padding of hoof on dirt. The rolling country led to the forests beyond as the small group progressed with jangling steps.

Upon reaching the edge of the forest, Demosyna saw it was nearly an even curve around the Fort from extensive maintenance performed by slaves. The group was halted by the commander, who removed the gold mask to speak. All the prisoners collapsed in breathless heaps at the order to stop.

"Thirty minutes rest. Then we proceed till dark," the first officer announced.

Demosyna looked up from her seated position and saw a narrow path worn through the trees. It was so thin and overgrown at the entrance that Demosyna would likely have walked right by it. The Wise-woman found a small comfort that the journey for Jui would be easier now than in the southern forest. Fleeing blindly through massive trees with the sounds of death at her heels was one of the only clear memories Demosyna had from those days.

As Demosyna glanced from Jui to Rrra, both of her fellow prisoners turned their gaze. Demosyna had to fight back tears and remind herself of the first night of imprisonment. It seemed like weeks ago, yet the promise she had made to herself still echoed in the apprentice's mind. Escape for her friends was once again the only desire Demosyna had.

Taking the offered skin from a soldier, each of the prisoners greedily drank some of the precious liquid.

"I'm sorry, Jui, for getting you into this," Demosyna whispered, almost to herself. "I will find a way to explain our situation to—"

Rrra cut her off, anger in his voice.

"Enough, Wizen. Last time you talked, we got seven years for your troubles."

Jui nodded painfully in agreement and glowered at Demosyna with fresh exhaustion. Demosyna knew their new sentence was her doing, just as her failure to protect her Wise Mother was.

My weakness resulted in them getting tortured for days, Demosyna thought numbly. *I would hate me too.*

With a resigned sigh, Demosyna nodded and turned to face the woods that stood over and around her. The soldiers near them said nothing to the prisoners and simply waited, scanning the pristine open fields. A commander stood with the animals as they drank water, nickering at one another.

During the short rest she was given, Demosyna tried to center herself and calm her mind. The proposition of being enslaved, even if it was legal, had no appeal to the apprentice. Demosyna tried to block out the memories of running free in the face of her new reality. Such dreams would not help her now, she thought as the cold metal shackles rubbed unrelentingly. This further served to remind Demosyna she wasn't free with her Empress, who promised equality in the Fist.

"Thoughts of flowers and warm beds are foolish," Demosyna chided herself, shaking her head and rocking. "I must be able to help somehow."

The rest of the daylight was spent walking single file between mounted guards along a smooth path. For hours, the party moved through the wild trees that sent playful leaves dancing. Demosyna barely noticed, as she was straining her mind to recount each detail of the previous day. She had freed their shackles during her outburst and analyzed the experience as she walked.

The chaos of that moment, from the fear of blindness to the sudden hope of the slaughter, made the memory unreliable. The smell of dirt, the sting of the cold tornado, and the sudden feeling of control that had accompanied the shackles falling—all were details Demosyna sought so desperately to understand and imitate.

I will try. No, Demosyna thought, determined to keep her promise, *no, I will free us. All it will take is me being a Wise-woman on purpose.*

Demosyna felt resolve fill her mind, but Jui fell, dragging the young woman into the dirt. The gold mask of the first officer approached the prone figures with other soldiers fanning out. Jui was gasping for breath and sweating while her arms shook trying to hold herself upright. Demosyna felt a heat rising from the woman and feared the worst when Jui didn't open her eyes.

"Are you able to stand?" the first officer asked.

Jui gave no response, and Rrra called out hoarsely, "Dear heart, are you here with me?"

Rrra's voice was a gentle rasp, and Jui did stir fitfully at his voice. Rrra called out with tears in his eyes, but a soldier placed a hand on his shoulder to prevent his crawling to Jui.

The commander knelt down to examine Jui before taking a key and dagger from the gleaming armor. The commander prodded Jui on a horn with the dagger, carefully watching the prisoners. The first officer slowly unshackled the helpless woman after only a moan escaped Jui.

"We will carry her to the river camp on my horse," the officer decided, removing her saddle.

"Thank you, ma'am," Rrra gasped. "She is so weak."

The commander said nothing and gestured her soldiers to put the unconscious Jui on. The first officer's golden mask was vaguely face shaped but had no emotion carved into the surface. Given the small blessing in hard times, Demosyna felt a shred of hope blossom in her heart.

"With just a bit of care, Jui will get better for sure," Demosyna convinced herself, wondering at the unfamiliar feeling. "I will get her healed, and we can survive together."

* * * * *

It did not take long for the prisoners to reach the camp the commander had mentioned. The sound of a river was heard before the trees parted to reveal a clearing with tents. A cold firepit and a hitching post sat away from the bank of the half-frozen river. Its flow was slow and choked with ice, yet it hadn't completely frozen over for the season. The river ran toward the ocean in the west, uncaring of the prisoners' plight.

Demosyna puffed clouds of fatigue as she was taken near the tents. The apprentice was chained by the horses with Rrra, who kept his eyes on his mate. The air had grown still, and the sound of Jui muttering was heard as the soldiers carried her.

Rrra was shivering with cold but refused to stand near Demosyna. Avoiding a fight, Demosyna retreated into her memories. Demosyna was only vaguely aware of the soldiers talking in hushed tones as the first officer started a fire. The smell of food reached her, and Demosyna was taken away from her meditations. Rrra, too, stood up from his defeated posture to watch the guards bring food.

Without responding to their gratitude, the soldiers brought a third bowl into the tent Jui slept in. As she tried not to burn herself, Demosyna watched them bring the full bowl back out. They shook their heads at the officer, who observed the feeding from the fire. She nodded, and the commander took the bowl for herself. Unhooking the ornate gold mask from its helmet, the first officer began eating too.

Rrra had already finished his portion, and Demosyna downed the chilling meal before the horses noticed. The steady lapping of the river was a welcome sound, having slept many nights with a rhythmic flow while sailing. A warm meal in her belly, along with the tiring march, caused Demosyna to feel overwhelmingly drowsy. Sitting with her back against a post, Demosyna let her arms hang above her horns.

As she drifted to sleep, Demosyna felt she was so close to finding the answer that it would be easy to escape. She smiled happily for the first time in days at the small light of hope. The apprentice was sound asleep minutes after finishing her meal, chained hands almost touching Rrra's. Even when it started snowing, Demosyna slept better than she had in days.

* * * * *

Morning came too early nevertheless, as the soldiers roused the prisoners after the sun crested the mountains. Stiff joints prevented either Rrra or Demosyna from moving quickly as the two brushed snow off themselves. They were brought to the tent where Jui had spent the night.

The commander opened the tent flaps to show the two prisoners Jui. She was lying on a bed of straw face down, and the wounds on Jui's back were infected. Her scales fell in uneven time as she labored for each cold breath. Rrra stifled a cry and turned to the commander with fear written on his orange face.

"Please, ma'am, let me tend to her," Rrra pleaded.

The officer considered in silence for what seemed like too much time, and Demosyna furrowed her brow. All soldiers were trained in basic first aid, as the apprentice knew from the lessons Klai gave, so the lack of action confused Demosyna. Rrra grew more distressed at the silence from the soldiers around them, the last of the snow drifting.

"It will cost too much to take her with us. We chain her here and will return once we deliver you," the gold mask said.

Rrra stood with Demosyna in stunned silence before calling out, "No. I beg you, ma'am. She will not survive alone."

Demosyna nodded in agreement and opened her mouth, but the commander raised a hand. The signal prompted all the soldiers to draw swords like deadly stingers ready to strike. Falling back in fear, Demosyna and Rrra dropped to the icy ground against the aggression. Demosyna felt an all-too-familiar feeling stab up her spine, freezing her nerves and revving her mind.

"It is likely she will die, yes," the commander said, causing Rrra to sob louder. "Perhaps we should simply end her suffering. I hate to see things languish without cause."

Before either prisoner could process this latest development, the first officer dragged Jui away. Jui's wrists were bound, and the unconscious woman was unaware of the threat. Rrra cried out in protest, but the commander didn't slow as she pulled Jui face down over the riverbank. Two soldiers held Rrra down, and his claws dug futilely in the cold ground as he tried to crawl to the brittle river ice.

The officer dropped the ankle shackles once the muttering Jui was on the bank. A gold mask looked at the feverish woman before shaking its head with puffs of steam pouring from the helmet. The soldier stomped on the ice with her metal boots while Jui tried to rise. Cracks formed under the feet of the officer, and the ice holding Jui gave way. Jui's green scales shone bright as the woman fell through the ice and into the freezing water.

Rrra screamed in desperation and clawed forward, dragging the soldiers with him. Demosyna tried to run toward the river but was also held by unforgiving arms. Her face was smashed into the frozen ground, and Demosyna felt blood from her nose fall to darken the snow.

"No," Demosyna yelled wildly, clawing at the hard ground for purchase. "You can't kill her."

Demosyna spun around, falling hard onto her back while using her powerful legs to kick. The soldiers pinning the Wise-woman lost their grips with angry cries. Demosyna sprang away, eyes big and searching for any sign of her friend. Green scales reflected the dim light of this fresh nightmare, and Demosyna tried to reach Jui.

Rrra saw Demosyna's success and spun onto his back while clawing with unrestrained fury. Demosyna didn't know how Rrra was faring and focused only on the fading head still bobbing above the surface. The first officer, who had turned to survey the disturbance, sprinted to intercept the leaping Demosyna. The soldier drew her sword and yelled toward the other elves.

"Restrain that prisoner. I will handle this one," the officer barked. "Halt in the name of the Empress."

The first officer skidded to a halt feet from the water, and a raised sword prevented Demosyna from helping. The tone of command sent chills through Demosyna, and she found her traitor legs stopping out of some deep response. In disbelief, Demosyna stared down the edge of the jeweled sword. It was held at eye level by the commander, and Helen laughed in the Wizen's mind. Demosyna withered from the murder in the soldier's eyes while feeling her body grow distant.

Rrra was still screaming loudly, and Demosyna heard a pained yelp before he quieted with distressing suddenness. Jui was now just a green dot in the clear, frozen river, and one of her clawed hands gripped a chunk of ice.

"Please let me save her. I can carry her the whole way," Demosyna pleaded with the gold mask from her knees. "It is not too late. You can double my sentence. I swear on my pathetic life, I will return with Jui. Just let me help this once!"

"No. You two may yet prove valuable, but she would not have been a good investment."

The commander took a dominating step forward.

Demosyna shrank away in reflex while holding back tears of fury. She was led to Rrra, who remained bleeding on the snowy ground. Jui was no longer visible after being carried along toward the ocean by the timeless river. One of the soldiers was bandaging long scratches across her face, courtesy of Rrra. The frigid lands of the Fist now took Demosyna into her own decisions and away from any life she had known.

CHAPTER 10

The sound of the river seemed deafening in her ears as Demosyna took one begrudging step after another. Thoughts seemed to fade away as each pace took her closer to the still form of Rrra on the ground.

Another reminder of my failures, Demosyna thought hopelessly, gritting her teeth.

If Demosyna started weeping, she might not stop, she knew, and would wind up the same as Jui. The casual way the first officer tossed a life away shook Demosyna down to her core. A creeping sensation traveled along her spine from tail to crown as the apprentice walked. Rrra lay where he had been beaten and twitched slightly as the soldiers mounted their horses.

Early-morning light glinted off the twisted inlay of her gold mask as the commander spoke.

"We march till dark and will reach the next camp after sundown. I expect you understand your position now, seeder," the first officer said with mild boredom.

Demosyna barely heard the barked instructions, nodding dully. The cold air in the new morning wasn't noticed, even with a night spent in the open. Demosyna watched Rrra be hauled to his feet and hated the sight of the soldiers' treatment. Groggily, he swayed for a moment before his eyes cleared. Rrra began frantically looking for his mate, but no sign of Jui remained in the wide river.

Demosyna reached out in a daze to try and calm the man, but the arm moved so slow it seemed to freeze halfway to Rrra's orange shoulder.

"What can I even say?" Demosyna asked herself, her arm falling back. "I failed again. I'm not strong enough to help anyone."

Closing her eyes in despair, Rrra's expression of pain was mercifully cut off for Demosyna. The apprentice sighed in resigned exasperation and felt her mind clear of petty desires. Only a feeling of powerlessness remained in the young woman, and Demosyna found the clearing dead silent. The scene around the Wise-woman was so clear that it seemed to flow slowly through her mind. A puff of her breath hung suspended before her eyes, and Demosyna glanced at the sky. Clouds drifted in place with leaves dotting the arching blue.

Dismay rolled over Demosyna as a wild surge of power rushed from the earth, arcing through her stiff body. Wind began whipping in a circle around Demosyna while taking up plumes of frozen dirt. The intensity forced the wind into a cyclone surrounding the apprentice, who was paralyzed from the surging power. Even though the wind whipped and swirled with a howling pitch, the young woman felt only a slight breeze. Outside of the cyclone, the scene continued to move at such a pace as to be nearly motionless from Demosyna's perspective.

Rays of the rising sun pierced through the scattered clouds and leafy treetops as Demosyna walked between them. She marveled at the alternating warmth and shadows cast by the sun, as they seemed to vibrate through the air to reach her eyes. Walking in a powerful daze, Demosyna's thoughts were simple and bold in her head. They were more ideas than anything coherent like ice floating in a pond.

The soldiers who were not mounted, having been wrestling Rrra, stood with a frozen look of worry. Demosyna walked calmly forward with her yellow eyes burning from power. Confidence flowed through her with each pulse that pounded into her soles, filling Demosyna completely. Overwhelming assurance that she could help, if only this time, overtook the Wise-woman.

"Please, please, please," Demosyna pleaded as the tornado touched a soldier. "Just once."

The pained eyes of the soldier were lost in the debris of rocks and ice. A hapless elf was lifted by the tornado and sent flying away, tumbling and screaming. Demosyna smiled and cried out something that was lost in the volume of winds. Light poured from her teeth and horns in ribbons of power, unbeknownst to the apprentice. Energy flowed from an infinite well underfoot, and Demosyna knew only to push forward in the frazzled brain left between burning horns.

The wind, already enough to send a soldier flying, increased in speed and intensity. It was centered on the purple-skinned Wizen, giving her peace in its eye. Demosyna blinked as the great buffeting wall sent the other soldier near Rrra flying. A cry escaped the elf, and her back bent in a horrible angle where she landed. Though they seemed to be moving slow, the riders ahead turned their horses. Their mounts were screaming in foamy terror, and the riders lowered their spears.

Rrra was huddled in panic with his eyes closed against the earth flying close to his head. With one final step, Demosyna was close enough to Rrra that he was sheltered in the spinning vortex. He looked up with a start at the sudden silence given by the eye of the storm. Demosyna tried to smile down at him, but Rrra shrank back upon looking at her. Uncontrolled waves of power still threatened to overwhelm, but Demosyna knew now was her time.

"Run!" Demosyna yelled at Rrra, her voice accentuated by dripping light from her mouth and eyes.

"Jui" was all Demosyna heard from Rrra.

Unable to focus on anything but the fresh surges of power she harnessed, Demosyna held her arms toward the horses. The young Wise-woman used all the remaining thought she possessed to focus.

Stop. Stop. Stop.

The simple desire coursed through Demosyna's mind, power increasing to painful levels. Crying out with strain, Demosyna fell to her knees, and her vision faded. All around the prisoners, the wall of spiraling air contracted to nearly touching the two. It swiftly rushed outward in a violent blast of force while accompanied by a sound like shattering glass. Trees bent, the tents were blown down, and the approaching riders were tossed back. After a hundred feet, the wall of screaming wind dissipated with a final roar. There was a ringing silence in the small clearing for just a moment, the airborne soldiers still flying away.

As the horses were thrown backward, all five riders were tossed off their saddles. Reins snapped and bodies twisted in the magical force. One horse landed on a heavily armored soldier with a bone-cracking smack that echoed in the quiet. Two soldiers and their mounts were flung toward the trees before breaking themselves on the trunks. Horses screeched in pain as those who could bolted after regaining their feet. The others were either dead or writhing in spasms on the ground.

Demosyna only heard these horrific sounds, as her vision remained obscured by a blackness that rolled and churned. Rrra was shaken out of his fear by the cries of the mounts, eyes searching for Jui. The small man saw Demosyna on all fours with one hand over her eyes, no longer radiating horrible power. Demosyna was overcome with nausea as she tried to clear her vision, to no avail. The sounds of the wounded had grown loud and urgent in her blinded mind, but the apprentice wasn't able to stand.

As Demosyna began to dry-heave wordlessly in the dirt, she sensed Rrra start sprinting toward the river. He was already to the water before Demosyna felt her stomach calm and her mind stop burning. Her vision came back in patches, as light streamed through fingers, while she stood on legs that belonged to a stranger.

The dryness of her mouth was terrible, and the Wise-woman had a headache from her nausea. Demosyna began to stumble toward the river just feet away, a slow mind pushing her along. Blessed freedom was promised if her body could carry her, and Demosyna ignored the soldiers' calls. Demosyna picked up speed toward the frozen escape, locking her eyes on the beautiful water.

As she ran, Demosyna noticed that her shackles were gone, and she could move freely. Unaware of when she had been loosed of the cuffs, Demosyna pushed her sluggish legs harder. All thought left the apprentice as she lost focus on Rrra, the soldiers, and even the sudden pain in her foot. Demosyna saw the glorious water expand and fill her vision with the orange dot signifying Rrra a distant thing.

Before the end of the shore, Demosyna jumped with all her strength, straining her back to push an exhausted body ahead. As she dived into freedom with a splash, the icy waters of the river barely registered with Demosyna. The sudden elation of escape was curbed as arrows sank into the water with gold filigree shining. Demosyna swam with the current, and only the thought of fleeing was able to remain in her mind.

After a time—the young woman didn't know how long—Demosyna stopped her swimming. The Wise-woman regained her senses in the river's embrace and began looking around for any sign of Rrra or Jui.

How far ahead could he be? I was swimming all out for what seemed like hours, Demosyna thought, letting the current carry her along. *I know he got to the river. I know it.*

The sun had nearly risen to its height, and the waters were clear enough to allow good visibility. An occasional chunk of ice obscured her view, but Demosyna swam farther before surfacing. The apprentice started taking in her surroundings after failing to see any sign of her friends underwater. The icy river was seeping into her bones, and a throbbing foot called Demosyna to stop.

As she slowly raised her eyes above the water, Demosyna spun in place as the current swept her along in icy arms. Trees densely lined the bank on either side yet were passable, which she judged while pushing a piece of ice away. The apprentice did not see any pursuit and listened with her ears straining. Demosyna swam toward a spot ahead on the bank, careful to use her arms to navigate.

Breathing steadily, Demosyna sat up and removed her soaked shirt before tossing it down. The remains of an arrow were embedded in her right foot, and Demosyna gasped in initial despair. Jagged wood remained jutting from the sole of her foot, broken during the swim. The icy river did well to dull the pain, but seeing the injury made Demosyna nauseous. She lay on her back as the clouds above her spun in dizzying circles, waiting for her stomach to settle.

The shivering Wise-woman flexed her toes carefully and found trying flared the dull ache. A grinding pain made her cry out to herself, and she covered her eyes with an arm. Tears of pain and frustration welled up in her eyes as she sat up again and took a steadying breath.

Narrowing her eyes and ripping her soaked shirt into strips, Demosyna went to the painful task. The chunk of wood impaling her foot was only the thickness of a finger but had broken at both ends and swollen from the long soak. Just touching the tender foot made Demosyna groan deep in her throat, but she gritted her teeth.

A single tug was all it took to remove the arrow, and Demosyna took short breaths as the pain exploded. Gripping her thigh tightly with a hand, Demosyna threw the wood away in disgust. She groaned loudly in the afternoon air and heard several birds call back in surprise. Warm blood ran down her foot, and the apprentice grabbed the pile of torn bandages. Sitting on the bank of the chilled river, Demosyna bound her right foot with practiced motions.

The bleeding stopped, and she replaced the bloody rag with a fresh one. For as far as she could see, Demosyna observed uninterrupted forest with no landmarks. No sign of how close to the ocean she was could be gathered, and the young Wise-woman sighed. With no maps to aid her, Demosyna was lost in her search for her friends. Wind kissed her chest and back, making her shiver as she removed her wet pants. She threw them over a nearby limb after finding a wind-shielded side of the tree.

Demosyna debated starting a fire, but fear of smoke being spotted filled her mind. Instead, the apprentice sat down under the tree, lowering her throbbing foot down slowly. The sun warmed her, but Demosyna was deeply chilled by her swim in the river. After her panicked escape from the soldiers, time had been meaningless in the flow of water.

Where can I go? Will the Wise-woman Orders even accept me now after escaping my sentence? Demosyna thought.

Demosyna knew panic was an enemy, and after more of such thoughts, she remembered her mission. The cold around her seemed to drop away as she rose in naked defiance of the wilderness. The apprentice knew she would find her friends and began limping around to gather her clothes. Her purple scales shone dry in the daylight as she threw the soiled rags and remains of her shirt into the water.

It had been a better top than the bandits' sack, but Demosyna found satisfaction in watching the fragments drift away from her life. The pants were dry enough to wear, she felt, and Demosyna found a walking stick. A great pain in her foot was swelling, even as Demosyna rested against a tree. After wrapping strips of clean fabric around her arms and wounded foot, she set off.

Demosyna could almost hear Klai's disapproving tone, as a simple healing spell would fix the issue outright. Smiling bitterly, Demosyna began shuffling along the thin bank. The direction of the flow laid a course for the young woman with the aid of her scavenged stick. Rough bark scraped her arm, but the pain in her foot was all the discomfort Demosyna needed to think about.

For hours, Demosyna labored next to the river with its icy fog sinking into her. The trees were parting slightly as she limped westward, but the terrain was as challenging as ever since crashing onto this land. Warm summer days were a distant memory for Demosyna as her feet and hands grew numb. Her shivering grew worse over the day, and Demosyna still had not seen any sign of her friends. Frustrated, Demosyna sat down and bit back tears at her predicament.

So many horrible things had happened so quickly that it was hard to recall each example. They smeared together in her mind into flashes of fear and exhaustion, red-and-blue images of pain. The apprentice's breathing quickened slightly as the memories flooded back in sharp clarity, nearly drowning her in cruelty. Standing up quickly, Demosyna ignored her bandaged foot and walked with her face set in a grimace.

"I will not give up. I can help someone. I can," Demosyna said aloud, repeating the words as a mantra.

The sun was setting when the bank of the river began to widen before Demosyna's eyes. The Wise-woman pushed herself along at too fast a pace with her foot singing from the speed. Red-golden light led the panting young woman over a rise to reveal a golden field of wild grasses. Grains swept out ahead of Demosyna, rustling with warm sound. A gentle slope of the sudden flat expanse gave Demosyna pause, and she gasped. Yards ahead, the river ended in a sudden waterfall that cascaded over the horizon, out of view.

The sound of water was distant as Demosyna walked into the knee-high grasses she found herself moving toward. A large sun was nearly directly in front of her, and she saw countless dancing rainbows. Dazzling, prismatic spray caught the light at the drop, exploding the air in frozen splendor. Demosyna felt tears welling in her eyes, and she walked slowly toward the cliff. Stopping short of the sloping edge, Demosyna saw the falls dropped into darkness.

She watched the water flow over the edge and vanish into the damp shadows for minutes, amazed at the water's playful toying with the last of the light. Demosyna looked over the cliff to see that much of the scene before her was cloaked in the mountain's shadows. A great land of forest and rolling fields expanded to the horizon while broken by tall peaks in the distance. Demosyna was awestruck by the uninterrupted view of frozen land while holding a hand to her mouth.

She felt so many conflicting emotions fighting for recognition that she turned from the valley. The apprentice felt no pain as she walked into the middle of the gently waving grasses. The previous day's trials seemed distant in the face of this wonderful meadow, Demosyna thought as she glided. Demosyna watched in amused silence as a grasshopper jumped from the shadows of the tall grasses. Transparent wings caught a ray of light, and Demosyna was struck by the image so violently that she stepped backward.

The delicate wings of the small grasshopper were fluttering away, but the image remained in Demosyna's eye as her heart began to ache. Any pain in her foot was mercifully forgotten, and memories of her imprisonment flooded over her. Bhreel hung in her mind, suspended by his wings on the cold stone walls, and Demosyna had watched helplessly. Everyone the apprentice had known was taken in that horrible span of days—first her Wise Mother, then her new friends Bhreel, Jui, and Rrra.

As she backed up another step, Demosyna began to cry. Large tears streamed down her frozen scales as all the events played in her mind on a loop. All the pain was fresh in her weary heart as she relived her trauma. The Wise-woman's sobs were low and nearly silent at first but quickly turned to loud and horrible shouts of anguish.

No words came to her as she railed at the empty sky, and Demosyna let the tears fall from her snout to litter the ground. Her cries echoed in the night, powerful and raw for the empty expanse. Demosyna held her arms across her wind-chilled chest and cried before a great rising noise broke into her sorrow.

Thousands of grasshoppers rose in a wave of rustling leaves and glinting wings. The setting sun was giving off its last rays of light, and Demosyna watched through horror-filled eyes. They rose all at once and sped off toward the waterfall. Each small grasshopper glistened different colors, and the mass flew through dancing rainbows over the river. The beauty and suddenness of the spectacle pierced the grief Demosyna felt swallowed by.

Tears flowed down her cheeks, and Demosyna wept as thousands of buzzing grasshoppers flew away.

"I am truly alone," she mused. "Can I still see this splendor after all that?"

Watching the insects fly into the darkness had given Demosyna a rare sense of wonder. After the attack on her ship, all previous love for the strange land of the Fist had been lost. Demosyna felt wonder swell refreshed in her heart from the beauty she had witnessed. As her emotions ebbed and the tears slowed enough to allow her to stand, Demosyna looked at the stars. Demosyna stood on her injured foot to witness the heavens and collapsed back to let her vision fill with a million jewels.

Demosyna began crying again, but she smiled hesitantly to herself. A new feeling of hope sprang bold and bright in her heart to join the delight already returning. The young apprentice laughed silently and cried tears of pain and loss into a cold, understanding night. The grasses shielded her from the wind, and the warmth quickly calmed her overstressed body. The apprentice had pushed herself beyond her limit to gain her freedom and let her muscles finally relax.

After the tears had dried on her face, Demosyna watched the stars twinkle and slept. For the first time in recent memory, a smile of hope formed on her lips, and Demosyna dreamed of a future with any promise.

CHAPTER 11

Welcoming sunrays warmed her face enough to rouse her, and Demosyna sat up with a start. The grasses that had housed her for the night waved a gold-and-green hello. For a moment, the apprentice glanced around in fear but saw only the pristine landscape. The frightened woman leaned back on her hands with a sigh lost in the roar of the falls. Pain had slowly woken her, and without a shirt, Demosyna was shivering.

Dried blood caked the bandage around her clawed foot, and as Demosyna uncoiled the rag, she found the wound swollen. After removing one of the cleaner bandages from her uninjured forearm, Demosyna covered the wound. The sound of the falls was a nearby distraction, but the peace of her soft field occupied Demosyna fully.

Morning sun warmed her scales, and she grinned a sharp smile. Grasshoppers sprung and glided all around, and Demosyna laughed at the simple beauty discovered here. Rainbows shimmered beside her, and Demosyna saw the falls dropped less than seventy feet. The river continued along its roughly western path after pounding into the riverbank below.

Several small islands, little more than mossy rocks, peeked out near the end of the falls. Demosyna saw the familiar sights of a town as her gaze followed the river. Many small shacks surrounded a cluster of larger, more ornate buildings to form the sight of civilization.

Fields spanned out from around a ringed wall, appearing as small patches of color among the forests.

Excitement nearly overcame Demosyna as she strained her eyes to see the distant town. The apprentice had to restrain herself from leaping toward the strip of water below her, laughing to herself giddily. The water, though churning from the drop, was fairly shallow directly below. Demosyna judged climbing would be the safer option while flexing her hands and stretching. Despite the slickness of the rocks, the Wise-woman felt confident enough in her climbing to get her down. So far, the wind had been absent, and Demosyna knew the conditions for climbing would not improve.

She had bandages left from recycling her shirt, and Demosyna wrapped one around each hand and her uninjured foot. While limping along the slope and surveying a path, Demosyna found her stomach beginning to complain. The thin meal provided by the soldiers had been better than stagnant water, but she was still hungry.

Demosyna patted her pink-scaled stomach and smiled to herself without humor, remembering shared meals on the boat. No place seemed ideal to her practiced eye, so Demosyna carefully felt for the nearest foothold. Demosyna tried to avoid using her injured foot out of habit, and this slowed her progress more than she liked.

Her snout faced the ground, and her strong tail balanced above as a dense purple aid. The path she was forced to take was grueling as the apprentice snaked face-first down the cliff. Demosyna risked coming close to the pounding falls beside her, needing to find another handhold. Halfway down the cliff, her hands aching with strain, Demosyna found a ledge to lay on and rest.

Spray of the water stung her eyes with its bite, and her exposed back was quickly numb. Flexing her hands slowly, Demosyna looked down to determine her progress. She had made a considerable amount, but Demosyna was still nearly thirty feet above the ground. The falls swept along in a river again just out of jumping range. Turning to her other shoulder on the ledge, Demosyna tried to chart her next path.

Nearly there now, she thought, the frozen mist shielding her descent. *I can do it.*

118

Her thick pants were soaked in the first few minutes of her aching climb, weighing the Wise-woman down with an icy touch. Holes appeared in the fabric pants as Demosyna continued in her rhythm of hands and left foot, courtesy of the jagged rocks. As the ground approached her, Demosyna was shocked into losing her grip. She slid forward sickeningly when the sudden sound of a horn blast thundered through the woods on the opposite bank of the river.

Fear clenched her heart as she fell through the wet air, and Demosyna let out a short yell. The unexpected sound of an imperial horn had panicked the woman into losing her clawed grip. Practiced hands found a hold after only dropping about a meter, yet Demosyna's right foot lashed out. A burning pain spread through her body as she caught herself and bit down to remain silent. Her legs were splayed wide, along with her arms, and the apprentice gripped for her life.

Before she could do more than ease her injured foot from the crevice, a second horn call sounded from above on the falls. Sheer panic blocked out any hope of continuing the dangerous climb. Demosyna looked around for any refuge from the horns and the soldiers they signaled. The morning light glittered through the water as it streamed down, and Demosyna saw the shadows shift. A bit of darkness moved just enough to reveal a shallow in the sheer cliff behind the thundering water.

She could not tell how deep the hollow went, but from her upside-down view, Demosyna knew it was enough. After shifting her weight, she swung and strained a shoulder to grab the ledge. Pausing only a moment to ensure her grip on the soaked rocks, Demosyna carefully pushed herself up. Her good left foot finished guiding the woman onto the natural ledge behind the waterfall, grimacing from fear.

Even over the deafening roar of the water near her head, Demosyna heard two more blasts of silver horns. Like the initial trumpets that had nearly doomed her, Demosyna heard one below and one above. She cowered in the shadowy alcove while shivering in cold and distress. How the soldiers had found her—and so soon— was overshadowed in her mind by the fact that she was trapped.

Halfway up the falls, Demosyna was finally cornered by the soldiers. Warm blood still soaked into her bandage, but she put the injury from her mind to face a more pressing threat. Voices called near the muffled space she found herself safe in, and Demosyna turned her head to make it out. The falls made the armored soldiers shout to be heard, and Demosyna was able to glean much of the discussion.

"Yes, ma'am, the remains of the shirt were found downriver," one of the soldiers called through cupped hands. "There is no sign of any of them yet."

A response from above was mostly lost in the hiss of the falls, but the last few words brought a cold hope to Demosyna's chest.

"Those tracks there?" a commanding voice called from above, and Demosyna recognized the first officer's tone.

A handful of soldiers below danced in grotesque patterns, and each began searching the shore. A pair went about the search with care while bending at the waist and scanning the muddy bank. Barely a heartbeat passed before the response from those below was heard.

"Tracks leading from the river here, claws and all," the soldier called excitedly. "We may get our bonus yet!"

Laughter from below made Demosyna's heart burn with anger, but she held her position. She slowly turned her body to see how far the indention would allow her to retreat after growing tired of hearing the officer. Much was covered in shadow, but Demosyna was able to see the alcove was more of a cave. A hollow led into the dark, glistening rock of the cliff with an opening big enough to crawl into. Turning onto her stomach was difficult in the cramped position, but Demosyna inched into the cave.

"Rrra, did you make those tracks?" Demosyna whispered as she left the daylight. "I can only hope you found Jui."

Demosyna climbed up a slight slope and dropped down into a cavern that expanded all around her. It echoed slightly with the roar of the falls outside but otherwise was deadly still. Glancing around in wonder at the discovery, Demosyna held back tears of gratitude. The cave was seemingly natural, as the flow of the walls would suggest, but it was dry in the bosom of the cliff. Moisture failed to reach inside with the angle of the entrance and made the weather tolerable.

As her eyes adjusted to the gloom of the cave, Demosyna saw several bundles. One of three spaced indents along the wall held shapes of mysterious objects. Demosyna moved with care for her newly screaming foot now warm with blood. A steady hum of the water cut off any more voices of the soldiers, she noticed absently. This was a small comfort, as now she was trapped behind the waterfall, and Demosyna let herself slide down the wall next to the objects.

A mortar and pestle lay on its side in a layer of dust despite the damp entrance to the cave. Even the air was dryer here, Demosyna noticed as she picked up the simple tool with amazement. The familiar shape in her hands made the woman smile, and Demosyna wiped the outside of a bowl onto her pants. Marble shone through the layer of dust removed, and Demosyna knew this little grinder would become invaluable.

Seeing the smear of dirt the forgotten tools had left on her ruined trousers caused Demosyna to remove them with disgust. Just having the soldiers so close made the rough fabric itch and chafe her leg scales. After she set aside the newfound treasure on soggy pants, Demosyna investigated the other shapes. A broken clay bottle that had long ago lost all liquid sat next to the mortar and pestle. Demosyna moved the shattered pottery aside while avoiding the jagged edges begging to open her fingers.

A small compass with a golden case was the last thing that Demosyna found among the shadows. Angling it toward the entrance, Demosyna saw that the face had a crack in the glass. Her shoulders drooped with disappointment, and she put the item aside. She could tell basic directions by sun and moon, as all Wise-women could, but Demosyna needed anything she could get right now.

"Who could have lived here, so high up the falls?" Demosyna wondered, as no markings shone on the abandoned items. "This place is perfect for me, out of reach of the soldiers. Even with my foot injured, I know I can still outclimb or outswim them. But I should wait them out in here so they don't know I am close."

No other items remained from the previous occupant of the hidden sanctuary, much to Demosyna's disappointment. She would not be able to thank her long gone savior for their cave, it seemed.

Dust that had covered the items told of the years they had spent alone with their owner failing to return.

A few times, she heard horn blasts. But if the soldiers discussed anything, Demosyna didn't hear it. No stalactites lined the ceiling, she noticed when a horn above her called ominously, and Demosyna explored the space with her dark-adjusted eyes.

Remains of a campfire were in the alcove to her right along the smooth wall, and Demosyna saw nothing in the alcove on the left. Demosyna used her hands and bottom to scoot toward the remains of the ancient campfire, leaving her right leg extended above the ground. An ache in her arms and shoulders was joining the chorus of complaints her body was leveling, but after a few short scoots, the apprentice reached the fire.

Black charcoal was all that remained, and Demosyna rubbed the silky powder between her fingers. A small fire would be all you needed in such a cozy space, Demosyna thought as she took any chunks left intact.

"The kindling is the bed the fire calls home, little Scale."

Bhreel's friendly words echoed sadly in her memory.

"Even wet wood is useful with patience."

Demosyna had always been amazed by how the resourceful Orc could start a kitchen fire with even frozen driftwood, as he had shown many times. A gleam of humor would dance in Bhreel's round eyes when watching the wonder on Demosyna's face. Recalling that made her heart ache with the loss of her old life, and Demosyna stifled tears with a steadying breath.

No more running scared, Demosyna thought, a sense of outrage replacing the panic in her mind. *It will not bring anyone back or help me in my search for Rrra and Jui.*

The young apprentice stood up, ignoring the pain from her injured foot, and shuffled toward the entrance. Medicine was first in her needs, Demosyna saw from her bandaging, and the woods patrolled by her captors held the herbs she required. Her belly protested the decision, but with a grimace of humor, Demosyna put hunger from her mind. There were fish in the river, but healing herbs were vital before satiating her appetite.

The angle of the entrance kept the moisture from filling the cave but also made exiting difficult with one foot incapacitated. Demosyna lay flat on her belly and slid down with her arms extending from the lip. Her left foot found the ledge, and Demosyna lowered onto her knees on the outcropping.

The cold of the spray immediately chilled her with its roaring fury. The last horn had been heard over two hours ago, Demosyna estimated from the cave. She saw no signs of soldiers from her distorted field of view and smiled in relief. Even when her body started shivering from the cold air, Demosyna sat waiting for any movement. The only motion she saw during her vigil was from birds and the trees swaying in the wind blowing from the mountains.

Waterdrops streamed down the still apprentice as she licked her wet lips. Moving quickly and steadily, Demosyna found the remainder of the trip almost easy compared to the first half. Her light-purple scales glistened as she jumped the last feet to the riverbank. Once again, she waited for minutes on end before moving from her position, slowly crawling into the forest when no danger presented.

Moving low through the dense forest, Demosyna limped along in hopeful search. Any plant she recognized in the remaining light was a treat to her eyes. Demosyna gathered handfuls of long grass as she snuck her way between the trees while tucking them under her arm. Demosyna brushed a stray leaf from her horn when she spied a plant that she sought and smiled in excitement. A small bush had leaves she knew would help, and Demosyna grabbed a handful of the bright flowers.

The pain in her foot was a distant thing as Demosyna continued gathering any useful forageable. In less than two hours, she had found enough for medicine, as well as berry bushes that the Wisewoman ate from greedily. With sticky juice running down her chin, Demosyna laughed at her good fortune. Demosyna turned back toward her waterfall home with arms loaded full of useful goods.

As she limped out of the trees, Demosyna sent her gaze toward the hidden alcove, and a dawning realization occurred. With her arms full and one foot injured, it would be almost impossible to climb the distance. Chiding herself for lack of forethought, Demosyna sat in the whispering grass to hide from view. Her purple scales shone in the dwindling light, and Demosyna paused to consider.

She rubbed absently at her right leg as the clouds drifted above and the river flowed noisily beside. Deciding to risk staying on the ground longer, Demosyna moved to the cover of the tree line. The young Wizen wove the tall grasses together into large square sheets. She worked quickly and without regard to the life span as long as it held during her ascent. After squares of rough woven grass were assembled, the remaining strands were used to make thin ropes. The apprentice used the cords to tie corners together, forming three small pouches.

After admiring her handiwork, Demosyna tested the bag with berries from a ripe bush. When the bag held against the weight, Demosyna was confident the other bags would suffice. Any remaining items, some flowers and herbs, were divided between the pouches. Her stomach grumbled as she walked back to the waterfall, and Demosyna knew she would need to venture for better food.

The daylight was fading as she made her mist-shrouded ascent, careful of the shadows that made judging distance tricky. The young Wise-woman's makeshift bags held as she reached the sanctuary and threw the prizes ahead into the cave. Demosyna sat atop her slippery porch and used sharp eyes to scan for signs of soldiers.

The climb up had not been difficult, yet the constant icy spray prevented her from surveying for long. A scramble up the incline deposited Demosyna in her snug hideaway with a newfound haul of treasure. A small smile spread over her thin lips as the young Wizen gathered the foraged supplies and set to work.

Demosyna had found while sitting out of proper lessons due to her lack of magic that alchemy and research were things that could allow her to contribute. Countless hours were spent in the enchanted library, poring through any tome legible. Golden light streamed through ornate windows to let her dive into the research. Medicine was a chief focus after helping a wounded Wizen with burns, but Demosyna delved into any topic of interest. Clawed feet would click as the energetic research led between subjects and shelves in the library.

Little had been available to her as an apprentice, but the Wise-woman digested all the information she could get her clawed hands on. A short preparation period before the trip north had given Demosyna time to review useful books. What she might encounter in the vastly unexplored mountains of the Fist had filled her mind with wonder initially.

Demosyna knew all too well from the frantic blind chase through the forest that mysterious plants existed, some vines having impaled those who fell onto poisonous thorns. She had only caught a glimpse during the flight from the wasps, but the vines writhed hungrily around the impaled victims.

Various plants that Demosyna gathered lay in orderly piles on the rough woven squares based on how she would combine them. The falls outside provided water to clean the old marble mortar and pestle, along with the few remaining strips of cloth. As the fabric dried in the darkness of her cave, Demosyna began mixing the precious medicines for her injured foot. A practiced hand made the tedious work speed along, and the sun lowered through the watery barrier that separated her from the world.

Once the medicinal ingredients had been exhausted, the remaining plants were prepared. Powders and pastes soon littered the makeshift worktable, and Demosyna sat back with a contented sigh. As she surveyed her work from the last hours, the remaining berries were a sweet reward for the tiring young woman. The powders were in no danger of blowing away, as the air in the cave was still despite the waterfall.

Like most Scales, Demosyna could see very well in the dark. The sun was nearly set in the sky while coating the water in crimson. Demosyna stooped over and gathered the sacks to begin fashioning them into a top. It was a simple matter to weave the squares of grass into a garment that hung from her shoulders, cinched with rope. The last of the light faded from the oval exit as Demosyna happily donned the clothing before climbing to the river.

An overcast sky provided no starlight during her evening hunt, forcing Demosyna to limp along slowly. She gathered grass and twigs that lay scattered in the forest with her breath puffing away in wisps.

After wrapping a large pile of sticks together with grasses, Demosyna left them under a tree with her clothes. Her strong tail helped her balance as she walked on her hands and good foot into the river while her belly and breasts nearly touched the ground.

The river, as she had noticed during her escape, was teeming with fish of various colors. Demosyna swam through the ice and water, ignoring the needles of cold all over her. Small yellow fish whetted her appetite as the purple-scaled woman swam through the water. She felt weightless and at home cradled in the river, and Demosyna smiled after catching another fish. It took barely a snap of her powerful jaws to snatch the larger fish, and Demosyna used her body to slice the water as a shadow.

Before losing sight of the waterfall's safety, Demosyna swam to the bottom of the river. The fish she had caught were gripped in her teeth, leaving her hands free. A strong current was steadily resisting her progress as she pulled herself along the bottom back to the cave. Every so often, Demosyna would pause to inspect a rock or note potential holes to noodle. A rock that satisfied the Wizen was found, and she finished her swim.

The frigid young woman gathered handfuls of seaweed before exiting the river and tying them to her horns. The wealth of resources in this wooded valley was a welcome surprise after so many days of fasting and running.

Demosyna noiselessly crawled from the river under the cover of the clouds, dripping ice onto the grass. It was only after returning to her cached supplies that Demosyna's good mood was spoiled. A wind was pushing the smell of a campfire toward her as she crouched, still and afraid, from farther downriver.

It's too close to be the town, Demosyna thought in near panic. *Are the soldiers still searching for us?*

No sign of the light from the smoke could be found, yet the frightened young Wizen dared not move from her spot. When no sounds of the soldiers could be heard, Demosyna put on her top and bundled up the spoils of her hunt. She strapped the sticks to her back before stringing the fish together through their mouths. The rocks she carried in her shaking hands as Demosyna faded through the darkness toward the waterfall.

The cold of the night was overshadowed by the distress the smell of the campfire had awakened in Demosyna. She ignored the shivers in her body from the swim and moved to the entry of the hidden cave. Even after reaching the lip serving as a porch, holding the small rocks in her mouth, Demosyna couldn't see any sign of fire. Lack of seeing the camp calmed the wide-eyed Wise-woman, and she dropped into her claimed home.

She was panting from panic and the climb, so Demosyna regained her composure before unpacking. Four fish, each the size of her forearm, were put atop the bundle of sticks. She tossed the jagged small rocks down with the seaweed before shuffling over to sit facing the entrance. Her breath hung in small clouds in the still of the cave while she applied medicine to her foot. A burn of the salve caused a sharp hiss to escape her gritted teeth, but Demosyna wrapped her foot with the last bandages.

At least my training is good for something, she thought, letting her aching muscles rest.

The bundle of sticks had been soaked during her climb to safety and needed to dry before a fire could warm her frozen scales. In the meantime, Demosyna began preparing the fish for cooking. Several of the ground powders served as seasonings, which the eager woman smeared on the wet scales. Seaweed was wrapped around each fish before she pushed a long stick through gaping mouths.

After the last fish was propped against the wall, Demosyna gathered the stones collected from the river. She tried different combinations till a spark showed when two rocks were struck together. Demosyna smiled widely to herself in the dark once finding all she needed in these frozen woods. A few pieces of charcoal formed the base of the fire, using dried grass and the smaller sticks as the tower. With the newfound striker rocks, Demosyna lit the humble fire and crouched over it gratefully.

Warmth washed over her wet face and chest as the embers grew into a cheerful blaze. The cave was illuminated by the small fire, and Demosyna gazed around at the place she would call home. Smoke from the tiny fire flowed out of the entrance and dissipated in the water to hide it from prying eyes.

After bringing the impaled fish over to the fire, Demosyna leaned them at angles above the flames. The smoked fish would last her days, she knew from experience, and the fire would provide her warmth for the night. She nearly cried from joy at the bounty of wealth she had acquired despite the danger, and Demosyna sat beside the crackling fire to await being found.

CHAPTER 12

Her next days were spent tucked away in the safety of the cave dwelling she had discovered. No sign of pursuit was found during the respite, either by horn or smell of smoke. The sound of the falls soon became a welcome hum for the young Wizen as the injured foot began to mend, with the aid of her alchemy.

Once a day, several hours before sunrise, Demosyna crept down the increasingly familiar falls to relieve herself. The crawling young woman would stop to clean the remains of her bandage in the icy river while always alert for danger.

Moonlight and starlight were all the cat-eyed woman needed in the frozen nights. Crude boots of grasses, along with her makeshift top, were refined into more serviceable garments. Demosyna also made a rough skirt during the first day she hid behind the waterfall. Boots were a great benefit during the dark chill each time she had to risk exiting her cave. The apprentice's feet no longer sank as deep into the frozen riverbank, and she was thankful.

Precious resources provided Demosyna something to do during the hours spent indoors with only the muted light the rushing water allowed. Berries, herbs, roots, mushrooms, flowers, and any useful ingredients were found by the trained eye of the young Wizen. Each was prepared in its proper fashion, as she knew from many tomes, with patience learned long ago. More woven pouches housed the growing reserve of ingredients, and lengths of rope were added to an expanding hoard of necessities.

Her small campfire, Demosyna noticed one night as she returned with forageables, was visible from the waterfall as a dancing dot. Watching in silent dread, the light swam obviously in the water before the woman's darting eyes. Demosyna took an involuntary step backward, looking around for danger, and held her breath that puffed in fright. After another step backward by her rebellious legs, the worry drained from her mind. The dancing firefly of light from her cave disappeared from halfway up the falls after Demosyna stepped back a third time.

A brief experiment revealed the firelight was only visible from near the waterfall and not for miles, as Demosyna feared. Her heart eventually slowed, and she risked a short laugh that dissipated into blackness. Fires were limited to daylight hours upon the discovery of the light it caused in the waterfall.

Blankets of scratchy leaves and grasses served to warm the solitary apprentice during the long hours of waiting for the sun. A pile of fish bones near the entrance grew during the days she recovered, chewing the smoked fish with delight. It was the first home-cooked meal she had eaten since starting her voyage, and Demosyna savored each bite of the wild fish. The soreness in her tail and snout faded as well, but the tip of Demosyna's tail remained forever bent where the slaver had crushed it.

Even after finishing the last morsel of cooked fish, Demosyna was not distressed about the lack of food. Her nightly excursions proved the bounty all around ripe for the taking. Though she was greatly tempted, Demosyna resisted the impulse to try magic and instead focused on disciplines she had successfully practiced. Memories of her panicked escape from her captors flowed through her mind like ribbons of uncertainty.

It was hard to focus on the memories for long, as though they were too bright to see. Power beyond her knowing had flowed through the helpless Wizen and had allowed her freedom from chains. Demosyna knew she hadn't been in control of the power that overtook her being and worried over the implications.

A rasp of the mortar and pestle faded with the memory of the wind that occupied the mind of the young woman. Demosyna pored over each detail of the escapes with an analytical eye. Raw rage and passion had accompanied the cyclone and eventually overwhelmed her, but Demosyna remembered the energy that poured from the dirt. It had felt as though nothing was impossible in those brief lucid moments, and Demosyna craved that feeling again.

"If I can just learn how to control the magic, I can help my friends," Demosyna mused to herself. "I haven't seen any sign of them, but I won't give up."

The Wizen had found herself absently fiddling for the nonexistent hoops that dangled from her horns for the initial weeks of her journey. It was a habit she had picked up during the later days of the voyage, when rare compliments about them were given. A sad sigh followed the memory of Demosyna's captors stripping her and her fellow passengers of their last remaining dignity.

A yawn split the woman's face, and she prepared to sleep as the sun rose. Demosyna took to dozing in the early hours of the morning, having spent the cold darkness working on her gathered resources.

Like the previous mornings, rest came fitfully from the ache in her foot. As she drifted in and out of sleep, hopeful dreams dared to surface. The smiling faces of Jui and Rrra swam temptingly through Demosyna's thoughts as she envisioned a reunion, safe in the halls of a Wise-woman Order. Demosyna saw Jui begin to mouth something, causing the dreaming Wizen to strain to hear the words. Jui's eyes rolled back to the whites, and frozen water poured from massive sockets. Before she could hear what her friend said, an explosion issued from Jui's gaping mouth to jolt Demosyna awake.

Moments of confused silence followed as Demosyna bolted upright. She dared not breathe as the sound of another explosion bloomed barely ten seconds after the first. A loud crash echoed across the woods and sent birds to protest as they flew. The past days had allowed a ray of hope into her heart, but fear gripped the apprentice as a third explosion sounded.

She sat as more resounding booms issued from beyond the glittering water hiding her, each around ten seconds apart. The orderly timing of the shots brought images of well-trained loading of a cannon, as Demosyna had seen firsthand.

If they have a cannon, it's not safe here, Demosyna thought wildly as the explosions continued. *How did they get it here?*

Demosyna fled her cozy home, flinching each time a thunderous boom met her ears, with only the clothing she slept in. A small grass pouch around her waist carried a few items, but she left all others behind. All thought was gone from her head as the terrified Wisewoman left the cave, knowing only to get away. Her woven clothes were glistening from the falls as the apprentice touched down on the riverbed, encouraged by the explosions. Ragged, puffing clouds drifted as Demosyna tried to calm her raging chest.

While running as fast as the bandaged foot allowed, Demosyna made her way to where the sounds originated. They were close to her waterfall and the safety that lay behind, so Demosyna needed to know what fresh danger lurked around the bend.

I can always use the water to escape, if it comes to that, Demosyna reassured herself as five more explosions shattered the morning with fear. *If they are firing from here, they must be shooting downriver.*

The volume of the explosions increased with each trembling step, yet she pressed on with newfound anger. The brilliant sun was only a few hours risen, and the cold of the night was still hanging thinly around the riverbed. Silence gripped the woods when the explosions ceased as suddenly as they started. Demosyna slowed but didn't pause her advance toward danger while ducking under a limb. She hadn't slept for long, but fear pushed all fatigue from her body like a whipcrack.

Woods along each side of the wide river did not allow Demosyna to see far, so the sounds of those ahead were heard first. Her journey downstream had taken mere minutes, and Demosyna slipped into the frozen river. Her mind was focused and clear with memories of capture bringing the world into vivid detail. After swimming to the bottom of the river, Demosyna darted between the clusters of seaweed.

No more explosions were heard while Demosyna swam around a sharp bend, viewing tiny islands poking above the water. Three figures could be seen in the blurry sun, and Demosyna stopped to watch. Her woven grass clothing hid her among the seaweed, so Demosyna waited patiently. Two figures were near the shore, having waded out to their hips. A third sat on an island with a large wood pole.

A smear of red hair waved as the seated figure called at the two milling in the river. His words were lost to her submerged ear, but the two swam farther into the icy river. With some distress, the apprentice saw the distant people dive toward the bottom. Each searched in different directions, and she remained as still as possible. Demosyna was too far away to see what they were doing, but if they were braving the river, it was likely something important.

Two minutes passed before the pair surfaced, and Demosyna took that opportunity to climb to the bank. Using her grass top as camouflage, Demosyna moved silently through the forest with the river in sight. Upon reaching a sight line from the trees, Demosyna saw no sign of any cannons. No smell of gunpowder could be discerned either, and Demosyna realized she hadn't smelled it when the explosions drove her here. For minutes, she scanned the area frantically, seeing only a tent and clothes near a fire.

No signs of armor or artillery were seen by the hidden apprentice while the two divers continued their search. The seated man remained silent and observed the divers. He was strong with long red hair tied back with a strip of cloth, which blew in the wind. He wore no clothes that Demosyna could see, and despite the cold, he sat in the spray of the river. A long wooden pole, smooth and hollow, was atop his knees, and he fiddled with it occasionally.

Fear melted into confusion as Demosyna pondered the scene. Both divers surfaced and returned to the shore with armloads of rocks. Each of the glistening divers was bald, and they looked extremely strong. Their muscles strained against the stones, but the men wordlessly walked to the seated man. A pile was made beside the crimson-haired human, and the two bowed before returning to the river.

Over twenty minutes passed before the two ceased their gathering and stood where Demosyna had seen them originally. They calmly waited in the river, even with their clothes left by the fire. Neither seemed put out by the frigid river and gazed at the wilds in silence. The sound of music broke through the calm, and Demosyna turned to see the seated man using the rod as a flute. Shocked and amazed, the apprentice listened to the melody drift through the woods. It was the first music Demosyna had heard in ages, and the sweet, hollow sound caught her off guard.

The red-haired man, while playing the long flute with one hand, picked up a rock from the pile. A blur registered to Demosyna's sharp eyes as the rock was hurled toward the two divers. Neither man moved as the projectile approached, and Demosyna gasped. The source of the explosions was made clear, and her confusion tripled when one of the pair kicked the stone in midair.

The rock exploded into pieces that flew skyward with a cracking boom. His kick had been nearly a blur as the man reduced the projectile to pebbles. Never before had she seen anything like the feat displayed, and Demosyna watched in wonder as the red-haired man reached for another rock. Never ceasing the music, he threw the second rock toward the two with lightning speed.

Nearly ten seconds had passed, and another explosion echoed as the younger man broke the rock. This continued for minutes, with the explosions timed as the music reached a crescendo. It was oddly beautiful, Demosyna thought as she crouched in the trees.

When the last boom rolled away from the river, the seated man put down his flute. He clapped enthusiastically and laughed with a loud, infectious voice. The two bald men remained in the water, stretching their powerful limbs, but smiled.

His words were lost at the distance Demosyna watched from, but the men swam to the middle of the river. They took deep breaths and dived beneath the icy surface before darting along the riverbed. Once the two had been under for a full minute, the seated man turned his head. Icy dread washed over the apprentice as he scanned the woods with his face a mask of stillness. He only moved his head and remained seated as he called out.

"Greetings, friend. You are welcome to join us. That you are," the man called loudly at the trees.

His voice carried a weight of authority, yet laughter seemed to hide below the surface. Cautiously, the young woman emerged from the trees. He glanced at her with sharp green eyes when she appeared but returned his gaze to the river with a smile. His bare chest and legs shone in the sun as Demosyna stood silently in the cold air.

"Our fire is yours, if you desire," the man hollered over the river. "It will warm your bones and your scales!"

Demosyna glanced toward the crackling fire nearby and back at the seated man. There were three piles of bright robes, along with a single tent, making up the tiny camp.

"Who are you?"

Caution laced Demosyna's voice, and her body was ready to run as she spoke.

"This one is but a simple tutor," he responded with his green eyes shining.

Two bald heads popped up to pant slightly before diving again. The red-haired man smiled at this before responding further to the frozen woman's query.

"You may call this one Vaash."

He placed a weathered hand on his scarred chest.

"It is a pleasure to meet you."

No sound but the river was heard for several heartbeats, and Vaash sat content on the wet rock. His flute was rolled casually against the man's thighs, and he watched the divers swim.

"My name is Demosyna," she finally responded, sensing no threat. "What are you doing here?"

Demosyna's eyes darted around the forest, expecting charging soldiers at any moment. But instead of danger, the laughter Vaash bellowed filled the air.

"We are enjoying the morning with training and song."

Vaash motioned to where the divers moved.

"It is a wonderful time to be in such a beautiful place. That it is."

Three piles of yellow-and-orange garments were crumpled near the firepit, and Demosyna recognized the colors as an Order of monks. The Order had been dismantled by the Empress, and yet like so many others, stragglers of this monk Order remained.

"Thank you for the kind welcome, Vaash," Demosyna said hesitantly. "Are you with the imperial army?"

This gave the man pause, and Demosyna was about to bolt from the odd situation when he responded.

"No, this one is not with the army."

His voice was flat as he spoke.

"We are here by our own wills, and nobody else's."

"I see," the young Wizen replied, considering his answer.

The bald divers resurfaced and noticed the apprentice standing on the tree line. One uttered a small squeal of surprise, but both swam away from Vaash and Demosyna. Watching the two frantically move away seemed to tickle Vaash, who laughed and stood. He was naked and unashamed before the shocked Wizen with the flute held behind his back. Vaash jumped effortlessly to the bank with powerful legs, feet sinking slightly upon landing. Demosyna watched his broad frame move to the small camp, and Vaash began to dress.

"Forgive those two, Demosyna," Vaash called from over his back. "They are shy young boys. That they are."

Vaash had numerous scars over his chest, and now Demosyna noticed that his back was also marked by wounds. Vaash seemed to be in his late thirties, but his smooth face made guessing hard. Demosyna turned slightly out of respect for his modesty yet dared not keep her eyes away long. He was dressed by the time her gaze found him again, and Vaash smiled warmly.

"It is a beautiful morning, friend. Please join us for a meal," Vaash offered with a wave of his hand. "We share what we have, if you desire company. Pardon, if you would."

Vaash turned and brought the two swimmers downriver their clothes as Demosyna walked one hesitant pace at a time. She hadn't realized how cold she was, first from fear blocking the cold, then confusion. The unexpected monks near her cave dulled the cold for her, but Demosyna was shivering.

As the apprentice crouched near the fire, the three men returned with their brightly colored robes belted. Vaash led the two along with a pleasant smile on his face.

"These two will prepare food while we talk, Demosyna," Vaash said from across the firepit. "Do you prefer fish, bread, or both?"

"I can't remember the last time I had fresh bread," Demosyna said, mostly to herself.

"Both it is, then."

Vaash laughed heartily as his fellows wordlessly prepared a meal.

* * * * *

Her eyes widened, and Demosyna smiled through the flames that the two bald men had put fish into. One of the two, the elder of the divers, handed the woman a loaf of bread with a nervous glance. Demosyna broke the bread into four pieces and passed three to Vaash. His eyes sparkled as he watched her do this, and Vaash smiled upon taking the pieces.

"Demosyna, we thank and welcome you."

Vaash passed all three pieces to the monks tending the fish.

"It has been months since we hosted a guest, so enjoy what these ones can offer!"

"I am glad to find a friendly face in these woods," Demosyna said, swallowing the delicious bread. "It seems like months since I've seen one."

Vaash raised his eyebrows slightly, but only for a moment before his smile returned. The elder of the two divers handed the apprentice a skewered fish.

"Thank you," Demosyna said and saw him blush.

The monk nodded his understanding after sitting and nervously avoiding Demosyna's gaze. She saw that the younger diver was behaving similarly, sitting close to Vaash and avoiding her direct eyeline.

"Forgive me, Demosyna, but these two are my students," Vaash exclaimed, putting his hand on the younger man's thigh. "They don't have names yet, but that one will soon."

Vaash nodded toward the elder diver, and the monk looked at Vaash with hope. The red-haired monk smiled widely at the student, who blinked back tears from young eyes. Both apprentices appeared to be her age, with the younger looking just over twenty, if Demosyna knew human ages correctly.

"Your Order gives up names until they finish training, if what I studied can be believed," Demosyna said as she bit into the warm, salted fish.

It lacked the fresh seaweed she had used, but the meat melted into flaky pieces. It was delicious, and Demosyna had to stop herself from diving face-first into the meal.

"Just so."

Vaash laughed.

"This one sees you are one of learning. Freeing oneself from a name is one step in the journey, as are the vows of silence taken initially."

Demosyna nodded with a mouthful of fish, understanding the other monks' silence better now. Vaash passed an untouched piece of fish to his students, who eagerly began tearing into the flesh.

"Allow this one to get water," Vaash said after minutes of voracious eating.

He was gone barely ten minutes, spent in silence with the young monks, and the simple meal was finished when he returned. Vaash handed a full waterskin to Demosyna and sat down next to his pupils. The younger diver leaned in, and Vaash put his arm around the young man's shoulders.

"We can enjoy more training tonight," Vaash said to the two, giving the younger a squeeze. "We will host our new friend, Demosyna, till then. That we will."

"Please, don't let me interrupt your training, sirs," Demosyna began, but Vaash smiled and shook his head.

"Never think it, Demosyna."

Vaash laughed softly and handed his long flute to the elder pupil.

"This one will fetch medicine for that wound. Continue the song, if you would."

The older student began haltingly playing the song Demosyna heard Vaash perform as he hurled rocks at his pupils.

"I have medicine, sir. You don't have to use your own," Demosyna called. "Besides, my foot is healing better these last days. Thank you for the concern."

"May this one look and see?" Vaash asked earnestly as he knelt with a small bag.

"If you insist. I did need a new bandage anyway," the young woman reasoned aloud, extending her foot. "Thank you so much, sir."

Vaash laughed at this and opened the bag.

"Please, friend, call this one Vaash if you would. It is our pleasure to help when possible. That it is."

Both of the wordless monks nodded, never meeting Demosyna's gaze as they scanned the sky. Demosyna gently unwrapped the medicated bandage while glancing at the still puckered wound. Healing had begun to take root, but swelling was still present and painful. Vaash looked intently at the wound before producing bandages and a jar of blue salve.

"This one has discipline in medicine from many years ago," Vaash told Demosyna in a calm voice and motioned to her foot. "May we try to help?"

Demosyna nodded, and Vaash gingerly lifted her leg by cupping the ankle to inspect the sole. She winced slightly, but the roaring pain in that foot had subsided to a dull ache. The young woman withstood the quick inspection, holding her breath the entire time.

"You have done very well," Vaash complimented, inspecting the soiled bandages. "Healing has begun thanks to your skill."

Demosyna blushed as Vaash applied the blue salve to a clean bandage. Catching her gaze, Vaash raised his eyebrows before wrapping her foot when Demosyna nodded. His thick medicine was soothing against the tender foot, and Demosyna sighed in relief when only a slight burn was felt.

"Finished," Vaash said as he packed the items.

The bandage was already numbing the throbs in her foot, and Demosyna smiled back while wiggling her toes.

"Thank you, Vaash," she said, her smile widening. "It already feels much better."

"We are happy to help, Demosyna. These woods provide all one needs, and this one will happily offer aid."

Vaash stood and deposited the medicine into the tent. His elder student stopped playing at the end of a bar and held the flute out for Vaash. The master monk took the long instrument and looked at the sun's position in the sky.

"Would you hear our purpose in these frozen trees?" Vaash asked with a glint of humor on his face. "So you may know how you find us by your river?"

"I am curious what such an ancient Order is doing here," Demosyna said, nodding, vaguely remembering tales running through her mind.

This seemed to please Vaash, and he settled against his young pupil while Demosyna stretched her legs.

"We have journeyed these woods for nearly a year," Vaash spoke in a slow, expressive voice. "Such is our way, as we embrace the ever-changing world that carries us. This one is perhaps the last of the Order, but these boys show a spark where it once had faded. It is this one's privilege to be master to such amazing men. That it is."

Both young men blushed in embarrassment at the praise, and Vaash smiled warmly.

"That one has studied for years before arriving here and has reached the apex of instruction."

Vaash motioned to the elder diver.

"You have found us at the end of that one's training as he out-grows the home he knew. Such is the heart of life, and this one loves all in life."

The younger monk giggled before regaining himself, and Vaash put his arm around his pupil's shoulders. Tears formed in his eyes, but Vaash beamed toward the elder pupil.

"It is a wonderful time to be here, Demosyna. That one has grown strong enough to stand alone, just as a child should move beyond their parent," Vaash exclaimed, and his green eyes sparkled. "That one begins his new path as this young one is welcomed into a family he chose. This one will always love these men and feels great pride at sharing life with them. Thank you for breaking bread with us as we live free. As you say, Demosyna, a friendly face is a welcome sight."

"Will you stay long here on the river?" Demosyna asked, searching the man's friendly face.

"The way of our Order is change, Demosyna," Vaash said simply, his voice ringing with conviction. "These ones will be here for now, but our journey leads ever onward."

"I see," Demosyna said, lowering her head to think. "I appreciate the warm welcome, Vaash. May I be honest with you? I feel I can trust you."

Vaash smiled widely and pushed a strand of red hair from his face.

"If that is what you wish, Demosyna. But if you wish not to speak of the arrow wound, you do not have to. That you don't."

Demosyna felt her heart beat in her throat before she was able to speak. A cloudy sky was bright and alive with the noonday sun as she began to speak of herself. The truth, Demosyna decided, would suit her best.

"I was attacked by slavers as I traveled to the Wise-woman Order in the north," Demosyna said, recalling the events. "My Wise Mother, along with my companion, Bhreel, was killed when I was taken captive. I was imprisoned for days, along with many of my shipmates. I finally escaped in the river with two friends when being taken into forced servitude."

Vaash put his hand over his mouth upon hearing this, and the other two monks widened their eyes.

"We were separated by the river, and I haven't seen them since," Demosyna continued after several minutes passed. "Jui was gravely ill, both with fever and wounds. I worry she may be dead even though she can breathe in the water. Rrra wasn't used to the cold, and I fear he didn't find his mate. I can't even know for certain he got to the river, for all I could think of was my own escape. I was so selfish, and I can't change what happened till I find them again."

Demosyna motioned to the river with tears in her eyes and watched as ice streamed past the small islands.

"Then about two days ago, the soldiers caught up to me. I was hiding in"—Demosyna paused and swallowed—"in the woods when I saw them searching the river. They found tracks leading into the trees, and I haven't noticed anyone since. I am afraid they will catch me, and all I want is to find my friends. I know we can still escape to my Orders once I find them."

Vaash sat in silence next to his pupils while Demosyna recounted her harrowing journey. Once she started, the apprentice found herself speaking freely despite her initial hesitation.

"I thank you, Vaash, for all you have done for me," Demosyna said, her horns casting shadows on her face. "But I don't want you to get involved and wind up like my friends. It is my fault they were imprisoned, and I don't want you to fall victim to my life. If I find Jui and Rrra again, I know I can get them to safety like I promised."

Demosyna held back tears as her emotions surfaced again, clear and powerful. A frustration at her own inability to be useful was a biting voice of doubt in the apprentice's mind. Despite the recent hope she had found in her cave, remembering the desperate times stirred the emotions into a roiling tornado.

Vaash, too, had tears falling from his eyes, and the other orange-clad monks stared at Demosyna. The young apprentice wiped her eyes and took a deep, calming breath.

"I'm sorry. I shouldn't have burdened you with all that," Demosyna told the men. "I just feel like I need to trust you. You are all so kind, and your friendly faces have reminded me of those I seek."

"Demosyna, we thank you for the trust you place in us," Vaash replied with a sad smile. "This one knows the feel of slavery all too well. Let it be clear, then, that you will find safety with my Order if you wish."

Demosyna was speechless when she heard Vaash's reply and searched his face for deception. His long red hair fluttered in the wind, yet Vaash's smile remained honest.

"These ones strive for balance in strength and, as such, avoid using our bodies against others," Vaash explained. "We cannot kill these soldiers for you, Demosyna. That we cannot."

"Kill them?" Demosyna asked, frowning. "No, I only wish to find my friends and get home to the Wise-woman Order."

A relieved smile crept onto Vaash's face, and he exhaled a sigh that floated away in a cloud.

"Forgive this one, then."

Vaash bowed his head.

"No insult was intended. Many call on the Lost Orders to use them for war or profit. These ones here have no interest in such."

Both of the pupils nodded their bald heads in agreement and looked at Demosyna with new respect.

"Demosyna, you will always be welcome to travel with these ones," Vaash said with a good-natured laugh. "This one will keep you from harm as long as you wish."

Tears of gratitude filled the apprentice's eyes as she smiled with her sharp teeth shining. She couldn't find the words, so Demosyna simply nodded her thanks. Vaash sat next to Demosyna as she wiped the last tears from her eyes.

"It is this one's pleasure, Demosyna," Vaash said softly to the young Wizen. "You need not think yourself weak, my friend. That you do not."

CHAPTER 13

Her day passed as Demosyna watched the young monks go about their duties. The apprentice tended the fire while the trio resumed training, feeling wonderful that she could contribute. The master sat on the island as the pupils gathered the necessary stones. Moving to the steady rhythm of the deep flute music, the two smashed rocks and gathered replacements for hours. Demosyna marveled at the endurance these men must have to push themselves to such extremes.

Vaash called a halt to the diving with hours of daylight left. A short rest was allowed as Demosyna limped over and offered water. After a nod from Vaash, the two accepted with grateful smiles.

"Demosyna, would you like to see us juggle?" Vaash asked the woman as she sat back down near the fire.

Demosyna had never been fortunate enough to see any of the mobile carnivals but often heard tales of acrobats, jugglers, and exotic creatures.

"Yes, please," Demosyna called to the human monks. "That would be wonderful."

After sizing the stones, Vaash tossed one to the elder of the training monks. The bald monk caught the heavy stone with one hand and tossed it to the younger. No sooner had he tossed the first than Vaash arced another to the elder student, who repeated the process.

As they continued juggling the first two stones, a third was thrown just as the first reached Vaash.

Vaash laughed as he caught the rock and juggled two stones in the air before sending one toward the elder. Before long, each man juggled three stones, all while passing a fourth. Demosyna laughed at the tremendous display of dexterity, but they added more stones to the routine. When each monk juggled six large stones, they moved backward, increasing the size of the circle.

Vaash stood with his robes soaking the spray as he stopped back-tracking and continued the hypnotic juggling. All three monks were smiling and performed with the cooling air of the evening. Amazed at the spectacle, Demosyna clapped with joy when the monks finally stopped their display.

All three men jumped into the air and flipped through the circle their stones made. Rocks tumbled to the wet ground, and they stood from their somersaults, bowing to an audience of one. Echoes of her enthusiastic clapping rang across the camp, and they joined Demosyna around the fire.

"That was amazing," Demosyna gushed at the men. "I've never seen anything like that. Or your flute practice!"

Vaash laughed and patted his flute with a worn hand. The other two monks set about preparing another meal in wordless efficiency.

"It is useful to have many disciplines, as this one was taught," Vaash told her with a distant look. "Music is a useful tool for training and for life."

In place of fish, the two monks produced long strips of jerky they warmed on the coals. Another loaf of crispy bread was enjoyed, and Vaash offered Demosyna a gourd-shaped flask of wine. The young apprentice accepted and ignored the painful memory of Jui and Rrra. Despite eating that morning, Demosyna found herself famished and ate heartily.

"A nighttime swim is in order," Vaash proclaimed after the meal was finished. "These two will enjoy a dip while they gather dessert."

Still shy around Demosyna, the bald monks undressed out of view behind a tree. They dived into the river with barely a splash rising from the frozen water. Each pupil swam at a steady pace against the current toward the bend and the waterfall beyond. Barely four minutes passed before they returned, and Demosyna herself might have had trouble swimming that quickly, she thought.

"Those boys always surprise me," Vaash told Demosyna. "This one loves them both as one's own children."

"You have children?" Demosyna asked, glancing at the man.

"This one had two children and a wife, but not anymore."

Sadness crept into the man's eyes.

"Those two are the last people this one can call family."

The bald monks appeared from the bend and turned for a third trip upriver, fighting the chilly water.

"I'm sorry, Vaash. I didn't mean to upset you," the young Wisewoman said, turning with concern.

"You have done nothing wrong, my friend," he replied as he regained his usual expression. "Do you have any children?"

His question took her aback, and she considered before answering. Demosyna was a young woman still, and thoughts of children had yet to truly enter her mind.

"No," the apprentice responded. "I haven't given it much thought, as I am still an apprentice. It might be nice, but children are for the future, if at all."

Vaash laughed loudly at this and nodded his understanding.

The two swimmers returned with grins and armloads of fresh shells. Clams and snails were dropped near the fire, and a light dessert was enjoyed. Vaash found vinegar to splash onto the seafood, and wet shells joined the fish bones in the fire. As before, the bald monks declined any wine, so Vaash and Demosyna passed the large bottle.

"It is late," Vaash said after the others supped, having only consumed wine. "If you desire, you may use the tent. You seem like you need a restful sleep, Demosyna."

Demosyna glanced upriver and considered her cold, fireless cave.

"I would like that, yes. I do not deserve your kindness, but thank you, Vaash. Thank you all."

The two young monks blushed meekly at her words, but Vaash bellowed his booming laugh.

"This one doesn't use the tent, and those two will be warm by the fire," Vaash exclaimed. "If you can ignore the clutter, the tent is yours."

Demosyna retired to the enclosure with a final thanks. The fire kept the tent warm enough for her to remove her top when she closed the flaps. Demosyna's grass skirt was a welcome bit of comfort, having felt great pride in the success of the cloth.

Inside, there was a collection of containers littering the floor around a cotton mat. A pillow and blanket topped the mattress and gave a nostalgic feeling of apprentice dorms. After clearing the piles from the bed, Demosyna fell asleep almost at once. A full stomach and soft blanket ensured the exhausted woman slept through the night.

* * * * *

Groggily, Demosyna donned her clothes before making her way outside. The midmorning sun shone brightly off her purple scales as she walked the camp. Their fire was out, little more than coals, and the garbage cleaned up. No sign of the monks could be found besides sets of footprints. Demosyna gathered firewood with slight confusion, and the blaze was rekindled.

It was another cold day in the lands Demosyna was adrift in, and she sat by the fire while waiting. Vaash finally appeared, leading the other two, from downriver with armloads of sticks. Vaash laughed upon seeing Demosyna nursing the fire, and the three dropped their bundles.

"Thank you, my friend," Vaash said to the seated woman. "Did you sleep well?"

"I overslept actually," Demosyna said with a yawn.

"These two will find you food if you are hungry," Vaash told the Wizen with a smile. "The supply of preserved food has nearly gone empty, but fresh game can be found!"

Demosyna shook her head and returned the smile.

"No, thank you. I am so full from yesterday that I likely won't eat for days!"

Vaash laughed loudly and shook his head with good humor. The other monks began taking down the tent. A large bundle of firewood was lashed atop each pack, and the bags bulged with the strain.

Seeing the wide eyes of the woman, Vaash sat next to Demosyna with feet tucked beneath him.

"These ones travel onward, Demosyna," Vaash said, his voice a soft invitation. "We are visiting the town ahead. That one has earned his citizenship, and the village will offer imperial services. The promise this one made you stands. That it does."

"Thank you, Vaash. I would love to walk with you," the Wise-woman replied with sparkling eyes. "I thought it over, and if I can search from town, it will be best. I promise not to be a burden."

All three robed monks smiled and finished the last of the breakdown. Steam hissed off the campfire as Vaash put out the blaze, and a column of white vapor rose steadily.

After each monk had taken a pack, stuffed to bursting, the four began walking at a leisurely pace. The two bald monks remained silent, and Vaash played a walking melody from the large flute.

Demosyna didn't worry about leaving her possessions in the hidden cave, as it had gone unnoticed for years. It would be a simple matter of following the river, in any case, if she decided to return. Her new friends gave the young woman confidence, and watching them train let Demosyna understand their protection meant a lot.

Trees began to fall back as they followed the course charted by the river. The dense land eased into valleys that Demosyna was grateful for, even considering the help the monks had given.

During the rest they took upon seeing the woods disperse, Vaash gave Demosyna a spare robe of bright yellow.

"If you wish, you may have this. It will warm you better than grass," Vaash offered, smiling kindly.

The apprentice Wise-woman wrapped her frame in the robe and found it was billowy in the wind. Demosyna felt embarrassed to have the ill-fitting robe whipping around, but none of the monks smiled with anything but warmth.

"It would take you many more fish to fill out that robe, my friend," Vaash said, laughing cheerfully.

"Or a hundred years of workouts," Demosyna joked back.

The younger monk giggled shortly before catching himself with a wide-eyed look at Vaash. Vaash pretended not to notice as he clapped the young monk on the shoulder.

Vaash passed a waterskin around the brightly clothed group, shielding his eyes against the sun.

"After tonight, we shall be only a day's walk from town," Vaash told the group after surveying. "Are you able to keep pace still, Demosyna? Do you need another bandage?"

"My foot feels fine since you treated it. I think it can wait till tomorrow. Thank you, though."

Demosyna flexed her foot to test it while saying this.

"As you wish, Demosyna," Vaash responded before securing the empty waterskin. "Let us move on, then."

Four yellow-robed travelers marched in line through wooded hillsides and muddy valleys. Insects chirped and birds flew through the brilliant sky, leaving Demosyna to daydream as she followed the music. Already, the apprentice was planning her coming days of searching for her friends.

It was an hour before sundown, and the shadows grew long behind the travelers. They made camp a stone's throw from the nearly frozen river after unloading their packs. Ice lining the banks had begun to take hold instead of breaking into chunks of bobbing ice. The air, too, had grown colder as they journeyed, and Demosyna was glad for the fire. The two bald pupils had the tent set up and the backpacks put away as Vaash gathered water from the river.

"Tomorrow evening, when we reach the town, these ones would be overjoyed if you join us for a meal," Vaash said after sitting with his pupils. "We have seen no sign of your friends, but this one knows you will find a way to help."

"I would love to celebrate his graduation, Vaash!" Demosyna replied with excitement, looking at the elder student. "It's the least I can do to repay your kindness."

Vaash shook his head.

"You owe us no debt, Demosyna. In fact, this one is glad not to beg you to join."

The other two monks smiled, and Demosyna laughed.

The area chosen as their campsite overlooked a valley that spread out into farmland. A fading sun prevented sighting the village, but Demosyna knew, from her teary gazes on the waterfall, that the false safety of town was close.

"Are you hungry, Demosyna?" Vaash inquired. "The walk was tiring, and these two pups are always hungry!"

"No, thank you, Vaash. I am not stuffed like before, but I am not quite hungry yet," Demosyna responded, grateful for her slow metabolism.

Despite the long walk, Demosyna still had energy to spare as the monks finished a few last chores. One gathered river stones for the fire while the younger began grinding grains. The quality mortar and pestle were taken from one of the bulky packs with bags of raw materials. Even salt was ground into a fine powder from a chunk of crystal, and Demosyna observed the monk with interest. He mixed in the leavening as the dough was kneaded with sure hand movements. The young monk noticed the curious gaze from the woman after putting the dough aside, blushing in embarrassment.

"Your technique is amazing," Demosyna said, smiling politely. "Did you cook the bread from earlier?"

The yellow-robed monk nodded with his face burning and continued baking. Demosyna offered her help in grinding or mixing the powders, but the silent monk shook his head.

"That one practices a simple skill. That he does," Vaash interjected as he observed. "If you wish to help, would you escort that one to gather?"

Vaash motioned to the elder of the students, who stood straighter when addressed.

"I would be happy to help, Vaash, but what would you need?" Demosyna asked, brushing her robe.

"You clearly have a firm grasp on alchemy," Vaash called as he looted the tent. "If you could assist, we will have enough to share with those in town. That one knows what to gather, so follow his example, if you would."

Demosyna nodded with energy at the thought of doing something she was good at. Vaash handed them several vials from the tent with cork stoppers.

"It is a long shot, but if any abandoned honey is found, please collect it," Vaash explained as he handed pouches over. "Such is a rarity, as wasps seldom leave their nests."

Saying nothing, Demosyna nodded and recalled the frantic flight through the woods. She hadn't noticed a nest, but fear had prevented much observation as everyone fled the airborne threat.

The young woman followed the monk into the woods in search of plants. They were still in sight of the camp when the monk produced a blade, bending down. He uprooted a flower before offering the knife handle to the Wizen. Demosyna accepted it with thanks before kneeling to gather more of the flowers, root and all.

Demosyna didn't know all the plants collected, but she followed the technique demonstrated. Harvesting each item he deemed suitable was a joy for the apprentice, and she marched happily along. Upon finding a bright-blue mushroom on the underside of a branch, the monk smiled. Demosyna observed the man's skill, for the mushroom was not bruised, and did her best to replicate the circular cuts.

The two finished their silent gathering and returned to the camp with full bags. The now familiar sound of the flute drifted as Demosyna saw Vaash and his pupil beside the fire.

"Thank you both," Vaash said, smiling brightly as they unloaded. "This will do nicely as a gift for the town."

One entire bag was devoted to wild grains that the silent monk had found with keen eyes. Vaash handed the sack to the seated monk apprentice before unpacking the rest. The young man began grinding the wheat into flour, as he had before, in preparation to make more bread.

"For this night's training, that one will have a few contests," Vaash told the group. "Three pillars of study are tested, proving one's self-mastery. Starting with an endurance challenge, we will show feats of strength and will."

Vaash stood and removed his outer robe, leaving his scarred chest exposed. The elder of the two pupils stood and moved behind a nearby tree. The bald monk moved quickly, holding his arms across his torso, to join Vaash in the water.

"A simple contest of self-control," Vaash called to the observing woman. "The winner is the one remaining submerged the longest."

Vaash took a deep breath and dived under with his bright pants waving. The elder pupil also dived after a gasp of air, and Demosyna watched from the warmth of the fire. Both remained still in the flowing water, only moving their arms to avoid the current. Nearly five minutes passed before the apprentice monk rose and gasped for air. Demosyna clapped in delight as the breathless monk swam behind a tree.

"That was amazing," Demosyna called to the dripping man.

He sloshed back to the camp and sat beside the fire without a word, blushing slightly. Demosyna glanced back to the river and saw Vaash still underwater, and his yellow pants waggled. She smiled as the elder pupil joined Demosyna by the fire, where he took the bread his fellow monk offered.

The sun was beginning to sink as the first arrow landed in the fire. A loud thunk resounded as the projectile sunk into the coals, and its feathers caught fire. Two more arrows landed in the soft earth, and the young Wizen found herself backing away. The two monks remained seated with their legs under them as more arrows planted themselves. An echoing horn bellowed through the still air, and Demosyna knew the imperial reckoning had found her.

Horses emerged from the woods with their hooves kicking up dirt. The elder of the monks turned his head toward the soldiers and casually snatched an arrow. A bolt was headed toward the younger pupil, but the elder plucked it lazily with two fingers from midair. Demosyna looked in a panic toward the river, but Vaash remained oblivious.

Demosyna cried out in terror as she retreated from the chaos around her. Arrows landed seemingly everywhere, and the gleaming armor drove the apprentice into near panic. Less than a minute after the first arrow, the camp was surrounded by mounted soldiers. A short figure riding on a gray horse dismounted and removed her helmet.

"In the name of my Empress, I make a claim," Sai Aeri bellowed to the yellow-robed figures. "Stand aside."

The elder of the two monks held the intricate arrow he took from its flight and stood to face the aggressor. Sai Aeri put a hand on the hilt of her sword but stood firm as the monk looked at the arrow. After a moment that seemed an eternity, the bald monk threw the arrow into the dirt with a sigh.

"Wise decision, boy," Sai Aeri barked as she glanced at Demosyna. "Found you, little liar."

Demosyna saw the fury in the small general's eyes and shrank against the glare. The setting sun cast a bloody light over the scene as soldiers enclosed the frightened Wise-woman. The younger of the bald pupils hid behind the elder as the aggressive soldiers marched, swords held in warning.

"Bind them all," Sai Aeri commanded.

Three of the soldiers found shackles before approaching the orange-robed monks. The younger monk was clinging in fear to the strong elder pupil, who stood boldly as the scene unfolded. Sai Aeri advanced on the cowering apprentice while her eyes burned with barely controlled rage.

"You think yourself smart now, little Wizen?"

Sai Aeri produced a club.

"You will pay for your lies."

Demosyna held her hand up in a placating gesture, but Sai Aeri dashed forward with lightning speed. Before any words of protest could be uttered, the leather-wrapped club struck Demosyna in the snout. A sickening crack echoed in her head, and blood began to leak from the Wise-woman's face. Demosyna cried out, falling backward onto the icy riverbank. Three guards shackled the passive monks with cruel iron, and Sai Aeri stood with a stony expression.

"Hiding out with these boy monks?" the imposing elf asked, using the club to push Demosyna over. "And lying about being an apprentice. You are too dangerous to transport under your own power."

Demosyna felt tears streaming, and her entire face was swelling after the blow. Once again, the apprentice raised an arm in an

153

attempt to halt the fury, but Sai Aeri swung the club to knock the hand away. Pain beyond reason exploded in the prone apprentice's right foot as Sai Aeri struck with the heavy club. Demosyna screamed in agony as her foot was crushed repeatedly and felt a warm pool of urine form. Demosyna's mind railed against the tidal waves of pain, unable to grasp the scope of it.

"There," Sai Aeri said after putting the bloody club onto her belt. "You will come with us, and once you are mobile again, you shall repay all debts I hold. Be thankful I only took a foot, as you can still be useful while missing a paw."

Demosyna lay in a shuddering heap in the oversized robes and saw that neither monk had moved to help. Sai Aeri motioned to one of her soldiers, who brought a muzzle and shackles. Iron was forced on the bleeding Wise-woman with no resistance, as the pain in her foot made the world spin.

"Who are you, and why do you harbor this fugitive?" Sai Aeri asked the two silent men once Demosyna was bound.

The elder monk glanced at the younger man and smiled before raising his chained hands. Deliberately and with a grin, the apprentice monk motioned to the river.

"I asked you a question, boy," Sai Aeri took a step and brandished her club.

Again, the monk nodded toward the river and smiled before sitting down. Sai Aeri narrowed her eyes and swung her club down at the elder of the monks. The blow landed on the side of the man's head, but he barely registered the impact. Two more strikes caused blood to coat the elder pupil's face, and Sai Aeri turned her furious eyes to Demosyna.

"I see your friends share your arrogance," Sai Aeri spit at the Wizen. "They can join you, then."

A muzzle prevented Demosyna from speaking more than a moan. Demosyna tried to rise despite her broken foot or to summon the desperate magic that had helped her escape. Her body seemed distant, however, and Demosyna lay in the cold of defeat. Demosyna knew such feelings all too well, and it seemed now that her foot was lost. The young Wizen wept with frustrated agony, seeing the world become unfocused. It was at that moment of despair that Vaash surfaced from his underwater ignorance.

Sai Aeri spun to face the brightly clothed man as Vaash waded onto the shore. He stopped well short of the camp and the bloody spectacle the soldiers had made.

"Greetings, friends," Vaash said, his voice calm. "Please share our fire, Sai Aeri."

The short elf's eyes widened as recognition took hold, and the soldier put her helmet on. Sai Aeri drew her sword in a flash of red-soaked armor, faster than the eye could track. Two of the elven soldiers held the tips of their deadly blades to the backs of the silent men. Demosyna found her breath had stopped in the escalating threat around the once welcoming campfire.

"Vaash of the Fist," Sai Aeri called in a shaking voice.

Demosyna, despite her pain-riddled body, saw fear springing into Sai Aeri's eyes. Even when facing the overwhelming odds in the Fort, Sai Aeri had barely changed her icy expression.

As Sai Aeri took a trembling step backward, Vaash advanced toward the grisly situation.

"Kill them," Sai Aeri commanded, her voice a squeak.

Demosyna watched in horror as both of the men were stabbed through the back by the soldiers, their imperial armor shining dark red. Despite the muzzle holding her mouth closed, Demosyna screamed her protest. The apprentice was too weak to rise and lay uselessly in her own blood and failure. The elder of the two monks remained calmly smiling as blood spilled from his chest, but the younger looked toward Vaash with tears.

"Papa," the man choked through blood, brown eyes full of pain.

Both men fell to the cold ground and lay still as pristine robes soaked their lifeblood. Sai Aeri continued her retreat while calling for her guards to advance. Vaash stopped in place when the pupils were executed and hung his head so that his wet red hair fell. Demosyna couldn't see his expression with her face in the dirt, but Vaash's entire body was twitching. Steam rose from his soaked pants, which seemed to whip and dance.

155

One of the tall soldiers charged the stationary monk and swung her filigreed sword. With a speed of motion that defied belief, Demosyna watched the sword miss Vaash. Vaash took a single step forward as the soldier tried to bring the sword back up. She cried out in pain as the monk grabbed the soldier's wrist and broke it, causing her to drop the sword.

"Enough," Vaash yelled in fury. "That it is."

Demosyna saw tears in the man's eyes as he threw the attacking soldier. Vaash's head twitched spastically, sending his red hair dancing, and all the muscles in his body spasmed. Vaash advanced past the helpless Wizen with his fingers and back muscles moving in twitchy patterns. Pebbles bounced off her face as he marched past, and Demosyna felt a feverish energy radiating off the monk. His clothes rustled wildly despite the still air, and a warm breeze seemed to push the ground aside as Vaash strode past.

From her position in the mud, Demosyna began to fade in and out of consciousness. Three soldiers rushed the lone figure, and Demosyna saw Vaash raise his arms. He caught the club in one hand while intercepting the sword with another. A third soldier spun behind the monk and slashed, but Vaash had taken a step forward. The force used when Vaash stepped was enough to first bend and then snap the thin blade.

Tears continued streaming down Vaash's face as the soldier wielding the club swung again.

"This one is going to break each of your limbs," Vaash said in a shaking voice at Sai Aeri. "That I will."

Demosyna saw Sai Aeri drop her sword and begin backing away faster from the vengeful man. The monk's face was hidden from her, but Demosyna saw the terror in Sai Aeri's eyes. Everyone in the bloody camp heard the conviction in the man's voice, and Sai Aeri whimpered in fear. Vaash raised his arm to intercept a club, and the rusty spikes sank into his forearm. Vaash was unfazed by the attack, and with one kick, he sent the soldier flying. The soldier didn't rise again, and Sai Aeri screamed orders.

Each remaining soldier rushed toward Vaash in their ornate armor, but Demosyna found herself losing grip on consciousness.

The last clear image of the frightful scene was Vaash steadily advancing on Sai Aeri, who cowered while her soldiers charged. His arms dripped blood onto the earth, and the twitching man sent the last of the soldiers flying away. Vaash didn't even touch them as the elves tumbled, shrieking in fading voices.

Demosyna fell into unfeeling blackness, her mind swirling as agonized pleas echoed in her nightmares.

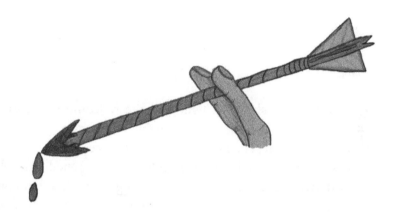

CHAPTER 14

emosyna felt sheltered light and the welcome touch of a blanket as the young woman regained her senses. The smell of cut wood reached the waking apprentice, and memories of soft beds from her youth surfaced. Demosyna opened her yellow eyes and saw brilliant rays of light pouring through a window. The dark wood was unadorned with carvings or decorations, and Demosyna felt confusion sweep over her.

"Wise Mother," the woman croaked into the plain room.

No answer came to the Wise-woman's call, and only her breathing was heard or seen.

Where am I? Demosyna thought, lying on a soft pillow. *Was it all a dream?*

Upon trying to sit up, the injured woman realized it was foolish to assume her memories were a nightmare. Pain had begun washing over the apprentice as soon as she opened her bright eyes, but she thought it lingered from dreams. A grimace formed on Demosyna's broken face and only served to send further discomfort through the woman. Demosyna grabbed at her right thigh tightly as the pain left any further sleep behind in a wave across her mind.

Tears formed in the young woman's eyes as she lay in paralyzing pain, fearing her unknown surroundings. One by one, the memories returned, and Demosyna pondered how long ago Vaash fought the soldiers.

I remember Sai Aeri beating me, Demosyna thought as she tried to avoid the degrading memories. *The last thing I remember clearly is Vaash coming from the river. Where is he, and how did I get here?*

Demosyna had no answers to these or any of the other questions that sped through her mind. She removed the blanket and saw a rough cast had been applied while she slept. The apprentice still wore the bright robes she recalled having, yet the front was now stained with dark patches of blood. There was also a circle around her crotch, and Demosyna remembered wetting herself out of fear.

Working with the pain, Demosyna shrugged out of the soiled robes and lay in her woven grass garment. Movement had excited her mangled foot, so the apprentice lay with her breath flying through the window. The tip of her tail still ached, and her arm was swollen as if broken. Demosyna's worst pains came from her face and foot, where the most brutal assaults had taken place.

She only tried moving her toes once after awakening, and the grinding pain it caused made the world spin. Birdcalls were the only sound the confused woman heard as she lay in the wooden sanctuary. Patience was something Demosyna had learned long ago, however, so she waited. Horses passed nearby while the young Wizen watched the light through the window, and a door opened. Footsteps stopped at the entry to the woman's room, and she craned a horned head toward the doorway.

"Who is it?" Demosyna called, fearing Sai Aeri's voice.

"Vaash," came the welcome reply as he entered.

His long red hair was shining in the afternoon light as Vaash put down a satchel and looked warmly at Demosyna. The apprentice returned his look with shock and lay her head back down on the soft pillow.

"I am sorry that you woke alone, Demosyna," Vaash said as he sat. "I was tending to a few errands that took longer than expected."

"Vaash, it's wonderful to see you. I thought I was done when Sai Aeri found me and that you were dead when I fainted," Demosyna said, tears filling her eyes. "How did we escape?"

Vaash didn't respond and sat with his eyes fixed on his hands. His normally jovial face was set in a hard and unknowable expression.

"The soldiers were no longer capable of pursuit after I was finished."

His voice took on a deadly tone Demosyna had never heard from the monk.

"It is a sad thing that happened. That it is."

Flashes of the terrible night rose in her mind, and Demosyna recalled the summary execution of the two monks. From her helpless position, Demosyna had seen the blood-covered swords protrude through their bodies and been unable to prevent anything. Demosyna wiped a tear from her cheek and winced when a finger brushed her swollen snout.

"Forgive me, my friend. I will give you this."

Vaash stooped and retrieved items from his bag. Demosyna barely noticed his change in speech with her pain-soaked body keeping most thoughts away. Vaash mixed a powder into a cup of water before helping the prone woman into a seated position. His strong arms eased Demosyna during the painful process, and she thanked Vaash with panting breaths. His arm was swollen badly, Demosyna noticed, but the monk seemed unbothered by it while helping.

"Are you hurt, Vaash?" Demosyna asked as he found bandages, noticing bruises and cuts.

"My body will heal," he replied simply.

"I'm so sorry I got you..." Demosyna began but was cut off when he shook his head.

"No, you have nothing to be sorry for, Demosyna."

Vaash looked her in the eyes with sorrow etched on his face.

"It was my choice to do what I did, just as it was Sai Aeri's choice to continue deciding others' fates for them. I know you have many questions, but for now, let me heal what I can."

Demosyna saw the pain in the man's face and was silent as Vaash applied salves to the bandages. A covering completely enclosed her foot, but Demosyna observed blood in spots. Vaash saw her shaking eyes and followed them to the foot before nodding.

"It is badly broken, Demosyna," Vaash said, placing a hand on her shoulder. "You must prepare yourself. I wasn't able to set all the bones yet, but you need to know something before I do."

"What?" Demosyna asked with a trembling voice.

"Sai Aeri caused so much damage to your foot that I wasn't able to save one of your toes," Vaash told the quivering woman with a gentle voice. "You deserve to know before I remove the bandage, if you want to see your foot. Know, too, however, that I will heal your foot, and you will walk on it again. That you will."

Tears fell from the Wise-woman's eyes as she nodded, not trusting her voice. Vaash removed a cloth cast, and Demosyna saw what remained after the crushing blows. All the toes sat at odd, crooked angles, and only the stub of a big toe remained. There were also large indents up and down the length of her foot where the thin bones had sunken. Demosyna cried at the sight of her foot and turned her eyes from the grisly appendage.

Vaash stood from the bed and sipped the water he had mixed before handing the cup to Demosyna.

"This will take almost all the pain away, I promise," Vaash said tenderly. "It should only take a few minutes to repair you. I know you are strong enough to take the healing, my friend. That you are."

Demosyna downed the cloudy drink with a painful grimace at the bitter taste, feeling warm blood in her nose. Vaash's potion went to work at once by numbing her mouth and spreading warmth to her body. Tense muscles relaxed as Demosyna felt her body melt away. The pain throughout her entire being seemed to fade, and the young apprentice smiled up at Vaash with tears of gratitude.

"Wow, that is so much better."

Demosyna's words came slow, as though from a distance.

"Thank you, Vaash."

"You are welcome, my friend," Vaash replied, tears in his green eyes. "Are you ready for me to set the rest of your foot, Demosyna? Your snout set cleanly, but your foot will take some finesse."

The young Wizen nodded and took a breath to rally against the coming pain. Her finger had broken once, and Klai set the crooked digit with a roll of her elven eyes. Demosyna knew that minor fracture paled in comparison and worried at the coming pain. Taking nearly a minute of contemplation, Vaash began to adjust the shattered bones. The rending pain of the fragile bones moving through her torn muscles caused Demosyna to groan through clenched teeth.

"I was only thirteen when accepted into my Order," Vaash said to the tortured Wizen. "Before that, I was raised in slavery, only knowing a master's desire to be my own. My mother died giving birth, so my slave master sent me to the Order due to my twitching ailments. I was still under the thumb of an owner during my training, subject to her will at any free moment."

Demosyna looked with confusion at the man instead of at her foot while Vaash moved the bones.

"I thanked them by using the strength the monks showed me for my own ends," Vaash breathed, tears flowing in his eyes. "They revealed how to calm my body spasms through grueling lessons over many years. I felt that joining the war raging in the Fist was the best way to use my newfound control."

Enormous pain caused by his strong hands faded as Vaash kept Demosyna's attention on the story.

"For years, I killed without care, using my body to control my surroundings. It came easy to me, as I found my will could be inflicted upon anyone. I grew to be a legend, famous for breaking bodies while keeping mine together long enough to do it again," Vaash said, rubbing a thick paste on Demosyna's foot.

A look of disgust formed on the man's hard face as Vaash said this, but his eyes remained thoughtful.

"My sons joined me in my bloodlust when my wife was killed, and we swam through carnage. They took to the life just as well as I, learning quickly how fragile a body can be."

Vaash paused for a moment, and Demosyna found herself sweating.

"Sai Aeri joined my legion after my actions earned her attention, and I trained her. We fought against armies beyond count, laughing together as we grew unstoppable."

Demosyna was shocked by this revelation but remained silent as a shooting pain from her pinky toe left her breathless. Warm blood ran in drops down her purple-scaled foot and stained the bedsheet scarlet. Demosyna closed her eyes as Vaash finished the adjustment and moved on to the other toes.

"I told myself I was helping, that I was able to by destroying those standing against my justice. I convinced myself and my children I was strong."

Vaash almost wept as he sat beside Demosyna.

"My youngest son was killed on the coast, and I saw my elder would face the same fate. He would have gladly joined his brother, following me blindly, and it would be my doing. The siege that took my son was the last act of violence I committed till Sai Aeri returned to my life. I had to show my boy a better way was possible, even for us."

Each time Vaash spoke, he went about the painful work of setting the bones of Demosyna's foot. The distant agony was held at bay by the potion and story as the apprentice observed the masterful first aid.

"I took my last son and fled to my order with its teachings of strength and peace. I spent years tempering the assassin I turned my son into and showing him the folly of my choices."

Vaash wiped a tear from his cheek before leaning back.

"He was so strong. He didn't question me, even when it meant leaving the only life he knew for the second time. He was stronger than me. That he was."

Demosyna put a hand on the man's shoulder, and Vaash wiped blood from his own before squeezing her hand. The apprentice shook her head slowly to clear it and took deep breaths through her broken nose. Her foot throbbed with each heartbeat, and Demosyna closed her eyes against the sensation. It had begun merging with the emotions rising in her heart, leaving the Wise-woman dazed.

"Was the younger apprentice your son, Vaash?" Demosyna asked, remembering the gurgled word to Vaash.

"No. He was mine, but that one wasn't my blood," Vaash replied, his voice full of pain. "The elder of the two was my child, the last of my wife left in this world."

Demosyna sat with that information in bewilderment before the renewed pain distracted her. Vaash expertly moved his hand between the sensitive areas, guiding splintered bones back in place as he did.

"After you fainted, I dispatched the soldiers and ran with you to this cabin. They were all badly broken, but I thankfully didn't kill any," Vaash said as he finished the last adjustments. "I rented it for the season last year, having planned to celebrate my boy's graduation here. It was the best place I could think of to let you heal."

"How long was I asleep?" the apprentice asked with slurred words.

Vaash turned and smiled warmly for the first time since starting his tale.

"You have been asleep for two days, more or less. You were out the night I carried you and slept through the first day here. When you developed a fever, I went into town to gather medicine. Once you were out of danger this morning, I got these final supplies for our recovery."

Demosyna still had many burning questions, but Vaash nodded at her foot.

"It is all done, Demosyna," the monk said with a final gentle testing. "I will make a solid cast, and you will keep the foot, my friend. I promise."

Vaash mixed ingredients in a bucket, adding water till a plaster was obtained. Demosyna noticed with satisfaction that her foot was already feeling considerably better thanks to the skill Vaash gave freely. Vaash cleaned the blood from her foot and applied a burning liquid. The apprentice had learned so many unprompted details of her new friend's life that it would take time to process.

His yellow-and-orange robes rustled as Vaash placed rolls of fabric onto the bed. Vaash gave the plaster a final stir, smiling with his wet cheeks. Demosyna hardly felt the fabric as he began wrapping the toes, pairing the remaining ones before securing them together. Barely any pain registered to the groggy Wise-woman as Vaash wrapped silky bandages up her ankle. The gentle pressure further eased the discomfort radiating from her foot, and Demosyna sighed.

Vaash produced metal rods and wrapped them in fabric before dipping it in plaster. After all the sticks had been soaked, he applied plaster bandages to Demosyna's foot. Layers of the icy fabric were wrapped, and Vaash used the rods as support.

Once he finished building the cast, Demosyna's toes were still exposed, and it encircled her leg up the calf. On each side of her ankle, a rod extended from the white plaster below her heel. It crossed at Demosyna's ankle with rods that extended toward her visible toes.

"Thank you, Vaash," Demosyna said. "I don't know what I would do without you."

Vaash smiled softly at the young woman.

"I am happy to help and that I can rectify my mistakes."

Demosyna frowned, pondering the words.

"It will dry fully in just hours, Demosyna," Vaash explained. "Try to avoid moving while the mixture sets and your bones knit. Your foot may feel hot, but that is normal as it dries. I will prepare a meal while we wait, if you are hungry."

Demosyna considered for a long moment, her thoughts coming as if through water. It had been days since the soldiers and Demosyna heard her stomach grumble. Even with her metabolism, the strain had awoken the Wise-woman's appetite again.

"Please," Demosyna rasped, her face stiff and swollen.

Vaash wordlessly gathered the scattered supplies before exiting the room.

The wood was a soothing bit of comfort for Demosyna as she sat with the cast drying in the evening air. Vaash took her soiled robe, and Demosyna maneuvered a blanket over her legs. Ragged grass clothes clinging to her body was a reminder of hardships faced, and Demosyna sighed as cooking smells reached her.

A potion she drank, combined with the ointments, let the persistent pain become more manageable. The woman reviewed years of information she received, much of which was disturbing. Vaash returned to offer a steaming bowl of broth, with bits of diced vegetables floating lazily. The young Wise-woman eagerly drank the bowl, and Vaash smiled as she ate.

"You will likely get very drowsy soon, my friend," Vaash told the full-bellied woman. "The potion will let you sleep deeply while your cast dries. I have to leave for a short time, but you are safe in this cabin. Have no fear, Demosyna, as I will be here when you wake. That I will."

Alarm turned to relief at Vaash's words, and Demosyna felt a wave of promised fatigue wash over her. Her room seemed to elongate, and Demosyna shifted to lay down on the soft bed. Using her sore tail to adjust the blanket, Demosyna found a comfortable position and soon drifted to blissful sleep.

Vaash watched the Wizen sleep for a few moments before leaving, locking the cabin as he ran impossibly fast into the murderous wilds.

CHAPTER 15

Demosyna didn't dream as she slept with her cast drying atop the pillow. Vaash was, as promised, back from his errand before the injured woman awoke. With his trademark smile on his face, Vaash offered the Wise-woman water after propping her to a seated position.

"Yes, please," Demosyna croaked.

Vaash inspected the cast while the apprentice drank deeply from a bursting skin. Already, the pain was rising in her newly conscious mind, and Demosyna paused with a belly full of water that sat heavy. Vaash saw beads of cold sweat form and dabbed at Demosyna's brow with a wet cloth.

"There, my friend. Be easy, and I will warm some soup for you," Vaash said in a gentle tone, muddy robes fluttering.

Demosyna began taking deep breaths to calm the nausea rising in her body. Her delicate toes were exposed where the cast stopped, wrapped together in pairs. The sight of the missing toe caused Demosyna to cry into her hands while she waited. Anger raced through her as she recalled Sai Aeri crushing her foot, with glee in the general's eyes.

"If the pain gets too great by this evening, I will give you more medicine."

Vaash handed her a bowl.

"In the meantime, I will need a cast on my arm. Can you talk to me while I do?"

"Of course, Vaash."

Demosyna set the empty bowl aside, rising slightly.

"I don't know what I would talk about, though. My life hasn't been interesting till the last few weeks."

The monk removed his outer robe to reveal a horribly swollen left arm, green-and-black bruises stretching the length. She gasped at the fracture, but Vaash smiled at her concern.

"Fear not. This is a clean break," Vaash explained, motioning to his arm's bones. "I will set the bone again, and we will both enjoy a cast. Let me fetch bandages and plaster."

Vaash came back with the supplies, and he stirred the plaster to consistency.

"Where did you go while I was sleeping?" Demosyna asked, broaching the topic she had wondered about.

"I went to bury those I just lost."

Vaash sighed after wiping a tear.

"It was the least I could do for such strong men. They took to my ways like prodigies, especially at the end."

"I'm sorry, Vaash. I tried to use magic, but I couldn't save them," Demosyna responded, her eyes filling with tears.

"No. Sai Aeri made her own aggressive choice that night, just as my boys did when they stayed passive and just as I did when stopping those soldiers with my fists."

Vaash finished mixing the plaster and stood.

"Will Sai Aeri come after us now?" Demosyna asked, her voice hushed with fear. "You said you didn't kill her."

"I did not, for I never again wish to kill," Vaash said, his eyes distant. "Do not worry over that one, for it will take her many months to recover from what I did. Sai Aeri will crawl back to her fort, as she was when I picked you up and ran. By then, we will have distance and winter to buffer us."

A sigh of relief escaped the young woman as she closed her eyes in celebration. The pain seemed to fade from her injuries, and Vaash tested his forearm before setting it.

"Let me tell you of the friends I'm searching for. I'm not sure I told you much about them yet," Demosyna said, gathering her thoughts. "I met them only days after beginning my boat trip, because we were required to fish for our meals. Rrra—he was mated to Jui, as I said—was taken aback by the fact that I always hunt without the weight of soggy clothes."

Vaash nodded his understanding as he steadied himself with a sigh. The monk's face didn't change, even when the bone visibly moved, while Demosyna continued.

"They were so open from the start, unlike many Wizen as I grew up," Demosyna recalled, thinking back on her lonely life in the Order. "Because I never showed any ability in magic, I was teased as a burden to the Wise-women. The things I could do rarely made money, and any I did was pathetic next to real Wizened."

Vaash looked up as he finished the painful movements.

"That is unfortunate, my friend. It can be easy to find fault, if you seek it in others."

Demosyna nodded and shook the memories from her head, bringing her focus to the present.

"We fished together every time after meeting, and Jui began teaching me about ledgers. Bhreel, our Orc companion, opened up to me when I gave him fish heads," Demosyna said, watching Vaash wrap his arm. "Rrra had been born into the wine trade and had excelled enough to procure tickets. Jui understood how to sell the liquor, so the two complemented since Rrra was terribly shy."

Demosyna felt a tear fall.

"They both had nothing to call their own except a barrel of wine and suffered through nights on our boat. They even had to borrow blankets, because Jui sold everything they owned. I was fortunate to be able to lend them my outer coat, as my Order issued blankets for our trip."

Vaash was sweaty but kept a stern expression.

"I assume they lost their wine when the boat sank?"

Demosyna paused at the question and remembered the harsh punishment doled out to the entire cabin.

"No. We reached a barricade of ice as we traveled. There was an accident, and it caused a lot of damage to the ship," Demosyna recalled. "The captain ordered all wood used for repairs, even the doors in each cabin."

Vaash nodded as he opened his green eyes.

"That does not surprise me, unfortunately. She owned them."

"That is what the sailors said, and people grew ill from the missing wood. The crew found the barrel, and the entire cabin was punished."

Demosyna remembered blood in the cold air.

"If I hadn't shared their wine, I wouldn't have gotten them into so much trouble. No wonder they started to hate me, along with the other passengers."

Vaash looked up from his wrapped arm before shaking his red-haired head. Demosyna recalled the increasingly hostile looks first Rrra, then Jui gave her as they endured dual imprisonments. A cloud of sorrow swept over her heart as Demosyna took a sip of water.

"I was overjoyed when my friends survived the boat, but they had begun to grow distant. Jui was already getting weaker from a whipping, so Rrra and I carried her into slavery."

Demosyna scowled at the memory.

"Bhreel had been so selfless, even risking his life protecting Klai and I. He was killed, along with my Wise Mother, when the slavers took us. All I did to help was stare. Rrra was taken with the men, and we only saw them once the slavers were done with them. I tried to keep her spirits up, but Jui worsened, and nobody cared.

"I spent a night trying to work out any way of escape, but Sai Aeri dealt with the bandits. I had never felt such anger as when I saw Rrra so helpless and knew freedom was all that mattered for my friends."

Demosyna frowned, seeing the flash of cloak.

"Even when I told her what had happened, the general wouldn't believe me. The magic that had overtaken me was something I can't control, and Sai Aeri sentenced us when I failed to prove myself."

"I have found elves to often be impatient when us lifers are involved," Vaash whispered, using the slang for *mortals*. "It can be hard for either to understand the other when their view on urgency is so different from the start."

Demosyna fell into silence, and Vaash completed the cast on his left arm. The process hadn't taken as long as her foot, and Vaash examined his work. Vaash seemed pleased and flexed his hand with a grimace.

"If there is a posting board in town, I can still search for them," Demosyna concluded with a small smile. "I won't let my foot hold me back, if they are still lost in the cold."

"Thank you, friend," Vaash said. "I am glad you shared yourself, as I did with you. I want no secrets between us, especially after my actions. Please do not think of me as a brute, for Sai Aeri learned cruelty from me. As I told you, we traveled miles together, and I showed her how to accomplish the impossible much as I can."

Tears formed on his cheeks, and Demosyna locked eyes with Vaash. The monk's words echoed in her mind, clear and horrible in their weight. A hatred in her heart for Sai Aeri threatened to join the respect Demosyna felt for Vaash in her mind. There were minutes of silence as unabashed sadness spilled from Vaash's eyes, and she knew he was a person of conviction.

No, Vaash isn't to blame for not stopping the attack, Demosyna thought and took a cleansing breath. *Sai Aeri is the one that deserves my anger.*

"You saved me, Vaash. I am in your debt."

Demosyna reached out a hand.

"I would be dead or worse if you hadn't stopped Sai Aeri. I'll never live down the loss of your boys, yet I will do my best to honor them."

Vaash took the offered hand.

"You owe me nothing, Demosyna. I got too emotional in the face of my past. Sai Aeri didn't recognize my son, and that likely is why she thought shackles could hold my boys. I could have carried you away once my students were gone, but I chose retribution. I saw my failures reflected in Sai Aeri's actions and found myself unable to face it. I was selfish and put you in danger with my choices."

A long moment passed as Demosyna and Vaash sat with their emotions. The man held tightly to Demosyna's hand while wiping tears with his plaster-wrapped arm. A sad smile formed on the young Wise-woman's face when a smear of plaster remained behind.

"Vaash, you are the kindest person I have met."

Demosyna wiped the grime off his cheek.

"You have done so much for a stranger like me without being asked. Thank you."

Vaash nodded, and tears fell from his eyes as the two tried to ignore their broken bodies. After several minutes, Vaash used his bright-orange top to dry the remaining tears. Vaash smiled down at the young woman before leaving to retrieve a large branch. The stick was nearly straight save at one end, where a horseshoe split formed in the grain.

"I will fashion a crutch if you wish to be mobile."

Vaash fished a knife from his satchel.

"The cast should be dry, and tomorrow, we can get you out of bed! The town will be beyond your reach, but I will be your errand boy while we heal. Till then, consider me your right hand, because that is the only one I can use."

Demosyna laughed, finding the jests a welcome distraction.

"I would love to be able to limp around, thank you. I don't know what I will need, but I'll let you know!"

The brightly clothed monk sat on the floor, using his feet to hold the stick, and shaved the bark. Vaash, with the delicate tip of his dagger, checkered a grip and carved Demosyna's name. He found strips of leather and wrapped the cup-shaped end of the crutch.

"Let us see if it will be the right length, as I guessed the size," Vaash said as he helped her balance.

She had never used a proper crutch before, and Demosyna swayed as she adjusted to the wooden foot. Vaash was smiling as Demosyna took slow steps around the bed with her breath panting jubilant vapor. Standing had caused the pain in her foot to grow worse, but Demosyna pushed it from her mind as she struggled.

"Very good, my friend," Vaash exclaimed, resting the crutch against the wall. "You have such determination. It is refreshing."

Demosyna shook her head, wincing.

"I am tired of being a burden, Vaash. I want to find my friends and get them to safety in my Order."

Vaash nodded his understanding.

"If speed is your goal, we should take the Empress's Highway. It covers the entire span through the wilderness, and we simply need money to pass the checkpoints. If we find work in town, that will not be an issue."

"I can mix potions or prepare ingredients," Demosyna explained, excitement in her heart. "I can also read and write elven, if any official letters need to be sent."

"Are you able to cook or bake with fire?" Vaash asked, his eyebrows raised.

"Yes," Demosyna responded with pride. "I cooked for my fellow Wizened when I failed out of the day's instructions."

Those memories were bittersweet, as Demosyna saw the potential her lonely hours provided her now.

"Excellent. Many of the vendors were offering baked treats. If we can set up outside the gate, we can earn enough to journey north."

Vaash stood and smiled.

"A baking permit is easy enough to purchase, especially if it is outside the walls. I will get the permits tomorrow, if you wish to aid in making quick profit."

CHAPTER 16

Demosyna sat in the outhouse near the humble cabin. Her crutch held the door open against the sluggish wind of the afternoon, crisp and fresh. Vaash had carried her the few times she needed to relieve herself, and Demosyna felt her face blush with embarrassment. Vaash had waited patiently to carry the helpless Wizen back, playing his flute to afford the woman privacy.

With the freedom provided by the crutch, Demosyna was able to make her own way along. Even though her foot burned with icy pain, Demosyna smiled to herself and watched the clouds drift.

Vaash had left over an hour ago to search out wild ingredients. Demosyna didn't bother closing the door to their isolated toilet and let the breeze bring new smells of the wild north. Before he left, Vaash made a pile of wood with the promise of assembling a trade booth.

Demosyna watched with idle wonder as two fuzzy mammals chased each other around the pile, darting into the woods that circled the cabin.

"Such energetic creatures," Demosyna sighed as she righted herself. "I should start dinner while Vaash finishes my errands."

Demosyna wobbled back into the single-bedroom cabin Vaash rented months ago, with a happier purpose in mind. The front door opened into the sitting room, and the kitchen was at the back of the snug building. The cabin's only interior door was to the left of the living room and led to a bedroom. Vaash had insisted the young Wizen take the bed, explaining he needed only meditation to rest.

The Wise-woman closed the door to stop wind from ruffling her robes, newly washed and clean.

Let's see what I have to work with, Demosyna thought as she caught her breath.

Even though it was new, Demosyna found the crutch to be an extension of her arm. The inclusion of her name had been a wonderful surprise, and the apprentice thought of Vaash's kind nature while searching. Despite his freely divulged past of mayhem, Vaash had yet to show anything but gentleness since he appeared in her life. After the heartfelt confessions each gave, Demosyna felt she knew Vaash better than anyone she had before.

Demosyna took any ingredients that she recognized from the cabinets, and a pile formed on the counter. Their small stove dominated a corner of the kitchen with a retractable cover secured to the wall. Demosyna added brittle sticks to the coals in preparation for cooking. Fire warmed the still air around the Wizen, who noticed a small leather pouch. Spare wood was piled near the stove, and she saw the bag once the shadows were pushed back.

The sack contained an off-white powder, along with pills that Demosyna recognized with a start. The young apprentice had seen the same pills during her time in the First Fort, filling up a barrel. Each day, she had watched teens being fed those tablets with wicked faces engulfing the slaves. Demosyna closed the drawstring and put it aside to begin chopping the food.

"What are they for?" Demosyna asked nobody, knowing she had no answer. "And why would Vaash have them?"

Her eyes would return to the pouch as she prepared the simple stew. Once the ingredients were diced, Demosyna decided to simply ask the man about the questionable bag.

"I trust him," Demosyna said aloud, recalling her early lessons. "All are lost without trust."

The living room consisted of thick pillows around a table, with barrels lining a wall. Demosyna filled a small cauldron with water while using the counter to transport the heavy pot. The metal was hung from a hook, and Demosyna added the dried meat and roots. She stirred absently at the soup while sprinkling herbs, and Demosyna daydreamed as the meal came together.

The door to the cabin opened while Demosyna was sampling the soup, and Vaash strode through. The monk was silhouetted from behind by deep-red light as he removed a pack before sitting on a pillow.

"Thank you for making a meal, Demosyna," Vaash said, untying his shoes. "I don't want you to strain yourself, though."

The spoonful that the young Wizen sampled tasted good, and she put the spoon down before addressing Vaash.

"It was no problem," Demosyna said, leaning on the crutch. "I wanted to make something warm for you and found these pills when I began cooking."

Demosyna motioned to the small pouch on the counter, and Vaash began blushing furiously when he saw it.

"I saw these pills when I was a prisoner, and the bandits were feeding it to the other slaves," Demosyna told the red-faced monk. "What are they, and what is the powder for?"

Vaash remained seated, his face burning.

"I am sorry that you found those, my friend. I did not mean to seem forward in having them. They are mine, of course, but I used its base powder to ease the pain when I fixed your foot."

Demosyna pondered his words, confusion replacing doubt in her mind. She had seen the man use an ivory powder for the potion and remembered Vaash tasting the drink before offering the medicine. The young Wizen took a pinch from the bag, finding the bitter flavor the same as the potion.

"I am truly sorry, Demosyna," Vaash whispered, his eyes wide. "I didn't mean anything by it, having the pills. I should have told you, and for that, I am sorry."

"Are you ill?" Demosyna asked, still in the dark. "What do you need them for?"

Vaash studied the young woman's face before responding.

"You don't know what they are?"

Demosyna shook her head and used her crutch to move into the living room.

"They are to prevent pregnancy in lifers," Vaash explained to the baffled young Wise-woman. "If I take them each day, it will stop me from making children with anyone."

"So why do you have them?" Demosyna asked again, further confusion swirling in her mind.

"Again, I am sorry for being too forward," Vaash told the Wizen, tears of embarrassment in his eyes. "I had assumed that you might want me as a man, as I have known that desire when staying with young women. I was just trying to be safe if you expected that of me. Having another child isn't something I desire right now. I never meant to deceive you, my friend. Forgive me."

The purple-scaled woman stood in painful silence, balancing on her good foot. Vaash broke eye contact after he apologized again, and red hair fell over his face. Demosyna had yet to feel much romantic attraction, but many lifers paired off to make offspring. Such was not the way the Wisest taught, with elven pairing preventing any possibility of children. Demosyna felt ignorant when looking at the unfamiliar pills and frowned in thought.

"I don't understand, Vaash," Demosyna said finally, looking at the humbled man. "You started taking the pills because we are sheltered together now?"

"It is my responsibility, yes," Vaash told the confused woman, with naked shame on his face. "Please don't think of me as just a pill chaser, Demosyna. I only wanted to be prepared if anything happened since a strong young woman has her needs. My owner showed me that before I became a citizen and left her clutches."

Demosyna shook her head in thought and took a deep breath before moving to the boiling soup. Vaash remained silent as the woman filled two bowls with the steaming liquid. The young Wise-woman had spent most of her life thus far in study, leaving little room for thoughts of affection. Demosyna, if she was honest with herself, had not truly desired that yet. The apprentice wondered what she had done to signal a flirtatious air while sighing in consideration.

Demosyna glanced at the man, and her heart melted in acceptance knowing the monk's intentions to be innocent.

"I am sorry for cornering you with this, Vaash, but I was worried when I recognized the pills," Demosyna told the monk, choosing her words in consideration of his feelings. "I didn't know what they were, and I feared a connection when you told me of your past. Forgive me, my friend, if you felt any pressure from being a man. I never expected anything from you, and the thought of you as anything but a true friend hadn't crossed my mind."

Vaash remained seated and wiped a tear from his cheek.

"Thank you for your understanding, Demosyna. I was too shy to tell you, but it seems my worries were foolish. It is a pleasant surprise to find someone like you so deep into these wild lands. My slavery taught me the cravings people can have when a pill boy is involved."

"Would you like supper?" Demosyna asked, tossing the bag and smiling.

Vaash caught it without breaking eye contact, smiling weakly as he answered, "I am famished, my friend. I would love some of that great-smelling stew!"

Even with many question still unanswered, Demosyna sat near her companion. She worried at the man's past but forgave him the slight deception. It didn't concern Demosyna if he took the pills since she wasn't interested in intimacy while searching for Jui and Rrra. The two seemed in agreement on that, and the sensitive topic was dropped.

Vaash stood and put the full bowls on the low table. Demosyna turned thoughts over in her mind but returned in her head once he finished. Rods poking from the dried plaster aided in keeping her foot elevated and slightly prevented bumping the toes. Demosyna hadn't made any bread, but Vaash eagerly slurped his bowl without complaint.

The sun finally faded, and Demosyna thanked Vaash as he took the dishes.

"I have brought back many things to prepare if we are to open a shop," Vaash muttered, cleaning the dishes. "Did you still wish to travel north with me?"

"Yes," Demosyna responded, looking gratefully at the monk. "I appreciate all the help, Vaash. Bring me the materials, and I'll grind till I drop!"

Vaash laughed at her jest and left the cabin to gather the packs he had dropped outside. He was still embarrassed by the personal nature of the pills, but Vaash stored the bag in his robes.

The remainder of the night was spent organizing, then preparing the gathered ingredients. Demosyna took the wild grains and ground them into flour while the strong monk provided a steady stream of plants. Empty clay jars were filled with processed ingredients, and Demosyna took a moment to let her aching arms rest.

"I will begin building the shop," Vaash said, gathering the nearly empty packs. "Feel free to keep grinding, but you should rest your foot soon."

Demosyna shook her head.

"If I am to help my friends, I must do whatever I can!"

The young Wizen set to work, smiling at Vaash as he left the cabin. She dared to dream of finding her friends and ignored the constant pain in her body. With each stroke of the pestle, Demosyna envisioned a bright tomorrow. The cold night outside the living room rang with sounds of production as Vaash labored in the stars.

Demosyna pushed through the heavy ache in her arms as balls of fresh dough were put to rise. The woman used a sharp knife to slice an *X* on the top, setting them on a tray to bake. The humble stove quickly cooked the bread, and Demosyna used a long fork to adjust them while baking.

Despite the big bowl of soup she had for dinner, Demosyna couldn't resist cutting a loaf and taking a bite. Her sharp teeth made quick work of the bread, and Demosyna smiled at the quality. It wasn't as good as the bread enjoyed with the lost monks, but Demosyna made her way outside to find Vaash. There were already frames leaning against a tree, and the monk hoisted the wood of another.

"Vaash," Demosyna called at the whistling man. "It looks like you've already made headway! Come try the bread I baked!"

Vaash fashioned a sling for his cast.

"It smelled really good from here, my friend. I would love to sample it."

The young woman smiled nervously as Vaash took the offered bread. It was steaming in the starry night, but Vaash eagerly bit into the warm loaf.

"That was very tasty, Demosyna," Vaash said after wiping his mouth of crumbs. "Thank you. I was famished still, and that was great baking!"

"My treat, Vaash," the Wise-woman responded, her eyes full of caution. "You really liked it?"

Vaash nodded as he, too, smiled.

"Indeed. If this is the quality we provide, I am sure anyone would be happy to pay several points apiece!"

Demosyna, while having been schooled in currency, had never been allowed any of her own. All had been provided by the elegant Wizened, so Demosyna was told she didn't need to concern herself with any currency. From her studies, Demosyna knew the large rounded piece was worth more than the small triangle coin but had no frame of reference for their value.

"A few points each?" Demosyna pondered aloud. "How much will we need to pay the tolls?"

"That will vary depending on the daily fee."

Vaash thought for a moment.

"But if we had perhaps two hundred points, it should get us north. The last time I used the Upper Highway, there were nearly a dozen tollbooths, but more are likely to have been added."

Demosyna did some rough calculations in her mind.

"I have a lot of baking to do, then! Thank you for building the shop, Vaash, and for getting ingredients. Would you like another loaf? There are more cooling in the kitchen!"

"No, thank you," Vaash replied as he retrieved a hatchet. "I wouldn't wish to take any more of your inventory, as we will need all the bread we can carry!"

Demosyna watched, wrapping herself tightly against the cold air, as Vaash used a hatchet to split wood. The large piece was taller than the man even though he was Demosyna's height, but he seemed indifferent to its size. He used only his good right arm, but the wood seemed to part like water.

With eager abandon, Demosyna began to bake loaf after dark loaf. There was plenty of firewood, and Demosyna filled the kitchen before fresh loaves spilled into the living room. Woven grass was used as mats for the food, which Demosyna sprinkled with extra herbs.

The exhausted young Wizen hadn't realized she had fallen asleep until an echoing silence replaced the sounds of construction.

* * * * *

Demosyna jolted awake, wincing from the pain in her foot. The groggy Wizen looked around at dark bread loaves that were piled on every available surface.

I remember using all the flour and sitting down from the pain in my foot, Demosyna thought, rubbing her leg. *I shouldn't have walked around so much, but it will be worth it once I get safely to my Order.*

She heard no sounds from beyond the cabin and tried to enjoy the comfortable surroundings with fresh pain. Her meditations helped focus the thoughts storming in her mind, and the Wise-woman felt the pain become distant. The excitement Demosyna had the last evening kept the discomfort at bay, but it plagued the Wizen anew as she rose.

"I refuse to allow this to hinder me," the woman hissed through clenched teeth. "I must not forget that Vaash is hurt too, so we have to work together."

Demosyna held back tears at the space where her big toe should be and turned toward the window to avoid thoughts of pity. The morning was cloudy, but the young woman doubted if rain would fall to spoil the day. Shadows drifted across the clearing, and Vaash sat with a peaceful smile while smacking a piece of clay. His wet hands shone in the bright, cold morning as Demosyna walked to her friend.

"Fair morning, Demosyna. Did you sleep well?" Vaash asked the Wise-woman.

She nodded, smiling at the man, before noticing a large piece of flat clay drying on a rock. The slab had taken on the gentle curve of the boulder, and Vaash wet his hands as he worked a large chunk.

"Are you hungry?" Vaash inquired. "I can make you something before finishing this serving tray."

"I am stuffed from our stew yesterday, thanks," Demosyna said, her voice filling with a hopeful tone. "That is a big serving tray. Will we use it for the shop?"

"Yes. Once I bundled the frame, I decided to make some clay dishes. A few cups would be nice, and perhaps plates as well," Vaash mused as he punched the clay. "I took a jog to the river and brought back plenty! Once the tray is done, I will make us flatware."

"You are amazing, Vaash!" Demosyna exclaimed, grinning broadly. "Thank you for working so hard and always thinking of me!"

Vaash laughed heartily and motioned for Demosyna to hold the lump of clay. The mass was heavy, so she sat on a dry rock before suspending the ball. With a series of pulling, tugging motions, Vaash used his good right hand to tease out a long ribbon. The monk quickly set aside even ropes, but Demosyna found her arms shaking. The man put aside a fifth string and took the lump of clay from Demosyna. Vaash used the longest of the cords of wet clay to make an oval. He centered this on the rectangle of clay nearby. Wide handles formed on opposite ends, and Vaash stood to smile widely.

"Would you want to help finish the last things?" Vaash asked the Wizen, seeing her eyes large and wondering. "I will move the frames and get a permit. The imperial office should be open, and I am eager to have your shop ready!"

Demosyna felt excitement bubble up, and she nodded.

"What would you like me to do, Vaash? I would be happy to finish the dish if you need to run errands for us!"

"It is a simple matter of pushing the wet clay together like this," Vaash explained. "The clay can spread with wet fingers and enough pressure!"

Demosyna watched as he demonstrated with two fingers, and she nodded.

"It looks simple enough, I suppose. How long will it take you to reach the town gate with all that wood you must carry?"

His pile of lashed-together wood looked unwieldy, but Vaash walked over to where it leaned with a chuckle. He used knotted straps to secure the bundle to his broad back. Vaash stood and balanced with the added weight but strode forward in his usual pace.

"I will be back in just over two hours," Vaash called as he marched along a path. "I will see you soon to help you over to where the shop is assigned. The bread you offer the lovely townsfolk will be popular. That it will."

Demosyna called safe travels to the man and rested her aching foot in the beautiful morning. Even though Demosyna had known Vaash only briefly, it was surprisingly lonely without his presence. He was quickly becoming a wonderful friend, and Demosyna smiled as she enjoyed the serenity.

After doing her requested task on the dish, Demosyna set to her routine for meditations. The sky soared above the gleeful woman, and she smelled clean air from the mountains. They were barely visible in the distance, but Demosyna knew she would see their peaks soon enough.

If Vaash intended to use the Empress's Highway, it would pass quite near mountains along its path. All the maps Demosyna had studied and lost during her trip were mostly incomplete. A northwestern edge was mapped due to the cities there, but a gigantic section in the middle simply remained blank. The Empress's Highway was the backbone of available maps, curving with the coast to reveal imperial lands.

The main reason for the lack of information was the natural barriers often barring passage and the deadly wildlife in stretches of ancient land. A gigantic mountain range that split the Fist cradled the mysterious wilds in a band of impassable spikes. The dwarf-wood forests in the south were a living barricade that defied any attempt to fell them from the Empress's cities.

Colonies in the northernmost peninsulas, often called the Fingers, were found on the only ground that wasn't sheer vertical cliffs. Ships had tried finding ways of sailing around, seeking entry into the free north without success. Tales of massive whirlpools, giant monsters, and luscious sirens warned other adventurers to use official routes.

Demosyna recalled the simple map she had reviewed, seeing the sliver of charted land that had islands just off the coast. One such island, New Empress City, was a large and fertile volcanic land within sight of the continent. Large green peninsulas poked from the north, with a cluster of tiny islands between two. This was a bustling center of trade for the Fist, and ships stopped in ports that dotted hundreds of islands.

Her map had been incomplete as well, but Demosyna had heard rumors as to what lay beyond the known mountains. Some told of an endless lake, with haunted shores and depthless waters. Others told of vast and impossible lands of glistening sand stretching forever.

"Giants lifted the mountains to hide their kingdom from us ants," one drunken gambler had raved on the ship. "They have staircases on the other side that let them watch us and laugh from paradise!"

Whatever the truth, Demosyna knew fanciful tales of monsters and treasure wouldn't aid her now except to entertain. She considered purchasing a map, but the coming shop would make the woman forget about following up on the idea.

The wind died down, and Demosyna heard a flute, still a distance away but approaching happily with notes of future hardships.

CHAPTER 17

Demosyna watched in fascination as travelers passed by along the road leading toward the town to her left. Vaash had returned to escort the injured woman just outside the town. Ever since viewing the buildings from her waterfall vantage point, Demosyna had felt a deep longing to see any city that could shelter with walls. The area around the road was barely wooded, and plots of farmland peeked from around the wall.

Despite the noon traffic being light, Demosyna wondered at the sheer number of new faces. She hadn't realized the volume of noise being close to a town could achieve, but the quiet days up till now let her hear with fresh ears. Its smell, too, was like a novel thing for the young Wizen as Vaash hammered together a booth. Horses would pass occasionally with shackled figures shuffling beside ornately dressed riders. Demosyna avoided drawing attention whenever such riders would pass, along with any soldier.

It was less than an hour before Vaash erected a stall, complete with a canopy. He smiled at the seated woman as he patted the wide counter.

"What do you think, my friend?" Vaash asked after drinking some water.

"It looks great, Vaash!" Demosyna exclaimed as she hobbled over. "Thank you."

Vaash laughed loudly and motioned to the bags near the assembled stand. Demosyna opened the nearest and began unpacking the dark, round loaves. Their trip had been slow due to her broken foot, but Vaash had remained smiling the whole way as he carried the serving dish and backpacks.

Demosyna used her crutch to drag the other sacks toward her, stowing them under the counter. One satchel of bread was set out in a pile atop the clay serving tray, and Vaash began playing his flute. A low song filled the air with familiar sounds as Demosyna sat on a log. The ache in her foot faded as Demosyna watched the song catch the attention of those on the road.

The first of those to listen was a woman with short black hair, and Demosyna vibrated as she walked over.

"What is this on top, Scale?" the large human asked, her voice rough from travel.

Demosyna took one of the topmost pieces and broke it into quarters.

"I sprinkled herbs onto the bread while it cooled, ma'am. Enjoy the sample, and let me know if you want to buy any!"

Demosyna's voice was watery in her own ears when she addressed the stranger.

"Have some water too, friend."

"That was surprisingly edible, scaled one. How much are you charging for these little beauties?" the woman saw the skin but shook her head with a grunt.

Demosyna looked frantically toward Vaash, who sat playing his flute with his right hand, before responding.

"Three points apiece," Demosyna said, almost a question, as she watched the woman pull her own skin.

"Three? Where have you been before now, Scale, if that is all you charge for bread?"

Bright-red wine dripped down the woman's chin. The dark-haired stranger fished a coin purse from her pants before dropping small triangles onto the counter. Demosyna smiled widely at her first sale and swept the money into her palm while the customer selected a loaf.

186

"Thank you, ma'am," Demosyna called while the woman walked away. "I will be selling here each day!"

A general murmur of the people gathering to hear the music overshadowed any response the woman called.

An average-looking woman was shadowed by two men, both of whom had shackles. The finely dressed woman inspected the pile of bread before taking the sample quarter Demosyna offered. When the apprentice held the last two wedges to the hunched men, the woman knocked the pieces to the dirty road.

"How dare you!" the tuxedo-haired Paw hissed at Demosyna. "These are my men, and you will not entice them."

Without another word, the lady stormed off with the men trying to keep pace. The woman left the city along the road, angry puffs trailing her. Demosyna had seen slaves all her life in the apprentice halls, yet now she had a new viewpoint on the people. She lowered her head, as the sight of the bands brought back memories of her imprisonment.

"Did you say three apiece?" a short man asked.

Demosyna broke apart a second loaf to allow the three gathered a sample.

"Yes, sir. I baked them myself!"

"It tastes fresh enough. Can we get some, Jessica?"

The man turned to a woman sniffing at the bread. Jessica wore a light-blue robe that sparkled in the afternoon light with inlaid silver and nodded after tasting. Demosyna smiled at the three before her and offered the nearly full skin to her potential customers.

"I suppose you won't have to bake bread for me tonight, then, eh, Lee?" Jessica joked with the man. "This is better than what you would have made anyway!"

Both men accompanying Jessica laughed and finished the wedges of bread they had accepted from Demosyna.

"Do you have any bags to carry these, purple scale?" Jessica inquired as she counted out coins.

Demosyna responded to the golden-haired woman with fear washing over her.

"I am very sorry, but I don't have any bags."

"That is why they are so cheap!" Jessica said, her voice filling with an understanding laugh. "No wonder if you don't even have bags. No matter. My boys will carry them while we visit our plot."

"I am sorry, ma'am. I simply didn't think of having bags, but I will have them tomorrow if you visit!" Demosyna said to Jessica as she put sets of three coins down. "Thank you for your purchase and your understanding."

"Sure, sure, my violet baker," Jessica said, having finished paying. "That should be ten loaves, then. You two, gather my bread, as I certainly won't be carrying them."

Her two men laughed as they grabbed handfuls of bread while following Jessica. Before one had taken more than a dozen steps, two loaves tumbled from his arms. Demosyna laughed to herself as she stood to gather fresh loaves. By the time she hobbled over to the man, trying to pick up the bread without spilling more, Jessica had returned with a frown.

"What is this now?" Jessica barked at the man. "How dare you waste my food."

"It was an accident, ma'am," Demosyna told the three standing around her. "Here, take these two instead!"

Jessica looked with a suspicious face toward the apprentice.

"So you can leech more from me? Not likely."

Demosyna shook her head.

"No, I meant you can have these since he dropped a couple. No charge. I just hope you visit again!"

Jessica scowled at Demosyna but nodded for the men to accept the replacement.

"Thank you, then. I didn't expect that from someone like you, but merchants can surprise me."

Demosyna smiled as Jessica turned on her heel and winked toward the man as he stood. He looked shocked, and the men carried their foodstuffs with more care. They followed Jessica around the corner of town, taking exaggerated steps.

Demosyna used her crutch to move back to the booth, and many of the gathered people noticed her foot. It had a bright-white cast and was obvious against her yellow robes and purple scales. A line of customers formed, and Demosyna took a deep breath to calm her nerves. The sight of nearly twenty people jostling about intimidated the young woman.

"Gather here, friends," Vaash called loudly, his voice booming down the road. "This one will entertain all here with music. The bread that one offers is delicious and a steal. That it is."

Demosyna smiled widely at hearing Vaash speak and also raised her voice.

"We can offer a loaf for three points each. Would anyone like a sample?"

Nearly every person in the line nodded, calling a cheerful affirmative, and Demosyna tore loaves apart. Vaash walked to the stall and smiled warmly down at the seated Wizen. He used a strip of cloth to tie back his long red hair before addressing Demosyna.

"The samples are a great idea, my friend."

He took wedges and walked down the line of waiting people. The first people chose their bread and paid the young woman, who deposited the coins in a pocket. Two of the people in line wandered off, snacking on the free sample, but everyone else moved forward. Demosyna sold over a dozen loaves while watching the customers flood by. Vaash came back to acquire more samples but returned to play a song Demosyna hadn't heard.

A general chorus of voices ebbed as the sun started to fall in the sky, and the traffic thinned. A mounted rider took the sample a young boy offered the figure as he ran beside. He wore bright-colored red-and-silver clothes, but they were without any sparkling ornaments. Without dismounting, the man threw a single coin to the boy. His boy ran to the stall and stood on his toes to place the large gold coin down.

It was very intricately crafted, Demosyna saw as she took the round coin, with a triangle hole through the center. Ornate waves covered both faces, but one side depicted a volcano on an end of the hole. The opposite side of the hole featured a styled letter *E*, and Demosyna knew it stood for *Empress*. The only other time she had seen a piece was when hiring Bhreel to guard her Wise Mother, but the apprentice tried to avoid such thoughts.

All the bread the woman had sold had been for the small triangle coins as people lightened the pile.

"How many would you like, sir?" Demosyna asked after staring at the gold. "I'm not sure how much this would get you if they are three points each."

Vaash looked over to the Wizen when she turned her worried gaze toward him. The monk took the coin and examined it before handing it back.

"This one saw the exchange to be low today. That it is," Vaash told the boy, who nodded silently. "It was posted at twenty points a gold piece."

Demosyna listened carefully and processed the information slowly, as she had only a vague understanding of the trade in this land. The rider nodded while looking at the young boy when he responded.

"It was the same yesterday too," he said in a very deep voice. "Very well. Give this boy six, and we will be on our way. Keep your points. I don't need change."

He opened a saddlebag on his black horse to remove an empty sack. Demosyna saw no chains on the toddler, but his attitude was the same as the other slaves the young woman had seen all day. The boy never made eye contact with Vaash or Demosyna as they helped him load the bread. Demosyna picked up two extra loaves and handed them to Vaash with a smile.

Vaash nodded and placed the extra bread into the nearly full sack. The boy's eyes widened at the gift, and he looked up with clear shock on his tiny face. Demosyna winked at the child with a sad smile, who turned to bring the purchase to his owner. The fading light of the day shadowed the man's face, but he thanked Demosyna.

"That is good business if ever I saw it!"

He laughed as he rode away into the town, stopping to show entry papers.

"That was very kind of you, Demosyna," Vaash said softly as he leaned against the booth.

"I didn't feel right letting the boy go without enough food since I can offer it!" Demosyna said to the monk, shielding her eyes to look. "Would you like some, Vaash? You have been playing for a couple hours now."

Demosyna broke one of the remaining loaves of herb-covered bread and offered half. He shook his head, laughing as Demosyna ate.

The road remained empty for twenty minutes, and the Wise-woman stood to stretch. Sitting on a stump had begun to wear on the woman, and her foot had started to scream. Vaash helped Demosyna to her feet and watched her walk down the road, finding a cluster of trees.

After relieving herself out of view, Demosyna divided the triangle coins among the pockets in her robes. A single pocket no longer bulged against her side, and Demosyna found Vaash playing his flute to the empty road. The clay dish held only a few loaves, so Demosyna opened one of the spare bags. After piling some bread carefully, the apprentice used the rest to make samples.

The sun had barely dropped and the torches were still being lit atop the wall when a series of bells sounded. A rising tide of noise reached the woman, who sat down again with excitement. From around both sides of the towering walls, large crowds of people began streaming toward the road.

Vaash picked up his flute and smiled.

"Get ready, my friend!"

Vaash began playing the wooden instrument as a mass of workers made their walk back into town. A majority of the exhausted people shuffled away without a glance at the lone stall. Another line formed near the booth that promised fresh bread. Demosyna smiled despite her trepidation as the first customer finished his sample.

"It is two points for a loaf," Demosyna called to the waiting line of workers. "Feel free to take a sample if you want some while you wait!"

The first dirt-covered man looked shocked at the announcement but grabbed handfuls of bread to pass back. Before long, the entire line was enjoying hefty wedges, and Demosyna took the payment from each figure. While several stayed to eat and enjoy the music, most of the gaunt faces disappeared into the city. Vaash took a few paces toward the booth while more curious faces joined the line.

The dark of the night was closing in, and torches danced in the breeze atop the wall. After opening the bag containing the last bread, Demosyna handed each customer their discounted purchase. When the wide clay dish had emptied of bread, the shuffling people put pairs of coins onto the tray.

Once the last ruddy face had gone into the city, Vaash stopped playing his flute and sat next to the woman.

"That was busier that I thought it would be, Vaash," Demosyna sighed wearily. "We nearly ran out of bread!"

"It is a good problem to have!"

Vaash lay in the grass to look at the stars.

"Thank you for dealing with the shop. This one has a shy heart sometimes."

Demosyna gathered the loose coins from the clay tray.

"Thank you for luring so many people here! We may need more bread tomorrow since people seemed to like it."

Vaash nodded as he stretched in the grass.

"This one will gather and grind once we return. Did you need anything else for the shop?"

Demosyna thought about his question and watched the guards being replaced for a night watch. This town had no moat, so the drawbridge was lowered onto the packed dirt road. Silvery armor worn by the soldiers flickered with the torchlight as the young Wise-woman turned back to Vaash.

"If you can get more of the herbs you found, along with tall grasses for weaving, it would be great!" Demosyna explained with excitement, "I can weave bags for the bread and bake it at the same time when we get back."

"This one will need to make a trip into town, but we can travel back once the errand is done," Vaash said as he rubbed his broken arm.

"Is there anywhere to give these last loaves?" Demosyna asked the monk as he grabbed his backpack. "I don't want them to be wasted if we are not hungry."

Vaash turned with a smile, and his green eyes danced.

"Of course, my friend. There are always those that need a kindness. This one will take them to the orphanage."

Crickets chirped, and the wind made the sparse trees around the young woman rustle with happy groans. The robed Wizen gathered empty bags and sipped from the remaining water in a skin as she waited. It took less than half an hour, and Vaash returned with a cart led by a pony. Demosyna widened her eyes at the unexpected sight and stood balancing as the man approached.

"Vaash, what a beautiful pony!" Demosyna exclaimed when she stroked its silky mane. "Where did you get it?"

Vaash laughed and petted the neck of the speckled beast.

"This one rented it from an employer to aid in a contract for firewood."

"Would you like to head to the cabin, Vaash?" Demosyna asked, her breath billowing into the dark.

Vaash nodded and loaded the narrow cart.

"The stall will be safe here, in sight of the town soldiers. Would you like to ride in the back?"

Demosyna agreed to the proposition and lay down on empty bags with Vaash walking the pony away. Darkness soon surrounded the trio, and they found the road empty. Demosyna looked at the stars with the cart gently rocking along, humming to herself. The aid of the pack animal allowed Vaash to navigate the wooded path to the cabin, and he unhitched the pony from the cart.

Demosyna took his hand and carefully exited the cart, thanking the man for his help. Vaash began brushing the pony with a coarse-bristled comb while the Wizen took the bags inside. The scent of bread still hung in the air of the house, and Demosyna rested her foot on a pillow with a grateful sigh.

A small wood table in the living room served for a surface as the Wizen unloaded the triangle coins. Dozens of pyramids sat on the table before Demosyna had emptied her pockets. The apprentice examined the larger rounded coin before her attention was drawn to the table.

Her piles of golden coins began moving, seemingly of their own accord. Fingertip-sized triangles seemed to vibrate off one another, slowly but all at once. Demosyna watched in silent wonder as the piles flattened out, and each coin distanced itself from the one beside. The whole process took less than a minute, and the table was left covered with even rows.

Amazement filled the young woman's mind, as such a display was new to her like the many things she endured in the north. Coins formed a grid of roughly twenty square, with missing spaces here and there. After counting the voids, Demosyna calculated nearly 150 coins on the table. Holding up the large round coin, Demosyna smiled to herself as the fire reflected on the gold.

Even after splitting this, it will only be days till we can start heading toward my Orders, Demosyna thought happily as she began dividing the coins.

When the Wizen moved the money, even numbers at a time to count, they formed grids when placed near other triangles. She marveled at the curious nature displayed, and the smooth golden triangles were easily divided.

"Vaash works so hard for me and never gives a word of complaint," Demosyna mused as her exhausted body relaxed. "All I did was sit there and sell things."

The apprentice eyed the rows of triangles and frowned, imagining Vaash as he searched the woods. His hard work was something that Demosyna desperately needed, being unable to gather them herself. She used her strong fingers to move a row of the rounded triangles. A scraping sound followed the action as the coins found a new equilibrium with one another.

The next half hour was spent in meditation, as Demosyna found the ingrained routine a comfort. The wildly varying emotions that had carried the woman through the day were calmed. Her lost friends rose in her mind, and Demosyna saw Jui and Rrra swim downstream, forever beyond her reach.

Sounds of Vaash returning awakened the woman, and Demosyna smiled as he opened the door. She had seen him return from the town, leading the welcome surprise cart, with a skin of wine.

"I think we should celebrate. That I do," Vaash exclaimed loudly, laughing and taking a drink. "Would you join me as we make more bread, my friend?"

Demosyna took the skin with thanks and sipped the strong drink. She returned the cap before the Wizen, along with Vaash, took a bag and unloaded the contents.

"I divided our earnings for the day, Vaash."

Demosyna motioned once he sat.

"If we keep this up for a week, I won't have any problem paying the tolls you mentioned."

Vaash looked at the rows of triangular coins.

"Are you sure you want to give me that much, Demosyna?"

Demosyna nodded at her friend.

"You did so much for me. I feel you earned each point there!"

"Thank you, my friend. You are very generous to give me so much!"

Vaash grinned and began to pick up the plain gold triangles from the smaller grid. Demosyna shook her head in mild amusement and pointed to the larger group of coins.

"I meant you take the bulk there, because you did a lot of difficult work."

Vaash paused in his collection and looked earnestly at the young Wise-woman.

"Are you certain, Demosyna? This is a lot of money you earned today."

"Without you, I would be lost in the woods to this day. I don't mean to pay you back with money. I mean you helped me where I was lacking, and I can never thank you enough."

Demosyna returned the man's gaze with open joy. Vaash's cheek showed tears as he hesitated.

"You have such a big heart, Demosyna."

The woman laughed with good humor as the monk gave her a leather pouch before gathering his profit. Both travelers soon had a nearly full sack of coins as Vaash cleared the living room.

Her mangled foot was elevated on a stack of pillows as Demosyna began weaving grasses into usable bags. Vaash went to the kitchen once the living room was mostly cleared and stoked the fire for baking. He removed a pouch from his robes and took a pill from the uncinched leather. Demosyna watched him take the dose with a swig of water and turned to the monk as he wiped his mouth.

"Is there any of the medicine you gave me left?" she asked. "My foot is hurting, and it would be nice to weave without such a distraction."

"You don't need to explain. If you wish for any, you need only ask!"

Vaash produced a wooden cup and paused before looking keenly at the woman.

"Are you going to share that wine with me tonight, Demosyna?"

Demosyna nodded, smiling with her sharp teeth shining, and Vaash measured a small amount. He sat next to Demosyna and filled the glass with water from a barrel. As before, when she had lain broken in bed, Vaash sipped the glass prior to offering the drink with a satisfied nod. Its bitter taste coated her tongue as Demosyna downed the potion. She had tried to avoid jostling her toes, wrapped together as they were, but moving about had made her foot hum with pain.

"I will keep baking for us whenever you need to sleep," Vaash said as he glanced around. "We can always make bread fresh at the stand. The permit I purchased includes a fire allowance before sundown."

"I am tired, more than I would have thought," Demosyna responded, her eyes moving to the piles of grass. "I wanted to make bags and need to grind salt and herbs once you are done with the flour."

Vaash grabbed the wine procured from the town and took a long pull. Demosyna began sizing up strands of grass as she was handed the wine. The potion she had taken was already making the pain in her foot distant, so Demosyna took a cautious drink. Her day had passed so quickly it seemed unreal, and Demosyna took another sip before passing the drink.

Vaash drank again before sitting to begin processing the grains. Demosyna deftly assembled bags from the grasses, pausing occasionally to braid a string, that would hold several loaves. Vaash used his viable arm to grind and pour flour into jars scattered about. The two friends passed the emptying wineskin as each processed their ingredients into useful shapes. Little talk was exchanged save for late in the evening, when the wine was nearly gone.

"Are you hungry, Demosyna?" Vaash asked the Wizen as he finished grinding. "I can make something if you are."

Demosyna shook her head from the current pouch.

"No, thank you. I am not hungry yet after all that excitement. Maybe tomorrow night, if you want to share a meal!"

Vaash moved to the kitchen.

"I understand. I often wait days between meals, but it is part of my training."

Demosyna paused her weaving and looked at the man.

"My appetites are like many among my kind—easily satisfied between long periods of famine."

Vaash laughed at the joke and rummaged through the spartan pantry. He chewed some jerky thoughtfully as he returned to sit next to Demosyna.

"I will trade in my points tomorrow for gold pieces while I am in town."

Vaash took out his coin bag and judged the weight.

"I can exchange yours as well, if you wish."

Demosyna looked with mild confusion at Vaash while she produced her own purse.

"Exchange them?"

Vaash sighed and took coins out before placing them on the table.

"The Empress embraces all people and needs us to put trust in her. The masses always bicker, but the Empress gives shelter and peace."

Demosyna shook her head, and she took the wine. Vaash leaned forward and moved a single triangle coin toward the others. Once the point got near, the stationary coins leaped away from the one Vaash pushed along.

"This proves these are genuine points at least," Vaash said, sending coins scooting across the table. "Can I see the gold piece?"

Demosyna found the round coin and put it on the table.

"How did they move like that? When I piled them up, they jumped off each other!"

Vaash smiled at the wonder on her face.

"The Empress knows we cannot abide one another, and only she can embrace us."

Vaash took the ornate gold coin and put it near the three triangular coins. The smaller coins were drawn toward and then stuck to the round coin after Vaash moved it close. He smiled at the display before taking the three triangle coins, leaving the round coin on the table. Vaash motioned for Demosyna to hold the large coin and took a single triangle in his hand.

"The Empress protects."

Vaash placed the triangle into the void at the center of the round coin. To Demosyna's amazement, the smaller pyramid-shaped coin clicked into place where the round coin had a hole. The coin that remained was seamless, the surface having fused in the merging. This new coin was noticeably heavier, and Demosyna laughed at the magical display.

"That is what I was taught when I was young," Vaash said as he watched the amazement on his friend's face. "It is simply magnetism, however, to explain the metaphor."

Demosyna nodded with understanding and held two of her triangle coins near each other. She felt a slight repulsion and smiled as she examined the newly whole coin. The ornate patterns that had covered the surface of the round coin were broken by the smooth triangle that now filled out the center.

"I have never heard that before," Demosyna said, prodding at the smooth central triangle.

Vaash took a sip of wine.

"It is a fun child story. But it lets one know their place surrounded by the Empress."

He held out his hand, and Demosyna placed the solid coin in his palm. Vaash used his thumb to push the triangle from the center and put the large coin back down.

"The Empress only takes a small token for her love," Vaash said, his tone suggesting an end of the fable. "I was taught that to let me understand the exchange system for a gold piece. It is simply a matter of knowing the current value of the coin, then adding a single point for an exchange tax."

Demosyna looked through the open hole in the coin to see Vaash finish the wine. His story was new to her, and Demosyna pondered the tale as she put a triangle into the round coin. A subtle click signified the two merging, and Demosyna used a claw to push the point out. She was vaguely aware of magnetism but had yet to be allowed access to such in her apprentice training save a compass.

"It will be easier to transport less coins, I suppose," Demosyna reasoned.

Vaash took the bag Demosyna tossed him with a smile.

"It is not a problem at all, my friend. I will be in town for my contract and can stop before I leave!"

Demosyna stood and went to the outhouse, as the wine was going right through her. Returning to the warm cabin, she saw the pile of woven bags signifying the progress she had made. There were nearly thirty bags, much to her relief, and Demosyna retired to the bedroom.

"I will keep weaving while I lay down, but I am getting very tired."

Demosyna yawned.

"I am sorry, but if you wake me early, I can help bake too!"

Vaash handed the woman the long grasses.

"No need to apologize, my friend. I will start the baking while you sleep, so have no fear about that."

Demosyna put the material under her arm as she moved into the bedroom, just off the living room. She sat on the bed after propping her foot on a pillow to continue making bags. The smell of baking bread crept under the door after nearly an hour of her solitary work. Demosyna smiled at the face reflected in her cup and wondered at her life, with its constant series of dubious changes.

CHAPTER 18

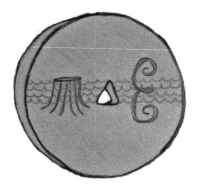

The next days were a blur of baking and hungry faces. Vaash, in addition to his flute, would attract attention from the passing figures when he chopped wood. Using one arm, he confidently swung the small hatchet into logs to split them. Seeing the brightly robed man, one arm in a sling, chopping wood with speed drew customers to the small bread stand. Vaash would leave the young Wizen alone when the traffic eased to deliver a full cart-load of wood to fulfill his contract.

The second day was less busy, and an entire bag of bread was delivered to the orphanage. Her foot was still an issue, but with the aid of a potion, Demosyna was able to continue baking. Vaash busied himself with preparation as well, and before long, the cabin had clay dishes stored in the cabinets.

On their third day selling, Vaash recommended bringing extra flour. It was the required day of rest tomorrow, Vaash explained, and many would purchase bread to last the weekend. Demosyna helped load the cart before sitting in the back as Vaash led the speckled pony. The man's prediction turned out to be spot-on, as the two sold all the bread well before sunset. Large bags sat empty and only a handful of woven sacks remained when Demosyna began baking bread fresh.

The smell of cooking dough drew even more customers, and Demosyna fought the pain in her body to thank each one. Vaash played his flute whenever the young woman took over the baking, even when the sun began to sink and the crowd hadn't dispersed. Despite the large jars the two took, Demosyna ran out of herb mixture to top the bread. When the samples ran out, many wandered off altogether, but the line was slow to move.

The moon had risen high when the flour was consumed, and Demosyna had to apologize to nearly thirty people. The number of travelers was shocking to Demosyna when hundreds of people strode by. Each pair of eyes scanned the booth to purchase a loaf of bread or sample the bread when it was available.

Pride swelled in the young woman's heart when she sat alone in the cold breeze, waiting for Vaash to return. Much of her short life was deemed useless, but Demosyna found her presence desired by Vaash and the townsfolk.

Each evening, Vaash journeyed into town to exchange their coin, using the cart to haul firewood with wheels squeaking away. The silence was deafening after the constant noise—from the idle talk of those in line to the general commotion of travelers.

A lone horsewoman trotted by, waving slightly toward the seated Wizen. Demosyna smiled and returned the greeting, using her crutch to stand and gaze toward town. She tried to pick out any sign of her friend among the buildings. Vaash returned with his normal smiling face, and the two traveled back to their cabin. Before he left for the evening to gather, Vaash gave the apprentice some bad news.

"The herbs I have been collecting have grown sparse."

Vaash filled a skin with water while he spoke.

"I do not wish to break the plant's natural grounds by taking it all."

His revelation troubled the Wizen, and she considered her options. Because they had gotten back so late, the night was cold as Demosyna pondered. It was a day of rest tomorrow, and she wouldn't be able to sell, even with herbs.

"If we don't have the topping, we will need a replacement," Demosyna thought aloud, touching her chin with a claw. "What else is being sold in town?"

Vaash considered a moment.

"Meat, along with many baked goods. Oh, and a lone produce stand as well. Bread, meat pies, and the like are offered by bakeries. There is only a handful, but they have similar products."

"There are no dessert vendors or sweet shops?" Demosyna asked after buzzing memories surfaced.

Vaash shook his head.

"Sugar is hard to get this far north, my friend. Molasses can be found, along with honey, but the wilds prevent much to be harvested normally."

"If I knew where honey was, could we use that to make sweet breads?" Demosyna asked, ignoring the terror the wasps ignited. "I had to escape giant wasps just after my boat was sunk."

Vaash widened his eyes and turned from his gathering.

"Wasp honey? That is dangerous not only to acquire but also to consume. That is why I asked my son to find an abandoned nest. It is destructive without refinement."

"I see," Demosyna said, furrowing her brow. "I didn't know that, and I certainly don't wish to harm anyone. I suppose that isn't an option. Besides, it was well past the grasshopper falls I found while fleeing Sai Aeri."

Vaash smiled widely, and his eyes sparkled.

"Grasshoppers? By boiling the honey, we leave only the sweet flavor and remove the harmful effects. If we cook the grasshoppers in honey, that would be an excellent option."

Demosyna nodded while hearing excitement in his voice.

"Yes, there was a waterfall upstream from where we met. The first night I found the falls, thousands of grasshoppers flew around the meadow. It was so beautiful after my bleak days locked in a cage or taken to my doom."

Tears formed in her eyes at the vivid memory, but Demosyna blinked them away. Vaash finished the final preparations for his trek and grinned down at the woman.

"If I am going that far, I will not be back till tomorrow at the earliest. It will depend on how fast I can find the nest," Vaash explained as he rubbed his broken arm. "I can smoke them docile and should get the honey without confrontation!"

Demosyna described as best as she could remember the location the huge wasps had attacked. Vaash nodded his understanding and locked the door behind when he left.

Demosyna was tired beyond words after the stressful day of trying to live up to the insatiable town. The bread that she and Vaash baked was popular beyond her hopes, and Demosyna smiled to herself at the good fortune.

"Be careful, Vaash," Demosyna called through the open window. "You are my right hand after all!"

Vaash laughed loudly at her joke from the tree line.

"I shall return, my friend. That I will."

Demosyna busied herself with meditating and organizing as she waited for Vaash. Her fatigue prevented her from doing more than locking up and collapsing the first night, but she awoke early. It had taken Demosyna days to travel from the coast, and she wondered how fast Vaash would return.

The light faded on the cold day of minor chores, and snow began to fall as Demosyna watched from the window. It was the first heavy snow the woman could recall since landing so abruptly in the Fist, and she marveled at the frozen world. Fat snowflakes drifted every which way as the young Wizen observed the sudden cold snap. Several times during her boat ride, the snow had piled up, but the steady progress of the ship forced any snow away. From her awestruck place in the warm window, Demosyna saw the world turn into diamonds.

Visibility was nonexistent as Demosyna saw the dazzling world of ice just beyond the rattling glass. The moon shone into the storm, casting vague and unhelpful light, but the young Wise-woman's sharp eyes seemed to catch each snowflake. She laughed to herself and waited for the storm to pass her little piece of happiness.

Hours later, the clouds broke after stilling the land in a white blanket. Demosyna wrapped the comforter around her shoulders with a wide grin. She had gotten a sudden impulse to feel the snow and stepped from her cabin. Despite the distant ache from her broken face, nearly healed with Vaash's aid, her grin widened upon crunching into snow. Watching the last ice dance, Demosyna felt the cold against her scales, and a clarity formed in her mind.

Each snowflake hung in the air, nearly motionless in their crystalline splendor, while Demosyna felt power surging through her grounded foot. A feeling of overwhelming assurance flooded over the woman as she watched the snow begin whipping around. A tornado of ice and dirt formed, launching itself into the sky with terrible speed.

Demosyna took a deep breath against a tidal wave of power and cried out with joy when the tornado slowed. It happened in the whisper the woman exhaled, and as her mind returned, Demosyna balanced on her left foot. She raised her crutch toward the twinkling night sky with a trembling hand.

"Yes!" Demosyna shouted into the dead void of night.

Her yell of triumph echoed over the snow as Demosyna felt warm tears coat her cheeks. The tornado responded to her joy by flaring up, and Demosyna had a moment of panic. Visions of horses writhing in agony sharpened the woman's mind enough to focus. The trembling Wizen spied the distant outhouse, narrowing her eyes. Instead of losing herself, as she had before, Demosyna used her disciplined mind to bend her will.

Upon lowering the crutch from its place of celebration, Demosyna pointed it at the outhouse. She stood balanced on her foot while the wall of wind contracted, lessening the magnitude of its fury. Demosyna used the crutch to further focus while filling her mind with a goal. Before her wondering eyes, the tornado moved forward along the path Demosyna saw in her mind.

As the wall of wind passed from behind the balanced apprentice, it barely seemed to rustle her, even with the howling gale it created. She took another steadying breath and attempted to push more energy into the whirling mass. Power flowed with an ease that delighted her, and Demosyna used the tip of the outstretched crutch to point. A smile of pure joy formed on the woman's lips as the icy whirlwind roared, growing as it darted away.

The crutch that Demosyna held forward began to vibrate against her hand and underarm, where she held the smoothed wood. She took her eyes from the powerful wind and focused just in time to see the cut end unravel. Like a frayed rope, the wood of the crutch split into gossamer strings before rapidly curling. Barely a second passed to the sharp eyes of the Wizen, but as wind struck the outhouse, her crutch burst into flames.

She cried out in shock, but the sound was lost when an explosion of wood echoed over the clearing. A spiraling force of magic reached the lone structure and leveled it without slowing. The purple scales of her face were lit up, and a ball of twisted wood sputtered fire. The apprentice threw the burning wood into the snow and looked toward the cyclone. The path it took was a dark line in the ice, and woods groaned from the impact against them.

Trees bent wildly, whipping thick trunks and sending snow flying, but the tornado dissipated. Hissing smoke rose from the doused torch, and Demosyna stood frozen with fear. A snaking line of devastation started from a ring around the woman, and she picked up the remains of her crutch. It was unusable to the apprentice now, as the charred tip was just under a checkered grip. Over half the length had been burned away in the aftermath of her first spell, and conflicting emotions rose in her heart.

The joy of knowing that the apprentice had finally summoned overshadowed any fear in her mind. Her cold left foot still seemed to dance beneath her skin as Demosyna hopped to lean against the cabin. The bark of a log wall steadied the tearful woman as she looked with thankful eyes at the stars. Through lazy snow, the tornado having stripped the trees of their coverings, Demosyna watched the lights applaud her.

"I did it! I can do magic!" Demosyna shouted again, her chest full of energy. "Vaash was right. I am strong!"

Her words rang out clear and true in the shadows of the deep night while Demosyna laughed without restraint. She laughed for nearly a minute before catching her breath, using a chilly sleeve to wipe her face. The jubilant woman made her way inside while using the wall to hop. After the door was locked, Demosyna knelt down on the nearest pillow and didn't notice her pain.

I felt the wind when I left the cabin, and I seemed to understand, Demosyna thought, remembering the feeling of certainty. *It was so alive when the blizzard played with the snow, I knew anything was possible.*

Any terror from her previous magical experiences faded as Demosyna meditated on the wonderful night. The blizzard had at last awoken the young apprentice, and she smiled at the thought of new progress. Years of impotence had convinced herself and all those around her that she was useless as a Wise-woman. Now she had first-hand experience with the wild power, and Demosyna knew she was capable in her own slow way.

The crutch unraveling had reminded the excited woman of Klai and the times the staff had broken. Demosyna pondered the implication long into the night, having too much energy to dream of sleeping. She would occasionally check the single window, but no sign of Vaash was seen. He escorted the rented cart back the previous day, and Demosyna confirmed she was still alone.

"It will likely be another day, then, at the earliest," Demosyna thought aloud to herself, having only vague knowledge of the distance. "I can at least keep the fire warm for whenever Vaash returns."

Furniture around the cabin served as her crutch while Demosyna drew some water. She sat on an empty barrel and listened to the wind increase its howl. Vaash had left a small amount of powder behind, taking the pills, so Demosyna used the amount he instructed to make a potion. Her drink did its quick work, and the agitated foot soon calmed. The woman was, to her own surprise, famished after the magic. Demosyna welcomed the drained feeling as she hopped into the kitchen.

There were only vegetables left in the cabinets, but she hummed as the young Wizen prepared a meal. The smell of food made her giddy, and Demosyna laughed as the water boiled. A last pinch of salt was being added when the door unlocked, revealing Vaash in the near-morning light.

"Vaash!" Demosyna cried out in happiness. "Welcome back!"

"Are you okay, Demosyna?"

His voice was urgent.

"I grew fearful when I saw that tornado."

Demosyna laughed nervously, remembering suddenly the destruction her magic caused. In her joy and wonder, Demosyna had forgotten the outhouse had been destroyed. The woman leaned against a counter before smiling sheepishly.

"I am fine, Vaash. Sorry to make you worry," Demosyna told the seated man.

"This one is just glad you are safe," Vaash replied, smiling up at the woman. "I feared the worst when spying the twister and sprinted the last hours to get here."

"I'm sorry, Vaash," the woman said, hanging her head slightly. "I didn't even consider who could see what I did in all my excitement."

"You made that cyclone?" Vaash gasped, his green eyes wide. "That is wonderful!"

"I did! I really did!" Demosyna gushed, tears forming in her eyes. "Everything just clicked, and I was able to direct the magic like I had always been taught! It was scary and wonderful, and I felt so great as the power danced through me. Oh, I ruined your crutch. I'm sorry."

Words came tumbling out of her mouth, and she grew more excited the longer she talked. Vaash stood and grinned, his red hair waving as he shook his head in amazement.

"Congratulations, my friend! That is fantastic news. I am so proud of you, Demosyna!"

Vaash took steps toward the woman, tears forming in his eyes as well.

"I always knew you could do it if you set your mind to the task!"

Demosyna nodded, forgetting her stew and opening her arms to Vaash. He embraced his friend, snow on his frozen clothes, and the two hugged tightly. Vaash leaned back slightly, not breaking the embrace, and looked into the woman's sparkling eyes.

"You are so driven, Demosyna," Vaash said to the overjoyed apprentice. "I am happy to be your friend and that you were not harmed by the tornado!"

Demosyna squeezed the monk once more, and the two stepped apart, laughing and wiping their faces. The joy she felt from her accomplishment redoubled upon seeing her friend equally excited. Demosyna had to gather herself as Vaash ladled soup, because she felt like giggling. New clay bowls held large portions of stew, and Demosyna joined Vaash to eat as the sun rose.

Demosyna told her friend, who sat awestruck, of the sudden blizzard that had enchanted her. She described the raw surges of energy felt when balancing in the snow and of a certainty that all was within her grasp. The apprentice saw nothing but fascination on Vaash's open face as she recounted the tornado tearing across the yard. Their outhouse remained in pieces, but little other evidence was left of her spell save the remains of the crutch.

The man took the splintered wood and examined it with interest, his hands tracing the damage. Vaash smiled in wonder at the charred wood before handing it back. Demosyna laughed as she told Vaash of the crutch catching fire and her overwhelming elation at the destruction.

"Even though it was terrifying, seeing the tornado toss aside the outhouse, I knew it was a good thing," Demosyna reasoned to the monk, smiling in thought. "I was there, I was finally alive, and I felt right in being."

"Of course you deserve to be, Demosyna!" Vaash said, a look of surprise crossing his face. "Never think otherwise, my friend. This evening, you proved what I see in you is correct—that you have a heart beyond limits!"

"I'm sorry for breaking the toilet, Vaash."

Demosyna half-smiled in embarrassment.

"It was an accident even if I am glad I did!"

Vaash laughed loudly at this, shaking his head.

"I am too, then! That I am. It is a wonderful thing you have done, Demosyna, and I am proud to celebrate the feat!"

Demosyna smiled warmly at the man.

"Thank you, Vaash. You are the best person I have known in all my days!"

Their excitement rang through the cabin, buzzing with an energy all its own. The two talked long into the morning, with Vaash listening intently about her spell casting. A newfound confidence in herself was coming to reshape her thinking, mocking Demosyna's past of failure. After describing the way her crutch served as a staff, Demosyna told the man of Klai.

"The first time I was showered with splinters from the explosion," Demosyna recalled, sunlight streaming through the window, "my Wise Mother healed me with my own staff, but it broke too. Klai was shocked when her magic was too powerful, and I, too, am curious how this can be. I am excited to try again but will not risk putting you or myself in danger."

"I see," Vaash replied, holding his chin with his good hand. "Then in place of opening shop, would you like to go into town and purchase a focusing charm?"

Demosyna tilted her head in confusion.

"Focusing charm? I have only used a staff when trying to do magic."

"Many of the Wise-women I have encountered use such," Vaash explained, smiling at the Wizen. "They last longer than wood and are easier to carry! There was a shop in town that sold rings and broaches to suit your purposes."

Demosyna nodded with enthusiasm.

"Please, Vaash! If I can begin training, it would go a long way to proving myself to my Order! How much would I need to take with us?"

Vaash pondered the question before responding.

"I can purchase the token for you. I do not want you to use your savings for frivolous things if my contract can cover it!"

Demosyna removed her purse and saw a handful of gold pieces rattling in the leather. She considered the generous offer, thinking of the Highway she must travel. Demosyna had nearly enough, she judged, to buy provisions and still pay the tolls. If the sweet grasshoppers sold as well as the bread, it would be only days till they could move on.

"I don't know, Vaash," Demosyna said finally. "If I can make up what I lose now, we can still move north soon. I don't feel right making you buy my apprentice supplies."

Vaash smiled at the seated woman.

"I understand. The offer stands or to split the cost. I am happy to help."

Vaash began unpacking the forgotten supplies. Neither had thought to unload the hard-gotten ingredients, having been engrossed in Demosyna's achievement. He shook his head when she offered to walk with him, smiling slightly.

"Your foot is mending well from what I can gather," Vaash said, inspecting her foot. "But we should use the cart."

Demosyna accepted his recommendation and found the minutes ticked by slowly. She had no clock but judged it to be noon when finally helped to the single-axle cart. Vaash laughed at her eagerness and gave the Wizen a blanket.

The snow-covered world passed before Demosyna's wide eyes as she saw her stall alongside the road. It had gotten a covering of ice and looked like a thing from a storybook. The crowd that passed her cart seemed cheerful, and Demosyna greeted many with a wave. The town entry hung over the woman as the cart creaked into the city she had longed to visit. Demosyna craned her neck to see above the cart and smiled at the sights of welcome civilization.

Buildings streamed by as the pony was led down streets by the yellow-clad monk. Heavily bundled figures swam into view, walking the icy streets in large boots. An ornate building passed that Demosyna saw was the imperial office and held back tears at the crest. Thankfully, the cart turned a corner, and the oppressive image was lost from sight. The young Wizen eagerly drank in all the sights and sounds of the city while Vaash halted the pony.

Narrow glass windows displayed finely crafted objects, including jewelry, mirrors, and candlesticks. Demosyna handed the earnings she had accumulated, smiling at Vaash.

"Do you prefer any type of ring? Gold? Silver? Jeweled?" Vaash asked.

"Just get me one of the cheaper ones, I suppose," Demosyna responded, hope rising in her heart. "Thank you, Vaash. I would love to practice my magic!"

"Good choice, as the crystal inlaid in the focusing charm is what matters," Vaash replied, thinking for a moment. "At least that is what the Wise Mother said when we spoke."

Demosyna was shocked at the proclamation.

"You met the Wise Mother of the northern Order?"

Vaash nodded, and his eyes glanced away for a moment.

"It was during my youth when this one sought conquest. She stood atop her broken towers and repelled my assault for weeks. It almost seemed a game to her after a while. It became clear this one wasn't going to break the powerful woman and called a truce. After meeting, we became fast friends instead of staying hateful."

Demosyna was speechless and watched as he entered the store. If Vaash had known the current Wise Mother, it might be easy for Demosyna to gain access to her Orders.

Demosyna found that time went by quickly as she began mentally preparing for making a sweet new product. Vaash told her the honey would be safe after boiling, and the grasshoppers remained perfect to sell in bundles.

If I use woven grass, it will take so long to make hundreds of tiny bags, Demosyna thought as she watched the traffic. *Perhaps we could buy paper to wrap them in.*

Vaash returned, his red hair tied back.

"This one has found a great deal. It is only from an apprentice, but she worked under the Wise Mother. They say her paws are the most skilled of anyone in the craft."

Demosyna clambered forward, minding her foot, and took the offered ring. It was a simple golden band, save for where a small rounded hourglass shape formed in the metal. A perfect ring of crystal wrapped around the plain surface, inlaid so that only a half circle protruded. Afternoon light sparkled off the prismatic crystal, and Demosyna saw a rainbow of colors inside the band.

"Thank you, Vaash. It is beautiful."

She laughed with excitement and put the ring on her thumb. Demosyna held her clawed hand up to examine the charm and grinned.

"You really like it?" Vaash asked cautiously. "It looks fine on your scales, my friend. We should head back to begin baking. That we should."

Demosyna could barely hold back her joy.

"It's such a nice thing, taking me to town for a selfish reason. I think this will really aid in my studies!"

Vaash shook his head.

"This one is glad to be able to help you. Onward!"

He shouted this last word with a laugh that Demosyna shared as the cart groaned into motion. She recognized no faces as the two left the town from those she had met selling bread. The ring fitted her thumb with a comforting weight, Demosyna observed as the pony carried her along. She turned it round on the digit with a content smile, finding the fiddling soothing. Demosyna was sorely tempted to try using magic right away but resisted.

"Don't forget the outhouse," Demosyna told herself, trying to avoid letting excitement overshadow logic. "I must go slow and experiment carefully like I always have. Besides, I should focus on the bakery to get back what this cost me."

Vaash helped her down and began brushing the speckled pony, leading it to a roofed hitching post. Demosyna balanced against the cart while letting the sun warm her face. The apprentice felt more sure of herself than ever, she mused with a mixture of wonder and pain, and it was due in no small way to Vaash.

I would still be hiding in that cave, looking for my friends with an arrow wound through my foot, Demosyna thought, frowning slightly. *It probably wouldn't be broken, but I would be much worse off without his mercy.*

Demosyna looked at her left hand and saw the multitude of colors sparkling in the pure crystal band. She had to squint her yellow eyes when the sun caught the gem just right. Of all the people who deserved a kindness, Demosyna decided, as the man brushed with his unbroken arm, that it was Vaash.

She closed her eyes to recall the items her vantage point had allowed as the sun shone through the shop window. There had been necklaces, but Vaash had never worn jewelry that Demosyna had seen. Demosyna considered what she knew about him while reviewing the window in her mind's eye. With a sudden grin spreading over her sharp face, Demosyna remembered seeing a small flute. Musical ability was one of the many things that she admired about Vaash and enjoyed his long wooden flute playing.

I didn't see a price, Demosyna thought as Vaash strode back. *I need to find that shop again once I have earned a few more gold pieces! I will work to thank him with more than words and company!*

Vaash saw the wide grin on her face and smiled back.

"I will fetch you a new crutch if you want to start processing these forageables."

The living room had been left cluttered with numerous things ran back from miles south. Vaash set bundles of grains beside the woman when she nodded eagerly. Like before, he worked the stick with the aid of his knife and used the leather from the ruined crutch to finish his work.

Demosyna laughed when he turned the crutch to reveal an addition to her name, gouged deep into the wood. Under the checkered grip were the words "Demosyna the Wise," using the title for a very powerful Wise-woman. Such a name would only be bestowed on someone who had mastered multiple disciplines, and Demosyna's eyes watered.

"Vaash, this is too much," she said, trying to keep her voice steady as she took the beautiful crutch. "I don't deserve such an honor, being called one of the Wise."

"Nonsense, my talented friend," Vaash exclaimed. "You are skilled in many things already. I know it will only take time for you to master this magic you have taken to!"

He motioned with his thumb at the ruins of the outhouse, invisible through the wall, and both laughed. They shared the first loaves of bread Demosyna prepared, and Vaash began pouring thick honey. Demosyna only baked thirty loaves before joining Vaash to observe with interest.

"Honey wasps can be nasty creatures," Vaash told her as he scraped the jar. "The honey they produce contains their own toxins, along with whatever dangerous plants they may have contacted."

As Demosyna watched, she noticed the murky brown color of the thick honey. There were also many suspended flecks throughout the sweet liquid, and Vaash poured water into the jar. The pot began boiling after Vaash added the slurry, topping off the mixture with a stir.

"Once we separate the honey from the addictive properties, we'll have a clear glaze for the grasshoppers!" Vaash told the wide-eyed young woman. "Can you hand me the strainer there?"

Demosyna handed him the tool he motioned to, a long-handled stick with a fine mesh square, and he began skimming. She had never worked with such a raw ingredient before, having typically been allowed an endless stock of supplies, and marveled at the process of refining. Demosyna grabbed a clean jar and put a cloth over the lid as Vaash poured. He used one knee to tilt the cauldron so that the burning liquid drained steadily.

After looking into the jar, Demosyna could see nearly straight through to the bottom.

"It looks so much clearer now. Is it ready to use yet?"

The excitement in her voice made the man grin.

"After we have done this once more, we can boil the insects, my friend!"

Vaash shook his head before pouring the jar of hot liquid back into the pot. She nodded her understanding and helped him pour, once it had been skimmed, into another clean jar. This time, the honey was nearly transparent with only the faintest shade of gold.

After boiling the viscous honey a final time, Vaash emptied the squirming bags of grasshoppers.

"These were right where you said they would be—atop the waterfall."

Vaash whistled as he ladled out a small jar of clear honey.

"These should sell even better than the bread! If my guess is right, many have never tasted honey in town."

"Thank you again for going and getting them, Vaash," Demosyna said as the honey thickened with grasshoppers.

Vaash nodded, motioning toward the pile of raw ingredients.

"Would you like to add cinnamon as they cool? I found some on my way back."

Demosyna ground the sticks to powder as Vaash laid a piece of woven grass on the counter. He sprinkled it with flour before pouring the honey-coated insects. The slow-pouring grasshoppers were the majority of the pot, but each was coated with a layer of honey. Vaash retrieved the ground spice and sprinkled it over half the quickly cooling insects.

"It shouldn't take long to be ready if you wish to try one," he told the Wise-woman.

The apprentice went back to weaving bags that would serve as dishes for the treats. When Demosyna did try the mostly cooled grasshopper, the taste exploded in her mouth. The cinnamon and honey combined so well with the crunch of the insect that she immediately took the second helping Vaash offered.

"This is so good and so sweet," Demosyna muttered at the man in amazement. "Did I really help make this?"

Vaash laughed with good humor as he, too, began weaving bags of the same size he saw Demosyna's. The two worked for hours before Demosyna broached the topic bursting at her lips.

"Will there be enough time to sell a few things tonight?" she asked the monk, wiping her forehead with a sleeve.

"That reminds me."

Vaash fished her purse from his robes.

"I never returned this, but yes, we can brush the snow from our shop and open if you wish."

Demosyna saw that there were still four gold pieces, along with a scattering of points, in the pouch. She smiled as the two packed the woven bags full of candied grasshoppers. In record time, the cart was loaded with goods, and the two found their stall. Vaash began chopping wood with his small hatchet while Demosyna tore the bread into samples. She sat down with a grin after loading the display tray with the fragrant rolls and avoided eating more candy.

After returning from delivering his first cartload of wood, Vaash found a long line waiting to visit their stall. Demosyna had watched, with a small bit of dread, as people formed a rough line to wait for a rumored free sample. She took a deep breath and trusted in herself as the apprentice sat alone behind the booth. Upon hearing there was candy, many more people joined the line.

* * * * *

It was just after sunset when Demosyna was opening the final bag of grasshoppers, having run out of bread completely. Vaash stopped playing his flute and called to the gathered masses.

"This one is nearly sold out for the night," he bellowed over the commotion of eager patrons. "We are truly sorry, friends, but we will have more tomorrow. That we will."

Cries of disappointment rang in the air, and Demosyna felt bad for turning away so many. When the last bag of grasshoppers sold, Demosyna sat in the snowy grass with a sigh Vaash mirrored. The two laughed as they cleared the booth and loaded the cart. Demosyna handed most of the tiny coins to Vaash before explaining her plan to him.

"I wanted to walk in town for a moment, Vaash," she told the monk as he produced a jar. "This new crutch is wonderful, and I want to try it out. I won't be gone long, and we can return to our cabin then!"

Vaash nodded and poured the last honey from a larger jar. The nearly clear liquid filled the container halfway, shown through the honeycomb-shaped glass set into the fat jar. Demosyna smiled at the man and put the pot into a satchel around her back. The apprentice took papers Vaash handed her before making her destructive way into town, a pocket full of pointy coins.

CHAPTER 19

An unfamiliar town swayed around Demosyna as she retraced the route Vaash had taken. With a joyous cry, Demosyna saw the shop had not closed and walked to the small trader. The shopkeeper greeted her, a short woman with long gray hair, and Demosyna motioned to the flute in the window.

"I saw that earlier and wondered how much it cost," Demosyna said with clear excitement. "I wanted to get my friend a present, and that would be perfect!"

The old woman grunted as she retrieved the pillow supporting the shiny silver flute. After sitting down on a stool, the woman produced a second flute, slightly larger than the first, and fitted them together. The result was a long metal tube that had over a dozen holes along the length.

"You have good taste, young Scale."

The woman coughed at Demosyna.

"This piece is one of a kind, having been crafted to be three instruments and one. I will sell it for thirty gold pieces and will even wrap it for one piece more!"

Demosyna sighed, her heart sinking at the quote.

"Is there any way I could barter for some of the cost? I don't have much, but I can offer you something, I'm sure!"

The woman looked with distaste as Demosyna removed items from her bag. A broken compass, long forgotten till now, and honey and a pocket of coins were placed down. The elderly woman examined the golden compass but looked disgusted at the cracked tool. Demosyna's jar of honey took her interest at once upon spying the vessel.

"Is this real honey?" the elderly human asked doubtfully. "How do you have this?"

"I help run a stall just outside the gates," Demosyna explained. "We just added grasshoppers but also sell fresh bread with—"

"Save the pitch, young Scale," the woman said shortly, picking up the jar and looking into the side. "This is honey, by all the luck!"

Demosyna nodded at the woman's excitement.

"Would you like to trade the honey for the flute, then?"

"A lousy, half-empty jar? No, you thieving Scale. Even with how rare it is, I…I will need these points as well."

The rising hope Demosyna felt was quickly squashed as the woman cackled. A stony expression formed on the saleswoman's face as she crossed her arms. The counter was covered with hard-earned triangles, and Demosyna considered in silence.

"I can't give you the jar, but the honey and coins are yours!"

The present was all Demosyna considered as she shook the trader's hand.

The gray-haired woman returned with a small dish that she filled with the thick honey. Demosyna stored the delicate jar back in her bag after the woman used a knobby finger to wipe any honey from inside. She sucked her finger, closing her eyes and sighing in ecstasy at the taste. Coins were collected before the flute was disassembled and wrapped in a patterned cloth bundle.

Her trip back passed in a daze, with the barely held excitement of a plan coming together making Demosyna grin. The pain in her shoulder from the crutch, along with the constant ache in her foot, was barely registered.

Vaash greeted her, informing the Wizen he had exchanged the points they had earned already. Demosyna smiled widely at the man, thanking him for the forethought. Several times, she craned her neck to look at the back of Vaash's head, imagining the surprise she would unveil.

Vaash began unpacking items from the cart as Demosyna secreted her present into the cabin. She sat, propping her foot on a pillow, and wove as she waited.

"That was quite the night, Demosyna," Vaash said after sitting. "These will be very popular, it seems."

"You had one bag left?"

He produced a bag of the sweet grasshoppers, and Demosyna smiled in surprise.

"I wanted to celebrate with you for finally reaching a goal in your training."

Vaash laughed, his eyes dancing.

"You are full of surprises, aren't you, Vaash? Thank you."

He also produced another full skin of wine, and Demosyna laughed as he took a long swig. She took one of the sticky insects and chewed, marveling at the spicy taste cinnamon added. After months of stews and fish, Demosyna found sugar to be nearly overwhelming. She had always enjoyed candies in her childhood, but this was the first consumed in months.

"We may need a lot of these, because I plan to eat a few pounds!"

Demosyna laughed, taking the wine and drinking. Vaash chuckled, covering his full mouth and nodding.

"I know what you mean. It is hard to not gorge on these!"

The two passed the skin and chatted, and as the night darkened, fresh bread was soon cooling. Demosyna paused the baking, unable to contain the excitement any longer.

"Vaash, I wanted to thank you for being unnervingly kind to me."

Demosyna smiled at the man, who raised his eyebrows.

"I got you this, and I hope you like it."

Demosyna took the bundle from under the table and motioned for Vaash to open it. His eyes widened when he saw the silver flute, and he looked at Demosyna with wonder.

"How did you afford this?" Vaash whispered, his eyes filling with tears. "I don't wish you to bankrupt yourself for me even if this is a marvelous instrument."

He picked the two shining tubes up and examined them closely, holding back tears as he did. Demosyna smiled widely, her own emotions rising, and sat back in relief.

"I didn't barter more than I could afford, Vaash," she told the monk. "Besides, you deserve more than a wooden flute to play your music with."

Vaash was silent for minutes as he looked at the two pieces of silver-crafted beauty. Finally, he set the gift back onto the cloth wrapping and smiled sadly at Demosyna.

"I cannot accept this, and I am sorry," Vaash said, a tear falling from his eyes. "I am but a simple monk and do not desire such luxuries. My music will bring joy despite the simple flute I play."

"Of course you can use this, my friend. This is a gift, not a possession. I want you to remember how kind you were to me each time you play this and how you always believed in a stranger! It is the least this one can do. That it is."

There was clear disappointment in his eyes, but Demosyna smiled. She had used wording picked up from her friend to express herself, and Vaash smiled with his eyes overflowing. He nodded and picked up the two-piece flute with a shaking laugh.

"I see, my friend," Vaash said, assembling the flute as he spoke. "In that case, I welcome the gift. Thank you, Demosyna. You are a true friend. I will make this flute sing of love and peace for all to hear, as you have reminded me."

The thin sound of music filled the cabin as Vaash tested the new instrument. Demosyna listened with rising happiness in her heart as Vaash used her gift to make beautiful notes. His resounding tones came to a stop, and Demosyna clapped as Vaash looked with wonder at the flute.

"This is a heartfelt gift, Demosyna," Vaash whispered through teary eyes. "Thank you. Thank you!"

Demosyna moved to put her hand on the man's shoulder.

"You are very welcome, Vaash. Let us enjoy the night and our time together!"

Vaash agreed with a deep laugh and passed her the wineskin before continuing the weaving.

Demosyna was too excited to sleep and spent the entire night making goods for their shop. Vaash left for two hours to meditate in the snowy field next to the pony, and Demosyna watched the sun rise through the window. Small bags were filled with insects, many sticking together from the honey binding them. Vaash played his new flute the entire way to the shop, and she sang along with any melody she knew.

Demosyna laughed upon seeing a line of people milling around the shop. Vaash helped her from the cart, and a tall man waved as he asked when the shop opened. Her day was busy, spent selling loaves of herbless bread and bags of insects. A line of people eagerly accepted the samples of bread, and gold triangles filled Demosyna's pockets.

To her relief, only five people had to be sent away with grumbles of complaint, and Demosyna fiddled with her new ring while waiting. The smooth gold band felt warm against her purple scales, and torchlight caught the brilliant crystal inlay.

After Vaash returned with the rented cart, the pair retired to their snug cabin. Demosyna was exhausted from the previous days and rested after a few hours of baking. Vaash wished her a pleasant evening, taking over the grinding using his working arm. Coins Vaash had exchanged were divided the next morning, with Demosyna insisting he take the majority despite his protests.

"I will have plenty after a few more days, Vaash," Demosyna explained as she packed a satchel. "We need to get north, but I don't want to take advantage of your kindness more than I have to!"

Vaash laughed and accepted the coins.

"Let us go, then!"

The day was overcast and threatened snow as the friends set up their humble stall. Travelers passing were drawn in by the silvery music Vaash played, and Demosyna thanked a stream of customers. It was a welcome change from the previous days of chaos, with lines clamoring for attention. Near the end of the daylight, when only half a satchel of candy remained, a line had begun forming. The apprentice shifted her weight on the stump, feeling the jangle of coins stuffing her pockets.

Soldiers were approaching the stall with a tall woman, parting the crowd with swords. Many of those waiting in line fled as the soldiers neared, and Demosyna watched with growing worry. They exchanged a few words, observing Demosyna as she sold bags of sweets, before marching over.

"Are you Vaash?" the tall woman asked, her voice snapping cold in the quieting air.

Demosyna shook her head, frowning in confusion.

"My name is Demosyna, ma'am. Would you like some glazed grasshoppers?"

Armored soldiers moved to surround the stall, readying their crossbows. The woman saw Vaash approaching, having stopped chopping wood, and faced the brightly clothed monk.

"Vaash, I presume?" she asked, putting a hand on her hip. "I am here to serve these papers."

Vaash took the scroll and unrolled it without responding. Demosyna glanced at the guards, who stood at attention with their crossbows held ready. She swallowed audibly and addressed the well-dressed woman in the road.

"Please, ma'am, what is the trouble?" Demosyna asked, her voice shaking at the sight of the soldiers.

Vaash finished reading the scroll, rolling it up with one hand.

"This one has infringed on the Traders Order contract for this settlement."

"That is correct, Vaash, and it appears you can read after all. The contract you signed specifies you will abide by market prices, which I am informed you have ignored. I represent the interests of the shopkeepers and carry the weight of their authority. This leaves your contract void, and your profits will be seized as restitution for their losses."

The severe woman nodded, her long brown hair fluttering.

Demosyna was speechless at the sudden turn and started to grab her crutch. The soldiers around her took a step forward while leveling their crossbows.

"Stay down, you Scale," one of the heavily armored soldiers called, motioning with a crossbow. "Don't give me an excuse, seeder."

Tension filled the roadside, and those remaining in line sped off to town. Vaash gave the rolled scroll back and raised his hands to let his sleeves fall down.

"Please, friends," Vaash called, "let this one speak on the charges. We would greatly appreciate it. That we would."

A moment of silence followed, and Demosyna held her breath against the rage swelling in her heart. She did her best to calm her breath, but it puffed away in fearful clouds to spite her.

"I have dissolved your contract, and you will cease all further business," the well-dressed woman said sharply. "There are even rumors of you selling raw honey, flaunting your bright robes around the square. If there was more evidence, I would throw you in shackles right now."

Demosyna felt her heart drop, remembering the jar she had bartered to the shopkeeper.

Have I doomed us again? Demosyna thought wildly, turning to her friend with fear etched on her face.

Vaash smiled calmly at the Wizen and addressed the official.

"Please, ma'am, have your soldiers stand at ease while this one withdraws."

An eternity passed as Demosyna saw snowflakes drift down while she waited to hear her fate. Finally, the woman's expression broke, and she smiled wickedly.

"You are a smart boy, aren't you?" she asked with a sneer. "Smart enough to exploit our small town. You are not welcome here, Vaash, and the seeder you travel with should be thankful I don't arrest you. You look like a fit male after all, and she would miss your company, I'm sure."

Demosyna glanced from Vaash to the tall woman, shame filling her mind.

"It was I that sold the honey, but it was not raw, because we processed it ourselves."

"An admittance of guilt. Excellent."

The woman turned to Demosyna at the outburst. The official used a piece of charcoal to write notes on a paper she carried. Vaash remained with his arms raised, smiling and stone-still in the evening breeze.

"You will turn over any illegal earnings," the official barked. "Soldiers, seize these criminals and my assets."

The soldiers surrounding Demosyna grasped her shoulders and hauled her from the stump. Armored women quickly restrained both Vaash and Demosyna as they searched the pockets of the robes each wore. The golden triangles that Demosyna had deposited in her clothes were piled on the counter. Vaash had no money and sat with his feet tucked under him once the soldiers had searched.

Demosyna was thrown to the ground after her pockets were emptied and gasped at the sudden pain. Soldiers bagged the coins before one marched back into town with the bursting sacks. Demosyna watched the hard-earned money disappear into the gloom and held back tears. One of the armored women held her crossbow ready while the other used Vaash's hatchet to smash the booth. Demosyna dared not move as the soldier laughed once the booth was little more than scattered wood.

"Take care of this litter before you leave, Vaash," the soldier mocked as she threw the hatchet into the snow. "Otherwise, I will have to fine you and your pretty friend there."

Vaash remained with his arms up despite the pain it clearly caused. Demosyna felt useless once again, having gotten Vaash into this mess. She didn't use magic, fearing escalating the banishment, and tried to avoid eye contact with the soldiers. The official watched with detached interest, making notes on her paper before calling the guards back.

"I think that will be all," the tall woman said, straightening her elaborate necklace. "You are barred from doing trade with our town, Vaash. I do not wish to see your smug face around here again."

Vaash smiled, lowering his hands and standing.

"Thank you, friend. This one will depart at once!"

The monk helped Demosyna to her feet and gathered the remains of their stall. Soldiers followed the official back down the road to town, laughing and counting some coin they pocketed.

Demosyna opened her mouth to apologize, but Vaash held his hand up before she could.

"No, my friend, you have nothing to apologize for," Vaash sighed. "This one overlooked details of the contract and is solely to blame."

"But I chose to sell so cheap," Demosyna said, tears forming in her eyes, "and bartered the honey that got us kicked out of the town."

Vaash smiled warmly and shook his head.

"The Traders Hall is unsupportive of a store that hasn't established itself. The official stores must pay their own soldiers, and to own a store, you must give dues to the Traders Hall."

Demosyna processed the information as the cart rolled sadly back to their cabin. After the two were seated in the warm walls, Vaash took a long drink of water from a skin.

"I am pleasantly surprised by how restrained those soldiers were," Vaash told the apprentice as she rubbed her leg. "It was fortunate that we sold for so long and that the soldiers only took our money for today!"

Demosyna fetched her purse and saw there were eight large gold pieces, along with dozens of points, contained in the pouch. With a weight seeming to lift off her shoulders, Demosyna let out a long sigh of relief.

"I have enough after all," Demosyna exclaimed with a grin. "I was worried I couldn't get us up the Highway. I'm sorry I have messed things up again, Vaash."

"As I said before, my friend, you have nothing to apologize for!"

Vaash stood and began packing the rations.

"We would have left soon in any case, but we have enough to share the cost of the tolls!"

Demosyna widened her eyes, having not considered Vaash sharing the cost. The generous offer took the young woman aback, and she nodded as Vaash smiled.

"Thank you, Vaash. What can I do to help get us moving?"

The young woman stood carefully with her crutch. The only items the two possessed lay where they had been using them for the shop. With a frown, Demosyna gathered the grinding tools and containers of ingredients. Any elation felt the previous days was gone, replaced with a shocked determination. The rapidity at which the day had turned for her was alarming, but Demosyna focused on the only path left.

Vaash made a corner for things they would leave, starting with the honey. Demosyna sorted the items they would take, leaving much behind in the cabin. Their cart was loaded with supplies as Demosyna felt anger rising in her heart. Lightning raced across her nerves, and Demosyna held her left hand out with a cry of frustration.

Vaash turned in surprise to watch a tornado rip across the clearing before breaking against the tree line. Demosyna panted from the magic but smiled as she examined the ring. It was slightly warm, but Demosyna wondered if it was her imagination as the air calmed her raging emotions.

"That was wonderful, Demosyna!" Vaash told the woman with pride in his voice. "You are really getting the hang of it! That you are!"

"Good riddance to this greedy town!" Demosyna yelled, laughing into the afternoon air defiantly. "We have miles to travel and won't be held back by details!"

Vaash laughed at her joke, helping her into the cart before playing a marching song. His silver flute shone in the sun, and Vaash used the smaller half to produce a high, sweet note. Clouds drifted by in the steady wind, and Demosyna saw the Empress's Highway looming out of the trees. The Highway was blocked from view whenever Demosyna visited the town, but Vaash swung the cart down a side road. She gasped in wonder as the enormous size of the Highway took her breath away.

It was the largest building Demosyna had ever seen, easily over a hundred feet tall, and it filled her vision. The shadow of the great road overtook the two, and a huge platform lowered down one of the slopes. Along both sides of the first gigantic section were even slants that ended atop the first level. Wooden platforms were used as elevators to get riders into the air and traveled up the slope.

A middle layer of the Highway formed a dome from the roof, arching up to a perfect half circle. Atop the domed tunnel of the second level was the third and final story, perched high enough above the apprentice to make her dizzy. The topmost level of the Empress's Highway was another perfect half circle but inverted to produce a flat top. The curves of the two half circles met at their apex and seemed to balance the massive stones impossibly into the sky.

Demosyna sat in silent wonder as a tiny square began to descend down the upper levels. After reaching the angled first floor, there was a lurch as the elevator moved to touch the snowy ground. Each story of the enormous structure was well over thirty feet tall, Demosyna guessed, yet the stones were over ten feet square. Vaash spoke to a soldier near the platform, and the elf pointed to the other side.

Vaash turned the cart to head slowly to an opposite edge of the Highway. As he guided the pony in a wide arc, Demosyna saw the Highway stretch forever. The colossal stone road drove straight ahead, and as far as the woman could tell, it didn't falter. The flat topmost story remained level the impossible length, never rising or falling despite the land being wildly mountainous. An image of the arrow-straight road was hard for Demosyna to grasp, and she shook her head as the cart passed the center.

The young woman craned her neck to see a square hole that was heavily guarded by armored soldiers. Two-story shacks were spaced on either side of the opening, and huge marble pillars crossed the entrance. The sight of so many armed figures worried Demosyna, but from the shadows, large tracks led straight north. Both the roof and floor of the closed-off first level were lined by tracks, perfectly straight and parallel.

Confusion formed while she sat back, and Demosyna watched a precisely angled side appear. This slant was the same as the other side but opposite to form a triangle. From her position, Demosyna saw the face of the Highway fade to the horizon and a huge wheel several paces away from the platform. Nearly fifty people were shackled to the metal wheel, which had large spokes jutting from a central pillar.

Armed soldiers milled around the slaves, calling orders or leaning against the slant of the Highway. Once the open platform was full of travelers, a trumpet sounded from behind Demosyna, and she jumped. Slaves immediately stood at the blast and began straining to turn the wheel. After barely half a turn, the platform began to rise along the sloped stone. Sorrow at the sight of the slaves filled Demosyna's heart, and much of the wonder turned dull.

It took minutes to reach the first level, and Demosyna was shaken from her thoughts. She could see for miles, it seemed to the Wise-woman, as the cart rattled from the angular journey. Trees formed a green-and-gold smear as far as she could see, and Vaash began playing his flute. Demosyna went to the cart's edge and sat with her left foot dangling. The town could be seen, a cluster of buildings dotting the landscape, and the Wizen drank in the wilderness anew.

Birds flew close by as the amazed woman felt a jerk, and the cart rose straight into the bright sky. The ground swam before her eyes, and Demosyna looked away from the growing distance with her stomach churning. She saw that the curved ceiling of the second floor had holes near the top spaced the entire length. There was also a large door that remained closed as the platform continued upward. The curve of the third floor seemed to flow toward the young woman, and the platform stopped with a clicking shudder.

Demosyna enjoyed the uninterrupted view as she waited for the cart to be led off. Miles of wilderness waved in front of the young woman, and she held back tears at the beauty. Mountains jutted large in the distance, and forests coated the land with happy colors of early winter. Her bright robes whipped in the wind, and Demosyna laughed as Vaash stopped playing to move the cart. Her excitement was nearly overwhelming as Demosyna watched the platform begin to drop once more.

Two large poles jutted from the first floor, suspending the platform high above the earth. As Demosyna watched the descent, the thick poles retracted into the stone with a twisting motion. Once the platform had reached the angled first floor, tracks carried it down the sharp slope. These tracks reminded Demosyna of the shadow-filled square, and she pondered at its purpose while the cart moved along.

Each stone that made up the Empress's Highway was wide enough for vehicles to travel, and her cart joined a slow line. The shadow of a checkpoint darkened the sky, and Demosyna turned to a large building blocking the flow. A two-story structure rose from the Highway to meet in the middle, making a wide entryway to the road. Clusters of armed soldiers processed the people, and barrels of coins shone in the sun as tolls were collected. Vaash joined her at the back of the cart while they waited for the traffic to move.

"If only I still had my spyglass, we could really look at the gorgeous land!" Demosyna said as she remembered her Wise Mother.

The excitement of the past week had driven thoughts of her friends and lost life away, and Demosyna reprimanded herself for the lack of empathy.

I must never forget my true goal here and not be too distracted by my own circumstances, Demosyna thought, looking at the view from her sky-top perch. *I have to trust that Rrra is alive and can hope he found his Jui.*

"This one can pay the first toll if you wish to cover the next."

Vaash leaned against the cart.

"That seems the best option between two friendly travelers. That it does."

"I agree, Vaash," Demosyna said with a smile. "Even with the slow pony, this highway will get us north faster than anything else!"

The vast land surrounding the two was beautiful, but travel would be slow at best when on foot. Woods and hills made walking a chore, and dangers in these mountains loomed in her mind.

Vaash shook his head but smiled as he responded.

"This one rented the cart from town and must return their property. Fear not. A new cart can be rented for your use!"

He had noticed the worry forming on Demosyna's face at the thought of walking thousands of miles, and the injured woman relaxed. Their wagon had become a welcome transport over the previous days, but Demosyna helped Vaash empty the bed. Soldiers motioned impatiently, yet Demosyna could only move so fast with her broken foot. Vaash shouldered the majority of the possessions, and Demosyna took her first steps along the Empress's Highway.

Hope bloomed in her heart as Demosyna sat beside the edge, and the journey seemed distant from her seat atop the world. A cold wind blew steadily across the smooth highway, and Demosyna watched small twisters form from snow. Demosyna smiled as the wind played with the ice and kept her friends prominent in her mind as a bloody path loomed ahead.

CHAPTER 20

A storm was felt by Demosyna as she drove the cart along the Highway, not close yet but approaching. Her broken foot was placed on the footrest, and the horse leading the cart was old beyond belief. The sky was a great, cold dome, brilliant blue as the Wizen marveled at the view. Their ancient horse knew the way, so Demosyna was able to let her gaze wander over the enchanting scenery. Smaller mountains passed close enough to see the icy peaks, and trees seemed dwarfed by the massive highway.

Demosyna didn't know how tall the Highway stood, but it was easily over a hundred feet into the sky. Some of the amazement was lost upon seeing how the elevators were powered, and more from the first snow. A storm came suddenly, and Demosyna had been in the back of the covered wagon when it hit. Vaash cried out, jumping from the driver's seat to secure the horse. The shocked young woman had looked out the back, seeing the drop-off mere feet away.

Wind blew with incredible fury, sending the cart scooting sideways. Demosyna launched herself from the wagon in terror, landing in a heap on her left side. Vaash materialized from the blizzard as bright yellow in the whiteout. Her foot seemed undamaged, and Vaash huddled with the apprentice after bracing the wheels. The side of the flat highway had no railings, and Demosyna now knew one edge of the sword that was the Empress's Highway. The other edge would cut shortly on the end of a rope and wound the young woman permanently.

"That first storm passed so quickly but was so violent," Demosyna recalled as the horse led her along. "I have to keep an eye out for clouds while we are exposed up here."

Demosyna glanced at the edge of the Highway and saw a dizzying drop-off. She could imagine falling from such a height, the ground screaming up to welcome you, and it made her head swim.

There was another tollbooth approaching in the north, and Demosyna peered into the back of the cart. Vaash was meditating, Demosyna having taken the reigns several hours prior.

"Vaash, it is my turn to pay the toll," the eager woman called. "I will stop the cart soon, if you need anything."

"This one must fill a few skins," the tanned human replied, opening his eyes with a smile. "That old mare drinks a lot more than the pony. That she does."

Both laughed, and Demosyna felt the horse stop without even touching the reigns. The bony animal shook its head and waited for Demosyna to grab her crutch. It seemed impatient at her dallying, and Demosyna limped to the gate. Previous tollgates had been simple wooden structures, but this one also had an elevator on either side. These wide wooden platforms allowed travelers and cargo to ascend into the heavens, able to stop at each floor.

A tall soldier, armored in metal, took the offered handful of triangles. The current price was posted above the entrance, so the young woman had the payment ready. Demosyna asked about water and was directed to a merchant near large barrels. Her mangled foot had been healing nicely, but she still used the crutch as the apprentice went back to her friend. Her own robes matched Vaash's, bright orange and yellow, and fluttered in the unbroken wind. Steps beside the cart let Demosyna access the driver's seat, and the horse began moving before the woman had fully sat.

Demosyna laughed as she was pushed into the seat, having grown used to the strict schedule the horse kept.

"I hate to make you late, but we need more water," Demosyna told the horse, a grin on her sharp purple face. "Please be patient with me!"

Vaash laughed quietly from the cart, and Demosyna felt wonderful as she enjoyed the travel.

The skins were filled for only a few points, and Demosyna put them with their belongings. After being banished from town, they had only taken a few days' worth of provisions. Vaash assured the woman that traders used the Empress's Highway, taking advantage of the constant stream of seeders. Vaash's words proved true once again, and barely a day passed when a seller failed to offer superior goods.

Her week atop the Highway seemed a dream, broken occasionally by a storm that halted their progress. Time became measured in tollbooths, save for when blizzards made that impossible. Days were mesmerizing to the young woman, but the nights took her breath away. A canopy of stars hung in the frigid dark, and Demosyna would lie on her back to swim in the beauty. The moon twirled across the star field, but the millions of winking lights captivated the young woman.

Twirling masses of tentacles and beaks drifted while powered by the moonlight, giving echoing calls as wild moon squid migrated. These glowing creatures were among the only beasts tamed in the Fist and served as a naval accessory. Trees had kept the stars from her view, unlike her fateful voyage had allowed. Her eyes had been filled with wonder as she saw stars reflected on still nights of sailing, letting Demosyna float in a dazzling void.

A trader stood beside the road, and Vaash shook his head when Demosyna mentioned it. She smiled and leaned back again, letting the horse move along. The woman noticed figures picking through the goods and that there was no horse near the stall. As she passed in the center of the road, the three barely seemed to care. Only after their cart had moved on did the figures peer at the retreating wagon. Demosyna didn't notice the three jog after, but Vaash did.

"Demosyna," the monk called with a hushed tone, "this one fears bandits approach."

The sudden news snapped the apprentice from her daydream, and she turned to look over the cloth top. One of the robbers loaded a crossbow, and the other two rushed forward with swords flashing. This distracted the apprentice from the figures that climbed over the edge, ropes tied around their waists. They let out a bellow as they reached the cart, and both climbers cut the horse free. It bolted at once, faster than a decrepit body would suggest, leaving the cart stranded.

Her heart raced, and Demosyna turned to see the wicked faces of the attackers. Vaash jumped from the cart with a calm smile on his face. His red hair blew in the wind while the monk stood blocking the advancing figures. Demosyna saw one of the swords swing at Vaash and reacted without thinking. She held her left hand south, and rage surged through her spine. Demosyna loosed a passionate yell, and a wall of force sprang forward.

Vaash withstood the gale, only taking a step to keep his feet, but all three bandits were thrown backward. Metal scraped on stone as the magic tossed them like leaves, knocking together in a cyclone. The climbers cried out in surprise and turned to flee over the sides. Demosyna grinned at one, seeing fear in the dirty woman's eyes, and held her hand up. She heard the bandit scream, and Vaash called toward her, but Demosyna felt power and confidence overwhelm her mind.

The force of the cyclone cast the climber into the sky until the rope around her waist snapped taut. Demosyna's magic buffeted the dark-clothed thief so that her back was twisted from the secure line. Blood poured from the human's mouth, and the only bandit still standing began screaming. It was seconds before the wind died down, and the broken body spun within the spell. Demosyna was hypnotized by the grisly spectacle, even when the bandit fell from the side of the Highway.

The apprentice's tornado stopped holding the body, and it dropped beyond sight over the edge. From behind Demosyna, the black-clad climber fell to her knees and wept. Vaash had rushed to the front of the cart, his green eyes wide and searching. Demosyna felt the smile on her face and tilted her head at Vaash. The master monk looked over the edge and closed his eyes when he saw the dead bandit hanging from a rope.

"You killed her!" the weeping climber yelled at Demosyna, raising a sword. "What did you do?"

Demosyna opened her mouth to respond but closed it again when no words came. Vaash put his hand on the woman's wrist, and the sword clattered to the ground.

"This one will help you," Vaash said, sadness in his voice. "Please leave this sword behind."

The other three bandits slowly approached, two of them with broken limbs. They all had fearful looks on their faces, and one of them raised a crossbow. Demosyna saw this and shook her head with narrowed eyes. A wave of terror passed over the short archer's face, and all three retreated south. Demosyna watched mismatched armor flee and felt no more danger from them. Vaash had begun hauling the body up, using his good arm to pull the rope. Numb stillness washed over Demosyna, and she felt oddly detached when the remains were rested on the Highway.

Before her acquisition of the focusing charm, Demosyna couldn't be sure if her magic had killed. Her memory had been overwhelmed by powerful magic twice, but she had felt it likely even if she was unsure. Now that certainty stared blankly at the apprentice from the cold stones of the Empress's Highway.

The weeping bandit refused Vaash's help in carrying the body and departed slowly back south. Vaash turned to the apprentice with tears in his eyes.

"Thank you for acting so quickly, my friend."

Demosyna stared dumbly at the man, tears threatening to spill from her eyes as well. The initial elation at acting when danger was present faded, replaced with sorrow. This confused the woman, and Demosyna furrowed her brow in thought. Many angry cries echoed in her mind, loud and overwhelming.

"I didn't mean to kill her, Vaash," Demosyna said finally, her voice barely a croak. "I didn't."

"This one understands. It can be easy to get carried away. That it can."

Vaash looked up at the woman, studying her face closely.

Demosyna broke the gaze as new and unknown emotions lit her heart. The dangers of the north had always scared the woman, but now Demosyna was terrified. If she could destroy with just a wave of her hand, the young woman knew she must never again simply react.

"Magic isn't just a fun toy to make flowers grow," Demosyna chided herself. "I could have hurt Vaash or smashed our cart now that I think of it."

A terrible price had been paid by a stranger, and Demosyna felt a heavy brow force her horned head down. Vaash sat beside the woman, warmly smiling and waiting. Over ten minutes passed while Demosyna wrestled with her conflicting mind and heart, letting tears fall from her eyes. She felt no shame at the display, and Vaash sat as always with understanding in his smile.

"I do not judge you, Demosyna," Vaash whispered as a figure approached from the south. "Nor do I blame you. Those women made their choices today. That they did."

It was barely any comfort to the distraught Wizen, but she nodded her understanding nevertheless. There was truth to what the man said, but Demosyna still felt the raw sting of emotion. A tear fell onto her wind-chilled face, and Vaash offered another handkerchief.

It took several minutes for the leisurely figure to reach their cart, and Demosyna had regained much of her composure. Before this solitary figure, there had been no other traffic, leaving the two alone with the apprentice's decisions in the open sky.

The dark-skinned human who approached was above average in height, with a long bow across her back. She wore supple leather armor studded with faded gold pyramids. Vaash rose to greet the stranger, and she bowed toward the two in the cart.

"Greetings, friend," Vaash called to the woman, climbing down. "Would you share a drink while you pass? It would please this one, and we have water to spare!"

"That depends. Was it you two that took care of those minnows?"

The dark-eyed woman put a hand on her hip and motioned with the other. Vaash looked back south, smiling slightly.

"It is unfortunate. That it is. They were repelled while springing an ambush with climbers."

Demosyna nodded, her eyes finally dry.

"I just reacted and took nearly all of them down before they could escape."

She hung her head, but Demosyna raised it again when the stranger laughed merrily. Vaash widened his smile and looked up at his seated friend. The woman rubbed her dense black hair and grinned widely.

"I like your style, ma'am."

The stranger laughed, shaking her head with cold eyes.

"Though if it were me, there would be a few less walking back!"

Vaash smiled and fetched the wine before pouring into two clay cups. They were the only mugs taken from the cabin, but Vaash had crafted sturdy glasses, and the women toasted.

"This one may be called Vaash," he said, capping the wine without indulging.

"I am Au Peirce, Vaash," she said after sampling the wine. "What do I call you besides Wise-woman? If you can take on five bandits with a broken foot, you are clearly a Wizen!"

Au Peirce sipped the glass as Demosyna responded.

"My name is Demosyna. It is nice to meet you, Au Peirce, but I am still an apprentice. You shouldn't call me Wise."

"I've never heard of such a powerful apprentice, but what do I know? I'm just an archer from a tiny island you've never heard of."

A shadow passed over the archer's face, and Demosyna frowned.

"I'm sorry, Au Peirce. I meant no offense," Demosyna said, her eyes wide. "I am still on edge from the attack and didn't mean to be short with you."

Au Peirce seemed taken aback, and her eyebrow raised.

"A Wise-woman apologizing? You must be an apprentice! I understand. Let us change the subject."

"Where are you headed, friend?" Vaash asked as he investigated the remains of the harness.

"I travel my Empress's Highway in search of a cousin," Au Peirce said as she finished her cup. "He got it into his fool head that he could start an entire trading empire. The last thing we heard from him was troubling, as he seemed to be in over his head. His obsession with legends drove him to seek any Orc tribes he could find."

Vaash spoke from his kneeling position.

"The Orc strongholds are the oldest in the Fist, more ancient even than the Highway itself, if such is possible!"

Au Peirce continued after thinking about that fact.

"It was nearly a year ago we last heard from him, but I have searched for months for sign of the fool to chart my path. I travel in hopes that word of him or any Orc tribe can be found. You haven't seen him on your travels, I am guessing."

"How would this one know him?" Vaash asked, standing and rubbing his broken arm.

"He rises to about my height with a large head of dark hair akin to those in my village," Au Peirce said, motioning to her own trimmed Afro with a slight grimace. "He always thought himself cute, but he took to putting gold piece flakes into his hair to turn it golden. He isn't as strong as Vaash here looks but is quite built for a boy. He also was never seen without his prized dwarven crossbow ever since it floated into town."

Both of the yellow-clad travelers combed their memories, thinking back on the sea of faces. Demosyna shook her head, and Vaash did too after a moment.

"I don't remember anyone with actual golden hair," Demosyna said, smiling as she imagined the costly hairstyle. "And I wouldn't know what a dwarven crossbow looked like. I'm very sorry."

"This one must apologize as well, Au Peirce," Vaash replied. "No such gentleman has been noticed."

"That's what I figured," the human woman said with a sigh of exasperation. "I have come to accept this land is so much bigger than I thought. The maps really don't have consistent scales around here by the way. How do you manage to get anywhere without accurate charts?"

Demosyna smiled and shared a laugh.

"At least you have a map. I forgot to get one before leaving the city! If you hadn't reminded me, I may never have remembered!"

Au Peirce took her long bow from her back, resting it against the cart.

"If you give me another cup of wine, you can have this one. It's not the worst map I've found, but I wouldn't trust it for more than cardinal directions. I personally know it to be off by a dozen miles in places, so be careful and only use it for the Highway if you can."

The leather-clad traveler searched as she spoke and handed a rolled map to Vaash. He unrolled the gift and smiled before offering the paper to Demosyna. The apprentice saw that the crudely drawn map was incomplete like all others as Vaash filled the glass. A crescent of mapped land was drawn with basic shapes to tell landmarks, and the entire southeast beyond the mountains was blank. Only a sliver of drawn waves showed a far-eastern edge of the known Fist, and the majority of the map was yet to be filled in.

"Thank you, Au Peirce!" Demosyna said, excitement filling her voice. "This will really help me search for my missing friends! Do you know where we are on this?"

The apprentice held the map flat for the woman to look. Au Peirce studied the page before peering at the sky with a calculating expression. Her mouth moved slightly without sound, and Au Peirce pointed along the slight curve the Highway formed on the map.

"We are about at this latitude," Au Peirce said, tapping the Highway about a third of the way up. "But the map shows more progress than you have actually made. You are just over a month away from the final stop since you have a cart. It took me over four months to walk down, and I am walking back north to keep looking for my thickheaded cousin."

"So you just got this far south?" Demosyna asked, her heart sinking. "You wouldn't have seen my friends, then."

Au Peirce shook her head, frowning.

"I doubt it. I haven't left the upper highway except to hunt. Unless your friends are deer or bears, I haven't seen any Wizened. They usually travel in the central level anyway since they can afford it."

"No, they weren't Wizen. They were with me on the last seeder boat," Demosyna said, shaking her head and describing her friends.

"I haven't found any sign of them in weeks but can still hold out hope!"

"I still can't help you, Demosyna."

Au Peirce sipped her full glass.

"The only Scales I have seen lately are you and a pair that were red and albino. They were walking north a few days ago if you want to try and catch up to them."

Demosyna looked north along the stone highway and nodded while deep in thought. The apprentice halls still seemed the best place to search from, and Demosyna sighed a puff of breath into the air.

"Thank you anyway, Au Peirce," Demosyna said, turning to the archer. "I will keep a lookout for your cousin and let him know you're here if we find him!"

"This one will fetch the horse," Vaash said, topping off Au Peirce from the skin. "It should not have gotten far."

Demosyna locked eyes with the man, who gazed with a question in his eyes, and nodded her comfort with Vaash leaving. Demosyna sat in silence after he walked away, studying the map. Au Peirce noticed the young woman's rapt attention and frowned while drinking. Vaash returned only minutes after disappearing, the elderly horse trotting behind.

"This one found it wandering back already!" Vaash said, patting the horse. "It wanted to finish the trip. Didn't you?"

Both women laughed at the horse's antics, and it stamped a hoof after it was reattached. Vaash offered to drive the cart, and Demosyna accepted with thanks. The sight of her foot gave Au Peirce pause when she helped the Wizen down but said nothing about the missing toe. Her sharp eyes went from foot to arm, and Au Peirce noticed that both travelers sported fresh casts.

Demosyna rested with her good leg dangling from the cart.

"Thank you for the help. Would you like to travel with us for a bit?"

Demosyna motioned to the half-empty cart shaded by the canvas top.

"I will walk behind your cart since I am going that route anyway," Au Peirce said, her voice singing in the afternoon air. "But I will say no to the ride, as it would be hard for me to shoot from inside there."

Au Peirce took her bow and held it beside her, the string tucked against her hip.

The cart began moving again, with the excitement of the attack fading behind. Vastly conflicting emotions rose in her heart as Demosyna left the murderous place. The apprentice felt unworthy of such happy company after her actions proved mortally dire. Demosyna pushed her own pain aside knowing it would take time to process what she had done. The apprentice put on a smile and rested, listening to Au Peirce tell of a hunt she had undertaken.

Au Peirce proved able to keep pace without any problem, her leather boots striding on the snow-slicked highway. Vaash assembled his silver flute and played songs while the trio traveled north. With a wild laugh, Au Peirce began singing a shanty to the tune Vaash played, and the night closed around their monitored journey.

CHAPTER 21

The sun had only just risen, but Au Peirce was already up and aiming her bow. Demosyna stirred from the back of the wooden cart, noticing the woman in the ruby sunlight. The archer loosed an arrow, and a gossamer string trailed behind the projectile. It was almost too thin to see, but the sun caught a shiny ribbon as the arrow impacted a bird. Au Peirce reeled the thin rope back in, drawing the bird to the woman's feet. Demosyna clapped at the wonderfully accurate display, and Au Peirce turned with a frown.

"I didn't know you were awake yet," the dark-skinned woman said, pulling her arrow from the bird. "If you want any, you'll still have to pay for it. Sky fishing is easier than normal bow fishing, but I won't just be giving my catches away."

Demosyna rubbed her eyes and smiled.

"That was a great shot, Au Peirce!"

Au Peirce narrowed her lips in the hint of a smile.

"Thank you, little Scale. This bow serves me well enough, ever since that bandit thought he could outshoot me! It took a few days, but I mastered this new weapon. As long as my steel cord doesn't break, I can fish in the sea or skies now! And the land creatures don't see me hiding. It can shoot from so far away."

Au Peirce stood admiring the finely crafted recurve bow. Its red wood was closely grained and shone with a polished surface that mirrored the world. As Au Peirce finished wrapping the cord, the Wizen

saw it was made of extremely fine threads. It was hung on the archer's belt, and the woman cleaned her arrow before putting it back in the leather quiver. Her arrow was simple, just flint and shaved wood, unlike imperial arrows that had wire or engravings. Like so many things in the Empress's world, the arrows were each handmade to be extravagant in their design.

The sight was still painful to the young woman, but Demosyna was learning to cope with having arrows shot nearby. Au Peirce had joined them only a day ago but already had displayed great skill in shooting. An arrow would twang into the unbelievable view atop the Highway, and each time, a meal would fall from the heavens. Vaash had paid the woman from his purse the first night, letting Demosyna enjoy a feast of roasted poultry.

"Fair morning, friends," Vaash called from the front of the cart. "This one will start breakfast if any are hungry."

Au Peirce perked up and nodded while plucking the fresh kill. Several feathers she kept in her breast pocket, but the rest were sent to scatter along the wind's discretion. The well-muscled archer hung the goose on the cart before sitting near the coals of a fire. Vaash had already put fresh wood on the embers, and a blaze soon warmed the archer's hands. Demosyna limped over, leaving her crutch, to rest against a wheel near the fire.

The last of their meat was warmed, having purchased some heavily peppered jerky along the way. Demosyna baked a large loaf of bread, and the three ate together in the dawn of a new day. After the travelers had eaten their fill, Vaash extinguished the fire and kicked the ashes over. The waste buckets were likewise emptied, and Vaash removed blocks from the wheels. Their desperately old horse had woken and blew its nostrils in judgment. Demosyna laughed as the three stretched before Vaash drove them along.

It was hours after noon when Demosyna emptied the last water from her skin. Au Peirce was moving behind the rickety cart, eyes always scanning for prey. When the archer turned from the south, Demosyna saw the war paint Au Peirce had applied. It was sparkly gold in hue and circled the woman's brown eyes with a line that met on her nose. The effect was startling, as Au Peirce's eyes seemed to blaze with light when the sun hit the paint.

"Would you like me to take over driving? We should reach the next tollbooth early tomorrow," the purple-scaled woman asked Vaash. "They seem to be spaced regularly even if they aren't marked on this map!"

"This one will need to stay here," Vaash said, his voice a warning.

Demosyna sat up in alarm, scanning the view she was allowed from the steep canvas cover. The cold air was still, and Demosyna heard horses approaching from the north. Au Peirce spun on her heel, crouching while moving to the front of the cart. Demosyna untied a section of the beige canvas to view the riders. They were two of the bandits from the previous attack, one with her arm in a sling. How they had gotten ahead of the group was a mystery, and Demosyna frantically scanned the Highway for climbers.

"Greetings, friends," Vaash called loudly. "Would you share a drink as you pass?"

"We will take all you have," the uninjured rider spit, leather armor creaking, "starting with you, pretty thing."

A crossbow fired at the brightly clothed monk, who remained smiling as the missile approached. A second arrow fired and then a third in rapid succession from Au Peirce's red bow. Even when the arrow reached his shoulder, colliding with one of Au Peirce's, Vaash remained motionless. The last of the arrows Au Peirce loosed struck a rider in the chest. It had all happened in a breath, but Au Peirce used one arrow to intercept a bolt while the other struck a bandit precisely.

Vaash nodded at Au Peirce.

"Thank you, friend. That was a very delicate shot."

The injured rider sounded a horn, trying to turn her horse. Au Peirce let another arrow fly, and it planted itself into the fleeing bandit with a thud. The robber yelled in pain before falling sideways from her horse, which kept running without a rider. Demosyna watched this play out over the course of several heartbeats, amazed by Au Peirce's eagle vision. She was going to exclaim her praise when both Vaash and the archer tilted their heads to listen.

Vaash reacted in a flash, shifting position to spin away from a bolt that sailed past his head. Au Peirce jumped toward the horse, firing more shots, while an arrow went under her feet. Demosyna turned to the approaching riders but saw one fall over the edge with arrows in her chest. A gurgling scream echoed over the Highway, drowned by thundering hooves. Five riders aimed crossbows, sending a rain of death toward Demosyna.

This sudden attack left Demosyna confused, and she retreated back in the cart as arrows landed. One missed her horn, its fletching brushing the black surface with a scream. Vaash rushed to the back of the cart as a blur of yellow and blocked an arrow with his cast. A metallic clang was heard, and he grimaced before turning wide eyes toward Demosyna.

"I'm okay, Vaash. Are you?" Demosyna called frantically, seeing the arrow protruding from his broken arm.

Vaash nodded, and Au Peirce shot back at the riders who were nearly upon them. Mismatched striped green armor the riders wore appeared from beyond the horizon but rushed forward with determination.

"We have to move," Au Peirce yelled, hopping onto the cart and crouching in front of Demosyna.

Vaash used his good hand to swat an arrow from the air before it could reach the women. He dashed to the driver's seat, the frightened beast nearly bolting at once.

That it stayed this long is a small miracle, Demosyna thought wildly as she braced herself with a free hand.

One of the riders was trampled by her fellows when Au Peirce shot true. Other bandits grew more furious and charged ahead while yelling war cries. Clouds of white hate swirled around their heads, and the riders grew closer to the slow wagon. Au Peirce turned back for a split second, a desperate look in her gold-rimmed eyes.

"A little help, Wise-woman?" the archer said shortly, moving aside to let Demosyna pass. "I can only kill so many today!"

Demosyna bit back the fear that the arrows caused and aimed her left hand at a cluster of horses. She stilled her mind with an effort, and the last image of the tethered rag doll faded. Vaash's words echoed, and Demosyna took a deep breath before casting her magic.

"Strength through balance," Demosyna muttered to herself. "I won't repeat my mistakes."

The apprentice strained her mind, focusing her will toward a controlled force of wind. A cyclone of unrestricted fury would only serve to harm, and Demosyna wished to protect. The young woman watched in acceptance as a bolt inched through the air, and she focused on halting it. A tornado formed behind the cart, centered where the apprentice focused, and caught the bolt. The harmless piece of wood was flung away in pieces, and Demosyna cried out in joy. As the cart moved along at far too slow a pace, the riders threw spears.

Au Peirce's arrow sailed past Demosyna's face, and it flew through the buffeting wall of wind to hit a rider. The man groaned in pain but raised a crossbow and fired back. The hostile bolt was useless, as the spears had been, and tumbled off into the woods. Au Peirce cursed, and another arrow flew by to pass through the tornado. This one found a home in the nose of a bandit, who convulsed off her horse with a rattle.

"Just like bow fishing, with the image refracting," Au Peirce said, hooting wildly and firing again. "The little fishy is never where they seem. Come meet your end, you guppies."

Another arrow finished off the shoulder-wounded bandit, who had been trying to pull the wood out. The riders fell back after another spear was splintered by the mobile wall. Demosyna sighed from the strain and nearly collapsed when the tornado spun itself apart. Even when the icy wind subsided, the riders remained at a distance. Vaash turned to check on the passengers before hurrying the horse along again.

"Once I get the last of them, I can salvage my arrows. I lost a few when they fell over, but most are scattered behind."

Au Peirce held her last three arrows.

"Then we can loot their useless bodies! Looking for my cousin takes a lot of money after all."

Demosyna saw the grin her archer companion gave and smiled in a toothy way that remained nervous. Her own purse would likely get her north, and looting corpses had not occurred to Demosyna. The idea that she would have access to bandit plunder hadn't crossed the young woman's mind, sheltered as she was.

For over an hour, the horse pushed itself, sensing the danger behind it. Great clouds of breath streamed from the beast, who set her eyes and ran.

Once during that frantic chase, the riders sent another volley, arching in the sky from a distance. Demosyna deflected them with a burst of winds, sending them flying like grass in a breeze. This time, the wind lasted only seconds, long enough to catch the projectiles before dissipating. Demosyna smiled in satisfaction while only panting for a moment from the strain. She flexed her clawed hand into a triumphant ball and laughed at the bandits.

"Leave us. We wish you no more harm," Demosyna yelled.

Each bandit responded with a string of curses, promising to rip her pretty scales off. One rider charged with a lance, a round shield raised. Demosyna turned to Au Peirce, who was already aiming one of the precious arrows. Au Peirce's arrow struck home in the animal's neck, and it crumpled with a cry. It fell behind as the cart moved forward, but the rider was pinned. An arm-mounted shield waved as the woman was crushed by the thrashing horse, and several riders stopped to help.

There were only six bandits still circling like vultures behind the cart, which had finally rolled to a stop. The horse was exhausted, and Vaash jumped down to offer water. It slurped noisily, and Au Peirce leaped from the cart to cover the south. Demosyna sat, tired but full of jittery energy, as she took deep breaths. The focusing charm was doing better than she could have dreamed after so long being unable to do magic. It was draining in ways she never would have guessed, and Demosyna meditated while trusting her friends for protection.

One rider remained lookout while the others retreated south, where the crushed bandit was visible. Perfectly level stones forming the Highway allowed an uninterrupted view, letting the group see no help was around.

Vaash took hurried steps as he joined the women. A bolt was lodged in his cast, but Vaash was only focused on the danger behind them.

"We have to keep moving," Au Peirce said, her eyes narrow. "I can fetch soldiers if you must use your cart."

Vaash considered, turning to Demosyna.

"This one agrees. We must keep moving."

Demosyna looked at the few possessions in the humble wood cart.

"I don't really mind leaving these things, I guess, but how fast can we escape with my foot?"

Her broken foot had gotten better but was still tender when Demosyna tried to walk for long. She knew running was out of the question, and frustration rose in her mind. Even with her magic, the apprentice was finding herself useless again. A cold helplessness threatened to swallow her, and Demosyna beat the feeling back with disgust.

I am strong enough to help, Demosyna raged to the depression looming over her. *I refuse to give up when I can do something this time.*

"I won't wait around much longer."

Au Peirce eased her bow, turning her head slightly.

"I only have two arrows and will soon have to run. Let me fetch the soldiers, and she can hold them off for you, Vaash. I can be back around nightfall, as I plan to sprint! I can't let you two claim all this salvage for yourselves after all."

Vaash frowned, looking north as he considered the options. He opened his mouth to speak, but the horse made the decision for everyone. It had finished resting, it seemed, and began sprinting north along the Highway. Vaash and Au Peirce looked shocked before running to catch up. Demosyna grabbed the side as it rocked and bumped with sudden speed, a crazed smile forming. The surprise on her fellows' faces made the apprentice giddy, and she was struck with laughter from the situation.

Demosyna's companions were focused to close the distance and didn't notice the riders regroup. Vaash moved with blinding speed and jumped into the seat. Au Peirce caught up and tossed the bow into the cart. Demosyna snatched the weapon and made room in the bed. With a cry, the archer landed in the cart, helped up by Demosyna's grasping claws. Riders approached once again, and Au Peirce took the bow in her skilled hands.

Both of the remaining arrows hit a bandit, sending the women to the cold stones. Puffs of snow showed where they fell, as the Highway was still lightly dusted. Au Peirce put the bow on her back before turning to the apprentice.

"It's up to you now, Demosyna," the dark-haired woman said. "I don't think they will give me my arrows back yet."

Demosyna nodded, meditating in preparation for the persistent riders. She tried to mirror the posture Klai had taken when focusing, and Demosyna felt her mind sharpen. A few more bolts were shot, but the Wizen blocked the assault with a wave of her purple hand. The bandits were growing furious at the ever calmer apprentice and threw their last spears. One sparked against the stones a foot from a wheel, but the rest were sent flying.

Vaash called out, and Au Peirce turned to see the dot of a checkpoint in the distance. Au Peirce let out a cry of victory, turning to mock the riders.

"You stupid wretches. Come and get us if you have the nerve. We killed so many of you already! Go lick your wounds, you cowardly squids."

Her taunt worked, and the riders spurred their mounts. Demosyna sent up more defensive tornadoes and knocked one horse from the race with a broken leg wet in the sun. The last riders reached the sides of the cart, only slowed by the restrained blasts Demosyna sent. Demosyna didn't wish to send a rider off the edge, and the horses' momentum pushed through the magic.

Vaash stood on the seat, turning to scan the scene before jumping. He kicked one of the riders in the face, landing next to the limp body. Demosyna crawled through the fabric tent, depositing herself in the driver's seat. A tollbooth was ahead, miles falling past as the bony horse strained itself along. The cart slowed as the gasping beast began stopping in sight of the booth, and one of the bandits hacked at the wheels. Demosyna blasted wind toward the rider, and the sword fell to the stone highway.

Soldiers had noticed the bandits, rushing forward with armor gleaming. One threw a spear, and the intricate wood drove straight into a horse. Blood flew into the air, staining the covered cart with gore. Demosyna sat in the halted cart, slouched from exhaustion, watching her breath join the savior horse's. The old mare's chest pumped at an alarming rate, having ran in terror for hours.

Those few bandits remaining were dispatched by the soldiers now securing the Highway. Even the unconscious ones Vaash dealt with were tossed unceremoniously over the side. Only one woke after they were thrown to their deaths, and she screamed in terror for seconds. The tall elven soldiers barked orders, calling for servants.

"This one is so glad you are not hurt, Demosyna!" Vaash exclaimed. "Are you also uninjured, Au Peirce? You were amazing with your bow. That you were."

Au Peirce shrugged, slapping Demosyna roughly on the shoulder.

"I was no big deal, Vaash. They had it coming, attacking me like that. I'm just glad this little Wizen was with us. Otherwise, things may have gone different."

Demosyna laughed nervously, a manic energy flowing through her body.

"Thank you. I am glad I can be helpful!"

Vaash smiled and leaned against the cart.

"You did so well, keeping the arrows at bay. This one feels safer traveling with you, for your magic is amazing."

Demosyna blushed but smiled to her fellow travelers. The three watched the area be cleared of horses and lightly armored corpses. Several slaves, their furry ankles shackled, used mops to clean up the blood. Their gray fur was patchy, and one of their pointy ears was nearly missing. Their faces sported flat noses, and they were often called Paws, having a resemblance to felines. Demosyna was often discounted as Scale, being of a reptilian appearance. Her youth had been spent with little thought of the lines drawn. Now Demosyna pondered why seeders like her were categorized in such a way.

They shivered in rags, but before fifteen minutes had elapsed, the Highway was pristine. Even the large horses were pushed over the side with a sickening series of branches snapping. The recovering Wizen looked back south, her terror already fading into confidence. Watching the cleanup had made her heart ache, but sheer fatigue left little room for thought.

Au Peirce backtracked along their route, calling a brief farewell.

"I am going to see what I can find back here," Au Peirce told the two yellow-robed travelers. "If you wait here, I will be back. Otherwise, have a good life, my strange piranhas!"

Vaash laughed heartily and waved along with Demosyna as the archer went to loot. The monk pulled the bolt from his cast and looked at the broken flint tip. An arrow had impacted one of the metal rods acting as support, stopping the bolt's progress. A shiny glint shone through the scar in the plaster, and Vaash threw the bolt over with a whistle.

"That was a close one."

Vaash laughed, shaking his head.

"It nearly went through my arm, and that would have been yet another setback for you!"

Demosyna sighed, glad her friend was unhurt. The assault hadn't come from nowhere, as Demosyna had recognized the bandit rider. This time, however, Demosyna felt swelling pride that she tempered herself with empathy. Each arrow deflected was a badge of honor in her memory.

Demosyna watched as Vaash followed the soldiers.

I'm glad it is his turn to pay the toll, Demosyna thought. *I am so tired, I may not be able to walk yet!*

Her stomach grumbled, but Demosyna pushed the hunger away. Demosyna's actions had saved her friend, with the help of Au Peirce and her golden eyes. This was so happy a thought that the young woman felt her heart swell, seeing an easy path north. Her own abilities felt more useful than ever, and Demosyna held back tears of happiness. She could help people with her life and not just kill or fail. The uplifting idea kept the apprentice warm in the face of a snowstorm forming over the distant mountains.

Demosyna sat drinking from a half-full waterskin, having guzzled nearly all the volume. She had been extremely parched upon passing the gate, and Vaash had found a water merchant.

Au Peirce returned after sunset, snows having started falling gently on the Highway. The human archer appeared riding a long-haired white horse while leading another laden with goods. The soldiers eyed Au Peirce suspiciously as she scattered eighteen loose points onto a table without slowing. Vaash was still looking at carts offering tradeables, at the young Wizen's request.

"We need to reward our hero here," Demosyna said, stroking the exhausted horse's mane. "If there are apples, I would love to treat this wonderful animal!"

Au Peirce leaned in close to Demosyna, her painted eyes sparkling with mischief.

"I found these horses just drifting without an owner. What luck, eh?"

Demosyna saw the sturdy horses were from among those who attacked them, the familiar saddles striped with green. A heaping collection of odds and ends the archer had retrieved was placed into the cart. Blades, shields, armor, and many personal effects nearly filled the back, leaving little room for Demosyna.

"Since I killed most of them, I will take the coins," Au Peirce whispered. "Don't worry, I know you helped a bit, and I am fair. We can split this and trade it as we go along if you don't want to use any. There are some good breastplates here, but a couple have arrow holes!"

Demosyna hadn't even considered asking for any currency the archer collected. Her own purse would last for her needs, and foraging was always an elevator away.

The various sundries were mostly ordinary, and Demosyna found nothing of interest. Au Peirce put aside a few weapons, pausing to let the young woman select from the pile. Thinking of Vaash and his tendency to put himself into danger, Demosyna put aside a breastplate. She also took a pair of armguards, all of which were dense leather stained yellow.

As Au Peirce moved more into her pile, Demosyna gazed at her broken foot. There were several boots, and the Wizen took two in thought of the journey ahead.

Vaash could use a pair too, Demosyna mused, trying the boot onto her left foot. *It fits well enough and will protect this foot till my other heals enough to wear one!*

The thick yellow leather was accented at the toe and heel by metal and laced up tight to fit on her clawed foot. It was still over-sized, but the extra room allowed her claws to move inside the toe. Closed-toe shoes had always felt restrictive for the apprentice, who favored saddles till donning these boots. Demosyna grinned at her prize, and Vaash returned with apples.

"Hey, monk boy, dive in and grab something!" Au Peirce said to the man. "Demosyna hasn't chosen much, but I claim whatever she turns down for our street cleaning! We did the heavy lifting after all."

Vaash nodded, laughing.

"This one is happy without those trinkets. Thank you, friends!"

Au Peirce raised her eyebrows, sending her war paint sparkling.

"Who are you two? A humble Wise-woman and an honest monk? I better travel to the next elevator with you to sell my extra horse, then. It'll be worth more in town, and you scalawags need someone to watch your backs!"

Demosyna finished her search and took the apples.

"I would be happy to travel farther with you, Au Peirce! What do you say, Vaash?"

"This one is always happy to share life, if that is what you wish," the monk said, turning to the archer as she bagged up her haul. "But know that this one travels for Demosyna."

Au Peirce nudged Demosyna.

"Right! I won't stand in the way, believe me. I just want to keep you from driving off the edge. I've seen how you don't steer that skeleton, little Wise-woman!"

Demosyna laughed and used her crutch to move next to the weary horse. The heroic animal sniffed the apples before widening its eyes. All four were quickly devoured, and the wiry hairs on her nose tickled as the horse sniffed for more. Demosyna giggled and rubbed its neck, feeling the animal that had saved her life.

"Thank you, brave friend," Demosyna whispered into the horse's ear. "You did so well. I am proud of you! I will get you more apples each stop from now on!"

She petted the determined beast once more and heard it drinking water as she left. Vaash passed with blankets as the young apprentice returned to her seat in the bed. There was more clutter in the back after the loot joined, but Au Peirce loaded the spare horse with her prizes. The archer mounted her long-haired horse, unslinging the red bow to hold the reigns. Snow was growing heavy, but the wind seemed to die out altogether as the group set off.

From her mounted position, Au Peirce soon downed another fat goose. She added the plucked bird to the cart, and Vaash played his flute as he drove. The rested horse pulled Demosyna along in the wagon, wearing a heavy blanket against the cold. Moonlight contrasted the stains on the canvas, and Demosyna meditated on the violence she hoped to leave behind. Demosyna's new boot dangled from the back of the half-loaded cart, but the extra weight seemed to energize the horse.

A half-hearted blizzard lasted all night and showed no sign of slowing after the sun rose. The frozen travelers stopped for a rest, starting a fire and gathering the horses around for warmth. Vaash took canvas from the cart to erect a lean-to, with the slanted roof sending snow off the side. It was big enough for all three travelers to sit and for the horses to keep their heads out of the snow. None of the animals minded the flames, and Demosyna smiled at their trained beasts.

The huddled people heard no travelers pass in the storm that froze the Highway for miles. A flat stone surface gathered snow in knee-high piles at places, burying the wheels in blown ice. Blankets served to cover the horses, and the three added more wood to the fire to keep warm.

Once the small fire had thawed the group, they shoveled the snow from the exposed cart. Demosyna insisted on driving for a time, letting the kind monk take cover in the back. The storm was still dropping snow, but the sun had begun to warm the stones. Groaning piles of snow melted with abnormal speed, pouring clear water over the sides. The melting ice crashed onto the ceiling of the middle level while flowing down to rain icy water. Holes spaced along the side drank in water, creating channels where the voids directed the flow.

By midday, the road only had a light covering of snow, and travel was less hazardous. The snow continued to fall heavily, but the sun acted with the stones to clear the Highway. Au Peirce clopped alongside the wagon occasionally, singing with Vaash's music as she led her loot. She paused once and spent some time trading.

A passing merchant stopped an eye-catching cart, calling out with promises of low prices. Vaash waved as the archer disappeared from view.

* * * * *

Night arrived, bringing a welcome end to the snow. Neither friend was hungry, so they passed wine over the fire. The apprentice found the leather armguards and handed them to Vaash, smiling widely.

"I thought you could use these," Demosyna said, sitting back down near the fire. "I also set aside a breastplate and pair of good boots, if you want new shoes."

Vaash thanked the woman, his eyes dancing with joy.

"This is a wonderful gift, my friend. You are too kind! It even matches this one's robes!"

The man seemed years younger as he put on the right guard. After lashing the buckles, Vaash flexed the leather with a straining creak. The dull remains of an imperial crest showed the bandit had repurposed a piece of low-ranked armor. Vaash smiled, but his eyes seemed sad as he looked at the dark-yellow leather. Demosyna widened her eyes, suddenly aware of what the gift might recall in the man.

"I'm sorry, Vaash," Demosyna said, putting her hand on his shoulder. "I only thought of you because you blocked the arrow with your arm. I didn't mean to upset you."

Vaash smiled warmly, and his eyes met hers.

"It is a wonderful gesture, Demosyna. Thank you. This one's past is just that, past. It remains of course, but this one can choose to grow beyond. Such is life, and this one loves all in life."

Vaash took the woman's hand and squeezed it slightly. The two sat holding hands, waiting for their new friend to find them. Au Peirce rode up eventually, scanning the night for any food. The horse she led was nearly empty, clopping lazily behind. Demosyna raised a hand in greeting while still grasping her friend's hand near the warm fire.

"Over here, Au Peirce," the fading apprentice called, sleepy eyes blinking. "It's good to see you again!"

Au Peirce dismounted and smirked at the two.

"It seems that way. I will leave you alone since you look busy."

Vaash blushed slightly and removed his hand before taking out his flute. He began playing a light tune, and Demosyna laughed.

"We are just good friends, Au Peirce, and nothing more," Demosyna told the archer. "I don't want you to get the wrong idea. He is the kindest person I have met, and I love being his friend!"

The archer frowned, considering as she brushed her horses. She joined the two at the fire after securing her mount to the cart. That answer seemed to satisfy the woman, and Au Peirce put her latest bird over the coals.

All the magic she had used days ago was catching up, and Demosyna wished her companions a good evening. Her blanket smelled vaguely of horse, but the Wizen barely noticed.

* * * * *

The next leg of her journey passed so quickly that Demosyna found herself approaching twin elevators. Au Peirce had ridden beside the cart, mostly silently as she scouted during that week. No more snow fell, and the cart creaked to a stop before the latest checkpoint.

After taking her turn to pay the toll, Demosyna asked Vaash to make a few purchases. He took a handful of coins Demosyna passed, careful of watching eyes.

"If you can find a pocket telescope or maybe a writing set," Demosyna requested. "I want to at least start penning letters to my Order since I've seen mail carts pass us. And as always, get some apples for our friend here!"

Vaash nodded, smiling.

"This one would be happy to help. The offerings are slim sometimes, however."

Au Peirce joined through the tollgate, moving off to allow traffic through. She spoke with the elevator operator, waiting for the rising platform, gesturing at the spare horse. After exchanging a few points, the archer walked over.

"The nearest town should be only a short ride away," Au Peirce said, looking slightly west. "I am going to sell the rest of this plunder and continue my search. It was interesting meeting you, Demosyna. Say goodbye to Vaash for me."

Demosyna nodded, smiling widely.

"I will, Au Peirce. Thank you for traveling with us for so long. I really enjoyed watching you shoot your bow and hope you find your cousin!"

"You may run into me again," Au Peirce said, smirking at the Wizen. "After I sell this nag, I will use my Empress's Highway to find that headstrong boy and knock some sense into him. I stay around each elevator for a day or two, checking the area before moving on. If you travel along the Highway again, I will likely see your bright robes a mile off! Lucky for you, I won't mistake you two for bandits, with your cute matching outfits."

Demosyna laughed, holding back tears from the parting of a potential friend. She didn't instantly click with Au Peirce as she had with Vaash, but Demosyna still felt a connection with the spirited woman. Her plight for a lost friend and her often stern outlook were understandable to the young apprentice.

The Highway proved a double-edged sword, and Demosyna felt stronger for having met Au Peirce along its endless lengths. It was the same with Vaash, whom she saw walking back, and Demosyna marveled at how she had grown. Vaash had allowed the woman to flourish in this cold land, and Demosyna would always love him for that.

CHAPTER 22

"I wanna see doggies!" a young child shrieked as he threw himself onto the stones. "Doggies, doggies, doggies!"

The boy's birthers picked him up, ignoring the tears streaming down his scaled face. He, along with his parents, was dressed in fine robes that were bold in the afternoon light. Large cloth banners, each displaying the same insignia, served to provide shade to those waiting atop the Highway. A checkpoint was within view, but Demosyna saw that the line was still barely moving.

Advertisements flapped between wooden supports, the Three Paw logo waving toward the traffic. Demosyna had been shocked to see the coverings over the Highway, enclosing the stones in a tall box. Before spying them appear over the horizon, wooden checkpoints had been the only landmarks. The tollbooth ahead was choked with traffic with hundreds of bodies and dozens of carts all waiting. The memory had been exciting, seeing a new sight on the unending gray highway, but Demosyna now felt terribly bored. She inched the cart forward for the hundredth time, and the ancient horse stamped a hoof.

Their line had seemed small, but the Wizen now saw the truth—that it was massively clogged. So many people wished to descend these elevators that on both sides of the checkpoint, crowds bustled. A general chatter had allowed Demosyna to gather the reason behind the delay. The town just off the Highway was famous for a canine circus, having formed from wealth the carnival provided. Demosyna had seen the town before entering the covered area and felt a pang at viewing the mock volcano centered in the city.

It had been a common sight, living as she had in the Empress's cities, for woven cloth to adorn buildings and resemble volcanoes. Banners would be attached to roofs, hanging in smooth curves till touching the bottoms of pillars. The effect was such that a plaza would appear as a mountain, the fabric patterned to be lifelike.

Chimneys from atop the central building puffed clouds of smoke, making the volcano seem ready to erupt. The false volcano Demosyna had spied from atop the Highway had been active, billowing clouds rising for all to see. It was an effective lure, as the carnival drew massive crowds that Demosyna now waited among.

A toll was posted at twenty-seven points, nearly twice the previous, and Vaash removed a round gold piece. Vaash was nearly able to pass the gated checkpoint and seemed eager to be done with the line as well. The wait to the elevators formed arcs, northbound and southbound traffic streaming to their respective elevator. Demosyna funded the refilling of water, and the two eventually led their wagon onto a platform. It was the first time they had left the Highway, and Demosyna gazed at a forest now dwarfing her. Vaash took them along the least trafficked road as the bony horse pulled the wagon with practiced grace.

Like the initial culture shock while selling bread, Demosyna was amazed at the sea of faces. Humans, Orcs, Paws, Scales, and ornately dressed elves streamed toward town, happy voices chattering away. Vaash expressed his desire to visit the carnival, and Demosyna agreed after seeing the man's excitement. The apprentice had known dogs while a child at her Orders but found them intimidating. Demosyna had been puny for a girl, and the stocky nursery dogs often overshadowed the girl. The keen eyes of the animals would seek her out, it seemed, and sharp teeth would fill the toddler's vision.

Those dogs never bit Demosyna, but the looming wolfish faces had left an impression on the young woman. She didn't classify the emotion as fear exactly but a healthy respect for the dangerous-looking beasts. Demosyna put her own unease away, wanting to treat her friend to a diversion. Her trip had been relatively dull, save meeting Au Peirce during the attacks, and Demosyna wanted to see anything but flat stones. The young apprentice had sold loot that Au Peirce didn't want and felt she had money to spare.

"I can watch the cart if you get tickets!" Demosyna said once they found a spot to park.

"This one is very grateful for the kindness, Demosyna."

Vaash was barely able to avoid looking at the entrance.

"This one can purchase a ticket if you wish."

Demosyna shook her head.

"It is my treat, Vaash. Take these and hurry back!"

The apprentice handed the beaming man three circular coins, and Vaash joined the line for admission.

Demosyna took out the crude map she had bartered from Au Peirce. They had been nearly halfway along the length when Au Peirce departed according to the roughly drawn map. Now the young woman put the progression at halfway, if not slightly over. Demosyna smiled to herself while watching the stubborn horse nibble grass.

Vaash was a yellow smear in the line, and Demosyna grabbed the writing set dug up from a trader. It was a simple collection of tools, having a pen and ink stored inside a wooden tablet. A cork strip at the hinged top allowed paper to be secured, letting the user write nearly anywhere. Demosyna used the light of the late afternoon to begin writing, gathering her thoughts as she did. The first was a general update regarding the disastrous outcome of her voyage. The apprentice felt it was her duty to relate the events to a Wise Mother, being the last Wise-woman able to complete the original mission. Demosyna detailed the events of the naval assault and the execution of her own Wise Mother.

The apprentice's recent magical proficiency was described, along with her monk friend. She ended the letter with a request for assistance and gave her approximate location along the Highway. Demosyna let the purple ink dry before rolling the page into a tube. She put the scroll into a chest pocket before starting the next letter. This page was filled with a description of Demosyna's lost friends, from their coloration to a time frame of their disappearance.

Demosyna wasn't talented at drawing but described her lost friends in detail. The apprentice paused after reviewing the text and added the reward of a gold piece for incentive.

That will have to do, Demosyna thought as Vaash was lost to view. *I have to hope they found each other.*

As the sun began to set, it cast the town in red shadows. Demosyna used the remaining light to write a final letter on her new tablet. This notice was a duplicate of the previous, offering a reward for the location of her lost friends.

The purple-scaled woman signed the letter Demosyna, feeling that calling herself Wise would be presumptuous. The powerful wind magic she had begun to master lifted the woman's spirits, but she resisted self-adulation.

I can defend with my magic, Demosyna thought, eyeing her missing big toe. *But I need more, like healing spells. If only I could heal my body at once like Klai did with her golden rings of magic.*

Demosyna shook her head of the saltwater-filled memory and focused on their landlocked position. The vibrant town was beyond sight of the ocean, with forests and hills blocking the view of the seas. Hopeful memories of strong magics would not serve the young woman here, and Demosyna rolled the dry poster.

"My mind and learned skills will have to be enough," Demosyna muttered to herself, watching the line march forward. "My foot still needs to heal, so I can't search myself. At least I am literate, unlike many that aren't elven."

Her orphan status had allowed Demosyna to be raised among the elite Wise-woman Orders, but she was a rarity considering the predominant elven alumni. Already, Demosyna found her education a benefit, as well as something to avoid flaunting.

"So what if I have read books about the Fist?" Demosyna mused, frowning slightly. "So much is waiting to be known. I have to accept there is more than I was taught."

The young woman used her carved, leather-wrapped crutch to move and tie cloth strips of canvas together. A covered frame shielded the items in their cart, and Demosyna unhitched the elderly horse. Using a length of rope, Demosyna let the noble horse graze nearby after securing the line. Vaash returned as the woman rested to watch the crowd pass.

"This one has purchased passes into the city," Vaash exclaimed, handing Demosyna a thick piece of paper. "Would you like to see the last family show of the night?"

Demosyna smiled and nodded.

"Lead the way, Vaash. I would love to enjoy a good performance!"

Vaash escorted the apprentice through the torchlit entry, hurried along by a stream of visitors.

Wooden shacks lined the roads while offering novelty goods with eye-catching colors. Ignoring these stalls, Demosyna followed the yellow-robed man past the imitation volcano. A round imperial tower was central to the sprawling town, and this allowed easy access to any road. The light was failing, but torches illuminated an amphitheater with dancing flames. An oval circuit was enclosed by stepped seating, and Demosyna sat with Vaash once he found a vacant space.

The packed dirt arena housed obstacles, from rings and tunnels to ladders and ponds, that would entertain the onlookers. A racetrack enclosed the entire field with low wooden fences making a loop. The bleachers were patrolled by elderly animals, and many children petted the beasts. Several of the animals were missing limbs, hopping on three legs as they braved the stairs. Those hounds seemed happy, receiving affection from the crowds, but Demosyna felt a pang upon seeing the old wounds.

Topless men wandered the seating, offering drinks and snacks with bashful smiles. Vaash was fixated on the ringmaster wandering the field, inspecting the area before the final show. A long-haired dog carrying a logo-stamped barrel on a collar sniffed blindly at Demosyna. The old hound was standing on three shaky legs and startled the young Wise-woman with its wet nose. Its once brown eyes were cloudy, but the fuzzy dog whined playfully. Demosyna patted the soft fur, smiling despite her trepidation at having a hungry grin next to her face. Vaash laughed loudly, turning to see the happy animal.

"What a good girl. That you are," Vaash gushed over the dog, who licked his face. "This one is glad to know you!"

The dog grew more excited, rolling onto a bony spine to expose a warm belly. Vaash dived in while rubbing the large canine as it squirmed. Sharp teeth shone, and Demosyna carefully patted the dog's head as it voiced happy barks.

"You aren't so scary, are you, girl?" the young woman asked. "You just want some love! You can't help having such big teeth, can you?"

The dog continued dancing on her back, stretching a remaining front limb and grinning. The injury that took the leg had long ago healed, and the animal was making do without it. Not all the retired dogs sported missing limbs, but enough did that Demosyna noticed one each time she scanned the bleachers. The crowds seemed to love the wandering attractions, and Demosyna sighed.

"They deserve love after losing a paw," Demosyna pondered as Vaash continued petting the animal. "I suppose it's a good thing, letting them be useful."

A small man, his chest exposed, caught the apprentice's attention with a tray. Demosyna held up two fingers, pointing to the small wooden cups of wine he offered.

"Thirty points, smooth scale," the man said, winking a bright-blue eye. "I wish I could do better for such a charming Scale, but alas, I cannot!"

Demosyna smiled at the flattery, handing over the coins. The young man departed with a sly smile while eyeing Vaash. The old dog stood, and her entire back side wagged from happiness. Vaash was grinning like a child, his face lighting up as he watched the dog.

"Thank you, Demosyna," Vaash said after taking a cup. "This one loves dogs and always has!"

"It's no problem, Vaash," the Wizen replied, sipping the diluted wine. "Looks like the final show is going to start!"

The elf pacing the field had found a place in the center, her gold-trimmed clothes shining a dark red. A cone helped the elegant ringmaster be heard over the ruckus.

"Gentlemen and ladies, thank you for joining us tonight for the best show in the Fist!"

Roars of agreement followed.

"We have a wonderful assortment of tricks that will captivate the most jaded hearts! Watch as crafty canines cavort and dancing dogs delight! We offer the widest array of talented tricks, of exotic entertainment, of death-defying demonstrations that will leave you dumbfounded and delirious!"

Applause blanketed the arena, Vaash clapping wildly and whistling, and the red-shirted elf continued.

"To begin this final show, we offer you a glimpse into the past."

The ringmaster motioned to a closed door.

"The crowd favorite has returned from retirement! Let them hear it, folks. It's the Terrifying Three-Pawed Trio!"

The metal door opened, releasing three wolves into the oval field. Each had a limb missing and hopped along as the crowd roared with delight. They were old gray wolves with sharp muzzles revealing predatory teeth.

From her seat midway up the stands, Demosyna saw the defeated animals trot out to the hoots of the masses. Each elderly wolf moved with stiff joints, but their eyes were sharp as the hunters circled. On a gesture from the statuesque elf, the wolves stood on their hind legs and howled. The powerful animals held a single forepaw to the sky, releasing a mournful call.

Vaash applauded with the rest of those attending, and Demosyna smiled at the display. The gray wolves balanced for nearly a minute while howling over the thundering adulation. They marched back through the door after righting themselves, using their remaining front leg to lope along.

The young Wise-woman had never seen live wolves, only having crude pictures and dry text to imagine them. Their muscular frames dwarfed the dogs in the stands, and Demosyna shivered at the sight of the predators. The Three Paw logo waved from banners around the stadium, and Demosyna better understood the meaning upon seeing the wolves.

Vaash sipped the small cup of wine and watched as the elf lit several rings with a torch.

"Next, my fine friends, feast your eyes on the fastest fleet of fur for five fortnights! The Greased Lightning Greyhounds!"

The ringmaster waved a tall hat in signal.

Children jumped in excitement, babbling as ten greyhounds were locked in the racetrack. A red-robed elf stood at the gate before raising a hand to produce a ball of blood. The trim dogs smelled the liquid and jumped toward the sphere. A Wizen laughed and sent the magic hurtling around the track, leading the foaming animals along. Her straight brown hair danced in the breeze, and the carnival's Wise-woman sent the dogs on another lap around the oval.

"Look at these magnificent, majestic marathoners! Such speed, such sleek and slender silvery sights!" the ringmaster said, whipping the crowd into a frenzy.

The greyhounds continued to chase the hovering orb of blood, and more dogs joined the show at a flourish from the booming elf ringmaster.

"Cripple Cavern hosts the Three Paw Park and lets me bring you such spectacular shows!"

The ruby-shirted elf held out an arm as a line of people joined the dogs.

"That is why I am proud to introduce the hardworking people of Cripple Cavern. Each one is provided a cute canine companion to complete the contract clauses! That's right, every employee of Three Paw Park gets an officially bred puppy!"

A stream of red-clothed people paraded around, smiling and walking dogs in a flashy display. Many of the dogs were medium-sized, long hair waving, but large and small dogs pranced around the ring. Several of the smaller dogs were carried by their owners, shivering in the noise, but the larger dogs held their humans on saddled backs. The crowd went wild, and a few dogs did tricks for the children. Greyhounds ran with determination after the tempting blood ball, lapping the slow parade as the crowd cheered.

The ringmaster's jet-black hair shone in the starlight, and the parade of employees marched through the metal door. Some of the greyhounds had lain down from exhaustion, but many pushed themselves into another lap. It was several more minutes of chase before the last animal collapsed. Applause sounded in happy waves, and Demosyna had to stand to see over the onlookers.

"Now for the main event, gentlemen and ladies! Our dogs are bred to be the smartest, the fastest, the most loyal animals to walk the Fist! Watch, my fine patrons, as our vast array of canines perform feats that will surely amaze! That is the Three Paw promise, for our dogs do more with three paws than others can with four!"

The crowd went wild at the slogan, and nearly fifty trilegged dogs flew from the open door. Greyhounds were carried off the outer racetrack, panting feverishly as they left. Nearly each of the fifty dogs was of a different breed with their coats flashing in the torchlight. They all hopped and ran along, using the playground constructed just for that purpose. Many of the dogs jumped into the ponds scattered around the field, splashing and howling with joy.

Several of the smaller dogs ran in frenzied paths between obstacles. They would run over a seesaw, balancing as the wood tottered, and dart through a tunnel of fabric. The grinning dogs would emerge from the opposite side before jumping over a series of rising bars. One canine failed to jump high enough to clear a final hurdle and yelped as it impacted the wood. The others continued their all-out running, leaving the limping dog to wander away.

A medium-sized dog, clean black hair waving, led a pack as he ran and jumped in excitement. The ebony-haired dog would run for several steps and then spring into the air with his legs tucked. He would sail through the flickering light while seeming to float above the dirt ground. Just before he would have fallen, the impish dog balanced on three legs to run forward again. He circled the field as the audience applauded, letting his momentum carry him through the air.

Demosyna laughed at the antics, watching the dog lead the followers as he pranced. He acted like a spry deer, bounding around the ring with strong legs pumping away. An initial worry at being near so many dogs faded, and Demosyna enjoyed the fantastic display.

More packs formed, chasing one another in playful barking groups. Several wrestled in the dirt, kicking up blooms of beige excitement. A group of red-robed employees joined the show while juggling three balls each. Nearly twenty of the chaotic animals noticed and ran to sit at the jugglers' feet. Bright-red balls sailed into the sky, the jugglers having thrown them one by one. Fifteen balls arced before the crowd with eager dogs sprinting after. The victorious dogs ran across the field, displaying their prizes in sharp jaws.

Dogs fetched and returned the toys with determined speed, panting into the echoing amphitheater. The ringmaster produced a silver whistle, making a grand show of blowing the signal. Many of the smaller dogs stopped their running, moving to sit before the elf. A series of notes caused the trained animals to jump over one another while circling the ringmaster. The agile canines sprang sideways, launching their small bodies over the dog standing next to them.

Some of the more energetic dogs did somersaults as they responded to the shrill whistle. The audience clapped, throwing purchased scraps of jerky into the arena. This caused dashes for the meat, and snarling teeth fought for any morsels. Many of the children took great handfuls of flesh, hurling them with high-pitched laughter. Some larger dogs barked to scare off the scrambling pack and eat the jerky themselves.

The tallest dogs limped over to the edge of the ring, straining their necks to catch treats. Snapping jaws seized the salty meat from midair before swallowing the food in a few bites. A long whistle drew the dogs' attention, and the ringmaster called loudly to the crowd once more.

"What a dynamic display!" the elf bellowed as the dogs gathered. "Watch now as they beg for their food!"

Each dog around the elf stood on their back legs, balancing carefully for those missing a hind paw. All the red-shirted jugglers fetched the jerky, shuffling over to the canines. After all the jittery dogs had a bit of meat on their snouts, the ringmaster did a slow pirouette.

The dogs waited with puffing breath clouding the scene, and the grand elf gave the signal. In a flurry of motion, each hound threw their piece of jerky behind their head. Arcs of red meat sailed, and rows of dogs ate the tossed treats. Nearly every dog got a bit of jerky, their trained antics enabling a rain of food to fall near each canine. The rings of dogs swarmed, devouring the scraps with wide eyes.

After the frenzy subsided, the energetic animals returned to their frivolities. For over half an hour, the dogs entertained the screaming mass, jumping and running to the cheers from raised stands. A pack of muscle-bound dogs began digging with their good front paws, sending rocks into the crowd. A pit of earth formed, and the pack wrestled in the newly dug hole. The ringmaster directed the dogs that jumped and danced around her, and the evening grew colder.

"Fear not, faithful friends! A final surprise awaits! Once these talented tripaws have left to dream, a unique treat can be enjoyed by any adventurous child! That's right. A fresh litter of certified Three Paw pups are eager to be taken home!"

A quartet of shrill tones called the dogs' attention when the brightly clothed ringmaster spoke. The mass of dogs was herded off the field while the ringmaster bellowed, tails wagging and howls calling. Every dog jumped through a burning hoop before leaving, barking as they avoided the flames. A few stragglers left swimming in ponds were hurried along with boots to the rear. The crowd laughed as the yelping dogs ran through the metal door standing at one end of the field. As Vaash watched with childlike wonder, over a hundred puppies were trotted out.

Large dogs were used to support baskets that teemed with squirming puppies. A few small bodies wiggled their way out, falling to the dust with helpless cries. After the caravan of young life reached the ringmaster, she turned to address the remaining people. Some of the onlookers had begun to depart, leading their children, who strained to see.

"The floor is open to any child that wishes to hold one of these purebred pups!" the raven-haired ringmaster exclaimed. "Come down and play with the next stars of the Three Paw Park!"

Fresh red-shirted employees joined the scene as streams of flailing children accepted the invitation. Rough lines were formed, and each child selected a ball of fur. A new form of chaos issued forth as children pranced about with their fuzzy new playthings. Red-clothed wranglers rushed here and there, but the seeder children petted and wrestled with the animals.

The small glass of wine she had purchased was empty, and Demosyna searched for another salesboy. The apprentice flagged one down as the children were being escorted off the field, some crying at being separated from the puppies. Demosyna exchanged a handful of coins to refill both cups, taking Vaash's from his hand. The show had been a wonderful alternative to the endless highway, and Demosyna stood sipping her drink. A stream of bodies was pouring from the stadium, their coats flashing in the torchlight.

"I wish to thank all the families that joined us today, because that is what makes the Fist great!" the ring leader called to the departing people. "Thank you to the fine people of Cripple Cavern, who work so hard to make Three Paw Park the best!"

The stone seating was emptying of families, young voices trying to convince their parents into a tour of the kennels. Demosyna sat down while watching the majority of the crowd depart through the arched doorways. Any dug holes were filled with shovels, and the arena returned to its generic state.

"We will take a short intermission to set up the evening show," the ornately clad ringleader shouted. "The betting halls are now open, and all free people are welcome to place a coin on the coming games!"

Vaash laughed with shining green eyes.

"That was an astounding show! Thank you for treating this one to such a wonder!"

Demosyna nodded, finishing her meager cup of wine.

"Did you want to watch the evening show?"

"Were you able to stay and watch? This one doesn't wish to pressure, but dogs are a welcome presence."

The monk scanned the freshly leveled arena. Demosyna smiled at the man.

"I need to stretch my leg, but we can watch the evening show once I limber up a bit!"

The pair left the stadium, passing booths to warm up at the mock volcano. A rounded imperial building held the kitchens required to produce the food sold and allowed chilly figures to huddle under the banners. Pleasing aromas hung in the air, making Demosyna's stomach growl. The young woman smiled, patting her belly, and knew she wasn't truly hungry. The apprentice had eaten the previous day and felt that the lingering smells of cooking were tricking her appetite.

Her night was full of stars, and Demosyna watched families exiting the town. Children carried balls of fur in their arms, laughing at the new pet. Their puppies squirmed, barely able to open tiny eyes while taken to a new home. Demosyna smiled, watching the adorable crowd mill through the gate set into the town's stone wall.

As the noise faded with the bulk of the tourists, rattling chains could be heard faintly as janitors began cleaning the streets. A collection of shackled humans, some wielding brooms, shuffled in the alleyways. Nobody noticed the line of people cleaning, and the seeders avoided eye contact with the townspeople. From her place under the volcano banners, Demosyna saw people walk right by slaves as they righted a potted tree. Even the children were too busy to bother, and the cuffed figures struggled along.

The process was fast, and Demosyna watched the slaves return the town to pristine order. Humans melted back into the shadows of an alley, and the young Wise-woman shook her head. It wasn't getting any easier for the young Wizen to witness such blatant captivity, and Demosyna held back a tear.

Both friends felt warmed by the roaring kitchen fires and returned to the stadium. The large open-air arena had been emptied of nearly all its crowd, leaving only clusters of adults on the steps. Topless serving girls joined the boys to offer refreshments, wearing brightly colored pants that clung to their figures. Now the wine offered was of a larger size, Demosyna saw with a grin, and many of the waiting audience purchased mugs. Vaash handed her a waterskin after sipping a bit, and Demosyna tipped the skin back with thanks.

"What can I get you, smooth scale? The show will begin shortly, so don't forget to place your bets!"

A tall elf walked up the stairs, smiling sweetly and motioning to a tray. Demosyna paid for the costly drinks, getting two glasses of red wine. Vaash accepted his with a smile, putting it beside him after taking a sip. The young Wise-woman didn't know what show was next but had no desire to place a wager. Demosyna had seen gambling on the boat and often witnessed the heartbreak it caused the losers in a bet.

I barely have enough for the tolls as it stands now, Demosyna thought as carts were wheeled into the arena. *This carnival is fun, but I should be more careful with how much I spend from now on.*

The attention of the audience was drawn to the racetrack, where red-robed Wizened unloaded carts. Cruel metal traps were placed along the length of the track, hinged jaws open wide. These dark iron bear traps dotted the outer circle and were randomly placed along the distance. The Wizened would wave a hand, opening the jaws with magical flair, to applause from the crowd.

"I can see a lot of eager faces out there tonight," the red-clothed ringmaster shouted. "Now that the track is complete, all betting is stopped."

Several Wizened returned to the stadium, and all five sent large fireballs into the night sky. Demosyna watched in wonder as the burning spheres spun around one another, exploding high in the air when one impacted its neighbor. The crowd cheered, stamping their feet in a frenzy of noise.

"That signals the first round of the Three Paw races!"

The elf's voice was an echoing call.

"Bring out the lucky racers!"

Five dogs were led to the large racetrack now strewn with dangerous obstacles. Demosyna gasped, dawning horror clouding her mind at the sight. Each of the dogs stood panting and slightly nervous at the booming stadium. One Wise-woman remained in the track, her red robes waving in the breeze. A great ball of flame was conjured at the ringmaster's signal behind the idle dogs. The crowd stood and yelled at the dogs, overpowering their cries of dismay.

All five racers sped away from the fire, sprinting on four legs with terror in their eyes. Each dog had a number painted on its side, and as the animals ran, wooden fences held them. The majority avoided the bear traps, but upon reaching the turn, one golden-haired dog stepped into the snare. A yelp of pain followed the metallic crunch when the trap was sprung.

Demosyna put her hand to her mouth, and Vaash went white at the poor animal's struggles. The carnival Wise-woman had been walking behind the fireball, urging the dogs to run. When the blood-robed Wizen opened the jaws enough for the dog to escape, it limped away with a crippled leg held close. The Wise-woman laughed, shaking her head in exaggerated frustration, and called the injured dog. It returned, crying and yelping with each step.

A fireball chased the other dogs around the bend, continuing the race while the elf knelt. The dog was licking its shattered leg, and the Wise-woman patted its head. A cloud of golden light surrounded the yellow dog, and its leg stopped bleeding. The dog looked with surprise at the paw, barking loudly over the laughing spectators.

The energy hadn't been uniform rings, but Demosyna recognized the magic for a healing spell. Fur was missing where the trap had ripped its flesh, but the dog was licking the carnival Wizen. The crowd cheered the dogs, and the rest ran the race without stepping in a trap. Number one finished her lap well ahead of the others, and the ringmaster led the frightened animal into the arena. The fireball rocketed upward after the last turn, exploding with a pointed finger from the Wise-woman. This lone firework signaled the end of the race, and many gamblers ripped their receipts up.

"That was horrible," Demosyna breathed, holding back tears as the gold dog was taken away. "The Wise-woman can heal the dogs at least, but I don't feel right about treating them like that. It seems unnecessary if people just want to bet on a race."

Vaash sat down after the race, holding his head in his hands. The young Wise-woman sat beside him, trying to be heard over those still applauding. Vaash was crying softly and wiped his eyes before turning to Demosyna.

"This one had no idea the race would be so brutal," Vaash said with terror in his voice. "How could people enjoy that every night? This one wished only for a race, not blood sports!"

Demosyna sipped at the half-full glass.

"I am sorry we had to see that, Vaash. I didn't expect the race to be so violent either! We should leave before the next one."

The monk nodded wordlessly, stifling his tears. Demosyna stood and grabbed her crutch before the ringmaster bellowed another announcement.

"What a race!"

The elf removed her tall hat and bowed.

"We are pleased to open betting again! For those that stay to watch our employees set up, I offer an opportunity! If anyone is able to catch our winning dog, they get to keep it! It's only a single gold piece to compete, so come on down and win a Three Paw winner!"

Demosyna had begun shuffling to the exit but turned to watch people scramble to the track. Many were still drinking from large cups, stumbling as they laughed. The dog with the large blue number 1 painted on its side was put into the track, and the assembled group was handed clubs.

A rising feeling of nausea swept upon Demosyna, seeing the laughing faces swinging the weapons. The dog that had won the race looked on with suspicion, trotting away slowly from those now armed with clubs. The young apprentice didn't realize her grip had gone slack, and the cup tumbled to the stone steps with a clatter. Her remaining wine spilled down rows of seating, and Demosyna raised a hand to her mouth.

The rowdy few who accepted the ringmaster's offer ran after the dog, laughing loudly. The dog barked and ran between the open traps with its long tail tucked in fear. One of the tipsy chasers threw his club at the dog, making it yelp when it struck the animal's ribs. The announcer was shouting to the crowd, but Demosyna didn't hear as a thin tone filled her head. Demosyna felt cold sweat form and closed her watery eyes.

A group had chased the dog once around the track and paused to catch their breath. None of the traps had been stepped in, but Demosyna had seen enough. She tried to hold herself together, but Demosyna found that her body had its own plans.

Dark vomit erupted from behind her shaking hand, and the apprentice felt waves of disgust fill her. Watching the show had upset Demosyna, but her contempt manifested through heaves of nausea. Vaash appeared beside the apprentice and rubbed her back with his good hand. Tears of embarrassment fell, and Demosyna felt the last wave of nausea subside. Several people had noticed the pair of brightly robed travelers and mocked them loudly as Vaash helped Demosyna from the stadium.

The apprentice passed a few chained figures carrying mops and mumbled an apology through a dizzy head.

"I'm sorry for the mess," Demosyna nearly whispered, shocking the slave into looking up.

A man in shackles blinked in clear surprise but went with his fellow servants to clean. Demosyna saw that the steps where she had purged were stained deep red in the torchlight. The janitors quickly had the stones cleared, and Demosyna walked with Vaash to the nearest tavern. She found a table with three chairs, and Vaash left Demosyna to order drinks. Demosyna sat in the noise, barely hearing it over the memories in her eye.

The apprentice used a chair to prop her foot up, sipping from the waterskin to get the taste from her mouth. Three Paw banners hung around the tavern, and Demosyna saw coasters that bore the insignia. Raw anger surged in her heart, and Demosyna turned the disc over to hide its logo. She sat in the splintery chair, fuming at the barbaric turn of events in the carnival. The apprentice wished to leave the town behind and waited patiently for Vaash to ask his opinion on continuing their warpath north.

CHAPTER 23

The two saddened travelers drank slowly from their cups, ignoring the logo. Midnight had come and gone, but Demosyna wasn't tired after witnessing the races. Anger burning in her body kept the apprentice wide awake, and Vaash sat silently beside her with his face still ashen. Loud fireballs exploded from beyond the tavern, and Demosyna knew they signaled yet more cruel races. First ten, then twenty explosions reverberated, and Demosyna stopped bothering to count.

The young woman considered purchasing a dog, if only to spare it such a life. Talk from within the bustling tavern dissuaded that thought, as Demosyna overheard the asking price for a single animal.

"Fifty gold pieces for a runty puppy?" one inebriated man exclaimed. "And they want thirty for a retired show dog! The show was great, but I'm not the Empress! How do they think anyone can afford that with the war on? I just wanted someone to take along during training, like a war hound, ya know?"

"No war talk. You promised!" his elf friend said, leaning on the bar. "You can find your sister once you join up with us! But tonight, we celebrate you signing a twenty-year contract!"

The elf was dressed in custom armor and purchased another drink for the man barely standing already. The two stumbled from the bar, laughing and boasting about previous feats. Demosyna had less than ten gold pieces left and felt that rescuing a dog was beyond her.

An elf of average height dressed in soiled green traveling gear smoked a pipe and tuned a harp. Demosyna had seen the elf sit, nursing a mug of dark beer once finding a chair. Her forest clothes were soggy at the cuffs, but the stranger had a pair of short swords that looked pristine.

> The Empress is so wonderfully kind.
> She gave the low her stony spine.
> Now we have no more excuse
> not to grab a sword and clean our boots.
>
> She gave law to the Fort once more.
> Let her name be spoken for all to adore!
> Bark your voices to the night
> and wag Three Paws in shows of might.
> The Fist remains within her sight,
> for she watches from our highway's heights!

The elf sang to the rowdy patrons of the tavern, overpowering the clinking glasses. She used her harp to pluck a melody, laughing to the audience. The bard played a solo on the harp after a mug was handed over and drank the ale before placing the empty glass on her head. Her song continued, and the cheers from the listeners filled the building. After more verses, the elf smiled and offered her cap for tips. Many of the people gathered dropped triangles in, drinking merrily.

"I know, I know!" the grinning bard yelled. "Calm down, you milkers. It's a work in progress! I put that bit about dogs for you people, but I will sing it again once I visit the next time! It should be done by then. But how about a classic Empress ballad in the place of my half-finished song?"

A loud affirmative from the drinkers led the musician to sing a long song about the Empress. She strummed and plucked with both hands, making a complex tune with the harp. Demosyna found the music enchanting, but the noise was giving her a headache. Vaash agreed to retire to their wagon, and the two exited the town with slow feet.

Demosyna looked idly at her new boot, its yellow leather capped with black iron.

"How much longer till I can remove this cast?" the woman asked, scratching her leg. "I don't want to stay here and need to be able to walk freely again."

The songs praising the Empress had raised images of cruel soldiers throwing a life away. Such behavior was contrary to all the apprentices had been told about the Empress. Anger still burned in her heart as Demosyna drank from the last full waterskin. Nearly all the soldiers encountered in the Fist had seemed bloodthirsty and callous, unlike the formal compliments from Demosyna's home Orders. Their wagon was set off the main road into town, surrounded by trees that the ancient horse slept under.

"This one can remove it next week since your toes are healing straight!" the gentle man responded after inspecting the foot. "You are doing so well, already able to walk on it! This one is proud of you, as always."

Demosyna smiled sadly, accepting the news with a sigh.

"That is promising, I suppose. Let's rest tonight and leave this town tomorrow!"

"While we are discussing your foot, my friend, would you like me to fashion you a prosthetic?"

Vaash gazed into the woman's yellow eyes.

"It would look like a toe, at least from afar. That it would."

Demosyna hadn't considered such a thing and frowned nervously.

"Will I need one to walk?"

Vaash shook his red-haired head.

"No. You may simply have to get used to a new balance without the cast. Once your cast is off, we can fit the metal to your foot."

The empty space next to her toes still gave the Wise-woman a start, never quite expecting to see the void. The sound of a replacement toe, fake though it would be, excited the apprentice. Demosyna watched the master monk gather tools from a pack, smiling happily as he rummaged. Demosyna nodded at the man, thanking Vaash for his kind thought.

"Vaash, can you train me to better control my magic?" Demosyna asked, having been considering requesting for days. "I am slowly improving, but is there anything you can teach me about balance? Or maybe control of myself?"

The human monk was silent for a long time, considering the question carefully. Vaash flexed the arm wearing the dark-yellow armguard with tears in his eyes.

"This one can teach you control, my friend!" Vaash exclaimed with a laugh. "The old Orders' ways are not ones of magic, but similar effects can be obtained."

To demonstrate, Vaash glanced about before helping Demosyna from the cart. The young apprentice stood a few paces away, swaying on her crutch, as Vaash took a low stance. His knees were nearly square with the ground, and Vaash used his good right arm to grab the wagon. A warm breeze seemed to push out from the man, and Demosyna felt the force of the wind. With a great bulging of his muscles, Vaash lifted the cart one-handed with a look of determination. It rose nearly a foot off the ground, creaking and clattering with the goods inside.

"This one was taught the ways of my Order long ago but still can do apprentice exercises!"

Vaash laughed, balancing the large cart in one hand.

"This is one level of discipline, but others exist as well. You witnessed such on the frozen river with my boys so many wonderful days ago!"

Slowly, with muscles straining, Vaash removed his hand from the cart. To Demosyna's wondering eyes, it remained inches from his outstretched arm. Sweat began to form on his brow, making the mysterious force buffet the apprentice again. Demosyna remembered pebbles hitting her and how Vaash seemed to writhe with power that desperate night. The grasses flattened in a circle around the man with each step, and the loaded cart floated before the crouched monk.

Vaash stood up as the wagon returned to the ground, exhaling a long breath into the sky. The powerful monk had moved the bulky wagon ten feet in their clearing, putting it facing the road. Nobody seemed to have noticed, and shadows helped to conceal the show. Demosyna laughed and walked over to where Vaash sat in the grass. The powerful winds had subsided, and she no longer felt the force from Vaash.

"As this one may have said, magic is beyond any learned skills thus far," Vaash said to the apprentice. "If you wish physical control, that is what this one will teach!"

"Thank you so much, Vaash!" Demosyna said as she lay next to the monk. "Can we start soon, once we reach the Highway again?"

"It will be possible when you travel in the back of the wagon, yes! This one can instruct while driving the horse if you wish to improve yourself."

Vaash laughed, his green eyes sparkling in the dim firelight. He seemed eager to teach again, whistling as he stoked the fire nearby.

A harp was heard as a green-clad elf approached the two lounging in the grass. Vaash stood and greeted her, offering a drink to the musician. The stranger accepted the gesture with a flourish of her instrument.

"My name is Plu Durrah, travelers. Pleased to make your acquaintance," the elf said, taking off her floppy cap and bowing. "I saw you at the races and again at the tavern tonight! Did you enjoy my songs?"

Demosyna nodded, smiling as she stood as well.

"My name is Demosyna, and this is Vaash. I did enjoy the harp music and the new song you premiered! It was a little empire heavy, but the melody was really good!"

"I see you, too, feel cautious about the Empress, my strange fellow," Plu Durrah said. "I only sing such trashy songs because it's what gets people to loosen their purses. These towns along the Highway are patriotic, and I find myself playing the same songs in every settlement!"

The relit fire shone on Plu Durrah's face, revealing a slight dark-orange tint. It was subtle, but it sparkled with a deep light when the fire hit the cheek just right. Plu Durrah's eyes were a brilliant silver, which Demosyna only now saw, as lighting in the tavern had been mere candles.

The apprentice didn't realize she had been staring, but Plu Durrah met her gaze with a raised eyebrow.

"I know. I have a bit of the old dwarf in me!" the elf said, rubbing her bald head. "Don't fear, though. I am nothing like those creatures of old. Lazy things they were. We are enlightened folks, and both know about books and covers."

Demosyna laughed softly, pondering the bard's words. The apprentice had heard that old saying, and it was used to refer to a lesser class. Having some dwarf in you was spoken with disdain, as elves professed a deep grudge toward the legendary people.

The lack of access Demosyna had in her apprentice library meant little information regarding Dwarves was available. Scattered references to a great and forgotten war formed the bulk of Demosyna's knowledge, along with named places in reference to Dwarves. The impassable dwarf-wood forest was one such example that came to the apprentice's mind. Due to the mythical sound of the Dwarves, Demosyna assumed they were things of tales or fables. Many she had crossed in her travels felt the same, lumping Dwarves in with goblins or trolls.

"I also noticed what you thought of the night races!" Plu Durrah said, laughing in a high voice. "Good form, Demosyna, good form! It was a great way to stick it to these carnival morons! Always prancing around, waving their little banners. It is enough to make you sick, the way they act!"

Demosyna blushed, thankful for the shadowy night.

"It was an accident. I was just not expecting the race to involve bear traps. It looked so gruesome, I lost my composure."

Plu Durrah shook her head.

"No need to explain, Demosyna. I approve either way. It looks like you two are traveling together. Which way are you headed when you depart? Up or down?"

Vaash had baked a loaf of bread earlier and handed a piece to the elf.

"This one will take the upper road all the way north."

Plu Durrah nodded as she chewed, and Demosyna saw that a large scroll was secured in her belt. Plu Durrah made a show of noticing the glance and slapped herself on the forehead dramatically.

"Silly me, leaving this plan out where anyone can see it!" Plu Durrah exclaimed, taking the scroll and unrolling it. "But if you want to help those dogs, I have an idea. I have posed as a simple musician in this overmanaged nightmare of a town. Really, I am the fastest mercenary in the Fist. Like always, they never even saw me coming!"

The firelight showed the hastily drawn map, with labels near the kennels and the ringmaster's office. With a pink-painted nail, Plu Durrah laid out her plan for the heist.

"These greedy people charge so much for these carnivals while keeping their animals and employees in horrible conditions," Plu Durrah explained, her voice hushed. "They may look all smiles and red clothes, but they are forced to live caged in the carnival too. That wouldn't be so bad, free housing and all, but the apartments are unlivable, and they're paid in Three Paw currency. They are paid well but are only able to spend their earnings at the company shops."

The elf flipped the two a coin each, watching the metal twinkle in the starlight. Demosyna saw the coin was light and silver with three paws stamped into the surface. It lacked the refinement of the Empress's currency and seemed cheaply produced with very little care or skill. The edges had grooves, showing where they had been stamped in bulk to leave rough burrs. Whatever common metal comprised the round coin was seemingly hollow when it clacked lightly against Demosyna's thumb ring.

"Nobody outside the town cares about those worthless bits of metal, and the employees are forced to buy overpriced garbage."

Plu Durrah spit into the fire, frowning in disgust.

"I am a killer, but even I have a heart still. Mostly. When I learned what the circus was up to, I knew only I could help. After I saw your less-than-accepting viewpoint, I felt it was safe to ask for your help. A Wise-woman with that focusing charm would be useful when I rob that elf blind!"

"I was curious why you were just letting us in on the plan," Demosyna said, smiling at the elf.

"I noticed your fine taste in jewelry! Don't forget that I am the fastest elf around, and you wouldn't even see me if I ran," Plu Durrah said, puffing her chest out in a grand display. "Secondly, if you limped to foil my scheme, the guards wouldn't believe some seeder. Plu Durrah might not even be my real name, and I still plan to hit their bank tonight. Having them on alert will only make the heist more exciting!"

Demosyna glanced at her ring, smiling.

"It's just my focusing charm, nothing too fancy."

Plu Durrah's eyes gleamed with a knowing look.

"I understand, you crafty young Scale. Friends can keep secrets, and we are becoming fast friends, I'd say!"

Vaash laughed with good humor.

"This one has no interest in stealing any money."

"Don't think of it as stealing, my buff friend," Plu Durrah said, smiling over her plans. "Consider the dogs you will aid by dealing a blow to the carnival's economy. How long can they continue without their earnings? We get rich, and the town returns to a fair rule with the Empress."

"The recent blizzard held their bank from sending the coins. They are sitting on hundreds of gold pieces, if not over a thousand," Plu Durrah exclaimed, her bright eyes alight. "All these people care about is their shiny gold, so let's hit them where it hurts by taking their only friends. The town will go on without any opportunistic nonsense, and we will be hailed as heroes of the Fist!"

The green-clad bard's words gave lovely images of gold and glory, but Demosyna smiled. Like Vaash seemed to feel, Demosyna lacked the often observed desire to hoard wealth. Many people would argue over such things, but Demosyna was fortunate to have been raised without the need to consider those matters. She had been isolated with an upper-class society, Demosyna came to realize, but nearly all others existed without such niceties.

"I also have no wish to steal, Plu Durrah," Demosyna said, sipping water. "I am tempted to try and help their plight. I won't deny it. But a grand bank heist won't help the people. Or the dogs, for that matter."

"Don't tell me a Wise-woman is worried about a few guards?" the elf asked slyly, winking. "I'm sure you could turn them into moon squid or do something equally effective! We can talk splitting the gold with the town, if you want to give them your share. Heck, I could even let the dogs free. It was always a distraction plan, but if we free them from their cruel masters, would you consider helping this humble musician?"

Vaash's ears were piqued.

"Can you truly free those dogs tonight?"

Plu Durrah smiled slowly.

"Of course. Vaash was it, my sharp fellow? I am the fastest pick around. Those kennels won't even see me coming!"

Vaash thought deeply, and Demosyna asked Plu Durrah a pressing question.

"If I help you, will you kill anyone? I have had enough of killing lately and don't wish to leave this checkpoint soaked in more blood."

"If all goes to plan, we will walk away without anyone being the wiser!" Plu Durrah claimed, smiling a toothy grin. "There will be a shift change after the last race of the night. I already procured some uniforms, and we will swipe their gold right out from under them! The only person that should be in the building is the ringmaster, having retired to roll in her gold no doubt. I've scouted for a month, and tonight is the perfect night!"

"I am just an apprentice, and only recently have I been able to perform magic," Demosyna explained, stretching her purple-scaled arms. "I seek to return to my Orders and journey with that goal. Murder and mayhem are things I wish to avoid if I do this."

"I knew my instincts were right in choosing you two for my assistants!"

Plu Durrah laughed.

"You seemed like decent, kind folks. Let me fill you in on the details if you wish to share my wine!"

The elf produced a wineskin, but both yellow-robed figures declined. Plu Durrah shrugged with a smile and drank a bit of the white wine. The plan the bard described was simple enough. They would be blending in as employees to procure the gold.

It was several hours before sunup when a series of fireballs let the scheming group know the races were concluded. They had been going off in the distance the entire evening, and the three had ignored the once joyful display.

Huge kennels were amassed along one side of the area displayed on the map, with the banking house marked on the opposite side of a wide cul-de-sac. A solid line represented the wooden wall surrounding the complex, and the arena took up one corner. The scale was inconsistent, but Demosyna saw well enough what the mercenary was outlining. Guards should be lazily patrolling the area, and if they remained unnoticed, the operation would run smoothly. Anger burned in her heart, and Demosyna nodded while the elf motioned around the map.

CHAPTER 24

Plu Durrah dressed in the employee outfit, complete with its floppy hat. The crafty elf showed the two how to wear the pins and sash and explained how to wave and smile just so. It was hours before sunup, and the loose plan was agreed upon. Dogs would be the primary concern, and they would create a major distraction for any soldiers. The pair of women would infiltrate the Three Paw complex, with Vaash as lookout from the canopy.

"Are you able to climb safely, Vaash?" Demosyna asked, changing next to the man. "I don't want you falling from a tree for this foolhardy mission. I would like to help those dogs, but not at the cost of a life!"

Vaash grinned, green eyes sparkling.

"Climbing was never a hobby, but this one will have no trouble balancing on a limb! Worry not of this one's safety, for you must be invisible and ever moving. To stop would be to die like a shark in the ocean. This one is fast but cannot teleport like some Wizen."

Demosyna nodded at the advice, pondering her coming challenges.

"I'm kind of excited helping this town. The dogs will be happier without being tortured. I know that without a doubt."

The conviction of her words felt bright and uplifting, and Demosyna steeled herself for the act she might have to perform. Plu

Durrah had explained some basic diversion plans should the two be seen slinking through the alleys.

"We've got the simple techniques," Plu Durrah had whispered, "the puke, the kiss, and the fight. They are fairly self-explanatory, I would venture. In the event of being spotted, one of those things should happen. Puke can be tricky, but it's effective when combined with faint. The guard will often think you are drunk and kick you a bit before leaving."

"So we are going to kiss or fight, then," Demosyna said, blushing and smiling. "Just don't step on my foot please!"

"Adventurous, I see!" Plu Durrah said, grinning as well. "Kiss it is, then. I thought a Wise-woman might want that option! Just don't fall in love, smooth scale. You'll never see me coming!"

Demosyna had kissed one or two people in her life, from the requested desire of another apprentice. Two had been the more acceptable females, but one was a trembling boy who ran away blushing. The elven Wizened, having no natural variety of gender, often found mating rituals foreign. Elves didn't procreate through biology but magic, if what Demosyna understood was true. It was vague and conflicted, but hints of cocoons or rebirths told of how new elves were born.

Lifers, however, would often mate to create an offspring to raise. Kissing was a semi taboo thing because of the disparity, and children were strictly regulated. Imperial cities frowned upon mating pairs being visible, and few were known from Demosyna's youth. The northern Fist was nearly entirely populated by seeder kind, and Demosyna often saw kissing along the Highway.

"I only meant it would be better than hurting myself with my broken foot."

Demosyna laughed, shaking her scaled head.

"It would be a good distraction if I can't put my finger down my throat in time! I'll kiss you the moment you're seen, songstress!"

The boast made the elf puff up in mock annoyance. Plu Durrah pretended to play her harp in frustration, muttering nonsense words and frowning.

"The very idea!" Plu Durrah exclaimed. "If anyone is going to get us caught, it's that one armed monk there. If the guards don't see him dangling from the treetops, they will surely hear your clanking cast in the shadows!"

Plu Durrah clapped the apprentice on the shoulder.

"Call me Plu. That is my name after all, and there is no need to hide that any longer. Adding Durrah just seems silly when we are blood bound now! However this goes, my conspirators, thank you for being good sidekicks!"

Vaash was given the simple spyglass by their mastermind elven friend, and Demosyna saw it was only one magnification. The telescope Demosyna had lost was crafted by Klai and contained multiple lenses to allow many stages of adjustment. She looked through the eyepiece when Vaash asked the apprentice's expert opinion on the tool.

"The lens is not cloudy," Demosyna noted, looking at the tree Vaash would climb. "That is a good sign, and there are no cracks or warps I can see. Each glass seems aligned correctly even if the metal is rusty. Will you be able to watch in the starlight?"

Vaash nodded with a smile.

"This one's eyes are sharp, ignoring age! Your eyes are sharper in the dark of course, but this one will have no trouble at all. Remember to keep listening for bird calls. You will do fine. That you will!"

The two burgling women wished the monk good fortune and marched through the city gate. Revelry was heard for hours as the group discussed their plan, but the town had grown quiet when morning neared. After entering the city proper, the two ambled toward the nearest alley. These handy side streets were seldom traveled by the guests, with slaves typically using them.

Deep shadows covered the crouching pair, and they slid their way through the buildings. Fires in the mock volcano were extinguished, and the two skirted the torchlight. The complex was beyond the metal door in the arena, and a collection of small booths served as cover. Demosyna's foot was aching, but the cautious pace Plu Durrah set was perfect. The young apprentice was able to lean against things the entire way, only having to walk on her foot a few times. Demosyna left her crutch at the advice of the elf, as it would draw attention.

A jittery energy filled the young woman, and Demosyna watched with anxious breath as her fellow robber picked the lock. Stories of bandits and adventure had filled her head as a child, but Demosyna found that the act was terrifying. Getting caught would mean imprisonment again, yet the plight of this town washed the fear nearly away. The young apprentice was determined to help her friends Rrra and Jui, and money would be a valuable asset. Everyone seemed fixated on wealth in the empire, and Demosyna knew how quickly things could happen with the flow of coin.

"If the Order needs help, I can give them aid with the funds as well," Demosyna told herself as the lock clicked open. "We haven't heard from them, so I may be the last Wise-woman in the northern Orders. Maybe that is why Klai was so worried about bringing those chests to the Fist."

Plu Durrah grinned in the moonlight, leading the nervous apprentice into the courtyard. Many wooden buildings were enclosed in a log fence, as the rough diagram had shown. What it hadn't shown was the animals streaming among the buildings, carrying things from one to the other. Only one soldier was stationed at the far end of the area, seeming to sleep in a chair near the kennels.

Some of the dogs looked at the two as they carefully approached the nearest cages. They seemed unimpressed by the sneaking figures and went about their hauling. The theme of the park extended to their shipping too, and Demosyna felt anger boil in her chest.

Many of the dogs were old or injured, freshly missing limbs making them stumble. Some carried ore, and Demosyna recognized the entrance to a mine. Demosyna knew her position and tried to lean against the building casually. The apprentice tucked her foot behind her leg while attempting to shield the cast from view. Demosyna removed a nearly empty wineskin and held it ready to drink.

Cages were clustered in stacks of fifty, allowing a show to release many dogs at once. A single lock let Plu Durrah crack open nearly a fourth of the visible cages, moving to the next lock with a hunched posture. The carrier dogs went about their duties without bothering the two, and Demosyna scouted. Most of the caged dogs were asleep at this late hour, but a few wandered out of the open kennels.

Some saw the cracked door to the arena and walked toward the playpen. Others sniffed around the courtyard, eager to explore. More of the locks clicked open, and Plu Durrah returned to the leaning apprentice.

"I will get the other side of the kennels after the bank," Plu said, glancing at the dogs. "If these dogs are noticed, we are finished!"

Demosyna shook her head, frowning.

"The goal is helping, not adding a few coins to our pockets."

There was silence between the two for a long moment, but Plu Durrah relented when more dogs left the cages. The mercenary hurried away, turning a corner around the kennels. A soldier seated at the end of the kennels stirred as one of the freed dogs sniffed her hand. Demosyna froze at the sight, ready to whistle, but the soldier waved a hand and snored.

The dog took the gesture in stride, trotting away to patrol the pointy wall. Demosyna exhaled a breath of relief, wiping her brow. The night was nearly silent with only the sound of tired dogs reaching the young woman's ears. Demosyna felt a giddy laugh bubbling in her chest and steadied herself with deep breaths. No danger was evident, and the apprentice tried to resist nervous movements while she served as lookout. The last few locks took less time than the first, with Plu Durrah returning after only a few minutes.

The pair grinned at each other, and the elf motioned to a distant building. Their targeted structure was secured with an iron door, and the two moved to cross the cul-de-sac. One curious dog followed Demosyna, sniffing the woman with interest. The apprentice flapped her clawed hand above the animal, sending it on its black-spotted way.

It carried a collection of scrolls and ran toward a doggy door set into a building. The house that the two scuttled toward was the only stone building, and they rushed across the empty street. They were briefly exposed in the flickering torchlight but made it unhindered into the shadows.

Demosyna leaned against the building as Plu Durrah picked the lock. Mere minutes passed, but the young woman felt sweat building. Demosyna was searching the grounds, fearful of an unexpected soldier discovering her plot. A sigh of success let the worrying pair know the door was open. Plu Durrah grinned and winked at the purple-scaled woman, vanishing into the building.

This was the most crucial part of the heist, and Demosyna limped to the half-open door. The apprentice took a drag from the wineskin while leaning against the porch. The only motion was the dogs shipping things between the wooden structures. Creaks of boards and muffled noises came from the banking house, and Demosyna waited.

Four red-clad workers emerged from the mine, brushing dust from their clothes. They loaded dogs with ore before marching slowly out the open metal door. Their weary bodies carried the workers along, and they barely noticed the seemingly relaxed Wise-woman. The one who did notice Demosyna waved, and the young woman returned the greeting as she was shown. Icy claws had gripped her heart, half expecting the employees to alert the sleeping guard, but Demosyna calmed her mind.

Demosyna took several paces away from the door, letting the shadows welcome her into their embrace. The young woman adopted her previous posture, pretending to drink from the wineskin. Only minutes passed before three bulky bags landed onto the porch. Demosyna knew her job here and slid the bags into the alleyway. The apprentice was expecting loose coins, but the gold pieces were packed inside canisters. Not wishing to be caught unawares, Demosyna resisted looking inside her pack. The new weight was uncomfortable on her back, and the odd handles dug into her ribs.

The red-clad woman leaned against the corner of the porch, waiting for more bags. Three more appeared after only a few heart-stopping minutes, and Plu Durrah carried them silently. The musical elf was holding bags already but grabbed the three she had tossed. After putting the hefty sacks in the alley, the elf returned to lock the bank door.

The creak of a hinge and scrape of a lock told that the heist was halfway over. Plu Durrah was grinning wickedly in the low light and took the bags Demosyna couldn't carry. The strong mercenary was swiftly carrying nine large backpacks, three on her back and the same in each hand.

"That will be a nice surprise for them in a day or two," the crouched musician whispered. "It's the day of rest tomorrow, so nobody will be checking on her! Now let's drink our way north! She thought she was so smart, but she never even saw me coming!"

Demosyna smiled and stifled a laugh before following. They swam through the shadows of the near-moonless night, barely a clink from the tubes carrying their stolen gold. They paused only to allow a quartet of soldiers to pass, holding hands over lips to cover their breath. Fear and excitement roiled in her heart, and Demosyna felt giddy when the soldiers remained oblivious.

The patrol had just passed, and Plu Durrah pulled a silver whistle from her pants. A flourish of her arm brought the instrument to her pink-painted lips, and Plu Durrah called her sleeper agents into the heist. The thieves were crouched behind a wide stall that had offered toys, hidden in the shadow near the outer wall.

Guards were standing just inside the archway, avoiding the biting wind from the dark clouds overhead. It took only moments for the whistle to work, and hundreds of dogs sprinted from the arena. Fur of every length and color formed a wave of barking energy, and the guards in the area ran to deal with the commotion.

"Not again," one of the taller guards exclaimed, kicking a barrel. "That's the third time this month. They need to get better locks on those cages."

The dread from the last hour melted away, and Demosyna had to stop from laughing. Any soldiers blocking the exit ran to deal with the canines, and Plu Durrah was gone in the blink of an eye. The elf was fast, even with the extra weight from her stolen gold pieces. The gate was over a hundred feet away, but the bard sprinted flat out to pass through in seconds.

The soldiers were distracted by the sea of dogs overtaking the town, and Demosyna walked along the wall to the unguarded gate.

Her backpack felt like a feather when the young woman stepped through the stone arch, and she laughed when Demosyna saw Vaash holding her crutch.

"Plu Durrah seemed in quite a hurry," Vaash whispered. "She ran straight past, heading to the cart."

Vaash took the bulky sack from the struggling woman, putting both straps over his shoulder.

A large pack of dogs emerged from the city, looking around with wide eyes at the forest. Their leader, the black-haired dog Demosyna had seen hopping like a doe, barked in joy. The other members of the pack howled in response, and the lead black dog bounded to freedom. Nearly fifty dogs of all types followed the canine, along with the old wolves, vanishing to their new life in the wilds.

Smaller clusters of dogs found their way outside and wandered toward the retreating thieves. They wagged and barked playfully, begging for attention. Demosyna shooed the dogs away, pointing toward where the large pack had gone. The trailing dogs hurried away, eager to please any command.

Vaash sighed while watching the dogs be swallowed by the forest, but his eyes glistened.

"The untamed wilds will be far better for those beautiful animals," Vaash said, turning from the scene. "That they will."

Demosyna agreed, and the two friends found their cart after a short walk. The crutch was a necessary addition to her escape, because the excitement made Demosyna's foot ache. Their campfire was still burning and revealed Plu Durrah next to the ancient horse.

A tree blocked her view, but as Demosyna rounded the trunk, a golden mask greeted her. Demosyna stopped dead, and her face drained of color as the armed soldier turned to see the young thief. The helmet bore a plain gold mask, and Demosyna nearly screamed at the sight of the first officer.

"What have we here?" the gold mask asked, a mocking tone in her voice. "What might you two be up to?"

Demosyna tried to step back, but Vaash was behind her, and she bumped his cast. The monk inhaled sharply but stood firm as the soldier marched forward. The sight of the gold mask was nearly enough to make Demosyna bolt, leaving all thought behind. The only thing that kept the young woman from fleeing the cruel memories walking forward was the sound of the stranger's voice.

It lacked the absence of mercy the last first officer's voice had. Only the commanding gold mask was the same. Her heart beat unrelentingly, and Demosyna's breath puffed away in terrified clouds. There was a moment of further tension before the elf removed her mask, laughing in a strong voice. The stranger was younger than the other first officer and sported a crooked nose from many fights.

"I never knew you worked with such pretty Scales now, Plu," the soldier said, her elven face split in a grin to reveal missing teeth. "I would have joined your little crew sooner if the perks were that good!"

Plu Durrah tossed a rolled cigarette into the fire before joining the victorious conspirators of her robbery. The bard had already changed back into her green traveling gear, complete with a tent backpack.

"I thought you would get a good scare from our friend here!" the sly bard said, clapping the soldier on the back. "I only kept her a secret because she is way too obsessed with Scales, especially pretty young things like you, Demosyna. She is the commander in this area and needs to be aware of any happenings. When I decided to liberate this town, I naturally informed our honorable soldier sister."

Plu Durrah handed the soldier a full bag of gold pieces, and the officer opened the pack. Inside were seven copper-colored tubes wrapped in leather, with glass windows showing thick coins. The commander used a curvy handle to remove a canister, unscrewing the top once the coins shone through the displays. After the cap was free of the threads, the soldier turned it over to remove an outer casing.

Three triangular prongs jutted up from a threaded cap, holding columns of gold pieces through the hole in each coin. The coins had been stacked on top of one another in the tube, but Demosyna marveled as each coin hovered above the previous. They separated as the tube was lifted away and vibrated as three pillars of gold coins were held aloft.

"I see you are still a woman of your word, Plu," the commander said, spitting on the ground. "Our deal stands, then. If you find your way back down, look me up! I always had issue with how your sister ran that place and am glad you came to me about it. Less paperwork that way, and bloodshed."

"I am shocked you would doubt my word, Xi Xi. I took care of our mutual issue while taking what's mine!" Plu Durrah said, spitting as well. "Try not to spend that all on those shows you like. Sorry, but there was a bit more gold than I let on, Demosyna! I didn't want you to get a big head, running in and ruining things without me!"

Plu Durrah turned to grin at the two newly redressed travelers. The pair had changed into the robes Vaash carried, with Xi Xi eyeing the apprentice with a side-eyed glance. Demosyna laughed, and Vaash smiled as he shrugged. They handed their borrowed red clothes back to Plu Durrah, who turned when the first officer replied.

"What would those poor Scales do without me?"

Xi Xi laughed, screwing the leather-bound tube down.

"Someone has to support those poor workers, paid mostly in tips!"

Vaash and Demosyna walked to the fire, the young woman shivering from conflicting feelings. The initial horror at seeing Xi Xi had awoken a primal terror, but a dawning excitement from the heist was rising. If the ranking soldier in the region was on their side, it seemed they had won. Elation coursed through the young woman, and a jittery sense of surety floated around Demosyna. Through a sight line in the woods, dogs could still be seen running from the town.

"Thank you for helping those animals, Xi Xi," Vaash said after a considering moment. "Would you share a drink with this one in celebration?"

Both Xi Xi and Plu Durrah spoke their agreement at the same time and laughed as they clasped shoulders. The elves moved to take the skin Vaash produced, and all four carnival robbers toasted their success.

"That was really exciting!" Demosyna said, seated to ease her foot. "I'm glad you found us, Plu and Xi Xi. Thank you for letting me help those dogs! I couldn't stand the sight of their cruel treatment and planned to leave them to their fates."

"Looks like you found some fresh lambs for your wolf pack, Plu."

Xi Xi laughed, eyeing Demosyna with a wink.

"I doubt this purple Scale has so much as cursed before. What a shame to corrupt something so innocent!"

Demosyna smiled sadly but spoke with good humor.

"I wouldn't go to that extreme, but it was the first major rebellion in my life! I now know who to seek out for my next coup, Madam Xi Xi!"

All three surrounding Demosyna laughed, passing the skin around. The soldier retrieved her pack from a tree limb, putting the cut onto an armored back. Plu Durrah walked over to the officer, handing the golden mask to Xi Xi. The two exchanged a few words, and Plu Durrah kissed the taller elf on the lips for several seconds.

They enjoyed the embracing kiss and unwrapped their arms after a few moments. Plu Durrah wiped pink lipstick from Xi Xi's mouth and looked with hungry eyes at the commander. Vaash had been strapping down the wagon for travel, and Demosyna watched the two embrace. They kissed passionately again before Xi Xi turned to walk into town with a wave.

"Don't forget about the little addition to our deal," Plu Durrah called. "I expect to see you at the elevator, Xi."

The strong officer raised a hand over her head in response, walking away without slowing. Vaash woke the bony horse with an apple as incentive, and the beast stiffly walked to the cart. Demosyna put out the fire, piling water and dirt on the coals before standing.

Demosyna rode in the bed, eyeing the large pile of backpacks hidden in the back. They had been put behind various random clutter, shielding the gold well from casual inspection. Plu Durrah walked beside the wagon with Vaash driving from the tall seat. The added backpacks prevented Plu Durrah from riding, and she grumbled when seeing the lack of space in the wagon.

Demosyna apologized, but the elf shrugged it off with a plucked song. Plu Durrah used her harp to make the short trip to the elevators a musical affair. The narrow road was only traveled by freed canines, and the Highway overshadowed the wagon once more. Vaash was delighted by the parade of dogs that gathered, and he laughed as they circled around the monk.

A few old hounds had been milling around the elevators when the group approached, and soldiers were bickering in confusion. One of the elves returned to the town, leading leashed dogs that struggled behind. The remaining two soldiers talked with Plu, who palmed a few coins to the smiling guards. A heavily laden cart was wheeled onto the elevator as the sole occupants waiting to ascend.

Demosyna walked to pet their noble guide, grabbing an apple from the wagon. The vast imperial trading networks assured a variety of goods available no matter the season. Apples were usually found near each checkpoint, and Demosyna was glad to treat the horse. Au Peirce had warned against too many sweets for their ancient mare, and the apprentice had taken the archer's advice.

"Only one more for now, my friend," Demosyna whispered. "We need to make our escape, and you are the only one for the job!"

Their rented horse stamped a foot before drinking some water Vaash left the animal.

The sun was showing signs of rising when the gold-masked officer returned with a pair of dogs. One of the leashed hounds was the fluffy three-legged dog Vaash had pet so happily. The other was a wide-chested, short-haired animal with a reptilian jawline from the breadth of its head. This bright-white dog was grinning sharp teeth at the yellow-robed apprentice, and the crocodile-toothed greeting reminded Demosyna of her nursery dogs.

Both canines were of a white coat dotted with spots, with the fluffy dog's spots being gray. The short, slightly bowlegged younger canine had brown spots that gave its face the look of eyebrows. The initial reaction to seeing the familiar snout gave Demosyna a start, but she laughed upon seeing the expression on the monk's face. Vaash practically ran over to the nearly blind gray dog, who licked his face and barked.

The barrel had been removed from its leather collar, and Xi Xi handed the leash to Vaash. Xi Xi's mask was affixed inside her helmet, and Demosyna took steadying breaths as it loomed gold in her vision. The commander handed the other dog off to the wide-eyed young woman, who nodded slightly while looking down at the gift.

"Thank you, ma'am," Demosyna called, her voice soft and near trembling. "I wasn't expecting to get a dog! Thank you!"

"You two left these mangy things in the town, drunken seeders," the emotionless mask barked in a severe tone. "I had to get them from the packs running wild in the city. I need you troublemakers to leave immediately. Take your lost animals and vacate my city!"

Plu Durrah was grinning slyly with her face away from the soldiers at the elevator. Demosyna lowered her head, adopting a humble posture with ease. She wasn't sure, but the young apprentice took the commander's anger to be a ruse. The gold mask nodded, and the soldier slapped Demosyna's shoulder with an armored glove. It was hard enough to jostle her, but Demosyna felt it was jovial in nature, as it didn't really hurt.

"I am Xi Xi, first commander of this city and all its lands," the shining gold mask called out. "Remember my name, you two seeders, if you ever expect to drink in my realm again."

Vaash had observed the situation and sat down, feet tucked under him. The dog also lay down, holding a remaining front paw out in front of its head. This caused Plu Durrah to grin wider, her eyes dancing with enjoyment. Her back was to the elevator, and the soldiers were clueless to Plu Durrah's mockery. The officer pointed at the teary-eyed mercenary, who regained her composure in an instant. The laughing smile was gone, replaced with a look of humility and slight fear.

"I need to have a few words with you before I can allow you passage," Xi Xi ordered, marching away without looking back.

The slightly hunched elf followed with dragging feet, clearly making a show of being humble. Demosyna marveled at the acting and watched Plu round a bend in the road.

Her shining white dog sat on the elevator, smiling widely up in joy. The apprentice held a clawed hand toward the dog in greeting, as Vaash had shown her recently. It stood and sniffed her knuckles with a wide-eyed expression, wagging its tail. It strained a flat head toward her face, breathing in Demosyna's laughing clouds. He licked a long pink tongue at the woman's scales, and the young Wise-woman let a cheek be kissed.

Unlike the elderly dog that Vaash petted while seated in the dirty road, Demosyna's had all four limbs. Demosyna saw no scars on its legs, and they twitched with strength as the dog balanced. The hound smiled inches from her face, looking with discerning eyes up at Demosyna. The apprentice continued petting its thick skull, watching his broad chest puff air into the morning sky.

Plu Durrah returned, smacking her lips with fresh pink color being applied. Vaash rose when the commander didn't appear, and the two stood beside the wagon. The three-legged old dog sat down beside Vaash with a long sigh, lowering its body in stages. Vaash used his good arm to stroke the tall dog's neck as the soldiers roused slaves chained to a wheel.

Her heart broke anew at the sight, and even the questioning eyebrows of her new dog barely lifted Demosyna's spirits. He sat down when the elevator jolted forward along the slanted portion of the Highway, looking up in worry. Demosyna turned away from the struggling figures below, bending to rub the animal's chest. His low whines of fear reached the apprentice's ears, and the young woman felt her heart open for the dog's concern.

The elevator rose smoothly, save when it started or stopped at a level. Gold light shot down from the cloudy sky, bringing the landscape to life in every direction. The horse was unimpressed, but the other animals gazed with startled faces at the vast forests leading to the mountains. The older dog barked, shivering before Vaash knelt to hug the animal. Her own dog whined, pressing its body against the Wizen's hanging left leg. Demosyna sat in the back of the wagon, smiling in triumph and petting her new friend to calm his fears.

"It's okay, my brave boy!" Demosyna called softly to the animal, who looked up. "Stick close to me, and I can keep you safe. Get used to this amazing view, pretty boy, since we are moving away from your cruel town!"

This seemed to still the animal, and he walked a few steps to peer over the elevator. Demosyna grasped his leash tightly, feeling his strong shoulders pull against the leather harness. The curious dog stopped short of the drop, glancing its wide head around with a grin. He barked once, a short farewell that carried over the green hills.

The ocean was out of view, but Demosyna knew it would be visible at times while they traveled. The Highway appeared straight to her keen eyes, as it never seemed to rise or turn along its northern path. Maps showed a steady, gradual arc that traveled much of the western Fist, however. This had troubled the apprentice at first, but the sheer length of the Highway prevented a traveler from seeing any curve. It was a small thing, but the idea that a perfectly flat highway was gently curving intrigued the young apprentice.

A final click let the party walk off the wood platform, which began to drop at once. They saw no other figures in the new day's light, and Demosyna moved from the wagon.

"That was fun, my sly assistants!" Plu said, slapping Demosyna's back. "I couldn't have asked for a better crew. I hope you like your bonuses, for those dogs are from purebred stock. You could even stud that young beast if you want to make some coin from his solid breeding."

Demosyna laughed, watching her dog mark the Highway.

"I suppose, but I am just happy giving him a better life! Thank you for the surprise, Plu. Vaash is taken with his already!"

Vaash laughed in agreement, rubbing the dog's belly.

"This one is overjoyed to see her again. She is the best girl. That she is!"

His dog smiled and wiggled atop the Empress's Highway, her cloudy eyes searching Vaash's face.

A random pack was opened, and Plu Durrah took one of the metal coin purses. The elf counted the visible coins, turning the cylinder to view all three windows. Plu Durrah sighed in frustration, shaking her head.

"It's just like her to skimp on the count," Plu Durrah exclaimed, rubbing her bald head. "But it looks like most of the stacks are correct, with fifty each. Now I will claim half our score since I orchestrated this little event. The administration fee was nonnegotiable since Xi and I go way back!"

Plu Durrah moved five of the backpacks to one side, leaving the other four bags in the left of the covered bed. Vaash seemed uninterested in the gold and walked his dog carefully to the edge. The monk held the leash taut, showing the deadly drop to the blind dog. She sniffed at the spots he motioned toward, and Vaash walked to the opposite side. The three-legged dog hopped stiffly along and lay beside the monk when he sat, feet dangling over the side, to take in the view.

"Even though Vaash doesn't want any, I would ask that he and I be given a pack each," Demosyna said, leaning against the wagon. "He is so kind and rarely seems to bother with possessions. I know he could use it, especially since he has a dog now! I will keep it safe for Vaash till he wants some."

Plu Durrah smiled crookedly.

"I am sure you will, my thieving Scale! They all should be about the same, give or take a few gold pieces. I stuffed seven tridents into each one, so choose any of the bags for yourself! You've earned about a thousand gold pieces each tonight, so enjoy them with my blessing!"

Demosyna was shocked by the proclamation and looked at the backpacks with glittering eyes. The few trinkets she had sold, taken as loot from bandits, had earned the apprentice around fifteen gold pieces. This fortune was inspiring, and Demosyna grabbed two heavy packs. Demosyna beamed at Plu Durrah and asked the mercenary what her plans were.

"Well, Demosyna, I was going to accompany you to your goal," Plu Durrah said, taking the last two bags for herself. "I trust you two now for the most part since Xi took a liking to you. She always had a nose for trouble and was impressed by you two! Tell me, woman to woman, where did you get that ring? Was it your parents?"

Demosyna shook her head, frowning as she held her left hand up.

"I got it from the city farthest south along the Highway, Plu. I needed a charm for my magic, and Vaash found it in a trade shop. I was war-orphaned into my Orders and never knew of my parents. Why do you ask?"

"I knew you were too young to know the old signs," Plu Durrah said, nodding to herself. "That is why I assumed it was an inheritance since you don't seem the thieving types. See the round hourglass bulges along the band? That's an old thief sign used to identify friendly sneaks. It's subtle enough to go unnoticed, as my former shadow master wanted it to look like an elven design."

Demosyna looked at the gold band with fresh eyes and saw the figure eight shape the metal had been cast with. The rest of the band was uniform, but a small pair of bumps formed an odd *m* shape on either side. They looked a bit like round eyes now that the young Wizen saw it for a signal.

"She would laugh so hard about the design," Plu Durrah reminisced, her silver eyes distant. "Us elves are so fond of that swirling, looping shape that she would giggle. The final form was to look like binoculars to remind we are always looking! It was fun times, but the shadow master decided to disband when the war kicked up again. Thieves have a harder time during war, she now knew, and we went our separate ways rich!"

Demosyna had often seen tapestries and carvings adorning ornate walls having a similar double-looped design. The elven form was more flowing, having long arcs and dips that formed a swirling ovular shape. The young Wizen saw the inspiration in the ring's design and the clever hidden sign for those in the know.

"Should I not wear it openly if it's a thief's sign?" Demosyna asked, her voice a hushed whisper. "I can get another focusing charm, I suppose, but this was kind of a gift, and I would like to use it!"

Plu shook her head, covering her seven bags with a tarp.

"As I said, we are disbanded in this land. We may come together again, but I doubt many will wish to leave their retirements! I travel now for the songs and the sport of the occasional heist. I try to be more charitable in my old age and only take from those that steal without good cause!"

"That is a noble code, Plu!" Demosyna responded, glad to display Vaash's gift. "Thank you again for letting me help those animals! It means a lot to me that I can do something for once and not just watch uselessly!"

Vaash stood from meditating over the view, and his fluffy gray dog milled along behind the man. Demosyna's dog had patiently sat while the ladies divided the spoils, his keen yellow-gold eyes scanning the horizon. The red-tinted sun had risen above the distant mountains, towering with unconquered peaks at the horizon and beyond.

Plu Durrah rested her wrists on the pommels of her swords, calling to Vaash as he wandered back.

"Hey, Vaash, I will drive for a spell if you want to walk with the dogs!" Plu Durrah said, elbowing Demosyna with a knowing wink. "I also have a present for these pups."

The mercenary took one of the sealed canisters from her pile, grinning at the puzzled man. Plu Durrah grabbed a handful of the stacked coins after unscrewing the container, offering them to the monk. Vaash paused before accepting them, but a smile crept over his face.

"For the dogs, you say?" Vaash asked, raising an eyebrow. "This one is grateful, Plu. The animals will be better off with coats and toys! And maybe cute little boots since the snows are setting in for the season."

Vaash went on talking to himself, petting his large companion's head and grinning. It was settled, and all three robbers laughed as Plu Durrah climbed into the driver's seat.

The cart rolled forward once more, heavy with treasure and a new traveler. Vaash walked with both dogs at first, but Demosyna's medium-sized animal found its way to the young Wise-woman. He sniffed at her dangling boot, and Demosyna laughed at the dog's expressive face.

They had been traveling mere minutes when loud howls pierced the calm morning air, sending birds flying toward the sea. Numerous dog calls responded to the loud signal, and the woods sang with the freedom the dogs possessed. Demosyna's heart felt full, nearly bursting, as tears of happiness fell momentarily from her eyes. The shining white dog seemed worried, but Demosyna smiled with her tears to calm the animal.

Vaash assembled his silver flute and played a marching song, with Demosyna sending her laughing group directly into the war raging ahead.

PART II

CHAPTER 25

Hark the true tale of the wise Tin Toed,
who saw such despair and took what was owed.
Under cover of bravery, a true heart aglow,
she stole into cages and set free all enclosed.

Her justice is sound and mind is top-notch.
She floats all around on her magical crutch.
Fear the gold in her eyes and the hardened pink skin
lest she sees through your lies and hasten your end!

She screams 'cross the Fist on a skeletal steed,
hooves catching ablaze with unparalleled speeds.
Packs of snarling wolves are at her command,
snapping through bone as Death's grinning band.
So for any in bondage, just raise your hand
for the freedom long promised in this brutal Fist
        land!

For those that are blue and fear their sad human lot,
trust in pink Scales while you clench your paws taut.
No colors remain in elfish faces, distraught,
while Orcs take what is ours to tear down what
        is wrought.

Let them all live in fear of the fate they have
  bought.
Blood, claw, and fur fly in the war to be fought.
Let no voice be silenced; a new balance is sought.

Plu Durrah sang loudly into the afternoon air in mockery of the storm clouds swirling overhead. Plu's voice was beautiful and carried over the flat stone highway she drove the cart along. Demosyna laughed wildly at the verses, nearly crying from the humor she found in the song. Vaash, too, was chuckling at the musician's newest lines, and his dog barked playfully from its furry gray face.

"Did you say magical crotch?" Demosyna called through fits of laughter. "And I only have nine toes now, not ten!"

"I said crutch, with a *u*. Magical crutch! You don't have a broom to ride on, so why would I say crotch, little Wise-woman? Everyone is always so critical. It's only the first draft!"

The musical elf stopped playing a complex melody on her harp, turning to face Demosyna. Demosyna redoubled in laughter, and the bald driver turned back around to laugh with good humor. The horse shook a bony head while clopping along steadily atop the Highway.

Vaash was playing a few bars he picked up from the tune but put his flute away with a grin.

"This one is pleased to hear the song, Plu!" Vaash exclaimed, laughing as his old canine panted. "It was a wonderful retelling of freeing our friends here. This one thinks it was tin with an *i*, Demosyna. Plu has watched the hammering of your new toe these past days!"

Vaash shook his long red hair in amusement, tossing Demosyna the metal tube. The apprentice caught it with a tear-filled face and wiped the streaming glee from her eyes.

The past days atop the Highway had seen Vaash shape a piece of light metal for a toe. He used a small hammer to bend the silvery material into a rough digit shape, filing the seam away. The sound of tools could be heard for hours each night as the monk worked by the firelight. He used heavy tongs to hold the metal as he filed, and Vaash soon had the workings of a big toe.

"At least someone can appreciate good art," Plu Durrah said, feigning a huff. "Although Ten Toed would work too. Good idea! You haven't done much yet worthy of song in any case, smooth scale. Talk to me again when you are my age, if we are both still around!"

Demosyna laughed heartily again, turning over her future prosthetic. It was light and smooth with holes punched into opposite sides near the base. There was even a pointy metal nail that seemed to flow from the top of the cylinder. It was amazing craftsmanship, but Vaash explained it was only half finished. Leather padding and filigree scales would still need to be applied.

"This one will also turn it a deep purple blue in the fire," Vaash told the mystified apprentice. "That way, it will blend better with your scales! The proper powders can be bought to get a specific temperature as the metal burns."

Demosyna didn't understand enough about metalworking to fully grasp the lesson but nodded in thanks. The apprentice tossed the work in progress back to the monk, smiling in the easy light of the afternoon. Storm clouds had been gathering for days and swirled ahead in troubling patterns.

The first lazy raindrops had fallen, splashing the party with ice. It wasn't actually raining, but as they marched north, the clouds had seemed ready to break. The wind picked up as well while the travelers progressed, and Demosyna practiced the lessons Vaash gave her.

"You have done very well to master defensive reactions," Vaash had explained, looking openly into Demosyna's eyes. "This one is very proud to see your dedication. To start control training, we must balance your body and mind to a goal. If the body cannot support what the mind needs, what good would it be? Likewise, if one treats their flesh indifferently, a mind withers with the body."

The young apprentice had nodded, beginning to let the lesson sink in. Vaash saw the understanding in Demosyna's eyes and smiled.

"Control is painful and exhausting sometimes," Vaash had warned. "It would be easy to break things down, but to stop something seldom involves force to the open mind. Begin by extending the time you are able to keep a spell active. Float this leaf in a handheld tornado for as long as you can."

So it had been for a few days now, as Demosyna rode in the wagon stuffed with stolen gold pieces. The canvas cover had been cleaned of blood and blocked the wind to allow the eager apprentice occasional practice. A broad golden leaf had been used to focus the magic, found fluttering along the Highway one morning.

Even with her recent success in holding the bandits back, Demosyna could vividly recall white bone against blue sky as a horse broke a leg. The cries rang through her mind sometimes, chilling the Wise-woman more than the frozen air. The apprentice was also quickly learning what Vaash had meant about tiring and uncomfortable.

It was thirty minutes of focus before the leaf fell again. The results were worth the sweat that Demosyna wiped, grinning over the feat. Her body was getting used to recovering after the intense drain, and Demosyna felt her energy returning. The apprentice sipped from the recently filled waterskin, having paid the previous toll.

Plu Durrah hadn't offered to pay tolls, and the two yellow-robed travelers didn't think to ask for a three-way split. They had always alternated paying, and their budgets were already planned as such. Nearly a month had passed since first setting foot on the Empress's Highway, and Demosyna felt confident in her growth as a Wise-woman. The carved title on her crutch served as inspiration for the weary young woman, and Demosyna picked up the leaf again.

The Wizen's muscular dog always watched the spinning leaf with interest, only breaking his concentration to scan the area. Demosyna grew fond of her pet and would half watch his intelligent eyes as she held the leaf aloft.

The few times that Plu Durrah tried to pet the animal, it would shrink away with his gold-yellow eyes wide. This drew laughs from the travelers, and the dog would often burrow his face behind Demosyna's legs. He didn't bark or bite, so Plu Durrah shrugged the animal's behavior away.

Demosyna found she couldn't practice when the older dog needed to rest, for it would paw and bite at the floating leaf. The apprentice used those downtimes when the elderly dog snored to meditate on the only magic she knew. Other Wizened, even the unfeeling ones from the racetrack, could perform multiple types of magic with ease. Healing magic was first on her mind even though Demosyna knew it was unlikely her toe would regrow. Her foot had nearly healed, and even without a big toe, the injury would soon stop slowing Demosyna down.

If I knew any healing, I could be out of this itchy thing today! Demosyna thought, scratching her calf. *And help in the future when the next injury occurs for me or my friends.*

The older dog was barking at Vaash as the monk walked along, his arm in a sling. Demosyna patted the space left in the wagon with a purple hand, and her dog jumped at once. It was a welcome warmth the animal provided in these unhindered winds, and Demosyna rubbed his chest. The strong beast rolled and folded his front legs, seeking more affection. Demosyna laughed at the needy dog and stroked his massive rib cage with a grin. She hadn't found a name for the dog, but he was still a near instant friend. No more trepidation about his wide jaws remained for the young Wizen, and she was glad for it.

"Watch this, my silky boy," Demosyna told the attentive dog, who tilted his head. "I will show you something great that I have learned!"

Demosyna held the leaf in her palm, backing away from the windy opening. The brittle leaf floated up while spinning in even patterns as a wind twisted. The feather-light blur sped up, rising and falling in a magical heartbeat. The apprentice tilted her left hand, sending the golden flotsam sideways. The tiny cyclone dissipated, and a new twister formed to catch the leaf in her right hand. It wobbled slightly, adjusting to the new winds, but remained hovering above the scaled palm. Wonderful feelings of pride and exertion mixed in her heart, and Demosyna laughed at her control. She passed the leaf between her open hands, making delicate wind magic to do so.

The dog's focused eyes followed the leaf, his long tongue hanging from a strong jaw. He rarely barked, save for alerting her about approaching figures, and Demosyna smiled at the watchdog. The tired animal rested his chin on crossed paws and closed his eyes when the Wizen grabbed the leaf. Demosyna felt rising joy while staring at the gold leaf, dry and fragile between her fingers. Never before had she dreamed such magic would be within her grasp, but Demosyna saw the proof in the delicate leaf she held.

Demosyna held the leaf as a badge of honor.

"Just wait. I will show everyone what I can do!"

Vaash slowed to join her behind the cart.

"What have you done, Demosyna?"

Even with her spent body, Demosyna showed the man her trick. For many long minutes, she passed the leaf between her palms, careful to not break the dehydrated structure. Vaash walked behind, smiling with dancing green eyes as Demosyna displayed her prowess. When the panting Wise-woman relented, snatching the gold leaf from the air, Vaash applauded.

"That was wonderful, Demosyna!" Vaash told the nervous Wizen, grinning in excitement. "You have nearly mastered that skill!"

Vaash studied the dry leaf for a moment, then crushed it in his strong hands.

"Send these lesser disciplines into the wind and move beyond them!" Vaash called loudly, throwing the leaf dust into the air.

Golden flakes drifted from Vaash's upraised hand, and Demosyna's vision slowed to nearly motionless. The young woman smiled, holding her left hand before sharp yellow eyes. Golden confetti was blown skyward when a streaming blast of wind shot from her, and Demosyna laughed. The apprentice had produced a tube of air, spinning and twirling the bits of leaf. A snaking torrent of magic sent the crumbled leaf into the distance with Demosyna yelling.

"I am not a failure," the purple-scaled woman called into the darkening sky. "Let this be the proof."

The tunnel of wind halted while freezing the leaf dust and rain in place. The young Wizen groaned but held the tube together as the cart moved. Her left thumb grew warm as the charm strained, and Demosyna swept her arms apart in a wide arc. Wind exploded from the magic, and color scattered over the Highway as the spell broke. A canopy of rainbows shielded the wagon from rain, blanketing the group in dazzling peace. Demosyna's dog gazed in wonder at the prismatic display while letting free a rare bark of joy.

Vaash laughed, gazing at the young woman.

"This one is humbled once more, Demosyna! You have taken to your goal like a bird to the wind! Rest easy knowing tomorrow, we take another step!"

Plu Durrah had been watching and clapped as well.

"Stop making things harder for me, violet! I am already chronicling your tale. How much should I need to rhyme? Tell me how to link rainbows and dead leaves! Maybe something about rain and boughs?"

Demosyna laughed from the wagon and nudged her dog to get down. He jumped from the wooden cart, shaking his fur off in the rain. The soaked gray dog was helped into the wagon, and the Wisewoman was drenched by fur-sprayed water. Rain had wet the fluffy dog, and she shook herself nearly dry with a wolfish grin. The cleanest rag was used to dry the young woman, and Demosyna rubbed the cloth on the wet dog.

"You didn't have to get me wet too!" the Wizen said, mopping the dog dry. "I only wanted to help."

Vaash was soaked but smiled.

"She is a princess!"

Plu Durrah wiped her face, calling back to the two.

"The storm is picking up. Someone else needs to drive for a bit! My strings are going to rust at this rate!"

Demosyna volunteered, having been practicing her magic for hours. Vaash gave her a leather cover, and Demosyna used it to shield her cast foot. The horse led the group with the purple-scaled woman driving the wagon again. The apprentice had never minded rain, often enjoying the warm caress of the water on her scales. This water was nearly cold enough to turn to snow, however, and Demosyna wrapped her robe tighter. The rain fell in heavier streams as lightning and fire illuminated the horizon.

Dark thunderclouds were lit with energy and rumbled in crashing rhythms. The sound of the storm overshadowed the battle, but the Highway revealed a bloody skirmish. As she approached, Demosyna heard unrelenting cannon fire from both sides of the Highway. The rain blocked most of the spheres, but the apprentice had sharp eyes and saw the volley. The western side of the Highway was filled with shining elven troops, many under cloth tents. Tall scaffolding was constructed on the east, where the Fist stretched into the mountains.

A sea of patchwork armor swept her vision into the distance, and Demosyna saw over thirty thousand rebels. There were many who rose as tall as elves, but the majority was of the seeder classes. The top of the Highway ahead was pitched in combat, turning the stones a fading pink.

Rebel climbers had made their way up the massive height of the Highway, using frames and climbing ropes. Orcs used their wings to fly atop the Highway while swinging huge weapons after landing. Shining elven soldiers swung swords and thrust spears, but the wave of rebels had gained a foothold. Demosyna stopped the cart well short of the hellscape and didn't wish to believe what her eyes knew was true.

Cannons were readied, and their sheer numbers ensured a constant stream of fire. By the time one row had fired, another had been reloaded. The checkpoint ahead had an elevator, and the western one was sending troops up. Arrows covered the eastern lift, but shielded rebels were moving to operate the crank. The slaves on that side had been killed, their bodies hanging from the wheel by chains.

Flags waved from windows in the checkpoint, and horns tried to be heard over the thunder and screams. Rain soaked the world nearly to the horizon, and weary soldiers exploded from whistling cannonballs. The elven side of the Highway surged forward in huge rectangles of soldiers with elephants heading to the elevator. The great beasts used the cover of the forest to advance, but many lay dead as gray mounds in the trees.

Cavalry hung back with the elven generals and Wizened patrolling the rear. The rebels had no mounted units and half as many cannons, but the forest teemed with bodies. One rebel was thrown off the Highway, screaming as she crashed down. Trees fell periodically, and others were set ablaze, even in the downpour. At the signal from an elven general, huge siege engines rolled, pulled by hundreds of slaves. The terrified figures strained against the hundred-foot-tall structure and moved the wooden building nearer the Highway.

A cannonball hit the edge, exploding in painful shrapnel. Soldiers from both armies fell, some into the darkness off the edge. The Empress's Highway was undamaged, and the blood atop its heights rained down. Troops marched to join the fray from the coast, and their armor shone in the setting sun. Neither side worried about clearing the battlefield and trod on the corpses instead. Lightning lanced down from the clouds, illuminating all the rebel faces in a flash. A tree was split vertically down its trunk, but the fire was quenched by rain. From west to east, soldiers of competing armies clashed for control of the checkpoint, filling the horizon.

Nearly all the cries were lost in the rain, but Demosyna heard plenty from her seat. Vaash noticed the battle with narrowed eyes, coming from around the cart. Both dogs had been put into the wagon during the storm, and Plu Durrah joined in silent observation. There were mounted elves running through the slaughter, but the majority was engaged in mortal close-quarters fighting.

The flat, slippery stones hindered everyone, and confusion swam among those atop the Highway. The storm was completely blocking the sky, and the light of the sun was nearly gone for the day. Torches were useless in this freezing rain, and Demosyna stepped down to talk over the thunder, from above and below.

"We can't cross this."

Plu Durrah was nearly shouting to be heard.

"Let's go back and take a path around. This could go on for weeks!"

"This one agrees, Demosyna," Vaash said, bending close. "You are in danger, for this one cannot defend against two armies. One maybe, but not two!"

Demosyna laughed at the joke, but her face was set.

"I don't see a way around for miles. The east army spans to the horizon. If we go down, how can we continue north?"

Frustration was clamping upon her heart, but Demosyna resolved to keep her mind alert. The battle was still a distance away, yet she felt exposed on the featureless highway. Demosyna had studied the battle for minutes already, and if they were noticed by either army, it would end in bloodshed.

Plu Durrah and Vaash discussed boats or imperial escorts, but Demosyna barely heard. The apprentice was watching the arrows and cannonballs fly in streams through the pounding rain and smiled very slowly.

"I will get us across," Demosyna said flatly, standing tall and flexing her left hand. "I can deflect whatever those armies throw at us if you two watch the animals!"

The faces of her two companions were drenched with rain but considered the option as they looked at the apprentice. Demosyna felt confident in the magic and knew in her heart this was a chance to help. The bandits' arrows and lances had been weeks ago, and the young Wise-woman had only refined her skills.

As if in agreement, her dog joined the Wizen and barked. He glared ahead through the water at the straight shot into chaos, standing boldly at Demosyna's knee.

Vaash looked with worry at the battle but nodded along with Plu Durrah.

"This one trusts you," Vaash said, looking at Demosyna with adoration. "Lead us onward, through the life we face together! None will harm those you put in this one's care. That they will not."

"This is a terrible idea, purple."

Plu Durrah laughed, pulling both swords.

"Rest assured, I will protect the gold. And Vaash if I have time! You they will notice, with your magic and all, but they won't even see me!"

Vaash took both dogs and waited beside the old horse, petting its neck. Plu Durrah exchanged the pack she wore for one of her loot bags, swinging twin swords to limber her body.

Demosyna stood atop the seat with her foot not hurting in the pouring sleet. It had gotten cold enough for the storm to become ice, and the apprentice ignored the needles. The massacre continued ahead, and Demosyna felt rage swell in her heart. So many were dead, and so many more rushed forward to die. Demosyna let her tears freeze in the wind. She had never imagined such bloodshed and held a trembling hand in response.

A tornado materialized around the apprentice, forty feet across and shooting into the dark sky. It rose so fast that it broke through the thunderclouds in seconds, roaring and twisting with passion. A disc of stars hundreds of feet wide beamed light onto the Highway, and the cyclone of magic held steady. Inside the eye of the magic, the rain was gone when the wall carried it away.

The horse jumped in surprise, but Vaash held the ancient animal's reins to calm the beast. Plu Durrah let out a loud curse, her silver eyes wide and wondering.

The cart moved forward slowly, and Demosyna closed her eyes to breathe deeply. After several breaths, the young apprentice opened her yellow eyes to see volleys of projectiles rising toward the tornado. Both sides of the road had turned their fire, and hundreds of cannons gaped wide. The storm was sliced in half as the tornado moved, and a ribbon of starlight was stretched across the sky. Calm breaths kept Demosyna focused, and she saw the first wave strike the barrier with clear vision.

"South, where it won't kill," Demosyna whispered to herself.

The spiraling tower responded to her will, picking up in speed and noise. Arrows and bolts were shredded to dust, forming streams of confetti. The cannonballs were flung behind the Wizen after orbiting in the force. Demosyna sent the deadly pieces hurtling into the south, where they wouldn't fall on either army. The dogs were walking with tucked tails after seeing the impacting projectiles.

For over a minute, the wagon made progress, shielded by a powerful magic. Cannons fired and arrows sailed, yet nothing but the sight of a battle made it through. Those fighting atop the Highway froze to look at the tornado, having appeared from nowhere. Many silvery-armored soldiers retreated into buildings, and rebels jumped onto the scaffolding to escape. Clusters of fighting resumed as all fled north, leaving bloody stains on the ground.

Two mounted soldiers charged, having spied the wagon. They rode full speed through the rain and bodies, ignoring the tornado. One waved an imperial banner and shouted words that were lost in the noise. A final volley was thrown easily away, and both sides stopped their shelling. The arrows stopped as well, and for another thirty seconds, the battle slowly lost momentum. Another minute of trotting got the group to the edge of the battlefield, on the top of the Empress's Highway.

The two mounted soldiers removed their helmets before saluting the tornado. Horns were heard without the cannons spoiling the night, and fighting stopped from each army. One of the riders dismounted to kneel formally before the twister. The rider's horse bolted in fear, but Demosyna looked around before lowering her hand.

The tornado blew outward in the blink of an eye, sending wood and rain to blanket the armies. More horns sounded, but there was near silence as the rain was stopped directly above. It was still pouring sleet on the east and west armies, but stars shone clear and bright in the snaking path. The hush that fell upon the night was deafening, and Demosyna looked down at the soldiers with a frown.

"Let us pass please, for we need to continue north," Demosyna called loudly, her voice ringing across stone.

The kneeling soldier saw Plu Durrah by the wagon and stood to address her. Plu still held both swords and marched forward with a smirk.

"Madam elf," the soldier said, "thank you for helping with that tornado. Can we escort you across our Empress's Highway once you finish these rebels?"

"You have a serious misunderstanding," Plu Durrah said, pointing one sword at Demosyna. "Bow to her and thank her purple scales you are not flung from the Highway. You may escort us if Demosyna desires, so ask our Wise-woman what she thinks, fool."

"Apologies, Wise-woman. Will you let us escort your party safely?"

The guard looked confused but saluted. The regal soldier bowed deeply, and the standard bearer blew a loud horn. Ten heavily armored soldiers marched from the buildings, carrying massive shields. A silver-masked commander led the soldiers in double time while donning a cape of authority. Spyglasses twinkled from both armies as they tried to get a view of the Highway, now free of tornadoes.

The young Wise-woman remained standing in the driver's seat as the commander removed its silver mask.

"Thank the Empress, a Wizen!" the soldier exclaimed, wiping blood from her armor. "I thank you for your assistance in fighting these seeder rebels!"

Demosyna shook her head, frowning.

"I want no part of this war yet, as I told your fellow soldier. You will escort us through the checkpoint so we may continue our way north! Please, ma'am, I don't want to see any more killing today."

There was a moment of silence, broken by the occasional horn or yell from the squads. The tank soldiers had formed up around the party before putting their shields facing the battle. A handful of rebels killed the last imperial soldiers while helping their fellows up the Highway. Lines of marching elves started pouring from the checkpoint, silver swords gleaming. The Highway was filling with soldiers, and those below grew restless.

"You are a citizen of this empire, and you cannot shirk your duty! These seeders need to be driven back!" the commander said, taking a step while drawing her sword. "Even as a Wise-woman, you serve our Empress!"

"I am just an apprentice," Demosyna explained. "I travel north to rejoin my Order and would appreciate an escort."

Demosyna's dog hunched low on his legs, growling loudly and glaring. The two horsewomen looked worried but drew their own swords and watched for further commands.

"If you are not a citizen, you have no choice!" the commander said, taking shackles from her belt. "Get down here and kill them, you Scale, or die with the rebels."

Passion rose in Demosyna's mind, and she used her left hand to send a tube of howling magic at the bindings. The aim was true, and the cruel iron cuffs were tossed away down the Highway. The commander looked shocked when the shackles were ripped from her grasp and lowered her sword.

"I will cross, soldier," Demosyna yelled, rage filling her voice. "Stand aside or help, but do it now. The eye of this calm I made is about to pass, and time is against us. Nobody will touch my friends, so keep your chains away!"

The soldier considered only a moment, sheathing her sword in a flash. The shield bearers formed a turtle shell of polished alloy, so Vaash and the dogs were blocked from view. The commander put her silver mask back on after bowing to Demosyna and grabbing the reigns.

"We can only escort a few at a time, so let us get your animals and boy across," the elf called through the mask. "Please, Wisewoman, wait here for our return."

The apprentice grabbed her crutch as she exited the driver's seat. No fighting had resumed, but the Highway was awash with tension. The air was still in a wide strip atop the road as more soaked rebels joined from below. A large, soggy banner was waved from the elven tents, and a squad had reached the top via elevator.

A dome of shields parted the lines forming up, and the cart was marched through the soldiers. Demosyna watched the lull in battle with hope, but Plu Durrah stretched her legs nearby in preparation. The cart was at the gate, having crossed nervously forming squads held back by spears. Vaash and the frightened dogs reappeared, and the escort began to move back when several Imperial Battle Wizen joined the fight.

Fire rocketed into the air, sizzling from rain pouring down on the west. Huge burning spheres sailed through the sky before splashing upon the eastern army. Bodies scattered in the force, breaking the peace in an instant. Balls of magically frozen rain were lobbed, shattering into millions of icy darts. Rebels yelled before surging forward to engage the elven militia. Fire exploded as cannons roared, sending fresh death across the fields. Magical lightning arced over the elevators in bold colors to dance between rebels as they climbed. Burning flesh and spilled blood filled the evening with black powder, and screams overlapped their presence.

Demosyna watched in horror as arrows began striking those battling atop the Highway. Their ancient horse trusted Vaash and only stamped a hoof from under the gateway. The monk tugged the dogs back, putting himself between a battle and the animals. Demosyna's white-haired dog locked eyes with her from across the span, muscles tense and teeth bared. Clanging swords rose in a chorus of mayhem, and Demosyna felt Plu Durrah nudge her with an elbow.

"Looks like we get to help after all!" the elf said, laughing wildly and cracking her neck. "I will clear a path to my gold if you want to follow with your magical crotch!"

"Please don't kill unless you have to, Plu!" Demosyna called, but the mercenary was already sprinting. "I can shield you while we cross."

The apprentice didn't know if she had been heard but limped on while making a small tornado. It roared into the sky for hundreds of feet but only remained around the purple-scaled woman. As before, when Demosyna protected the group, any projectiles were deflected away from the battle toward the southern horizon. Birds flew and trees fell from the streams of shrapnel flung back behind her while Demosyna let her mind absorb the scene.

Magic tore through the storm on both sides of the Highway as rebels began sending aggressive spells. The battle doubled in slaughter from when Demosyna arrived, and the magic was devastating to both armies. Entire squads of elven soldiers were smeared from the scene when trees were thrown over the Highway, glowing with spells. A broad elf clashed with a rebel near Vaash, who used his good arm to take both weapons in an instant. The monk didn't strike the two, simply plucked their swords from swinging hands. Both glanced from Vaash to each other and commenced to grapple on the cold stones.

Plu Durrah was sprinting between clusters of dueling armies, mostly avoiding the combat. The few who took swings at the elf met their end quickly, for Plu was extremely fast with both blades. An elf soldier stabbed a two-handed sword, but Plu rolled under the blade to thrust into ribs. Her short blade pierced the silvery armor, and Plu Durrah jumped away to continue. Rebels threw hatchets at the bald elf, but she slapped them away and laughed. A quick dash to the pair let Plu gut each one, leaving the rebels writhing near the edge. The merciless musician didn't engage in fights but dispatched elf and rebel alike in her journey.

A series of gigantic fireballs crashed into the tornado around Demosyna, and she felt the impacts move her cyclone. The winds sputtered for a moment but resumed their terrible dance with a roar. Nearly a hundred of each army were battling, clogging the Highway with bodies and curses. The groaning siege towers reached the edge of the stones, and a wooden ramp fell onto the Highway. Elven forces spread out, many with large shields covering the advance. A squad of crossbow soldiers tore into the rebels, sending bodies over the eastern side. This only served to enrage the rebel forces, and they streamed over their edge of the Highway with renewed passion.

Vaash was busy taking weapons from anyone threatening, and an elf noticed him disarming imperial soldiers. The commander motioned her crossbows to fire, and bolts sailed toward the monk. Two struck the wagon, but Vaash caught the others with speed that defied thought. The yellow-robed monk held the bundle of arrows in his right hand before tossing them over the edge. Vaash mouthed something to the elves, holding his hand up palm out, but Demosyna couldn't hear over the commotion. Her magical tornado erased a line of storm, and the combatants parted as Demosyna hobbled along.

The elven commander raised an axe, signaling her troops to charge. The serene monk tied his old dog's leash to the wagon before taking an unarmed step forward. Plu Durrah was slashing two throats at once, felling an elf and a rebel in one attack. Bolts flew toward Demosyna's friends, and she saw one hit near her dog's paw. Vaash grabbed numerous arrows from midair before pushing an armored soldier with his closed fist.

The force was enough to send the elf crashing into several advancing figures, and they fell in a heap. Plu Durrah emerged from the chaos to aid the monk, and Demosyna's faithful dog leaped to tear out a throat. The apprentice grew panicked when soldiers closed in on her friends and felt emotion threatening her reason. One rebel fell when Plu Durrah decapitated him, and an elf facing Vaash died when Plu stabbed through bone. Vaash was struck on the head by a club but carefully disarmed several elves as he glided around the battle.

Another volley of arrows narrowly missed the old gray dog, and Demosyna had seen enough. Her dog growled as a rebel kicked at the snarling animal, missing it by inches. The wide jaws of the canine tore into the rebel's face. Plu Durrah sparred with three elf soldiers.

All her friends stood blocking the gateway, feverishly battling both armies' rage for Demosyna.

"I will stop this madness myself," Demosyna shouted, her heart filled with revulsion.

The spiraling magic surrounding the young woman contracted, barely touching the bright-yellow robes. The battle nearly halted from her perspective, and Demosyna felt the tornado lift her off the Highway. She balanced on her left foot, and the cyclone held the frightened Wise-woman aloft. Terrified faces turned to view the roaring threat, and Demosyna smiled as light dripped from her teeth.

Focused tubes of wind exploded outward from the tornado, pinning dozens of people from both armies onto the Highway. Demosyna floated forward by using tunnels of wind as crutches to move her storm. Each soldier she pinned onto the Highway served as a stepping stone, and the radiant Wise-woman glided above everyone.

"I will not sit idle any longer!" Demosyna roared through a cyclone, her voice resonating across the sky. "I am Demosyna, and I am here!"

The cyclone tore the sky in agreement, and each person was left without air when her magic lifted from their bodies. Demosyna actually felt each lungful of breath leave her victims, joining the swirling fury protecting the woman. The tornado spun, and fifty legs of wind supported the feverish Wizen. Half of the battle atop the Highway was forcibly stopped, with many soldiers near Demosyna's friends sent breathless to the stones.

Vaash was dodging a spear, and Plu Durrah was yelling while plunging both swords into flesh. Demosyna's white dog was a streak of fur, lunging toward an elf near the older canine. Demosyna took a deep breath of frozen air, calming her mind and focusing her heart. The young woman ran like a spider and used numerous legs to support a cyclonic body. Demosyna fought back fatigue as she advanced, refusing to let harm befall her friends any longer.

The young apprentice hovered feet above the Highway with white light streaming from her eyes and mouth in painful gushes. Cannonballs and lightning crashed all around, but Demosyna ignored the screams of the dying. Her protective tornado sent all the aggressive projectiles south, and the apprentice screamed once she reached the wagon. All the soldiers surrounding the checkpoint, elf and rebel alike, were violently smashed to the bloody surface of the Highway.

"Stop!" Demosyna bellowed, burning tears falling from her eyes. "Please, just stop."

The apprentice's entire body radiated feverish light, streaming from her horns, nails, teeth, and eyes. She nearly lost herself to the anguish in her heart, but Demosyna lifted her head and shrieked her plea. No words were spoken, but a terrible and desperate cry issued forth from the Wizen. Demosyna's magic protection blasted away from the checkpoint, sending soldiers toppling and one siege tower crashing into another.

Vaash had begun scooping up both dogs in his strong arms, ignoring the broken limb. Plu Durrah was jumping into the driver's seat with her elven face coated in blood. Demosyna broke her focus on the tornado and drifted to the Highway with a final cyclonic growl. For half a mile on either side of the Empress's Highway, both armies were laid flat by magic. Trees whipped violently, and all were dazed when tossed to the ground.

Demosyna sent disappointment outward from her exhausted body, limiting her justice with mercy for life. Two elf soldiers crashed into the tilted siege tower, buckling planks to reveal more armored figures. Twenty rebels were sent into the wood scaffolding on the eastern side while grasping for purchase on the soaked framework. Vaash had deposited the canines, and Demosyna felt his burning grip on her robes. The apprentice was pulled backward, her monk friend steering an unresponsive body into the cart.

The stress of the magics had rendered Demosyna useless, and she sat in a wagon with numb thoughts forming her reality. The Wise-woman's body no longer pumped burning light, and Plu Durrah smacked the ancient horse into motion. Vaash ran backward behind the speeding wagon, jumping and snatching arrows from the air with expert precision. No soldier pursued the cart, turning instead to continue fighting one another once they stood.

Neither dog moved during the flight from the battle while remaining huddled together on top of the piled loot. Blood dripped from white jaws and green clothes as the orange-and-yellow-robed monk protected their retreat.

Demosyna faded from the world, hoping that the screams she caused didn't mean more death.

CHAPTER 26

Her strong white dog remained at Demosyna's side as she lay in the wagon for over a day. Vaash cleaned the blood from its fur, but the faithful animal refused to do much as it waited. The warm hound kept the young Wise-woman from shivering in the storm while the blankets and covered wagon left her dry. Both of her companions took turns driving the cart, the other guarding the back with drenched clothes. Lightning and blood twisted through her mind, but Demosyna rested without haunting nightmares. The battlefield was left in the distant south, and the group continued through the storm atop the Highway.

The young woman woke in the bright light of the afternoon, the wagon having left the storm covering the battling armies. Demosyna's loyal dog barked in happiness before licking her face with quizzical eyebrows. The apprentice sat up with a start, expecting a battle to greet her waking mind. Vaash grinned and laughed, his green eyes full of dancing light. Plu Durrah was driving and noticed the young woman waking from her magic-induced slumber. The cart moved steadily along, and no other travelers dared the Highway so close to a battlefield.

"Demosyna!" Vaash called, laughing. "This one is glad you are awake! You were so amazing, my friend! Thank you for saving our lives!"

"That was quite the tantrum, purple scale!" Plu Durrah exclaimed, smiling down at the Wizen. "Warn me next time you decide to turn into a millipede so I can run faster! Gross. Way too many legs!"

Demosyna sipped water to quench her burning throat, breathing heavy streams of vapor into the cold air. She was ravenous and still drained from her explosion of anger. The apprentice recalled gliding over dozens of squirming bodies, each one gasping for air as her tornado passed. The feeling of power and brutality had almost overtaken the woman, as it had when Demosyna escaped her captivity.

The love Demosyna felt for her friends and her newfound self had banished any desire to submit to ignorance in the moment. Seeing the armies slaughter hundreds with the wave of a hand had revolted Demosyna to her core, but her friends' peril cemented her will. She was finally strong enough to help, and Demosyna refused to allow anyone else to stop her from saving someone.

"Thank you two for fighting so hard," Demosyna panted, looking at both of her friends with tears. "I saw everything so clearly like it was a painting in a museum. I am so glad you are safe and didn't befall the fate other friends have."

"Sir Monk here didn't bother to kill anyone from what I could tell."

Plu Durrah laughed, turning back to keep driving.

"At least I actually stopped them, not just pushed them into their playmates!"

"This one is saddened violence was used," Vaash said, shaking his long red hair. "For never again does this one wish to kill! Force was applied with that goal in mind."

Demosyna searched the scattered containers before finding a long strip of jerky in a barrel. She tore into the peppered meat with sharp teeth, and the Wizen's stomach stopped screaming from under yellow-and-orange robes. The storm was a dark line over the southern horizon, and Demosyna tossed a strip of meat to her dog. The apprentice had fetched another large portion of dried flesh and ate the half she didn't feed her young pup.

Vaash offered a stale loaf of bread, having not baked while the storm had poured down. The young Wizen didn't complain about the dry crusts and simply gobbled the loaf with thankful eyes. Demosyna's white-haired dog jumped from the slow wagon, stretching its limbs from the long vigil.

"This good boy waited by your side as you slept!" Vaash said, petting the dog's wide head. "You are such a smart hound! That you are!"

The animal pranced in playful bounds, smiling and eyeing Demosyna with affection. Vaash's older dog sniffed at the canine, and the two animals trailed behind the wagon. Demosyna felt worlds better after her meal and drank more water from a nearly empty skin. The wagon must not have reached a checkpoint yet, so the young woman left water for her friends.

"Did anyone follow us?" Demosyna asked, letting her left boot swing from the cart.

Vaash shook his head, smiling at his matching-robed friend.

"The battle still rages, most likely."

The young apprentice sighed, leaning against the side of the covered wagon. Crisp, lightning-flashed images floated in her mind, and Demosyna closed her eyes against the setting sun. There was a slender strip of ocean visible from their height but ended nearly where the star was sinking. Red rays bathed the water and forests in blood as screaming faces bobbed in stormy visions. The battle had been fierce, but Demosyna felt pride that her anger hadn't burned out of control.

"What is the next stage of training, Vaash?" Demosyna asked after the sun had stopped stabbing her eyes. "I am eager to keep at it!"

"If that is what you desire, this one is happy to help!" Vaash exclaimed, scratching his broken arm. "Rest for tonight would be advised, but the next practice will involve balance and control. The daylight training can be done from the step behind the wagon, for you will balance in a stance while throwing. At night, this one would ask you do the same, but balanced on one foot at a time!"

Vaash demonstrated the stance he meant, with his knees nearly squared to the Highway. It was the same powerful, wide-leg posture that had helped the monk lift the wagon days ago. The stubborn old horse left the human behind for a moment while he posed, but Vaash caught up with a smile. Both dogs were sniffing the man when he returned, and Vaash pointed to a heavy backpack.

Demosyna hefted the bulky satchel to the edge of the cart, finding numerous stones of rounded colors. Plu Durrah had turned to observe the two and laughed when she saw Vaash's backpack full of river stones.

"Is that really all you own, Vaash? What would you even use them for?" Plu Durrah said, laughing into the sky. "I can lend you some pants. Or maybe a new robe? Both of you need a bath, so I am glad I am upwind!"

Vaash laughed as well.

"This one never knows when such could be useful. Until Demosyna finds a ball for her dog, she can use these as projectiles!"

The wide-shouldered monk chose two smooth stones, juggling them both in his good right hand. His fluffy old dog jumped and barked in excitement, but Demosyna's hound walked away to mark the Highway. Plu Durrah laughed at the man, seeing his dexterous trick from her periphery. Vaash gently tossed a stone toward the seated Wise-woman, and she caught it easily.

Her cast foot no longer hurt, so Demosyna let it dangle while catching the other rock. Both weighed about the same, Demosyna felt while holding them, but each was differently shaped. One was nearly spherical, with a chip missing to flatten a side, yet the other was wider and nearly flat. They would be much harder to hold in the air than a leaf, but Demosyna was ready for a new challenge.

Demosyna focused on the gentle breeze against her face, closing her eyes as the moon rose higher into the stars. Her first attempt only sent the rocks tumbling to the Highway after jumping from the Wizen's hands at the force used. Vaash laughed and stopped his dog from biting the stone in its long jaws.

The apprentice tried many more times before the group stopped for a meal and put the animals near the fire. Her robe was soaking her cold sweat away, but the young Wise-woman smiled from the task. Vaash had set up camp, as he usually did when they stopped, and Plu Durrah stretched from her long shift driving.

The smiling monk stood by the fire, sawing into his elbow with a long serrated knife. Vaash made a rough circle around the dirty arm cast, letting him move his left elbow again. The hard plaster cracked and fell from the joint before exposing Vaash's flexing muscles. He tested his forearm with calloused fingers and removed the cast with the jagged tool. His exposed arm was slightly paler than the other, and Vaash laughed as he moved the healed limb.

The monk's dog barked with a loud voice, her spotted tongue dangling from fuzzy jaws. Demosyna's cast was removed next, and the woman was overjoyed to see her foot. It was strong and whole; only the healed stump of the big toe told of the injuries. The teary-eyed Wise-woman thanked Vaash while carefully wiggling her toes once they were free.

It had been nearly maddening sometimes to not move her toes, but the disciplined apprentice let them heal undisturbed. The claws were long, having not clipped any, but no toes ached when Demosyna touched them. She had expected pain when gently prodding the foot, yet none flared as the young woman rotated her ankle. Even when Demosyna stood with hesitant balance, her foot seemed completely healed.

Plu Durrah noticed the missing digit wiggle as the stump was flexed, and Vaash tested the metal toe. It was still bright silver in shade, but the inlaid scales seemed to blend into the foot. The look of the prosthetic made her well up in tears, and Demosyna thanked the man for his devotion.

Demosyna took off her left boot, letting both soles feel the icy stones of the Empress's Highway. She walked in small steps at first, but the apprentice's leashed dog pulled the exuberant woman to go faster. The view was a spectacular sight for the Wizen, and Demosyna threw the remains of her cast into the forest below. They had smelled awful, and Demosyna was glad to be rid of the itchy weight on her leg. The stars glittered happily as Demosyna tested her foot by marching her dog around the camp for long minutes. He walked with his wide dog smile ever present, and the friends laughed as the meal was done cooking.

Demosyna twirled the ring on her thumb in thought, taking the bowl Vaash offered.

"How long to the next checkpoint? Does anyone know? Because they are not marked on this map here."

"That is quite the drawing, Demosyna!" Plu Durrah said, leaning over to look. "Did Vaash use his broken arm to doodle this? The Highway is in the right place at least!"

All laughed at Plu's jests, and Demosyna estimated they were near the end of the Empress's Highway. They couldn't see the large peninsulas depicted by the map, but the coast was frequently seen in the distance. The sun had shown the apprentice that they had indeed turned enough to be heading more easterly each day. The curve shown on the map was unseen by the minuscule travelers, and it was a marvelous feat of engineering.

Demosyna had begun marking the previous tollbooths along the map's highway, little purple lines near the long path. She also marked the place Demosyna thought her sunken boat lay with a question mark, just south of the First Fort. The young woman was tempted to draw where her waterfall cave might be but decided to keep the secret. Her new wealth allowed the woman dreams of renting a cabin in the city.

"I wanted to post more notices about my friends. I nailed a few up along the way at each checkpoint that allowed it but needed more paper!" the purple-scaled woman explained, barefoot in the starlight. "The battle made me worry about Rrra and Jui, alone while a war closes in. I can only trust the postings remain and aren't lost from fighting at a previous tollbooth."

Neither of the companions knew the distance, so Demosyna nodded and sighed.

The simple meal was enjoyed, and the animals were fed from their buckets. Vaash declined any wine, so Plu Durrah drank with a smile when Demosyna passed as well. The Wizen was busy trying to hold the heavy stones with her magic and stood on one bent leg by the fire.

Her thigh burned from the stance, but her strong tail aided Demosyna's balance. Her healed right foot took the stance without complaint, and the young Wise-woman grinned in the firelight. The travelers moved on at sunrise with Demosyna offering to drive after her long slumber. The apprentice meditated to regain her energy and saw the ruins of the checkpoint ahead once afternoon arrived.

There were no bodies and no sign of armies in the trees lining the Highway. Wooden wreckage smoldered in half-dead fires, so the smoke first alerted the party of danger. The old horse seemed unfazed by the lack of a checkpoint and stopped for Demosyna to investigate. It stamped an impatient hoof as the group cautiously walked to the splintered mounds.

A large metal gate was somehow in a tree on the eastern side, bending the trunk with its great mass. The two-story structure was leveled and burned some time ago, leaving nothing but splintered wood piled on the road. Vaash cleared several rubble hills to make a path while Plu Durrah searched for anything useful. A smashed barrel still held water, but Demosyna saw the mercenary pour it out. It was dirty with blood and ash, so the group found nothing of help from the ruined checkpoint. Their water was nearly gone, and without an elevator, the friends hoped it rained soon.

Demosyna touched the rolled papers in her breast pocket and gazed south with a worried brow. The wagon was moved along quickly, nobody wanting to risk camping anywhere nearby. The times when others drove let Demosyna stand on the bouncing step behind the wagon and crouch in straining focus. It grew much easier to balance on her toes, and Demosyna got used to the uncomfortable stance Vaash recommended. The monk would watch her while guarding the south with both dogs padding along peacefully.

"Control the weight. Don't just hold it up," Vaash advised as she improved. "As with physical lifting, use the bigger muscles first— back to shoulder, arm to hand. Each muscle supports the other, and enormous strength is found. This one could easily hold a weight up, but to control it at arm's length is another matter!"

A day passed with sore training, and Demosyna got an idea as she balanced on the cart. The apprentice made thin tubes of magic from each of her fingers, stretching about a foot from her hands. This proved better to hold the heavy river stones, and Demosyna was eager to refine this new skill. The flatter was pinched between magical digits, and Demosyna soon was rolling the spherical rock as her purple fingers wiggled.

The weight seemed to grow with the distance her magic sent the stones, and Demosyna felt her arms now strained with powerful legs. She slowly drew the training aids back, just before Demosyna couldn't hold her shaking arms up anymore.

* * * * *

Nearly another week passed before an intact checkpoint was seen using Plu Durrah's spyglass to prevent ambush. One more was found in ruins but had long since been abandoned. No fires burned in the wooden pieces without bodies, but some dried blood was found. The weather had been mild—no rain but with a persistent chill. Their last reserve of water was depleted, and the weary travelers marched along.

Demosyna found that walking was a treat after sitting around for nearly a month and explored with her healed foot. Both of the apprentice's feet matched now, and the dark-yellow leather rang from a capped heel and toe. Vaash wore both armguards, a dark-stained sunflower, but declined the thick leather breastplate that Demosyna had set aside.

"This one doesn't really need armor but loves the gift you have given," Vaash explained, admiring the matching bracers. "It will aid in defense, for another break would be an unwelcome diversion!"

Plu Durrah rode silently in the back of the cart, tying ropes together from all their gear. Plu had mentioned climbing down to get water, as many streams and ponds were visible from the Highway. But it appeared that repelling would not be necessary when Demosyna saw an approaching building rising above the road.

Leather-clad guards milled around while collecting a toll from the lone traveler ahead. The figure marched south, a hood hiding their face. It was a Paw and walked huddled in a large silver cloak with charcoal fur hands. Vaash greeted the solitary figure, but the cloak moved away without a word. The checkpoint stood empty of pilgrims, and only a few seeder guards were present.

They eyed Plu Durrah and Demosyna with suspicion when the pair approached, leaving Vaash with the wagon. One was a human woman, and the other two were Orc men, all dressed in studded leather. No toll was posted above the gate, and a lack of vendors surrounding the checkpoint gave Demosyna pause.

"The free people's toll is two gold pieces, strangers," the woman said, leaning against a wooden wall. "Each!"

Both Orcs stood in front of the closed gate, huge wooden poles clutched in their strong hands. Demosyna was gathering her coins, but Plu Durrah smiled wickedly.

"Free people toll, eh?" the elf said, wrists on twin swords. "That sounds like quite the hustle! I approve, you slippery fellows! What do you say to one gold piece for a sympathizing mind?"

The human shook her head and smiled, motioning her Orc companions forward. They raised their thick wooden weapons in aggressive manners, and the woman giggled.

"If you were as smart as us, you would have your own tollbooth," she said, drawing a dagger. "Maybe two coins would be the wrong toll judging from your loaded wagon! I think we will take what we want and let you pass after. Feel free to turn around, but the Highway in the south might prove a challenge! We are the only checkpoint for over a week. My boys made sure of that!"

A flash of metal was all Demosyna saw as the dagger lashed out, and she reflexively raised her left hand. It was slashed by the quick attack, opening the palm and several fingers. Blood ran down her wrist, and the young apprentice took a backward leap. Plu Durrah had already drawn both swords and parried a thrusting dagger.

The skilled mercenary did a flourish with her blades and removed both of the bandit's hands at the wrists. The leather-clad human shrieked in pain, falling to the Highway with a whimper. Both Orcs took a sword to the face while barely beginning to swing their poles. Demosyna didn't have time to cast magic, defensive or otherwise, before her deadly companion killed all three attackers.

Demosyna's dog had given a rare bark in concern, but Vaash patted the animal once the fight was won. Demosyna barely winced at the raw pain in her hand, wrapping the gash in a clean bandage. The apprentice had taken to carrying a couple of rolls of bandages after the battle and was glad for the foresight. The colorless cloth turned a bright red, and Demosyna held her hands flat together to apply pressure.

Plu Durrah was looting the bodies, tossing things over the edge as she checked pockets and armor.

"That was easy! This war must have taken the elves away, leaving only a skeleton crew, if those morons took a gate," the musician said, standing from her kills. "Let's see if there is water inside or maybe some extra gold! If they have been running this little scam for a while, we may get lucky! It was pretty bold, though, seizing a checkpoint from the empire with three people."

Demosyna called to Vaash the plan, and both women moved through the unlocked left door. They adopted a crouched posture, as they had when robbing the corrupt circus. Demosyna followed on all fours, able to use her foot again for sneaking. The apprentice had always favored a low-to-the-ground approach when playing as a child and balanced with her powerful tail. Plu Durrah glanced back once and smiled with wide eyes at the crawling young woman.

The large room comprising the first floor of the left building was empty, save a staircase and dining room. The matching wooden table and chairs took up a corner with stairs to the left upon entering. A small bookshelf held several books, but the women ascended the stairs with Plu Durrah's swords leading.

Her hand ached and left a smear of blood on the stairs, yet Demosyna ignored the small pain. The apprentice had endured the cruel hobbling by Sai Aeri, and pain was now vastly more relative.

The second floor was a hallway leading to the other side of the Highway, with doors on both walls. Four rooms stood closed ahead, and the two each took a different knob. Plu Durrah counted down five pink-painted nails, and they opened the doors together. Both were bedrooms with simple cots and empty chests as the only furniture. The other rooms proved the same, but a wardrobe held several sets of elven armor. It was of fine custom design and seemed to flow with metallic strength.

Demosyna had never seen the armor not on an elven soldier and was amazed it appeared like a cloth top. The thick metal shone and moved like silk, but Demosyna felt the armor's solidity between her claws. It seemed a hybrid between chain mail and plate armor, so Demosyna rolled up a top that looked her size. She tucked the prize into her wide orange belt, following Plu Durrah when the elf left empty-handed.

Stairs leading down to the rightmost building revealed a kitchen and secured armory. Iron bars made a cage of the right corner, and a simple stove with a cabinet served as a kitchen under wooden stairs. Windows had been in each bedroom on the second floor, and one was on each wall of the bottom floors. These had allowed flags to be waved during the battle days ago, and Demosyna sighed a cloud of relieved breath.

The checkpoint was empty of other bandits, and Plu Durrah sheathed her swords. A metal safe was locked behind the cage, along with various weapons lining the walls. Straight leaf-bladed swords leaned in their racks, and long spears stood beside lances, nearly touching the roof. Stacks of tall shields lay on the floor, but Demosyna didn't see anything she desired. The weapons might be valuable, but the young Wizen thought of her full wagon and left them.

Plu Durrah had both the cage and the safe open with her lock picks, revealing thirty bags of loose points and gold pieces. There were far more triangular coins filling the pouches, and the pair loaded their pockets with loot. Plu Durrah divided the bags without open-ing the drawstring tops, simply feeling the coins' shape and handing them over. Demosyna was nervous in the creaking wooden building, but the silence was unbroken as the two took the goods.

"I don't know where they hid the key, but at least this gold won't go to waste when the Empress takes this back!" Plu Durrah said, rub-bing her bald head and searching. "You should see what those books were, because there isn't any food worth taking. I will load these bar-rels if you want to visit their library!"

Fortune had been with the group, and three full water barrels were rolled out the open door. Vaash saw the mercenary push two barrels onto the Highway and secured the animals to help.

Demosyna walked back upstairs to move to the opposite side, reviewing the books with a practiced hand. The apprentice didn't bother sneaking anymore, and her boots clapped on the wood floors. Several of the tomes were useless logs of travel, detailing the daily tolls taken and any notable incidents.

Demosyna's eyes grew wide when they fell upon a gold-bound codex, heavy with dense pages of shaved leather. It was a cover style that Demosyna recognized, for it resembled books that were outside her apprentice level of access. Demosyna would often gaze into the official Wise-woman library, seeing the talented people busy studying ancient and powerful secrets.

Demosyna lifted the book with her uninjured hand, eyeing golden leaf script stamped into the cover and spine. It was clearly an elven text, and Demosyna opened the cover with bloody fingers. The contents list took the woman's breath away, for it covered several different types of magic. Healing was near the middle of the seven chapters, and the apprentice turned to let the window illuminate the pages.

As with all elven words, the meanings of the lines were complex and subjective. One symbol might need another to be legible, but both could also be used separately for different meanings. Demosyna had spent years studying the timeless language and could read most things she had encountered. This text was near gibberish, because it spoke more in the abstract from what the wide-eyed Wizen saw.

Diagrams and figures accompanied the symbols, showing what the confusing letters were to discuss. The apprentice wasn't terribly distressed, as she grasped the surface level of the text. When magic was involved, Demosyna knew from her dealings with elven people that things could easily be layered with ceremony.

A series of illustrations depicted different levels of flesh bodies, from skin to muscle to bone. The text referenced healthy and broken states, showing bones and organs in different levels of injury. Her studies had never encountered such ancient and mysterious works, so Demosyna carried the treasure back to the wagon.

The animals were drinking a small ration of water, eagerly lapping from the buckets Vaash filled. They had been dehydrated as well, the entire group having been forced to limit water for days. Plu and Vaash stood chatting over their clay water cups, and Demosyna failed to miss the crutch as she walked. Vaash looked with concern at her bandaged hand, but Demosyna smiled and shook her head.

"I found something that may help!" the young Wise-woman said happily, letting the monk examine the elven armor. "I will try this part here."

The young woman pointed a clawed finger at a diagram, but neither friend could read the intricate Wise-woman variant of elven. Plu Durrah studied the book while flipping through the pages with a grin.

"This is the junk you were schooled on?" Plu asked, eyeing the detailed gold ink. "I can see why most don't become Wise-women! These elven letters are all swirled around but still seem to form a thought. Odd."

Her focusing charm grew red-hot, and Demosyna hissed in surprise. She had directed her mind on the lessons the book described, trying to understand the symbolic meanings. A faint light shone from the depths of her ring, and Demosyna felt a painful tingle in her injured left hand. The wound didn't close entirely, but the flesh sealed enough to stop throbbing.

The apprentice was left breathless by the effort her healing took, grabbing the cart to steady herself. Vaash put a worried hand on her shoulder, but Demosyna smiled as she removed the bandage. The dagger cut was only an angry red line across her palm and fingers, slanting in the path the blade struck. Vaash smiled at the healing, seeing the clean wound was already beyond further need of help.

A vague golden mist had formed around the injury before seeping into the wound with sluggish waves. It was nothing like the solid rings that Klai had produced, but Demosyna was elated by the newfound magic. The burning charm was worrying to the inexperienced Wizen, yet she ignored the development as the gold band cooled.

Practice would be needed to master the spell, and Demosyna grinned with pride.

"At least something came from the lives lost here," the young Wizen said, eyeing the bodies Vaash had moved from the gate. "Let me know the next time anyone needs healing, because I intend to study hard on that subject for a while!"

"Knowing you, you'll be raising the dead before the hour is out!" Plu Durrah said, handing the book back. "Study away, smooth scale! We should move on in case any of their friends are around."

Everyone agreed, and Vaash's large dog barked in blind joy.

The wagon moved on with Demosyna reading from the driver's seat. The empty sky domed above the travelers, and flute complimented harp as songs were sung. Plu Durrah's newest song about Demosyna was recited, causing laughs from the yellow-robed friends.

A mountain moved aside as the laughing cart traveled, revealing a huge collection of buildings on the horizon. It was built against the side of a large mountain, and its sectors rose nearly to the first peak. Demosyna gasped at the sight of the mountain supporting the city, for it soared into the sky to a point before widening again to a flat top. A deep shadow fell over the city from the impossible mountain, which seemed to brace the stars with its heights. The hourglass shape formed by the mountain defied belief, as the stone colossus seemed to reflect itself from the frozen peak.

An interconnected city ascended the slope of the bottom mountain with a harbor in the west. A peninsula was seen jutting from the rolling landscape, but Demosyna didn't know which one she observed. The crude map showed a pair of triangles pointing toward each other, with a plateau just beside to depict the grandeur displayed. The symbols were near two fingers of land, so the Wisewoman was unsure about the actual location. Demosyna did know that she was nearly done with her perilous journey, for those icons were at the top of the Fist.

The city sparkling from the horizon was the closest to the north Orders and the most profitable city in the Fist. A bustling harbor and access to the Empress's Highway ensured this early colonized location was a major center of trade.

Demosyna didn't know much about the city, as the sight of the mountain was something that failed to come through the dry words of books. They often described a double mountain, or a flattop peak, when telling of the Wise-woman Settlement. Images of plateaus and crooked mountains leaning together had filled the apprentice's mind till now. The truth of the landscape was beautiful and disturbing, as the wide top balanced on a pinpoint of snow.

The mountains that trailed away from the city were all normal in the sense that they rose to a peak from the hills and forests. Rivers flowed from their snowcapped heights, rushing toward the endless sea. Her mind wanted to look anywhere but the illogical mountain on the horizon, as the dizzying sight brought tears to Demosyna's eyes.

Vaash and Plu Durrah joined the awestruck young woman while passing a spyglass to compensate for their weaker eyes. The sprawling metropolis was one of legend, being founded at the base of a great dwarven ruin. The tales told it was among the only remaining legacies the weavers had left, as no Dwarves were found in the Empress's world. The city clung to the towering mountain on gray domes with many clusters of buildings held within golden glass tops. Thin roads connected the city from its separate areas, winding across the mountain like snakes.

Instead of a large walled city like Demosyna had always known, this settlement was broken apart into grand bubbles of safety. The bottoms of the spheres were stone with some having small parks or farms under their massive yellow windows. The arching glass tops showed buildings and imperial volcanoes with smoke seen escaping a central hole above the townspeople. The gap was directly above the circular imperial square, giving the volcanoes' smoke an exit. It was an amazing display of form, for the sections of the city seemed to balance on their spherical bodies. The mountain nested the people living there, and the beautiful glass domes kept heat from escaping in the thin, brutal air.

Demosyna took in the sight while already planning in her sharp mind. Farms encircled the base of the mountain as colorful patches even in the midst of winter. It was the most plots of land the young

Wise-woman had seen, and thousands of chained figures were tend-ing the plants. Half was lost behind the mountain, but the ring of spaced farmland told the volume of work in the city.

Railroad tracks enclosed the farmland, swinging wide away from the harbor road. Train whistles carried across the fields for miles in all directions with the landscape free from the forests around the mountain. Whipped figures pulled huge wagons of cut trees, meet-ing a train to send the raw wood into the city.

She had a fresh and unwavering surety in herself and her new friends, but Demosyna knew her own limitations would hinder any rising ideals. The commander's ready chains had awoken a deep fire in her young heart, and Demosyna studied the magical book with desperation. As with the First Fort, her mind swam with half-formed ideas and possible solutions regarding a next step. The war was clearly getting more dangerous the farther north she led her friends, and the last bandit encounter had taken the Wizen by surprise.

Demosyna flexed her bandaged hand, noticing the dressing needed changing. The party moved on from the breathtaking view of their hard-sought goal, and Demosyna would soon have a loyal army to aid in her unceasing war.

CHAPTER 27

The next checkpoint the group reached was free of bandits, and the travelers browsed merchant booths with grins. Demosyna restocked her writing supplies after posting the last of her notices at the tollbooth. Plu Durrah refilled her dry wineskins and grinned as she carried back another barrel of wine for reserve. Vaash took some coins from the young Wise-woman before leaving to restock their foodstuffs.

She had spied a booth with toys and marched her furry knee-high companion around as Demosyna shopped. A pair of throwing balls was found, and Demosyna purchased a spare ball after thinking a moment. She took her three toys back to the wagon and laughed at the older dog's wide blind eyes. The show dog clearly wanted to play, so Demosyna tossed the dogs their new toys while her friends bartered. The apprentice had stored her crutch under fresh piles of gear in the cart, not wanting to throw the heartfelt gift away. Her foot was finally healed, and Demosyna could play with her dog more now.

The training that Demosyna practiced for hours each day and night now would use these dense leather spheres. Demosyna strained her legs and mind to throw them down the Highway, sending her panting dog to fetch. A second attempt to hold the ball sent it flying off the Highway, causing laughs from all who saw.

Several travelers were watching the display while laughing loudly at the misfortune. Demosyna laughed as well, pulling her eager dog from jumping after the ball. Vaash had assured her that he wouldn't fall off the edge, but Demosyna still worried about the loyal hound's safety.

"I've got a spare!" Demosyna called to the passing figures. "Safe travels!"

The two Scales waved their blue hands and marched farther up the Highway. Vaash was returning from his latest haul of food, smiling as he dropped the sacks into a near-full wagon.

"Three people really take up space!" Demosyna exclaimed, showing the dog toys to him. "At least I found these, so my dog and I can train together!"

Demosyna used a large gust of wind to hurl the ball back down the Highway, laughing as her dog bolted in pursuit. He grinned his toothy grin while sprinting atop the world, and sharp yellow-gold eyes tracked the dot. A streak of white fur caught the ball after a few bounces, and the dog avoided travelers on his return. Demosyna saw shocked and worried faces at the loose animal, with its huge jaws and muscular frame.

A few fearful visages turned upon seeing the magic, hurrying away to pass the checkpoint. The young Wizen frowned while grabbing her naked dog's harness from the wagon. It was a simple design but had several adjustable cinch points to fit the thick leather straps firmly. As the dog stood and allowed its fitting, Demosyna stroked the silky white fur. In place of a neck collar, a harness around the chest and front paws was needed for the powerful canine. The dog stood panting in joy with the ball held in proud display, so Demosyna praised him and took the toy.

"Good job, boy!" Demosyna said, kneeling and rubbing the dog's rear leg. "You got that ball so quickly! I'm proud of you, good boy!"

He seemed to really enjoy when the purple-scaled woman massaged his wide hips, often pressing into the rubbing hands with wide eyes. Demosyna laughed as he backed up into her massaging fingers and rubbed the dense muscles for another moment.

Plu Durrah was returning from her errands and plucked absently on a harp as she sauntered closer. Plu was singing the Tin Toed verses completed thus far with her melodious voice ringing out for all to hear. A few children, bundles of coats with tiny feet below, giggled at the music and pranced. Tips were collected in her floppy green hat, and Plu Durrah thanked all the onlookers.

"That's all for now, my generous listeners!" Plu Durrah called, leaning against the cart. "I will be in yonder metropolis for a while, so visit me in any of my favorite bars! Those other so-called musicians won't even see me coming!"

A few laughing spectators wandered away before paying the toll to pass the elven soldiers. This checkpoint was heavily defended with cannons atop the wooden building and lining the edge. Mounted patrols clopped in large groups, going single file when moving under the gate on the routes. The imperial banners hung everywhere, and Demosyna was glad to move on once Vaash paid the toll.

The monk tossed the ball to his old dog, laughing as she snatched it from midair. They played catch like this till the large animal grew tired, and she slept in the wagon with Plu. The long stretch of the Highway now had a set landmark in the distance, and Demosyna drove the cart slightly east as the city expanded. It was still so far away that it would take over a week to reach, but the superb view from the Highway let the friends see their destination.

Demosyna studied her map, wondering how many checkpoints remained. They had gotten less frequent as the apprentice traveled north, but none would be seen ahead till they rose from the horizon. Storm clouds were forming over the mountainous city, promising rain and snow sometime soon.

* * * * *

That evening, Vaash burned his hand on a hot cooking pot, and Demosyna rushed over with a gleam in her yellow eye. The apprentice reviewed a page of text one final time while breathing healing over the injury. Her wind magic had come naturally to the young Wise-woman, but this mending spell was painful when cast. It was like running her hand through broken glass—not cutting her but scraping painfully.

Demosyna hissed as a dim gold light barely touched the burned thumb, blown away in the steady wind. It was more successful than the dagger cut had been, and the burn faded after a few heartbeats.

The drain from the magic was horrible, so Demosyna sat down slowly to avoid fainting. Spots were forming in her vision, and Vaash gave the apprentice some water.

"Easy, Demosyna!" Vaash said, concern in his voice. "It was just a small burn. This one doesn't want you to push yourself to such extremes!"

Demosyna shook her head, smiling through her mental pain.

"I am happy to help, Vaash. I think I just need to get better at the spell. I can kind of remember the wind being painful at first too. It's all fuzzy and vague in my mind, though."

"Thank you, my friend," the monk said, standing to continue cooking. "This one knows you will find what you seek, if you truly devote yourself towards a goal! Nobody has been able to even slow you down. So passionate is your heart!"

Demosyna laughed, shaking her vision free of darkness.

"Think nothing of it!"

The yellow-robed Wizen meditated on the recent developments with her training. The good fortune felt at finding the book had faded. So difficult was the interpretation that she spent hours reading the same word. She felt as though she was mentally pushing against a huge weight each time she tried the magic. The willpower required to produce even a pathetic mist of health was taxing, and the grating feeling was worrying.

Demosyna pushed ahead with the practice anyway, healing small cuts and bruises as they traveled. Plu Durrah would laugh at the trembling state Demosyna was reduced to, shaking her bald head at the healed splinter or blister.

Traffic increased noticeably for a few days, but after leaving an elevator behind, it ebbed. One of the last checkpoints was littered with upturned carts, spaced as cover leading to the buildings. A recent battle had given the rebels control, and they were amassed in force to keep it.

Nearly sixty leather-armored soldiers milled in rough units, covering both sides of the gate. They were letting people pass after taking the coins, and Demosyna discussed the unexpected development with her friends.

"This one can scout if you wish," Vaash offered, judging the distant armed figures with squinted green eyes. "Their barricades may be hiding ambushes."

"You never know with those seeding rebels!" Plu Durrah said unhappily, crossing her strong arms. "Looks like they aren't just some bandits I can loot. Dang! I was hoping for some new swords, but nobody has any better than these! Alas, my search continues!"

"I would like to stick together, seeing the size of the squad ahead," Demosyna mused, thinking hard. "Would you watch the pets, Plu?"

"That great beast of yours doesn't really like me, Demosyna," the bard responded, wiping her bald head. "I guess I could, but Vaash enjoys it so much more! I would hate if he didn't smell like dog every day!"

The canine had gotten better about shying away from Plu Durrah but remained nervous and jittery if the elf was too near. Demosyna nodded, and Vaash smiled his normal serene expression.

"It is a wonderful view, and this one is happy to enjoy it with wet noses!" Vaash said, gathering the leashes. "Come, noble hounds! The city is a sight to behold. That it is!"

The elderly dog barked for nearly two minutes straight, pawing a ball in the wagon. The horse had to be carefully guided in a twisting pattern to narrowly miss the spaced obstacles. Several were large piles of rocks, but most were wooden stacks of clutter serving as walls.

They were halfway over the span to pay the toll when a horn sounded, sending a portion of the forces to investigate. Long spears and drawn bows were aimed at the halted group, and Demosyna stared at the response to their presence. Vaash watched from the ancient horse's side, and the two women stepped forward when a commander waved.

"What are you doing sneaking this elf into our free North?" the commander asked, rage in her voice. "Disguising her as a mercenary won't let it slide, Scale. Explain yourself!"

The young Wise-woman did after a moment of panicked musing. She was completely blindsided by the question, and Demosyna had to gather her thoughts.

"I am Demosyna, ma'am," the apprentice began, touching her chest with a ringed left hand. "These are my friends, who have joined my journey along the Highway."

Demosyna was taking a breath to continue, but many of the faces of rebel soldiers grew terrified at the name. Four actually took a step backward, their weapons shaking slightly. A whisper of discussion swam around the forty soldiers, and Demosyna heard her name spoken with terror and reverence.

"You split the sky in half!" one woman called, her wide blue eyes terrified. "I saw it myself!"

"She flung me off the Highway with her magic!" another shorter lady called. "I barely survived the fall."

"That Wizen saved me!" one young man yelled, staring at the woman in awe. "Her golden horns stopped three soldiers that would have impaled me. Murderous, grinning elves they were!"

"She will kill us all!" one hooded figure shrieked, running toward the wooden buildings. "She's a Wise-woman!"

A few more followed, leaving the squad's discipline broken. The commander tried to get order, but soldiers had begun closing around the two travelers. Plu Durrah drew her twin swords with practiced ease, but Demosyna held her hands up to talk over the noise.

"Stand down, soldiers. Please!" Demosyna called, using as calm a voice available. "We mean you no harm and wish all peoples free as you do! I travel to reach my Order, just ahead. Please don't stand against us, for I, too, hate the cruelty I see in the Fist!"

This drew a few disbelieving chuckles from the rebel soldiers, but the commander considered the scaled young woman carefully. Momentary order was hers, and the commander paced her troops before stopping at Plu Durrah.

"I am Yoila, first commander of these woods," the powerful woman said, her black scales shining in the sun. "I was told to hold this area against your kind. You will not be allowed through, but your friends can pass."

The commander had poked Plu Durrah several times in the chest with her sword point, but the musician was smiling. A turn of the fast elf's wrists disarmed the commander while a long elven sword fell to the stone highway. Plu Durrah didn't attack the woman, but Yoila took a step backward in shock. The dark-scaled woman wore a braided golden sash of command, adorned with imperial crests taken during battle. Yoila removed a needlelike dagger from behind the wide cloth while taking a guarded stance.

"I don't appreciate being prodded at, Scale!" Plu Durrah nearly spit at the woman. "I only travel with this purple Scale because it's fun. I don't care what you think of me or my kind. Just let us pass, and nobody has to die. Don't be stupid, you seeder. Just guard the wall like a good little girl."

Anger and hatred passed over nearly all the soldiers' faces upon seeing the elf casually crossing swords over her unarmored chest. Vaash had tied the dogs to the wagon and hoisted a piece of wreckage from beside the shared cart. The wood frame was twice the size of their own wagon, but the monk used both arms to toss the heavy wooden barricade over the edge.

It broke apart with great crashing notes, snapping living and cut wood alike. The monk was smiling widely and stretching his left arm, having moved the wood with ease. Open-mouthed shock and terror crossed half the soldiers' faces, and a few cried out in worry.

"Greetings, friends," Vaash said in a booming voice to be heard. "Would anyone wish to share water with this one before we pass by? None here wishes conflict, gentle people. That we do not!"

An arrow flew to hit the stone ground between the soldiers and travelers, shot from the roof of the gateway. It didn't hit anyone, but another struck down closer than the first to Plu Durrah.

"Enough. We will go back and walk across the country," Demosyna called as loudly as possible, because the noise of the angry soldiers had risen. "My goal is in sight, and we do not need to use your highway any longer. We will leave with our blessings to your fight, for none should be enslaved in the free North!"

"Pretty words from a murderous Wise-woman!" Yoila hissed, searching Plu Durrah for an opening. "I heard about you, Demosyna the Wise. You started the massacre during the battle when you used magic. The elves were avoiding it till then, because they knew we had more Wizened than them. You forced them to start using magic, thinking you were a rebel fighting atop the Highway."

Demosyna's eyes grew wide at the news, gasping at the knowledge of her continued hand in the slaughter. It was true, for Demosyna hadn't seen magic until her tornado drew attention from both sides.

"We would have taken the Highway without using magic!" Yoila yelled in fury, turning to Demosyna. "We wiped those greedy elves away but lost so many doing so it almost wasn't worth the victory. It would have taken longer if you hadn't shown up, sure, but we would still have our army!"

Yells of agreement reached the disturbed young Wise-woman, and she felt tears form in her eyes. It was information Demosyna put aside for later, when her life wasn't so immediately threatened.

"I am truly sorry for escalating the fighting," Demosyna said, a tear falling on her purple scales.

The apprentice's next words were lost in yells of accusation, and the soldiers pushed forward. None attacked, but Plu Durrah moved backward several steps. An arrow struck Demosyna in the chest, sinking into the elven armor under her robes. It knocked the surprised Wise-woman back slightly while bruising her ribs with its force.

It remained sticking from her side as Vaash rushed over, feeling the armor Demosyna had shown her friends already. It was light and thin enough to be an undershirt, so Demosyna smiled at the harmless arrow. Demosyna held up her hand, intending to give another plea to the soldiers, but the peace was lost. Another arrow was shot, but Vaash was ready, and the arrow stopped in midair before hitting a target.

A feverish wind was pouring off the monk, and the arrow was tossed over the Highway by his energy. Demosyna produced a focused tornado, shielding herself and her nearby friends in an instant. Unlike the painful healing magic, this was so easy Demosyna laughed in the face of her aggressors. The handful of arrows was torn to splinters by the raging winds, driving the mass of soldiers back.

It didn't take long for them to stop firing, but Plu Durrah had gotten impatient. The mercenary darted from the cover of the wind buffer and charged the group with a yell. Vaash nodded wordlessly when Demosyna looked her burning eyes toward the friend, knowing her request without words. The monk secured both dogs in the wagon while leading the group's noncombatants through the skirmish.

Many of the retreating soldiers fled into the buildings, but thirty remained fighting Plu Durrah. The squad of soldiers on the far side of the gate rushed away, fleeing the tornado and regrouping with their army in the Fist. They vanished over the horizon and left half their fellows to an unknown fate.

Plu Durrah fought with rage in her eyes, yelling curses and decapitating most she clashed with. Demosyna pushed a large pile of stones aside, sending them like sand on a beach, to clatter against the side of the Highway. The apprentice felt clear in her goal and walked with even strides behind Plu Durrah. Demosyna didn't engage any soldier, and when the arrows stopped firing, she dropped the shield. The horrible sight of the pinned soldiers' eyes was one reason, and the taste of their breath leaving flattened lungs was another.

The lightning-quick Plu had nearly killed everyone ahead as the commander fell back with an arm wound. Over twenty bodies lay scattered in a rough line toward the tollbooth, with many writhing or unconscious from their wounds. The sight of the wounded broke Demosyna's heart, but less than the sight of the chained slaves. Yoila was leading the frightened group of fifteen by their chains around a corner, away from the fighting. Many were bloodied elves dressed in rags, but several of the slaves were seeder kind.

A momentary hush fell over the Highway after Plu Durrah threw a sword into one retreating soldier's back. The leather-armored solider had been nearly through the door but fell forward inside the rightmost building. A caged armory was shown to be pried open and stood empty of the fancy elven weapons.

Demosyna knelt behind a wide barricade just before the gateway with rebel bodies surrounding the jittery woman. Vaash was busy watching for arrows from the upper floors, and Plu Durrah returned with only one of her swords held in a bloody fist. Plu had left the thrown weapon embedded in the soldier's back, not entering the shadowy building yet. None of them knew how many more were inside, and the tight quarters would be difficult to siege.

Vaash bent to hear the two while never taking his eyes from the second story of the checkpoint. Plu Durrah was furious but smiled as she wiped blood from her face. The warm fluid steamed in the cold air, making the elf seem to radiate waves of ire. Her tornado was dissipated again, and Demosyna hid from the carnage.

"Those stupid seeders! I gave them a chance."

Plu Durrah spit onto the ground, shaking her bald head.

"Are you wanting to take this place like we did from those bandits?"

Demosyna only had to consider for a moment.

"No. We will move on with my wind as a cover. I don't want any more killing, Plu. Please!"

Vaash voiced his agreement.

"This one has no issue with you two fighting, but these people have done nothing to deserve this. We must leave them to their war!"

"Killing these rebels won't help us and only hurt their cause," Demosyna said, nodding at Vaash's logic. "I want a better life for these free folks no matter what they think is true about us! I won't fight them here since I know I'm more useful as a Wise-woman than a soldier!"

"Don't sell yourself short, purple scale!" Plu Durrah said, laughing. "Just let me get my sword I dropped over there, and we can be on our way! Don't worry, they won't even see me coming!"

She was covered behind a tall wooden pile of food carts, stretching her legs, when the arrow pierced Plu Durrah's left eye. It gave a sickening thud as the bloody arrowhead pushed out from near the jaw. Demosyna screamed in horror, and Vaash looked to see the falling elf clad in bloody green clothes. Her sword was held tight in a hand, but Plu Durrah was falling into a heap on the Highway.

Vaash moved quicker than the mercenary herself to catch Plu, holding her head before it cracked against the stones. Demosyna

351

turned her eyes to see Yoila reloading a crossbow while peering from around a corner. Vaash had already expertly removed the arrow from her eye, and Plu Durrah lay bleeding onto the gray Highway. Demosyna watched with rising heartache as Vaash treated the head wound with a set expression on his face.

Neither noticed the arrows that struck the barricade as the monk tended to their fallen friend. Demosyna took deep breaths to maintain control of her mind but was only half successful. The apprentice's ring burned hot on her thumb after Vaash moved back from his limited healing.

"She is alive, but we must get her to safety," Vaash whispered with blood on his fingers. "You can heal her in the wagon as we flee!"

"No, I can help right now!" Demosyna yelled, placing her hand on the twitching elf's chest. "I can finally help!"

It was like her mind was being strained through diamonds, slicing Demosyna to pieces. She hammered herself against some unseen force as thoughts slowly fled the Wizen's mind. Tears dropped onto Plu Durrah's green shirt, but only a vague dusting of magic was seen. Some blood flow was slowed, yet Plu Durrah was draining of color and growing weaker before their eyes.

She cursed herself for her weakness, and Demosyna gripped tighter into the cloth shirt under her claws. Golden light began streaming from Demosyna's horns and eyes, causing the commander to duck her head behind the gate again. The young apprentice felt on the verge of losing herself to the grief and magic storming in her mind and let the tears flow freely in her dismay. Demosyna tried to focus and gritted her sharp teeth together.

Fear of losing her musical friend gave Demosyna all the strength she needed to endure the torturous casting. A final screaming push sent a bright ribbon of golden light into Plu Durrah's left eye, turning the silver pupil gold with the brilliance of the spell.

It streamed from Demosyna's curved horns before spiraling and twisting together into the wound like a needle. The arrow hadn't only gone through the eye but also slightly above in a horrible angle. Demosyna didn't know if the brain had been struck but felt burning tears fall on her purple-scaled hand. The energy from the spell was dripping from her eyes and falling in sizzling drops to scald the young Wise-woman's fist.

The magic lasted seconds, and the wind was the only sound besides Demosyna's triumphant yells. A golden ball of magic had formed from the energy flowing into Plu Durrah's eye, some light seeping out of the jagged exit wound. Plu Durrah coughed and stilled, but Vaash told the trembling Wise-woman she was sleeping. The last thing Demosyna knew for several minutes was a sudden pain in her hand, along with rage that seemed like it drowned the young woman.

The crystal band circling the gold ring cracked, sending pieces flying outward with the force. One stuck into a finger on her clawed left hand, and Demosyna's ring also sent a chunk to embed into Plu Durrah's breast. Neither woman noticed this, however, because Demosyna was swiftly crawling on all fours toward the gate. The arrow in her ribs snapped when she jumped onto the Highway belly first, strong limbs speeding the furious Wizen along. Demosyna didn't yell words, but a deep and primal scream carried for miles in the forests.

Several paces before reaching the open doorway on the right building, she swiped a flexed hand through the cold air. The entire wall facing Demosyna was torn away, revealing frightened rebels atop the stairs. Without pausing her run, the apprentice snaked her way to the closed left building. A swipe from a clawed hand sent half that structure into the forest below. Wood groaned from lack of support for the checkpoint, buckling it in places.

Demosyna rose onto her legs while opening her jaws wide to show waves of chaotic energy. The apprentice bit powerfully into the air, snapping her jaws as though to catch a fish. The second floor of the gateway crumbled like a rotted log while held in place by pointed teeth of magical rage. A jerk of the mindless apprentice's head sent bodies and rubble flying toward Vaash and the wagon behind a barricade.

Screams filled the air as limbs were broken from the fall, and others were crushed under beds or support beams. Vaash had a terrified expression but moved to aid the fallen soldiers with his bag of medicine. The monk set bones quickly, ignoring their cries and curses with his delicate manner. Demosyna didn't see this, because she turned back at once to slither through the open gate.

Yoila hastily fired an arrow at the crawling figure, but it sank into the armor on Demosyna's back. Slaves huddled near an elevator wheel with raw panic emanating from their chained helplessness. Demosyna hissed loudly at the commander before leaping and snapping her jaws in unfeeling anger. The commander was fast and rolled backward to avoid the bite at her neck.

Demosyna only caught a bit of cloth in her teeth, rolling in midair to tear it free. Yoila was drawing her dagger once more, but Demosyna rose to her feet without blinking. Her ears were ringing, and light pooled in the young Wizen's boots before dripping down the leather. Claws dripped poisonous light as Demosyna held a numb hand toward the commander, strips of Yoila's shirt in her mouth.

Fear roared from Yoila, who leaped forward and stabbed Demosyna's shoulder. The blade hit the armor and slid away but left a deep gash on the bicep. The armor had sleeves, yet the fabric had fallen back somewhat from the commotion. Demosyna felt the blade's sting and didn't fully come back to herself yet. Yoila had started holding Demosyna's throat with an armored hand when the grinning apprentice took a powerful step forward.

The dagger plunged again, clanging in stabs that only bruised Demosyna's chest. Confusion bloomed in Yoila's black eyes as her dagger bent from the attacks, cracks forming in the metal. Demosyna used her right hand to dig deep into the woman's face and block the commander's eyes from view. Blood streamed from the claws that held her face, and Yoila shrieked in pain.

"That knife won't help," Demosyna said, gurgling the words toward Yoila, barely forming thoughts. "You are mine."

A rock struck the frenzied apprentice in the head, bouncing against a glowing horn with a clack. Demosyna turned her burning eyes toward the slaves, who stood trembling with improvised weapons. The young Wise-woman ran forward toward the new threat while dragging the struggling commander by the face. Yoila was a Scale, so the top of her long snout was held fast with her eyes covered by a strong palm.

The bleeding commander stumbled behind Demosyna with her flesh pulling from the bone at each stride. A desperate slave swung a chunk of wood at the apprentice, but she ignored the blow from the wreckage clutter. The tall elf attacker was also gripped mercilessly on the face using Demosyna's free left hand.

Yoila had dropped the dagger to claw uselessly at Demosyna's hand but couldn't stop the blood from pooling in her eyes. The elf screamed as well, gripping Demosyna's wrist with cold hands. The elf fell to her knees, and the rags she wore soaked the blood Demosyna drew from the slave's face. The teeth in her mouth were almost too bright to see, and waves of energy poured from Demosyna's gaping jaws as she opened wide to bite.

That was when Demosyna regained control of her mind, snapping awake into a pain-riddled body. The last thing she remembered was trying to heal her gravely injured friend, yet the apprentice stood now above two helpless victims. Demosyna removed her blood-drenched claws from their faces before stepping back in confusion and panic. Vaash was approaching with his green eyes wide and frightened. Both women were sobbing through their bloody faces, holding their heads and screaming at the apprentice.

None of the slaves moved, their malnourished bodies shaking and collapsing. As Vaash walked calmly forward, Demosyna noticed the devastation she had caused anew. Groaning figures were littering the Highway beyond the ruined checkpoint, many with serious injuries threatening their lives. He had stabilized all he could, and Vaash stood beside Demosyna, burning like hot wind. Demosyna held back tears of sorrow, falling to her knees before the two injured women. The apprentice's face remained calm, set in a stern expression, while healing light swept over the two.

It was still enormously painful, but whatever had held her back was gone, and Demosyna needed to help. The five holes on each face closed, stopping the blood from where sharp claws had sunk in. Yoila wiped blood from her furious face while screaming at Demosyna.

"Who are you?" Yoila demanded, eyes full of pain.

Demosyna rose in silent thought, her heart breaking with a new idea. The apprentice looked at Vaash with a blank face while ignoring the cries of those she mutilated.

"Get the rest from inside and bring them out to watch."

Demosyna's voice was a monotone whisper, looking the commander dead in the eye.

"I am Demosyna. My magic is stronger than you, Yoila, and I will show you how strong. Once your soldiers are watching, I will show you all what my strength means."

Without waiting for a response from Vaash, the saddened young woman marched to her cart. The dogs were worried, but Demosyna grabbed her bag of gold pieces with a pat on their heads. Vaash stood in thought for only a moment before entering the crumbling building to escort soldiers into view. Demosyna sighed at Plu Durrah, comatose but no longer dying on the Highway. A line of treated soldiers was eyeing the Wise-woman in fear, but she stopped near the first with a sigh.

"I would have given you gold to let us pass, to aid your noble cause," Demosyna began, waving her hand over the soldier. "I asked for understanding, but you can't hear anything but violence. Now watch, everyone, while I try to make you hear me again."

Golden light washed over the huddled soldier, who let out a cry of dismay. Yoila yelled her own denial, a high shriek of despair in the cold sky. After healing the injured soldier, Demosyna moved on to the rest of her recent mess. Pain exploded each time she healed a soldier, and Demosyna was soon crying from the exertion. Blood began sweating from her body, running in streams down the apprentice's purple scales. Everyone had gone deadly still when she began casting magic, and Demosyna yelled at the commander again.

"You claim rebels desire freedom but keep each other in chains," Demosyna roared, healing a broken leg. "I will no longer stand by, for I have seen enough of this hypocrisy."

"How many did you kill before finding matching boots?" Yoila yelled, her face burning with bloody anger. "I saw the crest. You are just as bad as the traitors fighting for the Empress. Those boots and bracers were from our armies, you hypocrite. Kill me and end your delusions, smooth scale."

"My choice was taken by those more powerful than me, at least at those times," Demosyna reasoned, reaching the gate from her crucible. "I am now strong enough to make that choice for myself and for others if I deem necessary, just as you do with your slaves, for you think yourself strong with their forced submission. You are killing yourselves with your hate, and I offer you peace in its stead. I have made the choice for you, because I am stronger than you, Yoila. Let this be another proof."

Demosyna had finished healing the injured soldiers she attacked and turned to those whom Plu Durrah tore through. Many were gutted, lying nearly dead on the cold stones. The pain blinded Demosyna for a moment while finishing the last of the wounded that were missing limbs. The apprentice cried out but walked without sight through the ruined gate. Behind her, a cautious group of soldiers was helping the other healed to their feet. Demosyna wasn't able to regrow limbs but did what her magic allowed to heal her mistakes.

"I am sorry for the pain and death I caused today," Demosyna told the crowd of soldiers and slaves. "I cannot change what happened, but we can choose to move forward without holding on to hateful ways. Yoila, start by freeing those slaves."

Her vision was barely returned, but the chains falling away was unmistakable to the young Wise-woman's ear. Demosyna had used her magic to remove a heavy canister of gold pieces from her back, straining from the willpower needed after healing so many. The apprentice used her magic claws to give the money to the slaves once they were all freed of their bindings.

"Take this, friends, and join me if you wish," Demosyna said, tears falling from her weary eyes. "I cannot give you back your time as slaves but will promise freedom to any that desire it. None will stop you, and you will be free like you should have been already. If you wish to fight with the rebel soldiers to stop the Empress's armies, you have my blessing. Divide that with those chained below and start a new life."

Demosyna turned to the wondering commander with a calm look of surety in her eyes. Yoila was gaping at the Wise-woman, struck silent as the purple-scaled woman spoke.

"I will need your army, Yoila. You reminded me I cannot change anything without protecting what is precious in this life," the Wizen told the black-scaled commander. "Bring these to your leaders and tell them what I have done here. If they are serious about freedom for all of the Fist, let them find me in the city ahead. If they are not true believers in life, you may keep the gold for the damage I caused to your mission.

"I love you, friends, and wish only peace for all lives. I hold no grudge for you shooting Plu Durrah, Yoila. Fear no retribution from me, for I have enough to hate without adding to that ocean."

Nobody moved or spoke as Demosyna handed the stunned commander three tridents of gold, leaving three in the pack. Demosyna floated them over with her thumb ring burning, and Yoila grabbed each with slow hands.

"Free the slaves you hold in your armies and those on the elevators below—all of them across your entire lands," Demosyna commanded, wiping the tears from her face. "I will not allow it any longer. Give your captives anything they desire and let them be. When you are worthy of their devotion, people will build your cause without chains. I want to help you see this but will not abide needless cruelty to get there. Tell your masters that if they do not wish to help now, I will turn my eyes to them after I finish with the Empress. I truly wish we can bring an end to this madness together without chains and generational misery."

"If you are letting us go, Demosyna, then I will see you again soon," Yoila said, standing and moving to her troops. "Your desire will be upheld today, and I thank you for the mercy to my soldiers. I make no promises about all the rebel slaves, but we shall free those in the lands I control. That is all that is within my authority as commander, Demosyna. You have given me much to inform the generals, but you have my word, I will loose my slaves."

Vaash remained silent during the exchange and the healing display. An initial frown was replaced with his serene smile, and Vaash gently put Plu Durrah into the wagon. The ancient horse led the full cart through the wreckage of a checkpoint, watching the soldiers limp onto the elevator.

The hopeful slaves moved to start lowering the soldiers, but Demosyna shook her head at them.

"You too, friends," the exhausted Wise-woman called, summoning her magic a final time. "I will lower you down this time. You are free from your former lives, and I wish you only good days ahead in the lands of your choice. Remember my offer and seek me out if you wish to help me! I am Demosyna, soon a Wise-woman in the northern Order."

The wheel was enormously heavy, but Demosyna was determined to prove her case. Vaash joined her, straining against the long bars to slowly lower the elevator. Bloody faces dropped from view, and Demosyna lay in the driver's seat to pant air into the sky. The elevator reached the ground with a distant click, and the young woman was nearly sobbing again from nerves.

Demosyna hoped her desperate gamble would pay off and worried about Plu still unconscious in the wagon. The healing left eye kept shining with a gold light, but Vaash explained time was needed.

"What made you change your mind about killing those people?" Vaash asked, starting to lead the cart along. "You grew out of control for a moment, it seemed. I was worried for you, Demosyna."

"I don't remember doing that, Vaash, and it really scares me," Demosyna said, covering her face with a sleeve as she lay in the driver's seat. "I woke up killing a slave and knew I was bringing terror into the world. I just did the most selfish thing I could think of and used my strength to force others into action."

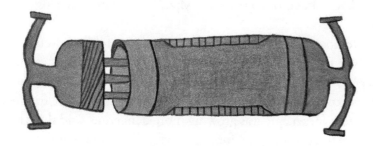

CHAPTER 28

Plu Durrah slept for hours after the ordeal, stirring occasionally but lying covered in the wagon the entire time. Demosyna's white-coated dog was by the injured elf's side, contrary to his previous behavior around the mercenary. The quiet hound waited patiently beside Plu as he had with Demosyna while she recovered.

Vaash walked behind the wagon, which wheeled across the sky, tending to the patient with expert care. Demosyna drove the cart while letting the stubborn old horse lead its own way along. It knew this highway, the group had discovered, better than anyone else and kept its own schedule most of the time. The welcome gift of steady apples had calmed the beast somewhat, but the mare was prideful in its job.

Demosyna was absently staring at a page of the recovered tome, rereading the same word for a thousandth time. It was a complex passage, but the young woman's mind was back to the southwest. She had lost control of herself and done so much damage it frightened the Wizen. Her magic was growing more dangerous, and these blackouts were not encouraging for Demosyna. The wind that the apprentice had mastered thus far was something like a dream, making her invincible and infallible. This new style of magic was overwhelming in its intense and painful channeling.

The young woman twiddled her broken ring on her thumb, drawing blood from a knuckle. Demosyna sucked the finger and endured the grating pain to heal the abrasion, sighing softly to herself.

Vaash insisted that he help Demosyna wash after the short rebel encounter, motioning to the numerous dried patches of blood on her exposed purple scales. Some was hers, from effort and injury, but the majority was others' crimson pain staining Demosyna's scales. There was nobody around—not that she cared much—so Demosyna removed the soiled robes and stood in the chilly evening air. The apprentice washed from a bucket with their water reserves while wiping the day away. Vaash cleaned Plu Durrah for several minutes, allowing Demosyna some privacy atop the featureless highway. The young Wizen turned toward her friend, icy body wet and bruised.

"Can you help with my back?" she asked, her teeth chattering slightly from the breeze. "My arms and legs are so sore, it's hard to move yet. Otherwise, I would do it myself."

Vaash blushed slightly but took the offered rag, his green eyes running over the naked friend before him. He was observing the swollen bruises dotting the woman's torso, front and back, but Demosyna wasn't shy around her friend. She had seen him training nude with his lost students, and the young Wise-woman had been seen shattered in bed by Vaash.

The monk touched several ribs that had been struck by arrows, searching her face for a reaction. Demosyna winced slightly but smiled back as he finished his inspection. Vaash was kneeling behind the young woman before looking at the bent tail tip and the minor cuts along its length. The cold water from the bucket was barely felt, and Vaash was gentle as he washed his friend's back and tail.

Demosyna turned when Vaash called he was finished, beaming at the man.

"Thank you. That helped a lot!"

She held out her hand, purple scales shining in the starlight, and Vaash gazed in wonder at the Wise-woman for a long moment. Demosyna tilted her head, smiling at the man and patiently waiting against the chilly air. Vaash took the offered palm and lifted himself to face Demosyna.

"I am always happy to help when I can!" Vaash said, tossing the dirty water over the edge.

"Let me return the favor, Vaash!" Demosyna said, half filling a bucket with water.

Vaash allowed his friend to wash his bloody face and arms. He did not get injured while helping the soldiers. The apprentice was grinning the entire time, for it was a simple but bonding show of love. Vaash, too, was grinning widely once his exposed skin was cleaned with red hair flying loose in the breeze. The monk had removed his robes, and Demosyna found no new injuries on the scarred body. The wind was picking up slightly, so the friends wrapped up their baths.

Vaash gave Demosyna the clean spare robes while motioning to his barely soiled clothes. He was the last defense for their wagon those past encounters and had hardly gotten involved enough to be grimy like the other two. Plu Durrah was stirring slightly, but the wagon moved on when the injured friend didn't rise.

The pair of robed travelers set up a small camp while resting for a few hours, watching the moon sink in the sky. The moon wasn't full enough for the floating squids to stream through the stars, and Demosyna missed seeing the native animals. A faint light was visible from the tied-down, covered wagon from the last bits of the magic forming Plu Durrah's eye. Demosyna had checked on the elf before eating and saw the sphere of light was fading. Neither friend knew if that was a good sign, and Vaash told the worried Wise-woman Plu Durrah was strong and would fight to return.

"You know how much she loves singing!" Vaash said, sitting next to Demosyna. "She wouldn't give up, not when there is gold to be had!"

"You've got that right, monk boy!" Plu Durrah muttered from inside the wagon. "You better not have touched my side of the pile here."

Demosyna's dog barked happily, and there was a short commotion inside the sealed cart. The white dog came bounding from the wooden bed while grinning and licking Plu Durrah. Vaash's old dog continued snoring from the man's knee, cloudy eyes closed and dreaming.

Demosyna rose with a tearful smile before walking over to the leaning bard. Plu Durrah was blinking her eyes and trying to focus her groggy head. The wound was healed, leaving only a jagged scar near Plu's jaw. The only other major visible change was the left pupil, which was now gold, and the other had stayed a shining silver. The image was jarring and slightly hypnotizing as the mercenary smiled.

"Where is MJ?" the elf asked, looking around the Highway. "Don't tell me she snuck off again to do a solo job."

"I don't know any MJ, Plu. It's just been us for weeks now!" Demosyna said, frowning and offering water. "Sit down and rest. You were really badly hurt today."

"It sure feels that way, Demosyna," Plu Durrah said, mumbling her thanks for the cup. "My head is killing me. How much did I drink last night? I can't remember anything from today, and it's already night again!"

"You don't remember Yoila or the last tollbooth?" Vaash asked from his seated place near the fire. "What do you remember?"

"We were fighting our way through this new war that just sprung up," Plu Durrah said, frowning and rubbing her bald head. "I just left my shadow master on an assignment and thought I was traveling with someone else. I must be confused. But didn't we meet on MJ's task?"

"You approached us about a job, Plu. Later on, you mentioned being a shadow hiding in the Fist but said they were disbanded years ago."

Demosyna felt her heart sink, fearing her friend was deeply damaged by the bolt.

"The master decided it grew too dangerous, and everyone retired with their riches."

"That's ridiculous. We only just started..."

A wave of emotion swept Plu Durrah's face.

"Oh, right, right. I remember now. Sorry. My head is just scrambled from wine and songs! I remember you now, Tin Toes!"

Demosyna's initial worry faded slightly, but Vaash looked intently at the recovering patient. Plu refused food, claiming nausea, and drank slowly from the cup Demosyna refilled. Plu Durrah darted her dual-colored eyes around the scene and took in details as she did. A barely registered look of panic was spread across Plu's mouth, but Demosyna patted the elf.

"I was so worried about you," the young apprentice said, a tear falling from seeing her friend. "Did you need more healing?"

"It must have been quite the battle if someone got a shot in on me. They should never see me coming after all."

The mercenary shook her head, smiling finally and removing a traveling harp. Plu Durrah scratched absently at her chest, near where the torn claw marks showed Demosyna's painful grip. The elf frowned, looking into her shirt at the offending object.

"There's crystal in my tit," Plu Durrah exclaimed in surprise. "Were you feeling me up while I was sleeping, purple scale? I see these claw holes. Just what were you up to last night?"

"No, that is from where I healed you," Demosyna said, her eyes widening while watching. "Are you okay? Did you need any help?"

The mercenary shook her capped head before pulling an arm through a shirtsleeve. There was a brief pained expression, but her hand emerged, holding a bloody piece of crystal. It was a shard from Demosyna's ring, and Plu held it between pink-painted nails. She had dug the shrapnel out with filed nails, frowning as the elf held the clear gem to the moon. The piece was sent flying into the darkness and tumbled in rainbows of starlight.

"That's better!" Plu said, sighing and leaning back. "That was getting really annoying. How much farther till we reach the Wisewoman Settlement? I am dying for some wine since we ran out yesterday! I hope we find some water soon. You already gave me so much!"

Demosyna laughed, assuming a joke.

"You bought barrels of wine just a few days ago. You actually loaded the water from those bandits, remember, Plu?"

"Oh, of course," the confused-looking elf said, glancing down at her missing sheath. "And then I threw my sword into that rebel's back. I remember now!"

Demosyna had forgotten all about the sword during her rage and healing and failed to retrieve it from the Highway. A cold sense of failure filled her heart for a moment, and the apprentice looked back the way they had come. The ruined checkpoint was far behind and left abandoned at Demosyna's orders.

"I'm sorry, Plu. I left it when we carted you away," Demosyna said, turning her wide eyes to her friend. "I didn't even think about it. I was so focused on my own magics. Do you want to go back with us and look for it?"

Plu considered but shook her head.

"Let's get you to the settlement first, and then I will decide what I want to do about this lost sword. Here, Vaash, you can use this till I find another matching pair. I can't fight well with one sword anyway. It just feels off!"

Vaash stood with wide eyes to take the belt and single sword attached. It was a short sword, about as long as a forearm, and of fine elven design. Demosyna had seen the elf use her blades with lethal precision, and the filigree shone in the moonlight. Musical bars swept from the pointed tip, waving and moving as though being played via instrument. Vaash ran two rough fingers along the edge while studying the balanced sword with fascination. The musical blade flashed through the air before landing in its matching sheath. The metal housing for the brilliant sword featured musical instruments carved into the surface, depicting flutes and harps and drums.

Both Vaash and Plu Durrah were known to play wonderful music, so the gift was perfect for the monk. He was speechless for many moments when handling the sword with trained hands. Demosyna left the two for a while, feeling elated that her friend was recovering. The apprentice needed to meditate and practice control with her leather fetch toys.

The Wizen's white dog was lapping some remaining water from a bucket, wagging when it saw the ball. Demosyna balanced her heels on the cold metal step and tossed the ball away with specific places in mind. This worked better than adjusting the force of magic since the Wise-woman's mind knew how to send the ball where her eyes looked.

Plu Durrah retired early while rubbing her head and yawning. The practicing Wizen gladly let the mercenary sleep, and Demosyna balanced on one leg near the fire.

* * * * *

They moved along at sunrise and watched the light display the world. Several ships were trading cargo at the docks, and Demosyna saw the golden glass doming the city sectors explode. Her sharp yellow eyes witnessed puff after puff of thick shielding turn into smoke, and Demosyna smiled. Even from the distance atop the Highway, huge crystals could be seen glowing above the faux volcanoes in each dome. Magic flowed from these towering crystals to turn the solid yellow glass into golden clouds of vapor. The wind took the smoke away from the stone flats, leaving the buildings and people exposed to the day.

That evening, Demosyna saw the opposite was done by turning billowing gold smoke into a dome of glass. It was slower than the dismantling, but near sundown, each sector of the sprawling city received a shining new window. The columns of smoke were laid down in rings around the sections of city, layering up a shield of magical glass. Demosyna had never seen transmutation, and her eyes danced at the sight of such powerful magic. Wonders seemed around every corner of the Fist, and Demosyna smiled over the pain in her heart.

Ahead was an elevator checkpoint, complete with rebel soldiers and slaves operating the wheel. Two carts were being escorted through the gate by weary traders heading to the city ahead. It had grown so close that you could almost smell the baking bread and sweaty bodies, so Demosyna pondered what to do. Her heart spoke the truth, and Demosyna focused her eyes on the task ahead.

If they only respond to force, so be it, Demosyna thought, breathing steadily in the late-afternoon air. *I will free the slaves and move on, letting anyone who wishes live.*

Demosyna loathed the thought of further violence but could no longer stomach the heartache from seeing slaves. The apprentice put herself aside, feeling for the plight of those chained to their fate. A black dot ran from the forest below and caught the sharp eyes of Demosyna's dog. The young Wise-woman noticed the pointing signal and followed his gaze to watch the figure jump to a slanted side of the Highway.

Yoila climbed the stones of the Highway with ease while jumping to the curved floors in minutes. She was lost from view when the soldier climbed the expanding curve, but Yoila clawed up the sheer stone highway. The commander stood panting with black-scaled hands on her blue leather armor.

"Just a moment, Demosyna," the woman said between deep breaths. "I don't want you to get the wrong idea. These lands are commanded by another, but I have been authorized to escort you to the city. Please, my Wise-woman, let me talk to them."

"That would be wonderful, Yoila. Thank you," Demosyna said, smiling slightly from relief. "I am glad you are here. And that was some great climbing!"

Yoila raised a scaly eyebrow but marched toward the soldiers watching with amused expressions. A few words were exchanged, and a rolled scroll was shown to the rebel soldiers. The talk grew more heated, resulting in Yoila rising tall to assert command. She personally unchained the slaves, and Yoila walked the newly freed figures to Demosyna. The group received a tube of gold from the dwindling supply, but Demosyna gave freely to the slaves.

"Where do you wish to go, gentle people?" Demosyna asked, practicing magic to hand the gold pieces over.

Many different places were called out by the shivering crowd, and soldiers gathered to escort them away. Plu Durrah plucked a cheery tune, and Vaash assembled his silver flute to play along. Demosyna waited for the singing and weeping slaves to descend, letting the rebel soldiers operate the wheel. The apprentice rode the final elevator down and only noticed the ruined highway ahead once on the ground.

The top continued for quite a while, but it, too, ended with melted and deformed stones. Both of the bottom two floors of the Empress's Highway were nearly demolished, leaving open gaps that yawned in shadows. The second level was decorated with torches and a wide red rug, central in the tunnel and patterned in the elven design. Broken troughs lined each side to catch any water that fell through cut holes in the middle floor's ceiling. The broken end was open to the elements, but as the tunnel went back southwest, it grew spotless.

Tracks emerged from the first story, clearly constructed after the Highway was broken. The newest rails were of a different metal yet were fitted well to the existing tracks. No trains were seen, here or at the beginning of her journey, and Demosyna wondered at their use. The apprentice hadn't heard trains till the Wise-woman Settlement, and the tunnel remained silent and endless.

The impenetrable stone of the Empress's Highway wasn't scattered around as if from an ancient battle. It was simply gone or melted from beyond the last elevator. More mysteries revealed their lures to the woman, and Demosyna had to pry her gaze from the final span of the Highway.

You took us so quickly to my Order, Demosyna thought at the towering stone monument. *Thank you for letting me heal and get stronger.*

This simple practice in humility, as with praising the animals, kept Demosyna focused on her task of helping anyone she could. Wizened she had encountered usually had an air of superiority about them, and Demosyna wished to avoid sinking to those stereotypes. Her life had been spent useless to many people, but now Demosyna was finding herself more helpful than her dreams revealed. Plu Durrah was walking proof of Demosyna's progress. The missing toe and arrow wound in her foot were further evidence.

The slaves at the bottom of the elevator were confused and afraid, and many didn't want to take the gold coins from the trident. Yoila assured them of their safety, using a key ring to toss their shackles to the dirt. The commander even apologized to each of the slaves while looking them in the eye and handing them a share.

Most of the seeder classes ran into the woods and didn't look back from the unusual situation. The rest were escorted onward, leaving the slow cart on the road with rushing, unshod feet. Each soldier had to push themselves to keep pace, and Yoila returned from the slaves. The reflected mountain was blocking the sky ahead, and the friends stopped at a clearing to observe. Golden glass was being finalized atop each separate cluster of buildings to let those living there be shielded from the dark. It was a fantastic magical display and Demosyna stood in deep thought about her future learning.

Five round dots surrounded Yoila's black-scaled face as remnants of Demosyna's claws days ago. The sight of the scars gave the young apprentice deep pangs of sadness, being visible proof of her deadly mistakes. Demosyna had watched the commander approach, jogging across the hills and roads, to kneel beside the young Wizen. Her delicate neck was bent forward in submission, and Yoila touched Demosyna's boots with clawed hands.

"The generals have told me to free any slaves you come across in their lands while they consider your proposition," Yoila said, her face nearly in the dirt. "I am to observe you as well but wasn't to tell you that. I defy my orders to follow my heart, Demosyna the Wise. You hold my flesh and heart in your hands. For as you said in your beautiful passion, I am yours now. I thank you for your marks, my Wise-woman, and await your next desire."

The black-scaled commander raised herself to seated and touched the puffy face scars with wondering eyes. Demosyna looked with a frown at the humbled woman, not fully grasping her words yet. Any help was needed for the young apprentice's growing idea of freedom, and Demosyna knelt beside the scaled commander. Demosyna locked eyes with Yoila, facing the woman with an open mind and heart.

"I welcome you, Yoila!"

Demosyna was nearly crying from joy.

"I didn't wish to scar your face but am glad you wear them without anger. My desire is love, but I fear death will be the path that is set for us to get there. We must always temper my strength with love and give everyone a choice for themselves. I have given you that choice and am proud to call you a friend if you help me!"

Tears fell from both scaled women's eyes, and the two embraced tightly on the dirt road. They cried and held each other for many minutes with their emotions ebbing and swelling. When Demosyna pulled away slowly, smiling at the woman, Yoila kissed the young Wise-woman on the cheek.

"Thank you, Demosyna. I am yours for all generations," the commander said, bowing her streaming eyes once more. "You have shown my weakness and your pure domination of will. For as long as you desire me, you will find me on my knee."

Plu Durrah laughed softly toward the two but continued tuning her harp atop the wagon.

Both dogs walked over, sniffing at the commander with hesitant posture. Yoila was helped to her feet by the sniffling Wizen, and together, they joined the wagon. Vaash smiled warmly at Yoila and offered her a rag and waterskin. Demosyna watched her friends say their hellos with the old gray dog barking in excitement on three legs.

The slaves were distant shapes on the horizon, and shadows cast by the mountain covered the land for miles. Lights danced under golden domes, showing carts and figures moving among the buildings. The sight was no less breathtaking from the ground, and the party let the ancient horse lead them along.

Plu Durrah didn't seem to remember—or care if she did—that Yoila had nearly killed the mercenary. A sigh of tension escaped Demosyna's nose, happy at avoiding the confrontation she had imagined. Yoila remained nearly silent during the trip and typically only spoke when directly asked something. Many soldiers acted with trained patience for an order, so Demosyna put the behavior from her worries.

The rolling hills were a near-novel thing after the perfectly level highway, and Demosyna's legs burned from travel once again. No more slaves were seen as the group reached the lowest visible sector, so Demosyna left the cart with Plu and Vaash. Yoila followed a step behind the young Wizen, and Demosyna strode into the city with a hopeful smile.

The stairs leading to the archway fell behind, and Demosyna's eyes adjusted to the torchlight inside the dome. The star and moonlight were dim and blurry, making the torches a main source of illumination. The imperial offices were sought by the young Wisewoman for directions, and Demosyna headed to the central volcano in the distance. The ringed streets were easy to follow, and few people were left outdoors at the late hour.

Demosyna had rounded a corner, tuning to move deeper into the sector, when she saw two rebel soldiers and several children. Two were young Orcs with their dense skin glistening in the greasy light. The third was a Paw, runty and matted, that was already bleeding on the ground. As the apprentice watched from the top of a street, both armed soldiers knocked the youths to the ground with yells of anger.

Demosyna was already moving, her robes swirling around as wind rose at her call. One of the soldiers pinned a terrified Orc to the ground and pressed the point of a sword into his chest. The blackhaired soldier leaned onto the sword and pushed the blade while the Orc whimpered. The other boy was kicked once by a blond-haired Paw soldier before they both noticed the approaching Wizen.

The runty girl who was bleeding on the road was already shackled with her furry hands behind her starved back. The blondhaired soldier picked the young girl up by the scruff and tossed her aside onto a raised step. The sound that the girl made would haunt Demosyna forever, for it was one of a broken animal dying in a trap.

A deep and guttural moan escaped the throat of the helpless girl while grinding and stuttering with misery beyond merciful thought. It lasted nearly a minute, and the final escaping gasp was a squeak that hung in the night air. The neck of the Paw was bent at a horrible angle, and the shuddering girl drew another breath to scream into the dust.

Neither soldier seemed affected, and the pinned boy struggled for breath as the sword crushed into his chest. The blond-haired soldier bent to shackle the remaining child and only glanced at the approaching yellow-robed woman. Demosyna was too numb to cry, because the sound of the paralyzed girl was too much to bear.

"You there, turn and see me," Demosyna cried at the heartless soldiers. "You are done."

"Please, it hurts," the sword-pinned young boy said, tears of pain in his compound eyes.

Tubes of wind struck the two soldiers and pinned them to opposite sides of the street with brutal force. Their leather armor ripped in places, and loose helmets and boots were flung away. Weapons were sent tumbling down the empty street, and Yoila gasped. Demosyna took a single step forward, switching the blasts of wind to her new-found claws of magic.

Her left hand was raised as the soldiers were dragged toward her, and Demosyna held her right over the rattling girl on the road. The guards reached Demosyna while gasping and straining against the gripping winds. Light flashed once from the apprentice's furious eyes, and welcome pain filled her mind.

The matted-fur Paw rolled over, and her distant eyes filled with light as bones straightened instantly. Each golden claw of magic cradled the girl's head, soothing the crying figure with warm healing. Both Orc children curled into themselves and cried with hands over their heads against the winds.

"Why have you done this?" Demosyna roared, her voice and tornado noticed for blocks around.

"They. Didn't. Heed. Me."

The blonde-haired soldier strained out against the rib-crushing magic.

Demosyna dropped the spell, and the soldiers fell to the stones. Her left arm hurt from pulling them from such a distance, and Demosyna turned away to consider the answer. A sigh of frustration escaped the Wizen while she thought but waved Yoila down when the apprentice saw her draw a sword. The commander obeyed at once and stood at attention once Demosyna turned back around.

Demosyna walked past the breathless soldiers to heal the two boys, who shied away at first in their restraints. They had seen the woman heal their friend, however, and were easy to convince to stand.

A small chip was taken from the pinned boys' chest, and Demosyna healed the exoskeleton with a groan of discomfort.

"Unbind that girl first," Demosyna commanded, watching the winded soldiers stand.

The blonde-haired soldier stepped forward in a rage, swinging a fist at Demosyna. The young apprentice met the aggression without moving and allowed the woman to strike her in the face. Demosyna felt a tooth fall from her mouth with fresh blood pouring from her lips. The woman struck twice more, but Demosyna absorbed the body blows with a grin. Confusion washed over the angry soldier's face, and she took a step back with furious eyes shifting over Demosyna's shoulder. Demosyna spit a tooth onto the road before turning to see, ignoring the blonde soldier completely.

A young seeder was sliding down the rooftop, her crossbow held in trembling hands. The guard slid down to the road, landing in a dusty roll to aim the crossbow. A bolt fired and struck Demosyna in the chest with a dull thud. Her already bruised ribs sang with pain, and the apprentice knocked the crossbow aside out of reflex. Demosyna whipped the weapon from the young soldier's hands with wind, marching with red and gold dripping from her chin.

"What do you think is happening?" Demosyna bellowed, resisting sending the terrified soldier through a building. "Are you under attack? Are things so terrifying you must kill without thought? Are you so worried about those children you must use such force? Why are you so scared you must act this way? Answer me!"

Demosyna had pointed at the children while she yelled, turning back to address the two other soldiers. Nobody spoke for several seconds, and the echoes of the Wizen's fury faded.

"I don't know," the young guard who shot the crossbow croaked, holding her head in sweaty hands. "I...I don't know."

"I am sorry," Demosyna said to the children and soldiers.

A small tornado flared again, gathering the three soldiers in a grasping wind. Demosyna marched the struggling armored figures out of the city with her heart calming. A following of late-night revelers watched in humor, cheering the apprentice on. Vaash and Plu Durrah rushed to join the Wise-woman once she threw the peo-

ple beyond an arched gate. They had been sitting around a fire but
jumped up when noticing the disturbance. The leashed dogs watched
from the wagon, and Demosyna addressed the writhing soldiers. The
young crossbow soldier was weeping, but the other two rose after a
moment.

"Leave now since you lost your choice today," Demosyna said,
lowering her tornado to be heard clearly. "I am Demosyna. I spare
your lives in the hope you can learn and grow beyond yourself."

The two furious soldiers took in the ill-favored scene, cursing
the Wizen as they limped away. The youngest of the three soldiers
rose to shaking legs, shiny from tears. All three guards stumbled into
the direction of the Highway and left Demosyna to explain with
her friends. It didn't take long, because Demosyna was burning with
anger still. The two nodded their understanding, and Vaash smiled
his approval at the restraint. Demosyna calmed herself with some
water but thanked her friends for their quick response.

"I still need to visit the imperial office tomorrow but will find
an inn with a stable!" Demosyna called, moving back into the sleeping city sector.

Demosyna walked the path she had previously taken, and her
weary body was sluggish and numb. The apprentice half expected
further cruelty to be revealed but found a suitable motel near the
edge of the outer road. The young Wizen returned to her waiting
friends, eager to visit the long-sought Wise-woman Order.

The children were nowhere in the street, so the Wise-woman
returned to her room. Demosyna rubbed her dog, feeling the leather
harness against his fur, as everyone settled in a shared closet-sized
room.

The young apprentice awoke early the next morning and was
anxious to see the glass turn to smoke from below. It was worth the
lack of sleep, and Demosyna marveled as her world opened with
magical wonder.

CHAPTER 29

Demosyna cooked a parting meal for her friends, nearly crying into the bread she was mixing. The young woman bit back the sadness to focus on the time she had shared with Vaash and Plu Durrah. The mercenary had been the first to bring up parting, and Vaash said the same once the subject was broken. It didn't come as a huge surprise, as both had only ever claimed to travel to Demosyna's Order. The emotions still felt raw, however, since it was the final day the apprentice would see her friends for some time.

The noon sun was shining on the uncovered buildings, and Demosyna smiled at her petty emotions. Demosyna had never minded being alone in her youth, being often by herself in the library, but knew her heart would miss the wonderful friends.

"My son's birthday is next month," Vaash told the slack-jawed Wise-woman. "And this one would visit the grave. It is in a beautiful clearing looking at the sea he loved."

"Of course, Vaash!" Demosyna said, selfish thoughts leaving at once. "It was so great for both of you to help me here. I don't have enough words to tell you. Thank you, my friends, and know I will always love you both! I will stay here and aid the people I feel suffering each day. Join me once you are able, and we will build something stronger than ourselves!"

"You gave me a great crowd-favorite song, Demosyna," Plu Durrah said, sipping her wineskin. "I may find my way back north once you settle things down somewhat up here! They don't seem too kind to me this far north, dwarf blood and all! I may look up an old friend I haven't seen in years. She is stationed in a small carnival settlement along the Highway!"

Vaash looked with a frown at Plu but turned back to Demosyna quickly.

"This one will return, Demosyna. A short walk each year to remember a life is all that is asked. We will travel together till Plu departs at Three Paws, so neither is in danger. You are strong enough to stand alone—that you are—just as one should outgrow their former days."

Tears fell from Vaash's and Demosyna's eyes while Plu went in search of a bar or blacksmith. The two friends sat in the room and talked for an hour, laughing and enjoying the roof. They walked their dogs together in the shining sun to let them run free in the endless fields. Simple joy filled the remaining daylight memories, and Demosyna told her friends she would make a feast. Both accepted with smiles.

Plu Durrah had found a new pair of swords. They were basic in design, no carvings or jewels on the metal, but balanced well enough for her needs, Plu claimed. Two entire birds, a duck and a large goose, were prepared with a huge salad of fresh greens. Demosyna had spent hours shopping and cooking, so all enjoyed the lavish spread. Demosyna also found jerky and fruit leather, presenting surprise ration bags for her friends once they ate. Plu downed half a bag of sweet fruit leather at once while laughing as she played harp with sticky fingers.

Yoila was quietly watching the friends' last meal, slowly eating the offered portions from a corner. The commander would sit, feet tucked under her thighs, until Demosyna addressed her or left the room. The black-scaled soldier was a silent shadow when the group ventured around the city, observing Demosyna carefully. Vaash eventually found a blacksmith willing to help and finished the toe by turning it blue purple.

A paste was applied to the shaped metal prosthetic, and the monk used long tongs to hold the tube in a furnace. Demosyna watched with fascination as the silver metal changed colors, sizzling the paste and glowing red-hot. Yellows, reds, and even green colors were seen rising in the metal, heated with expert care.

The final color was slightly darker than Demosyna's own scales, but the leather straps let the prosthetic seem to merge with the healed foot. Demosyna viewed the new toe with tears, grinning at Vaash while he washed from the forging. The leather caps on the metal left no chance of irritation, even when walking around the expansive sectors.

Demosyna tried to prolong her day with her friends, but soon, they gathered around the resilient horse leading their rented cart. It was well past midnight, and Plu Durrah was slightly drunk from her celebrations. Vaash smiled, leading Demosyna away several steps. The human monk wore the single sword gifted by Plu Durrah, leaving the empty sheath displayed on the cinched belt. It was a new accessory, but Vaash carried the sword as if he always had.

"I found your other bag of tridents when organizing the cart," Vaash said, out of earshot of the others. "Don't forget it, because you will need it here in the settlement. It can get very expensive in a harbor city."

Demosyna smiled, shaking her head.

"I claimed that for you, Vaash. I was going to use it on the dogs and maybe get you good meals with it! I just hadn't found the time to say so yet, but it's all yours for your trip now!"

Vaash's face had a cloud move over it, but he smiled again.

"You should have told me, my friend. I kept no secrets from you, but I understand. Let the matter drop, as it means little now. But I do worry about you—and Yoila that now serves you."

Demosyna frowned, shaking her head.

"I can defend myself if she is false about her intentions."

"I worry you may grow too violent and don't wish you to harden yourself. You are so loving, and I know you feel for all these people here," Vaash whispered, gazing into her eyes openly. "I know how strong you are, and that is why I worry for your kind heart. You could wipe out each soldier here, but I advise patience with our thick minds. Always remember what you found on the Highway, and stay this great till we meet again!"

Demosyna listened intently, taking the man's words for their wisdom. She, too, felt regret at losing control and had already determined to avoid that frenzy again.

Vaash continued and held her hand when Demosyna grabbed his.

"Yoila will likely desire intimate orders, for I see the way she gazes at you. She is smitten with you, Demosyna, and you do hold her heart. I know the look well since my own boy was killed beside my son," Vaash told the puzzled Wise-woman. "You have marked her, and Yoila takes that very seriously. I tell you only to enlighten you of the chance and don't wish to make you uncomfortable. You are my best friend, and I love you and this life we now share. Enjoy the time of solitude, and I will see you before you know it!"

"Thank you for the honesty, Vaash," Demosyna said, thinking for long minutes. "I agree with your worry and will always try to love those that are against me. It won't be easy or fun, but I have taken your balance to heart. As you know, I am not seeking intimacy yet in my life. What do I say if that is what Yoila wants?"

Vaash shook his head.

"Only you may know, if that time comes. Speak true and listen for what you desire in your heart. Worry not of this, Demosyna, as Yoila will not want to force the issue. If you ever do seek physical love in your life, she will be there waiting. If I judge her eyes correctly, that Yoila will."

His words were kind and honest, which the apprentice had always known from the monk. The friends embraced warmly and wet the other's clothes with tears.

Plu Durrah was watching the stars, and her dual-toned eyes gazed above with distant focus. Plu hugged the young woman as well once Demosyna moved over to the wagon, wiping her purple-scaled cheeks. Demosyna took a tube of gold pieces from her supply before handing it to Vaash at the back of the wagon. The two slowed as Demosyna motioned to the monk, leaving his old dog in the cart.

"I can't keep my dog with me here, Vaash. He will be in danger with how things are going," Demosyna said, looking sadly at her canine. "I want you to take him, and bring him back when you return. I know you will keep him safe, and he you! He seems to like being around Plu after the injury, and she needs help, I think."

Vaash nodded, frowning as well.

"I am honored you trust me with him, Demosyna! He will not want for anything as long as he is with me! I travel with Plu for that troubling reason as well and told her as much. She is not fully recovered, and I worry for her safety alone. I have no fears about you now since we understand each other so well! What is this gold for if you already gave me your hidden cache?"

Demosyna was still angry at her deception, even with the humor in his voice.

"I want you to put it in a secret cave I lived inside before meeting you. That was the only other lie I told you, Vaash, because I didn't hide from Sai Aeri in the woods. I am sorry for that deception too, but it was before I loved you as my best friend!"

Vaash laughed, shaking his long red hair.

"I see! I am glad we part as best friends, with no illusions remaining. I will do as you ask and find this cave you bunked within."

Demosyna described its location as just upstream of where she found the monk training. Vaash raised his eyebrows but smiled at the location's familiarity. The waterfall cave would be a perfect place to store a reserve of gold.

Demosyna waved her friends goodbye. They had been out of earshot during their brief chat, but Vaash easily caught up to the slow horse. Demosyna followed the wagon along the road for a moment but stopped to watch it fade into the darkness. The Highway was ahead on the horizon, waiting to lead her friends to their futures.

Yoila left the wagon and stood with the young Wizen while her black eyes sparkled at Demosyna's robes. Demosyna's dog mercifully didn't look back, keeping its watching eyes on Plu. The young Wizen sighed a steaming cloud into the stars while letting emotions swell in her chest. The loneliness wasn't as desperate as atop the grasshopper waterfall, but a few tears fell once Demosyna's friends were gone from sight.

Demosyna soon held her crutch as a walking stick, studying the crude map she owned. If the apprentice understood correctly, the lost northern Order was close to the sea, beyond the hourglass mountains. Nothing helpful was marked around a plateau on the map except the numerous islands in a bay.

Demosyna called her new companion over before motioning to the map with a claw.

"Do you know of where the Wise-woman Order would be on this map?" the apprentice asked, offering the paper to Yoila.

"Here, just south of the Wizen Bay," the scaled commander said, pointing, eager to be of use.

"But I must warn you, my Wise-woman. Reports tell of ruins leading into the sea, with none seen walking the castle. I understand the Wise Mother closed the area, limiting access for years now."

"Thank you, Yoila," Demosyna said, putting a question mark where the commander showed. "Did you need to prepare before we set out? I won't sleep tonight after saying goodbye and want to make progress toward the Orders."

"No, my Wise-woman," Yoila called, adjusting a small survival pack. "I will follow where you lead."

Demosyna smiled while nodding at the woman. The two began rounding the mountain's base by following the railroad tracks to sweep beyond the obstacle. A wide plateau had been blocked from their view on the Highway, but extravagant palaces topped the odd feature among the rolling hills.

It stood a few miles away from the mountain city with gold and marble shining in the starlight. Curvy iron gates and lushly tended gardens enclosed the sprawling manors atop the raised platform of rock. There was no fake volcano centered on the upper-class sector, and it lacked a golden dome of glass as protection. Each mansion held its own massive crystal, sending waves of colorful magic in bubbles over their grounds. The shields weren't solid for these massive houses but flowed with continual waves of opaque energy.

Magic lit up the plateau with a gallery of colors, each castle having a unique shade to display. The undulating domes were beautiful and distracting as a constant glowing beacon in the picturesque surroundings. Beyond the farmlands were gentle hills stretching to the horizon, where Au Peirce's island home lay in a frozen bay.

The ache in her feet was barely noticed, and neither was the chafing of her shoulders as the Wizen led her companion along. Both Scale women had cats' eyes and only needed natural light to traverse the forgiving terrain. Torches were spied as the hours fell away but remained distant to deny meeting any travelers.

Demosyna studied the map in the rising sun, letting Yoila rest under a rare shade tree. The distance was frustratingly off, and Au Peirce's words echoed in the Wise-woman's mind. No sign of the Bay was seen yet, nor the collection of islands farther out. The vast stretch of land had seemed small from the Highway, but Demosyna realized elevation and distance mistold the scale.

The Wizen rolled the map again, looking with an ache at the bright-yellow and orange robes she wore. No sign of the Highway was seen behind the two Scales, having fallen behind the horizon. The neon plateau and alarming mountain still provided distant landmarks, but green grasses flowed in all directions.

A light snowfall forced the two travelers to huddle inside a tiny tent that night while shivering out the storm. Demosyna awoke with Yoila's arm around her, warming both women by the embrace. The young Wise-woman smiled and lay beside someone she almost killed in a mindless rage. The black scales were smooth against her purple-hued flesh, and Demosyna turned to wake the woman.

"Are you hungry, Yoila?" Demosyna asked, moving Yoila's arm from her pink-scaled belly.

Yoila moaned weakly, waking with a slow yawn.

"Warm!"

The black-scaled soldier bolted upright, her eyes wide and alert. A blush formed on the sides of her face, and Yoila looked away quickly. Demosyna offered the embarrassed woman some water but took a drink herself when Yoila declined.

"It's good we can keep each other warm, with the snows falling!" Demosyna said, breaking the silence after a moment. "I don't mind if you want to sleep close, Yoila. It was nice to have someone near these last nights!"

"Thank you for the mercy, my Wise-woman," Yoila breathed, not looking at Demosyna. "I grew used to holding someone while sleeping from my former posting. That is how we stayed a squad, each soldier finding their partner. Or partners."

The two moved on without eating, watching the rolling hills spawn new vistas. Demosyna was glad for the nightly warmth when sharing a cozy blanket with a newfound friend. It took days to reach the Wizen Bay, named after the Wise-women who first settled the lands.

The frequent rest in the wagon was a sorely missed treat, but Demosyna pressed ahead once spying the remaining northern Order. The meandering path had left the travelers east of the Wizen Bay after cresting a hill to see the peculiar waters. Two different shades of blue formed the wide inlet with hundreds of islands poking from the estuary. Demosyna paused to rest and observe the tremendous sight with the ebony-scaled commander drinking deeply from the waterskin.

The darker blue of the ocean was cut nearly in half, leaving the icy southern bay a fresh white blue. Demosyna couldn't see any streams flowing into the Bay to form the line of brackish water but smiled at the natural wonder the Wizen Bay offered. Ships of all designs sped between the clusters of grassy islands, but the majority seemed to be pontoon boats. These wide ships cut through the water with twin prows and netting strung beneath carrying cargo. The largest trading ships lumbered around the tip of the peninsulas, huge pontoons with stacked metal crates.

Neither woman carried a spyglass, but the afternoon light gave both sharp-eyed travelers a perfect view of the towns. A larger of the islands, near the north edge of the icy bay, housed a real volcano that puffed slightly into the sky. The steam from the glowing mountain joined the storm clouds moving in from the east with consistency.

Demosyna blew a sigh into the frozen air, watching the faux volcano clouds join the real ones' emissions. Ships gave the active volcano a wide berth, and Demosyna's eyes followed one that traveled south in the Bay. The islands were uninhabited once reaching the freshwater portion of the Wizen Bay, and a towering dome of rock lay just off the southern beach.

"What is that?" Demosyna gasped, pointing two of her clawed fingers at the formation.

"That is the Order you seek, my Wise-woman," Yoila explained, smiling at Demosyna's wide eyes. "The Mother of the North moved the last of the Wise-woman castles into that geode. It was about ten years ago when she closed the borders to her lands after a lengthy siege. Many were forced to flee their island homes to honor the Wise-woman's decree."

"That sounds horrible," Demosyna said, frowning. "I will have to try and understand why once I talk with the Wise Mother!"

"She had the most profitable mine before she freed the slaves in her lands," Yoila said, motioning to the beach in the distance. "It was a wonderful day when she unbound thousands, but the Mother of the North remains in control of all the fresh waters. None have heard from the Wise Mother in a decade, but still, we obey her commands."

Demosyna could just see the tops of crystals jutting from a crack in the earth, glittering in various colors. The canyon was lost behind the massive rock dome rising from the fresh water, but the women could make out precious magical crystals filling the walls. No work was being done in the mine, and Demosyna twirled her broken ring in thought.

The apprentice's own focusing crystal was clear and polished where it wasn't cracked, but the distant raw gems had hues in various colors. Such a treasure would be worth a kingdom if enough focusing charms could be amassed from the mine. The broken walls making up the long-sought north Order were not visible from their line of sight; only the back of the geode and strip of mine were seen many miles away.

New energy flowed into the young Wise-woman, and Demosyna held back tears of happiness. The apprentice's future lay ahead, awash with conflicted frozen waters in the Wizen Bay.

"Let's get a few bites once we reach the water!" Demosyna exclaimed, smiling at Yoila. "Then I will rent a boat to head straight across the Bay. I don't want to walk the entire curve of the inlet!"

"I am not allowed into the fresh water, my Wise-woman," Yoila said, lowering her eyes. "Nobody is. You are a likely exception, but I do not know for sure."

This further troubled the young woman, but Demosyna knew questions would have to wait for meeting the Wise Mother. Mother of the North was a title Demosyna hadn't heard, and she pondered the revelations about the Wise Mother. It was the powerful Wizen herself who broke contact, it seemed, before the time of freeing all her slaves.

The hills were gone in the blink of an eye, letting Demosyna feel sand again once removing her iron-capped boots. The young woman laughed and ran with bright robes flapping like yellow wings. Yoila watched after sitting to guard the shed gear, a small smile forming. Life teemed below the frozen surface of the fresh water, and Demosyna wrapped the crutch with her clothes. Yoila's eyes grew wide, searching the purple-scaled young woman running free along the empty beach.

The waters were freezing, but Demosyna didn't mind in the slightest. The apprentice was weightless and free, pushing her body through currents with joyful abandon. The miles were cleaned off the young woman, and Demosyna surfaced, laughing and shivering. Yoila stood peering with a hand shading her eyes as steady clouds of breath flew away.

"How many fish can you eat, Yoila?" Demosyna called, splashing an ice chunk away.

"Any you catch will be fine, my Wise-woman!" Yoila yelled back, waving.

Demosyna had removed her metal toe, leaving it with her other possessions on the sand. The icy water felt odd against the stump of digit, like those lost nerves still felt the chill. The elation of fishing

swept Demosyna into her hunt while snapping thin spines with grinning jaws. Fresh seaweed was gathered, and Demosyna tied together
bundles of scaly meat.

Yoila had built a fire, gathering driftwood and dead grass, while
the young Wise-woman found them dinner. The commander was
lighting the kindling, trying to avoid staring as Demosyna dried her
frozen scales. A small hollow blocked much of the wind from the sea,
but it was difficult to get the spark bedded.

"Would you like your half of the fish cooked or raw?" Demosyna
asked the successful commander, sitting beside the fire. "I will smoke
some of mine, and they should keep a few days!"

"I can cook for you, my Wise-woman," Yoila said almost
hopefully.

"No need unless you prefer to!" Demosyna replied, wrapping
her catches in greens. "I enjoy cooking and don't mind making you
something!"

"As you wish," Yoila said, bowing her horned head. "Thank you
for allowing the food, my Wise-woman."

"Allow? I always want you to eat your fill, Yoila!" Demosyna
said with mild confusion, smiling over the fire. "Enjoy yourself while
we dine tonight, and I can rent a canoe from that port I saw north
along the beach."

"Is there any wine in those skins?" Yoila asked hesitantly, blushing slightly.

The night passed for the two, sharing the last of the wine and
chatting. Yoila had always known a soldier's life under the Empress,
she explained as the storm rolled in. The slight cavity the travelers
sheltered in kept the rain off their heads, and Demosyna listened
with dancing eyes.

The commander had joined the current swell of the ancient
war, leaving the imperial army to fight with the rebels. Yoila was now
serving Demosyna and hoping that the young woman could better
aid the Fist.

"I only wanted to save those I commanded, my Wise-woman.
But we have been hounded by the imperial army for years," Yoila

said, frowning. "Everyone proved unkind to my seeder soldiers, so we stole away with you and your beautiful vision."

Demosyna told her own short tale to the lounging woman, wiping a tear away once or twice. Yoila moved closer to the young Wizen as she spoke and held Demosyna's hand during the retelling of her brief slavery. The young Wise-woman skipped much of the weeks spent on the Highway, knowing she would have time later. What mattered now to the apprentice was freedom, and Demosyna felt strong enough to give it to everyone.

"I couldn't help those I saw along my journey, for the most part," Demosyna mused aloud, holding hands with Yoila. "So taking the First Fort should be our focus, I think. We can cut off the Empress in the south and begin taking the Highway from both directions!"

"Sai Aeri won't give up the lands easily," Yoila said, gazing into Demosyna's eyes. "But I know you could level the walls with your magic!"

"Perhaps, but I had a different plan in mind," Demosyna said, pointing toward the mountainous geode. "If I can mine enough crystals, we can let each soldier better defend themselves in battle! My winds must be taught to their Wise-women, and no rebel need worry over artillery or magic!"

"I would have to restructure the remaining forces but will begin preparations at once, my Wise-woman," Yoila said, taking a small notebook from her pack.

The rain let up, allowing Demosyna to stretch in the damp sand. Demosyna was tired but wished to sleep in an apprentice bed tomorrow and broke camp.

Yoila was jotting into her notebook while pausing to think occasionally as she marched faithfully behind Demosyna. Already, Demosyna had seen the commander's skill in drawing, watching Yoila doodle at camp each night.

Moonlight broke through the drifting clouds in a rhythm to set a pace for the sandy travelers. Nearly a mile after the slanted line of fresh water reached the shore, a tiny harbor rested on the beach. Several points were handed over, and Demosyna paddled toward the Wise-woman castle in the rising sun.

The Wizen Bay proved huge, stretching to the horizon with bustling travel. Demosyna sat in the back of the rented boat and paddled steadily toward a strip of beach. She didn't push herself, but the young Wise-woman powered the duo's water craft with skilled hands. The progress was slow while both women enjoyed the solitude together.

Yoila didn't sing or play instruments, but Demosyna listened while the woman spoke. The commander told of her first battle, thrust into the front lines by imperial spear point.

"I was punished for not killing anyone," Yoila recalled, spitting into the water. "I learned quickly how to hide the anger in my heart since that was met with whips as well. I killed my commanding officers before taking my troops into the wilds, promising them freedom and retribution. I never wanted to kill, and that is why I fail as a commander."

"You have kept that promise," Demosyna said, placing a comforting hand on Yoila's shoulder. "Your armies fight for themselves, and you have given them a better life. That is all I can do either sometimes—offer the chance at something new, if only to the few that hear me. I am proud to know you and am grateful you have joined me for the moment!"

"Let me take over if you would, my Wise-woman," Yoila said, rubbing her cheek on Demosyna's hand. "I can get you where you desire, if you want to meditate."

Yoila was several years older than Demosyna and in better physical condition from a life of violence. Vaash had helped the young Wise-woman strengthen her muscles, but they ached from the hours of paddling already. Demosyna accepted the offer while handing the oar forward with a smile. The crutch was balanced on Demosyna's knees, water hitting the carved title she bore with increasing truth.

Demosyna meditated on the approaching geode and its bottom that swallowed vast amounts of the fresh water. The path Yoila took was slightly less direct than Demosyna's by angling the canoe to land on a flat of beach. Massive crystals seventy feet tall supported the single building in the geode, wet from the surf. Other gems grew from the rock dome of focusing crystals and reflected in random angles against the light.

Magical crystals surrounded and enclosed the dwarfed tower, fading behind it in a uniform arc. Once the two made ground on the beach, Demosyna saw familiar jade walls in the broken hall. The apprentice halls were the only remaining evidence of any Wise-woman Order, and a mine dominated the land nearest the Bay. There were no ruins visible, in the canyon or on the surface, and Demosyna wondered at the missing grounds.

The apprentice halls were located near the center of a massive complex in her youth, but Demosyna spied no evidence of walls or aqueducts or even roads. Her journey to reach the top of the Fist was met with more curious turns, and the young Wizen marched toward the staircase above the water.

The great chasm she passed to reach the shore came to a point at one end but widened to a deep pit bathed in shadows. Crystals grew from the walls of the jagged rocks, almost forming steps in places. Ladders and ropes still clung to several large gems as rotting signs of former slave labor. Yoila had been correct, and no work was underway in the valuable mine. A few of the enormous crystals were diamond clear, glittering in the evening sun like Demosyna's shattered ring.

An offshore metal platform supporting a rotating crane stood massive in scale and holding a shaped orange crystal. Fiber and metal ropes held the crystal still, even in the breeze from another approaching snowstorm. There was no operator in the crane, and Demosyna saw no signs of life in the roofless rooms. The circular remains of the first-floor apprentice halls held several doorways, but one side was broken and missing completely. Open air filled the entire building with half a wall and no ceiling letting the elements into the pristine halls.

The sight saddened the young Wise-woman, but she wrapped her robes tight against the chill of surf and memory. Massive support crystals held the foundation of the ruin meters above the water, and the geode sparkled with fish and prisms. The mass of rock and crystal seemed to tilt from the bottom of the Wizen Bay, a near-perfect half sphere of defense.

Banded wood double doors stood locked high in the air with numerous holes in the walls giving proof of former battle. The world was quiet, however, for these lands were under strict lockdown. Boats remained distant, and no travelers were seen among the gentle hills.

"Greetings, Wise Mother!" Demosyna yelled, ignoring the surf soaking her robe hems. "I have traveled to your Order, seeking understanding with you!"

Yoila remained silent, wide eyes marveling at the sight. No answer came for minutes, and no movement was noticed from beyond the suspended walls. Even in the failing light, Demosyna's eyes caught a striped tail swish out from a shattered crevice above the doorway. It was long and slender, covered in tiger-striped fur that fluttered in the wind.

"You aren't welcome here," a woman called from the shadows, only a tail signaling her presence. "Leave. Celestria isn't home."

"Celestria? That is the Wise Mother for this Order?" Demosyna called, trying to see the Paw. "I am Demosyna and sought an audience with Celestria. I am from the southern Wise-women but wish to study here instead!"

A short, heavy woman rolled over into the light with a sigh. Her belly fell over the edge of her nook slightly, and the golden-furred woman eyed the pair. A long tail flicked in thought while the striped woman stretched a stubby leg.

"You aren't a Wizen," the woman said finally, resting in a crooked arm. "Leave before I banish you personally. I wish to sun myself while there still is one in the sky."

"I am, ma'am. My charm is broken, but I can still do two types of magic so far," Demosyna said, hoping that would be proof enough.

"So you bought a magic ring! You aren't a Wise-woman. You are an archer with your fireballs."

This caught the Paw's attention, and she sat up to glare at the two.

"I don't know any fire magic yet, only wind and some healing," Demosyna called, frowning. "Watch. Stand back a bit, Yoila."

Fingers of wind grabbed three rocks from the beach, tossing them each into the ocean. The brown-and-gold-furred woman watched intently while lying above the Bay. The stranger rose slowly and jumped to the ruined steps that curved below the doorframe. The tiger-furred woman wore no clothes, only a pair of armguards and an elaborate wide collar. Soft hair covered the figure, and sharp ears poked slightly above a whiskered face.

A simple red fabric was taken from the shadows of the door, and a shining magical staircase curved under her feet as the Paw wrapped a skirt. The stairs of light appeared with each lazy step and vanished into embers once the woman stepped forward.

"Now let me guess, you'll heal a small cut on your hand, right?" the woman said, mockery in her tone. "How about you heal your slave soldier from where you stand?"

Yoila remained at attention as the woman reached her, extruding a curved claw from a hairy finger. The sharp claw touched the commander's arm, and the Paw raised an eyebrow.

"If Yoila allows it, I can hold a stone and heal her from here," Demosyna said, tilting her horned head. "It's painful, but I will if it convinces you I am an apprentice!"

Vertical pupils scanned both travelers, and the skirted Paw grinned as she cut into a black-scaled arm. Yoila didn't register the small slice, and Demosyna quickly summoned her known magics. A stone was grabbed and held spinning in the young apprentice's left hand. Grating mental effort sent a substantial ribbon of gold healing toward Yoila, and the Paw squinted her eyes. Demosyna finished the display, letting the heavy stone fall to the beach.

"I don't see any other focusing charms, but you are wearing boots," the short woman said, thinking out loud. "I am Marrah the Jade, and if you are lying, I will kill you both. I just wanted you to know who ended you, so wait here if you are truly a Wise-woman."

Demosyna nodded before sitting on the sand while Marrah walked through the air on her magical staircase. Yoila stood behind the seated woman, rubbing her healed cut and beaming down at Demosyna. Marrah unlocked the heavy doors with a wave of her hand before rounding the cracked frame with no further words.

Marrah the Jade's bracers were adorned with a double row of focusing crystals, and Demosyna looked at the traders islands in consideration. If Demosyna was not allowed entry, other plans would have to begrudgingly be made. This disappointed the young Wise-woman, but she sighed in meditation while awaiting Marrah's return.

Over fifteen minutes passed in silent contemplation for Demosyna, and the sky darkened from the setting sun. Glowing stairs allowed the woman to descend once more, and the short Paw tossed a ring to Demosyna. It held a bright-orange crystal, sharp and straight in a setting. It didn't encircle the band, as Demosyna's did, but seemed to grow from the silver to be shaped into a gem.

"That should let you start a fire or maybe warm a tent," Marrah said, lying on the sand. "Toss me your ring and save your lives. Light a fire with the aid of that crystal, or your girl dies first."

"I cannot produce fire magic. Will the ring do it?" Demosyna asked, worry creeping into her voice.

"It will give you a taste of how to summon fire," Marrah explained. "Celestria made it before...well, when she still allowed people into our lands. I don't know any magic myself, but that is what she told me."

The puzzled young apprentice tossed the broken ring with a warning of the jaggedness, putting the silvery band in its place. Marrah used a claw to dangle the gold circle in the starlight, a keen eye watching Demosyna through the center.

Demosyna picked up several hollow logs to stack a hasty camp-fire. The apprentice meditated on the rough wood under her hands, and smoke began rising at once. The feeling of warm, crackling fire tingled in her hands, but the smell awoken by the ring was what Demosyna latched on to. It was the sudden memory of happy talk with friends relaxing over a fragrant wood fire that cast the magic.

Demosyna laughed, watching the fire catch on the brittle wood.

"That was really helpful. Thank you, Marrah the Jade!"

The two swapped rings again, and Demosyna put her gold ring in its place on her thumb. Marrah stood and tossed the young Wizen a stick, wrapping a cloth she took from a bag at her hip.

"Now make me a torch," Marrah said, putting away the silver ring.

Demosyna did so, remembering the way the smoke seeped into her robes each night. The warm smell would be there to greet her each morning from the cheery yellow robes Demosyna wore. Fire sparked to life where Demosyna focused, and Yoila breathed a sigh of relief. The torch lit the young Wise-woman's purple face, and Marrah smiled. Like healing magic, it was painful to cast, but Demosyna had grown used to the sensation.

"It was a nice touch, bringing a rebel uniform for your slave," Marrah the Jade said, taking the torch and looking closely. "But the ring gave you away, Demosyna the Wise. Using that tale to get yourself in was a fine idea, but I guard these doors now. That old sign was only to be used by my Order when it was active. You having this proves you are just another of those betraying Wizen, back with a new gamble."

"I speak true, ma'am. Plu Durrah told me of the sign, but I wear it only as a focusing charm," Demosyna explained, removing the ring. "I purchased it far in the south, at the start of my Highway travels. I don't know of any other Wise-women in the Fist, for I traveled with only my Wise Mother on a boat. Yoila here follows me to aid my goals, without chains or contracts binding the commander."

"My Wise-woman is correct," Yoila said, touching her claw scars. "I follow her because she showed me true strength by freeing me from my hateful ways. I unchained my slaves, each one that I owned, to be allowed to serve Demosyna. I do so willingly, as she holds my heart now instead of violence."

"Curious," Marrah said, thinking with her fuzzy tail twitching. "If the songs are correct, Demosyna is said to aid the slaves. I will believe you for now, because it matters not either way. Celestria isn't here, and I cannot grant you entry till she approves. The Mother of the North allows only me in her lands at the moment and has left me her keys."

The golden-chested woman held up the bracers, worn leather-wrapped guards sporting twelve gems apiece. Each one sparkled in a different color, and Demosyna leaned closer to view them. Marrah had used the gems to open the doors and likely to create the stairs up to her castle.

"Are you a slave, Marrah? I thought Celestria freed all her servants years ago!"

Demosyna had seen the wide collar on Marrah's neck and frowned.

"I can take you from here if you wish."

"No, silly Scale!" Marrah said, eyes full of wild amusement. "I am not bound against my desires! I wear this collar with honor, as a reminder to Celestria about her place!"

"Would you share a drink with us at least?" Demosyna said, nodding in response, sitting and pouring a cup. "I traveled so far. I at least want to look at the apprentice halls a bit longer!"

Demosyna had taken a mug from the wagon before it departed and smiled at the simple clay vessel. It reminded the young Wise-woman of Vaash, and she sighed herself back to the present.

"Thank you, Demosyna," Marrah said, sniffing the water. "I was thirsty after nearly killing you two! You seem harmless enough, but Yoila has quite the look in her eyes!"

The fire kept the three warm, and they chatted for several moments around the blaze. Marrah the Jade explained that the previous apprentices had left the northern Order, taking many of the remaining supplies with them. The war had given the students an opportunity, and they stole away with valuable books and treasure.

"They try occasionally to get someone back inside, but my beautiful Celestria moved our home into that eyesore," Marrah said, pointing at the massive geode. "She is away in New Empress City, delivering the latest order for her crystals."

"I saw many gems in the Wise-woman Settlement," Demosyna said, smiling. "Did Celestria make them all? That's amazing. She must be a skilled Wizen to produce such finery!"

"We do indeed!"

Marrah smiled, enjoying the adoration.

"She taught me a few things, but Celestria is a genius at growing crystals. The earth shook the morning she decided to move and produced that crystal mountain from the ocean floor. It lets me sun myself in peace but is gaudy with its scale, I say! The mine she made was a better addition to our lands, but who am I to complain?"

Marrah produced a jar of thick, clear fluid from a satchel and motioned at Demosyna's broken ring. The young apprentice handed the precious trinket over, smiling at the Paw as the stars shone down. A brush let the furry woman put sticky globs of gelatinous substance into the broken areas of the ring. The liquid sat quivering in the breeze, and Marrah frowned when nothing happened.

A blue gem glowed from its place on an armguard, and Marrah breathed onto the drying clear paint. Fresh crystals sprouted from the solidifying paste, remaining clear and square in the moonlight. Demosyna gasped while taking the repaired ring with trembling hands.

"That should hold you till Celestria returns any week now!" Marrah said, poking at the fresh-grown crystals. "You locked the band I made in the spell you cast. I'm surprised the structure let you use another magic."

"I did make a tornado initially with this ring," Demosyna whispered, thinking back. "Is that what kept me from healing?"

"I made that ring for a Shadow that couldn't do magic."

Marrah stretched, drinking more water.

"It was a virgin crystal and yearned for a spell to complete its purpose. If you tried other magic, it's no wonder the ring broke. The specific frequency of the crystal often tunes itself to one magic. That lets a strong Wise-woman make a specific enchantment, allowing anyone to cast a spell without tutoring. I saw the ease of profit and joined Celestria in making crystals after disbanding my Shadows."

"It was so trying, casting other magic," Demosyna said, putting the spiked ring on her thumb. "Thank you, Marrah, for mending my charm! Vaash said it was made by talented paws, and I see that is true!"

Marrah raised an eyebrow at the name but sipped her drink, golden-furred belly warmed by the flames. The fire was dimming, and Demosyna gathered more wood in the overcast night. A clawed purple finger rolled more fire into the embers, turning a jutting crystal orange. Several more gems remained clear, waiting for a tuning spell on the golden ring.

Demosyna gazed at the spikes of neutral minerals, and her yellow eyes filled with tears.

"Can I help you recover your stolen knowledge? I wish to repay this kindness, if only in a small way!" Demosyna asked, breaking her eyes from the marvelous ring. "If I must wait for Celestria to return, let me aid by retrieving the lost items while scouting the wilds."

"Be careful with these ones, Demosyna," Marrah warned, pointing to an eastern peninsula on the map. "They never took to magic but have many powerful artifacts and enchanted jewels left. Their leaders are twins that can make potions to rival magical effects and often dueled Wise-women with only their flasks. I've kept eyes on the sloppy deserters from the day they took off, as they unwittingly use my pawnshops to move the stolen loot! The real joke is, they can't read the books they stole since my Wise-woman always keeps so many secrets!"

"I will get the books back and any other property they may have with them," Demosyna said, eager to fill her time with adventure. "Thank you for visiting with us, Marrah the Jade! I will present a gift worthy of Celestria once I find those traitors."

"Just don't open any of the books, especially the blue-covered ones," Marrah called, ascending the magic stairs in the starlight. "Good luck, Demosyna. Don't let them see you coming."

Demosyna took turns with Yoila to row into the dark salt waters of the Wizen Bay. They rounded the massive metal crane, gazing up at the suspended crystal tied with cords. Steam was making mirages on the orange faces of the crystal, vapor blown around in the frozen wind. Twinkling torches approached in the gloom, and the thankful women rushed inside from the beginnings of a snowstorm.

The inn was nearly full, but a common room was still warm and inviting after the worsening waves. Yoila insisted on taking the first shift on watch, and Demosyna dreamed of crystal libraries.

The young Wise-woman was amused when Yoila didn't wake her up, the commander having watched the entire night. Demosyna made the woman rest in the canoe, and the young Wizen paddled east into the defenseless ocean.

CHAPTER 30

The frozen sea carried Demosyna along once more in a tiny wooden shelter among vast shipping lines. Yoila was snoring in the front of their canoe, letting Demosyna steer the rented craft. The larger pontoons had reinforced hulls to smash northern ice apart for the smaller boats with groaning crashes. Sluggish lines cut around the peninsulas, and Demosyna paddled east with sparkling eyes.

Marrah didn't know the precise cave the twin leaders claimed, but the majority of the last finger of land was riddled with submerged caverns. The Paws' network of spies traced the students to that area, yet Demosyna wasn't troubled about the vague location. The young Wizen could swim underwater nearly indefinitely and mentally prepared for long days searching in the icy waves.

Entire days passed for the two while sharing salted fish and trading with merchant boats. Demosyna purchased a wobbly spyglass and a small bag of citrus fruits from a passing pontoon. The frozen green treats were grabbed from the ice-covered nets holding perishable items, keeping them fresh during long voyages. The small canoe couldn't travel the deeper ocean, so the women kept the shore near at all times. The sea grew rough occasionally, but Demosyna spied towering waves in the north that rocked the giant cargo vessels. A light snowstorm convinced Demosyna to camp for an afternoon upon watching Yoila pretend she wasn't cold too.

Yoila fished after the third day of paddling and retrieved a large tuna with trembling arms. The prize took up much of the boat, covering the gear with oily fish smell for a week. They ate the raw meat in shifts when resting from powering the boat to snack on fresh ocean life. Yoila scraped salt off the canoe to season the tuna with ocean crystals. The peninsula on the east of the Wizen Bay faded, revealing their target.

Demosyna returned their canoe to walk on the beach and test her new telescope. Yoila sharpened her sword at their camp that night, maintaining one of her few carried possessions. No slaves were seen on the trip, and Yoila told of her generals favoring Demosyna's plans. Tens of thousands had been freed already, giving a needed boost to morale and troops all across the Fist.

"The Empress holds most territories in the Fist, with their slaves still waiting for your mercy," Yoila said, reading a missive of rebel communication. "I passed along your commands, my Wise-woman, and your wisdom has been understood. The last battle had many casualties, but the magical winds cut them in half from what we expected before."

"That is tremendous news, Yoila," Demosyna said, grinning. "Tell your armies to heal the Empress's forces after the battle as well. We must let them know a new era is dawning, and all can be welcomed without need of hatred. Once you have the First Fort, we can ship prisoners back south to rejoin their precious Empress."

"Can you give me any details about the fort since you were there?" Yoila asked, kneeling before Demosyna. "Please don't be upset, my Wise-woman, but any firsthand knowledge would save lives."

"You may ask me anything, Yoila."

Demosyna smiled down at the woman.

"That isn't a pleasant memory, to be sure, but I will draw you a diagram of the layout. You may find an entrance through the mine if a tunnel leads out to the harbor. I only saw the cells of the tower and have no idea what to expect on the other floors. I was there for days but only saw a few areas beside the disgusting courtyard."

"Thank you, my Wise-woman. I will pass your newest desires to my former generals," Yoila said, absently touching her facial scars. "Can I get you anything from the town ahead? I will ask any rebels about the twins you hunt if you wish to wait in camp. We will catch their scent soon, seeing as these lands are fully controlled by rebel armies!"

Demosyna only had a single trident of gold remaining, with tiny bags of points filling two pockets. The young Wizen shook her horned head while looking up from a half-filled page. Demosyna sketched a rough drawing of the First Fort, showing the mine, tower, and courtyard features. Scale wasn't of great concern, and Yoila bowed deeply after taking the simple doodle.

Demosyna had indicated where the mines she walked led, but the tunnels were ancient and sprawling. Yoila's drawings of Demosyna's travels always amazed the Wizen, but Yoila took the simple page with watery eyes. There was a good chance a shaft could be found in the hills or forests surrounding the Fort given the number of branching paths. A legend was added in a corner to allow the scribbles to be deciphered.

Both women were marching into the solitary town when Yoila asked for leave to run rebel errands. Demosyna nodded, smiling at the retreating commander, and walked the few streets in search of a spare focusing charm. A copper necklace was the only crystal found, and Demosyna paid thirty points from half of her coin bags. No posting board was located, and the yellow-robed young woman wandered back to the arched drawbridge.

The last of their tuna was handed to a traveling pack of families sharing a boat heading west. Demosyna was stuffed from days of dense fish. Yoila ate much more than the young Wise-woman, leaving Demosyna to adjust her fishing schedule slightly.

While waiting for Yoila to finish her tasks, Demosyna meditated on her current situation. Much of the plan would depend on in-the-moment decisions based on what was found in the hideout. Rest for the moment was needed, as well as more time to consider the options. There was no inn among the town buildings, and Demosyna scanned the horizon for likely campsites.

Yoila returned with no word on the twins, so together, the two bedded down for the night in sight of the village. The commander provided the tent, and Demosyna lit the fire with an ease that was astounding. After weeks of grinding struggle, the young apprentice was casting magic without a second thought. The healing was likewise free of agony and a clear gem turned a deep blue after the first blister was repaired.

The next days gave word of the eastern coast having sightings of the twins, and Demosyna marched across the rocky countryside with purpose that evening. Sheer cliffs dominated this side of the Fist as well, Demosyna saw through her glass, and a churning whirlpool stretched halfway to the horizon in the south. Demosyna knew tales of these destructive formations appearing along this edge of the north and witnessed the true phenomenon with wonder.

Ice swirled in the unending spirals the water formed, pulling the breaking chunks into the deep dark. The entire sucking mass vanished while the two watched and left a placid ocean in comparison.

"No wonder ships use the western routes," Demosyna mused aloud, laughing at the watery show. "That would swallow any ship whole without breaking stride!"

"Yes, none has ever mapped the whirlpools. It would be suicide to try, because they often appear directly under ships that sail those waters," Yoila said, nodding as another whirlpool appeared farther south.

That night, the moon was near absent, and the cloudy sky gave almost no light at all. Demosyna was sitting with her legs dangling off a cliff and letting Yoila sleep first. The camp was below, sheltered in a cluster of trees to break the wind that swept the bluffs. The rise she sat upon let Demosyna watch as a dark metal object tore through the ocean, sending a huge tail of spray in its wake.

The light was so poor that it was impossible to see detail, but the object moved fast enough to skip across the waves as though flying. Demosyna had never seen anything move so fast, not even the trains that rushed to keep deadlines and quotas. The purple-scaled apprentice stood, trying to get a better look, as a whirlpool formed under the speeding metal. She had been shining her chilly legs with a poor-quality cloth but dropped the fabric when Demosyna spied the dark streak.

The momentum achieved by the dark dot was sufficient to nearly clear the diameter, but the distant object started falling into the waves. Demosyna gasped as the tail of water doubled in size, pushing the mysterious spec out of harm's way. It sailed through the frozen air and vanished into the south without a sound. The whirlpools made distant rumblings, but whatever had just passed was too far away to hear.

The young Wise-woman rubbed her eyes in disbelief, unsure if she had actually seen anything in the tricky light. Yoila didn't know what it could have been either, and Demosyna pointed along the path it had taken in the eastern waters. Demosyna waited till her shift was over, not wanting to wake Yoila prematurely.

"It was gone in seconds, so fast it vanished before I could really catch a glimpse," Demosyna said breathlessly, shaking her head. "Look. There it is again."

The dull metal object was flying back toward the two, having just appeared out of a whirlpool. It rode the angle of a second swirling funnel and traveled once around the perimeter before continuing north. Yoila narrowed her eyes, and Demosyna fancied she saw a sparkle of gold from the metal object.

The two talked about the development with excited voices once the dot vanished on the northern horizon.

"Was it a creature? It was shiny, but it may have been metallic," Yoila thought aloud, stirring the campfire.

"I didn't see any shadows in the water, but it was so dark, I don't trust my eyes!" Demosyna said, laughing, twirling her regrown ring.

The two pressed on, making their way down the bluffs to a jagged beach. Yoila kept watch on their goods while setting up camp as Demosyna scouted for caves. The rising sun gave Demosyna the start of her time limit, swimming at night in the ocean being a dangerous idea. Hundreds of caves were explored, most only deep enough to catch her attention before she found them shallow.

Short breaks were taken to warm the frozen woman, but Demosyna explored for long hours without soggy clothes caking with salt. The first day proved fruitless, but Demosyna wasn't discouraged after watching the sun set with Yoila. The long stretch of beach was just starting to be explored, and both women slept their shifts with nervous energy.

Daylight still pierced the freezing water when Demosyna found the cave on the sixth day. A twisting intake tunnel left Demosyna in an echoing entry cave, and she saw nobody inside the small alcove. Yoila was ready to swim, having wrapped her clothes in leather to keep them dry. Yoila stood bare in the windy rocks while blushing and following Demosyna into the ocean.

Yoila grabbed the young woman's leg suddenly, halfway through the descending tunnel. A trip wire was pointed out, and Demosyna was amazed she didn't set it off when first finding the cave. The trap wasn't seen, but the sight of the wire slowed the two considerably. The entry cavern led the sneaking women into a large network of connected passages, most filled with currents of water. A huge chamber let the scaled women climb from the water, dressing in the still dark of the cave.

Torches lined some of the walls to send twisted shadows over the slaves chained underground. Demosyna marched to the sleeping figures while motioning Yoila to the other end of the line. They pried the chains from wet rocks with crowbars found nearby, quieting the waking slaves with hushed voices.

"Take them out and return once they are safe on the beach," Demosyna whispered to the group, grabbing Yoila's shoulder. "I will explore that passage ahead very slowly and find where the twins are hiding!"

"Be careful, my Wise-woman," Yoila said, kissing the purple hand. "That will not be the only trap here."

The trembling slaves had claimed they were the only servants here, so Demosyna watched the commander herd the group into the water. Many weren't Scales and had to be convinced to swim for minutes without air. Their former connecting slave chain was clutched by the captives with Yoila ready to pull them through the water to safety.

"I believe in you, Freebloods," Demosyna said, smiling with warm affection at each face. "You are stronger than you were taught, and I will let you see that from now on!"

The encouragement worked wonders, and Yoila grinned as she powered an escape from the earth.

Demosyna walked along the curving pathways leading into the cave system, seeing waterlogged tunnels spanning off from the floor. Damp smells reached her nose, and the Wise-woman inched along with all her senses reaching out. One room was devoted to alchemy and storage, with beakers and boxes stuffing the shelves full. None of the finished bottles was labeled, and Demosyna moved on without pocketing any.

Demosyna had placed the focusing ring on a toe inside her boots after dressing, wanting both hands free if crawling escape was needed. She could still summon her magic, but now the apprentice's left foot tingled in place of a hand when spells were cast. It poked into the toe beside with new crystals, but Demosyna crawled slowly to avoid detection.

The next natural room housed a kitchen and dining table, where Demosyna saw a few jeweled rings resting on the counter. She took them with a smile, hearing snores from the next room. The sleeping quarters had two beds and bookshelves holding scrolls and bound tomes. They would be stuffed, but Demosyna estimated she could take all of them in her new bag. She inched forward, almost scraping the ground with her robes, while Demosyna watched the twins with wide eyes.

Only the young Wizen moved in the quiet room when starting to load the stolen books into a leather sack. Demosyna had purchased it for this purpose and hoped the tightly sealed container would keep the knowledge dry.

"Let me carry the bag for you, my Wise-woman," Yoila breathed into an ear, slinking from around the corner. "You must be free to escape if they wake."

Demosyna handed the bursting pack to the commander, watching her black scales glisten from the rescue. A flooded tunnel led away from behind a potion-heavy shelf, and the two crept to the dark water. Both women missed a pressure plate in their vigilance, and a trap released heavy rocks from a shadow above.

Demosyna's tornado roared to life at the sound, but the eye of the magic didn't stop the tumbling stones. Each woman was knocked unconscious with a small crack forming in Demosyna's right horn when struck by a boulder. The twins woke from the commotion to find the helpless burglars under the piles of trap stones.

One went to find the slaves gone and returned with fury stamped on her elven face. Her twin elf sister took the bag of books, then stripped both women of their coats. The two worked fast to undress the prone Scales while taking Demosyna's copper necklace after spying the crystal.

"This stupid Wise-woman. They never think to look around, always stumbling about with their precious magics," a twin said, taking a drink from a potion. "Did you get back all of the volumes?"

"They took our slaves," the other elf said, tossing clothes onto the beds. "But they can take their places! This raven Scale looks strong. Get the thick chains."

Demosyna woke to her boots being untied with Yoila still down and already missing all her gear. The boots were the last clothing she wore. The elf slaver noticed the rising Wizen. Demosyna was seeing double, so quadruplets closed in with clubs held ready.

"Leave the Fist," Demosyna said, jumping to her feet. "I will not let you keep your slaves, so take your banishment in stride."

Both laughed loudly, stepping over the books and Yoila to advance. They each wore their loose underclothes, having been sleeping just moments ago, but were strong and had murder in their eyes.

"It's just like a Wise-woman—so full of herself she can't see she is beaten," the closer of the two elves spoke, swinging the club.

The attack was caught with wind hands, and Demosyna ripped it from the elf's grasp. The current in the water took the club from the fight, and Demosyna stepped forward with a smile.

"I am stronger than you both, so stop trying to hold on to your old ideals," Demosyna said, pushing the twins back a few feet with her magic.

"You aren't strong, Scale," the armed twin claimed, brandishing the club. "Take another step and see how moronic you sound."

Demosyna stopped at the challenge, searching the ceiling for more traps. None was visible, but the twins each drank a potion in the second of hesitation. Yoila stirred from her injured position, and a jar of oil was shattered onto the black-scaled commander. The twins moved in unison, one throwing the oil while the other sent a flame to ignite the liquid.

Demosyna threw up a tornado to shield her companion, and the oil was whipped into a howling tower of heat. Everything in the large room was blanketed with burning jelly, igniting the furniture with sticky globs of light. The pack of books was close enough it was in the eye, but their clothes were beyond Demosyna's reach and burned. The elf twins were coated with the fire, screaming and rolling on the blistering ground.

The world once again became all too vivid for the young Wisewoman. Demosyna smelled the burning faces, and fire consumed the shelves holding unlabeled potions. The fireball created when several jars smashed together was blinding and forced Demosyna to move with only memory as a guide. The apprentice closed her yellow eyes tight, swiping her wind claws at where the twins had been last.

A step forward let Demosyna touch the backpack, and she clutched the bag with calm hands, putting it on her back. Demosyna jumped onto her belly, finding Yoila and covering the woman's eyes with her searching fingers. Both women were still dazed, but Demosyna held the commander close while rolling to the smell of water. The pair of exposed Scale women splashed into the tunnel just behind the twins, with Demosyna healing Yoila's burns. The tornado of fire puffed out, and the alchemical explosion sizzled the water's surface.

Light from the fireball let Demosyna see well into the tunnel, and neither elf was moving as the current swept the four along. The young Wizen saw a split in the tunnel and grabbed out with her magic to catch both elves before they hit the sharp rocks. The current was strong in the underground river, and darkness loomed ahead when electricity crackled through the area. Painful lances of energy filled the space, sending all four swimmers into uncontrolled spasms.

Demosyna lost herself again while drifting with the current through darkness and time. Yoila was loosed from the young Wise-woman's arms and lost in a separate tunnel as the commander drifted. The elf twins were the first sight Demosyna remembered, and the darkness of the caves left her unsure if she was awake.

A cloudy night allowed the first sign of reality, rushing toward the apprentice. The twins were ahead and bobbing in the open ocean, where the flow had taken them. Demosyna recognized the area upon seeing a previous camp's grove of trees on the cliffs. All color drained from the young Scale's face, knowing a whirlpool would form at any moment. The waters were calm enough to allow Demosyna to inter-cept the floating elves, and the apprentice swam with all her might.

Her tail cut the freezing water with ease, and the shivering Wizen was beyond its reach when a whirlpool instantly formed. The roar lasted several minutes, and Demosyna dropped the elves onto a pointy beach without collapsing. Panting breaths escaped into the cloudy night, joining the fog around the beach from the latest ocean rescue.

Their clothes were burned in many places, along with their vis-ible skin, from the oil the twins had thrown. Demosyna judged their injuries hastily before placing a hand on each elf's stomach. Golden light flowed over the injured twins, and one vomited a great volume of seawater. Their burns healed, but wrinkled scars now showed on both deserting students.

Demosyna yelled over the ocean, calling for Yoila and straining to hear. Demosyna left the stabilized twins for a moment, combing the shore for any sign of her new friend. The freezing Wizen walked north while heading to the waiting camp she started the day from. Her boots allowed Demosyna to avoid cutting her numb feet, and her left thumb held the ring once more.

Demosyna puffed heat into her hands, using the crystal to send waves of warmth from her palms. The young apprentice walked while rubbing her tingling body, so cold she worried about injury. Demosyna didn't know how long she had been drifting underground, but her body sang of too much time for comfort. Demosyna wasn't concerned about the unconscious twins, knowing she could disable them if it came to that.

Electricity had taken all the swimmers out with the trap, and the young woman tried to recall what had triggered the magic. The colors of the lightning had made it clear they were spells, but the puzzled Wizen hadn't seen any crystals in the tunnel.

"Maybe in their underclothes or in the walls?" the woman puffed into the night. "Yoila! Yoila!"

The warming apprentice yelled periodically as she walked, letting her voice carry and fire magic thaw. The humble camp Yoila had erected the previous day was only a mile ahead, but Demosyna didn't carry any spare clothes in her pack. The apprentice wrapped herself in a blanket after lighting the fire with a pointed finger.

The light attracted the speeding dot approaching, sending a huge wave of spray behind. Demosyna shivered as the craft cut at an angle with a metal rudder vibrating. It was such an unfamiliar design that Demosyna gaped upon seeing hatches and seams running the entire curved body. No operator was visible, but the rudder steered with expert precision around any ice in the path.

"Hello, friend," Demosyna called to the vessel once it rested on the shore. "Would you share the fire or a drink with me?"

Pressure escaped the interior, and a regal man exited the complex wall of the water craft. Three panels slid back, smoothly revealing another figure, who remained seated inside. The air seemed to grow colder, and Demosyna nearly collapsed from a sudden wave of exhaustion. The man seemed affected as well and turned to the figure to give an elaborate circlet.

Even the water around the boat seemed to slow and freeze as a sphere of vacuum pulled all around the craft inward. Demosyna felt her energy flow out of her like it often did when practicing her magic for hours. This was not slow, however, and the magic reserves seemed to rip from deep within the young apprentice.

The shadowy figure placed the multicolored band on a short-haired head, and the drawing sensation lessened considerably. It was still present, but Demosyna was able to stop holding the tent for support. As their short chat unfolded, Demosyna would grow more weary from the odd effect the distant shadows seemed to radiate.

"Ahoy, stranger," the human said, stepping forward into better light. "What are you doing so far east?"

"I am keeping watch for a fellow traveler and thawing after a swim. Yoila and I were separated in the caves under the cliffs," Demosyna explained, sitting by the fire again. "I was so cold, I couldn't keep searching yet."

The man was powerfully built, with wide shoulders and strong legs, and wore ornate golden armor. It was like the elven armor Demosyna had rolled in a pack but much thicker and of a stranger metal. He also had a crossbow slung over his back, and Demosyna guessed it was a dwarven design. There were no strings or wooden arms to propel the bolt, and the long body was metal with three holes at one end. He sat with the blanketed woman, taking the cup Demosyna offered with frozen fingers.

"My name is Demosyna," the young apprentice said with chattering teeth. "I should soon be a Wise-woman in the northern Order. I will return west to the Wizen Bay once I find my lost friend."

"Really? That is impressive for one so young, Demosyna," the man said, placing a gold-nailed hand on his chest. "I am Au Cell, now a privateer after making my way in the Fist. It is a pleasure to meet you, as nobody normally ventures into my waters!"

"Are you cousins with Au Peirce?" Demosyna asked, struggling to keep her eyes open. "She travels the Highway searching for you, if the war hasn't halted her progress. Will you need me to leave your lands, sir? I don't want to trespass but do need to remain for Yoila."

Au Cell laughed, shaking his head.

"I know she seeks me out in the Fist, but she isn't ready to find me yet. My cousin still loves her Empress, but I have moved beyond such thoughts these last years. I see no more profit from murder and switched my fleets to cargo instead of pillaging. You sit on a small section of my lands, and even the lost Highway south of here is mine at last! I am not jealous like the Mother of the North with her lands and welcome you with a gift."

Au Cell removed a long purple top from a backpack and presented it to Demosyna. He had noticed her exposed body as they talked, and Demosyna stood to dress at once. The man laughed at her lack of modesty while lighting a long-stemmed pipe with an odd metal square. Au Cell balanced the device on the lip of his pipe, and flames shot from a hole in the metal.

Fragrant smoke filled the small camp, and Demosyna admired the fine silken thread. It was a plain color—no patterns or jewels stitched to the dark-purple shirt—that flowed over the young Wizen. It was a size that would fit the larger man and hung to cover the apprentice like a dress.

"Thank you, Au Cell!" the young woman said, sitting slowly from weakness. "Will you stay a moment to eat? That might keep me awake. I'm sorry, but I must be exhausted from my swim."

Demosyna yawned loudly, making Au Cell laugh.

"I must leave you soon, Demosyna. My associate isn't friendly to our kind, as we are feeling! You say you aim to join Celestria in her Order? If she decides to open her mine again, I will be golden to ship her merchandise like we used to. Let that headstrong elf know as much and that I will waive my fee if she lets me deal through you. You've got a free look in your eye, and I am glad to see it in someone so youthful! I will have a contract written if you wish to work with me as an intermediary."

Demosyna's thoughts were becoming sluggish, along with her aching body. Her head still hurt slightly despite the healing she had cast, and Demosyna had strained her back dragging the heavy elves.

Au Cell looked to the mountains and the uncharted lands beyond the purple-veiled walls.

"I will be gone for months yet, but if you visit my Highway, those living there will help. That shirt will be proof of your claims since I will release the design for sale once I return from my negotiations," Au Cell said, smiling at the fading Wizen. "The fabric I used is stored there, so enjoy the token and let me know what you think of the cut! If you need any seed money, talk with my assistant, and we can work something out."

"It is a thoughtful gift. Thank you, Au Cell!" Demosyna slurred, forcing herself to stay present. "Safe travels, sir! I hope we can meet again."

The man emptied the pipe into a dimming fire, standing to glitter with gold-red reflections. Golden paint surrounded the human's eyes, sending glittering light from his gaze akin to Au Peirce's. So much of Au Cell's financial talk had merely been absorbed by the young apprentice, not fully understanding it with her draining mind. The crutch allowed Demosyna to stand and wave farewell while swaying from effort to balance.

Much of that day had been like a dream, and the surreal vehicle closed around the two passengers with a whisper. The draining sensation faded as the craft rocketed away, a tall rudder propelling the black metal transport. Demosyna was left tired but no longer felt a sickening pulling from her mind that threatened to overwhelm.

It only took seconds for Au Cell to be lost from view, avoiding a whirlpool as he went south in the open ocean. Demosyna walked back to where the elves had been, but they were gone from the beach by that time.

The tide wasn't high enough to have taken the twins back into the sea, so Demosyna called loudly, but only the wind and surf answered. The apprentice refused to leave Yoila without a proper search and patrolled the beach with a torch as a beacon. Demosyna knew Yoila would return at any cost and continued her hopeful march to find the legendary woman.

CHAPTER 31

A small town near the bottom of the eastern peninsula was the lone established city in the area. Demosyna spied a broken sliver of the Highway as she explored tirelessly for Yoila. The vertical cliffs lining the eastern side of the Fist gave the apprentice a clear view for miles, and another small spec of the Highway was seen. Its western edge was crumbled like the Highway's end Demosyna saw, and it remained only a fraction as long as the Empress's Highway.

Au Cell's realm included the last finger of livable land, sweeping back to the mountains. Several houses were seen touching Au Cell's highway, but Yoila wasn't found for days. Snow on the second morning was blasted back with fireballs, and Demosyna hoped the flares would show Yoila her location.

No sign of the rescued twins was found, but Demosyna felt watched at points in her patient grid search. The few trees and many rocky hills barely hindered the seasoning traveler as Demosyna yelled during quiet moments. Grass-covered valleys carried her voice well, but Demosyna feared it was lost on the beach for any listening for rescue.

Daylight was spent combing a cave the young Wizen had exited, but the tunnels were scorched and ruined from the explosion. The bedroom had collapsed altogether, and the cave hideaway rang with silence in the other rooms. The young apprentice worked outward from this last known point of contact with Yoila, making wider circles in disciplined stages.

A cloudless third day let Demosyna use her tornado as a beacon and walked pondering in the eye of her passion. It would be seen for many miles, Demosyna knew, and looked at the open sky from the circle of calm. The crack in the apprentice's right horn was mended days ago when healing the twins but still showed a jagged line of gold. The young Wizen was furious at her lack of foresight and welcomed the sore body as punishment.

Yoila trusted me, and I let her down, Demosyna yelled into her own head. *I can fix this. I must.*

Demosyna saw the deadly mistakes clear in her memory, pacing Au Cell's lands while only stopping to sleep. Oil and gravity had been factors in her errors, the young Wise-woman accepted as she meditated. If she could not find Yoila, the apprentice would have to update the rebels on the weaknesses in her strategies. Demosyna could almost imagine battlefields splashed with fire and death at her ignorant command.

Demosyna's priority remained Yoila, but a ticking dread was building in the young Wizen's mind. A lone village held the rebel informants Yoila had used, but the apprentice saw squads moving through the distant lush fields. Au Cell's land held no slaves, and nearly all was empty of constructed landmarks for Demosyna to mark on her map.

Yoila was finally seen through the shoddy spyglass from a cliff overlooking the current campsite. The raven-scaled commander was clinging to the sheer rocks and inching above the water with trembling limbs. Demosyna jumped into the freezing ocean, tossing her telescope aside to start swimming south. It was a long cliff dive, over fifty feet, but Demosyna focused only on her friend.

The silk shirt seemed to push the water away, and Demosyna smiled, as the fabric didn't soak up the ocean. Demosyna didn't know how far Yoila had climbed naked from the south, but her trial was over. The exuberant young Wizen caught the woman, who let go of the cliff once seeing the rescue. Yoila was shaking uncontrollably from exposure, and Demosyna swam her friend to the beach. The

Wizen gave Yoila her dry purple shirt, clothing her friend before lifting her from the rocky shore.

Demosyna carried the half-conscious Yoila to their camp, using her practiced fire magic to heat the frozen scales. Injuries were knitted, and Yoila eventually stilled next to their roaring fire. Worry of saving wood was forgotten, and Demosyna piled the fire high with revitalizing heat.

Both blankets were wrapped around the two women, and Demosyna held Yoila so they faced the firepit. Tears fell from the young apprentice's eyes, and Yoila stirred to roll over. The weary commander tried to speak, but Demosyna kissed each claw scar tenderly to quiet the woman. Yoila was weeping from joy as well, and the two held on to each other for a long time.

Demosyna gave the feeble woman sips of clean water, and Yoila recovered that night under the young Wizen's loving care.

It was hours before Demosyna heard the harrowing tale, and Yoila's head lay on the apprentice's lap as she spoke. Demosyna stroked the smooth black scales of the commander's forehead, calming and soothing during the recounting.

"I woke up alone far to the south," Yoila began, shivering in the tale of her recovery. "I tried swimming north, but the whirlpools nearly killed me. I broke two claws gripping to the cliffs against the force until I saw your signals for me! I knew you lived and found the strength to crawl back to you, my Wise-woman!"

"I hoped you would see!" Demosyna cried, wiping tears from falling on the commander. "Thank you for finding your way back, Yoila!"

"Each time I almost fell into the whirlpools, a new signal would break through my pain," Yoila whispered, closing her eyes. "I climbed for days, watching your tornadoes and fire light my path home. You were all I thought of, and I thank you with all I am. I never want to be in the ocean again, my Wise-woman. I'm sorry."

"Then you won't have to, Yoila," Demosyna said, kissing the scars she caused on the commander's face. "Rest, my brave friend, and let me hold you a bit longer. We move camp shortly."

Yoila cried softly into Demosyna's legs, thankful for the safety the young Wise-woman offered. Demosyna couldn't imagine the terror of being sucked into a whirlpool and rocked the commander as they wept together.

The young Wise-woman easily adjusted their next path in her mind, favoring horseback to canoe. It would be faster by boat to reach the Wizen Bay again, but Demosyna banished the thought in light of Yoila's tale.

Demosyna had retrieved the books for Celestria, but a leisurely path would be needed for Yoila. Au Cell's offer was tempting, and Demosyna studied her map to add the new section of the Highway. Demosyna knew only that there was a gap in the Empress's Highway near the Wizen Bay and drew a separate line in the northeastern Fist.

Demosyna carried Yoila up the beach with the weak commander resting in warm arms. A new fire was made under a tree, and Demosyna moved the camp from sight of the ocean. Yoila was sleeping near the fire, twitching in her dreams at the sound of the surf. Demosyna spent the night in a sleepless daze, so great was her joy at recovering her friend. The young Wizen busied her restless body with training while careful to not wake the healing commander.

Her tornado's top was open to attack. Demosyna meditated and switched feet to balance again. The electricity that had rendered everyone in the tunnel helpless was worrying as well, but Demosyna focused on the known.

Once the commander woke late in the morning, Demosyna insisted she eat the last jerky. The two moved on lazily with the purple-topped Wise-woman leading in no hurry. Yoila had her blue leather armor to wear, giving the gifted shirt back to Demosyna. With no other clothes besides Demosyna's boots, the two were forced to wear the blankets while traveling. The recent snows hadn't lasted long, but ice still covered much of the landscape they traversed. Yoila offered to carry the unwieldy books, but Demosyna smiled while taking the burden for the moment.

Demosyna let the commander rest after the travel while renting a horse from the single town in Au Cell's region. It was a long-haired brown horse complete with saddle and stirrups to let Yoila ride in comfort. Demosyna was glad to put the books in saddlebags and walked with only her crutch and survival pack as gear. The sliver of the Highway in the south approached over the road-free lands, forcing any traveler to go cross-country. Once reaching the end elevator, nearest the ruined western side, Demosyna saw her lost friends Jui and Rrra.

The brightly colored Scale couple was milling around the wooden buildings lining the slanted first floor of Au Cell's Highway. The scale and design was identical to the Empress's Highway, and Demosyna felt it was connected at one point in the ancient past. The break in the uniform shapes of the three levels mirrored the smashed Highway near the Wizen Bay, with no rubble or sign of what happened. It was as though a section of the Empress's Highway had snapped like a twig and moved hundreds of miles, leaving both facing ends in ruins.

Demosyna's long-lost Scale friends didn't notice the Wise-woman leading the horse, focusing instead on a small plot of grapes. Rrra was tilling the soil, his orange scales moist from sweat in the cold sun. Jui was bringing her mate a cup with green hands missing several fingers. Rrra, too, had changed during their absence and was missing a horn nearly halfway down its curve. Demosyna felt tears fill her eyes and called out to the missing survivors.

"Jui! Rrra!" Demosyna cried, handing the reigns to Yoila. "You're alive!"

The couple looked up with a start, finding the waving young Wise-woman after a moment. Recognition took hold in both faces with slightly different emotions settling in their eyes. Jui was wide-eyed and shocked, but Rrra had rage building in his face. Demosyna was rushing over, leaving Yoila atop the horse, when the man ran and slapped the young Wizen. Rrra's open hand struck Demosyna's cheek, leaving a clawed handprint rising from the blow.

Yoila started to dismount with a shout of warning, but Demosyna held a hand up in signal. Rrra was crying and beating Demosyna's unarmored chest, the rolled mail too frigid to wear without underclothes. The young apprentice took the aggression, wrapping her arms tightly around Rrra.

"I hate you. I hate you."

Rrra was weeping, his struggles growing weaker.

"You did this to us."

"Yes, I did, Rrra," Demosyna whispered, closing her eyes. "I'm so sorry I wasn't stronger."

Jui had closed the distance, concern on her green-scaled face.

"Rrra, stop, my beautiful boy. You don't hate her. She helped us."

All three lost friends embraced together, Jui and Demosyna sandwiching Rrra in their arms. It seemed to work, but Rrra pushed both women away with a cry.

"I'll never forgive you, Demosyna," the man hissed, turning and going into his wooden shack. "Looks like you had an easy trip, riding horses wherever you wish. I hate you."

"Demosyna, I can't believe I get to thank you," Jui said, tears forming after the door slammed. "You kept me going through everything, even risking your life to help Rrra. Thank you, Demosyna. Rrra is just angry still, but I know he is grateful you freed us."

Demosyna hugged the woman tightly, having no words yet in the swirling emotions her heart sent. Jui fell to the ground with the young Wizen, laughing and crying from the reunion. A few people looked over, but Yoila kept watch for dangers from the leather saddle. The two friends sat and talked, wiping joy from their eyes with a cloth Jui offered.

"When did you get here, Jui?" Demosyna asked, marveling at the friend before her. "I couldn't find you after that river. I looked for days and left flyers when I had to move along."

"Rrra found me when you loosed his shackles," Jui explained, rubbing her missing fingers. "I only remember my pain and the cold and woke up in his arms. He found me in the river, saving me from a waterfall I was drifting toward. Rrra was so brave, but the river already took its toll. Frostbite is a small price to pay if you offered us our freedom like you promised!"

Jui showed the two travelers missing toes and fingers, wiggling the remaining digits with a sad smile. The stumps had long healed, and Demosyna sighed at being unable to help with her magic.

"So those were your messages, eh, Demosyna?" Jui said, laughing anew at the revelation. "Rrra was convinced it was Sai Aeri putting a bounty on our heads. A gold piece is quite the incentive for most folks we encountered, and we ran most of the way here. It grew dangerous to use the Highway, so we often had to wait days for troops to pass our hiding places."

"I am so glad to see you two again! Are you staying in Au Cell's realm for long?" Demosyna asked, her eyes dancing. "I planned to travel to the Wizen Bay but can stay if you wish to catch up!"

Jui looked for a long time at the closed door to her shack, where Rrra had stormed off to. A puff of regret escaped the green woman, and Jui shook her head in slow arcs.

"We will live here for now, because we both need rest while the field grows. Those bandits really hurt him, Demosyna," Jui said, wrapping her arms around scaled knees. "He had to keep taking those pills, because they overdosed him, and he grew reliant on the medicine. We spend much of our money on the lozenges, and I, too, have grown addicted."

Demosyna frowned, shaking her head.

"You take the pills too? I thought they were supposed to prevent pregnancy."

Jui blushed slightly but looked at her friend openly.

"He feels the medicine when taking it, and I get to feel it once he tries for a child. It works when I taste his seed too! It's so great, but I know we both need to slow down a bit. We can't afford this vice if we hope to keep our land or raise a family like we wish."

The shack the two used was near the patch of dirt Rrra had been working, a square of grapevines rising on wooden frames. The plants had taken root from the transplant, but with the cold still coming, Demosyna worried for the harvest.

Demosyna rose to get her spare backpack, returning to begin taking out the last trident she carried. Jui saw the handle of the tube, her eyes widening.

"Put that away, Demosyna. That is a fortune, and many would kill at the sight of half that much wealth!"

The green-scaled woman closed the top of Demosyna's bag, pushing it back at the Wise-woman. The apprentice nodded to find nobody was observing the seated pair of women.

"Sorry, but I was eager to give you some help with your winery!" Demosyna whispered, tapping the closed pack. "If you want it, you two can have every gold piece. I always wished you success in your business and will gladly help however I can! I don't have acreage for you to use, but what I have is yours."

"That is very generous, Demosyna," Jui said, frowning. "I wouldn't ask for such an amount, not even in a loan! We do need help even if Rrra won't admit the situation. If you had spare points, I can pay you back once these grapes ferment! Some methods can get us wine in weeks, but Rrra insists on specific aging! He's full of spirit, my beautiful boy!"

As if in response, Rrra opened the door and saw Demosyna chatting with Jui still. His orange face grew red, and Rrra called to Jui across the short distance.

"Are you coming in?" Rrra asked, closing the door without waiting for a response.

"Take your medicine, and I will be in soon!" Jui called to the door, winking at Demosyna.

"I'm sorry I upset Rrra so much. I just saw you and couldn't believe my eyes!" Demosyna said, twirling her pointy ring. "I will be staying near the Wizen Bay if you wish to visit or send a letter! You told me you were a bookkeeper during our trip, didn't you?"

"Among other things, yes!" Jui said, laughing. "We don't have paper, but I can visit next year after our first batch of wine is done! It was so great finding you in the wild Fist again, Demosyna! Let us stay in touch since I chose Au Cell's land for their safety with the rebels."

"We didn't talk long, but Au Cell seemed a kind and generous man."

Demosyna stood, tugging at her newest top.

"I may end up doing business with him depending on what my future with Celestria holds! Here, Jui, let me give you these few things to help before I go!"

Jui was clearly puzzled but followed the young Wizen to the horse.

"You met Au Cell? That is interesting. He hasn't been seen in years! They say he vanished one day after finding whatever he sought from his lands, leaving written commands as the only note. Au Cell wished any refugees or war survivors to be welcome in his eastern realm. That is why Rrra and I find ourselves here, knowing Au Cell's standing decrees!"

Demosyna made a small leather bag of supplies, putting paper, ink, and the last full bag of triangular points she carried. Jui watched with watery eyes and hugged Demosyna after taking the gifts. Jui's green scales were wet with tears when they parted, and Demosyna led the horse to a large golden wagon. Jui closed the door to her cottage, speaking to Rrra inside with muffled voices. Yoila had watched with her usual stoic silence, resting her overtaxed body on the horse.

The center of the Highway's village was a huge merchant cart repurposed as a town hall of sorts. Au Cell's assistant was handling the official business of the residents, and Demosyna waited her turn to see the man.

All six wheels of the gold-covered wagon served as a canopy for those in line, with the shelves now holding documents in place of wares. It was the first wagon Au Cell purchased to start his empire, a plaque claimed, and he once used it to travel the Highway in trade. Demosyna smiled in line, imagining the gold-armored human she met atop that chariot.

The attendant in the storefront of the wagon greeted Demosyna while eyeing the shirt with a raised eyebrow.

"Welcome, ma'am. You may call me Lark," the human man said, putting a pink hand out. "How can we help you this fine day?"

Demosyna introduced herself, explaining her need for a few supplies.

"Au Cell said to visit in preparation for his return. I don't have access to the mines he mentioned but wanted to introduce myself for future business."

"Of course, ma'am," Lark responded knowingly, bowing slightly. "I can see you bear the shirt our lord left with for his travels. Whatever we can offer in Au Cell's lands, you shall have, Wise-woman. Did he say when he might return, if you recall from your meeting?"

"Au Cell mentioned months as a time frame," Demosyna said, thinking a moment. "But he didn't speak more than that about it. Sorry. We only talked for moments, and worry over my friend kept me from focusing."

"Do you know Rrra and Jui?" Lark asked, his skin pale in the sunlight. "I saw you talking with Jui for a few minutes."

"They are good people, who I thought I lost in the south," Demosyna said, eyeing their house with tears. "Please be patient with Rrra. He has gone through a lot to get here! I ask you give them whatever they need. And their wine will be popular, I promise, because I tasted the drink myself months ago."

The middle-aged man was jotting notes and nodding, so Demosyna let him finish his sentences. Lark brushed the front of the simple purple robes, looking back at the young Wizen.

"Of course, Wise-woman. They will have whatever we can offer on your word," Lark said, handing a document for signature.

It was a simple contract entitling Jui and Rrra access to Au Cell's resources and the trade network he employed. Demosyna signed the paper with a smile, hoping this would further serve her friends.

"What is it you shall personally require from us? My apologies for sidetracking your business with town concerns," Lark said, drying the ink with a fan. "I have an inventory handy if you wish to see our stocks."

Demosyna listed the few items she needed for the days ahead, including paper and ink. Another horse was requested, along with spare clothes, food, and water for the party. Yoila came to mind, and Demosyna added a single pillow and a heavy blanket. The man wrote fast enough to have the list finished when Demosyna stopped talking, raising an eyebrow.

"Will that be all, Demosyna? Our stores of goods are vast, and we can offer nearly anything!" Lark said, peering at Demosyna over small glasses. "Au Cell himself allowed you access, so nothing is withheld for one with his favor. Will you be taking them now, or shall I ship them ahead while you ride?"

"I can manage the few things I need. Thank you, though," Demosyna said, smiling up at the man. "Also, please don't tell Jui or Rrra it was me that helped them. I wish to reveal that once we talk again. I know they can succeed and just need help sometimes."

"As you say, Demosyna."

Lark nodded, smiling back at the young woman.

"If these few items are all you need right now, I will return in moments. You estimate up to a week of travel, Wise-woman?"

It had taken days of rowing to Au Cell's peninsula, and the land would prove slower, which Demosyna knew from experience. Demosyna nodded, and Lark finished his notes with a flourish. A tall ladder allowed access to the half-enclosed second floor of the Highway, and it was full of shelves and crates. The red central rug, with golden elven swoops, was the only alley in the collection of goods.

Lark wandered away, judging bags and barrels as he went into the covered areas to the east. Demosyna reviewed a document he had written, nodding at the accurate list of items she was requesting. It was signed and drying when Lark returned, leading a worker, both carrying large sacks of provisions.

"Everything seems in order, then, ma'am," Lark said, glancing at the contract. "My associate will fetch a horse, if you care to wait with your companion."

The young worker had run off with her purple robes vanishing into the railed bottom level of the Highway.

Stables and barns filled the enormous cavity with the tracks providing a main street. A few larger houses dotted the ranches, but the majority of space was noisy animals that wandered in large pens. Soil boxes allowed the livestock to graze the fence line, and flowers provided color to the shadows. Light streamed through cracks or holes where they lived, and dozens of different farm animals enjoyed the impossible stone's protection.

Demosyna moved aside, letting those in line tend to their concerns. Yoila was gazing at the ocean, not visible on the horizon but still present in the commander's mind.

"It will only be a few moments, I think," Demosyna said, petting a grazing horse. "I will load the first supplies."

"Please, let me," Yoila said, hopping down quickly from the saddle. "I feel up to that, at the very least."

Demosyna nodded, walking with the shuffling commander as she loaded the rental horse. Grains for the horses and rations for the women were loaded into the deep saddlebags. A horse with long golden hair, large gold shoes clomping, was handed over to Demosyna. It was the largest horse she had seen, and Demosyna petted its silky shoulder from her height.

The size and power of the horse gave images of war animals, armored and charging into spears. The hay-colored horse was loaded with the remaining supplies and sniffed playfully at Demosyna's horns. It tried to nibble one, but Demosyna laughed and brushed the muzzle away.

"Three reams of paper, one magnum of violet ink, one feather pillow, one heavy sleeping blanket," the purple-robed young employee listed from a pad of paper, "one set of writing pens, one Au Cell thoroughbred, one barrel of fresh water, one week's feed for two horses, one week's food for two adults, four complete sets of winter clothes, complimentary return for madam's rental horse, and free Au Cell circlets with your purchases."

Demosyna smiled at the list, as it had sounded simple when talking with Lark. Hearing it read in sequence made both travelers laugh, and Demosyna signed the inventory list.

"Will you be inspecting the purchase before you leave, ma'am?" the young employee asked, bowing slightly. "I packed them myself, but feel free to verify you received all the goods! Those circlets let you pass freely in Au Cell's lands, so have a safe trip!"

Demosyna examined the tiaras with a smile upon taking them from the employee. Three different ribbons of metal swirled and intertwined, with gold, silver, and a dark, dense metal Demosyna didn't recognize. A golden sun would rest on the forehead once the circlet was put into its place. No other carvings or gems decorated the simple headband.

Demosyna handed the spare to Yoila with thanks.

"No need for that!" the young Wizen exclaimed, grinning. "Thank you for fetching the supplies for us. Good day to you as well, ma'am!"

A large barrel of water was latched behind the saddle, but there was still a free saddlebag on the giant horse. The precious recovered books were transferred once away from the Highway, and Demosyna rode the countryside with a sharp smile. Yoila was smiling from her smaller horse and pushing the stocky animal to keep pace.

The young Wise-woman let Yoila ride the new horse all the next day, laughing at the commander's enjoyment of the beast. It was extremely fast and had stamina enough to ride all day with the heavy cargo. Its long golden hair billowed in the wind, and he blew great clouds of steam in the expansive hills.

The clothes they acquired were blue and purple in tone, complete with underclothes, scarves, and gloves. Pants, shirts, and an outer coat let the travelers match somewhat. But Yoila kept her faded blue armor on over the garments. Demosyna wore the yellow-and-black boots from her travels and put the elven armor on once more under her coat. It had been left at camp when infiltrating the twins' complex and was among the last remaining items from a cherished time. The clothes were clean and new, matching Demosyna's scales wonderfully in their palate.

The travelers journeyed west while laughing and growing fonder each mile. Yoila had nightmares for weeks after her rescue, and Demosyna held the shivering woman each night she woke terrified.

The dark-scaled commander met a squad of rebel soldiers late one evening, galloping away while Demosyna made camp. Current intelligence was obtained, and Demosyna's cautions about her tactics were finally passed along. The apprentice hadn't found a plausible solution yet, but informing the rebels quickly saved lives in the next battles. The First Fort hadn't been taken, but forces were being assembled to plan the siege. It would likely be weeks, if not months, till all the pieces were in place for the Freebloods far in the southwest.

Demosyna spied a waiting figure idly smoking a rolled cigarette at the edge of Celestria's empire. The employee wore a purple Au Cell robe, offering to take the rented brown horse back to a stable. Yoila looked at her companion, and Demosyna explained her plan.

"Not yet, but thank you," the young Wise-woman called from her throne atop the horse. "If we don't return by sundown, where will you be staying?"

The inn she was bunked at was described, and Demosyna led Yoila toward the Wizen Bay.

It was late afternoon when the sparkling geode was sighted, and the travelers rode fast to beat the sun. Yoila watered the horses while Demosyna approached the suspended apprentice halls with heavy books slung on her back.

A large wagon stood on the beach as the two rode, and a tall elven warrior was unloading the back. Huge crates were floated through the air, cresting the broken wall to land inside the jade rooms. No horse was latched to the cart, and spiky crystal armor protected the figure in the distance.

"Hello. I am Demosyna," the young Wizen called, having to jump from the horse. "I bring a gift to seek an audience with the Wise Mother of this land."

The dark-silver elf approached after removing the heavy steel breastplate with a wave of her long fingers. It floated to join the steady stream of cargo sailing into the geode, and Demosyna stopped to observe. Only a worn steel helmet remained of her armor, with multiple-colored crystals growing from the metal like hair. A golden chain mail veil covered the bottom of the elf's face, but large eyes danced with a pearlescent color. Bright-red robes with blue under-layers featured gold thread woven into the fabric with no jewels sewn on.

"Demosyna the Wise?" the elf asked, her voice a stern melody. "My title is Mother, but you may call me Celestria. What have you found for me?"

The young Wise-woman floated the backpack over with magic, barely feeling the effort in her excitement. The books circled around the elf after being pulled one at a time from the sack. Each one caught fire in the air, and their ashes scattered into the cutting breeze. Demosyna was shocked, but the taller Wise-woman laughed as the fires circled.

"I should never have written that down. Thank you, Demosyna," Celestria said, smiling through her metal veil. "My recipes are not for everyone, and I can see you didn't read any! Good show, apprentice."

"Will you have me, then?" Demosyna asked, her voice shaking slightly. "It would be an honor to study with you, Celestria."

"A simple test first, but I feel so!" Celestria said, making a whip-cracking motion. "MJ tells me that you are determined to help, and I see the potential in your actions. Enlighten me, Demosyna. Did you kill the twins to obtain the books I just banished?"

The empty carriage sped away at the sound of the magic Celestria produced, leaving the horseless wagon steering toward a town. Demosyna smiled at the display but turned her focus quickly to the elf.

"No, ma'am," Demosyna said, locking eyes with her potential tutor. "I injured them through carelessness but healed both soon after. They were gone when I returned to check, but they were alive last I saw."

"Curious. Thank you for the gift, and I will see you in my castle," Celestria said, producing a chair from crystal in an instant. "Guide that horse you rode into the right center room there. It's fully enclosed by walls still."

Celestria sat on the magically grown chair to relax as Demosyna mounted her steed.

Yoila was watching the southern horizon, preferring to face away from the ocean. Demosyna asked her to wait, and the commander dismounted to start a fire. The lounging Wise Mother saw the commander's plan and snapped her dark-silver fingers several times. Wood flew to assemble itself, and fire erupted from the ground where the logs fell. Yoila jumped slightly but bowed in silent thanks to the elf.

Demosyna's horse sniffed the freshwater tide and let its gold-shod hooves get drenched without compliant.

"How can I make a ramp?" Demosyna asked, turning in her saddle. "I have never done that before."

"Good! That is how we can learn, right?" Celestria called, waving her hand at the beach. "What do you need here? A fire, a stream of moonlight, or a sturdy surface to walk on?"

A bright-red ramp appeared on Demosyna's right with beams diving into the water along the underside. The fresh water from the Bay rose to form the structure, turning into solid crystal once the shape was achieved. Demosyna gasped when watching the setting sun catch the opaque crystal bridge.

"Try forming a path of light first," Celestria advised, snapping her fingers. "Transmutation is more advanced but achieves a similar effect here. That is why many disciplines will be mastered if you wish to cross my bridge, Demosyna."

The ruby path turned back into water at the snap, splashing into the Bay with a foggy spray. Demosyna focused her mind on the stairs witnessed under Marrah, visualizing a smooth and even surface. The ramp Demosyna produced wasn't detailed with columns, but waves of purple light formed a path into the air. One of the raw crystals turned purple on her ring, vanishing into the shade of Demosyna's scales. The effort after focusing was nonexistent, and the young Wise-woman laughed when completing her first lesson.

Celestria clapped, standing to banish the crystal chair into the earth again.

"Good. Now do it once more before doing it again."

The Wise Mother moved to talk with Yoila, bending to lean closer to the seated commander.

Demosyna dissipated the glowing ramp while smiling and casting again with her left thumb. Five more times the apprentice summoned a glowing bridge with each one in a different place on an inner wall.

"Once more!" Celestria called, a spiky helmet silhouetted in the setting sun.

This continued for many minutes as Celestria spoke with Yoila in the distance. The graceful elf would call periodically at Demosyna, instructing locations for the ramp to strike along the walls. The color of the magic grew bolder while darkening and glowing brighter at the same time.

After nearly fifty ramps, Demosyna was told to cross the surface with clapping from both women watching. The young Wizen nudged her giant ride forward, and he walked up into the apprentice halls. There were three rooms on the right, with two large broken rooms forming the left of the round tower. Demosyna unsaddled her horse after leaving the magic bridge, laughing in the dark room. After shaking himself off, the horse walked the perimeter to see the space of his stable.

Demosyna made stairs to leave the room, adjusting their clumsy form to descend toward the sandy beach below. Her horse drank water from its bucket and was oblivious to Demosyna's absence. Celestria whistled from behind her veil, and Yoila grinned toward the Bay with eyes locked on Demosyna.

The three enjoyed the fire for a moment, and Demosyna took the gear from the rented horse. Yoila rode off to return the animal, and Celestria clapped Demosyna on the back.

"Good show, Demosyna! You even made stairs for yourself!" Celestria said, marching toward the Bay. "Your tomorrows will be difficult, but you seem up to a challenge. You two can have the closest room on the right, but the room in back is mine."

"Thank you, Celestria!" Demosyna nearly cried, grinning a sharp-toothed smile. "I will wait for Yoila, but we can let ourselves in, Wise Mother!"

Celestria laughed, shaking her veil in humor.

Demosyna sat atop the ruined apprentice halls and scanned the horizon for her friend. A new magic had been taught so easily by this Wise Mother that Klai seemed a novice teacher in comparison.

There was a row of green beds in the first complete rightly room, and Yoila snuggled on a mattress with the young Wise-woman. Sleep did come, but Demosyna didn't believe it when lying under a new blanket on a new bed. Demosyna rested and held the twitching commander against the muffled sound of the ocean.

CHAPTER 32

T he steamy workshop was the place Demosyna spent most of her time while training with Celestria. Huge metal vats of chemicals contained glowing liquids, and branching tubes connected the growing chambers. Demosyna was soon able to turn ten valves at once with the practiced magical claws of wind. Yoila was a near-silent assistant while fetching anything the two working Wisewomen needed. The jade walls of the crystal production room were broken on one side, letting the crane move the enormous finished gems.

Marrah was seldom seen, preferring to sun herself in the retirement enjoyed by the former thief. The large gold horse was walked down from the suspended castle to run, forcing the young apprentice to practice the new spell many times each day.

Demosyna stood on the thin wooden walkway serving as a second floor of the workshop, opening a valve to let water empty from the biggest of the vats. A huge crystal was being grown on the floor below, nearly ready for shipment. She had already learned so much about focusing gems that Demosyna didn't mind honing in on Celestria's preference as a starting point in training.

Her plan to shield the rebel armies with crystals was still in the works, but any knowledge gained was valuable in the young Wizen's ideas. Once a virgin crystal was used by a powerful enough spell, the gem would vibrate at that frequency from then on. Anyone could use the spell after that first casting as long as the gem was whole. Wise-women often regarded their skills as unique, but Demosyna saw anyone could cast magic with her help.

During her frequent breaks to let the horse run free, Demosyna studied the large mine that curved into a smile on the beach. The apprentice used her magical winds to pry crystals from the earth, leaving the fortune on the ground before talking with Celestria about permission. Demosyna's goal wasn't theft but testing the range and strength of her pulling ability.

If mining was required for the future, Demosyna wished to avoid using a pickax if possible. The biggest crystals might allow passage down into the canyon, but enough crystals poked from the top that such thoughts were set aside for later.

"This one has a small defect but will still hold the heating spell requested," Celestria called to Demosyna, inspecting the cooling crystal. "Make stairs to come and look, apprentice!"

This was an expected command, and Demosyna walked down a purple staircase of her magic. It grew easier by the casting, but the young Wise-woman still strained when supporting the huge horse with a ramp.

Much focus was directed to the quality of the gems, and Celestria was meticulous in the production. Mistakes were made by the inexperienced young woman, but Demosyna's newest Wise Mother never yelled or glared. Corrections were explained, and demonstrations of the proper technique were shown repeatedly. This small bit of decency let Demosyna thrive in the familiar environment, feeling right at home grinding and measuring.

"I can see the imperfections you meant," Demosyna said, taking the loupe from her tutor. "This will still heat the house without breaking?"

"Yes. It has been the most popular design I make. Next to the glassmaking crystals the towns utilize, of course."

Celestria nodded, flicking the crystal to listen at the note.

"With winter setting in, I have been so busy I hardly see my Jade anymore. It is a great boon you showed up, for without slaves or students, my production was nearly stopped."

"I understand you too are done with slaves," Demosyna said, broaching the topic she thought of those past weeks. "May I ask you why?"

"You just did, but I see your meaning!"

Celestria laughed, sending the loupe onto a shelf with magic.

"It was actually Marrah that showed me a better path. She returned a necklace that had been stolen years ago, and I fell in love with her wild spirit. It seems like yesterday when I was casually housing miners for my business, but Marrah convinced me of their true worth. I couldn't logically keep so many beings anymore and locked down my lands while deciding how to proceed. I will open my kingdom again once I have cooled off a bit!"

"It has been over ten years, Celestria!" Demosyna said, hearing the high note of the crystal with attention. "Can we let refugees use the fresh water if you must keep your lands secured still?"

"Ten years, you say? That seems right, as that is when I decided to make my crystal to order," Celestria said, lighting a candle with her finger. "You seem in a hurry, so I will say this. My lands are closed, but if you wish, I will give you control of the crystal mine I fashioned on the shore. I have refined my methods in the years since opening the chasm and only need this workshop now in place of slave labor to harvest my work!"

"You would let me mine the gems?" Demosyna gasped, smiling at her Wise Mother. "Thank you, Wise Mother! I want to help in this war for the Fist, and all free folk will benefit from your generosity."

"Yes, this newest uprising came so quickly it was jarring," Celestria said, motioning to the library in the next room. "My journals warned me, but it's hard to listen to my past when it's so full of hate. I suppose that's one curse of immortality—forgetting your past mistakes unless you write them down to actually learn something."

The dark-silver elf had given Demosyna access to her entire magical library shortly after the apprentice settled the first week. Large bookshelves had enchantments that summoned any book the Wise Mother owned as long as you knew the tome sought. Demosyna had been shy at first, but the personal diaries were offered freely by the powerful Celestria.

No details of the rebirths were told, but Demosyna saw the Wise Mother's life written on the pages. Dozens of different people seemed to pen the journals, as thousands of years were recorded. The personalities and desires changed over time, but all were in the same looping handwriting. It gave the impression that Celestria had lived different lives, each with their own unique dreams.

"I have no need of that mine anymore and will banish it soon if you don't want it," Celestria explained, making a chair from thin air. "Fetch me those setting crystals and bring me the water tome from my shelves, apprentice."

Excitement rose in the young Wizen's mind, already planning to use any resources the mine provided. She hadn't needed to ask about using the canyon, and Demosyna smiled while climbing the wood ladder. Smaller-growing chambers were secured into the wall of the exposed second floor, holding arm-sized crystals for sale. The large gems Demosyna had seen in each city section were popular, but need for mobile crystals was ever present. Without focusing gems, most Wise-women relied on disposable staffs or wands, and temporary casting charms seemed wasteful to many Wizened.

Demosyna snapped the raw grown crystals from their metal homes, sending them with magic toward Celestria. The enchanted shelves produced the thick book, and Demosyna grabbed the blue-bound tome.

"If you learn this fresh water channeling, you can set raw crystals to make drinking water," Celestria explained, illuminating the pages with a ball of magic light. "I will be ready soon, but my waters remain closed until I finalize my plans."

Demosyna found the spell easy once a few trials were undertaken, and a raw gem was enchanted to dribble clean water from its edges. This new magic darkened a crystal on her ring with yellow, locking that gem into the harmony of the spell. Demosyna didn't press the lockdown issue and thanked her Wise Mother for the mine access.

Celestria always wore a veiled steel helmet during the days, even when relaxing, while Demosyna rode her horse's energy away. Her voice would echo in the helmet, and the veil often frosted from the elf's breath. The worn crystal helmet was the only armor Celestria wore, with long blue or green robes completing her outfits. Her large elven eyes shone from the shadows of the armor, and Celestria seemed at ease in the heavy metal cap.

Weeks passed, and Celestria added weapon sparring to the young apprentice's training. A pinch of the Wise Mother's fingers revealed a magic closet containing honed weapons of every type. Yoila had been seen armed with a sword, and the Wise Mother was impressed by the black-scaled woman's skill. Demosyna had never fought with weapons before and was slow to grasp the discipline.

Yoila and Celestria would often pair off, swinging weapons and groaning from the strain. Celestria was untouchable in the sparring circle, easily fighting both women as they assaulted the Wise Mother feverishly. Much was learned over the weeks, and Demosyna grew lethal with her choice of weapons. A short sword and a sai became the favored pairing for battle, and Demosyna let her body adapt to the new reflexes required.

"I truly found myself on the battlefield," Celestria explained, parrying both Scales' attacks without looking. "Magic was worthless in the packed bodies, and all I had was this useless helmet and a sword. Let the tool be your arm, parting any that resist. Good show, Yoila. Demosyna, keep your limbs moving with your eyes."

Demosyna never felt she took to the martial arts but learned much to aid her in the war to come.

The young apprentice began wearing herself out entirely, studying in the day and enchanting crystals at night. Yoila would carry the woman to bed, having exhausted herself with magical channeling, to not let Demosyna sleep atop piles of gems. Hundreds of water crystals were made to allow the displaced residents access to clean water again.

Protective wind magic was set into many gems, and Yoila oversaw the shipments of fresh focusing charms for the rebel troops. Demosyna only worried over the magical gems' production, leaving the setting to be decided by its purpose. The tide of the war began shifting thanks to the added protection Demosyna provided to the troops.

In place of large, orderly squads facing off in a field, Demosyna's strategies required smaller numbers spaced farther away. The wind Demosyna offered freely was powerful and needed space to avoid harming nearby friendly soldiers. Most soldiers took to sending the magic straight ahead with laughs, tumbling the enemy in place of shielding themselves.

Units of three found home in the new style of war, with two crystal-powered soldiers helping an archer or shield bearer. Hit and run, along with crawling guerrilla-style skirmishes broke the grip the imperial army had in the Fist. Not each report Yoila read was favorable, but the rebels were now in loose control of the entire north of the Fist. Word of her continued to spread as Demosyna polished needed skills with Celestria, and migrations of slaves found their way to Au Cell's lands.

The learning woman was given a great gift one day, for Celestria taught Demosyna how to grow crystals from any surface. Yoila needed a house on the beach to store and process the thousands of charms Demosyna provided. The Wise Mother had grown crowded in her ruined castle and told Demosyna to summon a red crystal house near the mine.

The specific color had taken time to produce, but Demosyna gladly constructed a wide structure for her friend. Yoila managed Demosyna's affairs from the ground from then on, letting the young apprentice make stairs for daily sparring. Demosyna remained in the castle and learned all she could from the best Wise Mother of her long life.

Light magic was learned one stormy night when the Wisewomen needed illumination during a crucial step in growing a crystal. Demosyna gave up the tome she acquired on the Highway, and Celestria added the book to an endless single bookshelf. The purple-scaled woman hadn't read more than the middle healing chapters, and it seemed foolish to not keep the ancient leather pages safe.

Demosyna eagerly pored over each journal, absently setting gems in the starlight with Yoila, finding the personal tales of love and murder fascinating. Celestria had much knowledge and understanding about every discipline, it seemed, from thousands of years of combined history. The most recent books called the writer Celestria and detailed her impossibly fast rise to her position as Wise Mother.

"It was only eighty short years of work, but I am now the youngest Wise Mother ever," the journal told with large curvy letters. "I mastered everything and can work to remove the stain I placed on so many lives. It seemed like I was proud when I set the formula, but she was wrong. If the mountain opens to the current me, perhaps it isn't already too late. My Jade must be kept for generations yet, and I will start with her blood."

Many of the intimate pages told stories in such a way, referencing things that the author would know. Bits and pieces of information could be taken from the endless journals, but only after reading hundreds of volumes would there be a complete picture. Celestria was surprised by the apprentice's dedication, personally replacing dozens of slaves in the workshop.

The Wise Mother's crystal business took off again, and Demosyna worked for the experience with her Wise-woman tutor. Celestria raised her eyebrows when the apprentice declined a percentage and secreted away the profits for Demosyna in the future.

"Why did you put the windows facing the hills, Demosyna?" Celestria asked, slurring her words as she lit a pipe with a finger. "You finally got the light-red color right, so why not let Yoila watch my tides?"

The four were in Yoila's crystal house, sitting on chairs Demosyna grew from the smooth gem floor. Celestria insisted on celebrating after sending the latest crystal away on a ghost ship and produced a barrel of ancient wine. Marrah the Jade was sleeping next to Yoila, the two having stalemated a drinking competition. Demosyna was grinning loosely after finishing the latest glass of aged liquor.

"I didn't want to remind her of whirlpools."

Demosyna burped slightly, laughing and apologizing.

"I promised she wouldn't have to deal with the ocean anymore and tried to keep that in mind! My crystals are thick enough the sound doesn't come through. Thank you for teaching me so much! You are the best Wise Mother ever!"

"That may be true, Demosyna!"

Celestria laughed, petting Marrah's leg.

"I just want to let you lifers thrive again. It was cruel what we did, forcing their hands. Or maybe forcing your blood might be more accurate."

Demosyna poured both Wise-women more drink, blinking her eyes clear.

"Blood? What do you mean, Celestria?"

Celestria frowned, looking into the dark-red wine swirling in the crystal glass.

"Follow me, apprentice. I need some air, if you are to understand my arrogance."

The moon was nearly full, casting light on the empty landscape. Celestria puffed a short pipe while watching the smoke as the two walked slowly along her beach. Demosyna managed to keep her feet when swaying and sipping as she followed the Wise Mother. Numb tingling ran through hands and clawed feet, but Demosyna had grown used to the effects of wine during the Highway days.

"Before I was Celestria, Mother of the North, I worked on a Wise-woman project," Celestria said, conjuring more leaf for the pipe. "The idea was to limit the slaves' reproduction by keeping the males' seed docile. The Wisest feared their unchecked numbers and commissioned a solution that wouldn't be noticed. We worked only a few hundred years before I saw the answer and made this pill."

The Wise Mother removed an ivory tablet from her robes while floating the medicine in a ball of light. Demosyna recognized the pill since Vaash had often taken the magical capsule when housing with the young woman. Vaash had explained it kept children from being made, but Demosyna frowned with thought after taking the floating pill.

"The idea was, the magic lasted only while the powder remained in the blood," Celestria claimed, shaking her head sadly. "It is addictive, quick acting, and easy to produce with apiaries. The Wisest loved the idea, and for the last thousand years, all seeders have taken my poison. It made me absurdly wealthy, but generations are now born sterile. I have paved the path for extinction and need your help Demosyna. Please."

Celestria fell to her dark-silver knees with tears falling from her elven face. Demosyna knelt as well, trying to absorb the revelation with her drunken mind. The apprentice hugged her master while letting the elf weep her sorrow without restraint.

"I will help however I can, Celestria," Demosyna whispered, rocking with the Wise Mother. "There must be a solution if alchemy and magic are the problems."

"I've tried for generations now, Demosyna," Celestria said, her sobs quieting. "The numbers grow, but the fire I see in you may bring fresh eyes to my doom. Please, Wise-woman, don't let me exterminate the Fist. The love I have found with my Jade broke me, and I repent. I repent!"

Celestria yelled the last words into the frozen Bay, tears falling from her opalescent eyes. Demosyna cried with her Wise Mother while thinking of the terrible implications the pill brought to the world.

Marrah the Jade stumbled out of the nearly pink house, swaying on her fuzzy feet.

"How much did you drink, Cel?" Marrah croaked, having just woken from a stupor. "Stop repenting every time you open that wine! Take me to bed, love, and we can calm you down again."

Celestria smiled, wiping her snotty face behind the veil.

"Marrah! I didn't mean to wake you. You're probably right. I should turn in. Thank you, Demosyna, for being a sympathetic ear to an old fool. We can discuss this more tomorrow. Well after sunrise please!"

Demosyna hummed to herself, waving the two good night. Marrah plopped down in the sand before stretching her stubby limbs at Celestria. The Wise Mother laughed, summoning magic chains that bound wrists and ankles. Demosyna watched, her head tilted in surprise, as Marrah was carried through the air by the chains. The Wise Mother held the end of the glowing bindings when leading the helpless Paw into their castle. Both women were grinning drunkenly at each other, and Marrah seemed to enjoy the shackles as they flew into their bedroom.

Yoila was still snoring in the chair Demosyna had made with a cup lying empty on the table. The young apprentice covered her friend with the blanket, smiling while she tried to stay upright. Demosyna closed the crystal door and chuckled at the hinges grown from nothing. It was a simple shack but rose from the sand as a monument to many weeks of tireless study.

Demosyna was considering sleeping on the beach, for the weather was mild, and she was tipsy. The apprentice could still summon magical stairs but didn't want to fall into the water from stumbling over the steps. Demosyna watched the stars while thinking, and her shiny white dog came bounding over the horizon. The last glowing squid dived into the salty waters, dimming the light for the evening.

He didn't bark or howl as he sprinted toward the woman, but the dog grinned furiously with his huge, wide jaws. Demosyna gasped, hearing the approaching animal, and turned to see the running visitor. The apprentice rose to her knees, opening her arms wide to encourage the canine. In moments, he reached the delighted Wizen while tackling her to the sand and licking her laughing face.

Demosyna rubbed the short fur with the spots forming eyebrows dancing in excitement. She didn't see Vaash or Plu on the horizon, but Demosyna's dog was healthy and clean from his travels. Fatigue overcame the exhausted woman, and Demosyna collapsed from the surprise ball of warm energy. Her dog licked the smiling woman while Demosyna slept, watching Vaash approach from the southern hills.

The yellow-and-orange-robed monk observed the sleeping apprentice with her dog, laughing to himself. He didn't look in the shack, but Vaash walked the beach for a time to gather wood. The dogs stayed beside Demosyna, panting puffs of silent patience into the cloudless sky. A fire was made, and Demosyna woke with her friends grinning toward the groggy woman. The sun was warming the still air, rousing the purple-scaled woman from the bright rays.

"Vaash!" the apprentice exclaimed, drinking deeply from the offered water. "When did you get here? I thought I had dreamed seeing my dog again!"

"This one found you two relaxing on Celestria's beach!" Vaash said, petting his old dog. "Hush, noisy Rolls."

His large, fluffy dog had barked in excitement, but the monk had named and begun training the animal while away. It quieted obediently with her spotted tongue hanging from large teeth.

"Rolls? That is a great name for that squirmy beast!" Demosyna exclaimed, stretching her sore back. "Would you like some food after your trip?"

The two found Yoila in her house, knocking to wake the snoring commander. Yoila prepared a simple meal for the friends while watching the dogs mark their new territories through windows.

His trip was uneventful save for avoiding a battle once or twice, Vaash explained. After leaving Plu Durrah with Xi Xi, the monk had paid respect to his son in the wild south. The trip back atop the Highway had left the monk tanned, and his hair was nearly to his knees. Demosyna offered to braid his ruby tangle, and Vaash laughed as the mass was tidied into a single long strand. All the friends in the crystal house enjoyed a clear morning, snacking and waiting for Celestria to wake.

Celestria called from her geode eventually, imitating Vaash's deep voice.

"You will lay broken from this one's hands. That you will!"

"How wrong that was, Celestria!" Vaash responded, walking into the surf. "May this one enter your beautiful halls?"

"Naturally."

Celestria laughed, floating on her back in the air.

"I assume you can still jump after all these years! You look a bit frail these days, but the sword is a nice touch!"

Vaash wore the single short sword gifted by Plu Durrah around his orange belt and crouched into his square stance in the Bay. The stairs were nearly a hundred feet above the water, but Vaash leaped through the air to land on the bottom stone step. Demosyna gasped at the feat while Vaash jumped once more to reach the top of the broken walls. Celestria greeted the balancing monk by hugging him from her midair bobbing.

Demosyna led her horse down from the apprentice halls before tying a lead onto the hitching crystal she had produced. Until she grew a walled stable, the apprentice's horse would wander on a leash through the grassy hills. Demosyna could move the crystal in a moment and practiced her skills while letting the horse run.

"Care to see if you can still use a blade, Vaash?" Celestria asked, producing two metal rods from the air. "Apprentice, summon your weapons and get your commander! My headache will give you an advantage in the sparring, so use the opportunity, but don't yell please!"

A crystal short sword and sai were grown from her palms, and Demosyna found the commander organizing the latest boxes of donated charms. Some were set into shields, but most were shipped as smaller rings or necklaces. Yoila would receive the jewelry or armor from the rebels, letting her utilize the shaped gems Demosyna provided. The commander was finishing a bronze necklace but grinned at the chance to spar three on one.

"Maybe one of us will get a shot in on Celestria today!" Yoila called through the open window. "Let me find the sword in this clutter, my Wise-woman."

The sharp crystal weapons Demosyna felt comfortable using shone with purple light and were strong enough to stand against the elven metals the others used.

"My first blades barely withstood a single hit," Demosyna mused to herself as Yoila approached the surf. "But these latest models are so dense, like Celestria makes with her magic!"

Having things be around only temporarily was new to Demosyna, but her Wise Mother required the apprentice to banish things each time they finished using them. This let the young woman practice constantly and get used to simply growing or making things in the moment of need.

The keen edge of these fresh weapons shone with deep color, and Demosyna floated both women up on a disc of light. The stairs or ramps previously used were refined in the weeks before into this elevator, strong enough to carry everyone living with Celestria.

The dogs ran with the horse in the empty morning, and Celestria danced around all three fighters. The graceful Wise Mother spun and ducked, using her twin metal tonfas for defense. Celestria had been an Imperial Battle Wizen for generations and fought with weapon and magic together. Celestria sometimes floated inches above the ground in the practice combat, flipping and swimming around the sweating women. Vaash was faster than the elf, but Celestria outmatched the man with her physical skill. Whenever a swing was too fast to block, the Wise Mother used magic to foil Vaash's precise attacks.

"Sometimes, you can blind an enemy with blasts of light," Celestria instructed toward Demosyna, fighting Yoila and Vaash simultaneously. "Or set them aflame or freeze their blood or use crystals in your armor to constantly beam lightning. I found many interesting ways of killing, once sword and magic are in harmony. You have done well with your tools, but now you will combine reflexes with willpower, apprentice!"

Demosyna had been kicked across the circle in the library, nearly reaching the edge of the broken floor. The apprentice jumped back into the fight while stabbing the pointed sai to block Celestria's tonfa. Yoila moved like a shadow around Demosyna while fluidly turning and swinging an elven long sword. The two pressed their attack in tandem with Demosyna making water under Celestria's feet.

Vaash fenced with one hand behind his back, jabbing and slicing in a formal posture. The monk ripped a caught metal rod from Celestria's grasp with a laugh, but a newly summoned replacement joined the fray. The slick stones did cause the Wise Mother to slide several feet, but ice formed around the ornate boots she wore to stop the skid.

"Good show, Demosyna! You've backed me into a corner, so press the advantage!"

Celestria laughed, producing a rainbow of glowing light.

"Go for the legs since I froze myself in place and can't shift away yet. Yes, the joints in the knees. Perfect!"

Demosyna had already dropped to all fours in trying to stay out of reach of the tall master's weapons. The sai was held forward, but the purple sword was tucked flat against the young Wizen's forearm during the crawl. Both fists clenched their weapons, and Demosyna lashed out in quick jabs upward at armored knees. Celestria wore a full-plate armor during the sparring sessions, letting everyone use their real weapons without concern.

The pronged sai was like a long claw, Demosyna found during her training, and could pierce joints or plate armor with enough skill. The apprentice rolled onto her back to circle behind the stationary Wise Mother and gave the others room to fight. Even with her feet covered in ice, Celestria parried and ducked all three attackers' fury. Demosyna used her wind from behind the skilled warrior, sending her flying upward into the cold air. Celestria laughed loudly when floating ten feet above the sparring ring for a moment.

Enormous force blasted down onto the panting fighters below her, and Celestria seemed to increase the gravity inside the circle. Vaash remained standing, but Demosyna was flattened from her crawling position, along with Yoila. The monk jumped, his robes blowing with hot wind, as he clashed with Celestria. Demosyna pushed up slowly, straining against her heavy body to lift the two Scales into the air. An elevator caught Vaash too, and the group sparred in midair with the geode lighting the sky.

Vaash and Celestria fought for two hours once Demosyna lay panting next to her commander. Even through her fatigue, Demosyna studied the two masters during their extensive duel.

Marrah checked on the battle, shaking her tiger-striped head and frowning. She had brought juice for the weary group and called up to her mate, battling Vaash.

"Stop fooling around. The sun's only going to last so long," Marrah yelled, seeing the mess from the training. "We still have work to do, Cel. I'm sure Demosyna wants to learn more than how to stab things! You may like to poke things, but she came to do magic with you!"

The yellow-eyed Paw winked at the recovering Wizen, and Demosyna smiled through gasps for air. Yoila took two of the cups with a bow, and the young apprentice banished her platform of purple energy. Vaash remained floating in the air while crossing weapons with Celestria and laughing. The two sank down with ringing metal signaling their descent.

His feverish wind seemed to support the monk, and Celestria had crystals on each piece of her armor that allowed flight. Spare or backups were crucial, which Celestria had explained while displaying her custom armor the first sparring session weeks ago.

"Think of it as when and not if a crystal will break. I can always retreat thanks to the levitation crystals here and here and here and here!" the Wise Mother told the staring apprentice that day. "By ensuring an emergency casting will occur, you keep yourself alive, young apprentice. That is what I expect of you—survive to keep moving forward no matter what is taken or lost in battle."

Demosyna wore her flexible elven armor during the training but often ended up bruised and sore from the full contact lessons. It was yet another chance to practice her healing, and Yoila thanked Demosyna for the first aid magic by handing some juice over.

Vaash bowed deeply to his opponent before sheathing his music-themed sword to salute the duel. Celestria tossed her tonfa sticks into the air and turned them into flowers that rained onto the party. Neither master was sweating, a testament to their endurance during the intense sparring. Vaash jumped to the broken walls with his juice to check on the animals below while enjoying the view. The Wise Mother kissed Marrah in thanks before pinching the Paw as she left to nap.

"Very good effort today, Demosyna. You too, Yoila!" Celestria said, patting both scaled women's shoulder. "Apprentice, let Yoila get back to her duties so we can do the same! Vaash knows to not listen in on our secrets, so ignore that red braid waving at you, apprentice!"

"This one can't hear from this distance anyway!" Vaash called without turning to look. "Have no fears on that, my friends!"

Time seemed to vanish in a heartbeat, and Demosyna swam in a happy daze of learning. Vaash and Yoila lived on the beach, and Demosyna added a wing to the light-red house for the monk to sleep. Celestria helped with the large project one evening, and a field acres wide was fenced with dense crystals. The Wise Mother floated above the surveyed hills while directing the apprentice's effort to enclose her horse.

Vaash hadn't returned with a steed, and a simple yellow gem barn served as the large horse's dwelling. The mine that was given to Demosyna was huge, but the buildings were centered on the canyon to allow a small settlement to form.

Shipments were handled at the nearest towns, and fresh supplies were returned by Vaash or Yoila from the trips. Celestria still refused travelers in her lands, and the young apprentice respected the decision during the months of hard work. The Wise Mother offered to let Demosyna stay with her friends at night, but the student wished to follow tradition and stayed in the apprentice halls.

The troubling alchemy problem Celestria confessed to her apprentice was studied, and Demosyna knew it would be a daunting task. Formulas in the volumes the two reviewed were complex and magical, requiring expertise of many disciplines to understand. Both Wise-women settled into the project knowing progress would be sluggish, but Demosyna accepted the necessary challenge.

Demosyna did more one-on-one lessons as the days flew by, and her friends remained busy with their own interests. The apprentice still sparred with her balanced crystal weapons but also continued focus on tactics and history. The endless stream of ancient journals provided firsthand accounts of the past, fading back thousands of years of Celestria's lives. Reading about ancient battles in the Fist helped bring proven ideas to the rebel forces, and Demosyna wrote down any useful information to pass along.

The names the Wise Mother called herself during the passages weren't always present, but several were from a warlord's perspective. They were among the oldest Demosyna studied and recounted hundreds of strategies for successful conquests.

"I guess I did fight without magic at that point. Look at that!" Celestria exclaimed one morning, taking the book Demosyna offered. "It's easy to forget, as that was so long ago—at least a hundred generations if the horrible writing is legible enough to be believed!"

Celestria seemed unfazed by the forgotten lives of bloodshed, explaining she focused on crystals for this cycle of her life. Such was the elven way since the dawn of life in the world, the Wise Mother told the apprentice. Demosyna learned new schools of magic as necessary for the delicate crystal production she was mastering. Acid could scrub the tanks clean, and Demosyna learned to transmute glass like she saw in the mountain city.

Real windows were added to the grown buildings from the campfire smoke, and thick crystal panes were recycled as charms. The magic of pocket spaces was passed along by Celestria, and Demosyna soon made a crystal chest that stored her gold pieces. It was a rainbow of colors to show her skills but only accessed the hidden space with Demosyna's hand. Anyone could open and use the magic box, yet the currency would temporarily change places with the other contents when Demosyna opened it.

It was an astoundingly complex bit of channeling, for the objects would be destroyed if the magic wasn't perfect. The ruined walls of the apprentice hall held hundreds of such spaces and the Wise Mother allowed access to any Demosyna needed. Weapons, clothes, food, furniture, books, ingredients, and anything else the apprentice needed were found inside the remains of the northern Orders.

Any profit the purple-scaled woman made was secured in the heavy crystal safe tucked away beside her simple jade bed. Yoila had eventually insisted on paying for the hours Demosyna spent channeling power, and the two agreed upon a flat gold piece per gem. They would go for dozens more, but Demosyna refused to sell the water charms offered to the displaced people in the Wizen Bay.

"I can accept charging for certain crystals, but I will give whatever I can to help!" Demosyna explained as she debated with Yoila about sales. "If you wish to sell them once you buy them from me, go ahead, my friend. Know that I will continue to give most of my work away, however. I only ask you always help with your profits and don't charge more than half a gold piece as markup. With the volume I am producing, you can still earn a large sum from the modest price increase. All people are in need of help in this bloody war, and I wish to assist everyone, not just the rebel armies."

"It will be as you command, my Wise-woman," Yoila said, nodding her understanding. "Thank you for accepting my offer, and I will return with your earnings shortly!"

The idea for storing her tridents of gold came when Celestria showed the apprentice her vault. It was an enormous room with shelves and chests full of wealth, shining with jewels and precious metals. Decades of savings were magically sealed away, and Celestria explained the hoarding she was undertaking.

"I will buy that hourglass mountain south of here one day very soon!" Celestria said, walking through her treasure and daydreaming. "I seek the ancient secrets locked inside the flat peak and plan to purchase the realm in just a few more decades! You have changed everything, Demosyna, and we are in your debt. You have tripled the production with your tireless work, and Marrah says our goal is at hand! If you continue working this hard at my instructions, I will give you the Wizen Bay when I move into the city."

Demosyna had been inspecting a ruby-covered goblet and smiling at her reflection in the polished metal. The apprentice put the heavy platinum cup back into its chest and gaped at the tall elf. She had only been studying for months with Celestria, but already, Demosyna was being offered advancement.

"Are you done with my training, Wise Mother?" Demosyna asked, worry filling her eyes. "I have much to learn yet and love your instruction these last days. I don't need titles or lands. I wish to grow wiser under your hand!"

"No, I will just move while I study the entrance found generations ago. Your training is still in its beginnings, so don't think of getting away that easily!" Celestria said, summoning a journal from her shelves. "I only had a few years to study it initially, as the Wisest needed me for other things, as I told you. My lands here will be yours shortly, from the Wizen Bay to the start of the settlement realm I will own. It grows crowded for Marrah and I, even with your good company!"

"Thank you, Wise Mother!" Demosyna gushed, barely grasping the scope of the gift. "You are truly the wisest woman in the north! I can help so many people with these lands. Thank you!"

Millions of stacked tridents were locked away in Celestria's fabulous vault, and the loose treasure filled every corner. Demosyna had no way of estimating the value of such a hoard and shook her head as the room was locked away. If purchasing an entire section of the Fist was her goal, Celestria seemed well on her way to having the resources. The young Wise-woman took the advice to heart and began saving nearly all her funds in preparation for the unknown future. Demosyna only indulged her animals with toys and treats and wine for her friends with each weekly shipment.

Over two more months passed in weary discipline, and Celestria gave a short vacation to the diligent young woman. A stone from the broken walls was taken for purchasing the southern Wise-woman Settlement, hiding the vast fortune inside its magic surface. Yoila had a new home grown away from the beach near the horse rink, and Vaash took over the two-room dwelling near the Bay. The dogs shared one light-red room, and Vaash tended the grounds in the immediate area.

Demosyna didn't ask anything from her red-haired friend and let him help or wander as desired by the monk. The break in schooling was a welcome period of rest, and Demosyna spent more time training her reunited dog. The apprentice called him Jest for his eternal grin, and he needed hardly any instruction to loyally respond to hand or voice directions.

Vaash pointed out favorable hills for planting, and Demosyna's studies of botanical magics began in earnest. Growing plants was completely different from crystals—simple and repetitive in the gems' structure. Living plants were humming systems of growth all on their own, and Celestria's absence allowed practice in the skill. Water gems flowed freely from the Wizen Bay, but Demosyna knew food was the next thing she would provide the Fist. Armies protected the entire north half of the vast and wild Fist, allowing people access to a new home.

Fields of flowers were waving their colors in the rainy afternoon when Marrah the Jade returned to deliver a summons. Demosyna was called from the newly purchased mountain after many weeks of rest. Demosyna packed for the journey at once, letting her friends join the eager woman at their pleasure.

> I have secured the door to an ancient dwarf complex, apprentice. Come to my mountain, presenting yourself for new training and titles. The Wise-woman Settlement will hereafter be called Jade City, so find your way here at once!
>
> Marrah the Jade will guide you to our new manor, atop the highest dome of the city. Bring nothing but what is needed for travel, for we shall enjoy the fruits of our labor at the tip of the future!
>
> Yoila and Vaash are invited as well, so let them read this while you pack, apprentice! Safe travels, young Demosyna, and I await the progress with your gardening!
>
> Celestria, Mother of the North,
> the Jade in the Mountain

CHAPTER 33

The trip south to Jade City was a joyous affair, because all of Demosyna's friends joined the march. Demosyna took turns riding the golden horse and practiced her plant growth while walking beside the animal. Vaash used the larger half of his flute to make deep music atop the horse, and Yoila played with both dogs along the way. Marrah used her armbands to levitate while napping for long periods and exposing her golden belly to the sun for warmth.

It took days to spot the neon plateau on the horizon, dazzling the sky with color from the upper-class sector. The rolling land spread before the travelers, and Sai Aeri's army was seen departing Jade City. Marrah the Jade led the group straight across the realm with keen eyes judging a route past the army.

Thousands of soldiers marched toward the Highway, leading caravans back south across the Fist. Demosyna wasn't concerned by the imperial troops in the free north, as they left before she reached the mountain. Nights were spent setting crystals still from the heavy packs strapped to the tall horse. Demosyna had brought enough raw gems for several days but ran out once reaching her Wise Mother's mountain.

Yoila left the group to tend to rebel business, and Demosyna began traveling the winding mountain roads. The branching paths were steep and narrow in places, forcing the group to walk single file up the slope. The Empress's Highway had been a steady progression into the north, but these roads were swallowed by the mountain. The steep rises would snake wildly across the rocks, wearing on the foot-bound travelers.

Trees and jagged cliffs passed close enough to touch, and Demosyna marveled at the view allowed by the heights. Celestria hadn't locked the mountain range from use by the populace, and travelers hurried here and there during the trip. Only the topmost dome was forbidden to the masses, and Demosyna's party ascended toward the palace. Even with her strong horse, the pace left days behind as the group reached the top of the mountain.

The sprawling manor was the penthouse of Jade City and towered over the landscape in marble splendor. No servants tended the grounds, so Celestria greeted the weary friends with a smile.

"Apprentice! Welcome to Jade City," Celestria exclaimed, greeting each dirty traveler. "Rooms are prepared for all of you, so unload before dinner! I will ring the bell for supper, but enjoy the top of the world with me till then!"

The air was thin at that altitude, and Demosyna had to take breaks during the journey to catch her breath. She hugged her Wise Mother, smiling at the beaming elf, as the apprentice summoned a bundle of flowers. Celestria laughed before taking the welcoming gift and leading the party inside.

Demosyna washed the dirt from her scales using the ornate bathroom to bathe before dinner. Their animals had been left in the expansive fields atop the stone platform, enclosed by gold windows of glass.

Celestria cooked the party an extensive meal with courses flowing from the active kitchen. Meats and cheeses and vegetables and soups were all served to the famished travelers, filling their bellies.

"Thank you all for joining me on my mountain!" Celestria toasted, raising a glass as the meal wound down. "Will any accompany me in exploring the original ruins? I can now open the gates with my magic but need aid in securing the floors safely!"

"I am glad to help, Celestria," Demosyna said, wiping her snout with a napkin. "What do you need from your apprentice?"

"This one doesn't fully grasp the situation but will aid as needed," Vaash called, downing his cup. "Demosyna, this one remains your right hand. Use me as you will, for my strength is at your disposal."

"My Wise-woman commands my heart," Yoila claimed, taking Demosyna's hand. "I follow where she leads. This mountain won't best me, not when Demosyna walks its peaks!"

"How long will we be gone, Cel?" Marrah asked, leaning against the Wise Mother. "It's so cold on your mountain. I need your body to sleep soundly in this frozen height!"

"The ruins should be vast considering the size of the balancing mountain. I cannot scan into the rocks, so dangers likely will present themselves."

Celestria grinned behind her gold veil, manifesting a map on the table.

"If you join me in my quest, I promise adventure and knowledge from the journey! The Dwarves left many secrets, but I intend to unravel the weavers' threads to save you lifers I love!"

Demosyna spoke for the group, judging their faces before responding.

"Lead on, Wise Mother. I will assist you with the goal and follow your wise lead!"

Celestria banished the dirty dining table with a snap, laughing in eager joy as the group left the ornate castle. All the adventurers loaded themselves with gear while leaving their animals in the grassy fields of the palace. Marrah the Jade wrapped herself in charcoal fabric, and only her ears and fingers stayed exposed with her sharp eyes and fuzzy tail. Vaash tied down the single sword to avoid noise, putting the long braid into a top bun once he donned the heavy pack.

Massive metal doors opened to the staining Wise Mother's crystals, and the long-abandoned dwarven chambers appeared to the party. The towering doors stood at the peak of the upside-down mountain, allowing Demosyna to lead her friends into the dark unknown.

"Apprentice, remove your charms at once!" Celestria commanded, her voice echoing in the entry to a massive staircase. "Everyone else, halt!"

449

The interior of the balancing mountain consisted mostly of raw focusing crystal, solid and dense in its weight. Mind-boggling heights showed mile-high stretches of water-filled walls that held oceans worth of clean liquid. A circular central staircase ascended into the darkness, leading to floors in the shadows above.

Faces pushed out from the sheer surfaces of the expanding walls, subtle and serene in their expressions. Each was the same in its depiction, and Demosyna viewed a dwarf for the first time in recorded history. The young Wizen had obeyed her Wise Mother's instructions immediately, removing her focusing charms and casting them aside.

"Celestria, how should we proceed?" Demosyna called, her head swimming from the spectacle. "Should I grow weapons for myself?"

"Yes, but back out of the doorway, apprentice," Celestria replied, motioning everyone out. "I must make staves for our journey. Curious, this new development!"

Twisted magical trees in the courtyard provided the raw wood for their staves, and Celestria handed Demosyna an ornate staff ripe with symbols of power. It resembled Klai's patterned staff, and the young Wizen tested the balance while heeding the Wise Mother's cautions.

"Listen up, everyone. This is an unexpected setback," Celestria explained, rubbing her silver forehead. "My apprentice and I will be severely crippled during this journey, so take no chances with your safety. Marrah, you will know the exit, so flee if things get hairy, my love. Demosyna, follow my steps exactly as you are led. Yoila and Vaash will take the rear, moving slowly behind our footsteps."

All acknowledged their understanding while lashing long poles to each pack. Yoila always traveled in a disciplined manner, nothing loose or unpolished, and crouched behind Marrah in the middle. The crystal focusing charms were left behind, and Demosyna walked with a wooden staff once more. A staircase was made from the stone of the mountain, dark and solid in its design. The raw walls of the mountain faded outward as the party moved upward, enormous canisters of clear water fading above.

The thick stone housing the seas was invisible and showed the swirling titanic volumes of fresh water in their entirety. Vaash trailed behind the slow-moving adventurers as his watchful eyes scanned the darkness. Both Wise-women produced hovering spheres of light to aid the journey that were centered on their wooden staves.

Demosyna had grown her favored weapons out of purple crystal from outside and stored them on her wide blue belt. The apprentice still wore the gifted purple top from Au Cell, but hidden elven armor and purchased blue clothing finished the outfit. Celestria left her crystal armor while banishing the helmet gems with a sign of discomfort. The Wise Mother kept the veiled steel helmet on with a reassuring rub on the back from Marrah. All other magical possessions were left in a secure palace by the travelers walking headlong into the past.

None had entered these halls in countless years, and the air was stale with solitude. Footfalls echoed into the blackness after the Wise Mother closed the magical doors behind the party. Celestria led the group from the world, hoping for redemption in the ancient catacombs.

The first landing held empty stone rooms decorated at the seams with identical dwarven faces. Shadows flickered in the magical light, and the creeping party explored the barren first level. Each successive floor expanded in diameter, following the reverse mountain's flow. The second level of the vast deserted complex was lined with shelves holding dwarven crossbows. These metal and stone weapons stood in lines along each wall of a room, waiting to throw bolts with deadly accuracy. Demosyna motioned Yoila to take a few crossbows after Celestria nodded her approval.

A camp was made at the empty third landing upon seeing the stairs rise into the heavens without end. Vaash played his assembled flute into the empty air, lulling the jittery travelers to sleep for a spell. Demosyna tossed aside her broken staff after waking before grabbing a new one from the collection on her backpack. The illumination spells had ruptured the grains of the former staff, leaving both Wizen to exchange their wooden focusing rods.

Marrah the Jade found the first guardian when taking her leave one rest period.

"What the living hell was that?" Marrah called from around a corner, having left to relieve herself. "Cel, light the hallway!"

Celestria rose at once, casting spheres of light into the nearby walkway.

"Jade, to me!"

The tiger-colored woman ran from the hallway, adjusting her red skirt before clinging to Celestria. Nothing but an upturned bucket was found by the two Wise-women, and they returned to the group.

"Something knocked the bucket from under me!" Marrah explained, taking a steadying breath. "I fell on my tail and saw a flash of light."

"There, there," Celestria soothed, petting her mate. "Do you want to go back, my love?"

Marrah shook her cloth-wrapped head, and the mystified party moved on. Yoila armed herself with a salvaged crossbow, putting a wooden bolt in each of its three barrels.

Days passed for the exploring figures while camping as needed for rest. Most of the landings were barren of features and held empty rooms with dry stone doors. Demosyna asked Yoila to record their progress since the young Wizen had seen the commander's skill in drawing. The dark-scaled woman accepted the request with a smile, sketching the layout from any explored areas of the massive mountain.

Vaash pointed out the second sighting of a glowing guardian at the eighth level of the complex. It had dumped a pot of soup onto the human monk before flying off into the distance.

"Just there," Vaash called, pointing to the fleeing light. "At least the soup wasn't boiling anymore!"

Demosyna broke a staff healing his burns from the scalding food, and Vaash prepared another meal for the travelers. Yoila had fired a bolt toward the vanishing ball of light, but it had sunk halfway into the wall the guardian entered. The commander snapped the arrow in half, narrowing her eyes at the piece remaining in the stones.

"It merged with the wall, my Wise-woman," Yoila said, examining the fletching half of the arrow. "You must be careful if such power exists here!"

Celestria moved the group more cautiously after that, watching the stones for signs of light. The two darting balls of light had been different colors, but both were of a silver-brown hue that matched the stone walls.

The next incident met the party on the fifteenth floor, having stopped to set up a camp. Demosyna was walking through a doorway, lighting the room with her staff, when the stone door closed on her tail. A ball of beige light shot away and buzzed in a high-pitched tone.

Her fellow travelers found the sore woman, and Demosyna healed the smashed tail with a sigh. The empty room the apprentice was pestered in was full of water stored in tubes along the walls.

"I'm okay!" Demosyna panted, startled by the pain. "The stone swallowed the light in that corner."

Dwarven faces gave no clue in the corner, and Vaash stopped playing his flute nightly as the five moved skyward. Each figure drew a weapon for defense, with Demosyna holding the sai lightly against her leg. Dozens of floors fell away, and Celestria ignored a majority of the hallways.

"The peak will hold my salvation," Celestria called, marching up the endless spiraling stairs. "We must find the last floor and begin our search from there!"

Demosyna thought of her animals over the sunless days, hoping their rations would last the journey. Each night, the young Wizen meditated on her disciplines while feeling the walls around her groan in reaction. The raw mountain of crystal responded to any magic, and Demosyna saw the logic in leaving the focusing charms behind.

Each level seemed farther up than the last, but the sore travelers pressed on after the elf Wizen. Near what Demosyna judged as the middle of the fortress, a nursery was found made from the stones. Unmistakable tiny beds lined each wall of the rooms with stone pillows resting on each mattress.

"Let us move away from this place," Vaash said, putting out the cooking fire. "This one feels watched on this level."

The air continued to grow thinner as Demosyna rose into the sky, protected by the solid stone walls of the funnel she traversed. Celestria snatched a darting ball of brown light one morning by waving her staff suddenly over the firepit. The guardian had been heading toward an open wineskin, angling to tip it into the fire.

The Wise Mother flashed various colors of magic over the floating ball, but her staff shattered from the castings. Demosyna reacted with her wind fingers, snatching the splinters from the air before harm was done. Staffs were replaced for the searching Wizen, and Celestria took two poles in a hurry. Another ball of light had emerged from the current floor's walls and streamed toward the alert climbers.

Focused energy pinned the guardian from Celestria's dual staffs while lighting the target for Yoila. The commander fired the recovered crossbow at the shining sphere, crumbling a wooden bolt against the bright shell. Demosyna raised her staff and sent acid at the restrained light with a yell of warning.

"Back away!" Demosyna called to her friends, shooting death at the brilliant spec. "Shield yourselves."

Celestria worked with the young apprentice to shatter the gem floating before the group, trapped by the Wise Mother's magic. Diamonds flew in all directions while tinkling against the stone walls of the mountain. Demosyna's wooden staff caught fire, and she tossed it down the infinite staircase below.

It doused itself in shadows, and the last of Demosyna's carried staves was withdrawn. Vaash picked shards from his armguards, but nobody was injured in the guardian's assault. Demosyna had seen the jewel in her picturesque memory and told the group her vision.

"It looked like a sphere of crystal radiating light!" Demosyna said, glancing around nervously. "It was tough to destroy, so everyone, watch each other!"

Their sounds of travel were the only echoes that reached Demosyna's ears, and floors widened into the horizon while the party walked up the stairs. An armory was found with odd metal boxes containing stacked bolts of gleaming alloy. Yoila's dwarven crossbow responded to the ammunition by opening a slot in the surface to accept the arrows. Celestria studied a crossbow during downtimes, tapping and fiddling with the device after seeing the panel open.

Another shining guardian was trapped by the Wise Mother, and Yoila shattered it with the new bolts. They fired in rapid succession, throwing three heavy arrows into the glowing orb with a single pull.

"Everyone, grab a crossbow," Marrah said, stretching near a nightly fire. "I will get some of those arrows we saw below! Back in a flash."

"Should I go with her, Celestria?" Demosyna asked, rising to grab a staff. "If she needed my aid with the guardians."

"No need, apprentice!" Celestria replied, smiling at the shadowy Paw on the stairs. "My Jade can take care of herself!"

The short woman was gone several hours but returned unscathed from her sneaky mission. Each person held a heavy crossbow as they proceeded, armed with dwarven ammunition.

Celestria talked with her apprentice in low tones when they walked together, instructing the young woman in magic. The sight of the glowing gems flying in the catacombs awoke memories in the Wise Mother, and she wished to share the knowledge.

"That may be a pixie," Celestria whispered, eyes always moving, "or maybe an imp. They were said to be powerful and dangerous, often injuring ancient elves with their mischief. When the soup fell on Vaash, it was funny, and it clicked for me, apprentice. These creatures find it amusing to harass anyone around, and we know how tough the buggers are! Focus on trapping things with your staff, as you saw me do earlier."

"Yes, Wise Mother," Demosyna said, picturing the wavy energy that trapped the guardian. "I will devote my meditations to restraint magic!"

"Go very slow, apprentice. These walls are troubling, and any magic could sympathize with the mountain," Celestria advised, watching the water swirl. "Only ever cast what is needed, and restrain the power put into the channeling. I see you are able to limit your magics, so remember my words at all times, Demosyna! I wanted to train you more directly, but that must wait till we exit these resonance halls."

None attempted to track the days, and the lack of sky prevented hope of guessing the time. Yoila nearly ran out of sketching pads and used the blank pages of her shipping notebook to continue mapping. No more shining balls of mischief were sighted for long periods, as they seemed to know some were destroyed and remained elusive. Demosyna shot at one in the ceiling after a loose stone missed her horns. The three metal bolts vanished into the solid rock, leaving no trace of their passage.

Celestria tapped the spot with her staff, but the surface was rough and dense without give. The increasing floor space on each level quickly made searching impossible, and Celestria forbade anyone from wandering alone.

A rumbling was felt as the group neared the top of the stairs while growing dizzy from the repetitive turning. Dust shook from the stone and crystal walls, sending the held ocean into a vibrating frenzy.

Celestria called out loudly before jumping off the stairs to the previous level below. The others followed her command while falling in piles from the trembling steps. Nothing broke or fell apart, but Demosyna had never felt an earthquake. Demosyna clung to the smooth stone floor and waited for the rumbling to cease. Vaash's flute tumbled from his pocket, and a rare guardian shot toward the silver tube. The dark-silver ball of light knocked the instrument over the edge, leaving it to fall into infinity.

Demosyna's reflexes took over, and she shot two ribbons of her barely practiced holding magic. The dangling flute was captured over the void, and a shrill ball of light was held for a moment. Celestria saw the straining apprentice and used her own ornate staff to shatter the escaping sphere of diamond. Vaash took the flute back with a smile before tucking it inside a deeper pocket of his robes.

"You did well, apprentice," Celestria said, clapping Demosyna on the back. "I have taught you to focus on the enemy, not lost trinkets. That is why it wriggled from your grip. You tried to do too much without mastering the magic first. Remember for next time, but good show, Demosyna!"

"I am sorry, Wise Mother," Demosyna said, lowering her eyes. "I didn't think and just grabbed both. I will do better next time, I promise."

"Time and practice are required to have such reflexes, apprentice!" Celestria soothed with a hand on Demosyna's shoulder, smiling warmly. "Let yourself get there naturally and trust in my instruction. I have studied these things for many of your lifetimes and can guide your progress in the next years! Come, eyes up, apprentice!"

Demosyna obeyed and marched ahead while leaving her mistake in the past.

The last guardian before reaching the top was spied pouring the group's water down the stairs. Vaash had been on watch, and the man noticed the floating waterskin outside the firelight. Both Wisewomen pinned the creature, giving Yoila and Marrah a target to send deadly metal bolts into.

The shards of its struggling mass were sent falling toward Jade City miles below the party. Celestria watched the empty skin tumble down the stairs and praised her apprentice for the proper reactions. Yoila took stock of their supplies while the group divided a last remaining skin. Their food had been slowly taken at night, it seemed, and Celestria considered before pressing on.

The top was finally visible and slowly advancing as a flat expanse of raw crystal after the water-stealing guardian. Their supplies lasted till near the top, but hungry stomachs led the party into the topmost floor of the abandoned ancient complex. The final level of the reversed mountain was adorned with glowing symbols, having lights and panels on every wall. Tubes of dense metals flowed along the floor, warm with whatever the canisters housed.

The chill of the air made mirages at every turn, and Celestria halted the group atop the stairs. Her Wise Mother called for Demosyna, and they sent light into different directions while peeking over the landing. Nothing moved in the massive halls when the spherical spells shot away, but lights seemed to take energy from the passing magic.

Torches along the walls in places on the penthouse floor lit up, glowing with magical light to show the area. Celestria narrowed her large eyes and crouched forward as she circled around the stairs ahead of the group. The Wise Mother had stepped onto the landing and motioned the others to follow after a heartbeat.

"Nobody move from here for the moment!" Celestria whispered to her apprentice. "Demosyna, walk slowly behind me and be ready to retreat at any moment. No magic, no swords. Just retreat with me if I signal. Understand?"

Demosyna nodded silently while handing her near-broken staff to Yoila. The apprentice gave Vaash both of her crystal weapons and shrugged off the traveling pack to lighten herself. Celestria smiled after the apprentice was ready, winking at Marrah and leading Demosyna straight forward. Water could be faintly heard in the far walls, sloshing from the sudden tremor earlier. Rooms branched off the straight hallway the Wise-women explored, empty but for the metallic panels nearly covering the interior walls.

The torches were likewise metal, and the flames were housed in a beautifully shaped, clear crystal. Demosyna saw that the hollow gem seemed to move and swell with the fire inside, nearly touching the relic before catching herself.

"Wise choice, apprentice," Celestria whispered, observing the torch closely. "I wouldn't touch that without study. The wall torch appears simple, but I have never seen crystals like these! This is promising, Demosyna!"

Celestria sought the outer edge of the floor and began her search from the raw crystal walls. The ceiling was titanic and held waiting to smash the ants that walked under its limitless weights. Darkness had hidden the monster from her eyes, but Demosyna felt a shiver whenever glancing at the roof. The rest of the party was retrieved, warm and nervous, from the top of the stairs.

The piped flooring left the air humid, and Marrah had taken off her heavier wrappings. All marveled at the foreign markings as the group found the edge again when they changed and moved before their eyes. Patterns seemed to form from the waving lines of symbols, and the icons twirled around one another hypnotically. They took on a familiar design, and Demosyna pointed out the swirling elven forms the text made.

"I noticed that too. Curious," Celestria said, rubbing her ancient helmet. "I can't quite read it, but the pattern resembles a musical cipher of some sort. Good show, apprentice!"

Hours of searching left hundreds of empty rooms in their wake, and Marrah the Jade grew bored of the endless monotony. Their supplies of food were gone, and the water was quickly draining from each skin. Celestria studied the clear crystal walls, tapping the displays in thought of the water behind. Vaash offered to descend first, and Marrah agreed with the monk.

"We own this mountain, Cel!" Marrah called, cleaning her paws nervously. "Let us fetch more supplies and return later. We have all the time in my life, love!"

Celestria thought hard at the problem, looking at the room of ancient mystery.

"I will stay for a while longer, Jade. If Vaash brings more supplies, I promise only a month of study at a time!"

"This one would be happy to carry back more food!" Vaash said, nodding and smiling as he twirled the silver flute. "Will that be acceptable, Demosyna?"

"I would appreciate more rations, even with my slow appetite! Thank you, Vaash," Demosyna said, turning to Yoila. "What do you want to do, Yoila?"

"I am yours, my Wise-woman," Yoila said, touching her claw scars. "I won't leave your side unless you desire it!"

A few things were handed to the parting friends with Vaash carrying the crossbows and notes Yoila made along the journey. Celestria took the only kept crossbow, and Demosyna waved Marrah and Vaash goodbye.

"Check on the animals if you could, Vaash!" Demosyna called down, watching her friends jump away.

Two short blasts from a flute signaled acknowledgment, as echoes made yelling unreliable at such a distance. The two were skilled in their jumps, landing on the lower stairs to make great time. Marrah the Jade used all four limbs to hop and crouched before springing into the darkness below. Vaash was heard laughing softly as the pit swallowed him up, lightly stepping between ten-foot drops in the spiral stair.

The three remaining women all went about their searching while looking for a room that Celestria described.

"It should have pipes or maybe holes in the walls and floor. It will be a smallish room but very heavily detailed in the paneling," Celestria told the sneaking group. "All magic should have a focusing point or at least a way to activate the energies. We must find the nexus of this mountain, where all things flow to and from! Keep a sharp eye, apprentice, for we know we aren't alone here."

Another short quake rocked the mountain when Celestria found the central room, and the Wise Mother rushed to the stairs to call for Marrah. Two happy bars of flute music rose from the empty staircase, and the group sighed in relief. The two were already dozens of floors below, no doubt leaping through the shadows of ancient stairs.

No more guardians were seen during their short time in the mountaintop, but the Wise Mother slowly progressed back to the discovered room. Celestria spent over a day examining the panels, walking with her hands clasped behind a tall back. The two Scale women sat waiting to enter the room while enjoying the warm floors they rested on in silence. As the Wise Mother finished the first sweep of the room, all the walls on the top floor vanished.

The unobstructed view of the level was shocking to the seated women, who now rested next to a tiny shack in miles of empty stone. Yoila stood in a flash, drawing the elven sword from across her back. Celestria saw the empty darkness from beyond the doorless frame and dashed toward her apprentice. Demosyna sent a ball of light from her staff when the torches vanished with the branching stone walls. Echoing darkness stretched forever, and the stairs were seen to have instantly disappeared as well.

"Did anyone touch anything?" Celestria cried, large eyes scanning the dark. "Please, I must know for all our sake!"

Neither woman had moved in the hours of inspection, and they both shook horned heads. The roof of the central room bubbled as though in a boil, sending colorful blobs into the air. A tall, serene figure overshadowed the others with swirling chains from the wrists. The form appeared elven, with sharp cheeks and ears, but broader in proportion. The tallest figure was the dark silver brown of the stones, but dozens of animated silhouettes circled the dwarf.

Most were in profile, remaining dark and unseen, but two had lit up to show recognized models. An Orc outline was noticed, along with a long tail used to recognize a blacked-out Paw. Many were shapes nobody knew, but an elf and Scale were colored in with stone.

Opalescent waves covered the dancing elf, and the deep-purple Scale was also led by boiling chains of magic. It was like a maypole with dark forms bound to the central figure by helix-shaped ribbons of bloody light.

While the mesmerized women watched the display, the central figure shrank in size while the others grew. It took only seconds, but the thirty swirling portraits overshadowed the dwarf before the display vanished. The rock stopped boiling, and the silence held each living ear with ringing notes of emptiness. No sound had come from the projections, and only the colorful shapes showed the presentation.

"My stomach!" Demosyna cried as soon as the rocks settled. "Wise Mother, something is wrong!"

A thin liquid had begun pouring from Demosyna, spreading from her crotch to stain her blue pants. Yoila was there at once and knelt next to the trembling young Wizen. Celestria scanned the apprentice with magic upon seeing blood form in Demosyna's pants.

"Remove those trousers," Celestria called, bending down to help. "You may be injured, apprentice!"

Pain ripped through Demosyna's abdomen, and terrible clenching sensations paralyzed the Wise-woman. Another quake rocked the mountain as huge holes appeared on the outer walls of the top floor. Piercing wind rushed through the gaps, freezing the apprentice with thin atmosphere. Tears of agony fell from her eyes, and Demosyna felt contractions roar through her unsuspecting body.

"Help me!" Demosyna cried, completely unaware of what was happening. "It hurts, Wise Mother! Something is pushing out from inside me!"

"By the Empress, you are dilated!" Celestria yelled, pouring the last water onto Demosyna's mons pubis. "Apprentice, focus here at once!"

Pain surged inside the writhing young woman, but she forced her railing mind to obey. Yoila was gazing with wide eyes at the Wise Mother and holding Demosyna's clenching hand for support.

"Wise Mother, I am here," Demosyna panted, riding a wave of horrible stretching. "What do I do?"

"Push now, right now!" Celestria yelled, watching the water drain from the walls. "You have something here that is scalding you."

Demosyna found the strength within herself and bore down on the smooth surface of a crystal egg. Blood and diamond poured from Demosyna's vaginal lips while Celestria grabbed the ovular crystal with a rag. It was incredibly hot, and the Wise Mother passed the steaming object between burning hands. Demosyna was weeping in pain and confusion, cradled by her black-scaled friend.

A great rushing sound was heard from below as the walls emptied of their oceans to fill the pit. Torrents of clear liquid rose fast through the hollow mountain, sending air streaming out the spaced holes now open to the world. Pain became manageable for the shivering apprentice, and she looked at herself to see the damage.

Blood was covering much of her thighs, but Demosyna was healed by a soothing touch from her Wise Mother. Celestria petted the purple-scaled woman's head, sending golden mist over the injured apprentice. Demosyna gave birth on an empty floor atop the sky with a flood pushing up the levels to reach her. The view from the open windows showed the Wizen Bay far in the distance, and its volcano was erupting fire into the sky.

Great plumes of smoke issued from the far mountain, and molten rock spewed in all directions. Ash covered the Bay with a blanket of death, and Celestria handed the cooling egg to Demosyna. It was a dark purple, almost black, with no markings or visible inner details on the crystal egg.

"It's active? Now?" Celestria yelled over the wind and water trapped with them. "Marrah!"

A golden rocket was heading toward the open windows in the mountainside carrying crystal armor in tiger-striped arms. Marrah the Jade flew straight up toward the Wise Mother while throwing the armor into the air.

Celestria turned for only a moment before jumping, addressing her apprentice with a shout.

"Remember what I told you about loss, Demosyna!" Celestria yelled over the noise. "Survive and find me again, apprentice!"

The Wise Mother fell from the open window, catching her crystal armor and flying away with Marrah toward the Wizen Bay. Great orbs of magic surrounded the flying mates once Celestria cast again, and they danced around each other toward the volcano.

The earth shook again, and Yoila was terrified of the approaching ocean. Demosyna looked at the egg in her palm, and a deep instinct took over the young woman, who grabbed Yoila and ran. Demosyna tossed the birthed mystery into her mouth before closing her teeth tightly to protect the smooth diamond.

Water was pouring onto the top floor, and Yoila was shuddering with unparalleled fear. Demosyna got the woman's attention by holding up a makeshift blindfold for the commander. The cloth was wrapped around her streaming eyes, and Demosyna waited with her blind friend held tight in loving arms. The water was hot and pushed the two out of the mountain with a waterfall of force.

The two clutching women fell with the water, miles in the air but arcing down with tremendous speed. Jets of fresh liquid spewed from the top of Jade City, falling on the land for miles around and tearing the country apart with force.

CHAPTER 34

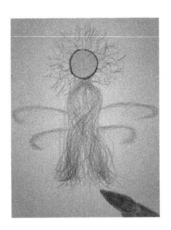

Warm water cradled Demosyna in the air, showing the morning sun and volcanic horizon. The image wavered and shifted as the woman fell for miles, clutching her blinded friend to spare her the sight. It was oddly terrific watching the land expand for minutes at a time in a jet of ancient water.

Her focusing charm was long left behind, and Demosyna held the weeping commander as doom approached from the Fist. The young Wise-woman didn't know how to stop the fall and held her friend tighter in defeat.

Yoila won't see the end coming, Demosyna thought, hypnotized by the sprouting trees in her vision. *That is a final mercy I can grant her at least.*

The volume of steaming water was impossible in its scope, and the force of the jets sent the columns of water miles from their issue points. Demosyna rode near the front of one, but there were over thirty powerful jets from the flat top of the reflected mountain. Even after the numerous waterfalls touched down, the water poured from the mountain for hours.

Hard ground was at hand, and Demosyna took a great breath to calm her screaming mind. The young apprentice turned on her back, looking at the sky as her jet hit the upper-class plateau. Demosyna shielded her unaware friend with a scaly back, taking comfort from the warm body as destruction rained all around. The force of the jet flattened each ornate castle easily before gouging into the earth under the foundations for dozens of feet.

Rivers were formed instantly when shallow ribbons pushed into the hills near Jade City. The earth now shook with magma and water as the force of the simultaneous water jets rocked the realm for miles. Each jet was at least fifty feet in diameter, a pressurized shovel that cleared a path for new rivers on the ground.

Demosyna rode in a channel made by the digging force supporting her, not daring to open her eyes yet. Debris and bodies jostled the women, but their water swept everything along toward the Bay. Nothing was left of the upper-class manors when the liquid reached the edge, falling over in a fresh waterfall. Another moment of sickening vertigo pushed the apprentice for miles in the torrent, and Demosyna opened her streaming eyes.

Death had passed by the two that day, and smoke against blue sky met the Wizen's gaze. Over half the distance back to the Wizen Bay had been traveled while riding inside the tube of plowing force. Demosyna had been knocked against stone earth many times during the panic in the water, but armor and experience kept the pain away. Demosyna felt the flow lessen slightly as distance calmed the raging forces of water. One arm held her paralyzed friend tight as Demosyna did a slow backstroke to leave the deadly river. The day was far too bright, and the entire northern horizon was ablaze with primal energy.

Demosyna spit the purple crystal egg onto the soggy ground, having carried Yoila away from the sound of rushing water. They were only hours from the Bay and smelled smoke on the horizon with each ragged breath. The commander had no color in her scales, and they would remain a faded gray from that day on. Stress had robbed Yoila of her dark-black hue, but Demosyna kissed each claw scar many times as the two recovered.

The young apprentice ignored the death in the Wizen Bay, letting her heart stop its frantic beating. Demosyna had tried to accept her end in those free-falling moments and was confused about how to feel yet. Some nervous energy remained, sourced from hope instead of fearful calm.

"Yoila, I'm taking off your blindfold. I'm sorry you had to be in the water again. I didn't wish to break my word!" Demosyna whispered to the stone-still woman. "Keep your eyes closed for a moment, but the river and bay aren't in sight! I promise."

"Wise-woman, where are we?" Yoila husked, sitting up very slowly. "Thank you, my master. You saved me again."

"I am proud of you, Yoila!" Demosyna said, embracing the pale-scaled woman. "I knew you were brave enough to withstand the blindfold!"

Yoila shook her head, looking at her new coloration without expression.

"Please, my Wise Mother, take me home away from the water! I thought only of you and our house you built while you held me. That got me through my torture, sucked away into the dark water again!"

"Of course, Yoila," Demosyna whispered, helping her stand. "I will move the house farther inland after dealing with that disaster."

Demosyna motioned to the distant cloud of ash darkening the sky, already considering her options as she ran north. The constant jets of water cut large wedges outward from Jade City and reshaped the lands for generations to come. The natural rainwater would divert to the fresh rivers in the coming years, stabilizing nearly each of the thirty freshwater streams.

Demosyna pocketed her warm violet crystal egg, not wishing to leave behind the only relic found in the mountain. Crossbows had been acquired, but Vaash carried those miles in the south. No answers had been found in the catacombs, and only new complications had resulted from the expedition.

"May I have the blindfold, my Wise Mother?" Yoila asked after running steadily, her voice shaking. "Your bay approaches. I smell it."

The path Demosyna took avoided sight of the virginal rivers or known ponds before reaching her new home. The blue cloth had been torn from Demosyna's outer coat and was silky and thick as a blindfold. Pale-gray scales contrasted with the deep blue of the fabric, but Yoila visibly relaxed after hiding her sight again. The talented commander followed with only her ears behind Demosyna, sprinting the last moments to reach the Wizen Bay.

Frenzied boats were evacuating the populated islands, but Demosyna saw many sunk or on fire from volcanic spray. The water had visibly risen in the Bay, nearly touching the lip of the crystal mines from the flood pouring out of Jade City. The steady flow had stopped some time ago, but the momentum would keep the water moving for days.

Demosyna left Yoila in the yellow crystal house near the empty horse fields. The blindfolded woman passed out nearly at once after curling up tightly in her golden bed. Demosyna ran the last distance to see Celestria moving the castle from the geode, magic pouring from each massive crystal inside. Marrah noticed the apprentice, letting out a happy cry over the volcano's latest eruption. The massive destruction was near the edge of the Bay, but the volcano continued to increase in power the entire journey north for Demosyna. An ash cloud was touching the beach, and Celestria shifted the massive castle down from its balanced heights.

Grinding stones echoed on the beach, and the apprentice halls relocated to south of the mine with Demosyna's village. Celestria took her helmet off, a rare event around anyone in the months Demosyna lived with her. Elation filled the Wise Mother's face, and all three friends embraced tightly on the ashy beach.

"Apprentice! I knew you would heed my words!" Celestria cried, her eyes dancing with colors. "Help me shift this geode. We will ride it to aid our people!"

A worn steel helmet was flicked by Celestria's long finger, and hundreds of crystals grew in a rainbow of colors. It was triple what had been on the armor previously, and Demosyna saw new crystals grow on every surface of the Wise Mother's other armor. The young apprentice produced ten rings of solid crystal, setting the bands with magic as she floated to the geode. Ten more rings were made, doubling each finger with enchanted focusing charms.

Power radiated from both Wise-women, and Marrah the Jade ran back to seek cover in the castle. Towering crystals eighty feet tall glowed and hummed with energy, tilting the enormous dome into the Bay. It crushed the metal crane flat and bobbed in the dual-colored waters of the Wizen Bay.

Like a bowl floating in a pond, the massive geode was supported by the churning seas. Demosyna laughed, but another fireball exploded from the volcano and sent chaos over the neighboring islands. Buildings were buried in feet of ash, rolling over the water like oil. Fires spread out of control with snaking rivers of lava pushing outward from the volcano.

Celestria pulled Demosyna's attention back from the devastation, snapping her fingers to begin activating dozens of crystals. The apprentice helped, and the ship of rock and gems leaped toward a burning bay. Celestria lightened the gravity; and Demosyna sprayed water, air, and fire behind to propel the two.

The Wise Mother aided the powering, and magical force pushed the unwieldy boat onward at greater speeds every moment. The young apprentice gripped tightly to the jagged rim of the geode before casting a sudden idea onto her yellow leather boots. An image of the water-resistant Au Cell shirt had risen clear as the Bay turned to salt water, and Demosyna tried a spell she had never heard of before.

Her looted boots were enchanted with what the young woman hoped would be water-walking when Demosyna applied the opposite channeling as fresh water gems. It was in that moment of creation that Demosyna's egg hatched, collapsing in on itself inside the pants cleaned of blood by the jets.

A bright-purple diamond flew out of the surprised woman's clothes, buzzing and darting around Demosyna's head. It was a perfect sphere of gemstone, flawless and shining from the fire lighting the sky. The fairy jumped to whiz around Demosyna's horns, sending tendrils of electricity dancing on matching scales. Its whiskers of light tingled in the rushing wind, and Demosyna lifted a pinky finger near the guardian. Celestria had seen the glittering orb but widened her eyes when it landed on Demosyna's claw.

Long, gossamer strands of magic radiated as the tiny sphere waved and clung, forming a flowing body like silk. The wisps of color were dozens of hues, but all were of a pink or purple spectrum to match Demosyna. Smaller hairs danced across the surface of the only solid part on the creature, a purple diamond of stunning clarity. Shimmering wings sprouted from the sides of the flowing torso, making the floating gem look like a head.

Double wings were dripping light likenesses of Orc wings, and the fairy floated over the scaled finger. The tickling robes the being was made of swished over the apprentice's hand, shocking her slightly with electric signals.

"Apprentice, be careful!" Celestria called, eyeing the approaching catastrophe ahead. "We near the volcano, and you must focus! Let that follow if you wish, but stop playing with that pixie."

Demosyna obeyed, moving the tiny creature onto her horn. She tried putting it safely behind her teeth again, but the tickling shocks numbed Demosyna's tongue. It clung upside down, using the wide base of the horn as a windscreen. Its wings seemed decorative, Demosyna noticed absently, and the fairy flew from the hovering gem forming a head. The strange new creature would stay glued to the horn for days while observing the events of the Wizen Bay unfold.

"Help those fleeing in the boats, apprentice!" Celestria yelled over the noise, hovering from the halted geode. "Meet me once they are safe inside here."

Five huge elevators followed the one Demosyna rode while streaming toward large boats in danger of sinking from fires. The young woman lowered her magic platforms to water level, scooping up all the struggling figures. Most recoiled from the glowing Wise-woman speeding toward them, but Demosyna bellowed her voice with magic.

"Climb to the discs, friends!" the apprentice called, using a magic learned months ago during a blizzard. "Safety awaits in the geode. Quickly!"

It took two trips to circle the boiling volcano, loading each platform with survivors to drop into the rocky half sphere. Demosyna couldn't fly like her Wise Mother but pushed herself along with the magical discs of purple light. Celestria was blasting water and ice from hundreds of crystals, trying to cool the surface of the molten rocks with battle armor. Demosyna joined her for hours and watched the land expand from the cooling magma.

The apprentice was taking a break and panting while her Wise Mother pressed on in the late afternoon. They had cooled half the surface, but it was quickly melting and boiling again to mock their fatigue. Demosyna took a final steadying breath while ignoring the heat and ash hanging in the air.

I can just walk there and rest my elevators for a moment, Demosyna thought, taking a step into the steaming ocean.

Her boots worked as planned when Demosyna ran onto the boiling salt water, and she was able to balance on the surface. The custom spell repelled water violently and seemed to push the young woman off the waves with ease. A massive tornado whipped around the skating apprentice, bending and turning to cover the volcano. A watery arc sucked red lava from the dome of the mountain before drawing the viscous material high into the air.

In minutes, the hook-shaped chunk of hot earth cooled from wind and water, solidifying and breaking into the tornado. The huge curve of steaming rock was flung north into the empty ocean before sticking from the water by its pointed tip.

The stench of sulfur was overwhelming, but squads of rebel soldiers began sending small blasts of air at the volcano. It was slow at first, yet the breeze built from steady use of the focusing charms on each shield. Natural winds in the Bay shifted completely during those days, and both Wise-women were able to keep helping for long stretches. Brave troops took hour-long shifts clearing the air, and hundreds of armored figures managed the evacuations.

Demosyna made more platforms, letting her Wise Mother take over after seeing the new tactic's success. No more ash flew into the sky, and glowing claws were sent flying into the north bay by Celestria's tornado. Most landed with their points splashing into the water, resembling broken talons of some titanic monster.

Those rescued from boats were flown to shore, escorted away by coughing soldiers. Demosyna let each climb on elevators from the geode while ignoring the occasional tickle from the fairy and its stinging whiskers. No more ships were launched, and all the islands had been evacuated by the time the sun went down. Neither Wise-woman knew how long the eruption had taken place before they noticed, having been inside the windowless mountain for days.

The tremors were a clue, but the danger grew as the water receded out of nowhere. Demosyna splashed into the Bay, stumbling from the drop in her floor while sending a twisted rock north. It was nearly boiling so close to the slowly expanding landmass of lava, and Demosyna frantically clawed toward the surface.

Demosyna stood again quickly, using a tornado to dry the steaming water from scalding her more. Her whole body felt on fire from the boiling salt, and the apprentice healed herself at once. An orb returned to a horn and hung from the absent earring holes with long electric strands.

The water level in the Bay continued to drop steadily, and Celestria swooped down to speak with her apprentice.

"You look unhurt. Good show, Demosyna!" the sweating Wise Mother said. "What is this fresh wonder? The hills are glowing too. Curious!"

Demosyna looked south at the radiance from over the edge of her vision, and it seemed to breathe with red light. Clouds of ash filled the night from the unrestrained volcano, but the rebel soldiers went back to clearing the sky. The Wise-women watched the boiled water drain alarmingly for minutes to rest and judge the scene.

"I don't see where the water is leaving, Wise Mother!" Demosyna called up at the floating elf. "It stopped, I think. What do we do now?"

The lowering of the Bay had revealed sections of each island within the inlet, expanding the real estate one more notch. An earth-quake signaled the start of more violent eruptions, and Celestria talked quickly.

"Make more rings, apprentice. Those are cracking," Celestria explained, pointing to the rivers of lava. "We milk the passion from the flow it gives us. Draw the hot rock into the Bay along the natural channels already carved. I will form break walls along the shore and join you after."

The apprentice had never moved liquid rocks, but Celestria had trained her to manipulate materials during their months of lessons. Stone and crystal had similar harmonics, and their spells were simple in their understanding. Demosyna hovered in the blistering heat, using wind to cool herself against the mountain's energy. The apprentice removed her coat and watched it burn away in the inferno, focusing on encouraging the sluggish flow from the cap.

It was like sliding hot dough over rocks when Demosyna urged the strands of heat into the water. All night, the two Wise-women helped the volcano safely move its bulk, eyes blurry from steam and smoke.

The fury had subsided as the sun crested the mountains, revealing Sai Aeri's ships sailing into the Bay.

* * * * *

Demosyna was panting on her bed in the apprentice halls when Celestria called for her. Precious water had been drunk, but their break had only lasted minutes.

"I already gave her the fees for purchase," Celestria mused, watching a squad of soldiers land on the beach. "Why does she bother me now?"

A short general marched from a lead ship, scanning the devastation from the last day. Sai Aeri walked with a tall metal pole arm showing a wide blade on top with imperial ribbons.

"I make a claim in the name of my Empress!" Sai Aeri bellowed, planting a flag in the crystal mine. "Demosyna is a fugitive, and her lands are mine!"

"Demosyna is my apprentice, Sai Aeri!" Celestria called from the high walls, summoning her breastplate with a snap. "You have no claim over any in my Orders. Leave her lands at once. I won't give a second warning."

The thirty imperial soldiers ashore drew swords at the challenge, and Sai Aeri marched painfully forward. Her limbs had healed, but she walked in crooked steps that hurt the general. Her legs were slightly bowed now, making Sai Aeri shorter than before. The close-cropped hair Sai Aeri sported wasn't visible with a helmet and mask in place, but her eyes burned with anger.

"She wasn't an apprentice when I issued an imperial decree!" the general called, holding the seven-year sentence. "Surrender the prisoner or forfeit your new realm as a traitor, Celestria!"

Vaash broke the tension on the scene when he came roaring over the southern horizon. The yellow-clad monk sped faster than a meteor across the hills, carrying both rescued dogs in his arms. Vaash ran and leaped so quickly that dust was kicked up thirty feet tall, and he glowed with a crackling white energy. The master monk smashed into the beach, lightning dancing around his body, and dropped his gray dog before Demosyna. The apprentice had joined her Wise Mother to face Sai Aeri, unafraid after her last months of living free.

"This one needs your help, Demosyna!" Vaash cried, lightning striking the tears on his face. "Rolls is sick from smoke and must be healed!"

The apprentice turned her back on Sai Aeri, falling to her knees at the unexpected arrival. Vaash's fluffy old dog was breathing in ragged, painful breaths from the sand. Fur had been burned from its body in numerous places, and its blind eyes stayed closed as she gasped for air. Jest was also missing fur in burned patches and half an ear from his time away from Demosyna.

Solid golden rings encircled the dying animal, lifting its frail body gently into the air. The apprentice poured all her energy into the casting, emotions rising at the threat of further death. Demosyna's healing worked, and the dog awoke to bark weakly up at Vaash. Jest walked over to receive healing of his own, knowing the golden light would help from previous minor injuries.

Jest's burns healed perfectly, and a wide grin surveyed the intruders to his beach. Vaash was sending overwhelmed tears into the fuzzy gray coat of his animal and thanked Demosyna profusely. Sai Aeri remained silent, slowly moving behind her numerous personal guards.

"Jade City is on fire, Celestria!" Vaash explained breathlessly. "Lava poured from the mountain once the waters stopped. These dogs herded the entire evacuation, and Rolls was injured from the smoky air! This one needs your help, Wise Mother!"

"Marrah, to me at once!" Celestria said, her voice ringing out with command. "Demosyna, I leave this rabble to your capable hands. Get them off your shores, apprentice! Wait for my word and remember what I have shown you."

Yoila had emerged from the distance with her tied blue blindfold waving in the breeze. Her pale-scaled friend drew a sword, tilting a horned head to find Demosyna in the sand. Celestria encased Marrah in glowing, magical arms, and a sonic boom blasted across the sand when they flew away.

Vaash left both dogs, and a white-hot electricity crackled from his muscles. Each step took the sprinting monk hundreds of feet, and both masters fled south to save Jade City. The entire situation took only minutes, and Demosyna stood to brush sand from her pants.

"Would you like assistance with these trespassers, my Wise-woman?" Yoila asked, easily navigating the terrain without sight.

"No, thank you, Yoila. Get any of your soldiers not cleaning the air for us," Demosyna said, growing her weapons with practiced ease. "Take the dogs inside your house, away from this beach, as you leave. I will show Sai Aeri what should matter to her."

A short sword was focused with acid, dark poison dripping from the razor edge. Golden light poured from the sai, shining with healing energies waiting to repair flesh and bone. Yoila obeyed the apprentice at once, leading the growling dogs to safety in the distance. The running commander began blasting loud horn calls into the empty hills, letting the sound alert any listening rebels.

Demosyna tore through the collection of soldiers to get to Sai Aeri, a calm expression on her sharp face. Her training had left the impression on Demosyna she lacked such skills, but the soldiers fell to her hands like leaves.

It's only because Celestria is so talented! Demosyna thought solemnly, healing soldiers by stabbing them with her sai. *I just seem slow in comparison to Yoila and Vaash!*

Demosyna would disarm with her sai, catching blades between prongs and rolling her whole body violently. Knees or ankles were slashed to disable, and the apprentice weaved around to heal the injury she just caused.

Those who did strike her torso found their blades bent on the elven armor, and Demosyna's eyes dripped golden healing light constantly. It was slow progress from the number of soldiers, but Demosyna saw growing fear in Sai Aeri's eyes the closer she walked. Wind and water knocked half the remaining soldiers aside, and Demosyna caught Sai Aeri's swung pole arm with a bare hand.

Blood and acid dripped from her straining fist while Demosyna melted the metal with burning magic. The gleaming blade dropped uselessly to the sand, bubbling with steaming liquid. Demosyna hadn't killed a single soldier, and they all rose painfully to arm themselves again. Most of their weapons had clashed with her acidic sword, leaving them warped and shattered.

Nearly twenty rearmed figures circled the two fighters, bright shields forming a wall. A purple disc of magic carried Sai Aeri away with Demosyna banishing her crystal weapons a few feet distant. The two sailed slowly through the air, and the apprentice ignored the angry general.

"Look, Sai Aeri. The lands we bicker in are on fire!" Demosyna yelled, pointing to the smoldering islands. "You must have seen the smoke. You aren't blind or dim! Stop this and help. Please!"

Sai Aeri responded with a dagger thrust, starting the fight again on the slow trip to the volcano. Demosyna grew only a sai and took a defensive stance to keep trying to convince the general. As if to signal the renewed battle, two towering pillars of lava shot from the east. One was near Au Cell's easternmost peninsula, but one was inside the Wizen Bay as it reached into the black sky.

Without both Wise-women stopping the ash, it had piled up in the air to choke the two hovering combatants. It took an hour of intentionally slow progress to the volcano, letting the rebels see the battle taking place over the Bay. More squads departed the fleet of ships in her bay, and Demosyna saw the crystal mines kick off in a full-troop battle. Yoila led a tiny group of rebel soldiers onto the beach, shouting orders in a blind blue fury.

All day long, Demosyna circled the volcano, pleading at Sai Aeri to stop and help. A battle on the crystal beach raged during that time with too many casualties on both sides. Each duelist was barely standing as the sun rose again, and twin columns of lava shot higher into the air. Soldiers rushed along the coast, marching the lands for the first time in decades.

Ship cannons boomed at the beach, but Demosyna melted their barrels with lightning from a distance. Sai Aeri was fast like memory told, yet Demosyna had honed her reflexes against the best in the Fist. Demosyna's goal was buying time and letting the general's anger burn with the ocean under the two.

Demosyna sent wind with one arm toward a collection of ships while letting a thrust hit the elven armor with indifference. A plume of deadly ash had reached the anchored ships, and the apprentice blasted the heavy smog into the sky. Imperial sailors swam to shore, coughing and dripping, to join the battle. Cavalry and hand-to-hand combat drenched the mines with blood even though Demosyna saw her orders followed regarding healing.

A series of turtle-style engagements let Yoila hold the mine with half the troops, and Demosyna smiled. The commander's blue blindfold signaled her presence, and Yoila slashed or blocked any imperial soldier near the furious commander. Sai Aeri paused her attack to watch the apprentice save the imperial ships, spitting blood from a punch to the face earlier.

Demosyna didn't have Vaash's restraint and defended herself with near-lethal force most times. Cuts and bruises covered both combatants, fighting atop their armies while everything suffered.

* * * * *

Around two days passed for the battle of the Wizen Bay with Demosyna straining beyond her breaking points. Hundreds of crystal rings were destroyed over the period, and replacements appeared at once for the apprentice. Nights were lit by boiling rocks, and the days were barely illuminated through the volume of ash.

The volcano erupted again, sending more lava than ever before to almost drench the airborne fighters. Demosyna rocketed the platform away at the sight of a tidal wave of fire, grabbing Sai Aeri when she slid off the smooth surface. A dagger pierced her arm, and Demosyna held the struggling general at arm's length with magic after that. Imperial Battle Wizened had joined the skirmish, and Demosyna jetted over to stop the slaughter.

"If you will not help me, you are out of chances!" Demosyna bellowed, throwing Sai Aeri down after healing the general. "We must move the geode to plug the volcano, and I need more Wise-women to manage it! If you don't decide now, I will be forced to banish everyone present. I granted you two days to think, so decide, because my patience runs thin."

Massive crystals in the mine lashed out with golden magic, forming whips that cracked with fifty individual threads. Celestria had shown her apprentice how to make these whips, shredding a log with powerful strikes to demonstrate. Each crystal could sprout a magical cord, and Demosyna made a final advantage for her rebels in the battle.

Demosyna's fairy flew from her horn when it glowed with passion; and teeth, eyes, and claws joined in pouring light into the dark. A massive tornado surrounded the floating purple elevator, and all the Battle Wizened took a knee before the trembling apprentice. Both armies did likewise, leaving Sai Aeri standing in furious silence on the blood-soaked sands.

Even with the sun gone, the air glowed with fire and smoke from lava. Sai Aeri stood alone, and all the Wise-women flew away on purple discs to lift the titanic geode. Demosyna shielded the group in her tornado and broke all her rings moving the weight. Rocks rained down from the geode while primal fury spit toward the Wise-women who were trying to quench its force. Howling cyclones did their practiced work, and sharp chunks of cooled lava failed to injure the struggling Wizen.

A final splash of magma ended the third day of struggle for Demosyna, and the volcano only gave a final earthquake before calming. The geode melted and fused with the lip of the massive volcano, creating a sparkling dome of ruined gems.

Au Cell came blasting from the southeast of the Fist at the last tremor, his small metal craft skipping over the waves. Demosyna sent the other Wise-women back to the crystal mines before moving to the vessel heading toward a distant magma pillar. The apprentice flew leagues to help the man with his lands, ash and wind stinging her nose with the speed of travel.

One peninsula fell behind, and the apprentice reached the lord's realm just after he did. His craft opened its panels, and Au Cell was jettisoned from the metal with a roar. Dark skin shone red in the light while Au Cell seemed to absorb the heat from the pillar he circled. The swirling mass of fire and rock slowed, breaking apart into a bay to drench the shore in tidal waves. Demosyna turned with the hovering man, sending air to throw the cooling chunks of death safely away.

He now wore a large cape over his golden armor, and Au Cell's skin crackled with subdermal magma as the jet of raw earth subsided. Demosyna saw fissures and channels of red energy pulsing inside the human's skin while rushing over to heal the lord.

"No, Demosyna!" Au Cell cried, his voice like an earthquake. "Stay back where you were. I will be golden in a moment."

Even Au Cell's eyes and mouth seemed to contain vast swirling pools of the lava he absorbed, Demosyna saw with horrified interest. The blistering man pointed at his empty craft below, and the cracks in Au Cell's skin faded at once.

The lord sighed a breath into the warmed air, calling over to Demosyna.

"Thank you, Demosyna! I came when I heard of the sudden trouble in my realm!" Au Cell roared, drifting back to his odd metal boat. "Do you need help with your Wizen Bay? Congratulations are in order since I kept in contact with my assistant while afar!"

"That would be wonderful, Au Cell!" Demosyna said, grinning sweaty joy at the assistance. "I appreciate the gesture, being neighbors now and all!"

Au Cell's laugh boomed with the absorbed energy of his pillar, causing a final halt in the crystal mine's battle at the thunder. It echoed over both eastern peninsulas with its power, and Demosyna followed Au Cell's black metal boat toward the Wizen Bay. Rebel troops were blasting healing magic over everyone on the sand during the lull, and Yoila organized the defense around the mine.

Au Cell flew around the second blinding tower of magma, helping the apprentice stop the last immediate threat to her bay. The man's skin peeled while the young woman's eyes dripped blood and healing from the long marathon.

"You are indeed a Wise-woman, Demosyna!" Au Cell called after his bursting skin returned to normal. "I see what Celestria draws from you is just hatching but is terrible in its grandeur!"

"Thank you for the hand, Lord Au Cell, and the flattery!" Demosyna said, blushing, watching him float nearer.

Au Cell removed a tiara from his belt as he approached, and the drain the apprentice felt from him lessened. It was similar to the free jewelry Lark provided Yoila and Demosyna after the recovered books were hauled back. The gold-armored human landed on the purple disc, shaking Demosyna's hand and smiling.

"Just being a courteous neighbor, as you say! I fear I must go, for my business wasn't finished when I took my leave to come here," Au Cell said, his eyes sparkling. "A final gift to celebrate your new position, Demosyna, and your timely assistance. Any you call family will be allowed to choose a horse from my stables, as I am told many you live with have no mounts yet. You may choose a full herd of whatever beast you desire from my ranches to start your realm properly. Seek out Lark at your leisure, my lady, and we will meet again very soon!"

Demosyna bowed to the man, smiling in weakness and gratitude.

"Safe travels, Au Cell! Our chats always seem brief, but I thank you with all my heart. You are welcome in my lands, and I will feast your return in my new halls!"

Au Cell sped off back into the dark whirlpools of the east, and Demosyna collapsed onto her platform with a deep sigh. No more fire poured like rain over the Wizen Bay, and both armies blasted the ash away from covering the sky. The halt in battle let Demosyna drift over undisturbed, watching the clouds begin to shift again.

Sai Aeri was standing at attention with her troops forming ranks of shining silver armor. Stairs appeared from the disc of magic, and Demosyna took Yoila's hand when she walked over to help the last trembling steps.

"If you truly wish to have peace talks, come to my fort in the south, Demosyna," the elven general said, signaling a retreat. "You have saved me and my soldiers' lives today, and you have my gratitude. I will have your sentence carried out, but we are at a stalemate today. If you accept a truce for the hour, I will withdraw to my realm, Demosyna."

"We will meet again, Sai Aeri," Demosyna breathed, leaning against Yoila for support standing. "Thank you for a merciful decision regarding the lives you command. Leave my shores, Sai Aeri, until you are invited again."

The black imperial ships sailed away past the claws, and Demosyna sent the rebel soldiers back to finish aiding any who needed help. Yoila held the spent young apprentice in strong arms, eyes wrapped from the sight of the Bay. The commander didn't see the glowing islands cooling in the ocean or the wind magic dissipating the clouds to show the stars.

"Thank you, Yoila," Demosyna rasped, barely able to stay present. "Thank you for letting me be so selfish while you fought for me!"

"I love you, Demosyna."

Yoila smiled, kissing Demosyna's cheek.

"You are my Wise Mother and will always be safe with your Yoila."

Demosyna looked up at the blindfold Yoila wore, and the commander stared down at her Wise-woman with pure love. Both were bloody and sweaty from days of battle, but neither cared as the moon shone down clear and bright. Yoila carried Demosyna into her golden bed, holding the Wizen till she recovered from fighting nature itself for everyone.

CHAPTER 35

It was a time of great change for the Fist after the battle of Crystal Beach, and Demosyna found herself in the center of the growth.

Thousands of evacuated islanders found new landmasses to call home after the apprentice magically covered the volcanic rock with flora. Lumber was felled in her vast forests, and Demosyna offered free houses to any who returned to an island in Lost Claw Bay. The estuary inlet was renamed for the numerous rock claws that remained standing, slowing shipping but offering tourism and protection. The young apprentice devoted personal land to crops and many acres to let her new dire hogs graze in luxury.

Celestria was absent for weeks on end while away south, tending to the destruction of Jade City. Demosyna waited for a summons with patient study, learning all she could while the Fist fled north.

"Please stop pestering Jest, you silly fairy!" Demosyna called, taking the dancing jewel in her hand. "I'm sorry, boy. Let's go outside."

Electricity laughed against the apprentice's scales, and she felt the tiny fairy giggle in its magical voice. It had taken patience for the mischief, but Demosyna had felt a primal connection with the fairy from the start. A deep tether between the two let desires be passed from whiskers of light, and Demosyna learned to understand its tongue somewhat.

The purple ball of light tugged on Jest's half ear, making the dog jump in surprise. The strong animal didn't growl, simply sniffed at the buzzing orb on his nose. The fairy flew around Demosyna's horn, and she led them into the sunlight. Crystal walls patched the broken apprentice halls, and Demosyna used them as her own small manor. Jest ran along the beach with a reptilian grin, splashing in the water and digging up sand. A favorite toy was thrashed mercilessly by Jest, the fairy playing catch with the stuffed bear.

Yoila was away on Demosyna's instruction, bringing the young Wizen's promotion recommendation. Hundreds of passing soldiers told Demosyna of the commander's bravery, the apprentice having opened the Bay to rebel combatants. Demosyna wrote a letter to the generals, telling them to promote Yoila upon her arrival in their camps.

Yoila would serve as the general of Lost Claw Bay, Demosyna explained, since the Wise-women held nearly half the Fist. The young woman needed a representative in her absence and finished the letter claiming Yoila a trusted intermediary. Yoila took the caravan of focusing gems into the south, using her remaining senses with the blindfold waving in the distance.

"This one has found a bounty for dinner, Demosyna!" Vaash called, his braided hair soaking the fresh water. "Catch, if you would!"

A huge swordfish was thrown toward the beach, but the fairy darted forward to knock it back into the water. It tried to swim away, yet Vaash was ready for the prank and tackled the meal again. The glowing purple orb dived under the water with a crackling splash, lifting the fish and monk through the air. They crashed into a flopping heap on the beach, almost falling into the open mine full of pointy crystals. With a sigh, Demosyna sat on a deep-purple disc to hover near the fairy.

Vaash broke the struggling fish's spine, and the patient Wizen put the orb onto a horn while descending. A glowing silken torso wavered and gyrated, laughing with audible vibrations of its tendrils.

"Are you okay, Vaash?" Demosyna called, shaking her head. "Sorry! Again."

"I am fine, only bruised from this great beast's wriggling!" Vaash said, wringing out his hair. "May I cook this while you walk the grounds after the last shipments?"

THE FROZEN FIST

Vaash was nude, having left his clothes on the private beach, as he wrestled his catch in the sand. Demosyna grinned, enjoying her empty lands for the night, as Vaash spoke without strict monk discipline. No wood buildings were on land yet, and the numerous fresh islands let Demosyna house any who reached her realm. The beach and surrounding miles were barren, being the personal acres for Demosyna's Wise-woman privacy. Magic could be dangerous in practice, Demosyna had found, and she refused to injure from accident whenever possible.

"I love your cooking, so yes!"

Demosyna laughed, tending to her evening duties.

"Thank you!"

Horses, livestock, and crops now needed oversight each day; and Demosyna shared that duty with Vaash most weeks. His years as a wandering monk gave the man great knowledge of life in the Fist, and Demosyna absorbed much from his wisdom. The apprentice continued growing crystals for Celestria in the workshop each morning, shipping them to Jade City for final approval of quality. It was slower without the Wise Mother's careful eye, but gems flowed steadily to the mountain each month. No word returned from the crates or letters Demosyna sent, so the young woman busied herself awaiting Celestria's next instructions.

Jest sniffed the noses of grazing dire boar, and Demosyna held the impish gemstone to avoid another stampede. The exercise was a welcome treat after hours of casting and study, so the apprentice ran in an open field with her fairy and canine laughing beside. This was one of her favorite spots in the growing manor, just between the animals and crops, where the entire bay was almost visible.

Gentle hills and lush grasses let the giddy Wise-woman frolic her cares away while viewing much of her realm from the rise in terrain. Demosyna did a cartwheel into the grass, laughing as the fairy tickled her cheek with light. Jest licked the fairy and Demosyna lightly before pointing toward the smell of food with his muscular body.

"Fine. Let's go eat!" Demosyna said, petting the short-haired dog.

The fairy didn't seem to consume anything, except maybe the cries of dismay from its painful antics. A dimming of the waving hairs signified a rest period for the creature, but they were rare in the weeks since it hatched from Demosyna's egg. Boundless energy seemed to flow from the fairy as it buzzed and circled the apprentice during her tasks each day. It could fly anywhere, air or sea, but seemed at home nestled in the young Wizen's horns.

"I put a salad on the table, Demosyna," Vaash said, glancing at the returning group. "The fish is almost ready. I just need to put the sauce on top!"

A meal was shared by the two friends, catching cups and bowls from tipping over with fairy light. Demosyna asked the monk if he wished a position in her expanding court, but he smiled and declined.

"I am here at your pleasure but don't wish an active combat roll," Vaash explained, wiping his face. "I sent burning pigs against elephants and felt others' tears on my hands in my youth. I would feel responsible for the pain caused if I advised your troops, Demosyna. I am sorry."

"No, Vaash, don't be sorry," the young woman said, taking her friend's hand. "I didn't mean in the rebel army necessarily but wished you to thrive in whatever you desired! I can finally help so many people and wish to spread the good fortune I have right now. I love you, Vaash, and want you to be fulfilled in our time together! That I do!"

Vaash thought for a long time on the answer while Demosyna cleared the table with a snap of her fingers. Jest had finished his crystal bowl of food, and the Wise-woman sat sipping her wine before Vaash spoke.

"When I left Plu Durrah on the Highway, the town was barely alive," Vaash said, tapping the sword he wore absently. "The dogs now gave bloodless shows, but I saw worse turnout than before we arrived at Three Paws. If I can help those dogs and the town after our misdeeds, I would like to try. I don't ask for money, but I know you can find a solution! You are wise, Demosyna, and I will accept the role you assign now that you know my heart."

"Thank you. I will think hard on the issue," Demosyna said, looking openly into his face. "I promise not to request violence from you, because I can see the strength in your Orders' balance. Your instruction is all that got me through facing Sai Aeri as I waged the battle from a balanced perspective. Let me find an answer, Vaash, if you wish to stay with me till then!"

"I would love nothing more, my truest friend!" Vaash said, covering her hand with his other. "I will watch your lands while you ponder my minor troubles. Thank you!"

The answer would come with the help of her fairy, but Demosyna received a summons before visiting Au Cell's Highway for the second time. The gifts of boar and horses had been herded back weeks before the summons, and Demosyna hadn't gotten to see Rrra or Jui in that moment.

Marrah the Jade hovered into the apprentice halls one random day, bearing a letter from Celestria.

> Apprentice, my mountain has been repaired of the volcanic disturbances. My fields await your progress in botanical magic, and official titles must be passed on. Bring the rainbow chest you made and the canine heroes of Jade City when you come.
>
> My tailor in the southern district will provide suitable clothing per my instructions. You left your ring in my palace, so bring a barrel of my wine when you come to collect it.
>
> New learning for us both begins with your arrival, so make haste, apprentice!
>
> Celestria, the Jade in the Mountain.

It had taken months for the summons, and the first signs of thaw were across the Fist. Vaash desired to stay on the grounds, so Demosyna packed only the chest and a few reading journals.

A hay-colored horse clopped along easily, leading the dogs and Marrah the Jade south past virginal streams. Fruit trees bloomed near huddled travelers' camps, letting Demosyna practice magic by freely giving food to the caravan lines.

Marrah the Jade spotted the mock battles first, being a seasoned thief and guiding the party along.

"The noise has been unbearable!" Marrah complained to Demosyna. "Cannons and construction for weeks before I found you. Even at the top of the mountain, the sound carries!"

Demosyna saw what the tiger-striped Paw meant, staring as thousands of rebel troops were flowing over the hills and streams. Cavalry practiced pincer formations, wedging itself against shielded lancers on foot. Amphibious squads forded the rivers, testing readiness for quickly crossing flowing water. Squares and rectangles of archers spent hours shooting and recovering arrows, marching in lines to maintain orderly ranks.

Commanders trained recruits in proper handling of powerful focusing charms, running along the lines bearing Freeblood standards. Boats patrolled the deeper rivers around Jade City, firing cannons periodically at empty carts or shacks. Wind and healing flew everywhere on the training fields, and Yoila rode a red Au Cell horse with her blindfold fluttering hello.

The majestic animal was huge like Demosyna's but shone a deep ruby red in the afternoon light. Its mane was jet-black, but Yoila had dyed it purple and pink before braiding the long hair. Each soldier Yoila passed to gallop toward Demosyna raised a smiling face, saluting the gray-scaled woman with respect. Some gave a cheer while yelling praises and calling her Ice Eyes.

"My Wise-woman, welcome to your army!" Yoila said, dismounting and bowing low. "It's about time you saw our progress since your Wise Mother hired a new general for her armies! He really turned things around for your troops, my Wise-woman, so inspect the soldiers at your whim!"

"Yoila! I have missed you these last weeks!"

Demosyna laughed, hugging the sightless woman tightly.

"How are you, and how goes your command?"

Yoila hung her head at the question, sighing deeply.

"I am well. Thank you for your kind worry, Demosyna. Any injury I suffer with my rebels is a welcome gift since you let me fight with all my heart! I failed you, however, and ruined the general's plans this last engagement."

Yoila had knelt in the dust, coating her blue leather armor in grime and humility. Demosyna let Marrah lead the animals away before sitting beside the tearful commander and taking her pale hand.

"Yoila, we will have time to discuss our mistakes on the walk up the mountain!" the apprentice whispered, standing Yoila up. "In the meantime, mount your horse, and I will show your troops their true leader!"

Yoila obeyed at once, not even using clawed hands to climb into the saddle. The commander had drawn her bastard sword, holding the double-edged blade into the sky with a yell. All troops snapped to attention as banners and horns signaled across the landscape at Yoila's command.

"Demosyna has arrived!" Yoila bellowed, near silence resounding after a moment. "Stand true and present arms!"

Over a hundred thousand soldiers thrust steel into the fading light, and magical fireworks lit miles of orderly squadrons. Lightning arced from crystal-rimmed cannons, dancing in harmless celebration of the announcement. Demosyna grinned with watery eyes at the love she felt but lifted Yoila high into the air on a purple disc of light.

"Here is where your praise belongs!" Demosyna bellowed, magically raising her voice to be heard. "Yoila has bled with you, has killed for me, and she deserves our love!"

Wet spots formed in the blue silk blindfold, and Yoila reared her horse into a dynamic pose on the floating platform. The cheers redoubled as Demosyna walked nearly each line of soldiers with a commander watching from above. It took hours, but the apprentice was overjoyed at the massive congregation of the free Fist. Yoila dismounted after returning to the ground, and Demosyna wiped tears from both of the Scale's cheeks with a soft laugh.

"Thank you all for giving yourselves to Yoila!" Demosyna hollered over the silent soldiers. "We stand together, seeking harmony with all in the Fist! I have seen the passion in each face and know our goal is just and true! I will break any ties to the slaver's empire and build a stronger future with every drop of blood given!"

Yells and cries beyond count roared into the stars, and both friends rose into the air on magical light. Yoila rode her ruby horse as Demosyna waved her gratitude over the disciplined army she had clawed into her life. The southern district rang with the renewed sounds of battle, and Marrah the Jade was clapping lightly once seeing the floating pair.

"Great speech, Demosyna!" the retired thief said, grinning in mockery. "Looks like you really inspired those rebels!"

"It was perfect, my Wise-woman," Yoila breathed, removing the blindfold with a few blinks at the light. "What is your next command, Demosyna? The generals have ordered my presence, but I walk at your pace!"

"I will meet you two up there," Marrah said, yawning widely and riding off toward a top-bound road. "You can find the tailor, I trust!"

The two reunited friends lazily walked their horses along the wide streets with Jest not being taken by Marrah. Her well-trained dog watched the hitched horses while Demosyna was fitted for a new set of robes. They were a heavy silk fabric and had dusty pink and purple colors layered with each piece of clothing. A deep molten red covered the trim of each robe while seeming to flow and move with primal energy.

Clean robes matched Demosyna's scales and fairy perfectly, and she admired the new look in a tall mirror. She still wore hidden elven armor next to the underclothes, but Demosyna felt like a true Wise-woman as she stared at the reflection.

Thin lines of silver had been woven vertically into the robes to create a subtle shine of pinstripes. The apprentice wore her enchanted yellow boots, invisible under the flowing formal outfit she belted tight. Even her tail had been tailored expertly into the robes, letting it hang free without being smashed down from heavy cloth.

Tiaras and crowns were offered, but Demosyna described her Wise Mother's chain mail veil adorning the ancient helmet. A blacksmith was found by the tailor, and Demosyna made a home for the fairy atop her head. The prankish orb had thrown sheers into the wall, laughing and dancing, so Demosyna commissioned a shielding for the creature.

It hung from the curved horns the woman had gracing her skull, forming a curtain of silver links that encircled above Demosyna's brow. The top was still exposed to show a faint purple glow, but the fairy was eager to enjoy the privacy afforded by the screen. Electric whiskers danced over the scales, and Demosyna's cranium hummed with giddy laughter while the gemstone explored the space.

All arrangements had been made by Celestria, so the two crafts-women bowed as Demosyna led her friend up the mountain. The chain mail crown was heavy in its solid construction, but the appren-tice loved the new armor and wore it for many years as a fairy den.

"I was told to take thousands of soldiers and sweep around a mountain," Yoila sighed, sitting with Demosyna at a nightly camp. "The other generals needed me in a three-part plan to engage the imperial army. I was ordered not to be noticed, being the surprise surge when both generals lured with a mock retreat."

The two travelers had stopped halfway up the mountain after moving from the thin road into the wild woods. Yoila hung her head when retelling her defeat, and Demosyna held the commander's pale hand in support.

"The day before the plan was to be realized, I reached a valley without any cover," Yoila explained, forming a fist in her anger. "My soldiers would have been seen if I crossed, but I needed to be in posi-tion before sunup for the plan to work. I took a side path but arrived hours too late to be effective, my Wise-woman. It was a slaughter, and all I could do was join the generals in a retreat. We fought for weeks to get back to Jade City, harassed by imperials without end."

"Yoila, I am sorry for your loss!" Demosyna said, hugging the furious woman. "I know you did what you could for your soldiers! You followed your orders well given the situation."

"The generals are not so forgiving, my Wise-woman," Yoila whispered, sorrow in her voice. "The summons they gave me leaves little doubt of their intentions, and I failed in my duty to you. Forgive me, Demosyna, for I wasn't strong enough to serve you."

"No, you are," the apprentice said, frowning, finishing the nightly meal with a stir. "You are so brave, Yoila! Don't forget, you are still mine and will serve me personally if the generals can't see your strength!"

Yoila smiled slowly at the hopeful words, nodding.

"You are too kind in the face of my inadequacies. Thank you, my Wise-woman. Let us face our summons together, hand in hand, against the unknown."

"As it should be!"

Demosyna grinned, handing her friend some stew.

"I have always felt safer when you are at my side, Yoila. Thank you for joining me and tempering my heart with your strength."

The remaining days to reach Celestria's palace were full of lazy talks, and Yoila blindfolded herself as the penthouse rose into view. Her dark-black eyes had gazed at Demosyna during the short trip, but the commander was more comfortable now with the blinder on.

An ornately dressed man was walking the topiary gardens while admiring the shapes trimmed into the bushes. Large fur cuffs adorned the steel-gray coat the man wore, and Yoila greeted the general with a salute. He carried a short baton with a silver tip and was nearly bald from age.

"Well, well, Demosyna at last!" the Paw man said, bowing in introduction. "I am Harol the Third, newly appointed general of Jade City. Did you find your troop's new discipline to your liking? Some didn't even bathe before I arrived, but I was having none of that! The Jade in the Mountain doesn't keep me to let troops fail after all!"

"It is nice to meet you, Harol the Third!" Demosyna said, returning the bow. "You say you helped train the rebel armies? Thank you, sir! Or do you prefer General?"

"I am Harol and proud of the name! Celestria fought beside my ancestors long in her past!" the patchy man said, handing a tiny dog to Yoila. "I am the third of my name, meaning three times three generations have passed while my Wise Mother supported the bloodline! My mind is trained for warfare, and I teach the newest lives discipline in order to survive this war. Learning to kill is only a part of what I impose when soldiers die from disease and starvation without strict refinement."

Demosyna had often seen miles of rebel caravans rolling steadily in support of soldiers guarding the provisions. Her recent delve into food for the rebels had shown Demosyna the volumes required, and much work was yet to be done in her mind. Yoila or Vaash often helped with the strict numbers, as Demosyna had little experience yet in bookkeeping or accounting. She was learning such each day, alongside her apprentice studies, in hope of being ever more useful to her realm.

"General, may I let your dog run with Demosyna's?" Yoila asked, cradling the shivering handful to her breastplate.

"Yes, yes, Yoila!" Harol said, waving a hand at the fairy tugging fur from his coat. "What is this now?"

"My apologies, Harol. Please return to me, fairy!" Demosyna called, raising a pinky finger. "Stay inside for a bit, if you would."

The purple orb returned in a jagged flight path, chirping electric laughter into the thin air. It lit up the silver mail covering Demosyna's horns while sending rays of pink light to form a halo of energy.

"Celestria spoke true, by my Wizen!" Harol exclaimed, laughing roughly before coughing. "What a prize you have, Demosyna! Such hasn't been seen in ages beyond telling. No wonder my Wise Mother keeps you close!"

"It is a marvelous surprise, I have found over time!" Demosyna said, walking with the bounding dogs. "It likes being called fairy, not pixie or imp, I've noticed! Other than that, I still am learning of this strange new life!"

The two chatted while circling the palace, and the apprentice marveled at the repairs Celestria had completed. Large channels were seen under spaced circles of melted rock, formed when the molten lava had poured over Jade City from above. Each winding path taken from the magma was turned into aqueducts, and freshly melted snow was sent all the way down the mountain.

Dozens of city bubbles were rebuilt with newly tilled fields waiting for Demosyna's hand. The mirrored mountains bore scars from the ordeal, but new life sprung from the destruction with fresh resolve.

As the three opened the large doors to the palace, Demosyna saw a grand chandelier heating the first floor with a crystal she grew.

"Celestria just installed similar heaters in each house in Jade City!" Yoila whispered, noticing Demosyna's stares. "She toiled day and night to rebuild her fallen realm and provided work for those without hope!"

A large orange heat crystal hung point down like a great sword that wept sky-blue gems from the hilt. Huge blue teardrops shed water into the reservoir below, catching the droplets the enchanted gems produced. This marvel hung from a metal hook with spherical heating crystals bunched like grapes to form a handle to the towering sword. The single chandelier allowed heat and fresh water for each home, Demosyna saw with wonder, and used the crystals she had sent for the construction. Tears formed in her eyes upon seeing such beautiful forms made from her hours of tiring work.

The dogs were quiet observers as the trio found the dining hall, lush with tapestries of Jade City and its double mountains. Harol's tiny canine gazed with silent, watery eyes, and Jest sat beside Demosyna's chair at a gesture from the young woman. Celestria was chatting with two generals clad in shining golden armor but excused herself once seeing her apprentice grinning across the hall.

The Wise Mother was much thinner than last Demosyna saw but beamed joyous energy while gliding over the marble floors. The old steel helmet was atop Celestria's head as always, and the linked golden veil shone in the torchlight.

"Apprentice! Welcome to the improved Jade City!" Celestria said, clasping Demosyna's hand tightly. "It seems you took your time with my instruction regarding Sai Aeri, but it sounded like fun! Good show, Demosyna! You make me ever more proud and deserve the titles you will receive shortly!"

Demosyna was tear struck at the praise, and the fairy danced above her head.

"Thank you, Wise Mother! I have come as ordered with the items you desired, Celestria."

"There will be time enough for that after dinner. You must be famished from that display I watched with your troops!"

Celestria laughed, snapping her fingers to start the meal.

There were three generals attending Celestria's feast, with Marrah, Yoila, and Demosyna rounding out the group. Harol sat with the golden-armored soldiers while discussing the latest reports from across the Fist. Celestria sat her apprentice at the right-hand position with Marrah the Jade sitting to the Wise Mother's left.

Long hours passed, and Celestria entertained the guests till the sun rose the next morning. Yoila sat in quiet dread until the sun signaled the generals into action, calling the pale-scaled woman to them. All three stood, reviewing a battlefield report from the disaster Yoila had told Demosyna of. Each of the generals was from a realm of the Fist, excluding Demosyna's newest lands of Lost Claw Bay.

Au Cell had a representative general, along with Celestria and Sai Aeri. These were the main realms of the Fist, but many smaller frontier settlements still existed in the vast wilds. Demosyna was surprised by Sai Aeri's general being present, but Celestria had called a peaceful talk with all the leaders fighting the war. Both armored generals wore jeweled platinum masks of authority, revealing nothing of their identities.

"Yoila, commander of our troops," Au Cell's general said, bearing a purple sash of silky material, "we have lost 23,000 soldiers from the failed attack on Sai Aeri's city. Your late arrival left our forces without the bulk to their support, leading to a costly retreat to Jade City."

"Why did you disobey orders, Commander?" Sai Aeri's general called, glaring at the blindfolded woman. "Those two laid out a strict timeline, but they tell me you missed the window by hours! Explain yourself."

"My orders relied on complete secrecy in taking position in the forest," Yoila said, bowing her head during the inquiry. "Sai Aeri's general had cavalry riding the valley, and I knew our cover couldn't be maintained if we engaged. Our troops outnumbered theirs greatly, but I couldn't ensure a complete routing and detoured those extra hours. I saw the remaining rebels once arriving, and covering the retreat was the only option left after seeing my failure."

"We will not abide disobedience from any soldier, commander or pawn alike," Sai Aeri's general growled, standing at ease before Yoila. "Your Wise-woman has chosen you as her personal general, but I doubt your ability to follow such complex strategies after seeing the attack I repelled. It would have driven me back, because your other generals know how to work within a chain."

"We also don't know every development that will occur and want those in command to adapt in the moment," Au Cell's general said, pacing slightly in thought. "You arrived without detection despite the 60,000 you commanded being late. My retreat was only possible due to your arrival, and you saved the remaining 10,000 soldiers I led to slaughter."

"Weather often stops any plan no matter how cunning," Harol mused, tapping the silver-tipped baton against his thigh. "Tell me, Yoila, why did you not try to finish the battle with your troops in that moment? You brought the numbers to finish Sai Aeri's forces but shielded the retreat instead. My soldiers would have been destroyed, but you would have secured our objective in little time. Why did you not keep with the original plan to conquer the city?"

Yoila considered a moment, and the room was nearly silent.

"Without soldiers, the war is lost. A city will be retaken without enough support, and I know Sai Aeri holds thousands in the lands around the target. I saw continuing the retreat was the only way to salvage both generals' armies and held the line myself in support of that decision."

"You did indeed hold your lines, Yoila," Sai Aeri's general said, eyeing the kneeling commander. "I am here to meet you off the battlefield, with Celestria holding the peace. After seeing you walk the trenches those long days, I know why Demosyna wants you as her own."

"We shall deliberate. Leave us, Yoila," Harol called, clapping the baton upon the table. "May we have the room, my Wise Mother, Celestria?"

Demosyna and Celestria had observed the debriefing, saying nothing as the generals grilled Yoila. The apprentice followed her Wise Mother outside to let Jest stretch his legs. Marrah was napping upstairs in the master bedroom and waiting for the sun to warm her golden belly.

A giant telescope was assembled in the sprawling gardens, and Celestria let her apprentice watch the morning training. The multiple lenses let Demosyna see crystal clear images at any magnification, and she watched a cannon fire toward a magically moving target. Eight rebels reloaded the artillery with precision, each one running clear after their job was done. Lightning crackled from crystal caps on each barrel and sent metal balls to shock the target into catching fire. The cannon had moved over five feet once fired, forcing several soldiers to adjust and aim the massive iron weapon before firing again.

Demosyna laughed as Celestria summoned jerky for the white dog, seeing all the tents and fires symbolizing the free armies.

"You have made a beautiful city, Wise Mother!" Demosyna said, watching the elf make Jest sit and roll over for the treat. "Do you know of Yoila's promotion? I didn't know of the defeat till arriving but still wish her as my representative."

"Those generals love their ceremony and strict codes!" Celestria exclaimed, laughing as Jest jumped high to snatch the jerky. "Yoila will be promoted, and she now understands the weight of being a general. The sun is up, so fetch your chest from that horse you tied off."

Over an hour passed in demonstrations of the apprentice's botanical magic, and Celestria tasted the produce after scanning them with spells. Pear trees were Demosyna's favorite to eat from, but she learned many types of edible crops in preparation for this reunion. Celestria cracked a pecan open with magic fingers, tasting the nut with a smile.

"Good show, apprentice. Can you make seeds yet or just grow a living plant?" the Wise Mother asked, turning the pecan shell to jerky.

Demosyna hadn't considered growing seeds and frowned.

"Only mature plants thus far, Wise Mother. It hadn't occurred to me to grow them naturally since I can produce a fruiting plant at once."

"It's as I thought. But no matter, apprentice. It isn't too difficult if you try," Celestria explained, leaning closer to Demosyna. "How did you make those boots I saw you using in your bay? It was a moment of understanding, correct?"

Demosyna nodded, displaying a boot from beneath her pristine robes.

"I knew I needed to rest at times and couldn't always use my discs. You taught me to improvise with magic during battle and use my armor as the final defense against threats. I took a gamble, but it paid off for me when I couldn't summon the elevators from fatigue."

"I noticed you design that spell and know you can learn this modification of botanical studies," Celestria told her apprentice, inspiring thoughts with her words. "Consider what the plant needs to become and impart that potential into a single seed! Focus now on compressing all the systems and growth into itself, and that is how you reach my goal, apprentice!"

Sai Aeri's general had come marching from the palace, bowing farewell to Celestria.

Demosyna walked her dog while meditating on the lesson, visualizing the new magic in her mind as she threw a ball with wind. Yoila returned to Demosyna's side, silent and nervous before the generals announced the decision. Sai Aeri's representative left before the coming declarations, but Demosyna stood by her friend when Harol spoke.

"We accept Demosyna's choice for general and welcome Yoila into our council," Harol said, handing a platinum mask to Yoila. "Rise, General Yoila!"

Yoila stood, taking the offered mask and handing it to Demosyna.

"Thank you, fellow generals. I will lead without that finery, for I only need my Wise-woman's blindfold to show myself to the enemy."

All cheered in the extravagant grounds, and Demosyna hugged her friend tightly in celebration. Celestria called the group over, having boarded a gold platform inside a sand garden. Demosyna walked the stone steps to lean on a handrail as the Wise Mother floated the group down the mountain on a golden chariot. Much of the free armies were gathered in the rising sun, and Jade City was emptied at Celestria's order to hear the announcements. Hundreds of thousands of free people cheered and applauded their leaders while Celestria boomed over the slowly silencing masses.

"I am Celestria, the Jade in the Mountain!" she proclaimed, spraying jade gemstones from open palms into the crowd feet below. "We have much to celebrate, my gentle people! Our city stands anew, and one of the rebels has risen to a place of honor!"

Thunderous noise seemed to rock the hovering gold platform since it flew close enough to let each face view the figures. Thousands of people held a valuable jade jewel above their heads while praising Celestria for the mercy. More jade blanketed the crowd during each speech, leaving over half the people with a sparkling prize.

"Yes, I present Demosyna and her general!" Celestria bellowed magically, gliding for miles before doubling back over new areas of the crowd.

Demosyna held Yoila's hand high into the air, smiling down at the figures passing with no words yet. Yoila raised her long sword aloft while shouting her victory to the troops below. Cheers of approval reached the generals, and many began chanting Yoila's name.

"Yoila! Ice Eyes! Yoila. Ice Eyes!" the crowd boomed.

The new general smiled through the tears wetting her blindfold, balancing on the railing in rare abandon. Demosyna sent fireworks into the morning air to signal thirty minutes of celebration among the swelling populace. Drums beat, horns called, and cannons roared life into the new day of progress.

Celestria smiled politely during the ruckus, bathing her people in wealth from her mountain. The other generals stood at attention with Harol occasionally waving or winking at the soldiers he commanded. Rolls barked herself hoarse from excitement in barely three hours. So great was the people's love for the rescue dogs.

"Let everyone see their faces and know their voices for the days ahead!" Celestria yelled, calming the crowd with her glance. "Yoila, general of Lost Claw Bay!"

Yoila planted the sword point down, letting Demosyna magically enhance her voice.

"I am not worthy of such an honor, but I promise to serve each soldier without fail from now on. You know me as a fellow rebel, but I ask you trust me now as a general! We will take what is ours no matter the cost, for my Wise-woman desires true harmony in our Fist! Demosyna took the last chain I shall touch from my hands and freed thousands with her mercy that day!"

Chaos erupted in the sea of jubilant faces, and Yoila touched her blade to any weapon the soldiers held up in salute. Demosyna wiped tears from her cheek and caught her fairy when it tried to push the new general off the railing. Yoila was knocked forward by the prank but balanced and spun to remain upright on the smooth railing.

Soldiers stamped their armored feet and laughed at the dexterous general, who smiled and continued tapping spears or swords along the trip. Even the citizens began chanting Yoila Ice Eyes into the air, catching the soldiers' energy after seeing the pale woman display her acrobatics.

"Thank you, Yoila," Celestria whispered to Yoila, raising her voice once more. "Now for my apprentice, Demosyna. She has been delivered to my care and will be titled Pegmatite at my word. Demosyna Pegmatite is now ruler of Lost Claw Bay, because she merges all around with her volcanic passion! Some have seen her along the Empress's Highway or in the eastern lands Lord Au Cell holds. Witness now, my free people, as Demosyna Pegmatite greets you as your lady!"

Celestria had reached the Bay residents when starting the speech to give the masses a view of the Scale. Demosyna was taken aback by her new title, having heard nothing of the name before now. It seemed fitting, for her goals were of uniting the lands, and fire would likely be the path. The crystals that magma formed often fused and melded together when growing, Demosyna knew, and wiped a tear at the thoughtful title her Wise Mother granted.

"I am Demosyna, first of the Pegmatite name! Thank you for braving something new and bold!" the purple-scaled lady called magically, holding her hands wide. "I try to always serve the needs of my people and offer my lands freely to any sharing my heart! Yoila will protect our realm, and she holds my trust completely. I study my magic still but already provide water and food to any selecting a new island residence in my bay. My Wise Mother gifted me this responsibility, and I love all who seek an end to forced bondage in our Fist!"

The crowd was cheering wildly, forcing Demosyna to pause before finishing her speech. Celestria was smiling while throwing magically summoned jade over her apprentice's population. Yoila had put her heavy sword away and stood beside her lady with formal attention.

"Much work must be done still, but I accept the challenge with an open heart!" Demosyna bellowed, sending flower petals into the wind with her magic. "The Empress cannot hold back the tide any longer, and I hear a swelling of change on the surface of the Fist! Jade City, Lost Claw Bay, and Au Cell's realm hold the entire northern lands from our enemy! Let us build something together that overshadows the Empress's realms now and for all generations to come! I am now Demosyna Pegmatite, apprentice to the Jade in the Mountain, and I give all I am for these free lands we love!"

"I have good news for your army, then, Demosyna Pegmatite," Celestria boomed, holding a trident of gold aloft. "What will you do with your earned profit from my empire? It is your duty to supply your armies, and you have many tridents waiting in my vault. I hold wealth entrusted to you from your sweat, so how shall I divide it?"

Demosyna frowned slightly but rose tall in her response.

"I give my gold pieces to aid the free rebels that protect us. Let each coin support our vision and fuel the progress I see coming over the horizon!"

"It is decided, gentle people!" Celestria exclaimed, clapping her hands in excitement. "Demosyna Pegmatite grants her tridents to the Fist that you may use them in good health! A final treat before our celebration truly begins, free folk! Rolls and Jest have returned and will greet Jade City as heroes for these days! Many were rescued by these dogs, and I present them for the festivities!"

At a signal from Harol, carts full of wine were rolled from the nearest city section to cheering crowds. Hundreds of gigantic wagons spread among the endless figures, filling skins and cups with celebration. Celestria nodded toward a spyglass in the city, and food joined the drink as the crowd thundered its adulation. Demosyna let her fairy dance slightly before the sea of faces, watching it fly circles in response to the huge volume of input. It didn't seem in the mood for pranks during her speech and only bobbed as Demosyna waved and cried in happiness. Jest barked several times into the crowd, licking the woman's cheeks and wagging feverishly.

"Good show, apprentice! One last thing, I think!" Celestria said before turning back to shower the crowd with jade. "Freebloods, hear my words! I have raised Jade City from the ashes, and Demosyna Pegmatite shall unite our lands with a gesture of peace! I shall let the lady of Lost Claw Bay sew my fields in a show of cooperation, proving harmony between realms can be achieved! Once she and I have planted the last of your crops, we shall have two days of celebration in both realms!"

A silence fell on the mountain as the hills rang with shuffling feet and held breath. Demosyna stepped forward, producing a handful of magic seeds for inspection. The apprentice had tried to produce what Celestria had instructed, and only three needed to be summoned again. Demosyna corrected the mistakes quickly, grinning in success when Celestria nodded wordlessly.

Her Wise Mother commanded Demosyna to make them till told to cease, and millions of seeds were thrown into the air by Celestria's magic. The plateau once adorned with upper-class manors now bore expanses of tilled earth and new ponds from the mountain's purge.

The fairy joined in, dancing and sending electric tendrils into Demosyna's scales. The power of the magical whiskers combined with Demosyna's, making the summoning much easier. The apprentice sent her thankful thoughts toward the fairy and felt a tickling laughter at helping with the goal.

Some of the seeds were burned away as inferior, but the majority Celestria planted over the course of an hour. Trees sprouted from each end of a row, and crops grew with magical swiftness from the fertilized soil. Demosyna watched in fascination as her seeds took root instantly, unfolding petals and leaves full of food.

The floating gold platform rose along the mountainside, dusting the city sectors with new plant life. Each waiting figure watched the magical display, barely a breath escaping the rapt faces. The generals remained at attention as they, too, circled the mountain as disciplined statues of authority for those below. Fatigue barely registered to the apprentice when Celestria clapped her shoulder to signal the young woman to stop planting.

Quakes that rivaled the volcano shook the land as over a million feet stamped the earth in celebration. Energy beyond measure overtook the people, and days of revel were enjoyed by all. Celestria took the golden chariot back to the mountain, leaving the free folks to their well-earned days of peace. Each general went back to their respective armies, but Yoila stayed at Demosyna's side as the party unfolded.

The young apprentice floated down the first day, joining Yoila in meeting much of the Bay's army. There was no way of remembering all the faces and names, but Demosyna tried to greet each who clamored for attention. Celestria spent the second day with her apprentice, praising the good work done with the crops. The Wise Mother toured the city sectors with Demosyna, drinking and laughing with any crossing their paths the second day. Salt fleas would soon devastate her bay for years, but Demosyna reveled in the days of ignorant happiness.

CHAPTER 36

Demosyna found diplomacy particularly tedious in the months of study in Jade City but pushed on with Celestria's instruction. The twin days of celebration had uplifted the spirits of half the Fist, and the bulk of each army returned to active duties. Hills and streams emptied of training squads, and Marrah the Jade welcomed the renewed peace in the air. Yoila took her new army north to Lost Claw Bay with the apprentice kissing five facial scars in private farewell. The two brave canines were cheered whenever roaming Jade City from that day on, trailing Demosyna with wolfish grins.

Celestria spent much time alone in the ancient catacombs she guarded, studying the cryptic top floor deeply when not teaching her apprentice. There were not many dignitaries in the Fist, and most lived in New Empress City, but Demosyna studied hard on the ceremonial subject.

"I know it can be daunting, apprentice. But the Empress has ruled for time beyond measure and wishes her world to behave in certain ways," Celestria explained patiently, seeing the bewilderment on Demosyna's face. "Table settings, proper titles, historical context of alliances, or correct dressage technique—so many things add up to a regal air, apprentice. We must uphold these values for tradition's sake, as the people need a royal figure to follow still."

"How goes your studies of the ruins?" Demosyna asked, turning a densely worded page. "Did the water damage the floors?"

"No, for the walls hold the memory of what the rooms should be!" Celestria said, her opalescent eyes sparkling. "It is astounding what the ancient weavers accomplished, and you saw the walls vanish before that projection. The entire mountain was preparing for the purging of water and hid the rooms outside physical space while the flood occurred. Only after the lava sealed the topmost floor did the water fill the walls again, leaving identical ruins behind. Even the crossbows we took have returned and those odd stone cradles."

"Have you found anything about my fairy, Wise Mother?" the newly appointed lady asked, watching the gem pull books from shelves. "It is still wild but in an infantile way."

"I have not, apprentice. That is something that bugs me still, for I have no idea where to start with that creature," Celestria said, fixing the mess with a snap. "That magical display may hold answers, but it likely will result in another flood if I try to duplicate it. I will study the top floor slowly and evacuate my city before trying anything major again. Marrah has suffered my absence enough lately, and I do not wish to deny her longer than necessary!"

* * * * *

Spring had finally arrived, and Rrra was satisfied with his latest batch of wine grown under Au Cell's Highway. Small barrels arrived in major cities, shipped far throughout the Fist using the human lord's trading empire. Demosyna had remained in written contact with Jui over the months, and the green-scaled woman eventually thanked the apprentice for her secret help.

Jui was smart and had deduced that the increased farm the pair was gifted had been Demosyna's doing. The resilient woman had been upset, but over the weeks of letters, Demosyna apologized for the deception. A last series of slow correspondence informed Demosyna she was welcome to visit and try the reserve Rrra had produced.

Celestria allowed the diversion, seeming eager for the extra time in solitude to pore over the ruins. Demosyna traveled alone with only the two faithful dogs keeping her company on the long journey. The purple-robed lady rode north initially, taking a slow path back to Lost Claw Bay. The apprentice was sidetracked for a day, escorting a family to the harbor, letting the children ride her massive gold horse.

Vaash was ecstatic when his three-legged dog came bounding over the beach, barking blindly at the yellow-robed man. Demosyna stayed the night to tell Vaash of her official position, and both marveled at the fortunate induction. The smiling monk led his old hound through Demosyna's personal acres, waving goodbye as she took Jest toward Au Cell's land.

Long stretches were becoming second nature to Demosyna, and the apprentice took a break from crystal growing on the way. The lady paid workers to mine in her absence while asking Yoila to oversee the operation between general duties. Thousands of raw crystals would greet the returning woman, but Demosyna enjoyed the solitude after being around so many in Jade City.

Jest sprinted along beside the horse, chasing golden horseshoes to run his energy away, and the fairy stayed content inside its metal house. After the surprise help the fairy had given Demosyna making seeds, it seemed to enjoy assisting in magic whenever it fancied. Whiskers of solid light would scrape against purple head scales, sending powerful energy coursing into Demosyna.

"Thank you, fairy! That was a very kind thing, helping my silly Jest," Demosyna called, seeing the creature heal Jest's cut paw with violet light. "Jest says thank you too!"

The knee-high dog gave a short bark, grinning and running with the ever friendlier fairy. Laughter carried the small group southeast, crossing undeveloped miles of woods and small mountains.

Au Cell had returned to his kingdom after many years of undisclosed travel with a vision. Any decrees issuing from his realm suggested great building was underway, but Demosyna only saw the projects once reaching Au Cell's Highway.

Acres of grapes were overseen by Rrra, his orange scales glowing from pride. Half of a massive winery complex was built already with clearly marked areas surveyed for expansion. Demosyna leashed her canine, dismounting to walk the last miles in observation.

Rrra greeted the lady, bowing formally before bursting into laughter.

"Demosyna Pegmatite, I remember you giving those fish heads to Bhreel and trying to dry yourself fast! It seems a lifetime ago, but my days are spent as they should be now! Wine is in my blood, my birthers always said!"

"Thank you for showing me your fields, Rrra! I have land yet to be sewn, if you ever wish to franchise into my bay!" Demosyna said, eating the offered grape. "Did you need help with anything today in your process?"

Rrra led the silk-robed young woman to a three-story barn, and both Scales used the crane to hoist barrels for aging. When Demosyna's muscles burned after hours of hauling and moving, magic shifted the final day's pressing of juices. Demosyna was able to easily transport dozens of casks at once, and Rrra watch in wide-eyed shock.

"Can you make rings for my workers that let them lift like that?" Rrra asked, looking at the gold ring Demosyna had retrieved from Jade City. "I see the advantages of magic now and would gladly purchase them for my workers! Jui can work out the details, but let's view the juicers next!"

The presses were corkscrew pillars set in the roof with wooden discs flush against massive barrels underneath. Demosyna offered to grow a series of crystal presses, and Rrra agreed without a second thought. Banded wooden tubs could develop leaks, Rrra explained, so Demosyna produced sturdy vessels with diamond hard presses atop. Spouts at the bottom let valves control the flow precisely, just as Demosyna was used to in her crystal workshop.

Jui had found the two from inside her office, hugging the young lady and watching the magic streamline their presses.

"I got your last letter, but you took your sweet time!"

Jui laughed, testing the screw function of a new press.

"I expected you two days ago. Did you get lost chasing your fairy?"

"No, I just walked the last leg to enjoy the view!" Demosyna replied, watching the purple fairy observe some grapes being loaded.

"It's so good to see each of you! It looks like things are taking off for your business! Congratulations, both of you!"

Demosyna had briefly told Jui about her fairy through the frequent letters passed along at mail stations.

Jui demonstrated the dumping of grapes from a bucket to the orb and laughed when it spilled half into the transparent crystal press. Rrra was measuring the surface of the round tubs, marking specific levels for future use with a leather ruler.

Workers moved to clean the spilled grapes, but the fairy dumped three buckets at once over the half-closed press. Loose fruit spilled everywhere, and the laughing fairy returned at Demosyna's call. The young apprentice helped clean the spillage with tingling giggles running across her skull.

"That's what I like about wine, Demosyna!" Rrra said over the central firepit in his home. "Now all we do is wait!"

Jui had said the same words almost at the same time as her mate. Laughter filled their wooden house, and Jui busied herself with papers and ink. Missing fingers made writing more difficult, but Jui's penmanship had improved at each successive letter those past months.

A fresh page was laid out, and Jui asked the details of Demosyna's offer to expand west.

"What will the annual rental for the acres be, Demosyna Pegmatite?" Jui began, starting to draw up a few lines. "And the tax on the production? Lord Au Cell gives a reasonable rate of 40 percent for the combined figures, and we offer him wholesale costs for his purchases."

Demosyna considered but smiled after a moment of thought.

"I charge nothing for use of the soil, and my lands only take taxes on purchased goods. Yoila and I worked out a trial structure, and all sold goods are taxed below 5 percent. I offer my own raw items, food or trees or water, for free through official channels! The only cost involved would be your harvesting or transporting fees, for the workers must be compensated! Your profits will be yours to keep, as I fund my realm with sales income and personal crystal profits."

"I have seen your prices are below market value as well. Interesting!" Jui replied, smearing ink on her green chin in thought. "Do you not want more than tax from our buying wood or grapes? That is an intriguing proposal, and I cannot pass it up! Rrra, we will need to pack soon to scout the Bay!"

Rrra and the fairy seemed bored of the dry financial discussion, and the orange-scaled man fetched a small barrel to share. Demosyna nodded at Jui's initial draft of the contract, and the two women joined Rrra outside. Midnight starlight lit the way for each sharp-eyed friend, and the three shared the refined wine Rrra had made.

It was superior in taste to the smuggled wine last year, and Demosyna toasted the man with a smile. Rrra's reserve was only for his family or select clients, like Au Cell and now Demosyna. The young lady asked for several barrels shipped to Lost Claw Bay and Jade City knowing Celestria and Marrah would enjoy the strong drink.

"What can you put as a down payment?" Jui asked, jotting down a quick purchase order. "Actually, those presses you made will do nicely! We can work out an exchange for their value later. I just want to finish this barrel! What do you say, Rrra?"

Demosyna was worried for a moment, for the lady carried no gold whenever she traveled. The rainbow chest was almost empty of coin, because funding a rebel army took considerable wealth. Little actual currency was owned by Demosyna, but such was her wish in giving what she could. The newfound magic her Wise Mother taught provided nearly any need, and Demosyna happily funded her realm out of pocket.

"That is good to hear, because I only carry three points lately!" Demosyna said, holding the triangular coins between clawed fingers. "It reminds me of my bakery, long destroyed in the far south. Celestria teaches creation as needed, and I have taken to that philosophy as her apprentice! I didn't even consider payments when I asked. Sorry, Jui!"

The misstep was waved away, and the fairy darted toward the ruins of the Highway with a buzz. Demosyna followed the creature, letting Jest wander on the long leash. Nobody was awake at the late hour, and the three revelers gaped at the fairy when it merged with Au Cell's Highway. Demosyna rushed forward, dropping her cup and clawing at the spot the crystal disappeared. No sign of the fairy remained, just a stone surface, as in the mountain ruins. The young apprentice ran here and there along the wall, but to no avail.

"No! Where could it have gone?" Demosyna said in a harsh tone, almost to herself. "I've seen it teleport twice before, but it flew straight into the rock like the guardians! No, no, no!"

"What?" Rrra asked, joining in on the search. "Guardians?"

Demosyna shook her head, focusing only on finding her lost fairy. The group had been walking and drinking for hours, and the sun would rise shortly. Lark opened the golden stall, and Demosyna sprinted over in near panic.

"Can you fetch Au Cell please!" the young Wizen panted, not taking her eyes from the stone. "It's urgent and regards his Highway!"

A strong horse was mounted, and Lark rode east at full gallop after seeing Demosyna's distress. Au Cell returned, flying fast across the black sky, to find Demosyna Pegmatite scratching at the stone.

"Lady Demosyna, how may I help?" Au Cell said, donning his tiara after landing. "Is something wrong with the Highway?"

"My fairy entered the stone comprising your highway, Lord Au Cell!" Demosyna panted, trying to calm her mind. "What do you know of this structure?"

Au Cell waved all the onlookers away while letting Lark usher them out of earshot. Jui and Rrra stopped their search, walking with Demosyna to hear the human lord.

"It stood long before any of our ancestors were born," Au Cell whispered. "Those I returned from talks with have knowledge of that very subject. I sought them out for that purpose, because I have joined the immortals in searching to master my realm. I cannot tell you more than that, Demosyna, for they are secretive by nature. I have yet to be allowed knowledge of dwarven relics, but that is what I was told the Highway is."

"That makes sense, Au Cell," Demosyna said, frowning. "I explored the mountain topping Jade City months ago and saw brown fairies vanish into the solid stone walls there too! That would confirm a relation if my fairy can meld with this rock. I was hoping you could open it or have greater know-how than I."

"I cannot do as you ask, Demosyna, since I study the secrets in my own ways," Au Cell said, moving into the stables. "I shall run the inside miles and look for any sign of your fairy. Lark, delay any business till further notice. Nobody is to disturb us here, so assemble a guard immediately!"

The violet-clothed assistant heard the shout from a distance and bustled off at Au Cell's command.

Demosyna hovered on her purple disc, letting Rrra and Jui join the flying search. None of the levels above the vanishing spot bore sign of the fairy, and Demosyna held back tears of frustration.

The sun rose and fell, leaving Demosyna without success in her frantic search. The young woman tried spells on the surface, hoping to lure or signal the trapped fairy. Nothing marred the color of the timeless stones, even when powerful lightning was blasted into the Highway in a rage.

"What is wrong with me?" Demosyna nearly shouted, ignoring the blood dripping from her hand. "I am still so useless. I lost it already!"

Jui saw the damage the grown band of crystal had done when the welding magic exploded the ring with its force. The apprentice's right hand was impaled by shrapnel, but Demosyna ignored the small pain. Jest whined in his throat, nuzzling against the furious Wizen with his tail tucked. Demosyna sighed deeply to calm herself, healing the cuts with weary magic.

Au Cell returned hours after sundown, sweaty and running back from miles of travel. No sign was reported by the lord, and Demosyna asked to stay till the fairy was recovered.

"I would assume nothing else, Demosyna," Au Cell said, nodding. "Stay as long as you wish. Both our harbors support new land for use thanks to our swift action. It would honor me to host the lady of Lost Claw Bay!"

Demosyna thanked her friends for their help.

"I will wait here if you wish to rest in your houses. Thank you, Lord Au Cell, and you, Jui and Rrra! I will not forget your kindness and will let Lark know of any further needs."

A deep rumbling came from below the broken tracks centered on the ranches, and Demosyna dropped to all fours instinctively. The quake was focused on the spot where the fairy vanished, and the earth began to open wide. It was several feet ahead of where the tracks broke apart, and Au Cell ran forward to investigate.

Jui and Rrra stayed behind at Demosyna's advice while the apprentice approached a large square of darkness. Tracks lined the floor of the pit, and both rulers gasped at the train resting on spotless rails. The metal resembled Au Cell's strange round boat but squared with geared wheels on top and bottom. Purple light approached from the rear, revealing empty metal boxcars with the fairy's brilliance. Demosyna jumped down at once before catching herself on a platform with a cry of joy.

"Fairy! Where did you go?" Demosyna whispered, letting the gem cartwheel along her arm. "I was really worried!"

Au Cell floated down, a dark-red cape fluttering slightly.

"What has your fairy uncovered? These tracks lead east and west, likely the length of the Fist! If it runs under the Empress's Highway too, we must maintain this secret, my lady!"

"Was there ever a train on the first-floor levels?" Demosyna pondered aloud, lighting the train with multiple spheres of magic. "I saw tracks in the Empress's like your Highway has in the ranches, but no locomotives!"

The lord shook his gold-flaked hair in response, sniffing the air and watching for traps. Au Cell seemed an adventurer in his posture, and Demosyna followed by crawling slowly along. Ten large cars left the pair facing an endless shot of tracks, perfectly straight east into the dark underground. No conductor room was found at either end, and Demosyna whispered to Au Cell in the echoing tunnel.

"I can fetch Celestria in only a few days' time!" the lady said, grinning a sharp-toothed smile. "That horse you bred is marvelous, Lord Au Cell!"

"I chose carefully and contracted the best breeder in the Fist!" Au Cell breathed, smiling. "If you have the resources, I found collecting what was needed easy with proper planning! It's the same with every aspect of my realm. I hire the best available to fill the role I may be lacking. Trusting in their wisdom for the craft is good business, and I typically submit to their recommendation for specifics. That is why Rrra has become a focus for me. His wine is golden for my tastes and sells well!"

Jui and Rrra peered over the edge, so Demosyna lowered the mates as they gawked. The empty subway seemed safe, because magic Celestria taught found no harmful energies. Empty squares served as windows in each car, and the fairy laughed during the second inspection. The walls of the metal train were uniform, without seams or decorations on the surfaces.

Lines of text were absent, but Demosyna steadied herself as the fairy woke the ancient railway. All four explorers grabbed for support as the train shot forward, moving west at an incredible speed.

"Fairy! Please stop the train!" Demosyna called, as the gemstone had vanished into the metal. "Come back from that wall please!"

Au Cell and the winemakers stared out the small windows, watching rock walls move past ten feet away. Wind rushed from the lead car through the empty doorway, and Demosyna grew a crystal to plug the hole. It was silent in its running, and all the passengers rode the train with wide eyes. No tales told of such inventions, and the fairy returned when the train began coasting. It laughed and flipped through the air above Demosyna's head when the subway stopped in near darkness.

"Where have you taken us, fairy?" Demosyna asked, scanning the range of her magic light orbs.

Stairs formed behind the caboose, and the party saw starlight pour into the tunnel. Au Cell and Demosyna led the way, and Lost Claw Bay was spotted in the north from the exit stairs. Vaash was sprinting toward the disturbance, as a slight rumble had occurred as the walls shifted into level stone stairs. The fairy returned to its chain mail screen, lighting a pastel crown from the links.

"Demosyna, can you tunnel with your magic now?" Vaash asked, looking at where the hole closed up. "That is amazing, my friend!"

Demosyna laughed, pointing at her head.

"The fairy discovered a wonder, Vaash! Would you like to ride a train underground? We would be the first in millennia, I have no doubt!"

"Let me fetch Celestria, if you would wait here. The stairs reverted, it seems, so nobody will stumble on it while I'm gone!" Au Cell spoke up, gazing toward Jade City.

The gold-armored human flew away, leaving the mystified party to discuss the events. Vaash was informed of all the known facts, and he listened with a furrowed brow. Theories were passed around, but Demosyna spoke up as the two rulers flew back from the double mountain.

"There is no way for us to know, unfortunately," Demosyna said, frowning at the mystery. "Let's see what Celestria has to say and maybe take the thing back to Au Cell's Highway."

"Show me this train!" Celestria called, making a crater where she landed. "Where is it, apprentice?"

Demosyna lifted the fairy from its perch, sending an image of thought in hope of communication. The stairs opened after a breathless moment, formed just like the image Demosyna held in her mind's eye. Celestria boarded the train, not caring about the others following.

"Curious," Celestria muttered, scanning the train with care.

The helmet the Wise Mother wore sprouted crystal in the eye-holes, their faces rotating during the inspection. Waves of light filled the ten cars, and Celestria tested the metal against hundreds of magics. The fairy laughed audibly the entire short exploration with tendrils vibrating in the dead, still air. Au Cell leaned against the wall, and Jui joined Rrra in preparing for another sudden start. Demosyna held the orb to the metal caboose, but it darted to the first car before vanishing.

"I see. Everyone, come quickly!" Celestria called behind her.

The train started moving as the last passenger entered the car, and Celestria was bent over, studying the fairy's entry point. A crystal had darkened black on a final raw gem, so Demosyna showed the thieves' sign band to her Wise Mother.

"Very interesting, apprentice!" Celestria said, poking the wall with an unset gem. "I saw the type of magic your pixie used, but it was so fast and strange. Let me try this!"

Their train was heading southwest along the Empress's Highway, streaming ahead at horrendous speeds. The Wise-women glassed over the windows and doors while leaving air holes in the back doorways. Celestria estimated mere hours passing before the last of the tracks was seen, huge marble pillars blocking an end of the line. They criss-crossed like the ones aboveground, and the fairy reappeared once the coasting ceased.

No sooner had it landed on Demosyna's head than the tunnel walls turned to glass, revealing the nearly rising sun. Guards and wag-ons marched in the air, visible through the solid rock separating the train. It was a one-way image, for after some worry, Au Cell noticed the lack of interest in a train appearing. Elevators rose and fell, and Demosyna saw the first southern stop along the enormous highway again.

"They are linked after all!" Celestria said, turning to Au Cell with a grin. "Just as we thought, Lord Au Cell!"

Demosyna felt an urge from the fairy and let it fly away toward the transparent stones. Pink light caressed the surface before color returned to the tunnel in a wave outward from the whisker.

"With this new transport, my shipping will be golden!"

Au Cell boomed laughter, clapping Demosyna's shoulder.

The trip back was powered by Celestria, who had observed the fairy and duplicated the magic after careful meditation. This tickled the fairy, who swung from a horn inside the metal home. Speeds were increased by Demosyna after feeling the magic flow into the metal caboose from Celestria's instruction. This allowed the train to travel nearly the entire Fist, from south to northeast.

Much talk was had by the lord and ladies in private, with the others walking the train carefully. What to do with the train was a problem, for it crossed all four major realms during its passage. Recent studies in diplomacy let the young apprentice keep pace with the plans, trying to find a viable answer to satisfy each ruler's needs.

"The stone walls are triangular on either side below as well," Celestria said, scanning the side of the tunnel. "That would make it a honeycomb shape overall, with the top floors being twin half spheres. Curious. The hollow basement walls are filled with water as well!"

Demosyna had images of falling for miles surface, imagining the tunnel flooding with water.

"Wise Mother, are we safe here? Your mountain flooded during our last exploration, and only three here can breathe underwater!"

"No, that's not true, apprentice," Celestria called, sitting down to rest. "It looks like Au Cell has extended life for himself at last! Neither of us should have trouble if it comes to that, so don't fear our peril! You or I could get Vaash to safety with our magics in a pinch. I also see no sign of a control room, and I feel it is just a train for the moment!"

"Good, because our armies can use this as near-instant ways to travel!"

Au Cell grinned, watching the tracks fly away behind.

"If we divide the carts between soldiers and cargo, we can move in silence anywhere we need! We will no longer need to bow and scrape to the Empress for transport and let my lands trade in safety!"

"My crystals will fit through the doors if I narrow their diameter," Celestria said, making paper for notes. "We can test the weight limits for the train, but I feel it will hold whatever we try to haul!"

"I want Vaash in charge of the subway, for he holds no ties, except maybe to me," Demosyna said suddenly, sensing the fairy talking about Jest. "He is the only free person I know who can be trusted not to abuse or turn sides with the knowledge. We should use the subway to reinvigorate Three Paws Park by turning it into a mobile circus once more! Wounded and any fleeing north can find cover in the guarded park, for each of our armies shall provide security for the train. Profit can be had by all involved, and safe travel for soldiers and freed slaves will be assured!"

"Yes, I can see the form this tide is taking!" Au Cell said, grinning with his golden-painted eyes shining. "If we have the civilian stops at my highway, Jade City, and Cripple Cavern, we limit the true scope of the subway in the public mind. Dogs are a wonderful cover for moving troops, Demosyna, for such a profitable carnival would need many guards! Families and covert soldiers will soon stream under the Fist, because I like what I hear!"

"That would be a grand gesture to the park, as the Empress still controls the region its contract allows," Celestria said, nodding in thought. "Word of our dedication to peace will spread, and I may be able to replicate these cars aboveground eventually. The tracks are there in your stables, Au Cell. We just need to utilize them! Good show, Demosyna Pegmatite. I see you are thinking as a true Wisewoman, ruling your realm with a careful hand!"

"Thank you, Wise Mother!" the young lady said, blushing. "Vaash had asked months ago to help in a peaceful way, and I finally found a solution! I'm sure details must be refined, but I know we can use this find to our advantage. A complimentary ticket will ensure slaves' safety, and all others will surely love the canines! We are coasting again. Maybe we have reached your highway, Au Cell!"

Celestria had experimented during the discussions by slowing and stopping the train at random times. Her understanding of the magic increased over the hours of travel, and Celestria grew a ring of dark crystal as a key. It was a similar color as the dark metal walls and was enchanted to fit Vaash's fingers only.

Demosyna and Celestria could power the train, but Au Cell trusted that they would leave the conducting to Vaash as agreed. Each ruler was on friendly terms that night and would amicably discuss the way ahead over the next days. Stairs appeared from the point of departure, and Jest bounded down with a bark of worry. Demosyna had nearly forgotten the dog in her exploration but calmed his shaking with affection for the beast.

"This one would be honored, Demosyna!" Vaash exclaimed, tears forming in his eyes. "Thank you, my friend! This would be a fitting retirement for my Order. That it would! Another with the spark may be found along my tracks, but this one loves whatever life brings! My way will not be truly lost if the ancient masters found it once before."

Vaash had seen the dismay caused by his words and reassured Demosyna with a smile. Au Cell dispersed the guards several hundred yards away, well outside sight or sound of the subway. Jui and Rrra promised their silence, and Jui told the apprentice she would send contracts soon.

Celestria floated the group toward Lost Claw Bay, forming a bubble of magic to fly northwest. Vaash was given the enchanted train key and wore the gift evermore on his left hand.

Au Cell stayed inside during the daytime talks but walked with the ladies across Demosyna's private beach at nightly negotiations. Yoila was summoned after weeks of discussion, and the generals were informed of the newest gift to the war in the Fist.

CHAPTER 37

The First Fort was the final major source of imperial influence in the continental Fist, and Sai Aeri ruled with unflinching control. Slaves dominated each city in the southern realm, polishing the aesthetics of traditional Empress lifestyle. Massive tracts of land reaching to Three Paws Park were under the general's command for eons, leaving Sai Aeri drowning in land and influence. The subway opened after many secret preparations, causing a massive increase in travel and trade north of Cripple Cavern. Xi Xi's city was the first stop on the rails, and Vaash walked the large cars with dozens of canine attendants.

Celestria announced the opening with Au Cell and Demosyna present, claiming the three built a subway for the Fist. It was a small lie, but Demosyna Pegmatite had to practice before the story became more true in her voice. The young lady saw little of Vaash after that opening day at Three Paws Park, watching him board the subway with the initial load of carnival goers.

The reveal of the tracks happened at that halfway point along the Empress's Highway, leading to further days of celebration across the Fist. Vaash set the guidelines for the carnival train, the lone monk running the entire operation without issue. Wealth came back to Xi Xi's town, and the elf commander sent a white flag north to Demosyna. The young lady would find her at the First Fort, the letter said, and Xi Xi marched most of her army south till her contract expired.

"Jui has begun surveying your lands, my Wise-woman," Yoila said, marking a note off her list of news. "She shall have what acres she needs, per your wishes. I have set aside a small island as their winery, near the beach in the freshwater half of your bay! Fresh shoes are needed for my cavalry, so I am hiring blacksmiths for the new forge on the capital island. Guards are no longer allowed more than clubs summoned by Wizen if needed in the field, as you commanded. Thank you, my lady, for continuing to set these crystals once your returned to your bay!"

Demosyna traveled between Jade City and her bay during the summer months, learning from Celestria and tending her realm in equal measure. The apprentice rode with whoever wished her company but often found Jest and her fairy the only companions under the stars.

Demosyna had returned early to spend a few weeks in her bay, letting the miners take their scheduled leave. They were kept on retainer and worked whenever the lady was summoned and couldn't grow crystals herself.

"Excellent, but make sure our fields expand with the growing needs!" Demosyna called, setting the crystals that floated around her. "Au Cell seems focused on Rrra's winery, but I wish to continue offering crops to any who can get here! I will help my friends, but not at the cost of my realm's needs. Continue sending the bulk to the soldiers and cities, selling what is needed to harvest and move the supplies!"

"Of course, my Wise Mother. Your cities swell with new citizens, reaching your lands with the neutral subway active."

Yoila nodded, writing notes on the stacks of papers.

"My troops occupy Cripple Cavern after its commander went south to reinforce Sai Aeri, and the park mostly moved to the subway. New Empress City and the First Fort are among the last remaining strongholds due to your generosity and love."

Celestria's general drove strict discipline into each person among the rebels, bringing soldiers together with trust and new tactics.

Battles dragged on at times from Demosyna's insistence on healing any injured during lulls in the slaughter. Casualties grew less a factor in the combat, and the rebels fought with endless supplies to keep them supported.

Au Cell and Celestria had vast stores of wealth at their disposal, and Demosyna paid her soldiers from profit at her bay. The young lady hadn't begun amassing tridents yet with her expenses but ignored the small issue while the war raged.

"You said the high command readies for the attack on the First Fort? Good!" Demosyna said, reading the letter from Celestria again. "I am allowed to help you in the battle, my Wise Mother writes! I am told to rely on our soldiers but aid as needed during the siege. That is great news, Yoila, since I have learned much over these last months from you and Celestria!"

"I agree, my Wise-woman, and would welcome your assistance. I, too, advise letting our war engine handle the Fort, however," Yoila said, kneeling in her yellow crystal house. "You have grown stronger than Sai Aeri, but it is my place to fight this war! I thank you for your presence for myself and the troops, Demosyna Pegmatite. They grow to love you as I do and fight with passion for your desires!"

Jest rolled on his back, and the fairy tickled the dog's belly with whiskers of purple light. Demosyna smiled, surrounded by peace and crystals each night she stayed in her bay. The fairy didn't set gems or conjure seeds but now helped Demosyna with energizing scrapes of lightning. It also grew fonder of Jest, and the two were seen running tirelessly while they played.

Yoila's newest house was on the edge of Demosyna's realm, away from any water, to mark a halfway point to Jade City. Demosyna let her dog run across borders of the realms, the far distant caravan lines ignored by the trained animal.

"I will leave a reserve to guard Lost Claw Bay, but we march to the subway after the last troops are moved south, my Wise-woman," Yoila said, walking with Demosyna back to her apprentice halls. "You will be told the week to prepare, but small numbers of soldiers already travel each night when the carnival closes. It won't take long to move the forces, with the speed Vaash achieves from his subway!

519

Hours are all that is needed to move down, not weeks as before the lords and ladies granted its use. All Freebloods thank you, my lady Demosyna Pegmatite."

The red trim glistened like magma, waving their purple-and-pink layers in the hot summer air. Demosyna regularly grew sweaty from the heavy silk fabric in her realm but withstood the discomfort out of pride at the robes. The young apprentice owned almost no possessions besides her clothes, having learned to make what was desired.

Her crutch, a broken compass, and the mortar and pestle Vaash returned with lined Demosyna's mantle. Little else was kept in the crystal-patched halls of Demosyna's manor save what was needed to cook food or grow gems in the workshop. Celestria took nearly all the hidden rooms to Jade City, leaving the bookshelf and workshop materials for the roaming apprentice. Packing was easy during the round-trip study the lady took to, and Demosyna wasn't interest in lavish decorations or finery like Celestria taught.

Vaash purchased rugs for the dogs usually around his house, and Yoila enjoyed hanging ocean paintings from the yellow walls of hers. The lady encouraged their comfort spending, from courtly income, seeing the pleasure each took from simple amenities. The monk returned from long stretches working the subway, taking the day of rest to visit Demosyna with his dogs.

Fall approached the warm waters of her bay, and Demosyna learned metal growing from Celestria. The Wise Mother attempted to duplicate the metal walls of the ancient train, teaching the apprentice specific metallic properties.

"Melting point and boiling point must be considered, apprentice. At this altitude, the numbers for such figures will change from those at sea level in your bay," Celestria instructed, making a huge new workshop in Jade City with Demosyna. "Some liquids will be boiling hot when running the pipes, and the tubes must heat without warping. Use an appropriate material for the job, because metal is easier than crystal to grow! I have gifted you the secret, but only we can grow crystals in the entire world!"

"That looks quite close to dwarven metal we have seen, Wise Mother! It is stunning work!" Demosyna observed, drawing lead from the walls in her lessons. "The alloy must be complex indeed if you struggle with the recipe. I will assist you whenever my skill improves enough to grasp that strange a material."

"I will retire for a month or ten soon to be with my Jade," Celestria announced, producing a red-tinted metal box that was almost right. "That is why I grant you leave to witness your army take the First Fort. These last days in my city have taxed me, so wait for my summons after the battle, apprentice. Continue this new branch of metallurgy study while I am secluded, and I expect progress in each type of natural metal in my journals!"

That day had been the last direct lessons Celestria passed on to the apprentice for some time, and Demosyna relished the extra days to visit her friends. Yoila was surprised from the weeks-early return but gave the apprentice reports as both tended the grounds. Demosyna had been daydreaming about metal lessons but returned when Yoila took the last crystals from the previous weeks of mining. Demosyna nodded, thinking a moment about the general's question.

"I can grow them crystal presses again if Rrra is free this week," Demosyna said, wiping her forehead with a rag from the focusing charm setting. "The design should be better than the first try, with glass seals and metal fittings! Let Jui decide what they are worth to her, and we can exchange for their reserve batch once value is assigned! Would you like a new sword, Yoila?"

"Would it have to be a simple blade, my lady Demosyna?" Yoila replied, fiddling with the blindfold in her pale hands. "I would challenge Sai Aeri with her own weapon if you can make a bladed pole arm! Any weapon you make will guide my hand to victory, but I wish to train with my enemy's tool to understand her."

Vaash was consulted on his day off, along with the master blacksmiths Au Cell recommended for Lost Claw Bay. Demosyna grew and forged a seven-foot-tall metal pole and used magic to fold the blade multiple times in the furnace. Yoila watched the day of forging, blue silk eyes following Demosyna as the young woman quenched the metal in her bay.

Diamond-filled stones honed and polished the weapon magically during the flight back. Demosyna stepped from her platform with a generational tower of command, gleaming with refinement. Three crystals were grown in the mirror finish, providing useful options Demosyna had found for battle.

"General Yoila, observe your new standard's functions," Demosyna said, presenting the finished metal before a personal guard of rebels. "Healing, acid, and wind. Acid will form on the blade, melting any assault. Healing will keep everyone whole, able to save your soldiers. I give you wind to save yourself so you will return to me with this arm I grant."

Demosyna planted the dense metal staff in the sand, activating the wind crystal with a finger near the point of balance. A tornado shot from the bottom, pushing Demosyna up with the powerful wind magic. By angling the long weapon, the tornado carried the lady any direction with strong arms controlling the inverted cyclone.

The user of the weapon needed great strength to hang with one arm on the magic, but Demosyna trained with Yoila and knew the woman's dedication. Jade City's balancing mountain had given the lady the idea, and she hovered feet above the kneeling general.

"I will train with you, General Yoila!" Demosyna said, lowering back down. "So all are prepared when facing Sai Aeri."

Yoila had not sparred with Celestria or Demosyna in months, busy with her command and travel. Martial discipline was still instructed before Celestria's temporary withdrawal, but Demosyna had missed the daily workouts. The rebel soldiers saluted their general, and Yoila accepted the refined pole arm with a bow. It was feet taller than the general, but the balance was perfect after months of practicing with master class weapons. Razor-sharp elven alloy spun through the air, and Yoila twirled the pole with skilled hands.

"Send word south. Lost Claw Bay will be ready for the siege in three weeks' time," Yoila called, using both hands to grasp the balancing point of wind. "I will take her fort using Sai Aeri's vile tools against the general! Let all the Fist know, Lady Demosyna comes with her Yoila and Freebloods!"

Demosyna didn't mind losing in the sparring practice, and Yoila refused to give up from being knocked to the dirt. The rebels watched the daily duels, cheering their general on with her unfamiliar weapon practice. Reach was a concern for Demosyna, and she struggled to close the seven-foot distance afforded to the pole arm.

Weaknesses were found in both women's tools for battle while reflexes developed to compensate during the weeks. Yoila had little option for close combat and used the pole for defense in those tight-quarter duels. Any who wished joined in the feverish practices, yet none could match their general's blindfolded skills but Demosyna.

"This one wishes you safe travels and will watch these lands each rest day!" Vaash said, helping the two Scales pack. "Demosyna, trust in your general, and she will secure your vision! This one will watch Jest till you return from the First Fort, so know he will be safe."

"I will meet you at the subway, my Wise-woman," Yoila called, leaving Demosyna in her manor. "Your fleet awaits you boarding west of Cripple Cavern, and I will see you inside the First Fort!"

Demosyna had worked with Celestria to armor the rebel fleets, leaving the ships low in the ocean with their decks nearly water level. Shipments of metal sheets flowed for weeks before the launch, grown with care by the ladies of the north. The young Wise-woman hadn't seen the newly fortified ships, but the short ride on Vaash's train deposited Demosyna at Cripple Cavern.

"Thank you again, Vaash!" Demosyna said, leaving Jest with the monk. "I will meet you at my bay in scant weeks' time!"

Cannons greeted from circular turrets, and Demosyna boarded the heavily armored lead ship waiting in the harbor. The ocean's sway took the apprentice south toward the First Fort, and she stood on deck the entire trip. No snow had fallen upon the Fist as the seasons cooled, but winter was creeping through the air again when the rebels surrounded Sai Aeri's fort. The fairy atop her head walked slow paths between her horns, and Demosyna had to watch as the rebels engaged Sai Aeri's troops.

Bloody ocean battles took Demosyna ever south, piercing into the blockades stationed as delays for the rebel navy. Wind and healing forced the imperial soldiers to swim to shore, with the apprentice summoning ferrous balls as ammunition for rebel cannons. Animals sped away once imperial riders were dispatched, and moon squid floated into the wilds again. Sails caught fire from lightning-coated shots while imperial ships sank into the ocean from the progression of Freeblood soldiers.

Rebel boats were lost along the campaign, and Demosyna rescued any overboard sailor with platforms and claws. Her clothing would drip from ocean rescues, and the apprentice saved all she could in the carnage. Sai Aeri had brutalized the green hills surrounding the Fort, making expanding redoubts from the stagnant moat. Magma now filled the ring enclosing the First Fort, bubbling and steaming with raw power.

Red light breathed a steady glow for a hundred yards, giving clear sight from atop the high courtyard walls. Hundreds of trenches connected the massive earthwork defenses, and soldiers scrambled in the muddy brawl. Demosyna saw chained figures for the first time in months but restrained herself from entering the combat on the land. The short general walked her fort's ramparts, a massive, ornate pole arm waving with banners. Cannons roared from the tree line, yet the rebels were held back by Sai Aeri's archers.

Strange imperial clockwork crossbows peeked from between stacked logs, sending bolts hundreds of yards with deadly precision. Shielded formations tried to push from the forests, but thousands of arrows drove through armor and momentum. Wind magic scattered the forceful projectiles while sheer numbers of archers, from many angles, ensured Sai Aeri's defenses.

Her trip to reach this strategic new stalemate took days, and Demosyna knew the battle raged during that time. A harbor before the apprentice was choked with rusty spikes, sunk on boats to prevent further passage by sea. Even the armored cruisers fell from the jagged obstacle, forcing the rebel fleet to disembark elsewhere.

Demosyna covered the fresh soldiers during the unloading, and the fairy laughed wildly at each projectile turned to profit. Wind caught the shot or iron balls from Sai Aeri's cannons, making solid gold spheres to fund the rebels they sought to destroy. Gold and silver were natural metals, and Celestria's journals had taught swapping of existing properties to the apprentice.

Cheers rang through the forest as thousands of supporting troops melted into the trees. Only pestering fire reached the troop ships after a few volleys, with Sai Aeri watching the mockery through a spyglass atop the tower. Armored cavalry made advances into the trenches, but the closest pit to the Fort dropped hundreds of feet to block mounted paths.

Slaves had strip-mined hundreds of square acres to achieve the defense, leaving wide ditches of bloody combat in the earth. Reports of the battle were galloped to Demosyna's ship, and Yoila was seen leaping over trenches while leading her command. The general pushed aside the dug-in soldiers, sweeping the massive pole arm to create space for rebels.

It was slow work, and the sun fell with Yoila only securing one new position feet from the last. No open space was left that Demosyna remembered from the previous year, only pits and long trenches full of slave soldiers. Harol and Au Cell's general directed from hidden wood towers in the trees, letting Yoila personally lead the rebels on the field.

Grueling inches gained each hour signaled a cease-fire from the Fort, and the rebels took the time to secure the closest southern trench. Yoila had reached the innermost redoubt after days of charging forward, melting the imperial cannons with acidic strikes. Shouts of challenge rose from the pale general, and Yoila's blue blindfold failed to handicap the woman's wrath.

Glowing magma stood as a final barricade, and the southern woods emptied into the trenches. Demosyna watched the meticulous operation, as hundreds of winding holes still held long-range archers. Rain would slow the progress further, but the weather held other than for a few watery hours.

"If Sai Aeri faces me, let the outcome bring a retreat for the losing army!" Yoila bellowed into the still air. "I will take Demosyna Pegmatite's forces north if I am bested, leaving the other generals to secure the victory! I have no more fear, because my Wise-woman sets my true path!"

An arrow was loosed by the squat general in the First Fort, but Yoila spun her bladed staff to knock the aggression into the mud. A short renewal of the battle left hours of starlight soaked in blood, and Demosyna hovered on a purple disc beside her battleship.

Thick plating only dented from the imperial cannons, and Demosyna stacked gold and silver balls on the deck in shining pyramids. The range of the sharpshooters along the high walls of the Fort far outmatched the rebels' bows, forcing the soldiers to press against the mud for cover. Yoila took the first tiered trench in a single day, blindly surging forward against the ornate imperial army.

Pockets of silver-armored soldiers still fought for weeks in the land surrounding the First Fort, but horns called from Yoila's position to signal a victory at hand. Sai Aeri marched the hourglass-shaped walls of her fort, seeing the closest trenches filling with rebel faces. Over ten thousand imperial soldiers remained in the deep pits, but the Fist swarmed from the tree line with unending support. Demosyna flew over to the waving of a white flag from Sai Aeri, landing with a purple halo glowing in fairy laughter.

Yoila walked the lowered drawbridge with her lady, and Demosyna stepped freely over the threshold to face Sai Aeri.

"No armor is allowed to slaves," Sai Aeri said, producing shackles for the two women. "Remove those ill-gotten metals before our talks, Demosyna."

"If I see those again, I shall level your tower, Sai Aeri," Demosyna said, calmly removing her outer coat with a touch of Yoila's shoulder. "We come in good faith of your surrender, so do not test my patience with pathetic threats."

The shining elven armor was exposed above her pinstriped pants, and Demosyna saw Yoila remove her blue leather armor in an instant. Sai Aeri motioned to a soldier, and Imperial Battle Wizened marched over the wide walls. Demosyna was folding her clothes, watching the new troops join the general, when she was stabbed through the heart.

Sai Aeri flashed a dagger with deadly speed, and it pierced through the silvery elven breastplate with ease. Yoila yelled in rage, but the fairy responded before anyone else. A shrill tone pierced into

Sai Aeri, shattering several teeth and exploding the dagger in a heartbeat. Demosyna collapsed to the ground, gurgling at the fairy as it flew to the wound.

Whiskers of light closed the gushing flesh for Demosyna, and the fairy pushed the metal armor together to patch the dagger hole. Yoila clashed pole arms with Sai Aeri while the apprentice slowly dusted herself off, adrenaline surging in her mind.

"Thank you, fairy!" Demosyna yelled into her head, tears streaming. "I am so proud of you!"

Demosyna let Yoila push the shorter general around the courtyard, letting loose her passion with skills hard learned. After several minutes of ferocious dueling, however, the young lady called Yoila off.

"Enough. I have come to talk terms," Demosyna roared, striding forward with her coat back on. "Lay down your arms, Yoila. If that is your attitude, Sai Aeri, I will break custom and remain armored."

The pale-scaled general knelt beside her lady, dropping the massive pole in obedience. Sai Aeri remained leaning on her own weapon, waving the streamers in a signal to the Battle Wizen. A volcano erupted underneath the First Fort, jetting lava into the deep earthworks nearest the moat.

Soldiers from all the battling armies burned, melting armor digging into bones with shrieks of dismay. Yoila rose at the fading noises, and the entire fort rocked west into the ocean. A massive dug foundation supported the tottering island while it sailed into the open waters with grinding crashes. The sunk barriers and scrambling rebel fleet were crushed under the weight of the mobile land, moved by volcanic propulsion.

"Yoila, I'm sorry, but you'll have to help those soldiers!" Demosyna yelled, ignoring the smell of crisping flesh. "Let me float you over to avoid swimming back."

"That won't be necessary, my Wise-woman. How far is the shore from here? It feels like we are moving," Yoila asked, standing on the drawbridge with her enchanted weapon.

Demosyna estimated the distance and watched the upside-down funnel of magic push from the pole arm. Yoila strained one arm to hover over the war-locked seas, landing on boiling earth in the receding view. General Yoila Ice Eyes drove herself into the fire, cooling the ground and healing any around with her weapon.

Fifteen Battle Wizened nursed magical lava from the exposed mine shafts, sending the First Fort north. The few ships able to move aside rushed to aid the battle, but most of the armored rebel fleet was sunk in groaning darkness. Slaves hurried to bring fresh focusing charms to the walls, and Demosyna called to Sai Aeri.

"Send your troops here to help the wounded, General!" the lady bellowed, magically raising her voice. "Let us speak alone, if you desire an end to this war. I can power this fort in their place."

"I accept your offer, Demosyna," Sai Aeri called, motioning her Battle Wizened south. "I have lost the lands, but this fort remains within my realm. My laws hold in these walls, and you do not give commands here, Lady Pegmatite."

"Thank you, and I apologize for overstepping in our negotiations."

Demosyna calmed herself as the Fort emptied of soldiers.

"I am new to diplomacy but will strive to restrain myself in the future. Lead on, General."

Sai Aeri led Demosyna through the nearly empty courtyard, pointing out the intricate carvings in each massive stone. Slaves tended the planters lining the walls, and Demosyna sighed when eventually asking for their freedom. Elven stories of colonies founded in every century were carved, detailing ebbs and swells of the timeless empire. They had decorated the walls when Demosyna was imprisoned before, but gore or banners hid them those dark days.

"What will it cost to free these people you keep, General?" the apprentice asked as the exterior tour wrapped up. "Will this suffice for the down payment?"

A heartbroken apprentice turned a cluster of grapeshot into gold balls stacked between wooden discs beside cannons. The pair stood on the two-story walls, watching the Fist coast by in the morning light. Demosyna would send bursts of molten rock as a jet of speed for the acres the Fort had left, replacing imperial soldiers. The entire trip took nearly a week of slow travel, and Demosyna listened most of the time as Sai Aeri negotiated.

"We are both ladies of powerful realms, so whatever you carry will serve as such leverage," Sai Aeri replied, bored of the interruption. "Free any you wish, but know I will tally each loss you bring to our talks."

Demosyna handed three points to the nearest clerk servant, letting her write the contracts with a smile. Chains fell away with a snap at each shuffling encounter, and Demosyna hovered the newly freed people to shore. A small bag of seeds would be handed over, with instructions to the malnourished people.

"The first harvest of these plants will have enchanted seeds!" the young apprentice explained. "Each after will be normal, but the magic seeds will instantly grow a plant in tilled dirt. If you keep some from each first harvest, you shall always have food in your home of choice! Join me in Lost Claw Bay if you wish, but enjoy the token for your new life, friends!"

The apprentice demonstrated by growing a pear tree in the courtyard, planting a seed to instantly sprout a tree full of traveling snacks. A second tree was grown magically from a seed Demosyna took from the ripe pear, loading each traveler with gifts. The general walked into the tower, and the former slave cages now held supplies of various sorts. Demosyna was glad to see no filth in the offset floor, and orderly crates took the place of slaves.

A library was in the basement of the tall structure, and stairs behind the mysterious door allowed travel between levels. Some slaves were studying on sofas among the shelves and asked to remain and learn from the knowledge they read. Demosyna allowed this, only taking them from captivity once departing at New Empress City. Sai Aeri skipped the kitchen, joking about needing to eat while sailing north.

Unenchanted shelves in the basement held thousands of volumes, rivaling the apprentice's earliest libraries. The general ran fingers along leather spines, detailing the knowledge of any book she personally had read. Demosyna spent hours in this vast collection of information, talking with the former slaves and their general. Many of the freed people were educated, the lady found, fluent in languages and understanding. Most of the talks were held in the ornate basement library, where the apprentice lounged on stuffed leather sofas.

Alchemy labs filled a third floor of the five-story tower, and Demosyna recognized several of the potions being produced by careful workers. Walls held nailed formula and diagrams, letting the lifers make powerful flasks for the empire. Celestria hadn't provided lessons yet on alchemy, but Demosyna understood from her lonely youth such disciplines.

Her fairy grew excited from peeking above the silver chain mail crown and tipped several beakers over before calming again. The apprentice apologized for the delay and remade the lost potion herself before following Sai Aeri. A nursery filled half the sleeping quarters on the fourth floor, and Demosyna let her fairy hover near Paw babies.

"You must be extra gentle with babies, fairy," Demosyna said, cupping the gem in restraint. "Such are vulnerable without help from others! There, just watch them squirm!"

The fresh litter had been delivered during the battle, and eight furry balls of mewing infant wriggled in a crib. Each baby had long white fur, and their parents beamed from a cot nearby. A short father wept onto Demosyna's clawed hand when freed, thankful for being allowed to stay with his babies. A weary mother fell back asleep while the fairy danced above the crib in excitement. Sai Aeri didn't care about the birth and simply waited for Demosyna to pry her fairy away before continuing their discussions.

Secured vaults lined the circular walls on the top fifth floor, and Demosyna sat on the roof to eat with Sai Aeri. Dinner was elaborate in presentation, for both dishes were placed silently onto golden china in tandem. Shadows in the doorframe hid the servants, but the chained figures would glide forward when tending the table.

The apprentice observed the known manners at the table, only breaking form to snap her fingers with metallic magic. Chains fell from wrists, and new slaves appeared to replace the freed people. Sai Aeri had an endless supply of servants, it seemed to Demosyna as the days fell away. The short general let Demosyna read written accounts of bringing civilization to the Fist, penned by Sai Aeri over hundreds of generations.

New Empress City appeared in the north, its polished marble splendor growing each hour. The final meal shared by Demosyna let her watch the harbors flow with golden ships, sending trade across the world. Au Cell employed hundreds of ships to run his trading networks, but New Empress City had harbors spanning entire leagues. Lost Claw Bay seemed a struggling port in comparison, and Demosyna watched patterned silk sails flutter bright colors for days before landing.

"I have shown you the progress my Empress has made in these lands, Lady Pegmatite," Sai Aeri said, toasting the approaching capital. "We have uplifted these people for centuries beyond count, and I have let you enjoy the benefits during our time here. We both understand order is needed for these wild lands and the barbaric seeders that inhabit the Fist. Our battle was a stalemate for everyone, for the Empress doesn't lose. She claims what is hers for the good of all, and we must respect that."

The apprentice remained silent, as she had most of the days sailing on liquid rocks. Another freed slave swam toward the shore, ignoring the conjured seeds as a parting gift.

"Our talks will end at New Empress City, but observe the straight roads or the golden-domed halls."

Sai Aeri motioned to districts of the elaborate city.

"Generations have refined these here and far south in Empress City that commands the world. I offer structure from experts in all fields bred for their minds. The Empress offers her subjects protection from an army undefeated within the recorded history of this war. You can be a ruler in the empire, after serving your amended sentence. My Empress's Highway can still unite the Fist for peasant and royals alike with simple handfuls of points."

Demosyna saw the new decree called for only five years in servitude, accounting for rounded-up time in the Fist already lived. Footnotes had been added concerning the purchasing of the slaves during the journey, and Demosyna returned the paper without signing.

"I have no interest in waiting five years to finish the war in the north," Demosyna said, leaning back in a plush dining chair. "You never had a true claim over me, because Klai escorted me into the Fist under her Orders' protection. My magic has awoken since landing, but I spoke truth in those chains you put on me. I am not impressed by your civilization, General. You have succeeded in confirming my beliefs—that potential is there for everyone living in the Fist. I will return to my bay and let you wage your losing battles from New Empress Island."

"I will not stop you since we have agreed to peaceful talks these past days," Sai Aeri said, grinning. "You likely won't have a home to return to, I am happy to say. While we drifted along and you funded my campaign, my personal Wise-women razed and salted your lands! I knew you couldn't resist taking this fort and led my soldiers in a massive diversion to you rebels. The tunnel I commissioned is nearly realized, so take the lands I abandoned while it is completed!"

"That may be true, Sai Aeri, but free soldiers will not let their homes be burned easily," Demosyna replied, not fully containing the fear rising in her eyes. "How many lives did we waste in that battle, and how much potential did you squander digging those pits? I can see the slaves from here, and New Empress City will be a new focus for me now! Thank you, Sai Aeri, for hosting me."

"The war you have joined lasts forever, little lady. Goodbye," Sai Aeri called, watching Demosyna hover southeast. "I have fought it for generations of your kind, and my will is woven into the Fist. My lands have been in this name since first landing these shores, and I will regain my southern holdings. I have done it before, so scurry back to the ruin I left you as a gift."

Home! Demosyna screamed into her own head. *I will find you at our home, fairy. Tell me what is left there please!*

The remaining thirty slaves joined the worried apprentice on a platform of magic, and the fairy teleported away at a thought from Demosyna. The young woman pictured the crystal mine clear in her head, holding the orb to her fresh chest scar. Purple light blinked from her sight, and Demosyna hoped the gem would understand the request. The rescued slaves flew back with Demosyna, who saw smoke on the horizon after miles passed in calculating silence. A bitter smile formed on her sharp purple face once touching down, and Demosyna Pegmatite set to work in Lost Claw Bay.

Printed in the USA
CPSIA information can be obtained
at www.ICGtesting.com
CBHW030736240724
11852CB00050B/87